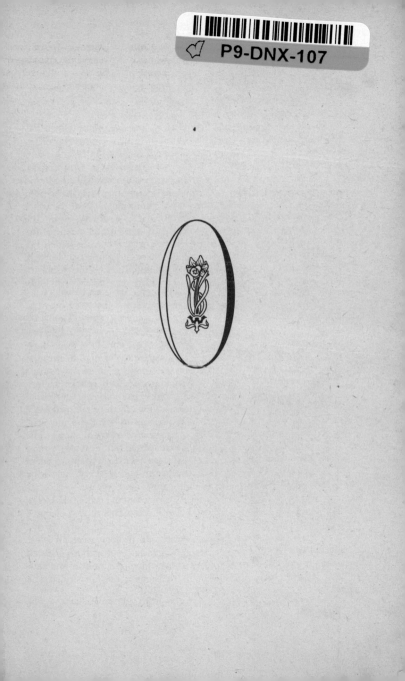

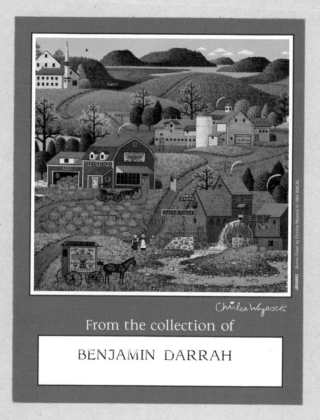

From the collection of

BENJAMIN DARRAH

THE HUNCHBACK
OF NOTRE-DAME
(Notre-Dame de Paris)

———◆———

Victor Hugo

WORDSWORTH CLASSICS

The paper in this book is produced from pure wood
pulp, without the use of chlorine or any other substance
harmful to the environment. The energy used in its
production consists almost entirely of hydroelectricity
and heat generated from waste materials, thereby
conserving fossil fuels and contributing little to the
greenhouse effect.

This edition published 1993 by
Wordsworth Editions Limited
Cumberland House, Crib Street,
Ware, Hertfordshire SG12 9ET

ISBN 1 85326 068 1

*Printed and bound in Denmark by Nørhaven
Typeset in U.K. by Antony Gray*

INTRODUCTION

THE HUNCHBACK OF NOTRE-DAME (*Notre-Dame de Paris*) is a dramatic historical romance set in medieval times, 1482, the year before Louis XI of France died. Victor Hugo's first great novel, it is centred on the life of the great Gothic cathedral of Notre-Dame on the Ile de la Cité in the heart of Paris - the focal point of French pride, religious life and ceremonial occasion. The principal characters are the beautiful La Esmerelda, a gypsy dancer who is in love with Captain Phœbus, Claude Frollo, the hypocritical and demented archdeacon, whose evil passion, fuelled by celibacy, for La Esmerelda causes him to denounce her as a witch, and most famous of all, the hero Quasimodo, the 'Hunchback of Notre-Dame', a deformed bell-ringer and creature of the cathedral, whose devotion to La Esmerelda saves her for a time, when she is confronted by a mob and seeks refuge and protection in the belfry of the cathedral. La Esmerelda is however doomed to meet a tragic end, while Quasimodo exacts a terrible revenge on Frollo on the pinnacles of Notre-Dame itself. Hugo was a champion, along with Charles Nodier and Madame de Staël, of Gothic architecture and Notre-Dame, begun in the rounded Romanesque period and finished in the pointed Gothic style, provided him with wonderful scope for the encyclopedic digressions for which he is famous, as well as a chance to expound his philosophical beliefs of democracy and evolutionary cultural advance. Hugo began writing *The Hunchback of Notre Dame* on 25 July 1830. Two days later there was a revolution on the streets of Paris, and on 28 July his fifth child, called Adèle after his wife, was born. Charles X was driven out in the revolution and the more constitutional Louis-Philippe came to the throne. Chateaubriand's rather apposite comment on this revolution was that Paris had seen 'yet another government fling itself from the towers of Notre-Dame.' After this interruption, Hugo began writing again in earnest in September and the book, of almost 200,000 words, was finished in just four-and-a-half months, by mid-January 1831 . Critics such as Prosper Mérimée and Goethe were not kind, but the public responded enthusiastically and 3,100 copies were sold in the 18 months following publication - a good seller by the standards of the time. *The Hunchback of Notre-Dame* first appeared in an English translation in August 1833. The novel had its own beneficial effect on the cathedral of Notre-Dame for, as the current Michelin guide to Paris puts it: 'Gradually the building began to fall into disrepair, until in 1841, in accordance with popular feeling roused by the Romantic Movement and Victor Hugo's novel *The Hunchback of Notre-Dame*, the July Monarchy ordered that the cathedral be restored.' The novel is the subject of a classic, black and white film starring Charles Laughton .

Victor-Marie Hugo (1802-1885) is one of the greatest writers in the illustrious Pantheon of French poets, playwrights and novelists. He was born at Besançon in eastern France, the third son of a major in Napoleon's army. Hugo père *went on to become a general and was created a count. Despite the peripatetic nature of life in army families, the young Victor-Marie received a good education in Italy, Spain and Paris. His literary talent showed itself at an early age and he won a prize for a poem at school, and in 1819 he co-founded the review -* Le Conservateur littéraire - *which established him as a leading figure in the Romantic movement in France. Victor Hugo's output was prodigious, ranging from twenty volumes of poetry, ten plays, nine novels, and a huge corpus of general writing on a wide variety of issues. His political creed was liberal and he was a firm believer in republicanism, universal suffrage, and free education for all. Despite his republicanism, Hugo retained a personal friendship with Louis-Philippe and honours were heaped upon him -* Chevalier de la Légion d'honneur *(1837), election to the* Académie française *(1841) and creation as a* pair de France, *equivalent to being elevated to the House of Lords in Britain, (1845). Following the revolutions* which shook France and much of continental Europe in 1848, Hugo became a member of the Constituent Assembly. However, he was a noted critic of the Second Empire of Louis Napoleon and he was forced into exile in Brussels, Jersey and latterly at Hauteville House in Guernsey where he remained with his wife Adèle and family, and with his mistress Juliet Drouet nearby, for 14 years. Swinburne described Hugo as 'the greatest writer born in the nineteenth century' while the frequently unsympathetic critic W.E. Henley opined that he was 'far and away the greatest artist in words that modern France has seen'. Hugo returned to Paris from exile in Guernsey in 1870, again serving as a deputy, and later becoming a senator in the Third Republic. His funeral was an occasion of great pomp and ceremony, his body lying in state beneath the Arc de Triomphe prior to burial in the Panthéon.

Further Reading

A Maurois: Biography of Victor Hugo (1956)
Also studies by E M Grant (1945), R B Grant (1968) and J P Houston (1974)

Contents

BOOK ELEVEN

BOOK ONE

I

The Great Hall

ONE MORNING, three hundred and forty-eight years, six months and nineteen days ago, the Parisians were awakened by a grand peal from all the bells, within the triple enclosure of the City, the University and the Town.

Yet the 6th of January, 1482, was not a day of which history has preserved any record. There was nothing remarkable in the event that so early in the morning set in commotion the bells and the bourgeois of Paris. It was neither a sudden attack made by Picards or by Burgundians, nor a shrine carried in procession, nor a student fight in the city of Laas; nor the entry of 'our most dread lord the King;' nor even a goodly stringing up of thieves, male and female, on the Place de la Justice. Nor was it a sudden arrival, so common in the fifteenth century, of some ambassador and his train, all belaced and beplumed. Only about two days ago, indeed, the last cavalcade of this kind, Flemish envoys commissioned to conclude the marriage treaty between the young dauphin and Margaret of Flanders, had made entry into Paris, to the great annoyance of Cardinal Bourbon. To please the king, his Eminence had undertaken to give gracious reception to the rough crowd of Flemish burgomasters, and to entertain them at his Hôtel de Bourbon with a 'very fine morality, burletta and farce,' whilst a beating rain was all the time drenching his magnificent tapestries at his portals.

But on this 6th of January, what 'set in motion the whole *populaire* of Paris,' as Jehan of Troyes, the old chronicler, phrases it, was the fact of its being a double holiday, united since time immemorial – the Epiphany, or Feast of the Kings, and the *Fête des Fous*, or Feast of the Fools. To celebrate such a day there was to be a bonfire kindled on the Place de Grève, a maypole raised at the Chapelle de Braque, and a mystery performed in the Palace of Justice. Proclamation had been made the evening before, to the sound of the trumpet, in all the public squares by the provost's men in fine coats of purple camlet, with great white crosses on the breast.

Crowds of people had accordingly been flocking all the morning, their houses and shops shut up, from all quarters of the town towards one of the three places appointed. Everyone had made his selection – the bonfire, the maypole, or the mystery. Thanks to the good common sense so characteristic of the Parisian sight-seers, the greater part of the multitude directed their steps either towards the bonfire, which was quite in season, or towards the mystery which was to be performed in the Grande Salle, or great hall of the Palace of Justice, well roofed and well sheltered – wisely leaving the poor, ill-garlanded maypole to shiver all alone under a January sky in the cemetery of the Chapelle de Braque.

The greatest crowds, however, were to be found on the approaches to the Palace of Justice, because it was known that the Flemish ambassadors, who had arrived two days previously, intended to be present, not only at the performance of the mystery, but also at the election of the Fool's Pope, which was likewise to take place in the Great Hall.

On that day it was no easy matter to make one's way into the Great Hall, then and long afterwards considered to be the largest covered apartment in the world (Sauval, the Paris historian, it is hardly necessary to state, had not yet measured the great hall in the chateau of Montargis) . The open square in front of the Palace, thronged with people, presented to the gazers from the windows the aspect of a sea into which five or six streets, like the mouths of so many rivers, every moment discharged fresh floods of human heads. The waves of this deluge, constantly increasing, broke against the angles of the houses that projected here and there, like so many promontories, into the irregularly shaped basin of the square. In the centre of the high Gothic façade of the Palace, the great triple-faced staircase, continually ascended and descended by the restless multitudes, with currents breaking on the intermediate landing or streaming over the two lateral slopes, flowed like a waterfall tumbling into a lake. In the square itself, the noise made by the shouting, laughing, tramping of these thousands of feet, great as it was, was redoubled every now and then, as something occurred to check, disturb or eddy the stream that surged towards the great staircase. At one time it was an archer clubbing somebody; at another it was the prancing horse of a provost's sergeant kicking right and left – the regular good old way to establish order, handed down from the *provostry* to the *constablery*, from the *constablery* to the *marshalry*, and from the *marshalry* to the *gendarmerie* of our Paris of to-day.

At the doors, at the windows, at the skylights, and on the roofs, swarmed thousands of good-natured *bourgeois* faces, looking calmly and quietly at the Palace, at the crowd, and asking nothing more to look at; for many honest Paris folks are quite content with gazing at the gazers, and can even regard a wall with intense interest when they think there is something going on behind it.

If we, men of 1830, could possibly mingle in imagination with those

Parisians of the fifteenth century, and enter with them, pulled, elbowed, crushed, into the Great Hall, that proved so small on this 6th of January, 1482, we should witness a spectacle at once interesting and charming, where everything would be so very old as to appear perfectly new.

If the reader consent, we shall cross the threshold of the Great Hall together. Let me endeavour to reproduce the impression made on his senses as we struggle through the surging crowd in frock, smock, jerkin, doublet, and every conceivable dress of the period.

At first our ears are stunned with the buzzing, our eyes are dazzled with the glare. Over our heads is the roof, consisting of a double vault of pointed arches, lined with carved wood, painted light blue, and sprinkled with golden *fleurs-de-lis*. Under our feet the marble floor, like a checkerboard, is alternated with black and white squares. A few paces from us stands an enormous pillar, then another, then a third, seven altogether, extending the whole length of the Hall, and supporting the central line that separates the double vaults of the roof. Around the first four are dealers' stands glittering with glass and tinsel ware; around the other three are oaken benches, worn and polished by the gowns of the layers and the breeches of those that employ them. Everywhere around the building, along the lofty walls, between the doors, between the windows, between the pillars, appears an interminable line of the statues of the kings of France, from Pharamond down – the sluggards, with arms pendent and eyes downcast, the warriors, with arms and heads boldly raised on high. In the long Gothic windows, the stained glass shines with a thousand colours. In the wide entrances the doors are richly and delicately carved. Everywhere all around – on vaults, pillars, walls, lintels, panels, doors, and statues – glows a rich tint of blue and gold, already a little faded, but even seventy years later, in spite of dust and cobwebs, Du Breul, the historian, will see enough to admire it from tradition.

If the reader now represents to himself this vast hall, visible in the pale light of a January day, filled with a motley and noisy mob drifting along the walls and eddying around the seven pillars, he will have some faint idea of the picture in general, whose curious details we shall now try to indicate more precisely.

It is certain, that if Ravaillac had not assassinated Henry IV, no documents of his trial would have been deposited in the Palace registry, no accomplices would have been interested in causing the said documents to disappear, no incendiaries would have been obliged, lacking a better method, to burn the registry in order to burn the documents, and to burn the Palace in order to burn the registry. Therefore there would have been no fire of 1618. The old Palace would be still standing, with its Grand Hall, and I could say to my reader, 'Go and look at it' – which would be a great convenience for us both; saving me from writing, him from reading, my imperfect description. Which goes to prove the novel truth: the results of great events are beyond calculation.

It is true that it is very possible that Ravaillac did not have any accomplices; secondly, that his accomplices, if by chance he had any, had nothing to do with the conflagration of 1618. There are two other explanations, both very plausible. According to the first it was set on fire and consumed by a shooting star, a foot wide and 2 cubit high, that fell on the Palace, as everyone knows, on the 7th of March after midnight. For the second is quoted the quatrain of Théophile:

> *Certes, ce fut un triste jeu*
> *Quand à Paris Dame Justice,*
> *Pour avoir mangé trop d'épice,*
> *Se mit tout le palais en feu.* *

But whatever we may think of this triple explanation, political, physical and poetical, one fact is unfortunately but too true – the burning itself. Thanks to this catastrophe, thanks especially to the various successive restorations which effectually finished up whatever little the conflagration had spared, we have hardly any remains to-day of this first abode of the kings of France, of this palace, the elder sister of the Louvre, already so old in the times of Philip the Fair that traces could then be found of the magnificent buildings erected by King Robert and described by Helgaldus. Almost every portion of it has disappeared. What has become of the chamber of the chancellery, where Saint Louis 'consummated his marriage?' The garden where he administered justice 'clad in a cotte of camlet, a surcoat of tiretaine without sleeves, and over all a mantle of black sendal, reclining upon carpets by the side of Joinville?' Where is the chamber of the Emperor Sigismond? that of Charles IV? that of John Lackland? Where is the staircase whence Charles VI proclaimed his gracious amnesty? Where are the flagstones on which Marcel murdered, before the young dauphin's eyes, the Marshals of Normandy and of Champagne? Where is the gate at which Anti-pope Benedict's bull was torn to pieces, and from which those who had brought it started on their procession through Paris, coped and mitred in derision, to make *amende honorable?* Where is the Great Hall itself with its gildings, its azure, its pointed arches, its statues, its pillars, its vast vaulted roofs all checkered and variegated with carvings? and the golden chamber? Where is the marble lion, kneeling at the

* It was certainly poor fun when Lady Justice set fire to her palace in Paris just because she had eaten too many *sugar-plums (bribes).*

4

gate, like the lions before Solomon's throne, head clown, tail between legs, in the attitude of humility that force should present when before Justice? Where are the beautiful doors, the splendid windows? Where the chiselled ironwork that threw Biscornette into despair? Where is Du Hancy's delicate cabinet-work? What has time, what have men done with these wonders? What has been given to us in exchange for all this Gallic history, for all this Gothic art? For art, we have the heavy flat arches of De Brosse, the tasteless architect of the portal of St. Gervais; and for history, we have the twaddling Souvenirs of the Big Pillar, still resounding with the Patrus' small gossip. Neither being much to speak of, let us return to the story taking place in the real Great Hall of the real old Palace.

The two ends of this gigantic parallelogram were occupied differently. At the west end could be seen the famous Marble Table, said to be of one single block, and so long, wide and high that 'no other such slice of marble was ever seen in the world,' as is recorded by the old chroniclers in a style that would have given an appetite to Gargantua. The east end contained the little chapel lately built by Louis XI, in which he had himself sculptured in stone kneeling before the Virgin, and to which he had also brought, without concerning himself with their two niches thus left vacant in the file of royal statues, the statues of Charlemagne and Saint Louis – two saints whom he supposed to be very much in favour in Heaven as kings of France. The little chapel itself, in all the charms of newness – it had hardly been built six years – was characterized all through by the exquisite taste in delicate architecture, wonderful sculpture and fine, deep carving, which, ending our Gothic era, is perpetuated to the middle of the sixteenth century in the fairy-like fancies of the Renaissance. The little *rosace à jour*, in particular, a wheel-shaped window over the portal, was a masterpiece of such lightness and elegance that it could be called a star of lace.

Towards the middle of the Hall, opposite the main entrance, a balcony covered with gold brocade, backed by the wall, and accessible by a private entrance from a corridor opening into the Gilded Chamber, had been erected for the special honour of the Flemish envoys and the other grand personages invited to the representation of the mystery.

This entertainment was to be given, according to ancient customs, on the Marble Table, where all the preparations had been made since the morning. The thick marble slab, scratched by the heels of the Basochians – a famous guild of lawyers' clerks – supported a solid construction of wood, sufficiently elevated, whose upper surface, high enough to be visible from the farthest parts of the hall, was to serve as the stage, while the interior masked with curtains, was to be the actors' dressing-room. A ladder, standing artlessly outside, was to connect dressing-room and stage, and help exits and entrances by its solid rungs. By this ladder and this only, actor the most unexpected, scene the most entrancing effect the most telling, was to gain access to the stage. Innocent yet venerable infancy of the mechanical resources of theatrical art!

At each of the four corners of the Marble Table stood a sergeant of the bailiff of the Palace to preserve order. The regular guardians of the people's amusements, whether on holidays or days of execution, there they now stood, stiff and motionless as statues.

The play was not to begin until the great clock of the Palace had struck the last stroke announcing noon. This was, no doubt, rather late for a mystery, but as ambassadors were to be present their convenience was to be regarded.

The most of the crowd had been waiting all the morning. A good many of these honest sight-seers had shivered on the grand staircase at daybreak; some even insisted that they had passed the night close to the great doorway so as to make sure of being the first to enter. The crowd, continually increasing, became by degrees too great for the room and, like a river overflowing its banks, began to rise along the walls, to swell around the pillars, and even inundate the window-sills, the tops of the columns, the cornices and every projection of the sculptures. As a matter of course, impatience, discomfort, weariness, the unrestraint of the occasion, the quarrels continually springing up from unavoidable causes – a sharp elbow, – a heavy heel, – the long day, – all these sources of discontent at last began to tell. The noise made by a crowd so squeezed, packed, crushed, trodden on, smothered, began to assume a tone of decided acrimony. Complaints and imprecations began to be plainly heard, against the Flemings, the Provost of the Merchants, Cardinal Bourbon, the Governor of the Palace Margaret of Austria, the sergeants with their rods, the cold, the heat, the bad weather, the Bishop of Paris, the Fools' Pope, the pillars, the statues, this closed door, that open window, – the whole to the great amusement of the bands of students and lackeys scattered through the crowd, who mingled with all this discontentment their teasing remarks and their malicious suggestions, and pricked the general ill humour with a pin, so to speak.

There was, amongst others, a group of these joyous rascals who, after breaking the glass of a window, had established themselves boldly upon the entablature, and from there cast their looks and their railleries alternately within and without, upon the crowd in the Hall and the crowd out of doors. From their mimicry of well-known personages, their flippant remarks exchanged with their comrades from one end of the Hall to the other, and their uproarious laughter, it was easy to see that these young clerks, far from participating in the general languor or vexation, were enjoying themselves heartily by making so much out of one spectacle that they never minded waiting for another.

'Upon my soul, it's you, Joannes Frollo de Molendino!' cried a friend in the crowd to a little blond with a pretty and malicious face straddled on an acanthus of the capital of one of the lofty columns. 'Hello! Jack of the windmill! You are well named to-day, anyway, for your two legs and your two arms keep moving like the four sails that go in the wind. How long have you been perched up there?'

'Four hours at least, by the devil's mercy,' answered Joannes. 'I hope they will be put to my credit in purgatory. I heard the beginning of the high mass sung in the Sainte Chapelle by the King of Sicily's eight chanters.'

'Sweet chanters they are too!' cried one of the students, 'with voices sharper than their pointed caps. Before founding a mass for Monsieur Saint John, the king would have done well to have found out whether Monsieur Saint John liked Latin psalmody with a Provençal accent.'

'It was all for the sake of employing those cursed chanters of the King of Sicily that he did it,' screamed bitterly an old woman in the crowd beneath the window. 'What think you of a thousand livres parisis for a mass, and charged, too, upon the farm of the saltwater fish of the fish-market of Paris!'

'Peace, old woman!' replied a grave and portly personage, who was stopping his nose at the side of the fish-seller; 'it was quite necessary to found a mass. Would you have had the king fall sick again?'

'Bravely spoken, Sir Gilles Lecornu, master furrier to the king's wardrobe!' cried the little scholar clinging to the capital.

A burst of laughter from the whole tribe of the scholars greeted the unlucky name of the poor furrier to the king's wardrobe.

'Lecornu! Gilles Lecornu!' said some.

Cornutus et hirsutus,' (horned and hirsute), answered another.

'Oh, to be sure,' continued the little imp at the top of the pillar; 'what have they to laugh at? Is not worthy Gilles Lecornu brother to Maître Jehan Lecornu, provost of the king's household, son of Maître Mahiet Lecornu, first gatekeeper of the Bois de Vincennes – all citizens of Paris – all married, from father to son?'

The gaiety redoubled. The stout furrier, without answering a word, strove to escape the looks fixed upon him from all sides; but he exerted himself in vain, for all his efforts served only to wedge more solidly between the shoulders of his neighbours his great apoplectic face, purple with anger and vexation.

At last one of these neighbours, fat, short, and reverend-looking, like himself, raised his voice in his behalf.

'Abominable!' he exclaimed, 'that scholars should talk thus to a townsman. In my time they would have been first beaten with a fagot and then burned with it.'

At this the whole tribe burst out afresh.

'Hello! who sings that stave? who's that ill-boding screech-owl?'

'Oh. I know him,' said one; 'it's Maître Andry Musnier.'

'Because he's one of the four sworn booksellers to the University,' said the other.

'All goes by fours in that shop,' cried a third; 'there are four nations, the four faculties, the four fêtes, the four attorneys, the four electors, and the four booksellers.'

'Well, then,' resumed Jehan Frollo, 'we must play four devils with them.'

'Musnier, we'll burn thy books.'

'Musnier, we'll beat thy lackey.'

'Musnier, we'll kiss thy wife – '

'The good fat Mademoiselle Oudarde – '

'Who's as fresh and buxom as if she were a widow.'

'The devil take you!' growled Maître Andry Musnier.

'Maître Andry,' said Jehan still hanging by the capital, 'hold your tongue, or I'll drop on your head.'

Maître Andry looked up, seemed to calculate for a moment the height of the pillar and the weight of the little rogue, multiplied in his mind that height by the square of the velocity, and was silent.

Jehan, master of the field, continued triumphantly –

'Yes, I would do it, though I am brother to an archdeacon.'

'Fine fellows, in truth, are our gentlemen of the University, not even to have taken care that our privileges were respected on a day like this: for here are a maypole and a bonfire in the Town; a mystery, a fools' pope, and Flemish ambassadors, in the City; and in the University, nothing at all!'

'And yet the Place Maubert is large enough,' observed one of the young clerks posted on the window seat.

'Down with the rector, the electors, and the attorneys!' cried Joannes.

'We must build a bonfire to-night in the Champ-Gaillard,' continued the other, 'with Maître Andry's books.'

'And the desks of the scribes.' said his neighbour.

'And the wands of the beadles.'

'And the spitting-boxes of the clans.'

'And the buffets of the attorneys.'

'And the hutches of the electors.'

'And the rector's stools.'

'Down, then,' said little Jehan, as counterpoint, 'down with Maître Andry, the beadles, and the scribes – the theologians, the physicians, and the decretists – the attorneys, the electors, and the rector!'

'This is then the end of the world,' muttered Maître Andry, stopping his ears.

'Apropos! the rector himself! here he comes through the Place!' cried one of those in the window seat.

Every one now strove to turn towards the Place.

'Is it really our venerable rector, Maître Thibaut?' asked Jehan Frollo du Moulin, who, as he was clinging to one of the internal pillars, could not see what was passing outside.

'Yes, yes,' answered all the rest, 'it is he – he himself – Maître Thibaut, the rector.'

It was, in fact, the rector and all the dignitaries of the University going in procession to meet the ambassadors, and crossing at that moment the Place of the Palace. The scholars all crowded together at the window, greeted them as they passed by with sarcasms and ironical plaudits. The rector, marching at the head of his band, received the first broadside, and it was a rough one.

'Good-day, monsieur le recteur! Hello! good-day to you!'

'How has the old gambler contrived to be here? has he really quitted his dice?'

'How he goes trotting along on his mule – its ears are not so long as his.'

'Hello! good-day to you, monsieur le recteur Thibaut! *Tybalde aleator!* (Tybald the gamester) – Ah! you old imbecile! you old gambler!'

'God preserve you! did you often throw double-six last night?'

'Oh! what a scarecrow countenance; leaden, wrinkled and battered through his love of dice and gaming.'

'Where are you going to now, Thibaut, *Tybalde ad dados* (Tybald of the dice) – turning your back on the University and trotting toward the town?'

'No doubt he's going to seek a lodging in the Rue Thibautodé *Thibaut aux dés*),' cried Jehan du Moulin.

'The whole gang repeated the pun with a voice of thunder and a furious clapping of hands.

'You are going to seek lodgings in the Rue Thibautodé, aren't you, monsieur le recteur, the devil's own gamester?'

Then came the turn of the other dignitaries.

'Down with the beadles! down with the mace-bearers!'

'Tell me, Robin Poussepain, who's that man there?'

'It's Gilbert de Suilly, *Gilbertus de Soliaco*, chancellor of the college of Autun.'

'Here, take my shoe – you're better placed than I am – throw it in his face.'

'*Saturnalitius mittimus ecce nuces.*' (We send Saturnalian nuts).

'Down with the six theologians with their white surplices!'

'Are those the theologians? I thought they were the six white geese that Saint Geneviève gave to the Town for the fief of Roogny.'

'Down with the physicians!'

'Down with the disputations, cardinal, and quadlibetary!'

'Here goes my cap at yon chancellor of Saint Geneviève – I owe him a grudge.'

'True – and he gave my place in the nation of Normandy to little Ascanio Falzaspada, belonging to the province of Bourges, because he's an Italian.'

'It's an injustice!' exclaimed all the scholars. 'Down with the chancellor of Saint Geneviève!'

'Ho, there! Maître Joachim de Ladehors! Ho! Louis Dahuille! Ho! Lambert Hoctement!'

'The devil smother the attorney of the nation of Germany!'

'And the chaplains of the Sainte Chapelle, with their gray amices, *cum tunicis grisis!*' (with gray tunics).

'*Seu de pellibus grisis furratis*' (or gray furred skins).

'Hello! the masters of arts! all the fine black copes; all the fine red copes!'

'That makes the rector a fine tail!'

'One would say a doge of Venice going to marry the sea.'

'Now, again, Jehan! the canons of Saint Geneviève!'

'The devil take the canons!'

'Abbé Claude Choart! Doctor Claude Choart, are you seeking Marie-la-Giffarde?'

'She's in the Rue de Glatigny.'

'She's making the bed for the king of the ribalds.'

'She's paying her four deniers, *quattuor denarios.*'

'*Aut unum bombum.*'

'Would you have her pay you in the nose?'

'Comrades, there goes Maître Simon Sanguin, elector of Picardy, with his wife on the pillion.'

'*Post equitem sedet atra cura.*' (Black Clare sits behind the horse man.)

'Stoutly, Maître Simon!'

'Good-day, monsieur l'électeur.'

'Good-night, madame l'électrice.'

'Now, aren't they happy, to be seeing all that?' sighed Joannes de Molendino, still from his perch on the capital.

Meanwhile the sworn bookseller to the University, Maître Andry Musnier, whispered in the ear of the king's furrier, Maître Gilles Lecornu:

'I tell you, monsieur, the world's at an end. Never were there seen such breakings-out of the students! It's the accursed inventions of the age that are ruining everything – the artillery – the serpentines – the bombards – and, above all, the printing-press, that other German pest! No more manuscripts – no more books! Printing puts an end to bookselling – the end of the world is at hand!'

'I can see it by velvets coming so much into fashion,' sighed the furrier.

At that moment it struck twelve.

'Ha!' exclaimed the whole crowd, with one voice of satisfaction.

The scholars became quiet.

Then there was a great shuffling about, a great movement of feet and heads, a general detonation of coughing and blowing of noses; each one arranged himself, posted himself to the best advantage, raised himself on his toes. Then there was a deep silence, every neck remaining outstretched, every mouth open, every eye turned toward the marble table – but nothing appeared. The bailiff's four sergeants still kept their posts, as stiff and motionless as if they had been four painted statues. All eyes then turned toward the gallery reserved for the Flemish envoys. The door remained shut, and the gallery empty. The multitude had been waiting since the early morning for three things, that is to say, for the hour of noon, for the Flemish embassy, and for the mystery; but only the first of the three had arrived on time.

This was really too bad.

They waited one – two – three – five minutes, a quarter of an hour – but nothing came. The gallery remained empty; the stage, mute. Meanwhile impatience was succeeded by displeasure. Angry words began to circulate, though as yet only in whispers. 'The mystery! the mystery!' was uttered in an undertone. The heads of the multitude began to ferment. A storm, which as yet only growled, was agitating the surface of that human sea. It was our friend Jehan du Moulin that elicited the first explosion.

'The mystery! and the devil take the Flemings!' cried he, with the whole force of his lungs, twisting himself, like a serpent, about his pillar.

The multitude clapped their hands. 'The mystery!' they all shouted, 'and let Flanders go to all the devils!'

'We must have the mystery immediately!' resumed the scholar; 'or my advice is that we hang the bailiff of the Palace in the way of comedy and morality.'

'Well said!' exclaimed the people. 'and let us begin the hanging with his sergeants!'

A great acclamation followed. The four poor devils of sergeants began to turn pale and look anxiously at each other. The multitude pressed toward them, and they already saw the slight wooden balustrade which separated them from the crowd bending inwards under the pressure.

The moment was critical.

'Bag them! bag them!' was shouted from all sides.

At that instant the hangings of the dressing-room which we have described above were lifted, giving passage to a personage, the mere sight of whom sufficed to stop the eager multitude, and changed their anger into curiosity as if by enchantment.

'Silence! silence!' was the cry from all sides.

The personage, but little reassured, and trembling in every limb, advanced to the edge of the marble table, making a profusion of bows, which, the nearer he approached approximated more and more to genuflexions.

Calm, however, was gradually restored. Only that slight murmur was heard which is always exhaled from the silence of a great crowd.

'Messieurs les bourgeois,' said he, 'and mesdemoiselles les bourgeoises, we shall have the honour of declaiming and performing before his eminence monsieur le cardinal, a very fine morality, entitled *The Good Judgment of Madame the Virgin Mary*. I play Jupiter. His eminence is at this moment accompanying the most honourable embassy from monsieur the Duke of Austria, which is at this moment detained by hearing the harangue of monsieur the rector of the University, at the Baudets gate. As soon as the most eminent cardinal is arrived, we shall begin.'

It is certain that nothing less than the intervention of Jupiter was necessary to save the four unhappy sergeants of the bailiff of the Palace. If we had had the happiness of inventing this true and veritable history, and had consequently been responsible for it before Our Lady of Criticism, it is not in this place, at all events, that we should have incurred any citation against us of the classical precept, *nec Deus intersit* (Ever let a god intervene), etc. Furthermore, the costume of Seigneur Jupiter was very fine, and had contributed not a little to quiet the irritated assemblage by attracting all their attention. Jupiter was clad in a brigandine covered with black velvet and gilded nails; his head-dress was a bicoquet ornamented with silver-gilt buttons; and but for the rouge and the great beard which covered each one-half of his face – but for the scroll of gilt pasteboard sprinkled with spangles and stuck all over with shreds of tinsel, which he carried in his hand, and in which experienced eyes easily recognized his thunderbolts – and but for his flesh-coloured feet, sandal-bound *à la Grecque* – he might have borne a comparison, for the severity of his aspect, with a Breton archer of the corps of Monsieur de Berry.

II

Pierre Gringoire

WHILE, HOWEVER, Jupiter was delivering his harangue, the satisfaction, the admiration unanimously excited by his costume, were dissipated by his words; and when he arrived at that unhappy conclusion, 'as soon as the most eminent cardinal is arrived, we shall begin,' his voice was lost in a thunder of hooting.

'Begin immediately! The mystery! the mystery at once!' cried the people. And above all the other voices was heard that of Joannes de Molendino, piercing through the general uproar, like the sound of the fife in a charivari at Nimes. 'Begin directly!' squeaked the scholar.

'Down with Jupiter and the Cardinal de Bourbon!' vociferated Robin Poussepain and the other young clerks perched in the window.

'The morality directly!' repeated the crowd immediately; 'go on! go on! The sack and the rope for the actors and the cardinal!'

Poor Jupiter, haggard, frightened, pale under his rouge, let fall his thunderbolts, took his bicoquet in his hand; then, bowing and trembling, he stammered: 'His eminence – the ambassadors – Madame Margaret of Flanders' – he knew not what to say.

The fact was, he was afraid he should be hanged – hanged by the populace for waiting, or hanged by the cardinal for not having waited – on either hand he beheld an abyss, that is to say, a gallows.

Happily, some one came forward to extricate him and assume the responsibility.

An individual who stood within the railing, in the space which it left clear around the marble table, and whom no one had yet perceived, so completely was his long and slender person sheltered from every visual ray by the diameter of the pillar against which he had set his back – this individual, we say, tall, thin, pale, light complexioned – still young, though wrinkles were already visible in his forehead and his cheeks – with sparkling eyes and a smiling mouth – clad in a garment of black serge, threadbare and shining with age – approached the marble table, and made a sign to the poor sufferer. But the other, in his perturbation, did not observe it.

The new-comer advanced another step forward.

'Jupiter,' said he, 'my dear Jupiter!'

The other did not hear him.

At last, the tall, fair man, losing all patience, shouted almost under his nose, 'Michel Giborne!'

'Who calls me?' said Jupiter, as if starting from a trance.

'I do,' answered the personage clad in black.

'Ah!' exclaimed Jupiter.

'Begin directly,' returned the other; 'satisfy the people, and I take upon myself to appease monsieur the bailiff, who will appease monsieur the cardinal.'

Jupiter now took breath. 'Messeigneurs les bourgeois,' cried he, at the utmost stretch of his lungs, to the multitude who continued to hoot him, 'we are going to begin directly.'

'*Evoe! Jupiter! plaudite, cives!*' (Well done, Jupiter! applaud, citizens!) cried the scholars .

'Noël! Noël!' cried the people. (That cry being the burden of a canticle sung in the churches at Christmas, in honour of the Nativity, whence, apparently, it was adopted by the populace as a general mark of approbation and jubilation as long as the season lasted.)

Then followed a deafening clapping of hands, and the hall still shook with acclamations when Jupiter had withdrawn behind his tapestry.

Meanwhile, the unknown, who had so magically changed the 'tempest into calm,' as says our old and dear Corneille, had modestly retired into the penumbra of his pillar, and would no doubt have remained there, invisible, and motionless, and mute as before, if he had not been drawn from it by two young women, who, being in the first line of the spectators, had remarked his colloquy with Michel Giborne-Jupiter.

'Maître,' said one of them, beckoning to him to approach.

'Hush! my dear Liénarde,' said her fair neighbour, pretty, blooming, and quite courageous by virtue of her holiday attire – 'it is not a clerk, it is a layman. You should not say *Maître*, but – *Messire*.'

'Messire!' then said Liénarde.

The unknown approached the balustrade.

'What is your pleasure with me, mesdemoiselles?' asked he impressively.

'Oh, nothing,' said Liénarde, all confused. 'It's my neighbour here, Gisquette la Gencienne, that wants to speak to you.'

'No, no,' rejoined Gisquette, blushing; 'it was Liénarde that said *Maître* to you – I only told her that she should say Messire.'

The two girls cast down their eyes. The gentleman who asked nothing better than to enter into conversation, looked at them, smiling:

'You have nothing to say to me, then, mesdemoiselles?'

'Oh, no, nothing at all,' answered Gisquette.

'Nothing,' said Liénarde.

The tall, fair young man made a step to retire; but the two curious damsels were not inclined to let him go so soon.

'Messire,' said Gisquette, with the impetuosity of water escaping through a sluice, or a woman taking a resolution, 'you then know this soldier who is going to play Madame the Virgin in the mystery?'

'You mean the role of Jupiter,' returned the unknown.

'Oh, dear, yes,' said Liénarde; 'is she not stupid! You are acquainted with Jupiter, then?'

'With Michel Giborne!' answered the unknown, 'yes, madam.'

'He has a grand beard!' answered Liénarde.

'Will it be very fine, what they are all going to say?' asked Gisquette, timidly.

'Very fine indeed, mademoiselle,' answered the informant without the least hesitation. "What will it be?' asked Liénarde.

'*The Good Award of Madame the Virgin* – a morality, if it please you, mademoiselle.'

'Ah! that's different,' returned Liénarde.

A short silence followed, which was broken by the stranger. 'It is a morality entirely new,' said he, 'which has never yet been played.'

'Then is it not the same,' said Gisquette, 'as was played two years ago on the day of the entry of monsieur the legate, and in which three beautiful girls performed – '

'As sirens,' interrupted Liénarde.

'And quite naked,' added the young man.

Liénarde modestly cast down her eyes. Gisquette looked at her, and did likewise. The other continued, smiling, 'It was a very pretty thing to see. But to-day it is a morality made on purpose for the Lady of Flanders.'

'Will they sing pastorals?' asked Gisquette.

'Oh, fie!' said the unknown. 'What! in a morality! We must not confound one kind of pieces with another. In a shepherd's song, indeed, it would be quite right.'

'That's a pity,' rejoined Gisquette. 'That day there were, at the fountain of Ponceau, savage men and women scrambling and making gestures, singing catches couplets and pastorals.'

'That which is suitable for a legate,' said the stranger, very dryly, 'is not suitable for a princess.'

'And near them,' continued Liénarde, 'played a number of bass instruments, that gave out wonderful melodies.'

'And to refresh the passengers,' resumed Gisquette, 'the fountain threw out, by three mouths, wine, milk, and hyppocrass, and everybody drank that liked.'

'And a little below the Ponceau fountain,' continued Liénarde, 'at the Trinity, there was a Passion performed without speech.'

'Oh, yes, how I remember!' exclaimed Gisquette; 'Our Lord on the cross, and the two thieves on each side of Him!'

Here the young gossips, warming in the recollection of the legate's entry, talked both at once.

'And further on, at the Artists' gate, there were other characters very richly habited' –

'And do you remember, at St. Innocent's fountain, that huntsman following a hind, with a great noise of dogs and hunting horns?' –

'And then at the meat-market, those scaffolds that represented the Bastile of Dieppe' –

'And when the legate was going by, you know, Gisquette, they gave the assault, and the English all had their throats cut' –

'And what fine characters there were over by the Châtelet gate!'

'And on the Pont-au-Change, which was all hung with cloth from one end to the other.'

'And when the legate crossed over, they let fly from the bridge above two hundred dozen of all kinds of birds. Was that not a fine sight, Liénarde?'

'There will be a finer to-day,' at length interrupted their interlocutor, who seemed to listen to them with impatience.

'You promise us that this shall be a fine mystery,' said Gisquette.

'Without doubt.' returned he. And then he added, with peculiar emphasis, 'Mesdemoiselles, *I* it is who am the author of it.'

'Say you so!' cried the young women, open-mouthed.

'Yes, in truth,' answered the poet, bridling a little – 'that is to say, there are two of us – Jehan Marchand, who has sawn the planks and put together the framework of the theatre; and I, who have written the piece. My name is Pierre Gringoire.'

The author of the Cid himself could not have more proudly said, 'My name is Pierre Corneille.'

The reader may have observed that some time must already have elapsed since the moment at which Jupiter retired behind the drapery and that at which the author of the new morality revealed himself thus abruptly to the simple admiration of Gisquette and Liénarde. It is worthy of remark that all that assemblage, who a few minutes before had been so tumultuous, now waited quietly on the faith of the player's promise – an evidence of this everlasting truth, still daily noted in our theatres – that the best means of making the audience wait patiently is, to assure them that the performance is about to begin.

However, the schoolboy Joannes was not asleep. 'Hello!' shouted he suddenly, amidst the peaceful expectation which had succeeded the disturbance. 'Jupiter! Madame the Virgin! you devil's boatmen! are you joking with one another? The piece! the piece! Begin! or it is we who will begin again!'

This was enough. A music of high and low-keyed instruments now struck up underneath the stage; the hangings were lifted, and four characters in motley attire, with painted faces, issued forth, clambered up the steep ladder already mentioned, and reaching the upper platform, drew up in line before the audience, whom they saluted with a profound obeisance, whereupon the musical sounds ceased and the mystery began.

The four characters, after receiving abundant payment for their salutations in the plaudits of the multitude, commenced, amidst a profound silence, the delivery of a prologue, which we gladly spare the reader. However, as is still the case in our own time, the audience paid more attention to the gowns they wore than to the parts they were enacting – and in truth they did right. They were all four clad in robes half yellow and half white, differing only in the nature of the material; the first being of gold and silver brocade, the second of silk, and the third of wool, and the fourth of coarse linen. The first character carried in the right hand a sword; the second, two golden keys; the third, a pair of scales; and the fourth, a spade: and in order to assist such indolent minds as might not have seen clearly through the transparency of these attributes, there might be read in large black letters worked at the bottom of the brocade gown, MY NAME IS NOBILITY; at the bottom of the silken one, MY NAME IS CLERGY; at the bottom of the woollen, MY NAME IS TRADE; and at the bottom of the linen garment, MY NAME IS LABOUR. The sex of the two male characters was clearly indicated to every judicious spectator by the comparative shortness of their garments and the *cramignole* (flat cap) which they wore upon their heads; while the two female characters, besides that their robes were of ampler length, were distinguishable by their hoods.

One would also have been very dull not to have discovered through the poetic drapery of the prologue, that Labour was married to Trade, and Clergy to Nobility, and that these two happy couples possessed in common a magnificent golden dolphin which they intended to adjudge only to the most beautiful damsel. Accordingly, they were going over the world in search of this beauty; and after successively rejecting the Queen of Golconda, the Princess of Trebizond, the daughter of the Cham of Tartary, etc., etc.; Labour and Clergy, Nobility and Trade, were come to rest themselves upon the marble table of the Palace of Justice, and deliver at the same time to the worthy auditory as many moral sentences and maxims as might in that day be expended upon the members of the faculty of arts, at the examinations, sophisms, determinances, figures and acts, at which the masters took their degrees.

All this was truly very fine.

Meanwhile, in all that assemblage upon which the four allegorical personages seemed to be striving which could pour out the most copious floods of metaphor, no ear was so attentive, no heart so palpitating, no eye so eager, no neck so outstretched, as were the eye, ear, neck and heart of the author, the poet, the brave Pierre Gringoire, who a moment before had been unable to forego the joy of telling his name to two fair damsels.

He had retired a few paces from them, behind his pillar; and there it was that he listened, looked and enjoyed. The benevolent plaudits which had greeted the opening of his prologue still resounded in his breast; and he was completely absorbed in that species of ecstatic contemplation with which a dramatic author marks his ideas falling one by one from the lips of the actor, amid the silence of a crowded auditory. Happy Pierre Gringoire!

It pains us to relate, this first ecstasy was very soon disturbed. Scarcely had Gringoire's lips approached this intoxicating cup of joy and triumph before a drop of bitterness was cruelly mingled in it.

A tattered mendicant who, lost as he was among the crowd, could receive no contributions, and who, we may suppose, had not found sufficient indemnity in the pockets of his neighbours, had bethought himself of roosting on some conspicuous perch from which to attract the attention and the alms of the good people. Accordingly, during the first lines of the prologue, he had hoisted himself up by means of the pillars that supported the reserved gallery, to the cornice which ran along the bottom of its balustrade; and there he had seated himself, soliciting the attention and the pity of the multitude by the display of his rags, and of a hideous sore that covered his right arm. He did not, however, utter a word.

His silence allowed the prologue to proceed without any disraction-and no noticeable disorder would have occurred had not, as ill luck would have it, the boy Joannes espied, from his perch at the top of one of the great pillars, the beggar and his grimaces. The young wag burst into an immoderate fit of laughter; and, regardless of the interruption to the performance, and the disturbance of the general attention, cried out in a tone of gaiety, 'See now! The mangy beggar there asking alms!'

Any one that has ever thrown a stone into a pond full of frogs or fired a gun among a flock of birds, may form an idea of the effect produced by these unseasonable words dropped in the midst of the universal attention. Gringoire started as if he had felt an electric shock. The prologue stopped short; and all heads were turned tumultuously toward the mendicant, who, far from being disconcerted, found in this incident a good opportunity of reaping a harvest, and began to cry out with a doleful whine, half shutting his eyes, 'Charity! if you please.'

'I say, on my soul,' cried Joannes, 'it's Clopin Troillefou. Hello! friend – so thy sore wasn't comfortable on thy leg, that thou'st changed it to thine arm?'

So saying he threw, with the dexterity of a monkey, a small white coin into the old greasy hat which the beggar held out with his diseased arm. The beggar received without change of expression both the alms and the sarcasm, and continued in a piteous tone 'Charity! if you please.'

This episode had considerably distracted the audience; and a goodly number of the spectators, with Robin Poussepain and all the clerks leading, merrily applauded this whimsical duet which had been struck up thus unexpectedly in the middle of the prologue, between the urchin with his shrill voice, and the beggar with his imperturbable drone.

Gringoire was grievously displeased. Having recovered from his first stupefaction, he shouted earnestly to the four characters or the stage, 'Go on! – what the devil! – go on;' without even deigning to cast a look of disdain at the two interrupters.

At that moment he felt some one pulling at the skirt of his coat; he turned round, not without some little annoyance, and forced with some difficulty a smile. Nevertheless he found it necessary to do so, for it was the pretty arm of Gisquette la Gencienne, which, extended through the balustrade, thus solicited his attention.

'Monsieur,' said the girl, 'will they go on?'

'Surely,' answered Gringoire, shocked at the question.

'Oh, then, messire,' she resumed, 'would you have the courtesy to explain to me – '

'What they are going to say?' interrupted Gringoire. 'Well – listen. '

'No,' said Gisquette, 'but what they have said already.'

Gringoire started as if touched to the quick.

'A plague on the little stupid, witless wench!' said he between his teeth.

From that moment Gisquette ceased to exist in his mind.

Meanwhile the actors had obeyed his injunction; and the audience, observing that they were once again trying to make themselves heard, had set themselves to listen – not, however, without having lost certain points of beauty in the soldering together of the two parts of the piece which had been so abruptly cut short. Gringoire reflected bitterly. However, tranquillity had been gradually restored; the schoolboy held his tongue, the beggar counted some coin in his hat, and the piece had resumed its sway.

It was really a very fine composition, and we think it might be turned to some account, even now, by means of a few changes. The performance, rather long indeed, and rather dry, was simple; and Gringoire, in the candid sanctuary of his own judgment, admired its clearness. As may well be supposed, the four allegorical personages were a little fatigued with travelling over the three known quarters of the world without finding an opportunity of suitably disposing of their golden dolphin. Thereupon a long eulogy upon the marvellous fish with numberless delicate allusions to the young prince betrothed to Margaret of Flanders – which young prince was at that time in very dismal seclusion at Amboise, without the slightest suspicion that Labour and Clergy, Nobility and Trade, had just been making the tour of the world on his account. The dolphin aforesaid, then, was young, was handsome, was vigorous, and above all (magnificent origin of all the royal virtues!) was son of the lion of France. I declare that this bold metaphor is admirable, and that dramatic natural history, on a day of allegory and of a royal epithalamium, finds nothing at all shocking in a dolphin the son of a lion. On the contrary, it is precisely those rare and pindaric mixtures that prove the popular enthusiasm. However, to have disarmed criticism altogether, the poet might have developed this fine idea in less than two hundred verses. It is true that the mystery was to last, according to the order of monsieur the provost, from noon till four o'clock, and that it was necessary to say something. Moreover, it was patiently listened to.

All at once, in the midst of a fine quarrel between Mademoiselle Trade and Madame Nobility, at the moment when Master Labour was pronouncing this predictive line:

Beast more triumphant ne'er in woods was seen

the door of the reserved gallery, which had until then been so inopportunely shut, opened still more inopportunely, and the stentorian voice of the usher, abruptly announced, 'His Eminence Monsieur, the Cardinal of Bourbon!'

III

The Cardinal

POOR GRINGOIRE! The noise of all the great double petards let off on Saint John's day – the discharge of a score of crooked arquebusses – the report of that famous serpentine of the Tour de Billy which, during the siege of Paris, on Sunday, the 29th of September, 1465, killed seven Burgundians at a shot – the explosion of all the gunpowder stored at the Temple gate – would have split his ears less violently at that solemn and dramatic moment, than those few words from the lips of an usher, 'His Eminence Monsieur, the Cardinal of Bourbon.'

It is not that Pierre Gringoire either feared the cardinal or despised him. He was neither weak enough to do the one, nor presumptuous enough to do the other. A true eclectic, as one would say now-a-days, Gringoire was one of those firm and elevated spirits, calm and temperate, who can preserve their composure under all circumstances – *stare in dimidio rerum* – and who are full of reason and of a liberal philosophy even while making some account of cardinals. Invaluable and uninterrupted line of philosophers – to whom wisdom, like another

Ariadne, seems to have given a skein which they have gone on unwinding from the beginning of the world through the labyrinth of human affairs. They are to be found in all times, and ever the same – that is to say, ever in accord with the times. And not to mention our Pierre Gringoire, who would be their representative of the fifteenth century if we could succeed in obtaining for him the distinction which he deserves, it was certainly their spirit which animated Father du Breul in the sixteenth, when writing these words of sublime simplicity, worthy of any age: 'I am a Parisian by birth, and a *parrhisian* by my speech; for *parrhisia* in Greek signifies liberty of speech, which liberty I have used even to messeigneurs the cardinals, uncle and brother to monseigneur the Prince of Conti, albeit with respect for their greatness, and without giving offence to any of their train, and that is a great deal to say.'

So there was neither hatred for the cardinal, nor contempt of his presence in the disagreeable impression which he made upon Pierre Gringoire. On the contrary, our poet had too much good sense and too threadbare a coat not to attach a particular value to the circumstance, that several allusions in his prologue, and in particular the glorification of the dolphin, son of the lion of France, would fall upon the ear of so eminent a personage. But personal interest is not the ruling motive in the noble nature of poets. Supposing the entity of a poet to be represented by the number ten, it is certain that a chemist, on analyzing and pharmacopœizing, as Rabelais says, would find it to be composed of one part of self-interest with nine parts of self-esteem. Now, at the moment when the door was opened to admit the cardinal, Gringoire's nine parts of self-esteem, inflated and expanded by the breath of popular admiration, were in a state of prodigious enlargement, quite overwhelming and smothering that imperceptible molecule of self-interest which we just now distinguished in the constitution of poets – a precious ingredient, by-the-way, a ballast of reality and humanity, without which they would never touch the earth. It was a delight to Gringoire to see and feel that an entire assemblage (of poor varlets, it is true, but what then?) were stupefied, petrified, and breathless by the immeasurable tirades which burst from every part of his epithalamium. I affirm that he himself shared the general beatitude; and that, quite the reverse of La Fontaine, who, at the performance of his play of *The Florentine*, asked, 'What poor wretch has written that rhapsody?' Gringoire would willingly have asked of his neighbour, 'By whom is this masterpiece?' It may, therefore, be supposed what sort of effect as produced upon him by the brusque and tempestuous arrival of the cardinal.

His fears were but too fully realized. The entrance of his Eminence disorganized the audience completely. All eyes were turned toward the gallery, and there was a general buzz: 'The cardinal! the cardinal!' repeated every tongue. The unfortunate prologue was cut short a second time.

The cardinal stopped a moment upon the threshold of the gallery; and while casting his eyes with great indifference over the assemblage the tumult redoubled. Each one wished to obtain a better view of him. Each one stretching his neck over his neighbour's shoulder.

He was in truth an exalted personage, the sight of whom was worth almost any other spectacle. Charles, Cardinal de Bourbon, Archbishop and Count of Lyons, and Primate of Gaul, was allied both to Louis XI, through his brother Pierre, Seigneur of Beaujeu, who had espoused the king's eldest daughter, and at the same time to Charles the Bold, through his mother, Agnes of Burgundy. Now, the ruling, the characteristic, the distinctive feature in the character of the Primate of Gaul, was his courtier-like spirit and his devotion to power. Hence, it may well be supposed in what numberless perplexities this double relationship had involved him, and among how many temporal shoals his spiritual bark must have tacked, to have escaped foundering either upon Louis or upon Charles, the Charybdis and the Scylla which had swallowed up the Duke of Nemours and the Constable of Saint-Pol. Heaven be praised, however, he had got happily through his voyage, and reached Rome without accident. But although he was now in port – and indeed, precisely because he was in port – he never recollected, without a feeling of uneasiness, the various chances of his political life, which had so long been both perilous and laborious. So, also, he used to say, that the year 1476 had been to him both a black and white year, meaning thereby that he had lost in that one year his mother, the Duchess of Bourbonnais, and his cousin, the Duke of Burgundy, and that mourning the one had consoled him for the other.

However, he was a very worthy man; he led a joyous cardinal's life; was wont to make merry with wine of the royal vintage of Challuau; did not detest Richarde-la-Gamoise and Thomasse-la-Saillarde; gave alms to pretty girls rather than old women; and for all these reasons was in great favour with the populace of Paris. He always went surrounded by a little court of bishops and abbots of high degree, gallant, jovial, and fond of good eating; and more than once had the good devotees of Saint Germain d'Auxerre, in passing at night under the windows of the Hôtel de Bourbon, all blazing with light, been scandalized by hearing the same voices which had sung vespers to them in the day-time, chanting to the sound of glasses, the bacchanalian proverb of Benedict XII, the pope who had added a third crown to the tiara – *Bibamus papaliter.* (Let us drink like the popes.)

No doubt it was this popularity, so justly acquired, which, upon his entrance, prevented any unpleasant reception on the part of the mob, who a few minutes before had been so dissatisfied, and so little disposed to pay respect to a cardinal, even on the day when they were going to elect a pope. (The Lord of Misrule was called the Fools' Pope.) But the Parisians bear little malice; and besides, by ordering the performance to begin by their own authority, the good citizens had had the better of the cardinal, and this triumph satisfied them. Moreover, Monsieur le Cardinal de Bourbon was a handsome man – he had on a vastly fine scarlet robe, which he wore in excellent style – which is to say, that he had in his favour all the women, and, consequently, the better part of the audience. Certainly it would be both injustice and bad taste to hoot a cardinal for being too late at the play when he is a handsome man, and wears well his scarlet robe.

He entered, then, saluted the company with that hereditary smile which the great have always in readiness for the people, and moved slowly towards his armchair of crimson velvet placed for his reception, looking as if some other matter occupied his mind. His escort – or what we should now call his staff – of bishops and priests, issued after him upon the gallery, not without exciting redoubled tumult and curiosity among the spectators below. All were busied in pointing them out, or in telling their names, each one striving to show that he knew at least some one of them; one pointing to the Bishop of Marseilles (Alaudet, if we remember right); some to the Dean of Saint Denis; others to Robert de Lespinasse, Abbot of the great neighbouring monastery of Saint-Germain-des-Prés, the libertine brother of a mistress of Louis XI – all their names being repeated with a thousand mistakes and mispronunciations. As for the students, they swore. It was their own day – their Feast of Fools – their saturnalia – the annual orgies of the *basoche* (Lawyers' clerks of the Parliament of Paris) and the schools. No liberty but was permissible that day. And then there were numberless wanton hussies among the crowd – Simone Quatre-livres, Agnès-la-Gadine, Robine Piédebou. Was it not the least that could be expected, that they should swear at their ease, and profane God's name a little, on such a day as that, in such a goodly company of churchmen and courtezans? And accordingly, they did not mince matters; but amidst the uproarious applause a frightful din of blasphemies and obscenities proceeded from all those tongues let loose, those tongues of clerks and scholars, tied up all the rest of the year by the fear of Saint Louis's branding-iron. Poor Saint Louis! how they set him at defiance in his own Palace of Justice! Each one of them had singled out among the newly-arrived company in the gallery some one of the cassocks, black, gray, white, or violet. As for Joannes Frollo de Molendino, and his being brother to an archdeacon, it was the red robe that he audaciously assailed, singing out as loud as he could bawl, and fixing his shameless eyes upon the cardinal, *'Cappa repleta mero!'* (Head, or hood, full of wine.)

All these particulars, which are thus clearly detailed for the reader's edification, were so completely covered by the general hum of the multitude that they were lost before they could reach the reserved gallery; though, indeed, the cardinal would have been little moved by them; so completely did the license of the day belong to the customs of the age. He had something else to think of, which preoccupation appeared in his manner – another cause of solicitude, which followed closely behind him, and made its appearance in the gallery almost at the same time as himself. This was the Flemish embassy.

Not that he was a profound politician, or concerned himself about the possible consequences of the marriage of madame, his cousin, Margaret of Burgundy, with monsieur, his cousin, Charles, Dauphin of Vienne – nor how long the patched-up reconciliation between the Duke of Austria and the French king might endure – nor how the King of England would take this slight toward his daughter. All this gave him little anxiety; and he did honour each night to the wine of the royal vineyard of Chaillot without ever suspecting that a few flasks of that same wine (revised and corrected a little by the physician Coictier), cordially presented to Edward IV by Louis XI, might possibly, some fine morning, rid Louis XI of Edward IV. The most honourable embassy of the Duke of Austria brought none of these cares to the cardinal's mind, but annoyed him in another respect. It was, in truth, somewhat hard, and we have already said a word or two about it in the first pages of this book, that he should be obliged to give welcome and entertainment – he, Charles de Bourbon – to obscure burghers; he, a cardinal, to a pack of scurvy sheriffs – he, a Frenchman and a connoisseur in good living, to Flemish beerdrinkers – and in public, too! Certes, it was one of the most irksome parts he had ever gone through for the *bon plaisir* of the king.

However, he had so perfectly studied his role, that he turned toward the door with the best grace in the world, when the usher announced in a sonorous voice, 'Messieurs the Envoys of the Duke of Austria!' It is needless to say that the entire hall did likewise.

Then appeared, two by two, with a gravity which strongly contrasted with the flippant air of the cardinal's ecclesiastical train, the forty-eight ambassadors from Maximilian of Austria, having at their head the reverend father in God, Jehan, Abbot of Saint-Bertin, chancellor of the Golden Fleece, and Jacques de Goy, Lord of Dauby, high bailiff of Ghent. A deep silence now took place in the assemblage, occasionally interrupted by smothered laughter at all the uncouth names which each of these personages transmitted with imperturbable gravity to the usher, who then gave out their names and callings, pell-mell and with all sorts of mutilations, to the crowd below. There were Maître Loys Roelof, Sheriff of the town of Louvain; Messire Clays d'Etuelde,

Sheriff of Brussels; Messire Paul de Baeust, Lord of Voirmizelle, president of Flanders; Maître Jehan Coleghens, burgomaster of the city of Antwerp; Maître George de la Moere, principal sheriff of the *kuere* of the city of Ghent; Maître Gheldolf van der Hage, principal sheriff of the *parchons* of the said city; and the Sieur de Bierbecque, and Jehan Pinnock, and Jehan Dimaerzelle, etc., etc., etc., bailiffs, sheriffs and burgomasters – burgomasters, sheriffs and bailiffs – all stiff, sturdy, starched figures, dressed out in Sunday clothes of velvet and damask, and hooded with black velvet *cramignoles* decorated with great tufts of gold thread of Cyprus – good Flemish heads after all, with severe and respectable countenances, akin to those which Rembrandt has made stand out with such force and gravity from the dark background of his picture of *The Night Watch* – personages on every one of whose foreheads it was written, that Maximilian of Austria was right in 'confiding to the full,' as his manifesto expressed it 'in their sense, valour, experience, loyalty and good prudence.'

There was one exception, however; it was a face, subtle, intelligent, crafty-looking – a mixture of the monkey and the diplomatist – toward whom the cardinal made three steps in advance and a low bow, but who, nevertheless, was called simply Guillaume Rym, counsellor and pensionary of the town of Ghent.

Few persons at that time knew aught of Guillaume Rym – a rare genius, who, in a time of revolution, would have appeared with *éclat* on the surface of events, but who, in the fifteenth century, was confined to the practice of covert intrigue and to 'live in the mines,' as the Duke de Saint-Simon expresses it. However, he was appreciated by the first 'miner' in Europe – he frequently lent a helping hand in the secret operations of Louis XI – all which was perfectly unknown to this multitude, who were amazed at the cardinal's politeness to that sorry-looking Flemish bailiff.

IV

Master Jacques Coppenole

AT THE MOMENT when the pensioner of Ghent and his Eminence were exchanging a very low bow, and a few words in a tone still lower, a man of lofty stature, large-featured, and broad-shouldered, presented himself to enter abreast with Guillaume Rym, looking something like a mastiff dog by the side of a fox. His felt hat and his leathern jerkin were oddly conspicuous amidst the velvet and silk that surrounded him. Presuming it to be some groom who knew not whither he was going, the usher stopped him.

'Hold, friend! you cannot pass.'

The man of the leathern jerkin shouldered him aside. 'What would this fellow with me?' said he, in a thundering voice, which drew the attention of the entire hall to this strange colloquy. 'Seest thou not that I am of the party?'

'Your name?' demanded the usher.

'Jacques Coppenole.'

'Your titles?'

'A hosier, at the sign of the Three Chains at Ghent.'

The usher shrank back. To announce sheriffs and burgomasters might indeed be endured – but a hosier! – it was too bad. The cardinal was upon thorns. The people were looking and listening. For two days his Eminence had been doing his utmost to smooth these Flemish bears into presentable shape, and this freak was too much for him. Meanwhile Guillaume Rym, with his cunning smile, went up to the usher. 'Announce Maître Jacques Coppenole, clerk to the sheriffs of the city of Ghent,' said he to the officer in a very low whisper.

'Usher,' then said the cardinal aloud, 'announce Maître Jacques Coppenole, clerk to the sheriffs of the illustrious city of Ghent.'

This was an error. Guillaume Rym, by himself, would have evaded the difficulty; but Coppenole had heard the cardinal's direction.

'No! by the Holy Rood!' he cried, with his voice of thunder: 'Jacques Coppenole, hosier. Dost thou hear, usher? Neither more nor less. By the Holy Rood! a hosier – that's fine enough. Monsieur the archduke has more than once sought his gloves among my hose.'

A witticism is quickly appreciated in Paris and this occasioned a burst of laughter and applause from the people below.

We must add that Coppenole was one of the people, and that the audience around him were of the people also; so that the communication between them and him had been quick, electric, and, as it were, on equal footing. The lofty airs which the Flemish hosier gave himself, while humbling the courtiers, had stirred in the plebeian breasts a certain latent feeling of dignity, of independence, which, in the fifteenth century, was as yet vague and undefined. They beheld one of their equals in this hosier, who had just borne himself so sturdily before the cardinal – a comforting reflection to poor devils accustomed to pay respect and obedience even to the servants of the sergeants of the bailiff of the Abbot of Sainte Geneviève, the cardinal's train-bearer.

Coppenole bowed haughtily to his Eminence, who returned the salute of the all-powerful burgher, formidable to Louis XI. Then, while Guillaume Rym, *sage homme et maliciex* (wise and malicious), as Philippe de Comines expresses it, followed them both with a smile of raillery and superiority, they moved each to his place – the cardinal thoughtful and out of countenance – Coppenole quite at his ease, thinking, no doubt, that, after all, his title of hosier was as good as another, and that Mary of Burgundy, mother of that Margaret for whose marriage he was to-day treating, would have feared less the cardinal than the hosier, for no cardinal would have aroused the people of Ghent against the favourites of the daughter of Charles the Bold; nor could any cardinal, by a single word, have hardened the multitude against her tears and prayers, when the Lady of Flanders came and supplicated her people on their behalf, even to the foot of the scaffold, while the hosier had only to raise his leathern elbow to cause both your heads to be struck off, most illustrious seigneurs, Guy d'Hymbercourt and Chancellor Guillaume Hugonet.

However, the poor cardinal had not yet finished penance; he was doomed to drain to the dregs the chalice of being in such bad company.

The reader has doubtless not forgotten the audacious mendicant, who at the time of the commencement of the prologue, had climbed up to the fringes of the dais reserved for the cardinal. The arrival of the illustrious guests had in no way disturbed him; and while the prelates and the ambassadors were packing themselves away like real Flemish herrings within the narrow compass of the tribune, he had made himself quite comfortable, with his legs bravely crossed upon the architrave. This insolence was extraordinary; yet nobody had remarked it at the first moment, all attention being fixed elsewhere. He, for his part, took notice of nothing in the hall; he was wagging his head backward and forward with the unconcern of a Neapolitan beggar, repeating from time to time, amidst the general hum, and as if by a mechanical habit, 'Charity, if you please!' and indeed, among all present, he was probably the only one who would not have deigned to turn his head on hearing the altercation between Coppenole and the usher. Now it so chanced that his hosiership of Ghent, with whom the people already were warmly in sympathy, and upon whom all eyes were fixed, went and seated himself in the front line of the gallery, just over the place where the beggar was sitting; and it excited no small amazement to see the Flemish ambassador, after scrutinizing the fellow beneath him, give him a friendly slap upon his ragged shoulder. The beggar turned. Surprise, recognition and kindly gratulation were visible in both faces; then, without giving themselves the slightest concern about the spectators, the hosier and the leper fell into conversation in a low voice, clasping each other by the hand; while the tattered arm of Clopin Trouillefou, displayed at length upon the cloth of gold that decorated the daïs had somewhat the appearance of a caterpillar upon an orange.

The novelty of this singular scene excited such wild gaiety among the crowd that the cardinal soon remarked it: he leaned forward; and as, from the point where he was situated, he caught only an imperfect glimpse of Trouillefou's ignominious garment, he figured to himself that the beggar was soliciting alms, and, shocked at his audacity, he exclaimed, 'Monsieur the bailiff of the Palace, throw me that fellow into the river.'

'By God's Cross! monseigneur le cardinal,' said Coppenole, without leaving hold of Clopin's hand, 'this is one of my friends.'

'Noël! Noël!' cried the mob. And from that moment Maître Coppenole had in Paris, as in Ghent, 'great credit with the people; as men of great stature have,' said Philippe de Comines, 'when they are thus presuming.' The cardinal bit his lip. He leaned toward the Abbot of Sainte Geneviève, who sat next him, and said in a half-whisper:

'Pleasant ambassadors, truly, monsieur the archduke sends us to announce the Lady Margaret.'

'Your Eminence's politeness,' returned the abbot, 'is wasted upon these Flemish grunters – *Margaritas ante porcus.*' (Pearls before swine.)

'Say rather,' rejoined the cardinal, smiling, *'porcus ante Margaritam.'* (Swine before pearls.) The whole of the little clerical court were in ecstasy at this play of words. The cardinal felt a little relieved. He was now even with Coppenole, for he too had had his pun applauded.

And now, such of our readers as have the power of generalizing an image or an idea, as we say in the style of to-day, will permit us to ask them whether they figure to themselves quite clearly the spectacle presented, at this moment when we pause to call their attention to the vast parallelogram of the great hall of the Palace.

In the middle of the western wall is a spacious and magnificent gallery hung with drapery of gold brocade, while there enters, in procession, through a small Gothic doorway, a series of grave-looking personages, announced successively by the clamorous voice of the usher; on the first benches are already seated a number of reverend figures enveloped in velvet, ermine and scarlet cloth. About this gallery, which remains silent and stately – below, in front and around – is the multitude and the noise. A thousand looks are cast from the crowd upon every face in the gallery – a thousand murmured repetitions of every name. The spectacle is indeed curious and deserves the attention of the spectators. But what is that down there, quite at the extremity of the hall – that sort of scaffolding, with four motley-attired puppets upon it, and four others below? And at one side of the staging, who is that pale-faced man in a long black sacque? Alas! dear reader, it is Pierre Gringoire and his prologue.

We had all utterly forgotten him.

That is precisely what he had feared.

From the moment at which the cardinal entered, Gringoire had been incessantly exerting himself for the salvation of his prologue. He had first enjoined the actors, who were waiting in suspense, to proceed, and elevate their voices; then, finding that no one listened, he had stopped them; and for nearly a quarter of an hour, during which the interruption had continued, he had been constantly beating with his foot and gesticulating, calling upon Gisquette and Liénarde, and urging those near him to have the prologue proceeded with – but all in vain. No one could be turned aside from the cardinal, the embassy and the gallery – the sole centre of that vast circle of visual rays. It is to be feared also, we regret to say it, that the prologue was beginning to be a little tiresome to the audience at the moment his Eminence's arrival had made so terrible a distraction. And after all, in the gallery, as on the marble table, it was still in fact the same spectacle – the conflict of Labour with Clergy, of Nobility with Trade; and most people liked better to see them in downright reality, living, breathing, elbowing and pushing one another in plain flesh and blood, in that Flemish embassy, in that episcopal court, under the cardinal's robe, under Coppenole's jerkin, than tricked out, painted, talking in verse, and stuffed, as it were, with straw, wearing the yellow and white gowns in which Gringoire had disguised them.

Nevertheless, when our poet saw tranquillity a little restored, he bethought himself of a stratagem which might have saved the performance.

'Monsieur,' said he, turning to one of his neighbours, of fair round figure, with a patient-looking countenance, 'suppose they were to begin again?'

'Begin what?' said the man.

'Why, the mystery,' said Gringoire.

'Just as you please,' returned the other.

This demi-approbation was enough for Gringoire, and taking the affair into his own hands, he began to call out, confounding himself at the same time as much as possible with the crowd. 'Begin the mystery again! – begin again!'

'The devil!' said Joannes de Molendino. 'What is it they're singing out at yon end?' for Gringoire was making the noise of four people. 'Tell me, comrades, is not that mystery finished? They want to begin it again, 'tis not fair.'

'No! no!' cried the students, 'down with the mystery! – down with it!'

But Gringoire only multiplied himself the more, and he bawled the louder – 'Begin again! – begin again!'

These clamours attracted the attention of the cardinal. 'Monsieur the bailiff of the Palace,' quoth he to a tall, dark man who stood but a few paces from him, 'are those knaves in a font of holy water that they make so much noise?'

The bailiff of the Palace was a kind of amphibious magistrate, a sort of bat of the judicial order, a compound of the rat and the bird, of the judge and the soldier.

He approached his Eminence, and with no small apprehension of his displeasure, he stammered forth an explanation of the people's refractoriness – that noon had arrived before his Eminence, and that the players had been forced to begin without waiting for his Eminence.

The cardinal laughed aloud. 'I' faith,' said he, 'monsieur the rector of the University should e'en have done as much. What say you, Maître Guillaume Rym?'

'Monseigneur,' answered Rym, 'let us be content with having escaped one-half the play. 'Tis so much gained.'

'May those rogues go on with their farce?' asked the bailiff.

'Go on – go on,' said the cardinal,' 'tis all the same to me; I shall read my breviary the while.'

The bailiff advanced to the edge of the gallery, and shouted, after procuring silence by a motion of his hand – 'Townsmen! householders! and inhabitants! – to satisfy those who will that the play should begin again, and those who will that it should finish, his Eminence orders that it shall go on.'

Thus both parties were obliged to yield, although both the author and the auditors long bore a grudge on this score against the cardinal.

The characters on the stage accordingly took up their text where they had left off; and Gringoire hoped that at least the remainder of his composition would be listened to. This hope, however, was soon dispelled, like the rest of his illusions. Silence had indeed been somehow or other restored among the audience; but Gringoire had not observed that, at the moment when the cardinal had given his order for the continuance of the play, the gallery was far from being full, and that subsequently to the arrival of the Flemish envoys there were come other persons forming part of the escort, whose names and titles, thrown out in the midst of his dialogue by the intermitted cries of the usher, made considerable ravage in it. Only imagine, in the midst of a theatrical piece, the yelp of a doorkeeper, throwing in, between the two lines of a couplet, and often between the first half of a line and the last, such parentheses as these:

'Maître Jacques Charmolue, king's attorney in the ecclesiastical court!'

'Jehan de Harlay, esquire, keeper of the office of the night-watch of the town of Paris!'

'Messire Galiot de Genoilhac, knight, seigneur of Brussac, master of the king's artillery!'

'Maître Dreux-Raguier, commissioner of our lord the king's waters and forests in the domains of France, Champagne and Brie!'

'Messire Louis de Graville, knight, councillor and chamberlain to the king, admiral of France, guardian of the Bois de Vincennes!'

'Maître Denis le Mercier, governor of the house of the blind at Paris!' etc., etc.

It was becoming insupportable.

All this strange accompaniment, which made it difficult to follow the tenor of the piece, was the more provoking to Gringoire as it was obvious to him that the interest was increasing, and that nothing was needed for his composition but to be listened to. It was, indeed, difficult to imagine a plot more ingeniously or dramatically woven. While the four personages of the prologue were bewailing their hopeless perplexity, Venus in person – *vera incessu patuit dea* (her step revealed the real goddess) – had presented herself before them, clad in a fine coat of mail, having blazoned fair upon its front the ship displayed on the escutcheon of Paris. She was come to claim for herself the dolphin promised to the most beautiful. She was supported by Jupiter, whose thunder was heard to rumble in the dressing-room; and the goddess was about to bear away the prize – that is to say, frankly, to espouse monsieur the dauphin – when a little girl dressed in white damask, and carrying a marguerite or daisy in her hand, (lucid personification of the Lady of Flanders,) had come to contend with Venus. Here were at once theatrical effect and sudden transformation. After a proper dispute, Venus, Margaret, and those behind the scenes had agreed to refer the matter to the wise judgment of the Holy Virgin. There was another fine part, that of Don Pedro, King of Mesopotamia; but amid so many interruptions it was difficult to discover his exact utility. All these personages climbed up the ladder to the stage.

But it was of no use; not one of these beauties was felt or understood. It seemed as if, at the cardinal's entrance, some invisible and magical thread had suddenly drawn away every look from the marble table to the gallery, from the southern extremity of the hall to its western side. Nothing could disenchant the audience; all eyes remained fixed in that direction, and the persons who successively arrived, and their cursed names, and their faces, and their dresses, made a continual diversion. The case was desperate Save Gisquette and Liénarde, who turned aside from time to time when Gringoire pulled them by the sleeve – save the patient fat man who stood near him – no one listened to, no one looked at, the poor abandoned morality. Gringoire, in looking back upon his audience, could see nothing but profiles.

With what bitterness did he see all his fabric of poetry and of glory thus falling to pieces! Only to think that this multitude had been on the point of rebelling against monsieur the bailiff through their impatience to hear his composition: and now that they had it, they were indifferent about it – that same performance which had begun amid such unanimous acclamation! Everlasting ebb and flow of the popular favour! Only to think, that they had been on the point of hanging the bailiff's sergeants! – what would he not have given to have returned to that blissful hour!

The usher's brutal monologue ceased at last; everybody had arrived: so that Gringoire took breath; and the actors were going on bravely, when Maître Coppenole, the hosier, rose suddenly, and Gringoire heard him deliver, in the midst of the universal attention to his piece, this abominable harangue:

'Messieurs the citizens and squires of Paris – by the Holy Rood! I know not what we be doing here. I do indeed see, down in that corner, upon that stage, some people who look as if they wanted to fight. I know not whether that be what ye call a mystery; but I do know that 'tis not amusing. They belabour one another with their tongues, but nothing more. For this quarter of an hour I've been waiting the first blow – but nothing comes – they're cowards, and maul one another but with foul words. You should have had boxers from London or Rotterdam. Aye! then indeed we should have had hard knocks, which ye might have heard even out upon the square – but those creatures there are pitiful. They should at least give us a Morris-dance or some other piece of mummery. This is not what I was told it was to be – I'd been promised a feast of fools with an election of the Lord of Misrule. We at Ghent, too, have our Fools' Pope; and in that, by the Rood! we're behind nobody. But we do thus: – a mob comes together, as here for instance, then each in his turn goes and puts his head through a hole and makes faces at the others; he who makes the ugliest face according to general acclamation, is chosen pope. That's our way, and it's very diverting. Shall we make your pope after the fashion of my country? At any rate it will be less tiresome than listening to those babblers. If they've a mind to come and try their hands at face-making, they shall be in the game. What say ye, my masters? Here's a droll sample enough of both sexes to give us a right hearty Flemish laugh, and we can show ugly mugs enow to give us hopes of a fine grinning-match.'

Gringoire would fain have replied, but amazement, resentment, and indignation deprived him of utterance. Besides, the motion made by the popular hosier was received with such enthusiasm by those townsfolk, flattered at being called squires, that all resistance would have been unavailing. All he could now do was to go with the stream. Gringoire hid his face with both his hands, not being so fortunate as to possess a mantle wherewith to veil, his countenance like the Agamemnon of Timanthes.

V

Quasimodo

IN THE TWINKLING OF an eye, everything was ready for putting Coppenole's idea into execution. Townspeople, students and clerks had all set themselves to work. The small chapel, situated opposite to the marble table, was fixed upon to be the scene of the grimaces. The glass being broken out of one of the divisions of the pretty rose-shaped window over the doorway, left free a circle of stone through which it was agreed that the candidates should pass their heads. To reach it they had to climb upon two casks which had been laid hold of somewhere and placed one upon another. It was settled that each candidate, whether man or woman (for they might make a popess), in order to leave fresh and entire the impression of their grimace, should cover their faces and keep themselves unseen in the chapel until the moment of making their appearance. In less than an instant the chapel was filled with competitors, and the door was closed upon them.

Coppenole, from his place in the gallery, ordered everything, directed everything, arranged everything. During the confusion, the cardinal, no less out of countenance than Gringoire himself, had, on pretext of business and of the hour of vespers, retired with all his suite; while the crowd, among whom his arrival had caused so great a sensation, seemed not to be in the slightest degree interested in his departure. Guillaume Rym was the only one who remarked the retreat of his Eminence. The popular attention, like the sun, pursued its revolution; after beginning at one end of the hall it had stayed for awhile at the middle, and was now at the other end. The marble table, the brocaded gallery, had each had its season of interest; and it was now the turn of Louis XI's chapel. The field was henceforward clear for every sort of extravagance; no one remained but the Flemings and the mob.

The grimaces commenced. The first face that appeared at the hole, with eyelids turned up to show the red, cavernous mouth, and a forehead wrinkled in like our hussar boots in the time of the Empire, excited such an inextinguishable burst of laughter that Homer would have taken all those boors for gods. Nevertheless, the Grande Salle was anything but an Olympus, as no one could better testify than Gringoire's own poor Jupiter. A second face, and a third, succeeded – then another – then another, – the spectators each time laughing and stamping their feet with delight. There was in this spectacle a certain delirious joy – a certain intoxication and fascination – of which it is difficult to give an idea to the reader of the present day and polite society. Let him imagine a series of visages, presenting in succession every geometrical figure, from the triangle to the trapezium, from the cone to the polyhedron – every human expression, from that of anger to that of lust – every age, from the wrinkles of the new-born infant to those of extreme old age – every religious phantasm, from Faunus to Beelzebub – every animal profile, from the jowl to the beak, from the snout to the muzzle. Picture to yourself all the grotesque heads carved on the Pont-Neuf, those nightmares petrified by the hand of Germain Pilon, taking life and breath, and coming one after another to look you in the face with flaming eyes – all the masks of a Venetian carnival passing successively before your eye-glass – in short, a sort of human kaleidoscope.

The orgie became more and more Flemish. Teniers himself would have given but a very imperfect idea of it. Imagine the 'battle' of Salvator Rosa turned to a bacchanal. There was no longer any distinction of scholars, ambassadors, townspeople, men, or women. There was now neither Clopin Trouillefou, nor Gilles Lecornu, nor Marie Quartre-Livres, nor Robin Poussepain. All were confounded in the common license. The Grande Salle had become, as it were, one vast furnace of audacity and joviality, in which every mouth was a shout, every face a grimace, every figure a posture – the sum total howling and roaring. The strange visages that came one after another to grind their teeth at the broken window were like so many fresh brands cast upon the fire; and from all that effervescent multitude there escaped, as the exhalation of the furnace, a noise, sharp, penetrating like the buzzing of the wings of gnats.

'Curse me,' cries one, 'if ever I saw the like of that.'

'Only look at that face.'

'It's nothing.'

'Let's have another.'

'Guillemette Maugerepuis, just look at that bull's muzzle – it wants nothing but horns. It can't be thy husband.'

'Here comes another.'

'By the pope! what sort of a grin's that?'

'Hello! that's not fair. You must show but thy face.'

'That devil, Perette Calebotte! She is capable of such a trick.'

'Nöel! Nöel!'

'Oh! I smother!'

'There's one that can't get his ears through' – etc., etc.

We must, however, do justice to our friend Jehan. In the midst of this infernal revel, he was still to be seen at the top of his pillar like a middy on a top-sail. He was exerting himself with incredible fury. His mouth was wide open, and there issued from it a shriek which, however, no one heard – not that it was drowned by the general clamour, all intense as that was – but because, no doubt it attained the utmost limit of perceptible sharp notes, of the twelve thousand vibrations of Sauveur, or the eight thousand of Biot.

As for Gringoire – as soon as the first moment of depression was over, he had regained his self-possession. He had hardened himself against adversity. 'Go on,' he had said for the third time to his players – who, after all, were mere talking machines – then he strode up and down before the marble table; he felt tempted to go and take his turn at the hole in the chapel-window, if only to have the pleasure of making faces at the ungrateful people. 'But no – that would be unworthy of us – no revenge – let us struggle to the last,' muttered he to himself – 'the power of poetry over the people is great – I will bring them back. We will see which of the two shall prevail – grimaces or belles-lettres.'

Alas! he was left the sole spectator of his piece.

This was worse than before; for instead of profiles, he now saw only backs.

We mistake. The big, patient man whom he had already consulted at a critical moment had remained with his face toward the stage; as for Gisquette and Liénarde, they had deserted long ago.

Gringoire was touched to the heart by the fidelity of his only remaining spectator; he went up to and accosted him, at the same time slightly shaking him by the arm, for the good man had leaned himself against the balustrade, and was taking a gentle nap.

'Monsieur,' said Gringoire, 'I thank you.'

'Monsieur,' answered the big man with a yawn, 'what for?'

'I see what annoys you,' returned the poet; 'all that noise prevents you from hearing comfortably; but make yourself easy – your name shall go down to posterity. Your name, if you please?'

'Renauld Chateau, Keeper of the Seals of the Châtelet of Paris, at your service.'

'Monsieur,' said Gringoire, 'you are here the sole representative of the Muses.'

'You are too polite, monsieur,' answered the Keeper of the Seals of the Châtelet.

'You are the only one,' continued Gringoire, 'who has given suitable attention to the piece. What do you think of it?'

'Why – why,' returned the portly magistrate, but half awake – 'in effect, it was very diverting.'

Gringoire was obliged to content himself with this eulogy, for a thunder of applause, mingled with a prodigious exclamation, cut short their conversation. The Lord of Misrule was at last elected.

'Nöel! Nöel! Nöel!' cried the people from all sides.

It was indeed a miraculous grin that now beamed through the Gothic aperture. After all the figures, pentagonal, hexagonal and heteroclite, which had succeeded each other at the window, without realizing that idea of the grotesque which had formed itself in the imagination of the people heated by the orgie, it required nothing less to gain their suffrages than the sublime grimace which now dazzled the assemblage. Maître Coppenole himself applauded; and Clopin Trouillefou, who had been a candidate, (and God knows his visage could attain an intensity of ugliness), acknowledged himself to be outdone. We shall do likewise. We shall not attempt to give the reader an idea of that tetrahedron nose – that horse-shoe mouth – that small left eye overshadowed by a red bushy brow, while the right eye disappeared entirely under a monstrous wart – of those straggling teeth with breaches here and there like the battlements of a fortress – of that horny lip, over which one of those teeth projected like the tusk of an elephant – of that forked chin – and, above all, of the expression diffused over the whole – that mixture of malice, astonishment and melancholy. Imagination alone can picture this combination.

The acclamation was unanimous; the crowd precipitated itself toward the chapel, and the happy Lord of Misrule was led out in triumph. And now the surprise and admiration of the people redoubled. They found the wondrous grin to be but his ordinary face.

Or rather, his whole person was a grimace. His large head, bristling with red hair – between his shoulders an enormous hump, to which he had a corresponding projection in front – a framework of thighs and legs, so strangely gone astray that they touched only at the knees, and when viewed in front, looked like two sickles joined together by the handles – sprawling feet – monstrous hands – and yet, with all that deformity, a certain awe-inspiring vigour, agility and courage – strange exception to the everlasting rule which prescribes that strength, like beauty, shall result from harmony. Such was the pope whom the fools had just chosen.

One would have said a giant that had been broken and awkwardly mended.

When this sort of cyclop appeared on the threshold of the chapel, motionless, squat, almost as broad as he was high – 'squared by the base,' as a great man has expressed it – the populace recognized him at once by his coat half red and half violet, figured over with little silver bells, and still more by the perfection of his ugliness – and exclaimed with one voice: 'It's Quasimodo the bell-ringer! It's Quasimodo the hunchback of Notre-Dame! Quasimodo the one-eyed! Quasimodo the bandy-legged! Nöel! Nöel!'

The poor devil, it seems, had a choice of surnames.

'All ye pregnant women, get out of the way!' cried the scholars.

'And all that want to be,' added Joannes.

The women, in fact, hid their faces.

'Oh, the horrid baboon!' said one.

'As wicked as he is ugly,' added another.

'It's the devil!' added a third.

'I have the misfortune to live near Notre-Dame, and at night I hear him scrambling in the gutter on the roof.'

'With the cats.'

'He always is on our roofs.'

'He casts spells at us down our chimneys.'

'The other night he came and grinned at me through my attic window. I thought it was a man. I was in such a fright!'

'I'm sure he goes to meet the witches – he once left a broomstick on my leads.'

'Oh, the shocking face of the hunchback!'

'Oh, the horrid creature!'

'Ugh!'

The men, on the contrary, were delighted, applauding loudly.

Quasimodo, the object of the tumult, stood in the doorway of the chapel, gloomy and grave, letting himself be admired.

One of the students (Robin Poussepain, we believe,) laughed in his face, rather too near. Quasimodo quietly took him by the belt and threw him half-a-score yards among the crowd, without uttering a word.

Maître Coppenole, wondering, went up to him. 'By the Rood! Holy Father! why, thou hast the prettiest ugliness I did ever see in my life! Thou wouldst deserve to be pope at Rome as well as at Paris.'

So saying, he clapped his hand merrily upon the other's shoulder. Quasimodo never moved. Coppenole continued: 'Thou art a fellow with whom I long to feast, though it should cost me a new douzain of twelve livres tournois. What say'st thou to it?'

Quasimodo made no answer.

'By the Holy Rood!' cried the hosier, 'art thou deaf?'

He was indeed deaf.

However, he began to be impatient at Coppenole's manners, and he all at once turned toward him with so formidable a grinding of his teeth that the Flemish giant recoiled like a bull-dog before a cat.

A circle of terror and respect was instantly made round this strange personage, the radius of which was at least fifteen geometrical paces. And an old woman explained to Maître Coppenole that Quasimodo was deaf.

'Deaf?' cried the hosier, with his boisterous Flemish laugh. 'Holy Rood! then he's a pope indeed!'

'Ho! I know him,' cried Jehan, who was at last come down from his capital to have a nearer look at Quasimodo; 'it's my brother the archdeacon's bell-ringer. Good-day to you, Quasimodo.'

'What a devil of a man,' said Robin Poussepain, who was bruised from his fall. 'He shows himself – and you see he's a hunchback. He walks – and you see he's bow-legged. He looks at you – and you see he's short an eye. You talk to him – and you find he's deaf. Why, what does this Polyphemus with his tongue?'

'He talks when he lists,' said the old woman. 'He's lost his hearing with ringing of the bells. He's not dumb.'

'No – he's that perfection short,' observed Jehan.

'And has an eye too many,' added Robin Poussepain.

'No, no,' said Jehan, judiciously; 'a one-eyed man is much more incomplete than a blind man, for he knows what it is that's wanting.'

Meanwhile, all the beggars, all the lackeys, all the cutpurses, together with the students, had gone in procession to fetch from the wardrobe of the clerks the pasteboard tiara and the mock robe appropriated to the Fools' Pope or Lord of Misrule. Quasimodo allowed himself to be arrayed in them without a frown, and with a sort of proud docility. They then seated him upon a parti-coloured litter. Twelve officers of the brotherhood of Fools, laying hold of the poles that were attached to it, hoisted him upon their shoulders; and a sort of bitter and disdainful joy seemed to overspread the sullen face of the cyclop when he beheld under his deformed feet all those heads of handsome and well-shaped men. Then the whole bawling and tattered procession set forth to make, according to custom, the inner circuit of the galleries of the Palace, before parading through the streets and squares.

IV

Esmeralda

WE ARE DELIGHTED to inform our readers that during all this scene Gringoire and his piece had held out. His actors, goaded on by himself, had not ceased spouting their parts, nor had he ceased to listen. He had resigned himself to the uproar, and was determined to go on to the end, not despairing of a return of public attention. This gleam of hope revived when he saw Quasimodo, Coppenole, and the noisy train of the Fool's Pope march with great clamour out of the hall. The rest of the crowd rushing eagerly after them. 'Good!' said he to himself – 'there go all the marplots at last!' But, unfortunately, all the hare-brained people composed the audience. In a twinkling the great hall was empty.

It is true there still remained a few spectators, some scattered about, and others grouped around the pillars – women, old men and children – exhausted with the crush and the tumult. A few students still remained astride the window seats looking out into the Place.

'Well,' thought Gringoire, 'here are still enough to hear the end of my mystery. They are few, but they are a select, a literary audience.'

But a moment later a symphony, which was to have produced the greatest impression at the arrival of the Holy Virgin, was missing. Gringoire discovered that his music had been carried off by the procession of the Fools' Pope. 'Do without,' said he stoically.

He approached a group of townspeople who seemed to him to be talking about his piece. Here is the fragment of their conversation which he heard:

'Maître Cheneteau, you know the Hôtel de Navarre, which belonged to Monsieur de Nemours?'

'Oh, yes – opposite to the Chapelle de Braque.'

'Well – the Treasury has just let it to Guillaume Alixandre, heraldry painter, for six livres eight Paris pence a year.'

'How rents are rising!'

'Well, well!' said Gringoire, with a sigh – 'but the others are listening.'

'Comrades!' suddenly cried one of the young fellows in the windows, 'Esmeralda! Esmeralda is in the Square!'

This word produced a magical effect. All who remained in the hall rushed toward the windows, climbing up the walls to see, and repeating 'Esmeralda! Esmeralda!'

At the same time was heard a great noise of applause without.

'What do they mean by Esmeralda?' said Gringoire, clasping his hands in despair. 'Heavens! it seems to be the turn of the windows now!'

He turned toward the marble table, and saw that the performance was interrupted. It was precisely the moment when Jupiter was to enter with his thunder. But Jupiter remained motionless at the foot of the stage.

'Michel Giborne!' cried the irritated poet, 'what art thou doing there? is that thy part? – go up, I tell thee.'

'Alas!' exclaimed Jupiter, 'one of the students has taken away the ladder.'

Gringoire looked. It was but too true. All communication between his plot and its solution was cut off.

'The rascal!' he muttered; 'and why did he take that ladder?'

'To go and see Esmeralda,' cried Jupiter in a piteous tone. 'He said: "Hello! here's a ladder nobody's using;" and away he went with it.'

This was the finishing blow. Gringoire received it with resignation.

'The devil take you all!' said he to the players; 'and if they pay me I'll pay you.'

Then he made his retreat, hanging his head, but the last in the field, like a general who has fought well.

And as he descended the winding staircase of the Palace, 'A fine drove of asses and dolts are these Parisians!' he muttered between his teeth. 'They come to hear a mystery, and pay no attention to it. They were occupied with everybody else – with Clopin Trouillefou – with the cardinal – with Coppenole – with Quasimodo – with the devil! – but with our Lady, the Virgin, not at all. Had I but known it, I'd have given you Virgin Marys, you wretched gapers! And I! for me to come here to see faces, and see nothing but backs! – to be a poet, and have the success of an apothecary! True it is that Homer begged his bread through the villages of Greece, and that Naso died in exile among the Muscovites. But the devil flay me if I understand what they mean by their Esmeralda. Of what language can that word be? – it must be Egyptian!'

BOOK TWO

I

From Charybdis into Scylla

THE NIGHT COMES on early in January. The streets were already growing dark when Gringoire quitted the Palace. This nightfall pleased him; he longed to reach some obscure and solitary alley, that he might there meditate at his ease, and that the philosopher might lay the first healing balm to the wounds of the poet. Philosophy was, indeed, his only refuge, for he knew not where to find a lodging place. After the signal failure of his first dramatic attempt, he dared not return to that which he occupied in the Rue Grenier sur l'Eau, opposite to the Port au Foin; having reckoned upon what the provost was to give him for his epithalamium to enable him to pay to Maître Guillaume Doulx-Sire, collector of the taxes upon cloven-footed beasts brought into Paris, the six months' rent which he owed him, that is to say, twelve pence of Paris, twelve times the value of all he possessed in the world, including his breeches, his shirt and his hat. After a moment's reflection, while sheltered under the wicket gate of the prison belonging to the treasurer of the Sainte Chapelle, as to what place of refuge he should select for the night, all the pavements of Paris being at his service, he recollected having espied, the week before, in the Rue de la Savaterie, at the door of a parliamentary counsellor, a footstone for mounting on mule-back, and having remarked to himself that this stone might serve upon occasion as an excellent pillow for a beggar or a poet. He thanked Providence for having sent him this happy idea; but as he was preparing to cross the Square of the Palace in order to reach the tortuous labyrinth of the City, formed by the windings of all those sister streets, the Rue de la Barillerie, Rue de la Vieille-Draperie, Rue de la Savaterie, Rue de la Juiverie, etc., which are still standing, with their houses of nine stories, he saw the procession of the Fools' Pope, which was also issuing from the Palace, and rushing across the courtyard with loud shouts, with great glare of torches, and with Gringoire's own band of music. This sight revived the blow to his pride, and he fled. In the bitterness of his dramatic misadventure, everything which recalled to his mind the festival of the day irritated his wound, and made it bleed afresh.

He turned to cross the Bridge of Saint Michel, where he found boys running up and down with squibs and crackers.

'A plague on the fireworks!' said Gringoire; and he turned back upon the Exchange Bridge. Attached to the front of the houses at the entrance of the bridge were three banners, representing the king, the dauphin and Margaret of Flanders; and six bannerets on which were portrayed the Duke of Austria, the Cardinal de Bourbon, and Monsieur de Beaujeu, Madame Jeanne of France and Monsieur the bastard of Bourbon, and I know not who else, all illuminated by torches – and a crowd admiring.

'Happy painter, Jehan Fourbault!' said Gringoire, with a heavy sigh, as he turned his back upon the banners. A street lay before him; and it seemed so dark and forsaken that he hoped there to escape his mental sufferings as well as the illuminations; he plunged into it accordingly. A few moments later his foot struck against some obstacle; he stumbled and fell. It was the bundle of hawthorn which the clerks had placed in the morning at the door of a president of the Parliament in honour of the day. Gringoire bore this new accident heroically; he arose, and reached the waterside. After leaving behind him the Civil Tower and the Criminal Tower and passing along by the high wall of the king's gardens, on that unpaved shore in which he sank to the ankles in mud, he arrived at the western end of the City, and stood gazing for some time at the small island of the Passeur aux Vaches (cow ferry-man), which has since disappeared under the bronze horse and esplanade of the Pont-Neuf. The islet appeared to his eyes in the darkness as a black mass beyond the narrow stream of whitish water which separated him from it. He could discern by the rays of a small glimmering light a sort of hut in the form of a beehive, in which the ferryman sheltered himself during the night.

'Happy ferryman!' thought Gringoire, 'thou dreamest not of glory! thou writest not wedding songs – what are the marriages of kings and Burgundian duchesses to thee! Thou knowest no Marguerites but the daisies which thy April greensward gives thy cows to crop! – while I, a poet, am hooted – and shiver – and owe twelve pence – and my shoe-sole is so transparent that thou mightest use it to glaze thy lantern! Thanks, ferryman! thy cabin gives rest to my eyes, and makes me forget Paris!'

He was awakened from his almost lyric ecstasy by a great double Saint John's rocket, which suddenly arose from the peaceful cabin. It was the ferryman also taking his share in the festivities of the day, and letting off his fireworks.

This rocket sent a shiver through Gringoire.

'Oh, cursed holiday!' cried he, 'wilt thou follow me everywhere – good God! even to the ferryman's hut!'

Then he looked into the Seine at his feet, and felt a horrible temptation.

Oh!' said he, 'how willingly would I drown myself – if the water were not so cold!'

Then he took a desperate resolution. It was – since he could not escape the Fools' Pope, Jehan Fourbaults' paintings, the bundles of hawthorn, the squibs and the rockets – to plunge boldly into the very heart of the illumination, and go to the Place de Grève.

'At least,' thought he, 'I shall perhaps get a brand to warm my fingers at the bonfire; and I shall manage to sup on some morsel from the three great shields of royal sugar that were to be set out on the public refectory.'

II

The Place de Grève

THERE REMAINS TO-DAY but a small and scarcely perceptible vestige of the Place de Grève (one of the places for public executions in the old city of Paris), such as it existed formerly; all that is left is the charming turret which occupies the northern angle of the Square, and which, already buried under the ignoble whitewashing which obstructs the delicate lines of its carving, will soon, perhaps, have totally disappeared, under that increase of new houses which is so rapidly consuming all the old *façades* in Paris.

Those who, like ourselves, never pass over the Place de Grève without casting a look of pity and sympathy on this poor little tower, squeezed between two ruins of the time of Louis XV, can easily reconstruct in their mind's eye the assemblage of edifices to which it belonged, and thus imagine themselves in the old Gothic Square of the fifteenth century.

It was then, as now, an irregular place, bounded on one side by the quay, and on the three others by a series of lofty houses, narrow and sombre. In the daytime you might admire the variety of these buildings, carved in stone or in wood, and already presenting complete examples of the various kinds of domestic architecture of the Middle Ages, going back from the fifteenth to the eleventh century – from the perpendicular window which was beginning to supersede the Gothic to the circular Roman arch which the Gothic had in turn supplanted, and which still occupied underneath the first story of that ancient house of the Tour-Rolland, forming the angle of the Place with the Seine, on the side of the Rue de la Tannerie. By night, nothing was distinguishable of that mass of buildings but the black indentation of their gables, extending its range of acute angles round three sides of the Place. For it is one of the essential differences between the towns of that day and those of the present, that now it is the fronts of the houses that look to the squares and streets, but then it was the gable ends. During the two centuries past they have turned fairly around.

In the centre of the eastern side of the Square rose a heavy and hybrid construction formed by three dwellings juxtaposed. The whole was called by three several names, describing its history, its purpose and its architecture; the Maison au Dauphin, or Dauphin's House, because Charles V, when dauphin, had lived there – the Trades House, because it was used as the Hôtel de Ville, or Town Hall – and the Maison aux Piliers (*domus ad piloria*) or Pillar House, on account of a series of heavy pillars which supported its three stories. The City had there all that a goodly town like Paris needs; a chapel to pray in; a court-room for holding magisterial sittings, and, when needed, reprimanding the king's officers; and in the garrets an arsenal stored with artillery and ammunition. For the good people of Paris, well knowing that it was not sufficient, in every emergency, to plead and to pray for the franchises of their city, had always in reserve, in the attics of the Town Hall, some few good though rusty arquebusses.

The Square of La Grève had then that sinister aspect which it still derives from the execrable ideas which it awakens, and from the gloomy-looking Town Hall built by Dominique Bocador, which has taken the place of the Maison aux Piliers. It must be observed that a permanent gibbet and pillory, a *justice* and a *ladder*, as they were then called, erected side by side in the centre of the Square, contributed not a little to make the passer-by avert his eyes from this fatal spot, where so many beings in full life and health had suffered their last agony; and which was to give birth, fifty years later, to that Saint Vallier's fever, as it was called, that disease which was but the terror of the scaffold, the most monstrous of all maladies, inflicted as it was, not by the hand of God, but by that of man.

It is consolatory, we may remark, to reflect that the punishment of death, which, three centuries ago, with its iron wheels, with its stone gibbets, with all its apparatus for torture permanently fixed in the ground, encumbered the Square of the Grève, the Market Place, the Place Dauphine, the Croix du Trahoir, the Pig Market, the hideous Montfaucon, the Barrière des Sergens, the Place aux Chats, The Gate of Saint Denis, Champeaux, the Baudets Gate, the Porte Saint Jacques – not to mention the innumerable pillories of the provosts, of the bishop, of the chapters, of the abbots, of the priors who dealt justice – not to mention judicial drownings in the river Seine – it is consolatory to reflect that now, after losing, one after another, every fragment of her panoply, her profusion of executions, her refined and fanciful penal laws, her torture, for applying which she made anew every five years a bed of leather in the Grand Châtelet – this ancient queen of feudal society, nearly thrust from our laws and our towns, tracked from code to code, driven from place to place, now possesses, in our vast metropolis of Paris, but one dishonoured corner of the Grève – but one miserable guillotine – stealthy – timid – ashamed – which seems always afraid of being taken in the act, so quickly does it disappear after giving its blow.

III

Kisses for Blows

WHEN PIERRE GRINGOIRE arrived at the Place de Grève he was benumbed with cold. He had gone over the Miller's Bridge to avoid the crowd on the Pont au Change and Jehan Fourbault's banners; but the wheels of all the bishop's mills had splashed him as he crossed, so that his coat was wet through; and it seemed to him that the fate of his piece had rendered him even colder. Accordingly, he hurried toward the bonfire which burned magnificently in the middle of the Place, a considerable crowd however, encircled it.

'You villainous Parisians!' said he to himself (for Gringoire, like a true dramatic poet, was addicted to monologues), 'so, now you keep me from the fire! And yet I've good need of a chimney-corner. My shoes are sponges in the water – and then, all those execrable mills have been raining upon me. The devil take the Bishop of Paris with his mills! I wonder what a bishop can do with a mill! Does he think, from being a bishop, to turn miller? If he only wants my malediction to do so, I heartily give it him, and his cathedral, and his mills! Let us see, now, if any of those lazy rascals will disturb themselves. What are they doing there the while? Warming themselves – a fine pleasure, truly! Looking at a hundred bunches of fagots burning – a fine sight, to be sure!'

On looking nearer, however, he perceived that the circle of people was much wider than was requisite to warm themselves at the bonfire, and that this concourse was not attracted alone by the beauty of a hundred blazing bundles.

In a wide space left clear between the fire and the crowd, a young girl was dancing.

Whether she was a human being, a fairy, or an angel, was what Gringoire, sceptical philosopher and ironical poet as he was, could not at the first moment decide, so much was he fascinated by this dazzling vision.

She was not tall, but the elasticity of her slender shape made her appear so. She was a brunette, but it was obvious that in the daylight her complexion would have that golden gleam seen upon the women of

Spain and of Rome. Her tiny foot, as well, was Andalusian, for it was at once tight and at ease in its light and graceful sandal. She was dancing, turning, whirling upon an antique Persian carpet spread negligently under her feet; and each time as she turned and her radiant countenance passed before you, her large black eyes seemed to flash upon you.

Every look was fixed upon her, every mouth was open in the circle about her; and, indeed while she danced to the sound of the tambourine which her two round and delicate arms lifted above her head – slender, fragile, active, as a wasp – with her golden girdle without a fold – her skirt of varied colours swelling out below her slender waist, giving momentary glimpses of her fine-formed legs – her round bared shoulders – her black hair and her sparkling eyes – she looked like something more than human.

'Truly,' thought Gringoire, ' 'tis a salamander – a nymph – a goddess – a bacchante of Mount Mænalus!'

At that moment one of he braids of the salamander's hair became detached, and a small piece of brass that had been attached to it rolled upon the ground.

'Ah! no,' said he, ' 'tis a gypsy.'

All illusion disappeared.

She resumed her dance. She took up from the ground two swords, the points of which she supported upon her forehead, making them whirl in one direction, while she turned in the other. She was indeed no other than a gypsy. Yet, disenchanted as was Gringoire, the scene, taken altogether, was not without its charm, not without its magic. The bonfire cast upon her a red flaring light, which flickered brightly upon the circle of faces of the crowd and the brown forehead of the young girl, and, at the extremities of the Square threw a wan reflection, mingled with the wavering shadows – on one side, upon the old dark wrinkled front of the Maison aux Piliers – on the other, upon he stone arms of the gibbet.

Among the thousand faces tinged by the scarlet light, there was one which seemed to be more than all the rest absorbed in the contemplation of the dancer. It was the face of a man, austere, calm and sombre. This man, whose costume was hidden by the crowd that surrounded him, seemed to be not more than thirty-five years of age; yet he was bald, having only a few thin tufts of hair about his temples, which were already gray; his broad and high forehead was beginning to be furrowed with wrinkles; but in his deep-set eyes there shone an extraordinary youth, an intense animation a depth of passion. He kept them constantly fixed upon the gypsy, and while the giddy young girl of sixteen danced and swung to the delight of all, his reverie seemed to grow more and more gloomy. From time to time a smile and a sigh met each other on his lips; but the smile was far more sad than the sigh.

The girl, breathless, stopped at last, while the crowd lovingly applauded.

'Djali!' cried the gypsy.

Gringoire then saw come up to her a little white goat, alert, brisk and glossy, with gilt horns, gilt hoofs and a gilt collar, which he had not before observed, because until that moment it had been lying crouched upon one corner of the carpet, looking at her mistress dance.

'Djali,' said the dancer, 'it's your turn now;' and sitting down, she gracefully held out her tambourine to the goat.

'Djali,' she continued, 'what month of the year is this?'

The animal lifted its fore-foot and struck one stroke upon the tambourine. It was, in fact, the first month of the year. The crowd applauded.

'Djali!' resumed the girl, turning her tambourine another way, 'what day of the month is it?'

Djali lifted her little golden foot, and struck six times upon the tambourine.

'Djali!' said the gypsy, with a new turn of the tambourine, 'what hour of the day is it?'

Djali struck seven strokes, and at that very moment the clock of the Maison aux Piliers rang seven.

The people were wonderstruck.

'There is witchcraft in all that,' said a sinister voice in the crowd. It was that of the bald man who had his eyes constantly upon the gypsy.

She shuddered and turned around. But the applause burst forth again and smothered the sinister exclamation.

Indeed, they so completely effaced it from her mind, that she continued to interrogate her goat.

'Djali!' said she, 'how does Maître Guichard Grand-Remy, captain of the town pistoliers, go in the procession at Candlemas?'

Djali reared on her hind legs and began to bleat, marching at the same time with so seemly a gravity that the whole circle of spectators burst into a laugh at this parody of the hypocritical devotion of the captain of pistoliers.

'Djali!' resumed the girl, emboldened by this increased success, 'how does Maître Jacques Charmolue, the king's attorney in the ecclesiastical court – how does he preach?'

The goat sat down on her haunches and began to bleat, shaking its fore-feet after so strange a fashion, that, with the exception of the bad French and the bad Latin, it was Jacques Charmolue to the life, gesture, accent and attitude.

The crowd applauded with all their might.

'Sacrilege! profanation!' cried the voice of the bald-headed man.

The gypsy turned round again.

'Ah!' said she, 'it's that ugly man!'

Then putting out her lower lip beyond the upper one she made a little pouting grimace which seemed familiar to her, turned upon her heel, and began to collect in her tambourine the contributions of the multitude.

Big pieces of silver, little pieces of silver, pennies and farthings were now showered upon her. In taking her round, she all at once came in front of Gringoire; and as he, in perfect absence of mind, thrust his hand into his pocket, she stopped, expecting something. 'Diable!' exclaimed the poet, finding at the bottom of his pocket the reality, that is to say, nothing at all; the pretty girl standing before him all the while, looking at him with her large eyes, holding out her tambourine, and waiting. Gringoire perspired from every pore.

Had he all the riches of Peru in his pocket, he would assuredly have given it to the dancer; but Gringoire had not the wealth of Peru – nor, indeed, was America yet discovered.

Fortunately an unexpected incident came to his relief.

'Wilt thou begone, thou Egyptian locust?' cried a harsh voice from the darkest corner of the Place.

The girl turned affrighted. This was not the voice of the bald-headed man; it was the voice of a woman – bigoted and malicious.

This cry, which frightened the gypsy, highly delighted a troop of children that were rambling about.

'It's the recluse of the Tour-Rolland,' cried they with uproarious bursts of laughter – 'it's the nun that's scolding. Hasn't she had her supper? Let's carry her something from the town buffet.'

And they all ran toward the Maison aux Piliers.

Gringoire had availed himself of this agitation of the dancer to disappear among the crowd. The shouts of the children reminded him that he too had not supped. He therefore hastened to the public buffet. But he little rogues had better legs than he, and when he arrived they had cleared the table. They had not even left one wretched cake at five sous the pound. There remained nothing but the bare decorations against the wall – the light fleurs-de-lis intermingled with rose-trees painted there in 1434 by Mathieu Biterne; and they offered but a meagre supper.

'Tis an unpleasant thing to go without one's dinner. 'Tis less gratifying still to go without one's supper, and not know where to sleep. Gringoire was at that point. Without food, without lodging, he found himself pressed by necessity on every hand, and he thought necessity very ungracious. He had long discovered this truth – that Jupiter created man in a fit of misanthropy, and that throughout the life of the wisest man his destiny keeps his philosophy in a state of siege. For his own part, he had never found the blockade so complete. He heard his stomach sound a truce, and he thought it very unkind that his evil destiny should reduce his philosophy by simple starvation.

He was sinking more and more deeply into this melancholy reverie, when he was suddenly startled from it by the sound of a strange but very sweet song. It was the young gypsy singing.

Her voice had the same character as her dance and her beauty. It had an undefinable charm – something clear, sonorous, aerial – winged, as it were. There was a continued succession of harmonious notes, of swells, of unexpected cadences – then simple strains, interspersed with sharp and shrill notes – then trills that would have bewildered a nightingale – then soft undulations, which rose and fell like the bosom of the youthful songstress. The expression of her sweet face followed with singular flexibility every capricious variation of her song, from the wildest inspiration to the most chastened dignity. She seemed now all frenzy, and now all majesty.

The words that she sang were in a language unintelligible to Gringoire, and which seemed to be unknown to herself, so little did the expression which she gave in singing correspond with the sense of the words. for instance, she gave these four lines with the most sportive gaiety:

> *Un cofre de gran riqueza*
> *Hallaron dentro un pilar,*
> *Dentro del, nuevas banderas*
> *Configuras de espantui.* *

And a moment after, at the tone which she gave to this stanza –

> *Alarabes de cavallo*
> *Sin poderse menear,*
> *Con espadas, y los cuellos,*
> *Ballestas de buen echar . . .* †

Gringoire felt the tears come to his eyes. Yet above all her song breathed gaiety, and she seemed to warble, like a bird, from pure lightness of heart.

The gypsy's song had disturbed Gringoire's reverie, but it was as the swan disturbs the water. He listened to it with a sort of ecstasy, and oblivion of all else. It was the first moment, for several hours, in which

---

* A coffer of great richness
  In a pillar's heart was found,
  Within it lay new banners,
  With figures to astound.

† The Moorish horsemen
  Without being able to move,
  With swords, and at their necks
  Ready cross-bows . . .

he felt no suffering.

The moment was short.

The same female voice which had interrupted the gypsy's dance, now interrupted her song.

'Wilt thou be silent, thou infernal cricket?' it cried, still from the same dark corner of the Place.

The poor 'cricket' stopped short, and Gringoire clapped his hands over his ears.

'Oh!' he cried, 'thou cursed, broken-toothed saw, that comest to break the lyre!'

The rest of the bystanders murmured with him. 'The devil take the nun!' cried some of them. And the invisible disturber might have found cause to repent of her attacks upon the gypsy had not their attention been diverted at that moment by the procession of the Fools' Pope, which, after traversing many a street and square, was now pouring into the Place de Grève, with all its torches and all its clamour.

This procession, which our readers have seen take its departure from the Palace, had increased on the way, having enlisted all the ragamuffins, the unemployed thieves and idle scamps in Paris, so that when it reached the Grève it presented quite a respectable aspect.

First of all marched the Egyptians. The Duke of Egypt was at their head, with his counts on foot, holding his bridle and stirrup behind them came the Egyptians, men and women, pell-mell, with their infants squalling upon their shoulders; all of them, duke, counts and people, covered with rags and tinsel. Then followed the kingdom of Argot, that is, all the thieves of France, arranged in bands according to the order of their dignities, the least important walking first. Thus marched on, four abreast, with the different insignia of their degrees in that strange faculty, most of them crippled in some way or other – some limping, some with only one hand – the shoplifters, the false pilgrims, the card sharps, the pickpockets, the tramps, the rogues, the lepers and those who wore false sores, and those of hidden lives – denominations enough to have wearied Homer himself to enumerate, and some explanation of which will occur as we proceed. It was with some difficulty that you could discern, in the centre of the band of wharf rats, archisuppôts, arch thieves, the King of Argot himself, the 'Grand-Coësre,' as he was called, sitting squat in a little waggon drawn by two large dogs. After the kingdom of the Argotiers came the empire of Galilee (gamblers). Guillaume Rousseau, Emperor of the empire of Galilee, walking majestically in his robe of purple stained with wine, preceded by mummers dancing Pyrrhic dances, and surrounded by his mace-bearers, his under-strappers and the clerks of the chambre des comptes. Lastly came the members of the basoche (lawyers' clerks), with their garlanded staffs, their black gowns, their music, worthy of witches' Sabbath, and their great candles of yellow wax. In the centre of this latter crowd, the great officers of the brotherhood of Fools bore upon their shoulders a stretcher, more loaded with wax-tapers than the shrine of Sainte Geneviève in time of pestilence; and seated upon this stretcher shone, crosiered and mitred, the new Fools' Pope, the ringer of Notre-Dame, Quasimodo the hunchback.

Each division of this grotesque procession had its particular music. The Egyptians sounded their balafos and their African tabours. The Argotiers, a very unmusical race, had advanced no further than the viol, the buglehorn and the Gothic rubebbe of the twelfth century. The empire of Galilee had made little more progress. You could but just distinguish in its music the sounds of the ancient rebeck of the infancy of the art still limited to the do, re, mi. But it was around the Fools' Pope that were congregated, in magnificent discordance, all the musical riches of the age; there was nothing visible but ends of rebecks of all sizes and shapes; not to mention the flutes and the cuivres. Alas! our readers will recollect that it was poor Gringoire's orchestra.

It is not easy to give an idea of the expression of proud and beatific joy which the melancholy and hideous visage of Quasimodo had attained in the journey from the Palace to the Grève. It was the first thrill of vanity that he had ever experienced. He had hitherto experienced nothing but humiliation, disdain at his condition, and disgust for his person. So, deaf as he was, he nevertheless relished, like a true pope, the acclamations of that crowd whom he had hated because he felt himself hated by them. What though his people were a gathering of fools, of cripples, thieves and beggars – still they were a people, and he was a sovereign. And he took in earnest all the ironical applause and mock reverence which they gave him; with which, at the same time, we must not forget to observe there was mingled, in the minds of the crowd, a degree of fear quite real; for the hunchback was strong; though bow-legged, he was active; though deaf, he was malicious – three qualities which have the effect of tempering the ridicule.

Moreover, that the new Pope of the Fools analyzed the feelings which he experienced, or those which he inspired, we can by no means presume. The mind that was lodged in that misshapen body, was necessarily itself incomplete and dull of hearing; so that what he felt at that moment was both vague and confused to him. Only, joy beamed through all, and pride predominated. Around that dismal and unhappy countenance there was a perfect radiance.

It was, therefore, not without surprise and alarm that all at once, at the moment when Quasimodo, in that state of semi-intoxication, passed triumphantly before the Maison aux Piliers, a man was seen to dart from the crowd, and, with an angry gesture, snatch from his hands the crosier of gilt wood, ensign of his mock papacy.

The person who had this temerity was the man with the bald head, who, the moment before, standing in the crowd that encircled the gypsy, had chilled the poor girl's blood with his words of menace and hatred. He was in ecclesiastical dress. The moment he rushed forth from the crowd he was recognized by Gringoire, who had not before observed him. 'What!' said he, with a cry of astonishment. 'Why, 'tis my master in Hermes, Don Claude Frollo, the archdeacon! What the devil can he want with that one-eyed brute? He will be devoured!'

A cry of terror proceeded from the multitude. The formidable Quasimodo had leaped down from his seat; and the women turned away their eyes, that they might not see him tear the archdeacon to pieces.

He made one bound toward the priest, looked in his face, and then fell on his knees, before him.

The priest snatched his tiara from his head, broke his crosier, and rent his tinsel cope.

Quasimodo remained upon his knees, bowed down his head, and clasped his hands.

They then entered into a strange dialogue of signs and gestures, for neither of them uttered a word. The priest, erect, angry, threatening, imperious; Quasimodo prostrate, humble, suppliant. And yet it is certain that Quasimodo could have crushed the priest with his thumb.

At last the priest, roughly shaking Quasimodo's powerful shoulder, made him a sign to rise and follow.

Quasimodo rose accordingly.

Then the brotherhood of Fools, their first amazement having passed, offered to defend their pope, thus abruptly dethroned. The Egyptians, the Argotiers, and all the Basoche, came yelping round the priest.

Quasimodo, placing himself before the priest, gave full play the muscles of his athletic fists, and regarded the assailants, gnashing his teeth like an angry tiger.

The priest resumed his sombre gravity, and making a sign to Quasimodo, withdrew in silence.

Quasimodo walked before him, scattering the crowd in his passage.

When they had made their way through the populace and across he Place, the crowd of the curious and idle wished to follow them. Quasimodo then placed himself in the rear, and followed the archdeacon backwards, looking squat, snarling, monstrous, shaggy, gathering up his limbs, licking his tusks, growling like a wild beast, and swaying backward the crowd by a mere glance or gesture.

At length they both disappeared down a gloomy narrow street, into which no one dared to follow them; so effectually was it entrance barred by the mere image of Quasimodo gnashing his teeth.

'All this is astonishing,' said Gringoire to himself; 'but where the devil shall I find a supper?'

IV

The Danger of Following a Pretty Woman in the Streets by Night

GRINGOIRE HAD SET himself to follow the gypsy girl at all hazards. He had seen her, with her goat, turn down the Rue de la Contellerie; and, accordingly, he turned into the Rue de la Contellerie likewise.

'Why not?' said he to himself.

As a practical philosopher of the streets of Paris, Gringoire had remarked that nothing is more favourable to a state of reverie than to follow a pretty woman without knowing whither she is going. In this voluntary surrender of one's free-will – in this fancy subjecting itself to the fancy of another, while that other is totally unconscious of it – there is a mixture of fantastic independence with blind obedience, a something intermediate between slavery and freedom, which was pleasing to Gringoire, whose mind, essentially mixed, undecided and complex, held the medium between all extremes in constant suspense amongst all human propensities, and neutralizing one of them by another. He compared himself willingly to the tomb of Mahomet, attracted by two lodestones in opposite directions, and hesitating eternally between the top and the bottom, between the roof and the pavement, between fall and ascension, between the zenith and the nadir.

Had Gringoire been living in our time, what a happy medium he would have maintained between the classic and the romantic!

But he was not primitive enough to live three hundred years; and 'tis a pity. His absence leaves a void which, in these days of ours, is but too sensibly felt.

However, nothing better disposes a man for following people in the street (especially when they happen to be women), a thing Gringoire was always ready to do, than not knowing where to sleep.

He walked along, therefore, thoughtfully, behind the young girl, who quickened her step, making her pretty little four-footed companion trot beside her, as she saw the townsfolk reaching their homes and the taverns (the only shops allowed opened on this festival) closing for the night.

'After all,' he had thought to himself, 'she must have a lodging somewhere – the gypsy women have good hearts – who knows?'

And there were some points of suspension around which he wove certain very charming and flattering ideas.

At intervals, meanwhile, as he passed before the last groups of people busy closing their doors, he caught certain fragments of their conversation which broke the chain of his pleasing hypotheses.

Now it was two old men accosting each other.

'Maître Thibaut Fernicle, do you know, it's very cold?'

(Gringoire had known it ever since the winter had set in.)

'Yes, indeed, Maître Boniface Disome. Are we going to have such a winter as we had three years ago, in the year '80, when wood rose to eight sols the measure, think you?'

'Bah! that's nothing at all, Maître Thibaut, to the winter of 1407, when it froze from Martinmas to Candlemas – and so sharp that the ink in the pen of the parliament's registrar froze, in the Grand Chamber, at every three words, which interrupted the registering of the judgments!'

Then farther on, two good female neighbours, gossiping to each other from their windows with candles in their hands that glimmered through the fog.

'Has your husband told you of the mishap, Mademoiselle la Boudraque?'

'No, Mademoiselle Turquant, what is it?'

'The horse of Monsieur Gilles Godin, notary at the Châtelet, took fright at the Flemish and their procession, and knocked over Maître Philipot Avrillot, lay-brother of the Celestines.'

'Really?'

'Assuredly.'

'A paltry hack-horse, too! It seems impossible – had it been a cavalry horse, now!'

And the windows were shut again. But Gringoire had nonetheless lost the thread of his ideas.

Luckily, he soon found it again, and easily tied it together, at the sight of the gypsy girl and of Djali, who were still trotting on before him, two slender, delicate and charming creatures, whose small feet, pretty figures, and graceful motions he gazed at with admiration, almost confounding them together in his contemplation; fancying them both young girls from their intelligence and mutual affection; while from their light, quick and graceful step, they might have been both young hinds.

Meanwhile, the streets were every moment becoming darker and more solitary. The curfew had long ceased to ring, and it was only at long intervals that a person passed along the pavement, or a light was seen at a window. Gringoire, in following the gypsy, had involved himself in that inextricable labyrinth of alleys, courts and crossings which surrounds the ancient sepulchre of the Holy Innocents, and may be compared to a skein of thread tangled by the playing of a kitten. 'Very illogical streets, in truth!' muttered Gringoire, quite lost in the thousand windings which seemed to be everlastingly turning back upon themselves, but through which the girl followed a track that seemed to be well known to her, and with a step of increasing rapidity. For his own part he would have been perfectly ignorant as to his whereabout, had he not observed, at the bend of a street, the octagonal mass of the pillory of the Halles (Principal Market), the perforated top of which traced its dark outline against a solitary light yet visible in a window of the Rue Verdelet.

For some moments past his step had attracted the girl's attention; she had several times turned her head towards him with uneasiness: once, indeed, she had stopped short, had availed herself of a ray of light that escaped from a half-open bakehouse, to survey him steadily from head to foot; then, after this scrutiny, Gringoire had observed on her face the little grimace which he had already remarked, and she had gone on without more ado.

This same little pout furnished Gringoire with a subject of reflection. There certainly was both disdain and mockery in that pretty grimace. And he was beginning to hang his head, to count the paving-stones, and to follow the girl at a rather greater distance; when, at the turn of a street which for a moment hid her from view, he heard her utter a piercing shriek.

He quickened his step.

The street was filled with deep shadows. Yet, a wick soaked in oil, which was burning in a sort of iron cage, at the foot of a statue of the Holy Virgin at the corner of the street, enabled Gringoire to discern the gypsy struggling in the arms of two men, who were endeavouring to stifle her cries, while the poor little goat, in great alarm, put down her horns, bleating.

'Hither! hither! gentlemen of the watch!' cried Gringoire; and he advanced bravely.

One of the men who had laid hold of the girl, turned toward him. It was the formidable visage of Quasimodo.

Gringoire did not fly – but he did not advance another step.

Quasimodo came up to him, and hurling him some four paces off upon the pavement with a backstroke of his hand, plunged rapidly into the darkness, bearing the girl, whose figure drooping over his arm was like a silken scarf. His companion followed him, and the poor goat ran behind with its plaintive bleat.

'Murder! murder!' cried the unfortunate gypsy.

'Stand, there! you scoundrels! and let go the wench!' was all at once heard in a voice of thunder, from a horseman, who suddenly made his appearance from the neighbouring crossway.

It was a captain of the king's archers, armed from head to foot with broadsword in hand.

He snatched the gypsy from the grasp of the amazed Quasimodo, laid her across his saddle, and, at the moment when the redoubtable hunchback, having recovered from his surprise, was rushing upon him to regain possession of his prey, fifteen or sixteen archers who followed close upon their captain, made their appearance each brandishing his two-edged blade. They were a detachment of the royal troop on extra duty, by order of Messire Robert d'Estouteville, Warden of the Provost of Paris.

Quasimodo was surrounded, seized and garroted. He roared, he foamed, he bit; and had it been daylight, no doubt his visage alone, rendered yet more hideous by rage, would have put the whole detachment to flight. But the darkness had disarmed him of his most formidable weapon, his ugliness.

His companion had disappeared during the struggle.

The gypsy gracefully gained her seat upon the officer's saddle rested both her hands upon the young man's shoulders, and looked fixedly at him for a few seconds, as if delighted with his fine countenance and the effectual succour he had rendered her. Then speaking first, and making her sweet voice still sweeter, she said to him:

'Monsieur le gendarme, what is your name?'

'Captain Phœbus de Chateaupers, at your service, my fair one,' said the officer, drawing himself up.

'Thank you,' said she.

And while Captain Phœbus was curling his moustache *à la Bourguignonne*, she glided down from the horse like an arrow falling to the ground and fled.

A flash of lightning could not have vanished more quickly.

'By the Pope's head!' exclaimed the captain, while he tightened the bands upon Quasimodo, 'I'd rather have kept the wench.'

'What would you have, captain?' said one of the archers. 'The linnet is flown – the bat remains.'

V

Continuation of the Danger

GRINGOIRE, QUITE STUNNED with his fall, lay stretched upon the pavement before the good Virgin at the corner of the street. By degrees, however, he recovered his senses. At first, he was for some minutes in a sort of half-somnolent reverie, which was not altogether disagreeable, and in which the airy figures of the gypsy and the goat were confounded in his imagination with the weight of Quasimodo's fist. This state of his feelings was of short duration. A very lively sense of cold upon that part of his body which was in contact with the pavement, suddenly awoke him, and brought his mind to the surface.

'Whence is this chill that I feel?' said he hastily to himself. He then perceived that he lay somewhat in the middle of the gutter.

'The devil take the humpbacked cyclop!' Grumbled he between his teeth, as he strove to get up. But he was too much stunned, and too much bruised, he was forced to remain where he was. Having, however, the free use of his hand, he stopped his nose, and resigned himself to his situation.

'The mud of Paris,' thought he, for he now believed it to be decided that the gutter was to be his lodging:

And what do in a refuge but to dream?

'the mud of Paris is particularly foul. It must contain a large proportion of volatile and nitrous salts. Such too is the opinion of Maître Nicolas Flamel and the hermetics....'

This word *hermetics* reminded him of the Archdeacon Claude Frollo. He reflected on the scene of violence of which he had just had a glimpse; that he had seen the gypsy struggling between two men; that Quasimodo had a companion; and the sullen and haughty countenance of the archdeacon floated confusedly in his memory. 'That would be strange,' thought he; and then, with this data and upon this basis, he began to erect the fantastic framework of hypothesis, that house of cards of the philosophers; then suddenly returning once more to reality, 'Oh, I freeze!' he cried.

The position was in fact becoming less and less tenable. Each particle of water in the channel carried off a particle of caloric from the loins of Gringoire; and an equilibrium of temperature between his body and the water was beginning to establish itself in the most cruel manner.

All at once he was assailed by an annoyance of quite a different nature.

A troop of children, of those little barefooted savages that have in all times run wild in the streets of Paris, with the everlasting name of *gamins*, and who, when we were children also, used to throw stones at us as we were leaving school in the evening, because our trousers were not torn, – a swarm of these urchins ran to the crossing where Gringoire lay, laughing and shouting in a manner that showed very little concern for the sleep of the neighbours. They were dragging after them some sort of a shapeless sack; and the noise of their wooden shoes alone was enough to waken the dead. Gringoire, who was not yet quite dead, half raised himself.

'Hello! Hennequin Dandèche! Hello! Jehan Pincebourde!' cried they at the top of their voices; 'old Eustache Moubon, the old junkseller of the corner, is just dead. We've got his straw mattress, and we're going to make a bonfire with it. This is the Flemings' day!'

Whereupon they threw the mattress precisely on top of Gringoire, whom they had come up to without seeing. At the same time one of them took a handful of straw, and went to light it a the lamp of the Blessed Virgin.

'S'death!' muttered Gringoire, 'am I going to be too hot now?'

The moment was critical. He was about to be caught between fire and water. He made a supernatural effort, such as a counterfeiter might have made in trying to escape when they were going to boil him to death. He rose up, threw back the mattress upon the gamins, and took to his heels.

'Holy Virgin!' cried the boys, 'it's the old junkman's ghost!'

And they too ran in the opposite direction.

The mattress remained master of the field of battle. Those judicious historians, Belle-fôret, Father Le Juge and Corrozet, assure us that the next morning it was gathered up with great pomp by the clergy of that quarter of the town and placed among the treasures of Sainte Opportune's church, where, until the year 1789, the sacristan made a very handsome income from the great miracle worked by the statue of the Virgin at the corner of the Rue Mauconseil, which, by its presence alone, in the memorable night between the 6th and the 7th of January, 1482, had exorcised the deceased Eustache Moubon, who, to cheat the devil, had, when dying, slyly hidden his soul within his mattress.

IV

The Broken Jug

AFTER RUNNING FOR some time as fast as his legs would carry him, without knowing, whither, headlong round many a corner, striding over many a gutter, traversing many a court and alley, seeking escape and passage through all the windings of the old pavement of the Halles, exploring in his panic what are called in the elegant Latin of the charters, *tota via, cheminum, et viaria* (every way, highway and by-way), our poet all at once halted, first because he was out of breath, and then because he was collared, as it were, by a dilemma which had suddenly arisen in his mind. 'It seems to me Maître Pierre Gringoire,' said he to himself, applying his finger to his forehead, 'that you are running all this while like a brainless fellow. The little rogues were no less afraid of you than you were of them – it seems to me, I say, that you heard the clatter of their wooden shoes running away southward while you were running away northward. Now, one of two things must have taken place; either they have run away, and then the mattress which they must have forgotten in their fright is precisely that hospitable couch for which you have been hunting since the morning, and which Madame the Virgin miraculously sends you as a reward for having composed, in honour of her, a morality, accompanied with triumphs and mummeries – or, the boys have not run away; in that case they will have put a light to the mattress, and there you have precisely the excellent fire of which you are in need, to comfort, warm and dry you. In either case – good bed or good fire – the mattress is a gift from heaven. The sanctified Virgin Mary that stands at the corner of the Rue Mauconseil perhaps caused the death of Eustache Moubon for the very purpose; and 'tis folly in you to thus hasten away, like a Picard running from a Frenchman, leaving behind what you are running forward to seek – and you are a blockhead!'

He then began to retrace his steps, and ferreting about to discover where he was – snuffing the wind, and with his ears to the ground – he strove to find his way back to the blessed mattress – -but in vain. All was intersections of streets, courts and blind alleys, amongst which he incessantly doubted and hesitated, more entangled in that strange network of dark lanes than he would have been in the labyrinth of the Hôtel des Tournelles itself. At length he lost patience, and vehemently exclaimed, 'A curse upon these crossroads! the devil himself has made them after the image of his pitchfork!'

This exclamation relieved him a little, and a sort of reddish reflection, which he at that moment perceived at the end of a long and narrow street, completed the restoration of his courage.

'God be praised,' said he, 'there it is! There is my blazing mattress!' And, likening himself to the boatman foundering in the night-time, *'Salve,'* added he, piously, *'salve, maris stella!'* (Hail, Star of the Sea.)

Did he address this fragment of a litany to the Holy Virgin, or to the straw mattress? We really are unable to say.

He had no sooner advanced a few paces down the long street or lane, which was on a declivity, unpaved, descending more abruptly and becoming more miry the farther he proceeded, than he observed something very singular. The street was not deserted; here and there were to be seen crawling certain vague shapeless masses, all moving toward the light which was flickering at the end of the street, like those heavy insects which drag themselves along at night, from one blade of grass to another, toward a shepherd's fire.

Nothing makes a man so adventurous as an empty pocket. Gringoire went forward, and soon came up with that one of the larvæ which seemed to be dragging itself along indolently after the others. On approaching it, he found that it was nothing other than a miserable cripple fixed in a bowl, without legs or thighs, jumping along with the aid of his two hands, like a mutilated spider, with only two of its feet remaining. The moment he came up to this sort of human insect it lifted up to him a lamentable voice: *'La buona mancia, signor! la buona mancia!'* (Charity, sir! charity!)

'The devil take thee!' said Gringoire, 'and me along with thee if I know what you mean.'

And he passed on.

He came up to another of these ambulatory masses, and examined it. It was a cripple, both in arms and legs, after such a manner that the complicated system of crutches and wooden legs that supported him made him look like a perambulating mason's scaffolding. Gringoire, being fond of noble and classical similes, compared him, in fancy, to the living tripod of Vulcan.

This living tripod saluted him as he went by; but staying his hat just at the height of Gringoire's chin, after the manner of a shaving dish, and shouting in his ears, *'Señor Cabarellero, para comprar un pedaso de pan!'* (Sir, Cavalier, something with which to buy a piece of bread!) 'It appears,' said Gringoire, 'that this one talks too; but it's a barbarous language, and he's more lucky than I if he understands it.' Then striking his forehead through a sudden transition of idea: 'Apropos! what the devil did they mean this morning with their Esmeralda?'

He resolved to double his pace; but for the third time something blocked up the way. This something, or rather this some one, was a blind man, a little man, with a bearded Jewish face, who, rowing in the space about him with a stick, and towed along by a great dog, whined out to him with a Hungarian accent, *'Facitote caritatem!'* (Give alms.)

'Well enough!' said Pierre Gringoire, 'here is one at last that talks a Christian language. Truly, I must have a most alms-giving mien, that they should ask charity of me when my purse is so lean. My friend,' said he, turning to the blind man, 'a week since I sold my last shirt that is to say, since you understand no language but that of Cicero. *Vendidi hebdomade nuper transita meam ultimam chemisam.*'

This said, he turned his back upon the blind man and pursued his way. But the blind man lengthened his pace at the same time; and behold, also, the cripple and the stump came up in great haste, with much noise of the platter that carried the one, and the crutches that sustained the other. All three, tumbling over each other at the heels of poor Gringoire, and singing their several staves:

'Caritatem!' sang the blind man.

'La buona mancia!' sang the stump.

And the man of the wooden legs took up the strain with, *'Un pedaso de pan!'*

Gringoire stopped his ears. 'Oh, tower of Babel!' he cried.

He began to run. The blind man ran. The wooden legs ran. The stump ran.

And then, as he hurried still farther down the street, stump men, wooden-legged men, and blind men came swarming around him – men with but a single hand, men with but one eye, lepers with their sores – issued from out houses, adjacent alleys, cellar-holes – howling, bellowing, yelping – all hobbling and clattering along, making their way toward the light, and wallowing in the mire like so many slugs after the rain.

Gringoire, still followed by his three persecutors, and not knowing what was to come of it all, walked on affrighted among the others, turning aside the limpers, striding over the stumpies, his feet entangled in that ant-hill of deformities, like the English captain who found himself beset by a legion of crabs.

The idea occurred to him of trying to retrace his steps. But it was too late, all this army had closed upon his rear, and his three beggars held him. He went on, therefore, urged forward at once by that irresistible flood, by fear, and by a dizziness which made it all seem to him like a sort of horrible dream.

At last he reached the extremity of the street. It opened into an immense square, where a thousand scattered lights were wavering in the thick gloom of the night. Gringoire threw himself into it hoping to escape by the speed of his legs from the three deformed spectres that had fixed themselves upon him.

'Onde Das, hombre?' (Whither goest, man?) cried the wooden legs, throwing aside his scaffolding, and running after him with as good a pair of legs as ever measured a geometrical pace upon the pavement of Paris.

Meanwhile the stumpy, erect upon his feet, clapped his heavy iron-sheathed platter over Gringoire's head, while the blind man stared him in the face with great flaming eyes.

'Where am I?' said the terrified poet.

'In the Court of Miracles,' answered a fourth spectre who had accosted them.

'On my soul,' returned Gringoire, 'I do indeed find here that the blind see and the lame walk – but where is the Saviour?'

They answered with a burst of laughter of a sinister kind.

The poor poet cast his eyes around him. He was in fact in that same terrible Court des Miracles, or Court of Miracles, where no honest man had ever penetrated at such an hour – a magic circle in which the officers of the Châtelet and the sergeants of the provostry when they ventured thither, disappeared in morsels – the city of the thieves – a hideous wart on the face of Paris – a sink from whence escaped every morning, and to which returned to stagnate every night, that stream of vice, mendicity and vagrancy which ever flows through the streets of a capital – a monstrous hive, into which all the hornets of society returned each evening with their booty – a lying hospital, in which the gypsy, the unfrocked monk, the abandoned scholar – the worthless of every nation, Spaniards Italians, Germans – of every religion, Jews, Christians, Mahometans, Idolaters – covered with painted sores, beggars in the daytime, transformed themselves at night into robbers – in short an immense cloak-room, in which dressed and undressed at that period all the actors in that everlasting drama which robbery, prostitution and murder enacted upon the pavements of Paris.

It was a large open space, irregular and ill-paved, as was at that time every square in Paris. Fires, around which swarmed strange groups, were gleaming here and there. All was motion and clamour. There were shrieks of laughter, squalling of children and shrill voices of women. The arms and heads of this crowd cast a thousand fantastic gestures in dark outline upon the luminous background. Now and then, upon the ground, over which the light of the fires was wavering, intermingled with great undefined shadows, was seen to pass a dog resembling, a man, or a man resembling a dog. The limits of race and species seemed to be effaced in this commonwealth as in a pandemonium. Men, women, beasts; age, sex; health, sickness; all seemed to be in common among this people; all went together mingled, confounded, superimposed, each participating in all.

The weak and wavering rays that streamed from the fires enabled Gringoire, amid his perturbation, to distinguish, all round the extensive enclosure, a hideous framing of old houses, the decayed, shrivelled, and stooping fronts of which, pierced by one or two circular attic windows with lights behind them, seemed to him, in the dark, like enormous old women's heads, ranged in a circle, looking monstrous and crabbed, and winking upon the diabolical revels.

It was like a new world, unknown, unimagined, deformed, creeping, swarming, fantastic.

Gringoire, more and more affrighted, held by the three mendicants as by three pairs of pincers and deafened by the crowd of vagrants that flocked barking round him – the unlucky Gringoire strove to muster sufficient presence of mind to recollect whether it was Saturday (witches' day) or not; but his efforts were vain; the thread of his memory and his thoughts was broken; and, doubting of everything – floating between what he saw and what he felt – he put the insoluble question to himself – 'If I am I, are these things then real? If these things be real, am I really I?'

At that moment a distinct shout was raised from the buzzing mob that surrounded him. 'Take him to the king! take him to the king!'

'Holy Virgin!' muttered Gringoire, 'the king of this place must surely be a goat!'

'To the king! to the king!' repeated every voice.

They dragged him along, each striving to fix his talons upon him. But the three beggars kept their hold, and tore him away from the others, vociferating, 'He is ours!'

The poet's frail doublet gave up the ghost in this struggle.

In crossing the horrible place his dizziness left him. After proceeding a few paces the feeling of reality returned. He began to adapt himself to the atmosphere of the place. During the first moments from his poet's head, or perhaps, indeed, quite simply and prosaically, from his empty stomach, there had risen a fume, a vapour as it were, which, spreading itself between him and surrounding objects, had allowed him a glimpse of them only in the incoherent mist of a nightmare in those shadowy dreams that distort every outline, and cluster the objects together in disproportioned groups, enlarging things into chimeras, and human beings into phantoms. By degrees this hallucination gave way to a less bewildered and less magnifying state of vision. The reality made its way to his senses – struck upon his eyes – struck against his feet – and bit by bit destroyed the frightful poetry with which he had at first fancied himself surrounded. He could not but perceive at last that he was walking, not in the Styx, but in the mud; that he was elbowed, not by demons, but by thieves, that not his soul but, in simple sooth, his life was in danger – seeing that he lacked that invaluable conciliator which places itself so effectually between the robber and the honest man – the purse. In short, on examining the orgie more closely and with greater calmness, he dropped from the witches' sabbath to the pot-house.

The Court of Miracles was, in truth, no other than a pot-house of thieves, but as red with blood as with wine.

The spectacle which presented itself to him when his tattered escort at length deposited him at his journey's end was little adapted to bring back his mind to poetry, though it were the poetry of hell. It was more than ever the prosaic and brutal reality of the tavern. Were we not in the fifteenth century, we should say that Gringoire had fallen from Michael Angelo to Callot.

Round a large fire burning upon a great round flagstone, and the blaze of which had heated red-hot the legs of an iron trivet empty for the moment, some worm-eaten tables were set out here and there in confusion, no lackey of any geometrical pretensions having conde-scended to adjust their parallelism, or see that, at least, they should not meet at too unaccustomed angles. Upon these tables shone a few pots dripping with wine and beer, around which were grouped a number of bacchanalian visages, reddened by the fire and the wine. There would be a man with a fair round belly and a jovial face, noisily throwing his arms round a girl of the town, thick-set and brawny. Then a sort of false soldier, a *narquois*, as they called him in their language, who whistled away while he was undoing the bandages of his false wound, and unstiffening his sound and vigorous knee, which had been bound up since the morning in ample ligatures. Beyond him there was a mumper preparing, with suet and ox-blood, his *Visitation from God*, or sore leg, for the morrow. Two tables farther on a sham pilgrim with complete garb was spelling out the lament of Sainte Reine, the psalmody and the nasal drone included. In another place a young scamp was taking a lesson in epilepsy from an old sabouleux, or hustler, who was teaching him the art of foaming at the mouth by chewing a piece of soap; while four or five women thieves, just by them, were contending, at the same table, for the possession of a child stolen in the course of the evening. All which circumstances two centuries later, 'seemed so laughable at court,' says Sauval 'that they furnished pastime to the king, and an opening to the royal ballet entitled "Night," which was divided into four parts, and danced upon the stage of the Petit Bourbon.' And 'never,' adds an eye-witness, in the year 1653, 'were sudden metamorphoses of the Court of Miracles more happily represented. Benserade prepared us for them by some very genteel verses.'

Coarse laughter, with obscene songs, burst forth on all sides. Each one held forth in his own way, carping and swearing, without heeding his neighbour. Pots rattled, and quarrels arose out of their collision, the smashing of pots thus leading to the tearing of rags.

A large dog, sitting on his haunches, looked into the fire There were some children mingled in this orgie. The stolen child was crying. Another, a bouncing boy four years old, was seated with his legs dangling upon a bench too high for him, with his chin just above the table, saying not a word. A third was gravely smearing the table with his finger in the melted tallow running from the candle. A fourth, a little one, squatting in the mud, was almost lost in a great iron pot which he was scraping with a tile, drawing from it a sound which would have made Stradivarius faint.

Near the fire was a barrel, and upon the fire barrel was seated one of the beggars. This was the king upon his throne.

The three who held Gringoire brought him before this cask, and the whole bacchanalia were silent for a moment, excepting the caldron tenanted by the child.

Gringoire dared not breathe nor raise his eyes.

'*Hombre, quita tu sombrero!*' (Man, take off thy hat) said one of the three fellows who had hold of him; and before he could understand what that meant, another of them had taken his hat – a wretched covering, it is true, but still of use on a day of sunshine or a day of rain. Gringoire heaved a sigh.

But the king, from the top of his barrel, put the interrogatory, 'What is this knave?'

Gringoire started. This voice, though menacing in tone, reminded him of another voice which that very morning had struck the first blow at his mystery, by droning out in the midst of the audience, 'Charity, if you please!' He raised his eyes – it was indeed Clopin Trouillefou.

Clopin Trouillefou, arrayed in his regal ensigns, had not one rag more or less upon him. His sore on the arm had disappeared. In his hand he held one of those whips with lashes of whitleather, which were, at that time, used by the sergeants of the wand to drive back the crowd, and were called boullayes. He had upon his head a circular coif closed at the top; but it was difficult to distinguish whether it was a child's cushion or a king's crown, so similar are the two things.

However, Gringoire, without knowing why, had felt some revival of hope on recognizing in the king of the Court of Miracles his cursed beggar of the Grande Salle. 'Maître,' stammered he, ' – Monseigneur – Sire – How must I call you?' said he at last, having mounted to his utmost stretch of ascent, and neither knowing how to mount higher nor how to come down again.

'Monseigneur – Your Majesty – or Comrade – call me what you like, only despatch. What hast thou to say in thy defence?'

'In my defence!' thought Gringoire. 'That is unpleasant.' He replied, hesitating, 'I am he – he who this morning – '

'By the devil's claws!' interrupted Clopin, 'thy name, rascal! and nothing more. Hark ye – thou art before three mighty sovereigns: me, Clopin Trouillefou, King of Tunis, successor to the Grand Coësre, supreme sovereign of the kingdom of Argot; Mathais Hungadi Spicali, Duke of Egypt and Bohemia, that yellow old fellow that thou seest there with a clout round his head; and Guillaume Rousseau, Emperor of Galilee, that fat fellow, that's not attending to us, but to that wench. We are thy judges. Thou hast entered into the kingdom of Argot without being an Argotier – thou hast violated the privileges of our stronghold. Thou must be punished, unless thou art either a capon, a franc-mitou, or a rifodé, that is to say, in the language of the honest men, either a thief, a beggar, or a vagrant. Art thou anything of that sort? Justify thyself tell over thy qualifications.'

'Alas!' said Gringoire,' l have not that honour. I am the author – '

'That's enough,' interrupted Trouillefou; 'thou shalt be hanged. It's a matter of course, messieurs the honest townsfolk. As you treat our people amongst you, so we treat yours amongst us. Such law as you mete to the Truands (vagabonds and outlaws) the Truands mete to you. It is but your fault if it be evil. 'Tis quite necessary that an honest man or two should now and then grin through the hempen collar – that makes the thing honourable. Come, friend, merrily share thy tatters among these young ladies. I'll have thee hanged for the amusement of the Truands, and thou shalt give them thy purse to drink thy health. If thou hast any mumming to do, there is yonder, in that mortar, a capital God the Father in stone that we stole from Saint Pierre aux Bœufs. Thou hast four minutes' time to throw thy soul at his head.'

This was a formidable harangue.

'Well said! upon my soul. Clopin Trouillefou preaches as well as any pope!' cried the Emperor of Galilee, smashing his pot at the same time to prop his table-leg.

'Messeigneurs the emperors and kings!' said Gringoire coolly (for I do not know how his resolution had returned to him, and he spoke quite firmly), 'you do not consider. My name is Pierre Gringoire – I am the poet whose morality was performed this morning in the Grande Salle of the Palace.'

'Ah! it is thee, master, is it? I was there, by God's head! Well, comrade, is it any reason, because thou tiredst us to death this morning, that thou shouldst not be hanged to-night?'

'I shall have trouble to get off,' thought Gringoire. However, he made another effort. 'I don't very well see,' said he, 'why the poets are not classed among the Truands. A vagrant! – why Æsopus was a vagrant. A beggar – Homerus was a beggar. A thief – was not Mercurius a thief?'

Clopin interrupted him. 'Methinks,' said he, 'thou'st a mind to matagrabolize us with thy gibberish. *Pardieu!* Be hanged quietly, man; and don't make so much ado.'

'Pardon me, monseigneur the king of Tunis,' replied Gringoire, disputing the ground inch by inch; 'it's really worth your while – Only one moment – Hear me – You'll not condemn me without hearing me?'

His unfortunate voice was in fact drowned by the uproar that was made around him; the little boy was scraping his kettle with more energy than ever; and, as a climax, an old woman had just come and set upon the redhot trivet a frying-pan full of fat, which shrieked over the fire with a noise like the shouts of a flock of children running after a masquerade.

Meanwhile, Clopin Trouillefou seemed to confer a moment with the duke of Egypt, and with the emperor of Galilee, who was completely drunk. Then he called out sharply, 'Silence!' and as the pot and the frying-pan paid no attention to him, but continued their duet, he jumped down from his barrel, gave the caldron a kick which rolled it and the child half a score yards off, gave the frying-pan another, upsetting all the fat into the fire; and then gravely reascended his throne, regardless of the smothered cries of the child, and of the grumbling of the old woman, whose supper was evaporating in a beautiful white flame.

Trouillefou made a sign; whereupon the duke, and the emperor, and the *archisuppôts* (receiver of stolen goods), and the *cagoux* (those living in hiding), came and ranged themselves about him in the form of a horseshoe, of which Gringoire, still roughly held, occupied the centre. It was a semi-circle of rags, tatters and tinsel – of pitchforks and hatchets – of staggering legs and brawny arms – of sordid, dull and sottish faces. In the midst of this round table of beggary, Clopin Trouillefou, as the doge of this senate, the king of this peerage, the pope of this conclave, dominated – in the first place, by the height of his cask – and then, by a certain haughty, savage and formidable air, which made his eyes flash, and corrected in his fierce profile the bestial type of the Truand race. One would have said a wild boar among swine.

'Hark ye,' said he to Gringoire, while he caressed his shapeless chin with his horny hand, 'I don't see why thou shouldst not be hanged. To be sure, thou dost not seem to like it, and that's but natural – you burghers aren't used to it. You have exaggerated its importance. After all, we don't wish thee any harm. There's one way of getting off for the moment. Wilt thou be one of us?'

One can imagine the effect this proposal produced upon Gringoire, who saw life about to escape him, and felt his grasp beginning to fail. He caught at it energetically.

'That I will – certainly, assuredly,' said he.

'Thou dost consent,' said Clopin, 'to enlist thyself among the men of the *petite flambe?*' (small banner).

'Of the *petite flambe* – exactly so,' responded Gringoire.

'Thou dost acknowledge thyself a member of the free *bourgeoisie?*' added the king of Tunis.

'Of the free *bourgeoisie.*'

'A subject of the kingdom of Argot?'

'Of the kingdom of Argot.'

'A Truand?'

'A Truand.'

'In thy soul?'

'In my soul.'

'I will just observe to thee,' resumed the king, 'that thou wilt be none the less hanged for all that.'

'The devil!' exclaimed the poet.

'Only,' continued Clopin, quite imperturbably, 'thou wilt be hanged later, with more ceremony, at the expense of the good city of Paris, upon a fine stone gibbet, and by honest men. That's some consolation.'

'Just so,' answered Gringoire.

'There are other advantages. As being a free burgher, thou wilt have to pay neither tax on the pavements, the lamps, nor for the poor; to which the burghers of Paris are subject.'

'Be it so,' said the poet; 'I consent. I am a Truand, an Argotier, a free burgher, a *petite flambe*, whatever you please – and indeed I was all that beforehand, monsieur the king of Tunis; for I am a philosopher; and, as thou knowest, *Omnia in philosophia, omnes in philosopho continentur* – ' (all things are included in philosophy – all men in the philosopher).

The king of Tunis knit his brows.

'What dost thou take me for, friend? What cant of a Hungarian Jew art thou singing us now? I don't understand Hebrew. Because a man is a bandit, he is not obliged to be a Jew. Nay, I don't even rob now – I'm above that – a cut-throat, if you like, but no cut-purse.'

Gringoire strove to slip in an excuse between these brief and angry ejaculations. 'I ask your pardon, monseigneur – it's not Hebrew, it's Latin.'

'I tell thee,' rejoined Clopin, in a rage, 'that I'm no Jew, and that I'll have thee hanged, *ventre le synagogue!* (by the stomach of the synagogue) as well as that little shopkeeper of Judea that stands by thee, and whom I hope to see, one of these days, nailed to a counter like a piece of bad coin as he is!'

So saying, he pointed with his finger to the little bearded Hungarian Jew, who had accosted Gringoire with his *Facitote caritatem!* and who, understanding no other language, was surprised to see the ill-humour of the king of Tunis vent itself upon him.

At length Monseigneur Clopin became calm. 'Varlet,' said he to our poet, 'then thou'rt willing to be a Truand?'

'Undoubtedly,' answered the poet.

'It is not alone enough to be willing,' said Clopin, surlily. 'Goodwill doesn't put one onion more into the soup, and is of no use but for going to heaven – and there's a difference between heaven and Argot. To be received in Argot thou must prove that thou art good for something; and to do that thou must rummage the mannikin.'

'I will rummage anything you like,' said Gringoire.

Clopin made a sign; whereupon several Argotiers detached themselves from the circle, and returned a moment later. They brought two posts, terminated at the lower extremity by two wooden feet, which made them stand firmly on the ground. To the upper extremities of these posts they applied a cross-beam; the whole forming a very pretty portable gallows, which Gringoire had the satisfaction of seeing erected before him in the twinkling of an eye. Everything was there, including the rope, which gracefully depended from the transverse beam.

'What will be the end of all this?' thought Gringoire, with some uneasiness. But a noise of little bells which he heard at that moment put an end to his anxiety; it proceeded from a stuffed figure of a man which the Truands were suspending by the neck to the rope, a sort of scarecrow, clothed in red, and so completely covered with little bells and hollow jingling brasses, that there were enough to have harnessed thirty Castilian mules. These thousand miniature bells jingled for a time under the vibrations of the cord; their sound dying away gradually into a profound silence, which resulted from the state of perfect rest into which the body of the mannikin was speedily brought by that law of the pendulum which has superseded the use of the water clock and the hour-glass.

Then Clopin, pointing to an old tottering stool beneath the mannikin, said to Gringoire, 'Get upon that.'

'*Mort-diable!*' objected Gringoire, 'I shall break by neck. Your stool halts like one of Martial's couplets – it has one hexameter leg and one pentameter.'

'Get up,' repeated Clopin.

Gringoire mounted upon the stool, and succeeded, not without some oscillations of his head and his arms, in recovering his centre of gravity.

'Now,' proceeded the King of Tunis, 'turn thy right foot round thy left leg, and rise on the toe of thy left foot.'

'Monseigneur,' said Gringoire, 'you are then absolutely determined that I shall break a limb!'

Clopin shook his head. 'Hark ye, friend,' said he, 'thou dost talk too much. It all amounts to this: thou must stand on tip-toe, then thou canst reach the mannikin's pocket, thrust in thy hand and pull out the purse concealed therein, and if thou dost all this without the sounding of a bell, well and good – thou shalt be a Truand. We shall then have nothing more to do but belabour thee soundly for a week.'

'*Ventre-Dieu!* I shall take good care,' said Gringoire. 'And if I make the bells jingle?'

'Then thou shalt be hanged. Dost thou understand?'

'Nay, I understand it not at all,' answered Gringoire.

'Hark ye once more. You're to put your hand in the mannikin's pocket and take out his purse. If one single bell stirs in the doing of it, you shall be hanged. Now dost understand?'

'Well,' said Gringoire, 'I understand that. What next?'

'If you manage to draw out the purse without making a jingle, you're a Truand, and will be soundly belaboured for eight days together. You understand now, I dare say.'

'No, monseigneur, I do not yet understand. Where is my advantage? To be hanged in one case, or beaten in the other!'

'And to be a Truand,' rejoined Clopin – 'to be a Truand! Is that nothing? 'Tis for thine own advantage we shall beat thee, to harden thee against stripes.'

'I am greatly beholden to you,' answered the poet.

'Come, hasten!' said the king, striking his barrel with his foot, which resounded like a big drum. 'Rifle the mannikin's pocket, and let's have done with it. I tell thee, once for all, that if I hear the smallest tinkle, thou shalt take the mannikin's place.'

The whole company of Argotiers applauded the words of Clopin, and ranged themselves in a circle round the gallows with so pitiless a laugh that Gringoire saw plainly enough that he gave them too much amusement not to have everything to fear. He had, therefore, no hope left but in the faint chance of succeeding in the terrible operation which was imposed upon him. He resolved to risk it; but he first addressed a fervent prayer to the stuffed figure whom he was about to rob, and whose heart was even more likely to be softened than those of the Truands. The myriad bells, with their little brazen tongues, appeared to him like so many asps open mouthed, ready to hiss and to sting.

'Oh!' said he, in a low voice, 'and can it be that my life depends upon the smallest vibration of the smallest of those bits of metal? Oh!' he added, clasping his hands, 'ye bells, tinkle not – ye balls, jingle not!'

He made one more effort with Trouillefou.

'And if there come a breath of wind,' demanded he.

'Thou shalt be hanged,' replied the other, without hesitation.

Finding that there was no respite, delay, or subterfuge whatsoever, he bravely set about the feat. He turned his right foot about his left leg, lifted himself on the toe of his left foot, and stretched out his arm; but the moment that he touched the mannikin, his body, which was supported only by one foot, tottered upon the stool, which had only three, he mechanically caught at the mannikin, lost his balance and fell heavily to the ground, quite deafened by the fatal vibration of the scarecrow's thousand bells; while the figure, yielding to the impulse which his hand had given it, first revolved on his own axis, and then swung majestically backwards and forwards between the two posts.

'*Malédiction!*' he exclaimed as he fell; and he lay with his face to the ground as if he were dead.

However, he heard the awful chime above him, and the diabolical laughter of the Truands and the voice of Trouillefou, saying, 'Lift the fellow up, and hang him promptly.'

He rose by himself. They had already unhooked the mannikin to make room for him.

The Argotiers made him get upon the stool again. Clopin came up to him, passed the rope round his neck, and, slapping him on the shoulder, 'Good-bye, friend,' said he; 'thou'lt not escape now, though thou shouldst have the digestion of the pope himself.'

The word 'Mercy!' expired on Gringoire's lips – he cast his eyes round, but saw no gleam of hope – all were grinning.

'Bellevigne de l'Etoile,' said the king of Tunis to an enormous Truand, who stepped out of the ranks, 'do you get upon the cross-beam.' Bellevigne de l'Etoile climbed nimbly up to the transverse bar; and an instant after, Gringoire, looking up, saw him with terror squatted just above his head.

'Now,' continued Clopin Trouillefou, 'as soon as I clap my hands do thou, Andry le Rouge, knock down the stool with thy knee; thou, François Chante-Prune, hang on the rascal's feet; and thou, Bellevigne, drop upon his shoulders, and all three at the same time do you hear?'

Gringoire shuddered.

'Are you ready?' said Clopin Trouillefou to the three Argotiers, about to throw themselves upon the poet. The poor sufferer had a moment of horrible expectation, while Clopin was quietly pushing into the fire with he point of his shoe some twigs which the flame had not reached. 'Are you ready?' he repeated, and he opened his hands to give the signal. A second more, and all would have been over.

But he stopped as it struck by a sudden idea. 'Wait a moment,' said he; 'I am forgetful. It is our custom not to hang a man without first asking if there be a woman who will have him. Comrade, it's thy last chance! thou gypsy must marry either a Truand or the halter.'

(This gypsy law, strange as it may seem to the reader, is to-day written out in full in the old English code. See Burington's Observations.)

Gringoire took breath. This was the second time he had come to life within half an hour, so that he dared not be too confident.

'Hello!' shouted Clopin, who had reascended his cask: 'hello, there! women! females! is there among you all, from the witch to her cat, ever a jade that will have this rogue? Hello! Collette la Charonne! Elizabeth Trouvain! Simone Jodouyne! Marie Piédebou! Thonne la Longue! Bérarde Fanouel! Michelle Genaille! Claude Rougeorielle! Mathurine Girorou! – Hello! Isabeau la Thierrye! Come and see! A man for nothing! Who will have him?'

Gringoire, in this miserable plight, was, it may be supposed, not over-inviting. The women displayed no great enthusiasm at the proposal. The unhappy fellow heard them answer: 'No, no – hang him! it will amuse us all!'

Three of them, however, stepped out of the crowd to examine him. The first was a large, square-faced young woman. She carefully inspected the philosopher's deplorable doublet. The coat was thread-bare, and had more holes in it than a chestnut-roaster. The woman made a wry face at it. 'An old rag!' muttered she; and then addressing Gringoire, 'Let's see thy cloak.'

'I have lost it,' said Gringoire. 'Thy hat?'

'They've taken it from me.'

'Thy shoes?'

'They've hardly a bit of sole left.'

'Thy purse?'

'Alas!' stammered Gringoire, 'I've not a single penny.'

'Let them hang thee – and be thankful,' replied the Truandess, turning her back upon him.

The second woman, old, dark, wrinkled, of an ugliness conspicuous even in the Court of Miracles, now made the circuit of Gringoire. He trembled least she should want to have him. But she only muttered, 'He's too lean,' and went her way.

The third that came was a young girl, fresh-complexioned, and not ill-looking. 'Save me!' whispered the poor devil. She looked at him for a moment with an air of pity, then cast down her eyes, made a plait in her skirt, and remained undecided. He watched her every motion – it was his last gleam of hope. 'No,' said the girl at last, 'no – Guillaume Longuejoue would beat me.' And she returned into the crowd.

'Comrade,' said Clopin, 'thou'rt unlucky.'

Then rising on his barrel, 'So nobody bids?' cried he, mimicking the tone of an auctioneer, to the great diversion of all – 'so nobody bids? Going – going – going – ' then turning toward the gallows with a motion of his head, 'gone.'

Bellevigne de l'Etoile, Andry le Rouge, and François Chante Prune again approached Gringoire.

At that moment a cry was raised among the Argotiers, of 'La Esmeralda! La Esmeralda!'

Gringoire started, and turned toward the side from which the shout proceeded. The crowd opened and made way for a clear and dazzling figure.

It was the gypsy girl.

'La Esmeralda!' said Gringoire, stupefied, in the midst of his emotions, by the suddenness with which that magic word linked together all his recollections of the day.

This fascinating creature seemed to exercise, even over the Court of Miracles, her sway of grace and beauty. Argotiers, male and female, drew up gently to let her pass by; and their brutal countenances softened at her look.

She approached the victim with her elastic step, her pretty Djali following her. Gringoire was more dead than alive. She gazed at him for a moment in silence.

'Are you going to hang this man?' said she gravely to Clopin.

'Yes, sister,' answered the king of Tunis, 'unless thou wilt take him for thy husband.'

She made her pretty little grimace with her under lip.

'I will take him,' she said.

Gringoire was firmly persuaded that he must have been in a dream ever since the morning, and that this was but a continuation of it

In fact, this sudden turn of fortune, though agreeable, was abrupt.

They undid the noose, and let the poet descend from the stool. His agitation obliged him to sit down.

The duke of Egypt, without uttering a word, brought forth a clay pitcher. The gypsy girl presented it to Gringoire. 'Throw it on the ground,' said she.

The pitcher broke in four pieces.

'Brother,' said the duke of Egypt, laying his hands upon their foreheads, 'she is thy wife – sister, he is thy husband – for four years. Go your ways.'

VII

A Wedding Night

IN A FEW MINUTES our poet found himself in a little chamber with a Gothic-vaulted ceiling, very snug, very warm, seated before a table which seemed to ask nothing better than to borrow a few articles from a hanging cupboard near by; having a good bed in prospect, and alone with a pretty girl. The adventure partook of enchantment. He began seriously to take himself for the hero of a fairy tale; now and then he cast his eyes around him, as if to see whether the fiery chariot drawn by two winged steeds, which alone could have transported him so swiftly from Tartarus to Paradise were still there. At intervals, too, he fixed his eyes steadfastly upon the holes in his coat, by way of clinging to reality, so as not to let the earth altogether slip from under him. His reason, tossed to and fro in imaginative space, had only that thread left to cling to.

The girl seemed to pay no attention to him. She was going back and forth, shifting first one article and then another, chatted with her goat repeating her little grimace every now and then. At length she came and sat down near the table, and Gringoire could contemplate her at leisure.

You have been a child, reader, and perhaps you have the happiness to be so still. It is quite certain, then, that you have more than once followed from brier to brier (and for my own part I can say that I have passed whole days in that manner, the best spent days of my life), on the brink of a rivulet, on a sunshiny day, some lovely green or azure dragon-fly, checking its flight at sharp angles, and kissing the tip of every twig. You recollect with what loving curiosity your thoughts and your looks were fixed upon that little whirl of whiz and hum, of blue and purple wings, in the midst of which floated an intangible form, veiled as it was by the very rapidity of its motion. The aërial creature confusedly perceptible amid the quivering of wings, appeared chimerical, imaginary, impossible to touch, impossible to see. But when, at last, the dragon-fly settled on the tip end of a reed, and you could examine, holding your breath the while, the long gauze pinions, the long enamel robe, the two globes of crystal, what amazement did you not feel, and what fear lest it should again fade to a shadow, and the creature to a chimera! Recall these impressions, and you will easily understand the feelings of Gringoire on contemplating, under her visible and palpable form, that Esmeralda of whom, until then, he had only caught a glimpse amid a whirl of dance, song, and the noise of the populace.

Sinking deeper and deeper into his reverie –

'This, then,' said he to himself; as his eyes vaguely followed her, 'is the Esmeralda – a heavenly creature! – a dancer in the streets – so much, and yet so little! She it was who gave the finishing blow to my mystery this morning – she it is who saves my life to-night. My evil genius! – my good angel! A pretty woman, upon my word! – and who must love me to distraction, to take me in this fashion. Now I think on't,' said he, suddenly rising up from his seat, with that feeling of the real which formed the substance of his character and of his philosophy, 'I know not quite how it is – but I am her husband!'

With this idea in his head, and in his eyes, he approached the young girl in so military and lover-like a manner that she drew back. 'What do you want?' she said.

'Can you ask, adorable Esmeralda?' replied Gringoire, in such impassioned tones that he himself was astonished at his own accents.

The gypsy opened her large eyes. 'I know not your meaning.'

'What!' rejoined Gringoire, growing more and more excited, and thinking that, after all, he was only dealing with the ready-made virtue of the Court of Miracles, 'am I not thine, sweet friend? – art thou not mine?'

And quite guilelessly he clasped her waist.

The girl's bodice slipped through his hands like the skin of an eel. She sprang from one end of the little cell to the other, stooped, and rose again with a small poniard in her hand, before Gringoire had time to see whence the poniard came – irritated and indignant, with swelling lips, dilated nostrils, cheeks red as crab apples, and her eyes flashing lightning. At the same time the little white goat placed itself before her, and presented a battle-front to Gringoire, bristling with two pretty gilded and very sharp horns. This was all done in the twinkling of an eye.

The damsel had turned wasp, with every disposition to sting.

Our philosopher stood crestfallen, looking confusedly, first at the goat and then at its mistress. 'Holy Virgin!' he exclaimed at last, as soon as his surprise permitted him to speak, 'here are two tricksters!'

The gypsy now broke silence. 'Thou must be a very bold rascal!' she said.

'Forgive me, mademoiselle,' said Gringoire, with a smile; 'but why did you marry me then?'

'Was I to let them hang thee?'

'So,' rejoined the poet, somewhat disappointed in his amorous expectations, 'you had no other intention in marrying me but to save me from the gibbet?'

'And what other intention dost think I could have had?'

Gringoire bit his lip. 'Humph!' said he, 'I am not yet quite so successful a Lothario as I thought. But then what was the use of breaking that poor jug?'

But Esmeralda's poniard and the horns of the goat were still on the defensive.

'Mademoiselle Esmeralda,' said the poet, 'let us compromise. I am not registering clerk at the Châtelet, and will not quibble with you about your thus carrying a dagger in Paris in the teeth of monsieur the provost's ordinances and prohibitions. You must know, however, that Nöel Lescrivain was condemned, only a week ago, to pay a fine of ten Paris pence for wearing a broad sword. Now that is not my business – and so, to the point. I swear to you, by my chance of salvation, that I will not approach you without your leave and permission. But pray, give me supper.'

The truth is, that Gringoire, like Despréaux, was 'very little of a voluptuary.' He was not of that cavalier and mousquetaire species who carry girls by assault. In a love affair, as in every other affair, he willingly resigned himself to temporizing and to middle terms; and a good supper, in comfortable tête-a-tête, appeared to him, especially when he was hungry, to be a very good interlude between the prologue and the issue of an intrigue.

The gypsy made no answer. She gave her little disdainful pout: drew up her head like a bird; then burst out laughing; and the dainty dagger disappeared as it came, without Gringoire's being able to discover where the bee hid its sting.

A moment later a rye loaf, a slice of bacon, some withered apples and a jug of beer were on the table. Gringoire set to with avidity. To hear the furious clatter of his iron fork upon his earthen-ware plate, it seemed as if all his love had turned to hunger.

The young girl, seated near him, looked on in silence, evidently preoccupied by some other thought, at which she smiled from time to time, while her delicate hand caressed the intelligent head of the goat, pressed softly against her knee.

A candle of yellow wax lighted this scene of voracity and reverie.

However, the first cravings of his stomach being appeased, Gringoire felt a twinge of shame at seeing that there was only an apple left.

'Mademoiselle Esmeralda,' said he, 'you do not eat.'

She answered by a negative motion of the head; and her pensive gaze seemed to fix itself upon the vaulted ceiling of the chamber.

'What the deuce is she thinking about?' thought Gringoire; 'it can not be that grinning dwarf's face carved upon that keystone that attracts her so mightily. The devil's in it if I can not at least bear that comparison.'

He raised his voice – 'Mademoiselle.'

She seemed not to hear him.

He repeated, louder still, 'Mademoiselle Esmeralda!' It was in vain. The girl's mind was elsewhere, and Gringoire's voice had not the power to bring it back. Luckily, the goat interfered. She began to pull her mistress gently by the sleeve. 'What do you want, Djali?' said the gypsy, briskly with a sudden start.

'She is hungry,' said Gringoire, delighted at an opportunity of entering into conversation.

La Esmeralda began to crumble some bread, which Djali nibbled daintily from the hollow of her hand.

Gringoire, however, allowed her no time to resume her reverie. He ventured a delicate question: 'You will not have me for your husband, then?'

The girl looked fixedly at him, and answered, 'No.'

'For your lover?' proceeded Gringoire. She pouted, and again answered, 'No.'

'For your friend?' then demanded the poet.

Again she looked at him fixedly; and, after a moment's reflection, said, 'Perhaps.'

This 'perhaps,' so dear to philosophers, encouraged Gringoire. 'Do you know what friendship is?' he asked.

'Yes,' answered the gypsy, 'it is to be like brother and sister – two souls meeting without mingling – two fingers on the same hand.'

'And love?' proceeded Gringoire.

'Oh! love!' said she – and her voice trembled and her eye beamed – 'that is to be two and yet but one – a man and woman blended into an angel – it is heaven!'

The street dancer, while saying this, was beautified in a way that struck Gringoire singularly and seemed to him in perfect harmony with the almost Oriental exaltation of her words. Her pure, roseate lips were half smiling. Her clear, calm brow was momentarily ruffled by her thoughts, as a mirror dimmed by a passing breath. And from her long, dark, drooping lashes there emanated an ineffable light, giving her profile that ideal sweetness which Raphael has since found at the mystic point of intersection of virginity, maternity and divinity.

Gringoire, nevertheless, continued.

'What must one be then to please you?'

'He must be a man.'

'And I,' said be, 'what am I then?'

'A man has a helmet on his head, a sword in his hand and gilt spurs at his heels.'

'Good!' said Gringoire; 'the horse makes the man. Do you love anybody?'

'As a lover?'

'Yes – as a lover.'

She remained pensive a moment. Then she said, with a peculiar expression, 'I shall know soon.'

'Why not to-night?' rejoined the poet, in a tender tone. 'Why not me?'

She gave him a grave look, and said: 'I can not love a man who can not protect me.'

Gringoire coloured and took the reflection to himself. The girl evidently alluded to the feeble assistance he had lent her in the critical situation in which she had found herself two hours before. This recollection, effaced by his other adventures of the evening, now returned to him. He struck his forehead. 'Apropos, mademoiselle,' said he, 'I ought to have begun with that – pardon my foolish distractions – how did you contrive to escape from the clutches of Quasimodo?'

At this question the gypsy started. 'Oh! the horrible hunchback!' said she, hiding her face in her hands, and she shivered as if icy cold.

'Horrible, indeed!' said Gringoire, still pursuing his idea.

'But how did you manage to escape him?'

La Esmeralda smiled, sighed and was silent.

'Do you know why he followed you?' asked Gringoire, striving to come round again to the object of his inquiry.

'I don't know,' said the girl. Then she added quickly, 'but you were following me also. Why did you follow me?'

'In good faith,' replied Gringoire, 'I do not know.'

There was a pause. Gringoire was marking the table with his knife. The girl smiled, and seemed to be looking at something through the wall. All a once she began to sing in a voice scarcely audible:

> 'Quando las pintadas aves
> Mudas eslan, y la tierra . . .' *

She suddenly stopped short, and fell to caressing Djali.

* When the gay-plumaged birds
Grow weary, and the earth, . .

77

'You have a pretty creature there,' said Gringoire.

'It is my sister,' answered she.

'Why do they call you La Esmeralda?' asked the poet.

'I don't know at all.'

'But why do they?'

She drew from her bosom a small oblong bag, suspended from her neck by a chain of grains of adrez arach (sweet-scented gum). A strong smell of camphor exhaled from the bag; it was covered with green silk, and had in the centre a large piece of green glass in imitation of an emerald.

'Perhaps it's on account of that,' said she.

Gringoire offered to take the bag, but she drew back. 'Touch it not,' she said, ' 'tis an amulet. Thou wouldst do mischief to the charm, or the charm to thee.'

The poet's curiosity was more and more awakened. 'Who gave it you?' said he.

She placed her finger on her lip, and hid the amulet again in her bosom. He tried a few more questions but could hardly obtain an answer.

'What's the meaning of that word, La Esmeralda?'

'I do not know,' she replied.

'What language does it belong to?'

'I think it is a gypsy word.'

'So I suspected,' said Gringoire; 'you are not a native of France?'

'I know nothing about it.'

'Are your parents living?'

She began to sing, to an old tune:

> 'A bird was my mother;
> My father, another;
> Over the water I pass without ferry.
> Over the water I pass without wherry;
> A bird was my mother;
> My father, another.'

'Very good,' said Gringoire. 'At what age did you come to France?'

'When very little.'

'And when to Paris?'

'Last year. A the moment we were coming in by the Porte Papale I saw the reed linnet fly through the air – it was at the end of August – I said it will be a hard winter.'

'It has been so,' said Gringoire, delighted at this beginning of conversation – 'I've done naught but blow upon my fingers. You have the gift of prophecy?'

She fell again into her laconism.

'No.'

'That man whom you call the duke of Egypt is the chief of your tribe?'

'Yes.'

'But was it he who married us?' timidly remarked the poet.

She made her usual pretty grimace – 'I don't even know thy name.'

'My name? – You shall have it if you wish: Pierre Gringoire.'

'I know a finer one,' said she.

'Cruel girl!' rejoined the poet. 'No matter – you shall not provoke me. Nay, you will perhaps love me when you know me better – and then, you have told me your history so confidingly that I owe you somewhat of mine. You must know, then, that my name is Pierre Gringoire, and that I am the son of a notary of Gonesse. My father was hanged by the Burgundians, and my mother ripped open by the Picards, at the time of the siege of Paris twenty years ago. At six years of age, then, I was an orphan, without any other sole to my foot than the pavement of Paris. How I managed to exist from six to sixteen, I do not know. A fruit woman would give me a plum, a baker would throw me a crust. At night I used to get myself picked up by the Onze-vingts (night watch), who put me in prison, and there I found a bundle of straw. All this did not prevent my growing tall and thin, as you see. In winter I warmed myself in the sun, under the porch of the Hôtel de Sens; and I thought it very ridiculous that the great bonfires on the feast of Saint John should be reserved for the dog-days. At sixteen, I wished to choose a calling. I tried everything in succession. I turned soldier, but was not brave enough. I then turned monk, but was not devout enough – and besides, I'm a poor drinker. In despair, I apprenticed myself to carpenters, but was not strong enough. I had more inclination to be a schoolmaster; true, I could not read; but that need not have hindered me. I perceived, at the end of a certain time, that I was in want of some requisite for everything – and so, finding that I was good for nothing, I, of my own free will and pleasure, turned poet and composer of rhymes. 'Tis a calling that a man can always embrace when he's a vagabond; and is better than stealing, as I was advised to do by some young light-fingered fellows of my acquaintance. Fortunately, I met, one fine day, with Dom Claude Frollo, the reverend archdeacon of Notre-Dame. He took an interest in me and to him I owe it that I am now a true man of letters, acquainted with Latin, from Cicero's Offices to the Mortuology of the Celestine fathers, and not absolutely barbarous either in scholastics, in poetics, or in rhythmics, nor yet in hermetics, that science of sciences. I am the author of the miracle play that was performed to-day, with great triumph and concourse of people, in the Grande Salle of the Palace. I've also written a book that will make six hundred pages, upon the prodigious comet of 1465, about which one man went mad. I have also had other successes; being something of an artillery carver, I worked upon that great bomb of Jean Maugue which you know burst at the bridge of Charenton the first time it was tried, and killed four-and-twenty of the spectators. You see that I'm not so indifferent a match. I know many sorts of very clever tricks, which I will teach your goat – for instance, to mimic the Bishop of Paris, that accursed Pharisee whose mill-wheels splash the passengers the whole length of the Pont aux Meuniers. And then, my mystery will bring me in plenty of ready money if they pay me. In short, I am at your service – I, and my wit, and my science, and my learning – ready to live with you, damsel, as it shall please you – soberly or merrily – as husband and wife, if you see fit – as brother and sister, if you like it better.'

Here Gringoire was silent, awaiting the effect of his speech upon the young girl. Her eyes were fixed upon the ground.

'Phœbus,' said she, in an undertone; then, turning to the poet, 'Phœbus,' said she, 'what does that mean?'

Gringoire, though not at all understanding what relation there could be between his address and this question, was not sorry to show his erudition. He answered, bridling with dignity, ' 'Tis a Latin word, that signifies the sun.'

'The sun!' repeated she. ''Tis the name of a certain handsome archer, who was god,' added Gringoire.

'A god!' repeated the gypsy; and there was something pensive and impassioned in her tone.

At that moment, one of the bracelets came unfastened and fell. Gringoire eagerly stooped to pick it up; and when he rose again, the girl and the goat had both disappeared. He heard the sound of a bolt. It was a small door, communicating no doubt with an adjoining chamber, which was fastened on the other side.

'Has she, at least, left me a bed?' said our philosopher.

He made the tour of the chamber. There was no piece of furniture at all adapted to repose, except a very long wooden chest; and the lid of that was carved; so that it gave Gringoire, when he stretched himself upon it, a sensation much like that which Micromegas, of Voltaire's story, would experience, lying at full length upon the Alps.

'Come!' said he, making the best of it, 'there's nothing for it but resignation. And yet this is a strange wedding night. 'Tis pity, too. That broken-pitcher marriage had something simple and antediluvian about it that quite pleased me.'

BOOK THREE

I

The Cathedral of Notre-Dame

THE CHURCH OF Notre-Dame at Paris is doubtless still a majestic and
sublime edifice. But, however beautiful it has remained in growing old,
it is difficult to suppress a sigh, to restrain a feeling of indignation at the
numberless degradations and mutilations which the hand of time and
that of man have inflicted upon this venerable monument, regardless
alike of Charlemagne, who laid the first stone, and of Philip Augustus,
who laid the last.

Upon the face of this ancient queen of French cathedrals, beside
each wrinkle we constantly find a scar. *Tempus edax, homo edacior* (Time
is destructive, man more destructive) – which we would willingly
render thus – Time is blind, but man is stupid.

If we had leisure to examine one by one, with the reader, the traces
of destruction imprinted on this ancient church, those due to Time
would be found to form the lesser portion – the worst destruction has
been perpetrated by men – especially by 'men of art.' Since there are
individuals who have styled themselves architects during the last two
centuries.

And first of all – to cite only a few leading examples – there are
assuredly, few finer architectural pages than that front of that cathedral,
in which, successively and at once, the three receding portals with their
pointed arches, the decorated and indented band of the twenty-eight
royal niches, the immense central rose-window, flanked by the two
lateral windows, like the priest by the deacon and sub-deacon; the lofty
and slender gallery of trifoliated arcades, supporting a heavy platform
upon its light and delicate columns; and lastly the two dark and massive
towers, with their eaves of slate – harmonious parts of one magnificent
whole – rising one above another in five gigantic stories – unfold
themselves to the eye, collectively and simply – with their innumerable
details of statuary, sculpture and carving, powerfully contributing to
the calm grandeur of the whole; a vast symphony in stone, if we may so
express it; the colossal work of a man and of a nation; combining unity
with complexity, like the Iliads and the old Romance epics to which it is
a sister-production; the prodigious result of a draught upon the whole
resources of an era – in which, upon every stone, is seen displayed, in a
hundred varieties, the fancy of the workman disciplined by the genius

of the artist – a sort of human Creation, in short, mighty and prolific like the Divine Creation, of which it seems to have caught the double character – variety and eternity.

And what we say of the front must be said of the whole church – and what we say of the cathedral church of Paris must be said of all the churches of Christendom in the Middle Ages. Everything is in its place in that art, self-created, logical and well-proportioned. To measure the toe is to measure the giant.

Let us return to the front of Notre-Dame, as it still appears to us when we gaze in pious admiration upon the solemn and mighty cathedral, inspiring terror, as its chroniclers express it – *quae mole sua terrorem incutit spectantibus* (which by its massiveness strikes terror into the beholders).

This front is now lacking in three things of importance: first, the flight of eleven steps which formerly raised it above the level of the ground; then, the lower range of statues, which occupied the niches of the three portals; and lastly, the upper series, of the twenty-eight most ancient kings of France, which filled the gallery on the first story, beginning with Childebert and ending with Philip Augustus, each holding in his hand the imperial ball.

As for the flight of steps, it is Time that has caused it to disappear, by raising, with slow but resistless progress, the level of the ground in the City. But while this flood-tide of the pavements of Paris devoured, one after another, the eleven steps which added to the majestic elevation of the structure, Time has given to the church, perhaps, yet more than it has taken away; for it is Time who has spread over its face that dark gray tint of centuries which makes of the old age of architectural monuments their season of beauty.

But who has thrown down the two ranges of statues? who has left the niches empty? who has cut, in the middle of the central portal, that new and bastard pointed arch? and who has dared to frame in that doorway the heavy, unmeaning wooden door, carved in the style of Louis XV, beside the arabesques of Biscornette? The men, the architects, the artists of our times.

And – if we enter the interior of the edifice – who has overturned the colossal Saint Christopher, proverbial for his magnitude among statues as the Grand Hall of the Palace was among halls – as the spire of Strasburg among steeples? And those myriads of statues which thronged the spaces between the columns of the nave and the choir – kneeling – standing – and on horseback, men, women, children, kings, bishops, warriors, in stone, in marble, in gold, in silver, in brass, and even in wax – who has brutally swept them out? It is not Time.

And who has substituted for the ancient Gothic altar, splendidly loaded with shrines and reliquaries, that heavy sarcophagus of marble, with angels' heads and clouds, looking like an unmatched fragment from the Val de Grâce or the Invalides? Who has stupidly fixed that heavy anachronism of stone into the Carlovingian pavement of Hercandus? Was it not Louis XIV fulfilling the vow of Louis XIII?

And who has put cold white glass in place of those deep-stained panes which made the wondering eyes of our forefathers hesitate between the round window over the grand doorway and the lancet windows of the chancel? And what would a precentor of the sixteenth century say could he see that fine yellow stain with which the Vandal archbishops have besmeared their cathedral? He would remember that it was the colour with which the hangman painted such buildings as were adjudged infamous – he would recollect the hôtel of the Petit-Bourbon, which had thus been besmeared with yellow for the treason of the constable – 'yellow, after all, so well mixed,' says Sauval, 'and so well applied, that the lapse of a century and more has not yet taken its colour.' He would believe that the holy place had become accursed, and would flee from it.

And, then, if we climb higher in the cathedral – without stopping at a thousand barbarities of every kind – what have they done with that charming little spire which rose from the intersection of the cross, and which, no less bold and light than its neighbour the spire of the Sainte Chapelle (destroyed also), pierced into the sky yet farther than the towers – perforated, sharp, sonorous, airy? An architect 'of good taste' amputated it in 1787, and thought it was sufficient to hide the wound with that great plaster of lead which resembles the lid of a porridge-pot.

Thus it is that the wondrous art of the Middle Ages has been treated in almost every country, and especially in France. In its ruin three sorts of inroads are distinguishable, having marred it to different depths, first, Time, which has insensibly made breaches here and there, and rusted its whole surface; then, religious and political revolutions, which, blind and furious in their nature, have tumultuously wreaked their wrath upon it, torn its rich garment of sculpture and carving, shivered its rose-shaped windows, broken its necklace of arabesques and miniature figures, torn down its statues, here for their mitre, there for their crown; and lastly, changing fashion, growing ever more grotesque and absurd, commencing with the anarchical yet splendid deviations of the Renaissance, have succeeded one another in the unavoidable decline of architecture. Fashion has done more mischief than revolutions. It has cut to the quick – it has attacked the very bone and framework of the art. It has mangled, dislocated, killed the edifice – in its form as well as in its meaning – in its logic as well as in its beauty. And then it has restored – which at least neither Time nor revolutions have pretended to do. It has audaciously fitted into the wounds of Gothic architecture its wretched gewgaws of a day – its marble ribands – its metal plumes – a very leprosy of egg-shaped mouldings, volutes and wreaths – of draperies, garlands and fringes – of stone flames, brazen clouds, fleshy Cupids, and lastly, cherubim – which we find beginning to ravage the face of art in the oratory of Catherine de Médicis, and destroying it two centuries after, tortured and convulsed, in the Dubarry's boudoir.

Thus, to sum up the points which we have here laid down, three kinds of ravages which to-day disfigure Gothic architecture: wrinkles and warts upon the surface – these are the work of Time; violences, brutalities, contusions, fractures – these are the work of revolutions, from Luther down to Mirabeau; amputations, dislocation of members, *restorations* – these are the labours, Grecian Roman and barbaric, of the professors according to Vitruvius and Vignola. That magnificent art which the Vandals had produced, the academies have murdered. To the work of centuries and of revolutions, which, at least, devastate with impartiality and grandeur, has been added that cloud of school-trained architects licensed, privileged and patented, degrading with all the discernment and selection of bad taste – substituting the gingerbread-work of Louis XV for the Gothic tracery, to the greater glory of the Parthenon. This is the kick of the ass at the dying lion. 'Tis the old oak, in the last stage of decay, stung and gnawed by caterpillars.

How remote is all this from the time when Robert Cenalis, comparing Notre-Dame at Paris to the famous temple of Diana at Ephesus, 'so much vaunted by the ancient pagans,' which immortalized Erostratus, thought the Gaulish cathedral 'more excellent in length, breadth, height and structure.' *

Notre-Dame, however, as an architectural monument, is not one of those which can be called complete, definite, belonging to a class. It is no longer a Roman, nor is it yet Gothic. This edifice is not a typical one. It has not, like the abbey of Tournus, the solemn and massive squareness, the round broad vault, the icy bareness, the majestic simplicity, of the edifices which have the circular arch for their base. Nor is it, like the cathedral of Bourges, the magnificent, airy, multiform, tufted, pinnacled, florid production of the pointed arch. Impossible to rank Notre-Dame among that antique family of churches, gloomy, mysterious, lowering, crushed, as it were, by the weight of the circular arch – almost Egyptian, even to their ceilings – all hieroglyphical, all sacerdotal, all symbolical – more abounding, in their ornaments, in lozenges and zigzags than in flowers – more in flowers than animals – more in animals than human figures – the work not so much of the

* The quotations in this paragraph are made by M. Hugo from Cenalis, *Gallican History*, Book II, Period III, fo.130, p. 1 – J. C. B.

architect as of the bishop – the first transformation of the art – all stamped with theocratical and military discipline – having its root in the Lower Empire, and stopping at the time of William the Conqueror. Nor can our cathedral be ranked in that other family of lofty, airy churches, rich in sculpture and stained glass, of pointed forms and daring attitudes – belonging to commoners and plain citizens, as political symbols – as works of art, free, capricious, lawless – the second transformation of architecture – no longer hieroglyphical, immutable and sacerdotal, but artistic, progressive and popular – beginning at the return from the crusades and ending with Louis XI. Notre-Dame of Paris, then, is not of purely Roman race like the former, nor of purely Arabic race like the latter.

It is an edifice of the transition period. The Saxon architect was just finishing the first pillars of the nave, when the pointed arch, arriving from the crusade, came and placed itself as a conqueror upon the broad Roman capitals which had been designed to support only circular arches. The Gothic arch, thenceforward master of the field, constituted the remainder of the church. However, inexperienced and timid at its commencement, we find it widening its compass, and, as it were, self-restraining, not yet daring to spring into arrows and lancets, as it did later in so many wonderful cathedrals. One would have said it was conscious of the neighbourhood of the heavy Roman pillars.

Indeed, these edifices of the transition from the Roman to the Gothic are not less valuable studies than the pure models. They express a blending in art which would be lost without them. It is the grafting of the Gothic upon the circular arch.

Notre-Dame, in particular, is a curious example of this variety. Every face, every stone, of this venerable monument, is a page not only of the history of the country, but of the history of science and art. Thus, to point out here only some of the principal details; while the small Porte Rouge attains almost to the limits of the Gothic delicacy of the fifteenth century, the pillars of the nave, in their amplitude and solemnity, go back almost as far as the Carlovingian abbey of Saint Germain des Prés. One would think there was an interval of six centuries between that door and those pillars. Even the hermetics find, in the emblematical devices of the great portal, a satisfactory compendium of their science, of which the church of Saint Jacques de la Boucherie was so complete a hieroglyphic. Thus the Roman abbey – the philosophers' church – Gothic art – Saxon art – the heavy round pillar, which recalls Gregory VII – the hermetical symbolism by which Nicolas Flamel anticipated Luther – papal unity and schism – Saint Germain des Prés and Saint Jacques de la Boucherie, all are mingled combined and amalgamated in Notre-Dame. This central and maternal church is, among the other old churches of Paris, a sort of chimera; she has the head of one, the limbs of another, the back of a third – something of all.

We repeat it, these hybrid constructions are not the least interesting to the artist, the antiquary and the historian. They show us in how great a degree architecture is a primitive thing – demonstrating (as the Cyclopean vestiges, the Egyptian pyramids and the gigantic Hindoo pagodas demonstrate) that the greatest productions of architecture are not so much the work of individuals as of society – the offspring rather of national efforts than the conceptions of men of genius, a deposit left by a whole people – the piled up works of centuries – the residue of successive evaporations of human society – in short, a species of formation. Each wave of time leaves its alluvium – each race deposits its strata upon the monument – each individual contributes his stone. So do the beavers – so do the bees – so does man. The great symbol of architecture, Babel, is a beehive.

Great edifices, like great mountains, are the work of ages. Art often undergoes a transformation while they are still pending – *pendent opera interrupta* (the interrupted work is discontinued), they go on again quietly, in accordance with the change in the art. The altered art takes up the monument where it was left off, incrusts itself upon it, assimilates it to itself, develops it after its own fashion, and finishes it if it can. The thing is done without disturbance, without effort, without reaction, according to a law natural and tranquil. It is like a budding graft – a sap that circulates – a vegetation that goes forward. Certainly there is matter for very large volumes, and often for the universal history of humanity, in those successive weldings of several species of art at different elevations upon the same monument. The man, the artist, the individual, disappear upon those great masses, leaving no name of an author behind. Human intelligence is there to be traced only in its aggregate. Time is the architect – the nation is the builder.

To consider in this place only the architecture of Christian Europe, the younger sister of the great masonries of the East, it presents to us an immense formation, divided into three superincumbent zones, clearly defined; the Roman zone, the Gothic zone, and the zone of the Renaissance, which we would willingly entitle the Grœco-Roman. The Roman stratum, the most ancient and the deepest, is occupied by the circular arch, which reappears rising from the Grecian column in the modern and upper stratum of the Revival. The pointed arch is found between the two. The buildings which belong exclusively to one or other of these three strata are perfectly distinct, uniform and complete. Such is the abbey of Jumièges; such is the cathedral of Rheims; such is the church of Sainte Croix at Orleans. But the three zones mingle and combine at their borders, like the colours of the prism. And hence the complex monuments – the edifices of gradation and transition. One is Roman at the base, Gothic in the middle and Græco-Roman at the top.

This is caused by the fact that it has taken six hundred years to build it. This variety is rare; the donjon tower of Etampes is a specimen. But monuments of two formations are more frequent. Such is Notre-Dame at Paris, a structure of the pointed arch, which, in its earliest columns, dips into that Roman zone in which the portal of Saint Denis and the nave of Saint Germain des Prés are entirely immersed. Such is the charming semi-Gothic chapter-house of Bocherville, which the Roman layer mounts half-way. Such is the cathedral of Rouen, which would have been entirely Gothic had not the extremity of its central spire pierced into the zone of the Renaissance.

However, all these gradations, all these differences, only affect the surface of an edifice. Art has but changed its skin – the conformation of the Christian temple itself has remained untouched. It is ever the same internal framework, the same logical disposition of parts. Whatever be the sculptured and decorated exterior of a cathedral, we always find beneath it at least the germ and rudiment of the Roman basilica. It unfolds itself upon the ground forever according to the same law. There are invariably two naves intersecting each other in the form of a cross, the upper extremity of which cross is rounded into a chancel forming the choir; there are always two side aisles for processions and chapels – a sort of lateral gallery communicating with the principal nave by the spaces between the columns. This settled, the number of chapels, doorways, steeples, spires, may be modified indefinitely, following the fancy of the age, the people, of the art. The performance of the worship being provided for, architecture is at liberty to do what she pleases. Statues, painted glass, rose-shaped windows, arabesques, indentations, capitals, bas-reliefs – all these objects of imagination she combines in such arrangement as best suits her. Hence the prodigious external variety of these edifices, in the main structure of which dwells so much order and unity. The trunk of the tree is unchanging – the foliage is variable.

II

A Bird's-Eye View of Paris

WE HAVE ENDEAVOURED to restore for the reader the admirable church of Notre-Dame de Paris. We have briefly indicated the greater part of the beauties which it possessed in the fifteenth century, and which are now wanting; but we have omitted the principal – the view of Paris as it then appeared from the summit of the towers

Indeed, when, after feeling your way for a long time up the dark spiral staircase that perpendicularly perforates the thick walls of steeples, you at last emerged suddenly upon one of the two elevated platforms inundated with light and air, it was a fine picture that opened upon you on every side, a spectacle *sui generis* some idea of which may easily be formed by such of our readers as have had the good fortune to see a Gothic town, entire, complete homogeneous – of which there are still a few remaining, such as Nuremberg in Bavaria and Vittoria in Spain – or even small specimens, provided they be in good preservation, as Vitré in Brittany and Nordhausen in Prussia.

The Paris of three hundred and fifty years ago, the Paris of the fifteenth century, was already a giant city. We modern Parisians are mistaken as to the ground which we think we have gained. Since the time of Louis XI, Paris has not increased much more than a third. She certainly has lost much more in beauty than she has gained in size.

Paris was born, as every one knows, in that ancient island of the Cité, or City, which is shaped like a cradle. The shores of this island were its first enclosure; the Seine its first moat. For several centuries Paris remained in its island state; with two bridges, one on the north, the other on the south; and two *tête-de-ponts* (bridge towers), which were at once its gates and its fortresses – the Grand Châtelet on the right bank of the northern channel of the river and the Petit Châtelet on the left bank of the southern channel. When, however, under the first line of French kings, Paris found herself too much confined within the limits of her island, and unable to turn about, she crossed the water. Then on each side, beyond either Châtelet, a first line of walls and towers began to cut into the country on both sides of the Seine. Of this ancient boundary wall some vestiges still remained as late as the last century; now nothing but the memory of it survives, with here and there a local tradition, as the Baudets or Baudoyer gate – *porta Bagauda*. By degrees, the flood of houses, perpetually driven from the heart of the town outward, overflowed and wore away this enclosure. Philip Augustus made a new embankment. He imprisoned Paris within a circular chain of great towers, lofty and massive. For upwards of a century the houses pressed upon one another, accumulated and rose higher in this basin, like water in a reservoir. They began to deepen – to pile story on story – to climb, as it were, one upon another. They shot out in height, like growth that is compressed laterally; and strove each to lift its head above its neighbours, in order to get a breath of air. The streets became deeper and narrower, and every open space was overrun by buildings and disappeared. The houses at last leaped the wall of Philip Augustus, and scattered themselves merrily over the plain, irregularly and all awry, like children escaped from school. There they strutted proudly about, cut themselves gardens from the fields and took their case. In 1367, the suburbs already extended so far that a new boundary wall became necessary, particularly on the right bank of the river; Charles V built it.

But a city like Paris is perpetually on the increase – and it is only such cities that become capitals. They are a sort of funnel, through which flow all that is geographical, political, moral and intellectual in a country – all the natural tendencies of a people – wells of civilization, as it were, and also sinks – where commerce, manufactures, intelligence, population – all the vigour, all the life, all the soul of a nation – filter and collect incessantly, drop by drop, and century after century. So the boundary of Charles V suffered the same fate as that of Philip Augustus. At the end of the fifteenth century, the Faubourg strides across it, passes beyond it, and runs farther. In the sixteenth we find it rapidly receding, and becoming buried deeper and deeper in the old town, so dense was the new town becoming outside it. Thus, in the fifteenth century – to stop there – Paris had already worn away the three concentric circles of walls which, in the time of Julian the Apostate, existed, so to speak, in germ in the Grand Châtelet and the Petit Châtelet. The growing city had successively burst its four girdles of walls, like a child grown too large for its garments of last year. In the reign of Louis XI were to be seen rising here and there, amid that sea of houses, some groups of ruinous towers belonging to the ancient bulwarks, like hill-tops in a flood – like archipelagoes of the old Paris submerged under the inundation of the new.

Since then, unhappily for us, Paris has undergone another transformation; but it has overleaped only one boundary more – that of Louis XV – the wretched wall of mud and spittle, worthy of the king who built it, worthy of the poet who sang it –

Le mur murant Paris rend Paris murmurant. *

In the fifteenth century, Paris was still divided into three wholly distinct and separate towns, having each its peculiar features, manners, customs, privileges and history – the City, the University and the Ville or Town properly so called. The City, which occupied the island, was the most ancient, the smallest, and the mother of the other two – sqeezed between them (if we may be allowed the comparison) like a little old woman between two tall handsome daughters. The University covered the left bank of the Seine, from the Tournelle to the Tour de Nesle, points which correspond today in modern Paris, the one to the Halle aux Vins or Wine Mart, and the other to the Monnaie or Mint. Its circuit embraced a large portion of that tract where Julian had constructed his baths, and comprised the hill of Sainte Geneviève. The culminating point of this curve of walls was the Porte Papale or Papal Gate, that is to say, very nearly, the present site of the Pantheon. The

* Play upon words, literally: The wall walling Paris makes Paris murmur.

Town, which was the largest of the three portions of Paris, occupied the right bank. Its quay, in which there were several breaks and interruptions, ran along the Seine from the Tour de Billy to the Tour du Bois, that is, from the spot where the Granary of Abundance now stands, to that occupied by the Tuileries. These four points where the Seine intersected the wall of the capital – on the left, the Tournelle and the Tour de Nesle, and on the right, the Tour de Billy and the Tour du Bois – were called, pre-eminently, the four towers of Paris. The Town encroached still more deeply into the country bordering on the Seine than the University. The most salient points of its enclosure (the wall constructed by Charles V) were at the Portes Saint Denis and Saint Martin, the sites of which are unchanged.

As we have just said, each of these three great divisions of Paris was a city in itself – but a city too individual to be complete – a city which could not dispense with the other two. Hence, each had its characteristic aspect. Churches abounded in the City; palaces in the Town, and colleges in the University. Leaving apart the minor eccentricities of old Paris, and the caprices of those who held the *droit de voirie*, or right of road, we make the general statement – and speaking only of the great masses in the chaos of the communal jurisdictions – that the island belonged to the bishop; the right bank to the *prévôt des marchands* or provost of the shop-keepers; and the left bank to the rector of the University. The provost of Paris, a royal and not a municipal officer, had authority over all. The City contained Notre-Dame; the Town, the Louvre and the Hôtel de Ville, and the University, the Sorbonne. Again, the Town had the Great Market; the City, the Hospital; and the University, the Pré aux Clercs (common). Offences committed by the students on the left bank, in their Pré aux Clercs, were tried in the Palace of Justice, on the island, and punished on the right bank at Montfaucon; unless the rector, feeling the University to be strong at that particular time, and the king weak, thought proper to interfere – for it was a privilege of the scholars to be hanged at home, that is to say, within the University precincts. Most of these privileges, it may be noted in passing, and there were some of greater value than the above, had been extorted from the kings by revolts and mutinies. Such has been the course of events from time immemorial. As the French proverb saith, *Le roi ne lache que quand le peuple arrache* (the king only grants what the people wrest from him). There is an old French charter which states the fact with great simplicity: speaking of loyalty, it says *Civibus fidelitas in reges, quae tamen aliquoties seditionibus interrupta, multa peperit privilegia* (the fidelity toward kings, which was nevertheless interrupted at different times – interrupted by seditious uprisings – preserved many privileges to the people).

In the fifteenth century, the Seine bathed the shores of five islands within the circuit of Paris; the Ile Louviers, on which there were then trees, though now there are only piles of wood; the Ile aux Vaches and the Ile Notre-Dame, both deserted, or nearly so both fiefs of the bishop (which two islands, in the seventeenth century, were made into one, since built upon, and now called the Ile Saint Louis); finally, the City, having at its western extremity, the islet of the Passeur aux Vaches, since lost under the esplanade of the Pont-Neuf. The City had, at that time, five bridges; three on the right – the Pont Notre-Dame, and the Pont au Change, of stone, and the Pont aux Meuniers, of wood – and two on the left – the Petit Pont, of stone, and the Pont Saint Michel, of wood all of them laden with houses. The University had six gates, built by Philip Augustus, which, starting from the Tournelle, came in the following order: the Porte Saint Victor, the Porte Bordelle, the Porte Papale, the Porte Saint Jacques, the Porte Saint Michel and the Porte Saint Germain. The Town had also six gates, built by Charles V, viz., beginning with the Tour de Billy, they were the Porte Saint Antoine, the Porte du Temple, the Porte Saint Martin, the Porte Saint Denis, the Porte Montmartre and the Porte Saint Honoré. All these gates were strong, and handsome withal – which latter attribute is by no means incompatible with strength. A wide and deep moat, with a swift current during the winter floods, washed the base of the wall around Paris; the Seine furnishing the water. At night the gates were shut, the river was barred at the two extremities of the town with massive iron chains, and Paris slept tranquilly.

A bird's-eye view of these three burghs, the City, the University and the Ville, presented each an inextricable network of strangely tangled streets. Yet a glance was sufficient to show the spectator that these three portions of a city formed but one complete whole. One immediately perceived two long parallel streets, unbroken, undisturbed, traversing, almost in a straight line, the three towns from one extremity to the other, from north to south, at right angles with the Seine, connecting and mingling them, and incessantly pouring the people of each into the precincts of the other, making the three but one. The first of these two streets ran from the Porte Saint Jacques to the Porte Saint Martin, and was called in the University, Rue Saint Jacques; in the City, Rue de la Juiverie (Jewery or Jewry); and in the Town, Rue Saint Martin. It crossed the water twice, under the names of Petit Pont and Pont Notre-Dame. The second, called, on the left bank, Rue de la Harpe; in the island, the Rue de la Barillerie; on the right bank, Rue Saint Denis; over one arm of the Seine, Pont Saint Michel, and over the other Pont au Change; ran from the Porte Saint Michel in the University to the Porte Saint Denis in the Town. However, under all these names, they were still but two streets; but they were the parent streets – the two arteries of Paris, by which all the other veins of the triple city were fed, or into, which they emptied themselves.

Independently of these two principal, diametrical streets, running quite across Paris, common to the whole capital, the Town and the University had each its own special street, traversing its length, parallel to the Seine, and intersecting the two *arterial* streets at right angles. Thus, in the Town, one went down in a straight line from the Porte Saint Antoine to the Porte Saint Honoré; in the University, from the Porte Saint Victor to the Porte Saint Germain. These two great ways, crossing the two first mentioned, formed with them the canvas upon which was wrought, knotted up and crowded together on every hand, the tangled Dædalian web of the streets of Paris. In the unintelligible designs of this network one distinguished likewise, on looking attentively, two clusters of great streets, like magnified sheaves, one in the University, the other in the Town, spreading out from the bridges to the gates.

Somewhat of this geometric plan still exists.

Now, what aspect did all this present viewed from the top of the towers of Notre-Dame in 1482? This is what we will endeavour to describe.

For the spectator, who arrived panting upon this summit, it was at first a dazzling confusion of roofs, chimneys, streets, bridges, squares, spires, steeples. All burst upon the eye at once – the formally-cut gable, the acute-angled roof, the hanging turret at the angles of the walls, the stone pyramid of the eleventh century, the slate obelisk of the fifteenth; the donjon tower, round and bare; the church tower, square and decorated; the large and the small, the massive and the airy. The gaze was for some time lost in the bewilderment of this labyrinth; in which there was nothing without its originality, its purpose, its genius – nothing but proceeded from art – from the smallest house, with its carved and painted front, with external beams, elliptical doorway, with projecting stories, to the royal Louvre itself, which then had a colonnade of towers. But these are the principal masses that were distinguishable when the eye became accustomed to this medley of edifices.

First, the City. The island of the City, as Sauval says, who, amidst all his rubbish, has occasional happy turns of expression – *The isle of the City is shaped like a great ship, stuck in the mud, and stranded in the current near the middle of the Seine.* We have already shown that, in the fifteenth century, this ship was moored to the two banks of the river by five bridges. This likeness to a vessel had also struck the heraldic scribes; for, it is thence, and not from the Norman siege, according to Favyn and Pasquier, that the ship emblazoned upon the old escutcheon of Paris comes. To him who can decipher it, heraldry is an algebra – heraldry is a tongue. The whole history of the second half of the Middle Ages is written in heraldry as that of the former half is in the symbolism of the Roman churches. They are the hieroglyphics of feudalism succeeding those of theocracy.

The City, then, first presented itself to the view, with its stern to the east and its prow to the west. Looking toward the prow, there was before one an innumerable collection of old roofs, with the lead-covered top of Sainte Chapelle rising above them broad and round, like an elephant's back laden with its tower. Only in this case the tower was the most daring, most open, most daintily wrought, most delicately carved spire that ever showed the sky through its lacework cone. In front of Notre-Dame, close at hand, three streets opened into the Cathedral Square, which was a fine square of old houses. The southern side of this Place was overhung by the furrowed and wrinkled front of the Hôtel Dieu, and its roof, which looks as if covered with pustules and wars. Then, right and left, east and west, within that narrow circuit of the City, were ranged the steeples of its twenty-one churches, of all dates, forms and sizes; from the low and worm-eaten Roman campanile of Saint Denis du Pas, *carcer Glaucini* (Prison of Glaucinus), to the slender spires of Saint Pierre aux Boeufs and Saint Laundry. Behind Notre-Dame were revealed northward, the cloister, with its Gothic galleries; southward, the semi-Roman palace of the bishop; and east-ward, the uninhabited point of the Terrain, or waste ground. Amid that accumulation of houses the eye could also distinguish, by the high perforated mitres of stone, which at that period were placed aloft upon the roof itself, surmounting the highest range of palace windows, the mansion presented by the Parisians, in the reign of Charles VI, to Juvénal des Ursins, a little farther on, the tarred booths of the Palus Market; and in another direction, the new apse of Saint Germain le Vieux, lengthened, in 1458, by a bit of the Rue aux Febves, and then at intervals, a square crowded with people – a pillory set up at some street corner – a fine piece of the pavement of Philip Augustus – magnificent flagging, furrowed for the horses' feet in the middle of the roadway, and so badly replaced in the sixteenth century by the wretched pebbling called *pavé de la Ligue* (pavements of the League) – some solitary backyard, with one of those open turret staircases, which were built in the fifteenth century, one of which is still to be seen in the Rue des Bourdonnais. Finally, on the right of the Sainte Chapelle, to the westward, the Palace of Justice rested its group of towers upon the water's brink. The groves of the royal gardens which occupied the western point of the City hid from view the islet of the Paseur. As for the water itself, it was hardly visible from the towers of Notre-Dame, on either side of the City; the Seine disappearing under the bridges, and the bridges under the houses.

And when the glance passed these bridges, the roofs of which were visibly turning green from mould, before their time, from the vapours of the water; if it turned to the left, toward the University, the first edifice that struck it was a large low cluster of towers, the Petit Châtelet, whose yawning porch seemed to devour the extremity of the Petit Pont. Then, if your view ran along the bank from east to west, from the Tournelle to the Tour de Nesle, there were to be seen a long line of houses exhibiting sculptured beams, coloured window-glass, each story overhanging that beneath it – an interminable zigzag of homely gables, cut at frequent intervals by the intersection of some street, and now and then also by the front or the corner of some great stone-built mansion, which seemed to stand at its ease with its courtyards and gardens, its wings and its compartments, amid that rabble of houses crowding and pinching one another, like a grand seigneur amidst a mob of rustics. There were five or six of these mansions upon the quay, from the Logis de Lorraine, which shared with the house of the Bernardines the great neighbouring enclosure of the Tournelle, to the Hôtel de Nesle, the principal tower of which bounded Paris on the side, and the pointed roofs of which were so situated as to cut with their dark triangles, during three months of the year, the scarlet disc of the setting sun.

This side of the Seine, however, was the least mercantile of the two; students were noisier and more numerous than artisans; and there was not, properly speaking, any quay, except from the Pont Saint Michel to the Tour de Nesle. The rest of the bank of the Seine was either a bare strand, as was the case beyond the Bernardine monastery, or a close range of houses with the water at their base, as between the two bridges.

There was a great clamour of washerwomen along the waterside, talking, shouting, singing, from morning till night along the shore, and beating away at their linen – as they do in our day. This is not the least of the gaieties of Paris.

The University presented a huge mass to the eye. From one end to the other it was a compact and homogeneous whole. The myriad roofs, dense, angular, adherent, nearly all composed of the same geometrical element, when seen from above, looked like a crystalization of one substance. The capricious hollows of the streets divided this pasty of houses into slices not too disproportioned. The forty-two colleges were distributed among them very evenly, and were to be seen in every quarter. The amusingly varied pinnacles of those fine buildings were the product of the same art as the simple roofs which they overtopped, being really but a multiplication of the square or cube, of the same geometrical figure. Thus they made the whole more intricate without confusing it, complete without overloading it. Geometry is harmony.

Several fine mansions also made here and there magnificent outlines against the picturesque attics of the left bank; the Nevers house, the house of Rome, the Reims house, which have disappeared; and the Hôtel de Cluny, which still exists for the consolation of the artist, but the tower of which was so stupidly shortened a few years ago. Near by Cluny, that Roman palace, with fine semicircular arches, was formerly the Baths of Julian. There were also a number of abbeys of a more ecclesiastical beauty, of a more solemn grandeur than the mansions, but not less beautiful nor less grand. Those which first attracted the eye were the monastery of the Bernardines, with its three bell-towers; Sainte Geneviève, whose square tower, still standing, makes us regret the rest so much; the Sorbonne, half-college, half-monastery, of which so admirable a nave still remains, the fine quadrangular cloister of the Mathurins; its neighbour, the cloister of Saint Benedict, within whose walls they have had time to knock up a theatre between the seventh and eighth editions of this book; the Cordeliers, with their three enormous gables; side by side the Augustins, whose graceful spire was, after the Tour de Nesle, the second lofty projection on that side of Paris, from the westward. The colleges – which are in fact the intermediate link between the cloister and the world – held the central point in the architectural series between the fine private residences and the abbeys, exhibiting a severe elegance, a sculpture less airy than that of the palaces, an architecture less severe than that of the convents. Unfortunately, scarcely anything remains of these structures in which Gothic art held so just a balance between richness and economy. The churches (and they were numerous and splendid in the University, and there displayed every period of architecture, from the round arches of Saint Julian to the Gothic ones of Saint Severin) – the churches rose above the whole, and like one harmony the more in that mass of harmonies, they pierced, one after another, the varied outline of gables, of sharply-defined spires, of perforated steeples and slender pinnacles, whose outline was but. a magnificent exaggeration of the acute angle of the roofs.

The ground of the University was hilly. The mountain of Sainte Geneviève, on the southeast, formed an enormous swell, and it was a sight well worth seeing, from the top of Notre-Dame, that crowd of narrow, tortuous streets (to-day the Latin quarter), those clusters of houses which, scattered in every direction from the top of that eminence spread themselves in disorder, and almost precipitously down its sides, to the water's edge, looking, some as if they were falling, others as if they were climbing up, and all as if holding on to one another. The continual motion of a myriad black dots crossing and recrossing each other on the pavement, gave a shimmering look to everything. These were the people in the streets, seen from a height and a distance.

Finally in the spaces between these roofs, these spires these innumerable and irregular structures, which so fantastically bent, twisted and indented the extreme outline of the University, one caught a glimpse here and there of some great patch of moss-covered wall, some thick round tower, or some crenellated town gate, resembling a fortress – this was the wall of Philip Augustus. Beyond extended the green meadows; beyond these ran the highways, along which were scattered a few more suburban houses which became more infrequent as they became more distant. Some of these suburbs were of considerable importance. There were first (starting from the Tournelle) the burgh Saint Victor, with its bridge of one arch over the Bievre; its abbey, in which was to be read the epitaph of King Louis the Fat – *epitaphium Ludovici Grossi*; and its church with an octagonal spire flanked by four small bell-towers, of the eleventh century (a similar one can be seen at Etampes; it is not yet destroyed). Next, the burgh Saint Marceau, which had already three churches and a convent. Then, leaving the mill of the Gobelins and its four white walls on the left, there was the Faubourg Saint Jacques, with the beautiful carved cross in its square; the church of Saint Jacques du Haut Pas, which was then Gothic, pointed and delightful; Saint Magloire, with a fine fourteenth century nave, which Napoleon turned into a hay-loft; Notre-Dame des Champs, where there were Byzantine mosaics. Lastly, after leaving in the open country the Carthusian monastery, a rich structure of the same period as the Palace of Justice, with its little gardens in sections and the ill-famed ruins of Vauvert, the eye fell to westward, upon the three Roman spires of Saint Germain des Prés. The borough Saint Germain, already a large community, had fifteen or twenty streets in the rear; the sharp steeple of Saint Sulpice indicating one of its corners. Close by it might be seen the square enclosure of the Saint Germain fair ground where the market now stands, then the abbot's pillory, a pretty little round tower, neatly capped with a cone of lead; the tilekiln was farther on as well as the Rue du Four, which led to the common bakehouse, with the mill on its knoll – and the lazaretto, a small, detached, and half-seen building. But that which especially attracted the eye, and long held the attention, was the abbey itself. It is certain that this monastery, which had an aspect of grandeur both as a church and as a seigniory, this abbatial palace, in which the bishops of Paris deemed themselves happy to sleep a single night – this refectory, upon which the architect had bestowed the air, the beauty, and the splendid rose-shaped window of a cathedral – this elegant chapel of the Virgin – this monumental dormitory – those spacious gardens – the portcullis and drawbridge – the circuit of battlements which marked its indented outline against the verdure of the surrounding meadows – those courtyards where gleamed men-at-arms intermingled with golden copes – the whole grouped and clustered about three tall spires with their semicircular arches solidly planted upon a Gothic apse – made a magnificent outline upon the horizon.

When at length, after long contemplating the University, you turned toward the right bank towards the Town, the character of the scene was suddenly changed. The Town was not only much larger than the University, but also less uniform. At first sight it appeared to be divided into several portions, singularly distinct from each other. First, to the East, in that part of the Town which still takes its name from the marsh in which Camulogenes mired Cæsar, there was a collection of palaces, which extended to the waterside. Four great mansions almost contiguous – the Hôtels de Jouy, de Sens, and de Barbeau and the Logis de la Reine – mirrored their slated roofs broken by slender turrets in the Seine. These four edifices filled the space from the Rue des Nonaindières to the abbey of the Celestines, whose spire formed a graceful relief to their line of gables and battlements. Some sorry, moss-grown structures overhanging the water in front of these sumptuous mansions did not conceal from view the fine lines of their fronts, their great square stone-framed windows, their Gothic porches loaded with statues, the boldly-cut borderings about their walls, and all those charming accidents of architecture which make Gothic art seem to begin again its series of combinations at every fresh building. Behind these palaces ran in every direction, in some places cloven, palisaded and embattled, like a citadel, in others concealed by large trees like a Carthusian monastery, the vast and multiform circuit of that wonderful Hôtel de Saint Pol, in which the French king had room to lodge superbly twenty-two princes of the rank of the dauphin and the Duke of Burgundy, with their trains and their domestics, without counting the grands seigneurs and the emperor when he came to visit Paris, and the lions that had a separate residence within the royal establishment. And we must here observe that a prince's lodgings then consisted of not less than eleven principal apartments, from the audience-chamber to the oratory; besides all the galleries, baths, stove-rooms and other 'superfluous places,' with which each suite of apartments was provided; not to mention the private gardens for each of the king's guests; besides the kitchens, cellars, pantries and general refectories of the household; the servants' quarters, in which there were two and-twenty general offices, from the bake-house to the wine cellars; games of different kinds, as mall, tennis, riding at the ring, etc.; aviaries, fish-ponds, menageries, stables, cattle-stalls, libraries, armouries and foundries. Such was, at that day, a royal palace – a Louvre – a Hôtel Saint Pol; a city within a city.

From the tower upon which we have placed ourselves, the Hôtel Saint Pol, though almost half hidden by the four great dwelling-houses of which we have just spoken, was, nevertheless, very vast and very wonderful to behold. One could clearly distinguish in it, although they had been skilfully joined to the main building by means of long windowed and pillared galleries, the three residences which Charles V had thrown into one, together with his former palace; the Hôtel du Petit-Muce, with the openwork balustrade so gracefully bordering its roof; the hôtel of the abbot of Saint Maur, having the aspect of a stronghold, a massive tower, bastions, loop-holes, iron cornice, and over the wide Saxon gateway, the abbot's escutcheon between the two grooves for the drawbridge; the residence of the Count d'Etampes, whose donjon-keep in ruins at the top, looked rounded and indented, like the crest of a cock; here and there three or four ancient oaks, forming a tuft together like enormous cauliflowers; swans disporting themselves amid the clear waters of the fish-ponds, all rippling with light and shade; numerous courtyards afforded picturesque glimpses; the Hôtel des Lions, with its low-pointed arches upon short Saxon pillars, its iron portcullises and its perpetual roaring; through all this the scaly spire of the Ave Maria; on the left, the house of the provost of Paris, flanked by four turrets delicately moulded and perforated; and, in the centre in the background the Hôtel Saint Pol, properly speaking, with its multiple fronts, its successive embellishments since the time of Charles V, the hybrid excrescences with which the fancy of the artists had loaded it in the course of two centuries; with all the apses of its chapels, all the gables of its galleries, its endless weathercocks, turned to the four winds, and its two contiguous towers, the conical roof of which, surrounded by battlements at its base, looked like cocked hats.

Continuing to mount the steps of this amphitheatre of palaces spread out afar upon the ground, after crossing a deep fissure in the roofs of the Town, which marked the passage of the Rue Saint Antoine, the eye travelled on to the Logis d'Angoulême, a vast structure of several different periods, in which there were some parts quite new and almost white that did not harmonize with the rest any better than a red patch on a blue doublet. However, the singularly sharp and elevated roof of the modern palace, bristling with carved gutters, and covered with sheets of lead, over which ran sparkling incrustations of gilt copper in a thousand fantastic arabesques – that roof so curiously damaskeened, darted upwards gracefully from amid the brown ruins of the ancient edifice, the old massive towers of which were bellying with age into the shape of casks, their height shrunk with decrepitude, and breaking asunder from top to bottom. Behind rose the forest of spires of the Palais des Tournelles. No view in the world, not even at Chambord nor at the Alhambra, could be more magical, more aerial, more enchanting, than that grove of spires, turrets, chimneys, weathercocks, spiral staircases, perforated lanterns, which looked as if struck out with a die, pavilions, spindle-shaped turrets, or tournelles, as they were then called – all differing in form, height and position. It might well have been compared to a gigantic stone checkerboard.

To the right of the Tournelles, that group of enormous inky black towers, growing, as it were, one into another, and looking as if bound together by their circular moat; that donjon tower, more thickly pierced with loop-holes than with windows; that drawbridge always raised; that portcullis always lowered; that is the Bastille. Those black muzzles, peering from the battlements, and which, at this distance, you would take for gutter spouts, are cannon.

Within gunshot below the terrible edifice is the Porte Saint Antoine, almost buried between its two towers.

Beyond the Tournelles, as far as the wall of Charles V, spread out in rich compartments of verdure and of flowers, a tufted carpet of garden-grounds and royal parks, in the midst of which one recognized, by its labyrinth of trees and alleys, the famous Dædalus garden that Louis XI gave to Coictier. The doctor's observatory rose above the labyrinth, like a great isolated column with a small house for its capital. In that small study terrible astrological predictions were made.

Upon that spot now stands the Place Royale.

As we have already observed, the region of the Palace, of which we have endeavoured to give the reader some idea, though by specifying only its most salient points, filled up the angle which Charles V's wall made with the Seine on the east. The centre of the Town was occupied by a pile of houses for the populace. It was there, in fact, that the three bridges of the City disgorged upon the right bank; and bridges lead to the building of houses rather than palaces. This collection of common dwelling-houses, pressed against one another like cells in a hive had a beauty of its own. The roofs of a great city have a certain grandeur, like the waves of the sea. In the first place, the streets, crossed and intertwined, diversified the mass with a hundred amusing figures, around the Halles, it was like a star with a thousand rays.

The Rues Saint Denis and Saint Martin, with their innumerable ramifications, rose one after the other, like two great trees with intermingling branches; and then crooked lines, the Rues de la Plâtrerie, de la Verrerie, de la Tixeranderie, etc., wound in and out among the whole. There were also fine edifices lifting their heads above the fixed swell of this sea of gables. There, at the entrance of the Pont aux Changeurs, behind which the Seine was seen foaming under the mill-wheels at the Pont aux Meuniers, there was the Châtelet; no longer a Roman tower as under Julian, the Apostate, but a feudal tower of the thirteenth century, of a stone so hard that, in three hours' work, the pick would not remove a piece the size of a man's fist. Then there was the rich square steeple of Saint Jacques de la Boucherie, its sides all encrusted with sculptures, and already worthy of admiration, although it was not finished in the fifteenth century. (It lacked particularly those four monsters which, still perched on the four corners of its roof, look like four sphinxes giving modern Paris the riddle of ancient Paris to solve. Rault, the sculptor, only placed them in position in 1526; and received twenty francs for his trouble.) There was the Maison aux Piliers, overlooking that Place de Grève of which we have already given the reader some idea. There was the church of Saint Gervais, which a large portal *in good taste* has since spoiled; that of Saint Méry, whose ancient pointed arches were still almost rounded; and that of Saint .Jean, whose magnificent spire was proverbial; besides twenty other structures which disdained not to bury their wonders in this wilderness of deep, dark and narrow streets. Add to these the carved stone crosses, even more abundant at cross-roads than gibbets; the cemetery of the Innocents, whose architectural wall was to be seen in the distance, over the house-tops; the market pillory, the top of which was visible between two chimneys of the Rue de la Cossonnerie; the 'ladder' of the Croix du Trahoir, with its cross-roads always black with people; the circular buildings of the wheat-mart; the broken fragments of the old wall of Philip Augustus, distinguishable here and there, buried among the houses – towers over-run with ivy, ruined gateways – crumbling and shapeless pieces of wall; the quay with its countless shops, and its bloody knackers' yards; the Seine covered with boats from the Port au Foin to the For-l'Evéque; and you will have a dim idea of the appearance, in 1482, of the central trapezium, or irregular quadrangle, of the Town.

Together with these two quarters, the one of princely mansions, the other of ordinary houses, the third great feature then observable in the Town, was a long belt of abbeys bordering it almost in its entire circumference, from east to west, and, behind the line of fortification by which Paris was shut in, formed a second inner circle, consisting of convents and chapels. Thus, close to the park of the Tournelles, between the Rue Saint Antoine and the old Rue du Temple, there was Saint Catherine's, with its immense grounds, bounded only by the wall of Paris. Between the old and the new Rue du Temple there was the Temple itself, a sinister group of towers, lofty, erect and isolated in the midst of a vast, battlemented enclosure. Between the Rue Neuve du Temple and the Rue Saint Martin, in the midst of its gardens, stood Saint Martin's, a superb fortified church, whose girdle of towers, whose tiara or steeples, where second in strength and splendour only to Saint Germain des Prés. Between the two streets of Saint Martin and Saint Denis were the precincts of the convent of the Trinity. And between the Rue Saint Denis and the Rue Montorgueil was that of the Filles Dieu. Close by might be seen the decayed roofs and unpaved enclosures of the

Court of Miracles. This was the only profane link in this pious chain of convents.

Lastly, the fourth division, clearly outlined in the conglomeration of roofs upon the right bank, formed by the western angle of the great enclosure, and the banks of the river down stream, was a fresh knot of palaces and great mansions crowding at the foot of the Louvre. The old Louvre of Philip Augustus, that immense structure – the great tower of which mustered around it twenty-three principal towers, besides all the smaller ones – seemed, at a distance, to be set within the Gothic summits of the Hôtel d'Alençon and the Petit Bourbon. This hydra of towers, the giant keeper of Paris, with its four-and-twenty heads ever erect – with its monstrous cruppers covered with lead or scaly with slates, and all rippling with glittering metallic reflections – terminated with wonderful effect the configuration of the Town on the west.

An immense mass, therefore – what the Romans called an insula or island – of ordinary dwelling-houses, flanked on either side by two great clusters of palaces, crowned, the one by the Louvre, the other by the Tournelles, bounded on the north by a long belt of abbeys and cultivated enclosures – blending and mingling together as one gazed at them – above these thousand buildings, whose tiled and slated roofs stood out in such strange outlines, the crimped, twisted and ornamented steeples of the forty-four churches on the right bank – myriads of cross-streets – the boundary, on one side, a line of lofty walls with square towers (those of the University wall being round), and on the other, the Seine, intersected by bridges and crowded with numberless boats – such was the Town in the fifteenth century.

Beyond the walls some few suburbs crowded to the gates but less numerous and more scattered than those on the University side. Thus, behind the Bastille, a score of mean houses clustered around the curious carvings of the cross of Faubin, and the buttresses of the abbey of Saint Antoine des Champs; then there was Popincourt, lost amid the corn-fields, then, La Courtille, a jolly village of taverns; the borough of Saint Laurent with its church, whose steeple seemed, at a distance, to belong to the pointed towers of the Porte Saint Martin; the Faubourg Saint Denis with the vast enclosure of Saint Ladre; beyond the Montmartre gate the Grange Batelière, encircled with white walls; behind it, with its chalky declivities – Montmartre, which had then almost as many churches as windmills, but which has kept only the mills, for society no longer demands anything but bread for the body. Then, beyond the Louvre, could be seen, stretching away into the meadows, the Faubourg Saint Honoré, even then of considerable extent; La Petite Bretagne, looking green; and the Pig Market, spreading itself out, in the centre of which rose the horrible cauldron used for boiling alive coiners of counterfeit money. Between La

Courtille and Saint Laurent, the eye noted on the summit of a hill that crouched amid a desert plain, a sort of structure, which looked at a distance like a ruined colonnade standing upon foundations laid bare. It was neither a Parthenon nor a temple of the Jupiter Olympus; it was Montfaucon.

Now, if the enumeration of so many edifices, brief as we have sought to make it, has not destroyed as fast as we constructed it, in the reader's mind, the general image of old Paris, we will recapitulate it in a few words. In the centre the island of the City, shaped like a huge turtle, extending on either side its bridges all scaly with tiles, like so many legs, from under its gray shell of roofs. On the left, the close, dense, bristling, monolithic trapezium of the University; on the right, the vast semicircle of the Town where houses and gardens were much more mingled. The three divisions – City, University and Town – veined with countless streets. Through the whole runs the Seine, 'the nourishing Seine,' as Father du Breul calls it, obstructed with islands, bridges and boats. All around an immense plain, checkered with a thousand different crops, strewn with beautiful villages; on the left, Issy, Vanvres, Vaugirard, Montrouge, Gentilly, with its round tower and its square tower, etc.; and on the right, twenty others, from Conflans to Ville l'Evêque. In the horizon a border of hills arranged in a circle, like the rim of the basin. Finally, in the distance, to eastward, was Vincennes, with its seven quadrangular towers; to southward, Bicêtre, and its pointed turrets; to northward, Saint Denis and its spire; to westward, Saint Cloud and its donjon. Such was the Paris seen from the top of the towers of Notre-Dame by the crows who lived in 1482.

And yet it is of this city that Voltaire has said, that *before the time of Louis XIV it possessed only four fine pieces of architecture:* – that is to say, the dome of the Sorbonne, the Val de Grace, the modern Louvre, and I know not what the fourth was, perhaps the Luxembourg. Fortunately, Voltaire was none the less the author of *Candide*; nor is he the less, among all the men who have succeeded one another in the long series of humanity, the one who has best possessed the *rire diabolique*, the sardonic smile. This proves moreover, that a man may be a fine genius, and yet understand nothing of an art which he has not studied. Did not Molière think he was doing great honour to Raphael and Michael Angelo when he called them 'those Mignards of their age?'

Let us return to Paris and to the fifteenth century.

It was not then merely a handsome city – it was a homogeneous city – an architectural and historical production of the Middle Ages – a chronicle in stone. It was a city composed of two architectural strata only, the bastard Roman and the Gothic layer – for the pure Roman stratum had long disappeared, except in the Baths of Julian, where it still pierced through the thick crust of the Middle Ages. As for the Celtic, no specimen of that was now to be found, even when digging wells.

Fifty years later, when the Renaissance came breaking into that unity so severe and yet so varied, with the dazzling profuseness of its fantasies and its systems, rioting among Roman arches, Grecian columns and Gothic windows – its sculpture tender and imaginative – its fondness for arabesques and acanthus leaves – its architectural paganism contemporary with Luther – Paris was perhaps more beautiful, though less harmonious to the eye and to the mind. But that splendid period was of short duration. The Renaissance was not impartial. Not content with building up, it thought proper to pull down – it is true it needed space. Thus Gothic Paris was complete but for a moment. Scarcely was Saint Jacques de la Boucherie finished before the demolition of the old Louvre began.

Since then this great city has been daily sinking into deformity. The Gothic Paris, under which the Roman Paris was disappearing, has disappeared in its turn; but what name shall we give to the Paris that has taken its place?

There is the Paris of Catherine de Medicis at the Tuileries;* the Paris of Henry II at the Hôtel de Ville – two buildings which are still in the best taste; – the Paris of Henry IV at the Place Royale – brick fronts with corners of stone and slated roofs – tricoloured houses, – the Paris of Louis XIII at the Val de Grace – of architecture crushed and squat – with basket-handle vaults, big-bellied columns and a hump-backed dome, the Paris of Louis XIV at the Invalides – grand, rich, gilded and cold; – the Paris of Louis XV at Saint Sulpice – with volutes, knots of ribbons, clouds, vermicelli and chiccory, all in stone; – the Paris of Louis XVI at the Pantheon – Saint Peter's at Rome ill-copied (the building stands awkwardly, which has not bettered its lines); – the Paris of the Republic at the School of Medicine – a bit of poor Greek and Roman taste, as much to be compared to the Coliseum or the

---

* It is with grief mingled with indignation that we learn of a proposition to enlarge, reconstruct and make over, that is, destroy this admirable palace. The architects of our day do not possess the lightness of hand necessary to touch the works of the Renaissance. We continue to hope they will not dare to undertake the task. Furthermore, the present destruction of the Tuileries is not only a brutal proceeding of which a drunken Vandal would blush but it is an act of treason. The Tuileries is not only a masterpiece of sixteenth century art, but a page from the history of the nineteenth century. This palace is no longer the property of the king, but of the people. Leave it as it is. Twice has our Revolution branded it upon the forehead. On one of its two façades are the bullets of the 10th of August; on the other those of the 29th of July. It is sacred. – Paris, 7th April, 1831. – *(Note to the Fifth Edition).*

Parthenon as the constitution of the year III to the laws of Minos; it is called in architecture, *le gout messidor* (the tenth month of the French republican calendar, from the 19th of June to the 18th of July), – the Paris of Napoleon at the Place Vendôme – this is sublime – a bronze column made of cannon; – the Paris of the Restoration, at the Bourse or Exchange – a very white colonnade, supporting a very smooth frieze; the whole is square, and cost twenty million francs. To each of these characteristic structures is allied, by similarity of style, manner and disposition, a certain number of houses scattered over the different quarters, which the eye of the connoisseur easily distinguishes and assigns to their respective dates. When one knows how to look, one finds the spirit of a century and the physiognomy of a king even in the knocker on a door.

The Paris of to-day has therefore no general physiognomy. It is a collection of specimens of several different ages, and the finest have disappeared. The capital is increasing in houses only – and what houses! At the rate at which Paris moves it will be renewed every fifty years. Thus, also, the historical meaning of its architecture is daily becoming effaced. Its great structures are becoming fewer and fewer, seeming to be swallowed up one after another by the flood of houses. Our fathers had a Paris of stone – our sons will have a Paris of plaster.

As for the modern structures of the new Paris, we would gladly be excused from enlarging upon them. Not, indeed, that we do not grant them the admiration they merit. The Sainte Geneviève of M. Soufflot is certainly the finest Savoy cake that was ever made of stone. The Palace of the Legion of Honour is also a very distinguished piece of confectionery. The dome of the Corn Market is an English jockey-cap on a magnificent scale. The towers of Saint Sulpice are two great clarinets; a good enough shape in its way; and then, the telegraph, crooked and grinning, makes a charming ornamentation upon the roof. The church of Saint Roch has a doorway with whose magnificence only that of Saint Thomas d'Aquin can compare; it has also a crucifix in relief in a vault, and an ostensary of gilded wood. These things are fairly marvellous. The lantern of the labyrinth at the Jardin des Plantes, too, is vastly ingenious. As for the Palais de la Bourse, which is Grecian in its colonnade, Roman by the circular arches of its doors and windows and Renaissance by its great elliptic arch, it is undoubtedly a very correct and pure structure; the proof being that it is crowned by an attic such as was never seen at Athens, a fine straight line gracefully intersected here and there by chimney-pots. Let us add, that if it be a rule that the architecture of a building should be so adapted to the purpose of the building itself; that the aspect of the edifice should at once declare that purpose, we can not too much admire a structure which, from its appearance, might be either a royal palace, a chamber of deputies, a town-hall, a college, a riding-school, an academy, a warehouse, a courthouse, a museum, a barrack, a mausoleum, a temple, or a theatre – and which, all the while, is an exchange. It has been thought, too, that an edifice should be made appropriate to the climate – and so this one has evidently been built on purpose for a cold and rainy sky. It has a roof almost flat, as they are in the East; and, consequently, in winter, when it snows, the roof has to be swept – and it is sure roofs are made to be swept. As for that purpose of which we were just speaking, the building fulfils it admirably. It is an exchange in France, as it would have been a temple in Greece. True it is that the architect has had much ado to conceal the clock-face, which would have destroyed the purity of the noble lines of the façade; but to make amends, there is that colonnade running round the whole structure, under which, on days of high religious ceremony, the schemes of money-brokers and stockjobbers may be magnificently developed.

These, doubtless, are very superb structures. Add to these many a pretty street, amusing and diversified, like the Rue de Rivoli; and I am not without hope that Paris, as seen from a balloon, may yet present that richness of outline and opulence of detail – that diversity of aspect – that something grandiose in its simplicity – unexpected in its beauty – that characterizes a checker-board.

However, admirable as you may think the present Paris, recall the Paris of the fifteenth century; reconstruct it in thought; look at the sky through that surprising forest of spires, towers and steeples spread out amid the vast city, tear asunder at the points of the islands, and fold round the piers of the bridges, the Seine, with its large green and yellow slimy pools, more variegated than the skin of a serpent; project clearly upon a blue horizon the Gothic profile of that old Paris. Make its outline float in a wintry mist clinging to its innumerable chimneys; plunge it in deep night, and observe the fantastic play of the darkness and the lights in that gloomy labyrinth of buildings; cast upon it a ray of moonlight, which shall reveal it dimly, with its towers lifting their great heads from that foggy sea – or recall that black silhouette; enliven with shadows the thousand sharp angles of its spires and gables, and make it stand out more indented than a shark's jaw upon the glowing western sky at sunset – and then, compare the two.

And if you would receive an impression from the old city which the modern one can never give you, climb on the morning of some great holiday, at sunrise, on Easter, or Whitsunday – climb to some elevated point whence you overlook the whole capital – and assist at the wakening of the chimes. Behold, at a signal from heaven – for it is the sun that gives it – those thousand churches starting from their sleep. At first you hear but scattered tinklings, going from church to church, as when musicians are giving one another notice to begin. Then, of a sudden, behold – for there are moments when the ear itself seems to see – behold, ascending at the same moment, from every steeple, a column of sound, as it were, a cloud of harmony. At first the vibration of each bell mounts up direct, clear, and, so to speak, isolated from the rest, into the splendid morning sky; then, by degrees, as they expand, they mingle, unite, are lost in each other, and confounded in one magnificent concert. It is no longer anything but a mass of sonorous vibrations, incessantly sent forth from the innumerable belfries – floating, undulating, bounding and eddying, over the town, and prolonging far beyond the horizon the deafening circle of its osculations. Yet that sea of harmony is not a chaos. Wide and deep as it is, it has not lost its transparency; you perceive the windings of each group of notes that escapes from the chimes. You can follow the dialogue, by turns solemn and shrill, of the treble and the bass; you perceive the octaves leaping from one steeple to another; you observe them springing aloft, winged, light and whirring, from the bell of silver; falling broken and limping from the bell of wood. You admire among them the rich gamut incessantly descending and reascending the seven bells of Saint Eustache; and you see clear and rapid notes, running criss-cross, in three or four luminous zigzags, and vanishing like flashes of lightning. Yonder is the abbey Saint Martin's, a shrill and broken-voiced songstress; here is the sinister and sullen voice of the Bastille; at the other end is the great tower of the Louvre, with its counter-tenor. The royal peal of the Palais unceasingly flings on every side resplendent trills, and upon them fall, at regular intervals, heavy strokes from the belfry of Notre-Dame, which strike sparks from them like the hammer from the anvil. At intervals, you see passing tones, of every form, coming from the triple peal of Saint Germain des Prés. Then again, from time to time, this mass of sublime sounds half opens and makes way to the stretto of the Ave-Maria, which flashes and sparkles like a cluster of stars. Below, in the heart of the harmony you vaguely catch the chanting inside the churches, exhaled through the vibrating pores of their vaulted roofs. This is, certainly, an opera worth hearing. Usually, the murmur that rises up from Paris by day is the city talking; in the night it is the city breathing; but here it is the city singing. Listen, then, to this chorus of bell-towers – diffuse over the whole the murmur of half a million of people – the eternal lament of the river – the endless sighing of the wind – the grave and distant quartet of the four forests placed upon the hills, in the distance, like immense organ-pipes – extinguish to a halflight all in the central chime that would otherwise be too harsh or too shrill; and then say whether you know of anything in the world more rich, more joyous, more golden, more dazzling, than this tumult of bells and chimes – this furnace of music – these thousands of brazen voices, all singing together in flutes of stone three hundred feet high, than this city which is but one orchestra – this symphony which roars like a tempest.

BOOK FOUR

I

Good, Honest Souls

SIXTEEN YEARS PREVIOUS to the period of this story, on a fine morning of the first Sunday after Easter – called in France, Quasimodo Sunday – a living creature had been laid, after mass, in the church of Notre-Dame, upon the wooden bed fastened into the pavement on the left hand, opposite to that great image of Saint Christopher, which the carved stone figure of Messire Antoine des Essarts, knight, had been contemplating on his knees since the year 1413, when it was thought proper to throw down both the saint and his faithful adorer. Upon this bed it was customary to expose foundlings to public charity; whoever cared to, took them. In front of the bed was a copper basin for alms.

The sort of living creature which lay upon that board on Quasimodo Sunday morning, in the year of our Lord 1467, appeared to excite, in a high degree, the curiosity of a very considerable group of persons which had gathered around the bed. It consisted, in great measure, of individuals of the fair sex. They were nearly all old women.

In the first row, and bending the farthest over the bed, were four, who by their gray *cagoule* (a sort of cassock), appeared to be attached to some religious community. I know not why history should not have handed down to posterity the names of these discreet and venerable damsels. They were Agnès la Herme, Jehanne de la Tarme, Henriette la Gaultière and Gauchère la Violette – all four widows, all four dames of the Etienne Haudry chapel, who had come thus far from their house, with their mistress's leave, and in conformity with the statutes of Pierre d'Ailly, to hear the sermon.

However, if these good Haudriettes were for the time being obeying the statutes of Pierre d'Ailly, they certainly were violating, to their heart's content, those of Michel de Brache and the Cardinal of Pisa, which so inhumanly enjoined silence upon them.

'What ever can that be, sister?' said Agnès to Gauchère, as she looked at the little exposed creature, which lay yelping and wriggling upon the wooden bed, frightened at being looked at by so many people.

'What is to become of us,' said Jehanne, 'if that is the way children are made now?'

'I am not learned in the matter of children,' resumed Agnès, 'but it must surely be a sin to look at such a one as this!'

' 'Tis no child at all, Agnès.'

' 'Tis a misshapen baboon,' observed Gauchère.

'It is a miracle,' said Henriette la Gaultière.

'Then,' remarked Agnès, 'this is the third since Lætare Sunday; for a week has not passed since we had the miracle of the mocker of pilgrims divinely punished by Our Lady of Aubervilliers; and that was the second miracle of the month.'

'This pretended foundling is a very monster of abomination,' resumed Jehanne.

'He brawls loud enough to deafen a chanter,' added Gauchère; 'hold thy tongue, thou little bellower.'

'To think that Monsieur of Rheims sends this monstrosity to Monsieur of Paris!' exclaimed La Gaultière, clasping her hands.

'I believe,' said Agnès la Herme, 'that it's some beast, or animal – the fruit of a Jew and a sow – something not Christian, in short, and which ought to be thrown into the water or into the fire.'

'I truly hope,' resumed La Gaultière. 'that nobody will offer to take him!'

'Oh, heavens!' exclaimed Agnès, 'those poor nurses yonder in the foundling asylum at the bottom of the alley, going down to the river, close by the lord bishop's; what if this little monster were carried to them to suckle! I'd rather give suck to a vampire.'

'Is she not a simpleton, that poor La Herme?' rejoined Jehanne. 'Do you not see, my dear sister, that this little monster is at least four years old, and would have less appetite for your breast than for a roast.'

In fact, the 'little monster' (for we ourselves would find it hard to describe him otherwise) was no new-born infant. It was a little, angular, restless mass, imprisoned in a canvas bag marked with the cipher of Messire Guillaume Chartier, then bishop of Paris – with a head coming out at one end. This head was a misshapen enough thing; there was nothing of it to be sell but a shock of red hair, one eye, a mouth and some teeth. The eye wept; the mouth bawled; and the teeth seemed only waiting a chance to bite. The whole lump was struggling violently in the bag, to the great wonderment of the increasing and incessantly renewing crowd around it.

Dame Aloise de Gondelaurier , a wealthy and noble lady, holding by the hand a pretty little girl about six years of age, and trailing after her a long veil attached to the golden horn of her head-dress, halted as she passed the wooden bed, and looked for a moment at the unfortunate creature; while her charming little daughter, Fleur-de-Lys de Gondelaurier, clad in silk and velvet, spelled out with her pretty little finger, the inscription hanging on the wooden framework: For Foundlings.

'Really,' said the dame, turning away with disgust, 'I thought they exhibited here nothing but children.'

She turned her back; at the same time throwing into the basin a silver florin, which rang among the liards, and made the poor good women of the Etienne Haudry chapel stare.

A moment afterward the grave and learned Robert Mistricolle, king's prothonotary, passed by, with an enormous missal under one arm, and his wife under the other (Damoiselle Guillemette la Mairesse), having thus on either side his two regulators, spiritual and temporal.

'Foundling!' said he, after examining the object; 'yes – found, apparently, upon the banks of the river Phlegethon!'

'It has but one eye to be seen,' observed Damoiselle Guillemette; 'there is a wart upon the other.'

'That is no wart,' replied Maître Robert Mistricolle; 'it is an egg, which contains just such another demon, who bears upon its eye another little egg containing another devil – and so on.'

'How do you know that?' asked Guillemette la Mairesse.

'I know it for very sufficient reasons,' answered the prothonotary.

'Monsieur the prothonotary,' asked Gauchère, 'what do you prognosticate from this pretended foundling?'

'The greatest calamities,' answered Mistricolle.

'Heaven save us!' said an old woman among the bystanders; 'withal that there was quite a pestilence last year, and that they say the English are going to land in great company at Harfleur!'

' 'Twill perhaps prevent the queen from coming to Paris in September,' observed another; 'and trade so bad already!'

'In my opinion,' cried Jehanne de la Tarme, 'it would be better for the commoners of Paris if the little sorcerer there were lying upon a fagot rather than a board.'

'A fine flaming fagot!' added the old woman.

'It would be more prudent,' said Mistricolle.

For some moments a young priest had been listening to the arguments of the Haudriettes and the oracular decrees of the prothonotary. His was a severe countenance, with a broad forehead and a penetrating eye. He silently put aside the crowd, scrutinized the *little sorcerer* and stretched out his hand over him. It was high time; for all the devout old women were already regaling themselves with the anticipation of the 'fine flaming fagot.'

'I adopt this child,' said the priest.

He wrapped it in his cassock, and bore it away; the bystanders looked after him with frightened glances. A moment later he disappeared through the Red Door, which then led from the church to the cloister.

When the first surprise was over, Jehanne de la Tarme whispered in the ear of La Gaultière:

'I always said to you, sister, that that young clerk, Monsieur Claude Frollo, was a sorcerer.'

II

Claude Frollo

CLAUDE FROLLO was in fact no common person. He belonged to one of those families of middle rank called indifferently, in the impertinent language of the last century, high commoners or petty nobility. This family had inherited from the brothers Paclet the fief of Tirechappe, which was held of the Bishop of Paris, and the twenty-one houses of which had been, in the thirteenth century, the object of so many suits before the judges. As possessor of this fief, Claude Frollo was one of the one hundred and forty-one seigneurs, claiming manorial dues, in Paris and its suburbs; and in that capacity his name was long to be seen inscribed between that of the Hôtel de Tancarville, belonging to Master François Le Rez, and that of the college of Tours, in the records deposited at Saint Martin des Champs.

Claude Frollo had, from infancy, been destined by his parents for the ecclesiastical state. He had been taught to read in Latin; he had been trained to cast down his eyes and to speak low. While yet a child, his father had cloistered him in the college of Torchi, in the University. There it was that he had grown up, on the missal and the lexicon.

He was, moreover, a melancholy, grave and serious boy, who studied ardently and learned quickly; he was never boisterous at play; he mixed little in the bacchanalia of the Rue du Fouarre; knew not what it was to *dare alapas et capillos laniare* (to give blows and to pull out hair); nor had he figured in that insurrection of 1463, which the annalists gravely record under the title of 'Sixième Trouble de l'Université.' (Sixth trouble of the University.) It did not often occur to him to annoy the poor scholars of Montaigu upon their *cappettes* (little hoods), from which they derived their nickname; nor the fellows of the college of Dormans, upon their smooth tonsure and their parti-coloured frock, made of cloth, gray, blue and violet – *azurini coloris et bruni* (of a blue and prune colour), as the charter of the Cardinal des Quatre Couronnes expresses it.

But, on the other hand, he was assiduous at both the great and the small schools of the Rue Saint Jean de Beauvais. The first scholar whom the abbot of Saint Pierre de Val, at the moment of beginning his reading on canon law, always perceived, glued to a pillar of the school Saint Vendregesile, opposite his rostrum, was Claude Frollo, armed with his inkhorn, chewing his pen, scribbling upon his thread-bare knee, and, in winter, blowing on his fingers. The first auditor whom Messire Miles d'Isliers, doctor of decretals, saw arrive every Monday morning, quite out of breath, at the opening of the doors of the Chef Saint Denis schools, was Claude Frollo. Thus, at the age of sixteen, the young clerk was a match, in mystical theology, for a father of the Church; in canonical theology, for a father of the Council; and in scholastic theology, for a doctor of the Sorbonne.

Theology passed, he plunged into the décret, or study of decretals. After the 'Master of Sentences,' he had fallen upon the 'Capitularies of Charlemagne;' and had successively devoured, in his appetite for knowledge, decretals upon decretals; those of Theodore, Bishop of Hispala: those of Bouchard, Bishop of Worms; those of Yves, Bishop of Chartres, then the decretal of Gratian, which succeeded the Capitularies of Charlemagne; then the collection by Gregory IX; then the epistle, *Super specula* (on Imitations), of Honorius III. He gained a clear idea of and made himself familiar with that vast and tumultuous period when the civil law and the canon law were struggling and labouring in the chaos of the Middle Ages – a period which opens with Bishop Theodore, in 618, and closes, in 1227, with Pope Gregory.

Having digested the decretals, he rushed into medicine and the liberal arts. He studied the science of herbs, the science of unguents. He became expert in the treatment of fevers and contusions, of wounds and sores. Jacques d'Espars would have admitted him as doctor of medicine; Richard Hellain, as a surgeon. In like manner he ran through all the degrees of licentiate, master, and doctor of arts. He studied the languages, Latin, Greek, Hebrew; a triple shrine, then but little worshipped. He was possessed by an absolute fever for the acquiring and storing of knowledge. At eighteen, he had made his way through the four faculties; it seemed to the young man that life had but one sole aim: knowledge.

It was about this period that the excessive heat of the summer of 1416 gave birth to the great plague which carried off more than forty thousand souls within the viscounty of Paris, and among others, says John of Troyes, 'Maître Arnoul, the king's astrologer, a man full honest, wise and pleasant.' The rumour spread through the University that the Rue Tirechappe was especially devastated by the pestilence. It was there, in the midst of their fief, that the parents of Claude resided. The young scholar hastened in great alarm to his paternal mansion. On entering, he round that his father and mother had both died the preceding day. A baby brother, in swaddling clothes, was yet living, and lay crying abandoned in its cradle. It was all that remained to Claude of his family. The young man took the child under his arm, and went away thoughtfully. Hitherto, he had lived only in science; he was now beginning to live in the world.

This catastrophe was a crisis in Claude's existence. An orphan, the eldest head of the family at nineteen, he felt himself rudely aroused from scholastic reveries to the realities of this world. Then, moved with pity, he was seized with love and devotion for this infant, his brother; and strange at once and sweet was this human affection to him who had never yet loved anything but books.

This affection developed itself to a singular degree; in a soul so new to passion it was like a first love. Separated since childhood from his parents, whom he had scarcely known – cloistered and immured, as it were, in his books – eager above all things to study and to learn – exclusively attentive, until then, to his understanding, which broadened in science – to his imagination, which expanded in literature – the poor scholar had not yet had time to feel that he had a heart. This little brother, without father or mother – this little child which had fallen suddenly from heaven into his arms – made a new man of him. He discovered that there was something else in the world besides the speculations of the Sorbonne and the verses of Homerus – that man has need of affections; that life without tenderness and without love was but dry machinery, noisy and wearing. Only he fancied – for he was still at that age when illusions are replaced by illusions – that the affections of blood and kindred were the only ones necessary; and that a little brother to love sufficed to fill a whole existence.

He threw himself, then, into the love of his little Jehan, with all the intensity of a character already deep, ardent, concentrated. This poor, helpless creature, pretty, fairhaired, rosy and curly – this orphan with none to look to for support but another orphan – moved him to the inmost soul; and, serious thinker as he was, he began to reflect upon Jehan with a feeling of the tenderest pity. He cared for him and watched over him as over something very fragile and very precious; he was more than a brother to the infant – he became a mother to it.

Little Jehan having lost his mother before he was weaned, Claude put him out to nurse. Besides the fief of Tirechappe, he inherited from his father that of Moulin, which was a dependency of the square tower of Gentilly; it was a mill upon a hill, near the Château de Winchestre, since corrupted into Bicêtre. The miller's wife was suckling a fine boy, not far from the University, and Claude himself carried his little Jehan to her in his arms.

Thenceforward, feeling that he had a burden to bear, he took life very seriously. The thought of his little brother became not only his recreation, but the object of his studies. He resolved to consecrate himself entirely to a future for which he made himself answerable before God, and never to have any other wife, nor any other child, than the happiness and prosperity of his brother. He accordingly became more than ever attached to his clerical vocation. His merit, his learning, his quality as an immediate vassal of the Bishop of Paris, threw the doors of the Church wide open to him. At twenty years of age, by special dispensation from the Holy See, he was ordained priest; and served, as the youngest of the chaplains of Notre-Dame, at the altar called, on account of the late mass that was said at it, *altare pigrorum*, the altar of the lazy.

There, more than ever buried in his dear books, which he only left to hasten for an hour to the fief Du Moulin, this mixture of learning and austerity, so rare at his age, had speedily gained him the admiration and respect of the cloister. From the cloister his reputation for learning had spread to the people, among whom it had been in some degree changed, as not unfrequently happened in those days, into reputation for sorcery.

It was when he was returning, on the Quasimodo Sunday, from saying his mass of the slothful at their altar, which was at the side of that gate of the choir which opened into the nave, on the right hand, near the image of the Virgin, that his attention had been aroused by the group of old women chattering around the bed for foundlings.

Then it was that he had approached the unfortunate little creature, the object of so much hatred and menace. Its distress, its deformity, its abandonment, the thought of his little brother – the idea which suddenly crossed his mind that, were he to die, his dear little Jehan might also be cast miserably upon the board for foundlings – all this rushed into his heart at once – a deep feeling of pity had taken possession of him, and he had borne away the child.

When he took the child from the bag, he found it to be very deformed indeed. The poor little imp had a great wart covering its left eye – the head compressed between the shoulders – the spine crooked – the breastbone prominent – and the legs bowed. Yet it seemed to be full of life; and although it was impossible to discover what language it babbled, its cry proclaimed a certain degree of health and strength. Claude's compassion was increased by this ugliness; and he vowed in his heart to bring up this child for the love of his brother, in order that, whatever might be the future faults of little Jehan, there might be placed to his credit this piece of charity performed on his account. It was a sort of investment of good works in his little brother's name – a stock of good deeds which he wished to lay up for him beforehand – in case the little rascal should one day find himself short of that coin the only kind taken at the toll-gate of Paradise.

He baptized his adopted child by the name of Quasimodo; whether it was that he chose thereby to mark the day upon which he had found him, or that he meant to characterize by that name how incomplete and imperfect the poor little creature was. Indeed Quasimodo, one-eyed, hump-backed and knock-kneed, could hardly be considered anything more than a sketch.

III

Immanis Pecoris Custos, Immanior Ipse *

Now, IN 1482, Quasimodo had grown up, and for several years had been ringer of the bells of Notre-Dame, thanks to his fosterfather, Claude Frollo; who had become Archdeacon of Josas, by the grace of his suzerain, Messire Louis de Beaumont, who had become Bishop of Paris in 1472, on the death of Guillaume Chartier, by the grace of his patron, Olivier le Daim, barber to Louis XI, king by the grace of God.

Quasimodo was, therefore, ringer of the chimes of Notre-Dame.

With time, a certain bond of intimacy had been established, uniting the bell-ringer to the church. Separated forever from the world by the double fatality of his unknown birth and his deformity – imprisoned from his infancy within that double and impassable circle – the poor wretch had been accustomed to see nothing of the world beyond the religious walls which had received him under their shadow. Notre-Dame had been to him, by turns, as he grew and developed, egg – nest – home – country – universe.

And it is certain that there was a mysterious and pre-existing harmony between this creature and the edifice. When, while yet quite little, he used to drag himself along, twisting and jerking in the gloom of its arches, he seemed, with his human face and his bestial members, the native reptile of that damp, dark pavement, upon which the shadows of the Roman capitals projected so many fantastic forms.

And, later, the first time that he grasped mechanically the bell-rope in the towers, hung himself upon it and set the bell in motion, the effect upon Claude, his adoptive father, was that of a child whose tongue is loosed and who begins to talk.

Thus it was that his being, gradually unfolding, took its mould from the cathedral – living there – sleeping there – scarcely ever going out of it – receiving every hour its mysterious impress – he came at length to resemble it, to be fashioned like it, to make an integral part of it. His salient angles fitted themselves (if we may be allowed the expression) into the retreating angles of the edifice, and he seemed to be not only its inhabitant, but even the natural tenant of it. He might almost be said to have taken its form, as the snail takes that of its shell. It was his dwelling-place – his hole – his envelope. There existed between the old church and himself an instinctive sympathy so profound – so many affinities, magnetic and material – that he in some sort adhered to it,

* Huge the guardian of the flock, more huge he.

like the tortoise to its shell.

It is needless to inform the reader that he is not to accept literally the figures of speech that we are here obliged to employ in order to express that singular assimilation, symmetrical – immediate – consubstantial, almost – of a man to an edifice. It is likewise needless to allude to the degree of familiarity he must have attained with the whole cathedral during so long and so intimate a cohabitation. It was his own particular dwelling-place. It had no depths which Quasimodo had not penetrated, no heights which he had not scaled. Many a time had he clambered up its front, one story after another, with no other aid than the projecting bits of carving; the towers, over the exterior of which he was frequently seen crawling like a lizard gliding upon an upright wall – those twin giants – so lofty, so threatening, so formidable – had for him neither vertigo, fright, nor sudden giddiness. So gentle did they appear under his hand, so easy to scale, one would have said that he had tamed them. By dint of leaping, climbing, sporting amid the abysses of the gigantic cathedral, he had become something of both monkey and chamois – like the Calabrian child, which swims before it can walk, and plays with the sea while still a babe.

Moreover, not only his body, but also his mind, seemed to be moulded by the cathedral. In what state was that soul? what folds had it contracted, what form had it taken, under that knotty covering, in that wild and savage life? It would be difficult to determine. Quasimodo was born one-eyed, hump-backed, limping. It was with great difficulty and great patience that Claude Frollo had taught him to speak. But a fatality pursued the poor foundling. Bell-ringer of Notre-Dame at fourteen years of age, a fresh infirmity had come to complete his desolation – the sound of the bells had broken the drum of the ear; he had become deaf. The only door – that nature had left wide open between him and the external world, had been suddenly closed forever.

In closing, it intercepted the sole ray of joy and light that still penetrated to the soul of Quasimodo. That soul was now wrapped in profound darkness. The poor creature's melancholy became as incurable and as complete as his deformity; add to which, his deafness rendered him in some sort dumb. For, that he might not be laughed at by others, from the moment that he realized his deafness, he determined resolutely to observe a silence which he scarcely ever broke, except when alone. He voluntarily tied up that tongue which Claude Frollo had worked so hard to set free. And hence it was that, when necessity compelled him to speak his tongue was heavy and awkward, like a door the hinges of which have grown rusty.

If now we were to endeavour to penetrate through this thick and obdurate bark to the soul of Quasimodo – could we sound the depths of that ill-formed organization – were it possible for us to look, with a torch, behind these untransparent organs – to explore the darksome interior of that opaque being – to illumine its obscure corners and absurd blind-alleys – to throw all at once a strong light upon the Psyche chained in the depths of that drear cavern – doubtless we should find the poor creature in some posture of decrepitude, stunted and rickety – like those prisoners who grow old under the Leads of Venice, bent double in a stone chest too low and too short for them either to stand or to lie at full length.

It is certain that the spirit becomes crippled in a misshapen body. Quasimodo barely felt, stirring blindly within him, a soul made after his own image. The impressions of objects underwent a considerable refraction before they reached his apprehension. His brain was a peculiar medium; the ideas which passed through it issued completely distorted. The reflection which proceeded from that refraction was necessarily divergent and astray.

Hence, he was subject to a thousand optical illusions, a thousand aberrations of judgment, a thousand wanderings of thought, sometimes foolish, sometimes idiotic.

The first effect of this fatal organization was to disturb the view which he took of external objects. He received from them scarcely any immediate perception. The external world seemed to him much farther off than it does to us.

The second effect of his misfortune was to render him mischievous.

He was mischievous, indeed, because he was savage, and he was savage because he was deformed. There was a logic in his nature as in ours.

His strength, so extraordinarily developed, was another cause of mischievousness, *malus puer robustus* (the wicked boy is strong), says Hobbes.

We must, nevertheless, do him justice; malice was probably not innate in him. From his very first intercourse with men he had felt, and then had seen, himself repulsed, branded, despised. Human speech had never been to him aught but mockery and curses. As he grew up, he had found around him nothing but hatred. What wonder that he should have caught it! He had contracted it – he had but picked up the weapon that had wounded him.

After all, he turned towards mankind reluctantly – his cathedral was sufficient for him. It was peopled with figures in marble – with kings, saints, bishops – who, at all events, did not burst out laughing in his face, but looked upon him with calmness and benevolence. The other statues, those of monsters and demons, had no hatred for him, Quasimodo. He was too much like them for that. Their raillery seemed rather to be directed toward the rest of mankind. The saints were his friends, and blessed him; the monsters were his friends, and guarded him. Accordingly, he used to have long communings with them; he would sometimes pass whole hours crouched before one of these statues, holding solitary converse with it; if any one happened to approach, he would fly like some lover surprised in a serenade.

And the cathedral was not only his society, but his world – it was all nature to him. He dreamed of no other hedgerows than the stained windows always in bloom – no other shade than that of the stone foliage which spreads out, loaded with birds, in the bushy Saxon capitals – no mountains but the colossal towers of the church – no ocean but Paris, murmuring at their feet.

That which he loved above all in the maternal edifice – that which awakened his soul, and made it stretch forth its poor pinions, that otherwise remained so miserably folded up in its cavern – that which even sometimes made him happy – was, the bells. He loved them, caressed them, talked to them, understood them. From the chimes in the central steeple to the great bell over the doorway, they all shared his affections. The belfry of the transept and the two towers were to him three great cages, in which the birds taught by himself sang for him alone. It was, however, those same bells that had deafened him. But a mother is often fondest of that child which has cost her the most suffering.

It is true that their voices were the only ones he was still capable of hearing. On this account, the great bell was his best beloved. She it was whom he preferred among this family of noisy sisters that fluttered about him on festival days. This great bell was named Marie. She hung in the southern tower, where she had no companion but her sister Jacqueline, a bell of smaller dimensions, shut up in a smaller cage by the side of her own. This Jacqueline was so named after the wife of Jean Montagu, who had given her to the church – a donation which, however, had not prevented him from figuring without his head at Montfaucon. In the second tower were six other bells; and finally the six smallest inhabited the central steeple, over the transept, together with the wooden bell, which was rung only from the afternoon of Holy Thursday until the morning of Holy Saturday, or Easter eve. Thus Quasimodo had fifteen bells in his seraglio; but the big Marie was his favourite.

It is impossible to form a conception of his joy on the days of the great peals. The instant the archdeacon let him off with the word 'go,' he ascended the spiral staircase quicker than any other person could have gone down. He rushed, breathless, into the aerial chamber of the great bell; gazed at her for a moment attentively and lovingly; then began to talk to her softly, patted her with his hand, like a good horse setting out on a long journey. He pitied her for the labour she was about to undergo. After these first caresses, he called out to his assistants, placed in the lower story of the tower, to begin. The latter then hung their weight upon the ropes, the windlass creaked and the enormous cone of metal moved slowly. Quasimodo, with heaving breast, followed it with his eye. The first stroke of the tongue against the brazen wall that encircled it shook the scaffolding upon which he stood. Quasimodo vibrated with the bell. 'Vah!' he would cry, with a mad burst of laughter. Meanwhile, the motion of the bell was accelerated, and as it went on, taking an ever-increasing sweep, Quasimodo's eye, in like manner, opened more and more widely, phosphorescent and flaming. At length the grand peal began – the whole tower trembled – rafters, leads, stones – all shook together – from the piles of the foundation to the trefoils of the parapet. Then Quasimodo boiled and frothed; he ran to and fro, trembling, with the tower, from head to foot. The bell, let loose, and in a frenzy turned first to one side and then to the other side of the tower its brazen throat, from whence issued a roar that was audible at four leagues' distance. Quasimodo placed himself before this gaping throat – he crouched down and rose with the oscillations of the bell – inhaled that furious breath – looked by turns down upon the Place which was swarming with people two hundred feet below him, and upon the enormous brazen tongue which came, second after second, to bellow in his ear. This was the only speech that he could hear, the only sound that broke for him the universal silence. He expanded in it, like a bird in the sunshine. All at once the frenzy of the bell would seize him; his look became wild – he lay in wait for the great bell as a spider for a fly, and then flung himself headlong upon it. Now, suspended over the abyss, borne to and fro by the formidable swinging of the bell, he seized the brazen monster by the ears – gripped it with his knees – spurred it with his heels – and redoubled, with the shock and weight of his body, the fury of the peal. Meanwhile, the tower trembled; he shouted and gnashed his teeth – his red hair bristled – his breast heaved and puffed like the bellows of a forge – his eye flashed fire – the monstrous bell neighed panting beneath him. Then it was no longer either the great bell of Notre-Dame, nor Quasimodo – it was a dream – a whirl – a tempest – dizziness astride upon clamour – a strange centaur, half man, half bell – a spirit clinging to a winged monster – a sort of horrible Astolpho, borne away upon a prodigious hippogriff of living bronze.

The presence of this extraordinary being seemed to infuse the breath of life into the whole cathedral. There seemed to issue from him – at least according to the growing superstitions of the crowd – a mysterious emanation, which animated all the stones of Notre-Dame, and to make the very entrails of the old church heave and palpitate. To know that he was there was enough to make one think the thousand statues in the galleries and doorways moved and breathed.

The old cathedral seemed to be a docile and obedient creature in his hands; waiting his will to lift up her mighty voice; being filled and possessed with Quasimodo as with a familiar spirit. One would have said that he made the immense building breathe. He was everywhere; he multiplied himself upon every point of the structure. Sometimes one beheld with dread, at the very top of one of the towers, a fantastic dwarfish-looking figure – climbing – twisting – crawling on all fours – descending outside over the abyss – leaping from projection to projection – and diving to ransack the belly of some sculptured gorgon; it was Quasimodo dislodging the crows. Again, in some obscure corner of the church, one would stumble against a sort of living chimera, crouching and scowling – it was Quasimodo musing. Sometimes one caught sight, under a belfry, of an enormous head and a bundle of ill-adjusted limbs, swinging furiously at the end of a rope – it was Quasimodo ringing the vespers, or the angelus. Often, at night, a hideous form was seen wandering upon the frail open-work balustrade which crowns the towers and runs around the top of the apse – it was still the hunchback of Notre-Dame. Then, so said the good women of the neighbourhood, the whole church assumed a fantastic, supernatural, horrible aspect – eyes and mouths opened in it here and there – the dogs, and the dragons and the griffins of stone, that watch day and night, with outstretched necks and open jaws, around the monstrous cathedral, were heard to bark. And if it was a Christmas eve – while the big bell, that seemed to rattle in its throat, called the faithful to the blazing midnight mass, the gloomy façade assumed such an aspect that the great doorway seemed to swallow the multitude, while the rose-window above it looked on – and all this came from Quasimodo. Egypt would have taken him for the god of this temple – the Middle Ages believed him to be its demon – he was its soul.

So much so that, to those who know that Quasimodo once existed, Notre-Dame is now deserted, inanimate, dead. They feel that something has disappeared. That vast body is empty – it is a skeleton – the spirit has quitted it – they see its place and that is all. It is like a skull, which still has holes for the eyes, but no longer sight.

IV

The Dog and his Master

THERE WAS, HOWEVER, one human creature whom Quasimodo excepted from his malice and hatred for others, and whom he loved as much, perhaps more, than his cathedral: this was Claude Frollo.

The case was simple enough. Claude Frollo had taken him, adopted him, fed him, brought him up. While yet quite little, it was between Claude Frollo's knees that he had been accustomed to take refuge when the dogs and the children ran yelping after him. Claude Frollo had taught him to speak, to read, to write. Claude Frollo, in fine, had made him ringer of the bells – and to give the great bell in marriage to Quasimodo, was giving Juliet to Romeo.

Accordingly, Quasimodo's gratitude was deep, ardent, boundless; and although the countenance of his adoptive father was often clouded and severe – although his mode of speaking was habitually brief, harsh, imperious – never had that gratitude wavered for a single instant. The archdeacon had in Quasimodo the most submissive of slaves, the most tractable of servants, the most vigilant of watch-dogs. When the poor bell-ringer became deaf, between him and Claude Frollo was established a language of signs, mysterious and intelligible only to themselves. Thus the archdeacon was the only human being with whom Quasimodo had preserved a communication. He had intercourse with only two things in this world – Notre-Dame and Claude Frollo.

Unexampled were the sway of the archdeacon over the bell-ringer, and the bell-ringer's devotion to the archdeacon. One sign from Claude, and the idea of pleasing him would have sufficed to make Quasimodo throw himself from the top of the towers of Notre-Dame. There was something remarkable in all that physical strength, so extraordinarily developed in Quasimodo, and blindly placed by him at the disposal of another. In this there was undoubtedly filial devotion and domestic attachment; but there was also fascination of one mind by another mind. There was a poor, awkward, clumsy organization, which stood with lowered head and supplicating eyes before a lofty and profound, a powerful and commanding intellect. Lastly, and above all, it was gratitude – gratitude pushed to its extremest limit, that we know not to what to compare it. This virtue is not one of those of which the finest examples are to be met with among men. We will say, then, that Quasimodo loved the archdeacon as no dog, no horse, no elephant ever loved his master.

V

Claude Frollo, Continued

IN 1482, QUASIMODO was about twenty years old, and Claude Frollo about thirty-six. The one had grown up; the other had grown old.

Claude Frollo was no longer the simple student of the Torchi college – the tender protector of a little boy – the young dreaming philosopher, who knew many things and was ignorant of many. He was a priest, austere, grave, morose – charged with the care of souls – Monsieur the Archdeacon of Josas – the second acolyte of the bishop – having charge of the two deaneries of Montlhéry, and Châteaufort and one hundred and seventy-four of the rural clergy. He was a sombre and awe-inspiring personage, before whom the choir-boys in albs and jaquette, the precentors, the brothers of Saint Augustine, and the matutinal clerks of Notre-Dame trembled, when he passed slowly beneath the lofty arches of the choir, majestic, thoughtful, with arms folded and head so bent upon his breast that nothing could be seen of his face but the high bald forehead.

Dom Claude Frollo, however, had abandoned neither science nor the education of his young brother, those two occupations of his life. But in the course of time, some bitterness had been mingled with these things once so sweet. In the long run, says Paul Diacre, the best bacon turns rancid. Little Jehan Frollo, surnamed Du Moulin (of the mill) from the place where he had been nursed, had not grown up in the direction which Claude had been desirous of leading him. The elder brother, had reckoned upon a pious, docile, studious, creditable pupil. But the younger brother like those young plants which baffle the endeavours of the gardener, and turn obstinately toward the quarter whence they receive air and sunshine – the younger brother grew up, and shot forth full and luxuriant branches, only on the side of idleness, ignorance and debauchery. He was a very devil – very unruly – which made Dom Claude knit his brows – but very droll and very shrewd – which made the big brother smile.

Claude had consigned him to the same college de Torchi where he had passed his early years in study and meditation- and it grieved him that this sanctuary, once edified by the name of Frollo should now be scandalized by it. He sometimes read Jehan very long and very severe lectures upon the subject, which the latter bore undaunted. After all the young scapegrace had a good heart – as is always the case in all comedies. But the lecture over, he nevertheless quietly resumed his dissolute and turbulent ways. At one time it was a yellow-beak (as a new-comer at the University was called), whom he had plucked for his entrance-money – a precious tradition, which has been carefully handed down to the present day. At another he had instigated a band of students, *quasi classico excitati* (to make a classic attack) upon some tavern – then had beaten the tavern-keeper 'with offensive cudgels,' and merrily pillaged the tavern, even to staving in the casks of wine in the cellar. And then there was a fine report, in Latin, which the sub-monitor of Torchi brought piteously to Dom Claude, with this dolorous marginal note – *Rixa; prima causa vinum optimum potatum* (quarrels, primary cause, most excellent wine drunk). And, in fact, it was said – a thing quite horrible in a lad of sixteen – that his excesses oftentimes led him as far as the Rue de Glatigny (then famous for its gambling-houses).

Owing to all this, Claude, saddened and discouraged in his human affections, had thrown himself the more eagerly into the arms of Science – that sister who, at all events, does not laugh in your face, but always repays you, though sometimes in rather hollow coin, for the attentions bestowed upon her. He became more and more learned – and, at the same time, by a natural consequence, more and more rigid as a priest, more and more gloomy as a man. There are in each individual of us certain parallelisms between our intelligence, our habits and our character, which develop without interruption, and are broken off only by the greater disturbances of life.

As Claude Frollo had, from his youth, gone through almost the entire circle of human knowledge, positive, external and lawful he was under the absolute necessity, unless he was to stop *ubi defuit orbis* (at the end of the world), of going farther, and seeking other food for the insatiable activity of his intellect. The ancient symbol of the serpent biting its own tail is especially appropriate to science; and it would appear that Claude Frollo had experienced this. Many grave persons affirmed that after exhausting the *fas* (lawful) of human knowledge he had dared to penetrate into the *nefas* (unlawful). He had, they said, successively tasted every apple upon the tree of knowledge; and, whether from hunger or disgust, he had ended by tasting the forbidden fruit. He had taken his place by turns, as our readers have seen, at the conferences of the theologians at the Sorbonne; at the meetings of the faculty of arts at the image of Saint Hilaire, at the disputations of the decretists at the image of Saint Martin, at the congregations of the physicians by the holy water font of Notre-Dame, *ad cupam nostrae dominae* (to the font of Notre-Dame). All the viands, permitted and approved, which those four great kitchens called the four faculties could prepare and serve up to the understanding, he had devoured; and satiety had come before his hunger was appeased. Then he had delved deeper – underneath all that finite, material, limited science; he had perhaps risked his soul, and seated himself in the cavern, at that mysterious table of the alchemists, the astrologers, the hermetics, headed by Averroes, Guillaume de Paris and Nicolas Flamel, in the Middle Ages, and which extended in the East, under the light of the seven-branched candlestick, up to Solomon, Pythagoras and Zoroaster.

This is, at least, what was supposed, whether rightly or not.

It is certain that the archdeacon often visited the cemetery of the Holy Innocents, where, it is true, his father and mother had been buried, with the other victims of the plague of 1466; but he seemed far less interested in the cross at the head of their grave than in the strange figures upon the tomb of Nicolas Flamel and his wife Claude Pernelle, which stood close by it.

It is certain that he had been seen often walking along the Rue des Lombards, and furtively entering a small house at the corner of the Rue des Ecrivains and the Rue Marivault. It was the house built by Nicolas Flamel, in which he had died about 1407, and which, uninhabited ever since, was beginning to fall into ruins, so greatly had the hermetics and alchemists of all countries worn away its walls merely by scratching their names upon them. Some of the neighbours even affirmed that they had once seen, through an air-hole, the archdeacon Claude digging and turning over the earth in the two cellars, whose supports had been scrawled over with innumerable couplets and hieroglyphics by Nicolas Flamel himself. It was supposed that Flamel had buried the philosopher's stone in these cellars; and for two centuries, the alchemists, from Magistri to Father Pacifique, never ceased to worry the soil, until the house, so mercilessly ransacked and turned inside out, ended by crumbling into dust under their feet.

Again, it is certain that the archdeacon had been seized with a singular passion for the symbolical doorway of Notre-Dame, that page of conjuration written in stone by Bishop William of Paris who has undoubtedly been damned for attaching so infernal a frontispiece to the sacred poem eternally chanted by the rest of the structure. Archdeacon Claude also passed for having sounded the mysteries of the colossal Saint Christopher, and of that long enigmatical statue which then stood at the entrance to the Square in front of the cathedral, and which the people had nicknamed Monsieur Legris. But what everyone might have noticed was the interminable hours which he would often spend, seated upon the parapet of this same Square, in contemplating the carvings on the portal – now examining the foolish virgins with their lamps reversed, now the wise virgins with their lamps upright – at other times calculating the angle of vision of that raven clinging to the left side of the doorway, looking at some mysterious spot in the church – where the philosopher's stone is certainly concealed if it be not in Nicolas Flamel's cellar. It was a singular destiny (we may remark in passing) for the church of Notre-Dame, at that period, to be thus beloved in different degrees, and with such devotion, by two beings so dissimilar as Claude and Quasimodo – loved by the one, a sort of instinctive and savage half-man, for its beauty, for its stature, for the harmonies which emanated from its magnificent whole – loved by the other, a being of cultivated and ardent imagination, for its signification, for its myth, for its hidden meaning, for the symbol lurking under the sculptures on its front, like the first text under the second in a palimpsest – in short, for the enigma which it eternally propounds to the understanding.

Furthermore, it is certain that the archdeacon had established himself, in that one of the two towers which looks upon the Grève close to the belfry, in a small and secret cell, into which no one entered – not even the bishop, it was said – without his leave. This cell, contrived of old, almost at the top of the tower, among the crows' nests, by Bishop Hugo de Besançon ('Hugo II de Bisuncio,' 1326-1332), who had practised sorcery there in his day. What this cell contained no one knew. But from the strand of the Terrain there was often seen, at night, to appear, disappear and reappear at short and regular intervals, at a small dormer window at the back of the tower, a certain red, intermittent, singular glow, seeming as if it followed the irregular puffing of a bellows, and as if proceeding from a flame rather than a light. In the darkness, at that height, it had a very weird appearance; and the housewives would say: 'There is the archdeacon blowing! Hell is making sparks up there!'

There were not, after all, any great proofs of sorcery; but still there was quite enough smoke to make the good people suppose a flame; and the archdeacon had a somewhat formidable reputation. We are bound to declare, however, that the sciences of Egypt – that necromancy – that magic – even the clearest and most innocent – had no more violent enemy, no more merciless denouncer before the officials of Notre-Dame, than himself. Whether it was sincere abhorrence, or merely the trick of the robber who cries Stop, thief! this did not prevent the archdeacon from being considered by the wise heads of the chapter as one who risked his soul upon the threshold of hell – one lost in the caverns of the cabala – groping his way among the shadows of the occult sciences. Neither were the people deceived thereby; to the mind of any one possessed of the least sagacity, Quasimodo passed for the demon, and Claude Frollo the sorcerer; it was evident that the bell-ringer was to serve the archdeacon for a given time, at the expiration of which he was to carry off the latter's soul by way of payment. Thus the archdeacon, despite the excessive austerity of his life, was in bad odour with all pious souls; and there was no devout nose, however inexperienced, but could smell him out for a magician. And if, as he grew older, he had formed to himself abysses in science, others had likewise opened themselves in his heart. So at least they were led to believe who narrowly observed that face, in which his soul shone forth as through a sombre cloud. Whence that large bald brow – that head constantly bowed – that breast forever heaved with sighs? What secret thought wreathed that bitter smile about his lips, at the same instant when his lowering brows approached each other fierce as two encountering bulls? Why were his remaining hairs already gray? What internal fire was that which shone forth occasionally in his glance, to such a degree that his eye resembled a hole pierced in the wall of a furnace?

These symptoms of a violent moral preoccupation had acquired an especially high degree of intensity at the period to which our narrative refers. More than once had a choir-boy fled affrighted at finding him alone in the church, so strange and fiery was his look. More than once, in the choir, during divine service, his neighbour in the stalls had heard him mingle, in the full song *ad omnem tonum* (note for note), unintelligible parentheses. More than once had the laundress of the Terrain, who was employed 'to wash the chapter,' observed, not without dread, marks of nails and clenched fingers in the surplice of Monsieur the Archdeacon of Josas.

However, he became doubly rigid, and had never been more exemplary. By character, as well as by calling, he had always held himself aloof from women; and he seemed to hate them more than ever. The mere crackling of a silken corsage brought his hood down over his eyes. On this point so jealous were his austerity and reserve that when the king's daughter, the Lady of Beaujeu, came in December, 1481, to visit the cloister of Notre-Dame, he gravely opposed her entrance, reminding the bishop of the statute in the Livre Noir or Black Book, dating from the vigil Saint Bartholomew, 1344, forbidding access to the cloister to every woman 'whatsoever old or young, mistress or maid.' Whereupon the bishop having been constrained to cite to him the ordinance of the legate, Odo, which makes exception in favour of certain ladies of high rank – *aliquae magnates mulieres, quae sine scandalo evitari non possunt* (certain great ladies who cannot be excluded without scandal) – the archdeacon still protested; objecting that the legate's ordinance, being dated as far back as the year 1207, was a hundred and twenty-seven years anterior to the Livre Noir, and was consequently abrogated by it. And he refused to make his appearance before the princess.

It was also remarked that, for some time past, his abhorrence of gypsy women and zingari had been redoubled. He had solicited from the bishop an edict expressly forbidding the gypsies from coming to dance and play upon the tambourine in the *Place du Parvis;* and for the same length of time he had been rummaging among the mouldy archives of the official in order to collect together all the cases of wizards and witches condemned to the flames or the halter for having been accomplices in sorcery with he-goats, she-goats or sows.

VI

Unpopularity

THE ARCHDEACON AND the bell-ringer, as we have already said, were but little esteemed among the small and great folks of the environs of the cathedral. When Claude and Quasimodo went forth together, as frequently happened, and they were observed in company traversing the clean, but narrow and dusky, streets of the neighbourhood of Notre-Dame, the servant following his master, more than one malicious word, more than one ironical couplet, more than one insulting jest, stung them on their way; unless Claude Frollo – though this happened rarely – walked with head erect, exhibiting his stern and almost august brow to the graze of the abashed scoffers.

The pair were in that quarter like the 'poets' of whom Régnier speaks:

> All sorts of folk do after poets hie,
> As after owls the tomtits shriek and fly.

Occasionally an ill-natured body would risk his skin and bones for the ineffable pleasure of running a pin into Quasimodo's hump. Again, a pretty girl, more full of frolic and boldness than became her, would rustle the priest's black gown, singing in his face the sardonic ditty: 'Nestle, nestle, the Devil is caught.' Sometimes a squalid group of old women, crouching in line down the shady side of the steps of a porch, grumbled aloud as the archdeacon and the bell-ringer passed, or called after them with curses this encouraging greeting: 'Ho! here comes one with a soul as crooked as the other's body.' Or a band of school-boys and street urchins playing at hopscotch would jump up together and salute them classically with some cry in Latin, as *'Eia! eia! Claudius cum claudo!'* ('Ah! ah! Claude with the cripple.')

Generally, the insult passed unperceived by the priest and the bell-ringer. Quasimodo was too deaf and Claude too deeply absorbed in his thoughts to hear these gracious salutations.

BOOK FIVE

I

Abbas Beati Martini *

DOM CLAUDE'S FAME had spread far and wide. It procured for him, about the period he refused to see Madame de Beaujeu, a visit which he long remembered.

It was on a certain evening. He had just withdrawn, after divine service, to his canon's cell in the cloister of Notre-Dame. This cell, with the exception perhaps of some glass phials, relegated to a corner, and filled with a certain equivocal powder which strongly resembled gunpowder, offered nothing extraordinary or mysterious. There were, indeed, here and there, several inscriptions upon the walls, but they were merely sentences relative to science or religion, and extracted from good authors. The archdeacon had just seated himself by the light of a three-beaked copper lamp, before a large cabinet loaded with manuscripts. He leaned his elbow upon the open volume of Honorius d'Autun, *De Prædestinatione et libero arbitrio* (on predestination and free will,) and he was turning over in profound meditation the leaves of a folio which he had brought in with him, the only product of the printing-press which his cell contained. In the midst of his reverie a knock was heard at the door. 'Who is there?' cried the sage, in the gracious tone of a hungry dog who is disturbed at his bone.

A voice replied from without: 'Your friend, Jacques Coictier.' He went to open the door.

It was, in fact, the king's physician, a person of some fifty years of age, whose harsh physiognomy was only corrected by his crafty eye. Another man accompanied him. Both wore long slate-coloured robes, furred with minever, belted and buttoned, with bonnets of the same stuff and colour. Their hands disappeared in their long sleeves, their feet under their robes and their eyes beneath their caps.

'God help me, gentlemen!' said the archdeacon, showing them in, 'I was not expecting so honourable a visit at such an hour' – and while speaking in this courteous manner he cast an anxious and scrutinizing glance from the physician to his companion.

'It is never too late to visit so distinguished a scholar as Dom Claude

* Abbé of the Blessed Saint Martin.

Frollo de Tirechappe,' replied the Doctor Coictier, whose Franche-Comté accent caused all his phrases to drag with the majesty of a court-train.

Then began between the physician and the archdeacon one of those congratulatory prologues which preceded, according to the custom of the time, all conversation between men of learning, and which did not prevent them detesting each other in the most cordial manner in the world. However, it is the same to-day, the lips of each wise man who compliments another sage are like a cup of honeyed gall.

Claude Frollo's congratulations to Jacques Coictier referred principally to the numerous temporal advantages which the worthy physician, in the course of his much envied career, had succeeded in extracting from each malady of the king, the operation of an alchemy better and more certain than the pursuit of the philosopher's stone.

'In truth, Monsieur le Docteur Coictier, I had great joy in learning of the bishopric granted to your nephew, my reverend seigneur Pierre Verse. Is he not Bishop of Amiens?'

'Yes, Monsieur Archdeacon, it is a favour and mercy from God.'

'Do you know that you made a very fine figure on Christmas day at the head of your company from the Chamber of Accounts Monsieur President?'

'Vice-President, Dom Claude. Alas! nothing more.'

'At what point is the work on your superb house in the Rue Saint André des Arcs? It is another Louvre. I like exceedingly the apricot-tree which is carved over the door with the pleasant play upon the words à L'ABRI COTIER.'

'Alas! Master Claude, all that masonry is costing me heavily. In proportion as the house rises I am ruined.'

'Ho! Have you not your revenues from the jail and the bailiwick of the Palace, and the rents of all the houses, butchers' stalls and booths of the enclosure? 'Tis a fine cow to milk.'

'My Poissy castellany has brought me nothing this year.'

'But your tolls of Triel, of Saint James and of Saint Germain en Laye are always good.'

'Six score livres, and not even Paris livres.'

'You have your place as king's counsellor, that is fixed.'

'Yes, Brother Claude, but that accursed manor of Poligny, about which they make so much noise, is not worth to me sixty gold crowns to the year, good or bad.'

There was, in the compliments which Dom Claude addressed to Jacques Coictier, that satirical, biting and mocking accent combined with that cruel, sad smile of a superior but unhappy man who for a moment's distraction plays with the fat prosperity of a vulgarian. The other did not perceive it.

'Upon my soul,' exclaimed Claude, finally, pressing his hand, 'I am glad to see you in such good health.'

'Thanks, Master Claude.'

'By the way,' said Dom Claude, 'how is your royal patient?'

'He does not pay sufficiently his physician,' replied the doctor, glancing at his companion.

'Think you so, friend Coictier?' said his comrade.

These words, uttered in a tone of surprise and reproach, drew the attention of the archdeacon upon the unknown personage, which, to tell the truth, had not been diverted from him a single moment since the stranger had crossed his threshold. It had even required all the thousand reasons which he had for conciliating Doctor Jacques Coictier, the all-powerful physician of King Louis XI, to induce him to receive the latter thus accompanied. Hence, his mien was but little cordial when Jacques Coictier said to him: 'By the way, Dom Claude, I bring you a colleague who has desired to see you on account of your renown.'

'Does the gentleman belong to science?' asked the archdeacon, fixing his piercing eye upon Coictier's companion. He found beneath the brows of the stranger a glance no less piercing or less defiant than his own. He was, so far as the feeble light of the lamp permitted one to judge, an old man about sixty years of age, of medium stature, who appeared somewhat sickly and broken down. His profile, though commonplace in outline, was still strong and severe; his eye flashed from beneath an overhanging brow like a light from the depths of a cave; and under the cap that was well drawn down and fell upon his nose, one recognized the broad expanse of a brow of genius.

He took it upon himself to reply to the archdeacon's question:

'Reverend master,' he said, in a grave tone, 'your renown has reached my ears, and I wish to consult you. I am but a poor provincial gentleman, who removeth his shoes before entering the presence of learned men. You must know my name. I am called Friend Tourangeau.'

'Strange name for a gentleman!' thought the archdeacon. Nevertheless he felt himself in the presence of a character both strong and serious. The instinct of his own lofty intelligence enabled him to recognize a no less able mind under the furred bonnet of Friend Tourangeau; and as he contemplated that grave countenance, the ironical smile, which the presence of Jacques Coictier had called to his gloomy face, faded slowly away as twilight upon the evening horizon. He had reseated himself, stern and silent, in his great arm-chair, his elbow in its accustomed place upon the table and his forehead in his hand. After a few moments of meditation, he beckoned to his visitors to be seated, and addressed Friend Tourangeau.

'You come to consult me, master, and upon what science?'

'Your reverence,' replied Friend Tourangeau, 'I am ill, very ill. You are said to be a great Æsculapius, and I am come to ask your advice in medicine.'

'Medicine!' said the archdeacon, tossing his head. He appeared to meditate for a moment, then resumed. 'Friend Tourangeau, since that is your name, turn your head and you will find my reply already written upon the wall.'

The Friend Tourangeau obeyed, and read, engraved upon the wall over his head, the following inscription: *Medicine is the daughter of dreams.'* – JAMBLIQUE.

Meanwhile, Doctor Jacques Coictier had heard his companion's question with a displeasure which Dom Claude's reply had only redoubled. He leaned down to the ear of Friend Tourangeau and said to him, softly enough to escape the hearing of the archdeacon: 'I warned you that he was mad. You insisted on seeing him.'

'But it is quite possible that he is right, this madman, Doctor Jacques,' replied the Friend, in the same tone and with a bitter smile.

'As you please,' answered Coictier, dryly. Then, addressing the archdeacon: 'You are a quick workman, Dom Claude, and you have as little trouble with Hippocrates as a monkey does with a nut. Medicine a dream! I doubt me the pharmacopolists and the master physicians would feel it their duty to stone you, if they were here. So you deny the influence of philters upon the blood, of unguents upon the flesh! You deny that eternal pharmacy of the flowers and the metals, which we call the world, and which was expressly made for that eternal invalid we call man!'

'I deny,' said Dom Claude, coldly, 'neither pharmacy nor the invalid. I deny the physician.'

'Then it is not true,' continued Coictier, with warmth, 'that the gout is an internal ringworm; that a bullet wound can be cured by the application of a roasted mouse, and that young blood, properly infused, restores youth to aged veins; it is not true that two and two make four, and that emprostathonos follows opistathonos?'

The archdeacon replied calmly: 'There are certain things upon which I think in a certain manner.'

Coictier became red with anger.

'There, there, my good Coictier, let us not get angry,' said the Friend Tourangeau. 'Monsieur the archdeacon is our friend.'

Coictier calmed down, muttering in a low tone, 'After all, he is mad!'

'*Pasquedieu,* Master Claude,' resumed Friend Tourangeau, after a silence, 'you embarrass me greatly. I had two subjects for consultation with you; one touching my health, the other touching my star.'

'Sir!' responded the archdeacon, 'if that be your object you would have done as well not to have wasted your breath in climbing my stairs. I do not believe in medicine; I do not believe in astrology.'

'Indeed!' replied the stranger, with surprise.

Coictier gave a forced laugh.

'You see obviously that he is mad,' said he in a low tone to Friend Tourangeau. 'He does not believe in astrology.'

'What reason to imagine,' pursued Dom Claude, 'that each ray from a star is a thread that touches the head of a man!'

'And what, then, do you believe?' cried Friend Tourangeau. The archdeacon rested a moment uncertain, then upon his lips appeared a sombre smile which seemed to give the lie to his response: '*Credo in Deum.*'

'*Dominum nostrum,*' added Friend Tourangeau, making the sign of the cross.

'*Amen,*' said Coictier.

'Reverend master,' resumed Tourangeau, 'in my soul am I rejoiced to find you of such religious mind. But have you reached a point, great savant that you are, of no longer believing in science?'

'No,' said the archdeacon, seizing Father Tourangeau by the arm, and a light of enthusiasm illumined his dull eye, 'no, I do not deny science; I have not crawled so long upon my belly with my nails in the earth amid the countless mazes of the cavern without perceiving, far away beyond me at the end of the obscure gallery, a light, a flame, something, a reflection, doubtless of the dazzling central laboratory, where the patient and the wise have taken God by surprise.'

'But, after all,' interrupted Tourangeau, 'what do you hold to be true and certain?'

'Alchemy.'

'*Pardieu,*' exclaimed Coictier, 'alchemy has its good without doubt, Dom Claude, but why blaspheme medicine and astrology?'

'Naught is your science of man, naught is your science of the stars,' said the archdeacon, imperiously.

'That is making short work of Epidaurus and Chaldea,' replied the doctor, sneeringly.

'Listen, Messire Jacques. This is said in good faith. I am not the king's physician, and his Majesty has not given me the garden of Dædalus in which to observe the constellations . . . – do not get angry, but listen to me. What truth have you derived – I will not say from medicine, which is too foolish a thing, but from astrology?'

'Do you deny,' said Coictier, 'the sympathetic force of the collarbone and the cabalistics which are derived therefrom?'

'Error, Messire Jacques. None of your formulas end in reality while alchemy has its discoveries. Do you dispute such results as these? Ice imprisoned under ground for a thousand years becomes rock crystal. Lead is the father of all metals. For gold is not a metal; gold is light. Lead requires four periods of two hundred years each to change successively from the state of lead to that of red arsenic from red arsenic to tin, from tin to silver. Are not these facts? But to believe in the collar-bone, in the great circle and in the stars is as ridiculous as to believe with the inhabitants of Grand Cathay that the golden oriole turns into a mole, and that grains of wheat turn into fish of the carp species.'

'I have studied hermetics,' cried Coictier, 'and I insist – '

The fiery archdeacon did not allow him to finish: 'And I have studied medicine, astrology and hermetics. Here alone is the truth' (and as he spoke thus he took from the cabinet a phial full of the powder of which we spoke above), 'here alone is light! Hippocrates is a dream; Urania is a dream; Hermes is but a thought. Gold is the sun; to make gold is to become God. Behold the unique science. I have sounded the depths of medicine and astrology, I tell you! They are naught, naught! The human body, shadows! the planets, shadows!'

And he fell back into his arm-chair in commanding and inspired attitude. Friend Tourangeau observed him in silence. Coictier forced a sneer, and imperceptibly shrugging his shoulders, said in a low voice: 'A madman!'

'And,' said suddenly Tourangeau, 'the splendid goal, have you attained it – have you made gold?'

'Had I made it,' replied the archdeacon slowly articulating, like a man who is reflecting, 'the king of France would be called Claude and not Louis.'

The stranger frowned.

'What do I say?' continued Claude, with a smile of disdain. 'What would the throne of France be to me, when I could rebuild the empire of the Orient?'

'Very good,' said the stranger. 'Oh, the poor fool,' murmured Coictier. The archdeacon continued, appearing to reply only to his thoughts.

'But no, I am still crawling. I bruise my lace and my knees upon the stones of the subterranean way; I see dimly, I do not contemplate the full glory, I do not read, I spell!'

'And when you can read!' demanded the stranger, 'will you make gold?'

'Who doubts it?' said the archdeacon.

'In that case, Our Lady knows that I am in sore need of money, and I would gladly learn to read in your books. Tell me, reverend master, is your science hostile or displeasing to Our Lady?'

To this question of Tourangeau, Dom Claude merely replied with calm dignity:

'To whom am I archdeacon?'

' 'Tis true, my master. Will it, then, please you to initiate me? Teach me to spell with you.'

Claude took the majestic and pontifical attitude of a Samuel.

'Old man, it takes longer years than rest to you to undertake the voyage through mysterious things. Your head is very gray! One leaves not the cavern but with whitened hair, and their locks must be dark who enter it. Science alone knows well how to hollow, wither and wrinkle human faces; she needs not that old age should bring her features already furrowed. If, however, the desire possesses you to submit yourself to discipline at your age, and of deciphering the formidable alphabet of the sages, come to me; it is well – I will make the effort. I will not tell you, poor old man, go visit the sepulchral chambers of the Pyramids, of which the ancient Herodotus speaks, nor the brick tower of Babylon, nor the great white marble sanctuary of the Indian temple of Eklinga. I, no more than you, have seen the Chaldean masonry constructed in the sacred form of Sikra, nor the temple of Solomon, which is destroyed, nor the stone doors of the sepulchre of the kings of Israel, which are broken. We will content ourselves with the fragments of the book of Hermes, which we have here. I will explain to you the statue of Saint Christopher, the symbol of the Sower, and that of the two angels which are at the door of the Sainte Chapelle, one of whom has his hand in a vase and the other in a cloud –'

Here, Jacques Coictier, who had been nonplussed by the archdeacon's impetuous replies, regained confidence and interrupted him with the triumphant tone of a savant who corrects another: '*Erras amice, Claudi* (thou errest, friend Claude). The symbol is not the number. You take Orpheus for Hermes.'

'It is you who are in error,' replied gravely the archdeacon. 'Dædalus is the basement; Orpheus is the wall; Hermes is the edifice, – the whole. Come when you will,' continued he, turning toward Tourangeau, 'I will show you the particles of gold which remained at the bottom of Nicolas Flamel's crucible, and you may compare it with the gold of Guillaume de Paris. I will teach you the secret virtues of the Greek word, '*peristera.*' But before all, I will make you read, one after the other, the marble letters of the alphabet, the granite pages of the book. We shall go from the portal of the Bishop Guillaume and of Saint Jean le Rond to La Sainte Chapelle, then to the house of Nicolas Flamel, Rue Marivault, to his tomb which is at the Holy Innocents, to his two hospitals, Rue de Montmorency. I shall make you read the hieroglyphs which cover the four great iron dogs at the door of the hospital of Saint Gervais and of the Rue de la Ferronnerie. We will spell out together the façade of Saint Come, of Sainte Geneviève des Ardents, of Saint Martin, of Saint Jacques de la Boucherie –'

For some time, Friend Tourangeau, intelligent though his glance was, had obviously failed to follow Dom Claude. He interrupted.

'*Pasquedieu!* What sort of books are these, then?'

'Here is one,' said the archdeacon.

And opening the window of his cell, he pointed to the vast church of Notre-Dame, which outlining darkly its two towers against the starry sky, with its stone flanks and its enormous back, appeared a gigantic two-headed sphinx crouching in the midst of the city.

For some time the archdeacon considered the enormous edifice in silence, then with a sigh, extending his right hand towards the printed book which lay open upon his table, and with his left hand extended towards Notre-Dame, his eyes sadly wandered from the book to the church. 'Alas!' he said, 'this will kill that.'

Coictier, who had eagerly approached the book, could not repress an exclamation: 'Why! But what is there so terrible in this: *Norimbergæ, Antonius Koburger*, 1474. This is not new. It is a book of Pierre Lombard, the master of Maxims. Is it because it is printed?'

'You have said it,' responded Claude, who appeared absorbed in a profound meditation, and stood with his forefinger resting upon the folio which had come from the famous press of Nuremberg. Then he added these mysterious words: 'Alas! Alas! Small things overcome great ones, the Nile rat kills the crocodile, the swordfish kills the whale, the book will kill the edifice.'

The curfew of the cloister sounded the same moment that Doctor Jacques repeated to his companion in low tones his eternal refrain: 'He is mad!' To which his companion this time replied: 'I believe that he is.'

It was the hour when no stranger could remain within the cloister. The two visitors withdrew.

'Master,' said Friend Tourangeau, in taking leave of the archdeacon, 'I love wise men and great minds, and I hold you in singular esteem. Come to-morrow to the Palace des Tournelles and ask for the Abbot of Saint Martin de Tours.'

The archdeacon returned to his chamber dumbfounded, under-standing at last who this Friend Tourangeau was, and recalling that passage from the cartulary of Saint Martin de Tours: *Abbas beati Martini*, SCILICET REX FRANCÆ, *est canonicus de consuetudine et habet parvam præbendam quam habet sanctus Venantius et debet sedere in sede thesaurarii.* *

It is affirmed that since that time the archdeacon had frequent conferences with Louis XI when his Majesty came to Paris, and that the influence of Dom Claude quite overshadowed that of Oliver Le Daim and Jacques Coictier, the latter of whom, as was his wont, roundly took the king to task on this account.

* The abbot of Saint Martin, namely, the King of France, is canon according to custom and holds the office of prebendary which Saint Venantius holds and should sit in the seat of the Treasurer.

II

One Shall Destroy the Other

OUR FAIR READERS will pardon us if we pause a moment to search for the hidden meaning of those enigmatic words of the archdeacon: 'The one shall destroy the other. The book will kill the edifice.'

In our opinion this idea might present two aspects. In the first place, it was the thought of a priest. It was the alarm of the priest in the presence of a new agent, printing. It was the horror and astonishment of the man of the sanctuary before the dazzling results of Guttenberg's press. It was the pulpit and the manuscript, the spoken word and the written word taking fright at the printed word: something similar to the stupor of the sparrow who should see the angel Legion unfold its six million wings. It was the cry of the prophet who already hears the roar of emancipated humanity, who beholds in the future intelligence undermining faith, opinion dethroning belief, the world at large shaking Rome. It was the prognostic of the philosopher, who sees human thought volatilized by the press, evaporating from the theocratic recipient. It was the terror of the soldier who examines the brazen battering-ram and says the town will fall. It signified that one power was succeeded by another. It meant, 'The press shall kill the Church.' But under this thought, without doubt the first and the most simple, there was in our belief another, more new, a corollary of the first less easy to perceive but more easy to contest, a view equally philosophic and not confined alone to the priest, but shared by the savant and the artist. It was the presentiment that human thought in changing its form would also change its mode of expression; that the dominant idea of each generation would no longer be written with the same material and in the same manner; that the book of stone, so solid and so enduring, was about to make way for the book of paper, more solid and still more enduring. In this relation the archdeacon's vague formula had another meaning, it signified that one art would dethrone another art. 'Printing would kill architecture.'

Indeed, from the origin of things down to and including the fifteenth century of the Christian era, architecture is the great book of humanity, the principal expression of man in his various stages of development, both as regards force and intellect.

When the memory of the first races felt itself surcharged, when the load of recollections which mankind had to bear became so heavy and confused that language, naked and simple, risked its loss by the way, men wrote them upon the ground in a manner most visible and most natural. They sealed each tradition beneath a monument.

The first monuments were mere fragments of stone, 'which iron had not touched,' says Moses. Architecture began like all writing. It was at first the alphabet. A stone was placed upright, it was a letter, and each letter was a hieroglyph and upon each hieroglyph reposed a group of ideas, like the capital upon the column. Thus did the first races everywhere simultaneously over the entire surface of the world. We find the 'standing stones' of the Celts in Asiatic Siberia: in the pampas of America.

Later on they made words; they placed stone upon stone, they coupled these syllables of granite; the verb essayed a few combinations. The Celtic dolmen and cromlech, the Etruscan tumulus, the Hebrew galgal, are words. Some of them, particularly the tumulus, are proper names. Sometimes even, where there was plenty of stone and vast coast, they wrote a phrase. The immense pile of Karnac is a complete sentence.

Finally men made books. Traditions had created symbols, which hid them as the leaves hide the trunk of a tree. All these symbols in which humanity had faith, continued to grow, to multiply, to intersect, to become more and more complicated: the first monuments were not sufficient to contain them, they overflowed them on every side; scarcely did these monuments still explain their original tradition, like themselves simple, naked and prone upon the earth. The symbol must needs expand into the edifice. Architecture then developed with the human thought, it became a giant with a thousand heads and a thousand arms, and fixed all that floating symbolism in an eternal, visible, palpable form. While Dædalus, who is force, measured; while Orpheus, who is intelligence, sang: the pillar, which is a letter; the arcade, which is a syllable; the pyramid, which is a word, set in motion alike by a geometric and poetic law, grouped themselves, combined, amalgamated, descended, arose, were juxtaposed upon the ground, ranged themselves in stories in the sky, until they had written under the general dictation of an epoch, those marvellous books which were likewise marvellous edifices: the Pagoda of Eklinga, the Rhamseion of Egypt, the Temple of Solomon.

The generating idea, the word, was not alone at the foundation of all these structures, but also to be traced in their form. The temple of Solomon, for example, was not only the binding of the holy book, but was the holy book itself. Upon each one of its concentric walls, the priest could read the Word, interpreted and manifested to the eye; and thus they followed its transformations from sanctuary to sanctuary until they seized it in the inner tabernacle, in its most concrete form, which was still architectural, the Ark itself. Thus the Word was concealed within the edifice, but its image was upon its envelope, like the human form upon the sarcophagus of a mummy.

And not only the forms of these buildings, but the sites that were chosen for them, arouse the thought they represented. According as the symbol they expressed was graceful or grave, Greece crowned her mountains with a temple harmonious to the eye; India disembowelled hers to chisel therein those deformed and subterranean pagodas supported by colossal ranks of granite elephants.

Thus during the first six thousand years of the world, from the most immemorial pagoda of Hindustan to the cathedral of Cologne, architecture has been the great handwriting of humankind. And this is so far true that not only all religious symbol, but also all human thought, has its page and its monument in this immense book.

All civilization begins with a theocracy and ends with a democracy. This law of liberty succeeding unity is written in architecture. For, and let us insist upon this point, masonry must not be thought powerful alone to erect the temple, to express the myth and sacerdotal symbolism, to transcribe in hieroglyphs upon its pages of stone the mysterious tables of the law. If it were thus, – as there comes in every human society a moment when the sacred symbol is worn and becomes obliterated under the influence of free thought, when man escapes from the priest, and when the excrescences born of philosophies and systems devour the fair features of religion – architecture could not reproduce this new state of the human mind; its leaves so crowded upon the face would be blank on the back; its work would be mutilated; its book incomplete. But no. Let us take for example the Middle Ages which period we can regard with clearer insight, being nearer to us. During the first half, while theocracy was organizing Europe, while the Vatican rallied and reclassified around it the elements of a Rome made with the Rome that lay in ruins about the Capitol, while Christianity was seeking among the rubbish of former civilizations all the various stages of society, and rebuilding with its fragments a new hierarchic universe with priesthood as the keystone of the arch, a solution is arising out of this chaos, one sees – appearing little by little, under the breath of Christianity, out of barbarian hands, from among the litter of dead architectures, Greek and Roman, we see arising that mysterious Roman architecture, sister of the theocratic masonries of Egypt and India, the unchanging emblem of pure Catholicism, the immutable hieroglyph of Papal unity. All the thought of the time is written in that sombre Roman style. There is felt everywhere, authority, unity the impenetrable, the absolute, Gregory VII: everywhere the priest, never the man; everywhere caste, nowhere the people. But the Crusades arrive. It is a great popular movement, and every great popular movement, whatever be its cause or its end, releases the spirit of liberty from its final precipitate. New ideas come to light. Here begin the stormy days of the Jacqueries, the Pragueries and the Leagues. Authority is shaken. Unity is divided. Feudalism insists upon sharing with theocracy, in awaiting until the people shall inevitably rise and, as usual, seize the lion's share: *Quia nominor leo* (because I am called lion). The nobles force their way through the ranks of the priesthood, the people those of the nobles. The face of Europe is changed. Well! the face of architecture is also changed. Like civilization she has turned her page, and the new spirit of the time finds her ready to write as it dictates. Architecture has come back from the Crusades with the pointed arch as the nations returned bringing liberty. Then while Rome is gradually dismembered Roman architecture dies. The hieroglyph deserts the cathedral and goes forth to emblazon the donjon and give prestige to feudalism. The cathedral, that edifice before time so dogmatic, is henceforth invaded by the commoners, by the masses, by liberty, escapes from the priest and falls into the power of the artist. The artist builds to his fancy. Farewell to mystery, myth and the law. Welcome fantasy and caprice. Provided the priest has his basilica and his altar, he has nothing to say. The four walls belong to the artist. The architectural book belongs no longer to the priesthood, to religion, to Rome; it is the property of imagination, of poetry, of the people. Hence the rapid and innumerable transformations of this architecture which endures only three centuries, and which is so striking after the stagnant immobility of the Roman period covering six or seven. Art, however, marches with giant strides. Genius and the originality of the people do the task formerly performed by the bishops. Each race as it passes leaves its line upon the great book; it erases the old Roman hieroglyphs from the frontispiece of the cathedral, and only here and there can be perceived the dogma penetrating through the stratum of new symbolism which covers it. The popular covering leaves scarcely visible the religious framework. It is impossible to form an idea of the liberties which the architects then took even towards the church.

We find capitals of columns interlaced with monks and nuns shamefully paired, as in the Hall of the Fireplaces, in the Palace of Justice, Paris, the adventures of Noah, sculptured with all detail, as under the great door of Bourges; or some bacchic monk with ass's ears, glass in hand, laughing in the face of an entire community, as in the lavatory of the abbey of Bocherville. There existed at that epoch, for thoughts transcribed in stone, a liberty, comparable only to the present freedom of the press. It was the liberty of architecture. This freedom goes to great lengths. Occasionally a portal, a façade, an entire church, is presented in a symbolical sense entirely foreign to its creed, and even hostile to the church. In the thirteenth century, Guillaume de Paris, in the fifteenth Nicolas Flamel, both are guilty of these seditious pages. Saint Jacques de la Boucherie was a church of opposition throughout.

This was the only freedom of expression at that period; it could inscribe itself within those books which we call edifices, freedom of thought would have been burned in the public place by the hand of the executioner in the form of manuscript, had it been so imprudent as to choose that form of expression; thoughts engraved over the door of a church would have witnessed their own execution when printed upon the pages of a book. Thus having alone in masonry a channel of expression, it left no opportunity neglected. Hence the immense number of cathedrals which covered Europe – a number so prodigious as to seem almost incredible, even after it had been verified. All the material forces, all the intellectual forces, converged towards the same point, architecture. In this manner, under the pretext of building churches to God, art developed in magnificent proportions.

Then, whosoever was born poet became architect. Genius, scattered through the masses, compressed on all sides by feudalism, as under a *testudo*, of brazen bucklers, found its only issue through the medium of architecture, burst forth through this art, and its Iliad took the form of cathedrals. All other arts obeyed and placed themselves under the discipline of architecture. They were the workmen of the great work. The architect, the poet, the master, embodied in its person the sculpture, which chiselled its facades, the painting which illumined its windows, the music which set its bells in motion and breathed into its organs. As for poetry, properly so called, there was none that obstinately refused to vegetate in manuscript form, but was compelled, in order to be of value, to find its place in the church as a 'hymn' or a 'prose;' the same role, after all, which the tragedies of Æschylus had played in the sacerdotal festivals of Greece, Genesis in the temple of Solomon.

Thus, down to the days of Guttenberg, architecture is the principal, the universal writing. This book of granite, begun by the Orient, was continued by Greek and Roman antiquity; the Middle Ages wrote the last page. Moreover, this phenomenon of an architecture of the people succeeding an architecture of caste, which we have just observed in the Middle Ages, repeats itself with every analogous movement in the human intelligence in the other great epochs of history. Thus, in order to enunciate here only summarily a law which it would require volumes to develop: in the upper Orient, the cradle of the primitive races, after the Hindu architecture came the Phœnician, that opulent mother of the Arabic style: in antiquity, after the Egyptian architecture, of which the Etruscan form and the Cyclopean monuments are but one variety, came the Greek architecture, of which the Roman style is only a prolongation, surcharged with the Carthaginian dome: in modern times after the Roman architecture, the Gothic. And by separating these three series we find again in these three elder sisters, Hindu architecture, Egyptian architecture, Roman architecture, the same symbol; that is to say, theocracy, caste unity, dogmatism, the myth, God: and for the three younger sisters, Phœnician architecture, the Greek and the Gothic and whatever may be the diversity of form inherent in their nature, the same signification in each, that is to say, liberty, the people, man.

In all the masonry of the Hindu, Egyptian or Roman, one feels always the priest, nothing but the priest, whether he be called Brahmin, Magian or Pope. It is not the same in the architectures of the people. They are more rich and less devotional. In Phœnician one recognizes the merchant; in the Greek, the republican; in the Gothic, the citizen. The general characteristics of all theocratic architecture are immutability, horror of progress, the conservation of traditional lines, of primitive types, a constant bending of all the forms of nature and mankind to the incomprehensible caprices of symbolism. They are books of darkness which only the initiated can decipher. Furthermore, every form and even every deformity has here a sense which renders it inevitable. Do not ask the Hindu, Egyptian or Roman structures to change their design or improve their statues. Any attempt at perfecting would be impious. In these architectures it would appear that the severity of the dogma seems to overlie the stone like a second petrifaction. On the contrary, the general characteristics of the masonries of the people are truth, progress, originality, opulence, perpetual movement. They are sufficiently removed from their religion to give thought to beauty and to cherish it; to correct and improve continually their ornamentation of statues and arabesques. They are of the century. They have a human sentiment mingled with the divine symbolism under whose inspiration they are still produced. Hence these edifices, open to every soul, to every intelligence, to every imagination: symbolical still, but easy of comprehension as the face of nature. Between theocratic architecture and this one there is the difference that exists between a sacred language and a vulgar one, between hieroglyphs and art, between Solomon and Phidias. If the reader will review what we have hitherto briefly, very briefly, indicated, omitting countless proofs and also a thousand objections, we are led to this conclusion: that architecture up to the fifteenth century was the principal register of humanity; that during this period, not a single thought of a complicated nature appeared in the world but was transformed into masonry; that all popular ideas as well as all religious law had its monuments; and finally, that mankind possessed no important thought which has not been written in stone. And why? It is because every thought, be it religious, be it philosophical, seeks to perpetuate itself; it is that the ideas which have moved one generation desire to move other generations likewise, and to leave their trace. Indeed, what immortality is more precarious than that of a manuscript? How much more durable, solid and lasting is a book of stone! To destroy the written word, the torch and the Turk have proved sufficient. To demolish the builded word, a social revolution, a terrestrial revolution is necessary. The barbarians have passed over the Coliseum; the deluge, perhaps, over the Pyramids.

In the fifteenth century all changes.

Human thought discovers a medicine by which to perpetuate itself, not alone more durable and more resisting than architecture, but still more simple and easier. Architecture is dethroned. To the letters of stone of Orpheus are about to succeed the letters of lead of Gutenberg.

'Alas! Alas! small things overcome great ones; the Nile rat kills the crocodile, the swordfish kills the whale, the book will kill the edifice.'

The invention of printing is the greatest event in history. It is the mother of revolution. It is a total renewal of the means of human expression: it is human thought which divests itself of one form and takes on another; it is the complete and definite changing of the skin of that symbolical serpent which since Adam has represented Intelligence.

In its printed form thought is more imperishable than ever; it is more volatile, more intangible, more indestructible. It is mingled with the very air. In the time of architecture it made itself a mountain and took powerful possession of a century, of a place. Now, thought is transformed into a flock of birds which scatter themselves to the four winds and occupy at once every point of air and space.

We repeat it, who does not perceive that in this manner it is far more indelible? From a state of solidity it has become animated. It passes from duration to immortality. A mass can be demolished; how extirpate ubiquity? A deluge comes; the mountain would have disappeared beneath its waves long before the birds ceased to fly above it, and if a single ark should float upon the surface of the cataclysm, they will alight thereon, will float with it, watch with it the going down of the waters, and the new world that shall emerge from this chaos will see soaring above it the thought of the submerged world, winged and alive.

And when one observes that this mode of expression is not only the most conservative, but also the most simple, the most convenient, the most practicable of all, when one considers that it does not drag after it a bulky baggage, and requires no cumbersome apparatus; when we compare the thought requiring for its interpretation in a building, to put in motion four or five other arts and tons of gold, a mountain of stone and a forest of timber as well as a whole population of workmen; when one compares to it the thought becoming a book, needing only a little paper, a little ink and a pen, why be surprised that human intelligence should have quitted architecture for printing? Cut abruptly the original bed of a river by a canal dug below its level, the stream will forsake its channel.

Behold how, beginning with the discovery of printing, architecture gradually declines, withers and becomes denuded. How one feels the water sinking, the sap departing, that the thought of the time and the people is departing from it. The indifference is almost imperceptible in the fifteenth century; the press is yet too weak and can only draw off somewhat of the superabundant life of mighty architecture. But beginning with the sixteenth century the malady of architecture becomes visible: it no longer is the essential expression of society; it transforms itself into a miserable classic art; from being Gallic, European, indigenous, it becomes Greek and Roman, from the true and the modern, it becomes pseudo-antique. It is this decadence which is called Renaissance. Magnificent decadence, however; for the ancient Gothic genius, whose sunsets behind the gigantic press of Mayence, for some time longer penetrates with its last rays that range of hybrid Latin arcade and Corinthian columns.

It is the setting sun which we mistake for an aurora.

However, from the moment when architecture is an art like any other, when it is no longer art in totality, the sovereign, the tyrant, architecture has no longer the force to retain the other arts. They emancipate themselves, break the yoke of the architect, and go each its own way. Each of them gains by this divorce. Isolation enlarges all. Sculpture becomes statuary. Imagery becomes painting. The pipe becomes music. One might compare it to a dismembered empire at the death of its Alexander, whose provinces become kingdoms.

Hence Raphael, Michel Angelo, Jean Goujon, Palestrina, those splendours of the dazzling sixteenth century. At the same time as the arts, thought emancipates itself in all directions. The heresiarchs of the Middle Ages had already made large breaches into Catholicism. The sixteenth century shatters religious unity. Before printing reform had been merely a schism, printing converted it into a revolution. I take away the press; heresy becomes unnerved. Be it fatality or the work of Providence, Gutenberg is the precursor of Luther.

Be this as it may, when the sun of the Middle Ages is completely set, when the genius of the Gothic is forever extinct upon the horizon, architecture gradually becomes dim, loses its colour and little by little fades away. The printed book, the gnawing worm of the edifice, sucks and devours it. Architecture decays, crumbles and becomes emaciated before the eye. It is poor, it is cheap, it is null. It expresses nought, not even the souvenir of the art of the past. Reduced to itself, abandoned by the other arts because it is abandoned by human thought, it summons journeymen instead of artists. Window-glass replaces the coloured panes. The stonecutter succeeds to the place of the sculptor. Farewell all sap, all originality, all intelligence. It debases itself like a lamentable workshop mendicant from copy to copy. Michel Angelo, who, no doubt, even at the beginning of the sixteenth century had felt that it was dying, had a last idea, an idea of despair. That Titan of art piled the Pantheon upon the Parthenon, and made Saint Peter's at Rome. Great work which is deservedly unique, the last originality of architecture, signature of a giant artist at the bottom of the colossal register of stone which was closing forever. Michel Angelo dead, what becomes of that miserable architecture which outlives itself in a shadowy, ghostly state? It takes Saint Peter's at Rome, copies it, parodies it. It is a mania. It is pitiable. Each century has its Saint Peter's of Rome. In the seventeenth the Val de Grace; in the eighteenth Sainte Geneviève. Each country has its Saint Peter's of Rome. London, St. Petersburg, Paris has two or three. Trifling inheritance, last dotage of a great art which becomes decrepit and falls into infancy before it dies.

If, instead of the characteristic monuments we have just described, we examine the general aspect of the art of the sixteenth and seventeenth centuries, we shall see the same phenomena of decay and phthisis. From the time of Francis II the architectural form diminishes more and more in the construction, leaving visible the geometrical character, like the bony framework of the emaciated invalid. The fine lines of art make way for the cold inexorable forms of geometry. An edifice is no longer an edifice, it is a polyhedron. Architecture, however, still struggles to conceal this nudity. Look at the Greek pediment inscribed within the Roman, and vice versa. It is always the Pantheon within the Parthenon, Saint Peter's of Rome. Here are the brick houses with stone corners dating from Henry IV in the Place Royal, in the Place Dauphine. Here are the churches of Louis III, heavy, squat thick-set, crowded, loaded with a dome as with a hump. We have the Mazarin architecture, the bad pasticcio Italian of the Quatre-Nations. Witness the palaces of Louis XIV, long barracks for courtiers, stiff, cold, tiresome. Finally we come to the style of Louis XV, with its chiccory and vermicelli ornament, the warts and fungi which disfigure that decrepit, toothless, coquettish old architecture. From Francis II to Louis XV the evil has increased in geometrical progression. Art has nothing but skin and bones left. It perishes miserably.

Meanwhile, what becomes of printing? All the life which abandons architecture is absorbed by it. In proportion as architecture dies, printing swells and grows in power. The capital of energy which human thought once expended upon buildings is expended henceforth upon books. Indeed, from the sixteenth century the press, lifted to the level of diminished architecture contends with it and conquers it. In the seventeenth century the press has gained such an ascendancy, such a triumph, such a victory over its rival as to give to the world the feast of a great literary age. In the eighteenth, having reposed for a long time at the court of Louis XIV, it again seizes the old sword of Luther places it in the hands of Voltaire and rushes forth tumultuously to the attack of ancient Europe, whose architectural expression it has already destroyed. At the close of the eighteenth century, it has destroyed everything. In the nineteenth it begins to reconstruct.

Now, we ask, which of the two arts has really represented human thought during the past three centuries? which translated it? not expressing alone its literary and artistic vagaries, but its vast, profound, universal movement? Which superposes itself, constantly, without rupture or gap, upon the human race, ever progressing like a monster with a thousand feet? Architecture or printing? It is printing. Let one here make no mistake; architecture is dead, irrevocably dead, killed by the printed book, killed because less lasting, killed because of greater cost. Each cathedral represents millions. Let the reader now imagine the capital necessary to rewrite the architectural book, to raise again the myriad edifices; to return once more to the time when the throng of monuments was such, in the words of an eye-witness, 'that one would have said that the world had shaken off its old habiliments in order to clothe itself in a white garment of churches.' *Erat enim atsi mundus, ipse excutiendo semet, rejecta vetustate, candidam ecclesiarum vestem indueret.* (For it was as if the world shaking itself had cast aside its old garments to clothe itself with a shining white vestment of churches) – *Glaber Radulphus.*

A book is soon made, costs but little and can go so far! Why should there be surprise that all human thought glides through this channel? This does not imply that architecture shall not yet here and there produce a fine monument, an isolated masterpiece. It is yet possible, from time to time, even under the reign of printing, I suppose, for an army to make a column of melted cannon, as we had during the reign of architecture. Iliads and Romanceros, Mahâbhâratas and Nibelungenlieds, made by a whole people out of combined and collected rhapsodies. The great accident of an architect of genius may occur in the twentieth century as that of Dante in the thirteenth. But architecture will not again be the social art, the collective, the dominant art. The great poem, the great edifice, the great work of humanity will no longer be constructed: it will be printed.

And if, henceforth, architecture should again rise by accident, it will never be mistress. It will be subservient to the law of literature, formerly subject to it. The respective positions of the two arts will be reversed. It is certain that during the domination of architecture such rare poems as appeared, resembled the monuments. In India, Vyasa is as complex, strange and impenetrable as a pagoda. In Egypt poetry has, like its buildings, both vastness and repose of line; in ancient Greece beauty, serenity and calm; in Christian Europe, the majesty of the Catholic faith, the simplicity of popular taste; the rich and luxuriant vegetation of an epoch of renewal. The Bible resembles the Pyramids, the Iliad the Parthenon, Homer, Phidias. Dante in the thirteenth century is the last Roman church; Shakespeare in the sixteenth, the last Gothic cathedral.

Thus, to sum up what we have thus far stated in a manner necessarily incomplete and mutilated, humanity has two books, two registers, two testaments; masonry and printing, the Word in stone and the Word in paper. Without doubt when one contemplates these two testaments, laying so broadly before us the history of the centuries, it is permissible to regret the visible majesty of that granite record, those gigantic alphabets of colonnades, of pylons, of obelisks, this species of human mountains which cover the world and the past, from the Pyramid to the steeple, from Cheops to Strasburg. The past as recorded upon these marble pages should be read again and again. This great book of architecture should have our incessant perusal and admiration; but we must not refuse to acknowledge the grandeur of the edifice which has in turn been raised by printing.

This edifice is colossal. I do not know what statistician has made the calculation that, were all the volumes which have issued from the press since Gutenberg's day piled one upon another, they would fill the space from the earth to the moon; but this is not the sort of greatness of which we desire to speak. However, when one tries to collect a comprehensive image in one's mind, of the total product of printing down to our days, does this image not take the form of an immense construction based upon the entire world and upon which humanity labours without ceasing and whose monstrous crest is lost in the mists of the future? It is the anthill of human intelligence. It is the hive where all the creations of imagination, those golden bees, arrive with their honey. The edifice has a thousand stories. Here and there upon its landings we see the openings to the gloomy caverns of science which cross each other in the profound depths. Everywhere upon its surface the eye is gratified by an artistic luxury of arabesques, rose-windows and delicate lace carving. There each individual work, however capricious and isolated it may seem, has its place and its importance. Harmony results from the whole. From the cathedral of Shakespeare to the mosque of Byron, a thousand belfries crowd each other pell-mell above this metropolis of universal thought. At its base have been written again some ancient titles of humanity which architecture had failed to preserve. At the left of the entrance, fixed in the wall, is the antique bas-relief in white marble of Homer; at the right the Bible of all languages rears its seven heads. The hydra of the Romancero, with the Vedas and Nibelungen, mingled with other hybrid forms, can be descried farther on. But the immense building is never completed. The printing-press, that giant machine which pumps unceasingly all the intellectual sap of society, perpetually vomits forth fresh materials for its work.

The whole human race is upon the scaffolding. Every mind is a mason. The most humble may stop a hole or place a stone. Rétif de la Bretonne brings his hod of plaster. Each day a new course rises. Independently of the original and individual product of each writer, there are collective contingents. The eighteenth century gives the *Encyclopædia*, the revolution gives the *Moniteur*. Assuredly, it is a construction which grows and piles up in spirals without end; there also are confusion of tongues, unceasing activity, indefatigable labour, the heated rivalry of all humanity; a refuge promised to intelligence from another Deluge, against an overflow of barbarians. It is the second tower of Babel of the human race.

BOOK SIX

I

An Impartial Glance at the Ancient Magistracy

A RIGHT ENVIABLE PERSONAGE, in the year of grace 1482, was the noble gentleman Robert d'Estouteville, knight, Sieur of Peyne, Baron of Ivry and Saint Andry in Marche, councillor and chamberlain to the king and keeper of the provostry of Paris. Already it was nearly seventeen years since he had received from the king, on the 7th of November, 1465, the year of the comet *, that fine place of Provost of Paris, which was considered rather as a dignity than an office – *Dignitas*, says Joannes Lœmntœus, *quæ cum non exigua potestate politiam concernente, atque prærogativis multis et juribus conjuncta est* (a dignity, to which is joined no small influence in affairs of state and many prerogatives and rights). It was an extraordinary thing in 1482 for a gentleman to hold a commission from the king whose letters of institution dated as far back as the time of the marriage of the natural daughter of Louis XI with monsieur the bastard of Bourbon. On the same day that Robert d'Estouteville had taken the place of Jacques de Villiers in the provostry of Paris, Maître Jean Dauvet succeeded Messire Hélye de Thorrettes in the first presidency of the court of parliament, Jean Jouvénel des Ursins supplanted Pierre de Morvilliers in the office of Chancellor of France, and Regnault des Dormans relieved Pierre Puy of the post of master of requests in ordinary to the king's household. Over how many heads had the presidency, the chancellorship and the mastership travelled since Robert d'Estouteville had held the provostry of Paris! It had been 'granted into his keeping,' said the letters-patent; and well had he kept it forsooth. So closely had he clung to it, so completely had he incorporated himself, identified himself with it, that he had escaped that mania for change which possessed Louis XI, a suspicious, tormenting and toiling sovereign, bent upon maintaining, by frequent appointments and dismissals, the elasticity of his power. Nay, more – the worthy knight had procured the reversion of his office for his son, and for two years past the name of the noble gentleman Jacques d'Estouteville, Esquire, figured beside his own at the head of the register of the ordinary of the provostry of Paris. Rare, indeed, and

* This comet against which Pope Calixtus, uncle of Borgia, ordered public prayers, is the same which reappeared in 1835.

signal favour! True it is that Robert d'Estouteville was a good soldier; that he had loyally raised the banner against 'the league of the public weal;' and that he had presented the queen, on the day of her entry into Paris in the year 14—, a most wonderful stag, all made of sweetmeats. He had, moreover, a good friend in Messire Tristan l'Hermite, provost-marshal of the king's household. Thus Messire Robert enjoyed a very smooth and pleasant existence. First of all, he had a very good salary; to which were attached and from which hung extra bunches of grapes from his vine, the revenues of the registries, civil and criminal, of the provostry; plus the revenues, civil and criminal, of the Auditoires d'Embas, or inferior courts, of the Châtelet; to say nothing of some little toll at the bridge of Mante and Corbeil, the tax on all the onions, leeks and garlic brought into Paris, and on the corders of firewood and the measurers of salt. Add to all this the pleasure of displaying, in his official rides through the town, in contrast with the gowns, half red and half tawny, of the sheriffs and police, his fine military dress, which you may still admire sculptured upon his tomb at the abbey of Valmont in Normandy, and his richly embossed morion at Montlhéry. Besides, was it nothing to have entire supremacy over the sergeants of the police, the porter and the watch of the Châtelet – *auditores Castelleti* (auditors of the Châtelet) – the sixteen commissaries of the sixteen quarters, the jailor of the Châtelet, the four enfeoffed sergeants, the hundred and twenty mounted sergeants, the hundred and twenty sergeants of the wand, and the knight of the watch, with his watch, the under-watch, the counter-watch and the rear-watch? Was it nothing to exercise high and low justice, to exercise the right of interrogating, hanging and drawing, besides the jurisdiction over minor offences in the first resort – *in prima instantia* (in the first instance), as the charters have it – over that viscounty of Paris, to which were so gloriously appended seven noble bailiwicks? Can anything more gratifying be conceived than to issue orders and pass judgment, as Messire Robert d'Estouteville daily did in the Grand Châtelet, beneath the wide elliptic arches of Philip Augustus; and to go, as was his wont, every evening to that charming house situate in the Rue Galilee, in the purlieus of the Palais Royal, which he held in right of his wife, Madame Ambroise de Loré, to rest from the fatigue of having sent some poor devil to pass the night in 'that little lodge in the Rue de l'Escorcherie, which the provosts and échevins of Paris were wont to make their prison; the same being (according to the accounts of the estate, 1383) eleven feet in length, seven feet four inches in width and eleven feet in height?'

And not only had Messire Robert d'Estouteville his particular court as provost and viscount of Paris, but also he had a share, both by presence and action, in the grand justice of the king. There was not a head of any distinction but passed through his hands before it fell into those of the executioner. It was he who had gone to the Bastille Saint Antoine to fetch Monsieur de Nemours from thence to the Halles; and to conduct to the Grève Monsieur de Saint Pol, who clamoured and resisted, to the great joy of monsieur the provost, who did not love monsieur the constable.

Here, assuredly, was more than enough to make a life happy and illustrious, and to deserve some day a notable page in that interesting history of the provosts of Paris, where we learn that Oudard de Villeneuve had a house in the Rue des Boucheries; that Guillaume de Hangest bought the great and the little Savoie, that Guillaume Thiboust gave his houses in the Rue Clopin to the nuns of Sainte Geneviève; that Hugues Aubriot lived in the Hôtel du Porc Epic; and other domestic incidents.

And yet, with all these reasons for taking life patiently and cheerfully, Messire Robert d'Estouteville had waked on the morning of the 7th of January, 1482, in a very surly and peevish mood. Whence came this ill-temper? He could not have told himself. Was it because the sky was gray? or because the buckle of his old Montillery sword-belt was badly fastened, and girded too militarily his provostal portliness? or had he beheld ribald fellows marching through the street, four by four, under his window, jeering at him as they passed by, in doublets without shirts, hats without crowns, and wallet and bottle at their side? Was it a vague presentiment of the three hundred and seventy livres sixteen sols eight deniers which the future king, Charles VIII, was to deduct the following year from the revenues of the provostry? The reader can take his choice; we, for our part, are much inclined to believe that he was in an ill-humour simply because he was in an ill-humour.

Moreover, it was the day after a holiday – a tiresome day for everyone, and above all for the magistrate whose business it was to sweep away all the filth, whether literally or figuratively, that a holiday accumulated in Paris. And then he was to hold a sitting in the Grand Châtelet. Now we have noticed, that judges in general contrive matters so, that their day of sitting shall also be their day of ill-humour, in order that they may always have some one upon whom to vent it conveniently, in the name of the king and the law.

However, the audience had begun without him. His deputies, civil, criminal and private, were acting for him, according to custom; and since the hour of eight in the morning, some scores of citizens, men and women, crowded and crammed into a dark corner of the lower court-room of the Châtelet, between the wall and a strong barrier of oak, were blissfully looking on at the varied and exhilarating spectacle of the administration of civil and criminal justice by Maître Florian Barbedienne, auditor at the Châtelet, deputy of monsieur the provost, in a somewhat confused and utterly haphazard manner.

The room was small, low and vaulted. A table, studded with fleurs-de-lis, stood at one end, with a large arm-chair of carved oak for the provost, which was empty, and, on the left hand of it a stool for the auditor, Maître Florian. Below sat the registrar, scribbling. Opposite were the populace; and in front of the door, and in front of the table, were a number of sergeants of the provostry in their sleeveless jackets of violet camlet with white crosses. Two sergeants of the Parloir aux Bourgeois, or Common-hall, in jackets of Toussaint half red and half blue, stood sentry before a low closed door, which was visible at the other end, behind the table. A single arched window, deep set in the massive wall, cast a ray of pale January sun upon two grotesque figures: the fantastic demon carved 'upon the keystone of the vaulted ceiling, and the judge, seated at the extremity of the chamber, upon the fleurs-de-lis.

Picture to yourself, in fact, at the provostal table, between two bundles of papers – leaning on his elbows, with his foot on the train of his gown of plain brown cloth, and his face in its framing of white lamb's wool, from which his eyebrows seemed to stand out – red – harsh-looking – winking, bearing majestically the load of his fat cheeks, which met under his chin – Maître Florian Barbedienne, auditor at the Châtelet.

Now, the auditor was deaf. A slight defect for an auditor. Maître Florian delivered judgment, none the less, without appeal and quite competently. It is certainly quite sufficient that a judge should appear to listen; and the venerable auditor the better fulfilled this condition, the only one essential to strict justice, as his attention could not possibly be distracted by any noise.

Moreover, there was among the audience a merciless censor of his deeds and gestures, in the person of our friend Jehan Frollo du Moulin, the little student of the previous day – that 'stroller' who was sure to be met with everywhere in Paris, except before the professor's chair.

'Look you.' said he in a low tone to his companion Robin Poussepain, who was tittering beside him, while he commented on the scenes that were passing before them; 'yonder is Jehanneton du Buisson. The beautiful daughter of the lazy dog at the Marche Neuf! – On my soul, he condemns her too, the old brute! He must have no more eyes than ears! Fifteen sous four deniers parisis for having worn two rosaries – 'tis rather dear. *Lex duri carminis* (harsh law of invocation) – Who's that? – Robin Chief de Ville, hauberk-maker. For having been passed and admitted a master of the said trade. That is his entrance-money. So, ho! two gentlemen among these rascals – Aiglet de Soins, Hutin de Mailly. Two esquires! – *Corpus Christi!* – Ha! they've been dicing. When shall we see our rector here? A hundred livres parisis (fine) to the king! Barbedienne hits like a deaf man – as he is! – May I be my brother the archdeacon, if that shall hinder me from gaming; gaming by day, gaming by night, gaming while I live, gaming till I die, and staking my soul after my shirt! Holy Virgin! what a lot of girls! – one after another, my lambs! Ambroise Lécuyère! Isabeau la Paynette! Bérarde Gironin! I know them all, by my fay! Fine 'em! fine 'em! That will teach you to wear gilt belts! Ten sols parisis, you coquettes! – Oh, the old snout of a judge! deaf and imbecile! Oh, Florian the blockhead! Oh, Barbedienne the dolt! There he is at the table – he dines off the pleader – he dines off the case – he eats – he chews – he crams – he fills himself! Fines – estrays – dues – expenses – costs – wages damages – and interest – torture – prison and jail and stocks with expenses – are to him Christmas spice-cake and marchpanes of Saint John. Look at him, the hog! Now then! Good! – another amorous wench! Thibaude la Thibaude, neither more nor less! – For going out of the Rue Glatigny! – What's this youth? Gieffroy Mabonne, gendarme bearing the cross-bow – he's been cursing the name of the Father. A fine for La Thibaude! a fine for Gieffroy! a fine for them both! The deaf old fool! he must have mixed up the two cases! Ten to one but he makes the girl pay for the oath, and the gendarme for the amour! Attention, Robin Poussepain! What are they bringing in now? Here are plenty of sergeants, by Jupiter! all the hounds of the pack. This must be the grand piece of game of all – a wild boar, at least! 'Tis one, Robin – 'tis one! and a fine one, too! – Hercle! 'tis our prince of yesterday – our fools' pope – our ringer – our one-eyed – our hunchback – our grin of grins! 'Tis Quasimodo!'

It was he indeed.

It was Quasimodo, bound, girded, roped, pinioned and well guarded. The detachment of sergeants that surrounded him were accompanied by the knight of the watch, in person, bearing the arms of France embroidered on his breast, and those of the Town on his back. There was nothing, however, about Quasimodo, excepting his deformity, to justify all this display of halberts and arquebusses. He was gloomy, silent and tranquil; only now and then did his single eye cast a sly and wrathful glance upon the bonds which confined him.

He cast the same glance about him; but it was so dull and sleepy that the women only pointed him out with their fingers in derision.

Meanwhile, Maître Florian, the auditor, turned over attentively the document in the complaint entered against Quasimodo, which the clerk handed him, and having glanced at it, appeared to reflect for a moment. Thanks to this precaution, which he was always careful to take at the moment of proceeding to an interrogatory, he knew beforehand the name, titles and misdeeds of the accused, made premeditated replies to answers foreseen; and so contrived to extricate himself from all the sinuosities of the interrogatory without too much exposing his deafness. The written charge was to him as the dog to the blind man. If it so happened that his infirmity betrayed itself here and there, by some incoherent apostrophe or unintelligible question, it passed with some for profundity, with others for imbecility. In either case the honour of the magistracy did not suffer; for it is better that a judge should be reputed imbecile or profound than deaf. So he took great care to disguise his deafness from the observation of all; and he commonly succeeded so well that he had come at last even to deceive himself. This, indeed, is easier than one would imagine. Every hunchback walks with head erect; every stammerer harangues; every deaf person speaks low. As for him, he believed, at the most, that his ear was a little refractory. It was the sole concession in this respect that he made to public opinion, in his moments of frankness and self-examination.

Having, then, well ruminated on the affair of Quasimodo, he threw back his head and half closed his eyes, by way of greater majesty and impartiality; so that, at that moment, he was blind as well as deaf – a double condition, without which no judge is perfect. It was in this magisterial attitude that he commenced the interrogatory:

'Your name?'

Now here was a case which had not been 'foreseen by the law,' that of one deaf man interrogated by another.

Quasimodo, receiving no intimation of the question thus addressed to him, continued to look fixedly at the judge, and made no reply. The deaf judge, receiving no intimation of the deafness of the accused, thought that he had answered, as accused persons generally did; and continued, with his mechanical and stupid self confidence:

'Very well – your age?'

Again Quasimodo made no answer to this question. The judge thinking it replied to, went on:

'Now – your calling?'

Still the same silence. The bystanders, however, were beginning to whisper and to exchange glances.

'Enough!' added the imperturbable auditor, when he supposed that the accused had finished his third reply. 'You are accused before us – firstly, with nocturnal disturbance; secondly, with dishonest violence upon the person of a foolish woman – *in prejudicium meretricis* (as an example of a prostitute); thirdly, of rebellion and disloyalty toward the archers of the guard of our lord the king. Explain yourself on all these points. Clerk, have you taken down what the prisoner has said thus far?'

At this unlucky question a burst of laughter rose from both clerk and audience – so violent, so uncontrollable, so contagious, so universal, that neither of the deaf men could help perceiving it. Quasimodo turned round, shrugging his hump with disdain; while Maître Florian, equally astonished, and supposing that the laughter of the spectators had been excited by some irreverent reply from the accused, rendered visible to him by that shrug, apostrophized him indignantly.

'For that answer, fellow, you deserve the halter. Know you to whom you speak?'

This sally was not likely to check the explosion of the general mirth. It seemed to all present so incongruous and whimsical, that the wild laughter spread to the very sergeants of the Parloir aux Bourgeois, a sort of pikemen, whose stupidity was part of their uniform. Quasimodo alone preserved his gravity; for the very good reason that he understood nothing of what was going on around him. The judge, more and more irritated, felt obliged to proceed in the same strain, hoping thereby to strike the accused with a terror that would react upon the bystanders, and bring them back to a proper sense of respect:

'So, this is as much as to say, perverse and thieving knave that you are, that you presume to be lacking in respect to the auditor of the Châtelet; to the magistrate in charge of the chief police courts of Paris; appointed to inquire into all crimes, offences and misdemeanours, to control all trades and prevent monopoly; to repair the pavements; to put down hucksters of poultry, fowl and wild game; to superintend the measuring of firewood and other sorts of wood; to cleanse the town of mud and the air of contagious distempers; in a word, with attending continually to public affairs, without wages, or hope of salary. Know you that I am called Florian Barbedienne, monsieur the provost's own proper deputy, and, moreover, commissary, inquisitor, comptroller and examiner, with equal power in provostry, bailiwick, conservator. ship and presidial court?'

There is no reason why a deaf man talking to a deaf man should ever stop. Heaven knows where and when Maître Florian would have landed, thus launched at full speed in lofty eloquence, if the low door behind him had not suddenly opened and given entrance to monsieur the provost in person.

Maître Florian did not stop short at his entrance, but, turning half round upon his heel, and abruptly directing to the provost the harangue with which, a moment before, he was overwhelming Quasimodo:

'Monsieur,' said he, 'I demand such penalty as it shall please you upon the accused here present, for flagrant and aggravated contempt of court.'

And he seated himself; utterly breathless, wiping away the great drops of sweat that fell from his brow and moistened, like tears the parchments spread out before him. Messire Robert d'Estouteville frowned, and made a gesture to Quasimodo to attend, in a manner so imperious and significant that the deaf one in some degree understood it.

The provost addressed him sternly: 'What hast thou done to be brought hither, varlet?'

The poor devil, supposing that the provost was asking his name, broke the silence which he habitually kept, and in a harsh and guttural voice, replied: – 'Quasimodo.'

The answer matched the question so little that the loud laugh began to circulate once more; and Messire Robert cried out, red with wrath: 'Dost mock me too, thou arrant knave?'

'Bell-ringer of Notre-Dame,' answered Quasimodo, thinking himself called upon to explain to the judge who he was.

'Bell-ringer!' returned the provost, who, as we have already said, had got up that morning in so bad a humour that his fury needed not to be kindled by such unaccountable answers – 'Bell-ringer, indeed! I'll make them ring a peal of rods on thy back through every street in Paris – dost thou hear, rascal?'

'If you want to know my age,' said Quasimodo, 'I believe I shall be twenty next Martinmas.'

This was too much The provost could endure it no longer.

'Ha! so you jeer at the provostry, you wretch! Messieurs the sergeants of the wand, you will take me this knave to the pillory in the Grève, and there flog him and turn him for an hour. He shall pay for his impudence, 'Sdeath! And I order that this present sentence be proclaimed by four sworn trumpeters, in the seven castellanies of the viscounty of Paris.'

The clerk instantly fell to work to record the sentence.

'Zounds! but that's a good sentence,' cried the little schoolboy, Jehan Frollo du Moulin, from his corner.

The provost turned and fixed his flashing eyes once more on Quasimodo. 'I believe the fellow said Zounds! Clerks, add a fine of twelve deniers parisis for swearing; and let one-half of it go to the vestry of Saint Eustache – I have a particular devotion for Saint Eustache.'

In a few minutes the sentence was drawn up. The tenor of it was simple and brief. The common law of the provostry and viscounty of Paris had not yet been elaborated by the president, Thibaut Baillet, and Roger Barmue, king's advocate; it was not yet obscured by that lofty hedge of quibbles and procedure which the two jurisconsults planted in it at the beginning of the sixteenth century. All was clear, expeditive, explicit; one went straight to the point – and at the end of every path was immediately visible, without thickets and without turnings, the wheel, the gibbet, or the pillory. One at least knew whither one was going.

The registrar presented the sentence to the provost, who affixed his seal to it, and departed, to pursue his round at the several auditories, in a frame of mind which seemed destined to fill every jail in Paris that day. Jehan Frollo and Robin Poussepain were laughing in their sleeves; Quasimodo gazed on the whole with an indifferent and astonished air.

However, at the moment when Maître Florian Barbedienne was in his turn reading over the judgment before signing it, the registrar felt himself moved with pity for the poor condemned wretch; and, in the hope of obtaining some mitigation of the penalty, he approached the auditor's ear as close as he could, and said, pointing to Quasimodo: 'That man is deaf.'

He hoped that a sense of their common infirmity would awaken Maître Florian's interest in behalf of the condemned. But, in the first place, as we have already observed, Maître Florian did not care to have his deafness remarked, in the next place, he was so hard of hearing that he did not catch a single word of what the clerk said to him; nevertheless, he wished to appear to have heard, and replied: 'Ah! ah! that is different – I did not know that. An hour more of the pillory, in that case.'

And he signed the sentence thus modified.

' 'Tis well done!' said Robin Poussepain, who cherished a grudge against Quasimodo, 'that will teach him to handle people roughly.'

II

The Rat Hole

WITH THE READER'S PERMISSION we shall conduct him back to the Place de Grève, which we quitted yesterday with Gringoire, to follow La Esmeralda.

It is the hour of ten in the morning. The appearance of everything indicates the morrow of a festival. The pavement is strewn with rubbish, ribbons, rags, feathers from tufts of plumes, drops of wax from the torches and fragments from the public banquet. A good many of the townspeople loiter about – turning over with their feet the extinct brands of the bonfire – going into raptures before the Maison aux Piliers at the recollection of the fine hangings of the preceding day, and now contemplating the nails that fastened them, the only remnant of the ravishing spectacle. The venders of beer and cider are trundling their barrels among the groups. Some busy passers-by come and go. The shopkeepers chatter and call to one another from their thresholds. The holiday, the ambassadors, Coppenole, the Fools' Pope, are in every one's mouth; each striving to crack the best jokes and laugh the loudest. And yet, four sergeants on horseback, who have just posted themselves at the four sides of the pillory, have already gathered around them a good part of the populace scattered on the Place, which condemns itself to immobility and fatigue in the hope of a small execution.

Now, if the reader will, after surveying this lively and noisy scene which is being enacted in all parts of the square, turn his eyes toward that ancient half-Gothic, half-Roman building, the Tour Roland, which stands at the western corner next the quay, he will observe, at the angle of its façade, a large public breviary richly illuminated, protected from the rain by a small penthouse, and from thieves by a grating, which, however, permits of the leaves being turned. Close by this breviary is a narrow, arched window-hole, guarded by two iron bars placed crosswise, and looking toward the square – the only opening through which a little air and light are admitted into a small cell without a door built on the ground-floor, in the thickness of the wall of the old house – and filled with a stillness the more profound, a silence the more dead, inasmuch as a public square, the most populous and the noisiest in Paris, is swarming and clamouring around it.

This cell had been celebrated in Paris for nearly three centuries, since Madame Rolande, of Roland's Tower, in mourning for her father who died in the Crusades, had caused it to be hollowed out of the wall of her own house, to shut herself up in it forever, keeping of all her palace only this wretched nook, the door of which was walled up, and the window open to the elements, in winter as in summer – giving all the rest to God and to the poor. The disconsolate damsel had, in fact, awaited death for twenty years in this premature tomb, praying day and night for the soul of her father, sleeping in ashes, without even a stone for her pillow, clad in black sackcloth, and living only upon such bread and water as the pity of the passers-by deposited upon the edge of her window-place – thus receiving charity after she had given it. At her death – at the moment of her passing into the other sepulchre – she had bequeathed this one in perpetuity to women in affliction, mothers, widows or maidens, who should have occasion to pray much for others or for themselves, and should choose to bury themselves alive in the greatness of their grief or their penitence. The poor of her day paid her the best of funeral rites in their tears and blessings; but, to their great regret, the pious maiden had not been canonized, for lack of patronage. Such of them as were a little inclined to impiety, had hoped that the thing would be done more easily in heaven than at Rome, and had frankly besought God, instead of the Pope, in behalf of the deceased. Most of them, however, had contented themselves with holding the memory of Rolande sacred and converting her rags into relics. The City, on its side, had founded, in honour of the lady, a public breviary, which was fastened near the window of the cell, in order that the passers-by might halt there from time to time, were it only to pray; that prayer might remind them of alms; and that the poor recluses, inheriting the stony cave of Madame Rolande, might not absolutely die of famine and neglect.

Moreover, this sort of tomb was not so very rare a thing in the cities of the Middle Ages. There might often be found, in the most frequented street, in the most crowded and noisy market-place – in the very midst – under the horses' feet and the wagon-wheels, as it were – a cave – a well – a walled and grated cabin – within which a human being prayed day and night, voluntarily devoted to some everlasting lamentation or some great expiation. And all the reflections which that strange spectacle would awaken in us to-day – that horrible cell, a sort of intermediary link between the house and the tomb, the city and the cemetery – that living being cut off from human community, and thenceforth reckoned among the dead – that lamp consuming its last drop of oil in the darkness – that remnant of life flickering in the grave – that breath, that voice, that everlasting prayer, encased in stone – that face forever turned toward the other world – that eye already illumined by another sun – that ear glued to the wall of the sepulchre – that soul a prisoner in that body – that body a prisoner in that dungeon and under that double envelope of flesh and granite, the murmur of that soul in pain – nothing of all this was noted by the crowd.

The piety of that age, unreasoning and far from subtle, did not see so many sides in an act of religion. It took things in the gross; honouring, venerating and hallowing, at need, the sacrifice; but not analyzing the sufferings, nor feeling any depth of pity for them. It brought some pittance, from time to time, to the miserable penitent; looked through the hole, to see if he were yet living; knew not his name; hardly knew how many years ago he had begun to die; and to the stranger, who questioned them about the living skeleton rotting in that cellar, the neighbours replied simply, 'It is the recluse.'

Everything was then viewed without metaphysics, without exaggeration, without magnifying-glass, with the naked eye. The microscope had not yet been invented, either for material or for spiritual things.

However, the instances of this sort of seclusion in the heart of cities, though they raised but little wonder, were, as we have already observed, in reality frequent. There were in Paris a considerable number of those cells of penitence and prayer; and nearly all of them were occupied. It is true that the clergy did not care to leave them empty, as that implied lukewarmness among the faithful; and that lepers were put into them when penitents were not to be had. Besides the cell on the Grève, there was one at Montfaucon, one at the charnel-house of the Holy Innocents, another we hardly recollect where – at the Clichon House, we believe – and others still at many spots, where traces of them are found in traditions, in default of memorials. The University had also its own. On the Montagne Sainte Geneviève, a sort of Job of the Middle Ages sang for thirty years the seven penitential psalms, upon a dung-heap at the bottom of a cistern, beginning anew when he had come to the end – singing louder in the night time, *magna voce per umbras* (a loud voice through the shadows); and the antiquary still fancies that he hears his voice, as he enters the Rue du Puits-qui-parle, or street of the talking well.

To confine ourselves here to the cell in Roland's Tower – we are bound to declare that it had scarcely ever lacked for recluses. Since Madame Rolande's death, it had rarely been vacant even for a year or two. Many a woman had come thither and mourned until death over the memory of her parent, her lover, or her failings. Parisian malice, which meddles with everything, even with those things which concern it least, affirmed that it had beheld but few widows there.

According to the manner of that period, a Latin inscription on the wall, indicated to the lettered passer-by the pious purpose of this cell. The custom was retained until the middle of the sixteenth century, of placing a brief explanatory motto above the entrance of a building. Thus in France one still reads over the wicket of the prison belonging to the seigniorial mansion of Tourville, *Sileto et spera* (Be silent and hope); in Ireland, under the escutcheon placed above the great gateway of Fortescue Castle, *Forte scutum, salus ducum* (Strong shield, the safety of lords); and in England, over the principal entrance of the hospitable mansion of the Earls Cowper, *Tuum est* (It is thine). In those days every edifice embodied a thought.

As there was no door to the walled-up cell of the Tour Roland, there had been carved, in large Roman capitals, over the window, these two words:

TU, ORA*

Hence the people, whose common-sense sees not so many subtleties in things, but readily translates *Ludovico Magno* into *Porte Saint Denis*, gave to this dark, damp, dismal cavity the name of *Trou aux Rats* (signifying rat-hole) – an explanation possibly less sublime than the other, but more picturesque.

* Pray, thou

III

The Story of a Wheaten Cake

AT THE TIME OF WHICH this story treats the cell in the Tour Roland was occupied. If the reader wishes to know by whom, he has but to listen to the conversation of three fair gossips, who, at the moment that we have called his attention to the Rat-Hole, were proceeding toward the same spot, going up the river-side from the Châtelet toward the Grève.

Two of these women were dressed like good bourgeoises of Paris. Their fine white ruffs; their petticoats of linsey-woolsey, with red and blue stripes; their white knitted stockings, with clocks embroidered in colours, pulled well up over the leg; the square-toed shoes, of tawny leather with black soles; and above all, their head-gear, that sort of tinsel horn, loaded with ribbons and lace, still worn by the women of Champagne, in common with the grenadiers of the Russian imperial guard, announced that they belonged to that class of rich tradeswomen which holds the middle-ground between what the lackeys call *a woman* and what they term *a lady*. They wore neither rings nor gold crosses; but it was easy to see that this was not from poverty, but simply from fear of a fine. Their companion was decked out nearly in the same manner; but there was that indescribable something in her dress and bearing which suggested the wife of a country notary. It was evident, from the shortness of her waist, that she had not been long in Paris; add to this a plaited tucker – knots of ribbon upon her shoes – her skirt striped across instead of downward – and various other enormities which shocked good taste.

The first two walked with the step peculiar to Parisian women showing Paris to their country friends. The provincial one held by the hand a big, chubby boy, who held in his a large, flat cake. We regret to be obliged to add that, owing to the rigour of the season, his tongue was performing the office of his pocket-handkerchief:

The boy was being dragged along, *non passibus æquis* (unequal steps), as Virgil says, stumbling every moment, with many exclamations from his mother. It is true that he was looking more at the cake than upon the ground. Some serious reason, no doubt, prevented him from biting it (the cake), for he contented himself with looking at it affectionately. But the mother ought surely to have taken charge of the cake herself; it was cruel thus to make a Tantalus of the chubby-cheeked boy.

Meanwhile the three damoiselles (for the epithet of dame or lady was then reserved for noble women) were all talking at once.

'Let us make haste, Damoiselle Mahiette,' said the youngest, who was also the lustiest of the three, to her country friend. 'I am much afraid we shall be too late; we were told at the Châtelet that they were to put him in the pillory forthwith.'

'Ah, bah! what are you talking about, Damoiselle Oudarde Musnier?' interrupted the other Parisian. 'He will stay two hours on the pillory. We shall have time enough. Have you ever seen any one in the pillory, my dear Mahiette?'

'Yes,' said the provincial; 'at Rheims.'

'Ah, bah! what's that, your pillory at Rheims? A paltry cage, where they turn nothing but peasants. A fine sight, truly!'

'Nothing but peasants?' said Mahiette. 'In the cloth-market! at Rheims! We've seen some very fine criminals there – people who had killed both father and mother! Peasants, indeed! What do you take us for, Gervaise?'

It is certain that the country dame was on the point of taking offence for the honour of her pillory. Luckily, the discreet Damoiselle Oudarde Musnier gave a seasonable turn to the conversation.

'By-the-by, Damoiselle Mahiette, what say you to our Flemish ambassadors? Have you any so fine at Rheims?'

'I confess,' replied Mahiette, 'that it's only at Paris one can see Flemings such as they.'

'Did you see, among the embassy, that great ambassador who is a hosier?' asked Oudarde.

'Yes,' said Mahiette; 'he looks like a very Saturn.'

'And that fat one, with a face like a round paunch? And that little fellow with small eyes and red lids, as ragged and hairy as a head of thistle?'

'Their horses are the finest sight,' said Oudarde; 'dressed out as they are in the fashion of their country.'

'Ah! my dear,' interrupted the rustic Mahiette, assuming in her turn an air of superiority, 'what would you say, then, if you had seen, in '61, at the coronation at Rheims, eighteen years ago, the horses of the princes and of the king's retinue! Housings and trappings of all sorts; some of Damascus cloth, fine cloth of gold, garnished with sables – others of velvet, furred with ermine – others all loaded with goldwork and great gold and silver fringe. And the money that it all cost – and the beautiful boy-pages that were upon them!'

'That does not alter the fact,' dryly responded Damoiselle Oudarde, 'that the Flemings have very fine horses – and that yesterday they had a splendid supper given them by monsieur the provost-merchant, at the Hôtel de Ville; where they served up sweetmeats, hippocrass, spices, and such like singularities.'

'What are you talking about, neighbour?' cried Gervaise – 'it was with the lord cardinal, at the Petit Bourbon, that the Flemings supped.'

'No, no – it was at the Hôtel de Ville.'

'Yes, yes, I tell you – it was at the Petit Bourbon.'

'So surely was it at the Hôtel de Ville,' returned Oudarde sharply, 'that Doctor Scourable made them a speech in Latin, with which they seemed mightily pleased. It was my husband, who is one of the licensed booksellers, who told me so.'

'So surely was it at the Petit Bourbon,' returned Gervaise no less warmly, 'that I'll just tell you what my lord cardinal's attorney made them a present of – twelve double quarts of hippocrass, white, claret and vermilion; four-and-twenty cases of gilt double Lyons marchpane; as many wax-torches of two pounds each; and six half-casks of Beaune wine, white and red, the best that could be found. I hope that's decisive. I have it from my husband, who is captain of fifty men in the Commonalty Hall, and who was making a comparison this morning between the Flemish ambassadors and those of Prester John and the Emperor of Trebizond, who came to Paris from Mesopotamia, in the last king's time, and who had rings in their ears.'

'So true is it that they supped at the Hôtel de Ville,' replied Oudarde, not a whit moved by all this display of eloquence, 'that never was there seen so fine a show of meats and sugar-plums.'

'But I tell you that they were waited on by Le Sec, one of the city guard, at the Hôtel du Petit Bourbon – and 'tis that has misled you.'

'At the Hôtel de Ville, I tell you.'

'At the Petit Bourbon, my dear! – for they illuminated the word *Hope* which is written over the great doorway, with magical glasses.'

'At the Hôtel de Ville! at the Hôtel de Ville! – for Hussen le Voir was playing the flute to them.'

'I tell you, no.'

'I tell you, yes.'

'I tell you, no.'

The good plump Oudarde was making ready to reply; and the quarrel might perhaps have gone on to the pulling of caps, if Mahiette had not suddenly exclaimed, 'See those people, crowding together at the end of the bridge! There's something in the midst of them that they are looking at.'

'Surely I hear the sound of a tambourine,' said Gervaise. 'I think it's little Smeralda, doing her mummeries with her goat. Quick, Mahiette – make haste, and pull your boy along. You are come here to see the curiosities of Paris. Yesterday you saw the Flemings – to-day you must see the little gypsy.'

'The gypsy?' exclaimed Mahiette, turning sharply round and grasping tightly the arm of her son. 'God forbid! She would steal my child – Come, Eustache!'

And she set off running along the quay toward the Grève, until she had left the bridge far behind her. But the boy, whom she dragged after her, stumbled and fell upon his knees; she stopped out of breath. Oudarde and Gervaise now came up with her.

'That gypsy steal your child!' said Gervaise; 'that's an odd notion of yours!'

Mahiette shook her head thoughtfully.

' 'Tis singular,' observed Oudarde, 'that the Sachette has the same notion about gypsy women.'

'What's the Sachette?' inquired Mahiette.

'Hey!' said Oudarde, 'Sister Gudule.'

'And what is Sister Gudule?' returned Mahiette.

'You are indeed from your Rheims – not to know that!' answered Oudarde. 'She is the recluse of the Rat-Hole.'

'What?' asked Mahiette; 'the poor woman to whom we are carrying the cake?'

Oudarde nodded affirmatively.

'Just so. You will see her presently, at her window on the Grève. She looks as you do upon those vagabonds of Egypt who go about tambourining and fortune-telling. Nobody knows what has given her this horror of zingari and Egyptians. But you, Mahiette, wherefore should you take to your heels thus at the mere sight of them?'

'Oh!' said Mahiette, clasping with both hands the chubby head of her boy; 'I would not have that happen to me which happened to Pâquette la Chantefleurie!'

'Ah! you must tell us that story, good Mahiette,' said Gervaise, taking her arm.

'I will gladly,' answered Mahiette; 'but you must, indeed, be from Paris – not to know that! You must know, then (but we need not stop while I tell you the story), that Pâquette la Chantefleurie was a pretty girl of eighteen when I was one too, that is to say eighteen years ago; and that it's her own fault if she is not at this day, as I am, a good, hearty, fresh-looking mother of six-and-thirty, with a husband and a boy – but alack! from the time that she was fourteen years old, it was too late. She was the daughter of Guybertaut, a boat-minstrel at Rheims – the same that played before King Charles VII at his coronation; when he went down our river Vesle from Sillery to Muison, and, more by token, the Maid of Orleans was in the barge with him. The old father died while Pâquette was quite a child, so she had only her mother, who was sister to Monsieur Matthieu Pradon, a master-brazier and coppersmith at Paris, Rue Parin Garlin, who died last year. You see she came of good family. The mother was unluckily a simple woman, and taught Pâquette little but to make finery and playthings, which did not hinder the little girl from growing very tall and remaining very poor. The two lived at Rheims, by the riverside, Rue de Follo Peine – mark that! for, I believe 'tis that which brought ill-luck to Pâquette. In '61, the year of the coronation of our King Louis XI, whom God preserve! Pâquette was so gay and so pretty, that everywhere they called her La Chantefleurie (the song blossom). Poor girl! What beautiful teeth she had! and she would laugh that she might show them. Now a girl who likes to laugh is on the high-road to weep – fine teeth are the ruin of fine eyes. Such was La Chantefleurie. She and her mother had hard work to earn their bread – they were fallen very low since the minstrel's death – their needle-work brought them scarce more than six deniers a week, which is not quite two eagle farthings. Where was the time when father Guybertaut used to get twelve Paris pence, at a coronation, for a single song! One winter (it was in that same year '61), when the two women had neither logs nor fagots, the weather was very cold, and gave such a beautiful colour to La Chantefleurie, that the men called her "Pâquette" – some called her "Pâquerette" (a daisy) – and then she was ruined – Eustache, let me see you bite the cake, if you dare! – We saw directly that she was ruined, one Sunday when she came to church with a gold cross on her neck. – At fourteen years of age! think of that! First it was the young Viscount de Cormontreuil, whose castle is about three-quarters of a league from Rheims; then Messire Henri de Triancourt, the king's equerry; then, something lower, Chiart de Beaulion, sergeant-at-arms; then lower still, Guery Aubergeon, the king's carver; then Mace de Frépus, monsieur the dauphin's barber; then Thévenin le Moine, the king's first cook; then, still descending, to men older and less noble, she fell to Guillaume Racine, viol-player – and to Thierry de Mer, lamp-maker. Then, poor Chantefleurie, she became common property – she was come to the last sou of her gold-piece. What think you, my damoiselles? At the coronation, in the same year '61, it was she that made the bed for the king of the ribalds! – That self-same year! – '

Mahiette sighed, and wiped away a tear that had started to her eyes.

'Here's a story,' said Gervaise, 'that's not very uncommon; and I do not see that it has anything to do with either gypsies or children.'

'Patience!' resumed Mahiette – 'As for a child, we shall soon come to it. In '66, sixteen years ago this month, on Saint Paul's day, Pâquette was brought to bed of a little girl. Poor creature; she was in great joy at it – she had long wished for a child. Her mother, poor simple woman, who'd never known how to do anything but shut her eyes; her mother was dead. Pâquette had nothing in the world to love and none to love her. For five years past, since she had gone astray, poor Chantefleurie had been a wretched creature. She was alone, alone in the world; pointed at, shouted after, through the streets; beaten by the sergeants; mocked by little ragged boys. And then she had seen her twentieth year – and twenty is old age for light women. Her wantonness was beginning to bring her in scarcely more than her needle-work had formerly. Every fresh wrinkle made a crown less in her pocket; winter became again a hard season; again wood was scarce on her hearth, and bread in her cupboard. She could no longer work; for in giving way to pleasure she had become idle, and she suffered much more than formerly, because when she became idle she longed for pleasure. At least, it is thus that monsieur the curé of Saint Remy explains how it is that such women feel cold and hunger more than other poor creatures do, when they are old – '

'Yes,' interrupted Gervaise; 'but the gypsies?'

'Wait a moment, Gervaise!' said Oudarde, whose attention was less impatient; 'what should we have at the end, if everything was at the beginning? Continue, Mahiette, I beg. That poor Chantefleurie! – '

Mahiette continued:

'Well, then – she was very sorrowful, very wretched, and her tears wore deep furrows in her cheeks. But in the midst of her shame, her folly and her debauchery, she thought she would be less shameful, less wild and less dissipated, if there were something or some one in the world that she could love, and that could love her. It must be a child, for only a child could be innocent enough for that. She was aware of this after trying to love a thief, the only man that would have anything to say to her – but in a little time she had round out that the thief despised her. Those women of love require either a lover or a child to fill their hearts. Otherwise they are very unhappy. Not being able to find a lover, all her wishes turned toward having a child; and, as she had all along been pious, she prayed to God continually to send her one. So the good God took pity on her and gave her a little girl. I can not describe to you her joy – it was a fury of tears, kisses and caresses. She suckled the child herself; she made it swaddling-clothes out of her coverlet, the only one she had upon her bed; and no longer felt cold or hungry. She became beautiful once more in consequence of it. An old maid makes a young mother. Gallantry claimed her once more; men came again to see La Chantefleurie; she found customers for her wares, and out of all those horrors she made baby-clothes, capes and bibs, lace robes and little satin caps – without so much as thinking of buying herself another coverlet – Master Eustache, I've already told you not to eat that cake – It is certain that little Agnès – that was the child's name: its Christian name – for, as to a surname, it was long since La Chantefleurie had ceased to have one! – certain it is that the little thing was more swathed with ribbons and embroideries than a dauphiness of Dauphiny. Among other things, she had a pair of little shoes, the like of which King Louis XI certainly never had. Her mother had stitched and embroidered them herself; she had lavished on them all her skill as an embroideress, and all the embellishments of a robe for the Holy Virgin. They were the two sweetest little pink shoes that ever were seen. They were no longer than my thumb; and unless one saw the child's tiny feet slip out of them, one would never have believed they could have gone in. To be sure, the little feet were so small, so pretty, so rosy – rosier than the satin of the shoes! When you have children, Oudarde, you will know that there is nothing prettier than those little feet and those little hands.'

'I wish for nothing better,' said Oudarde, sighing; 'but I must wait the good pleasure of Monsieur Andry Musnier.'

'Besides,' resumed Mahiette, 'Pâquette's child had not pretty feet only. I saw her when she was but four months old; she was a little love. Her eyes were larger than her mouth, and she had the most beautiful, fine, dark hair, which already curled. She would have made a superb brunette at sixteen! Her mother became more and more crazy about her every day. She hugged her – kissed her – tickled her – washed her – dressed her out – devoured her! She lost her head over her; she thanked God for her. Its pretty little rosy feet above all were an endless source of wonderment; they were a delirium of joy! She was always pressing her lips to them, and could not recover from amazement at their smallness. She put them into the little shoes, took them out, admired them – wondered at them – held them up to the light – would pity them while she was trying to make them walk upon her bed – and would gladly have passed her life on her knees, putting the shoes on and off those little feet, as if they had been those of an infant Jesus.'

'The tale is fair and very good,' said Gervaise, in an undertone, 'but what is there about gypsies in all that?'

'Why, here,' replied Mahiette. 'One day there came to Rheims a very odd sort of gentry. They were beggars and vagabonds, who were roving about the country, headed by their duke and their counts. They were swarthy, their hair all curly, and rings of silver in their ears. The women were still uglier than the men. Their faces were darker, and always uncovered; they wore a sorry kirtle about their body, an old cloth woven with cords, bound upon their shoulder; and their hair hanging like a horse's tail. The children wallowing under their feet would have frightened an ape. An excommunicated gang! They were all come in a straight line from lower Egypt to Rheims, through Poland. The Pope had confessed them, it was said, and had ordered them by way of penance to wander for seven years together without sleeping in a bed; and so they called themselves penancers, and stank. It seems that they were once Saracens; so they must have believed in Jupiter, and demanded ten Tours pounds from all archbishops, bishops and abbots that carried crosier and mitre. It was a papal bull gave them this right. They came to Rheims to tell fortunes in the name of the

King of Algiers and the Emperor of Germany. You can readily imagine that no more was needed for them to be forbidden entrance to the town. Then the whole band encamped of their own accord near the gate of Braine, upon that mound where there's a windmill, close by the old chalk-pits. And all Rheims went to see them. They looked into your hand, and told you marvellous prophecies – they were equal to predicting to Judas that he would become Pope. Nevertheless, there were ugly rumours about their child-stealing, purse-cutting and eating of human flesh. The wise folks said to the foolish ones, "Don't go there!" and then went themselves by stealth. It was an infatuation. The fact is, that they said things fit to astonish a cardinal. Mothers boasted loudly of their children after the gypsy-women had read all sorts of miracles in their hands, written in Turkish and Pagan. One of them had got an emperor – another a pope – another a captain. Poor Chantefleurie was seized with curiosity – she had a mind to know what she had got, and whether her pretty little Agnès would not some day be Empress of Armenia, or of elsewhere. So she carried her to the gypsies, and the gypsy-women admired the child, fondled it, kissed it with their black mouths and wondered over its little hand – alas! to the great joy of its mother. They were particularly delighted with the pretty feet and the pretty shoes. The child was not yet a year old. She had begun to lisp a word or two – laughed at her mother like a little madcap – was plump and quite round – and had a thousand little gestures of the angels in paradise. But she was frightened at the gypsy-women, and fell a-crying. Her mother kissed her the harder, and went away overjoyed at the good fortune which the sooth-sayers had told her Agnès. She was to be beautiful, virtuous and a queen. So she returned to her garret in the Rue Folle Peine, quite proud to carry with her a queen. The next day she took advantage of a moment when the child was asleep on her bed (for she always had it to sleep with herself), gently left the door ajar, and ran to tell a neighbour, in the Rue de la Séchesserie, that the day was to come when her daughter Agnès was to be waited on at table by the King of England and the Archduke of Ethiopia – and a hundred other marvels. On her return, hearing no sound as she went up the stairs, she said to herself, "Good, the child is still asleep." She found her door wider open than she had left it – the poor mother, however, went in and ran to the bed. The child was no longer there – the place was empty. Nothing remained of the child but one of its pretty shoes. She rushed out of the room, flew down the stairs, and began to beat her head against the wall, crying, "My child! who has my child? who has taken my child?" The street was deserted – the house stood alone – no one could tell her anything about it; she went about the town – searched all the streets – ran hither and thither the whole day, wild, mad, terrible peeping at the doors and windows like a wild beast that has lost its little ones. She was panting, dishevelled, frightful to look upon – and in her eyes there was a fire that dried her tears. She stopped the passers-by, and cried, "My daughter! my daughter! my pretty little daughter! – he that will restore me my daughter I will be his servant – the servant of his dog, and he shall eat my heart if he likes." She met monsieur the cure of Saint Remy, and said to him, "Monsieur le cure, I will till the earth with my fingernails – but give me back my child!" It was heartrending, Oudarde – and I saw a very hardhearted man, Maître Ponce Lacabre, the attorney, that wept. Ah! the poor mother! When night came she went home. During her absence, a neighbour had seen two gypsywomen steal slyly up stairs with a bundle in their arms; then come down again, after shutting the door, and hurry off. After they were gone, something like the cries of a child were heard in Pâquette's room – the mother laughed wildly – ran up the stairs as if on wings – burst in her door like a cannon going off, and entered the room. A frightful thing to tell, Oudarde! – instead of her sweet little Agnès, so fresh and rosy, who was a gift from the good God, there was a sort of little monster, hideous, shapeless, one-eyed, with its limbs all awry, crawling and squalling upon the floor. She hid her eyes in horror. "Oh!" said she, "can it be that the witches have changed my child into that frightful animal!" They carried the little club-footed creature away as quick as possible. He would have driven her mad. He was the monstrous offspring of some gypsy-woman given over to the devil. He seemed to be about four years old, and spoke a language which was not a human tongue – there were words that were impossible. La Chantefleurie flung herself upon the little shoe, all that was left her of all that she had loved. There she remained so long motionless, speechless, breathless, that they thought she was dead. Suddenly she trembled all over – covered her relic with frantic kisses, and burst out sobbing, as if her heart were broken. I assure you we all wept with her. She said, "Oh, my little girl! my pretty little girl! where art thou?" – and it wrung your very heart. I weep still when I think of it. Our children, I can tell you, are the very marrow of our bones. My poor Eustache! thou art so handsome! If you did but know how clever he is! Yesterday he said to me, "I want to be a gendarme, I do." Oh, my Eustache, if I were to lose thee! – All at once Chantefleurie sprang up and ran through the streets of Rheims, shouting: "To the gypsies' camp! to the gypsies' camp! Bring guards to burn the witches!" The gypsies were gone – it was pitch dark. No one could follow them. On the morrow, two leagues from Rheims, on a heath between Gueux and Tilloy, the remains of a large fire were found, some ribbons which had belonged to Pâquette's child, drops of blood and some goat's dung. The night just passed happened to be a Saturday night. There could be no further doubt that the Egyptians had held their Witches' Sabbath on that heath, and had devoured the child in company with Beelzebub, as the Mahometans do. When La Chantefleurie learnt these horrible things, she did not weep – she moved her lips as if to speak, but could not. On the morrow her hair was gray. On the second day she had disappeared.'

' 'Tis in truth a frightful tale!' said Oudarde; 'enough to draw tears from a Burgundian!'

'I am no longer surprised,' added Gervaise, 'that the fear of gypsies should haunt you so.'

'And you had all the reason,' resumed Oudarde, 'to flee with your Eustache just now, since these, too, are gypsies from Poland.'

'Not so,' said Gervaise; ' 'Tis said that they come from Spain and Catalonia.'

'Catalonia! – well, that may be,' answered Oudarde; 'Polonia, Catalonia, Valonia – those places are all one to me. There's one thing sure, they are gypsies.'

'Who certainly,' added Gervaise, 'have teeth long enough to eat little children. And I should not be surprised if La Smeralda ate a little, too, for all her dainty airs. That white goat of hers has got too many mischievous tricks for there not to be some wickedness behind.'

Mahiette walked on in silence. She was absorbed in that reverie which is a sort of prolongation of a doleful story, and which ends only after having communicated the emotion, from vibration to vibration, to the very last fibres of the heart. Gervaise, however, addressed her: 'And so it was never known what became of La Chantefleurie?' Mahiette made no answer – Gervaise repeated her question, shaking her arm and calling her by her name. Mahiette seemed to awake from her reverie:

'What became of La Chantefleurie?' said she, mechanically repeating the words whose impression was still fresh in her ear. Then, making an effort to recall her attention to the meaning of the words – 'Ah,' she said sharply, 'it was never known.'

After a pause she added:

'Some said she had been seen to quit Rheims at nightfall by the Fléchembault gate; others, at daybreak, by the old Basée gate. A poor man found her gold cross hanging on the stone cross in the field where the fair is held. It was that trinket that had ruined her in '61 . It was a gift from the handsome Viscount de Cormontreuil, her first lover. Pâquette would never part with it, even in her greatest wretchedness – she clung to it as to life. So when we saw this cross abandoned, we all thought she was dead. However, there were people, at the Cabaret les Vautes, who said they'd seen her go by on the Paris road, walking barefoot over the stones. But then she must have gone out through the Porte de Vesle, and all that did not agree. Or rather, I believe, that she did actually go out by the gate of Vesle, but she went out of this world.'

'I do not understand you,' said Gervaise. 'The Vesle,' answered Mahiette, with a melancholy smile, 'is the river.'

'Poor Chantefleurie!' said Oudarde, with a shiver; 'drowned!'

'Drowned,' replied Mahiette. 'And who could have foretold to the good father Guybertaut, when he floated down the stream under the Tinqueux bridge, singing in his boat, that his dear little Pâquette should one day pass under that same bridge, but with neither song nor boat!'

'And the little shoe?' inquired Gervaise.

'Disappeared with the mother,' answered Mahiette.

'Poor little shoe!' said Oudarde.

Oudarde, a fat and tender-hearted woman, would have been quite content to sigh in company with Mahiette. But Gervaise, more curious, had not yet come to the end of her questions.

'And the monster?' said she all at once to Mahiette.

'What monster?' asked the other.

'The little gypsy monster left by the witches at La Chantefleurie's in exchange for her child. What was done with it? I hope you drowned it, too.'

'Not so,' answered Mahiette.

'What? burned it then? I' faith, that was a better way of disposing of a witch's child.'

'Neither the one nor the other, Gervaise. Monsieur the archbishop took an interest in the child of Egypt; he exorcised it, blessed it, carefully took the devil out of its body, and sent it to Paris to be exposed upon the wooden bed at Notre-Dame as a foundling.'

'Those bishops!' muttered Gervaise; 'because they're learned, forsooth, they can never do anything like other folks. I just put it to you, Oudarde – the idea of placing the devil among the foundlings – for that little monster was assuredly the devil. Well, Mahiette, and what did they do with him in Paris? I suppose no charitable person wanted him.'

'I don't know, indeed,' answered the native of Rheims. 'It was just at that time that my husband bought the place of notary at Beru, two leagues from the town; and we thought no more of all that story – particularly as right by Beru there are the two hills of Cernay, which quite hide the spires of Rheims cathedral.'

While talking thus, the three worthy bourgeoises had arrived at the Place de Grève. In their preoccupation they had passed the public breviary of the Tour Roland without stopping, and were proceeding mechanically toward the pillory, around which the crowd increased momentarily. Probably the sight, which at this instant attracted every eye, would have made them completely forget the Rat-Hole and the halt which they intended to make there, if the sturdy six-years-old Eustache, whom Mahiette led by the hand, had not suddenly reminded them of it. 'Mother,' said he, as though some instinct warned him that the Rat-Hole was behind them, 'now may I eat the cake?'

Had Eustache been more adroit, that is to say, less greedy, he would have waited a little longer; and not until they had reached home, in the University, at Maître Andry Musnier's, in the Rue Madame la Valence, when the two channels of the Seine and the five bridges of the City would have been between the cake and the Rat-Hole, would he have hazarded that simple question – 'Mother, now may I eat the cake?'

This same question, an imprudent one at the moment when it was put by Eustache, roused Mahiette's attention.

'By the way,' she exclaimed, 'we are forgetting the recluse! Show me your Rat-Hole, that I may carry her the cake.'

'At once,' said Oudarde, 'for 'tis charity.'

This was not at all to Eustache's liking.

'Oh, my cake!' said he, rubbing both ears alternately with his shoulders, which in such cases betokens supreme discontent.

The three women retraced their steps; and as they approached the house of the Tour Roland, Oudarde said to the other two:

'We must not all three look into the hole at once, lest we should frighten the Sachette. You two pretend to read the Dominus in the breviary, while I take a peep at the window-hole. The Sachette knows me a little. I'll tell you when you may come.

She went to the window alone. The moment that she looked in profound pity took possession of every feature, and her frank, gay visage altered its expression and colour as suddenly as if it had passed from a ray of sunshine to a ray of moonlight; her eyes grew moist, and her mouth quivered as if she were about to weep. A moment later, she put her finger to her lips and beckoned to Mahiette to come and look.

Mahiette, much moved, joined her silently and on tip-toe, like one approaching a deathbed.

It was in truth a melancholy sight that presented itself to the eyes of the two women, as they gazed through the grated window of the Rat-Hole, neither stirring nor breathing.

The cell was small, broader than it was long, with an arched ceiling, and, seen from within, looked like the inside of a huge bishop's mitre. On the bare flag-stones that formed its floor, in one corner, a woman was sitting, or rather crouching. Her chin rested on her knees, which her crossed arms pressed closely against her breast. Doubled up in this manner, clad in brown sackcloth which covered her loosely from head to foot, her long, gray hair pulled over in front and hanging over her face, down her legs to her feet – she seemed at first only a strange form outlined against the dark background of the cell – a sort of dusky triangle, which the ray of light entering at the window divided distinctly into two tones, one dark, the other illuminated. It was one of those spectres half light, half shade, such as are seen in dreams, and in the extraordinary work of Goya – pale – motionless – sinister – crouching over a tomb, or leaning against the grating of a dungeon. It was neither woman nor man, nor living being nor definite form: it was a figure, a sort of vision, in which the real and the fanciful intermingled like twilight and daylight. Beneath her hair, which fell to the ground, the outlines of a stern and emaciated profile were barely visible; scarcely did her garment permit the extremity of a bare foot to escape, which contracted in the hard, cold pavement. The little of human form that was discernible under that mourning envelope caused a shudder.

This figure, which looked as if riveted to the flag-stones, seemed to have neither motion, thought, nor breath. In that thin sackcloth, in January, lying on a stone floor, without fire, in the darkness of a dungeon, whose oblique loophole admitted only the chill blast and never the sun – she appeared not to suffer, not even to feel. She seemed to have been turned to stone like her dungeon, to ice like the season. Her hands were clasped; her eyes were fixed. At the first glance she seemed a spectre; at the second, a statue.

At intervals, however, her blue lips were parted by a breath and trembled, but as dead and mechanical as the leaves which the wind sweeps aside.

Meanwhile those haggard eyes cast a look, an ineffable look, a profound, lugubrious, imperturbable look, incessantly fixed on one corner of the cell, which could not be seen from without; a gaze which seemed to concentrate all the gloomy thoughts of that suffering spirit upon some mysterious object.

Such was the creature who was called from her habitation the *recluse*, and from her coarse garment the Sachette.

The three women (for Gervaise had come up to Mahiette and Oudarde) peered through the aperture. Their heads intercepted the feeble light in the cell, without the wretched being whom they thus deprived of it seeming to pay any attention to them. 'Let us not disturb her,' whispered Oudarde; 'she is in her ecstasy; she is praying.'

But Mahiette was gazing with an ever increasing anxiety at that wan, withered, dishevelled head, and her eyes filled with tears.

'That would indeed be singular!' muttered she.

Passing her head through the bars of the window, she contrived to get a glimpse of the corner upon which the unfortunate woman's eyes were invariably riveted.

When she withdrew her head from the window her cheeks were bathed with tears.

'What do you call that woman?' said she to Oudarde.

Oudarde answered, 'We call her Sister Gudule.'

'And I,' returned Mahiette, 'call her Pâquette la Chantefleurie.'

Then, laying her finger on her lips, she motioned to the amazed Oudarde to put her head through the aperture, and look.

Oudarde looked and saw, in the corner upon which the eye of the recluse was fixed in that gloomy absorption, a tiny shoe of pink satin, embroidered with countless gold and silver spangles.

Gervaise looked after Oudarde; and then the three women, gazing upon the unhappy mother, began to weep.

But neither their looks nor their tears disturbed the recluse. Her hands remained clasped; her lips mute; her eyes fixed; and to any one who knew her story, that gaze of hers upon that little shoe was heartrending.

The three women had not yet breathed a word; they dared not speak, even in a whisper. This profound silence, this great grief; this entire oblivion of all but one thing, had upon them the effect of the high altar at Easter or Christmas. They were silent, absorbed, ready to fall upon their knees. It seemed to them as if they had just entered a church on the Saturday in Passion-week.

At length Gervaise, the most curious of the three, and therefore the least sensitive, tried to make the recluse speak: 'Sister! Sister Gudule!'

Thrice did she repeat this call, raising her voice every time. The recluse stirred not – there was no word, no look, no sigh, no sign of life.

Oudarde in her turn, in a sweeter and more caressing voice, said to her, 'Sister – holy Sister Gudule!'

The same silence, the same immobility.

'A strange woman!' exclaimed Gervaise, 'and one who would not start at a bombard.'

'She is perchance deaf,' said Oudarde, with a sigh.

'Perchance blind,' said Gervaise.

'Perchance dead,' observed Mahiette.

It is certain that if the spirit had not already quitted that inert, torpid, lethargic body, it had at least retired within it, and hidden itself in depths whither the perceptions of the external organs no longer penetrated.

'We shall have to leave the cake on the window-sill,' said Oudarde; 'and some lad will take it. What can we do to rouse her?'

Eustache, whose attention had until that moment been diverted by a little cart drawn by a great dog, which had just passed, noticed all at once that his three conductresses were looking at something through the hole in the wall; and curiosity taking possession of him in turn he climbed upon a stone post, raised himself on tip-toe, and thrusting his red, chubby face through the opening, cried out, 'Mother, let me see, too.'

At the sound of this childish voice, clear fresh and ringing, the recluse started. She turned her head with the sharp, abrupt movement of a steel spring; her two long, thin hands brushed back the hair from her forehead; and she fixed upon the child a look of astonishment, bitterness and despair. That look was but a flash.

'Oh, my God!' she exclaimed suddenly, hiding her head upon her knees – and it seemed as if her hoarse voice tore her breast in passing – 'at least do not show me those of others!'

'Good-day, madame,' said the boy, gravely.

But the shock, however, had, as it were, awakened the recluse

A long shiver ran through her entire frame, from head to foot her teeth chattered; she half raised her head, and said, pressing her elbows to her sides, and clasping her feet in her hands, as if to warm them:

'Oh, how cold it is!'

'Poor creature,' said Oudarde, with deep pity, 'would you like a little fire?'

She shook her head in token of refusal.

'Well,' resumed Oudarde, offering her a flask, 'here is some hippocrass, that will warm you. Drink.'

Again she shook her head, looked at Oudarde fixedly, and replied: 'Water!'

Oudarde insisted: 'No, sister; that is no January beverage. You must drink a little hippocrass, and eat this leavened cake of maize, which we have baked for you.'

She put aside the cake, which Mahiette offered her, and said, 'Some black bread!'

'Come,' said Gervaise, seized with a charitable impulse in her turn, and unfastening her woollen mantle – 'here is a cloak something warmer than yours – put this over your shoulders.'

She refused the cloak as she had the flask and the cake, and answered, 'Sacking!'

'But surely,' resumed the kind-hearted Oudarde, 'you must have perceived, I should think, that yesterday was a holiday.'

'I am aware of it,' said the recluse. ' 'Tis two days now since I have had any water in my crock.'

She added, after a pause, ' 'Tis a holiday, and they forget me – they do well. Why should the world think of me, who think not of it? When the fire goes out the ashes are soon cold.'

And as though fatigued with having said so much, she dropped her head on her knees again. The simple and charitable Oudarde who fancied that she understood from her last words that she was still complaining of the cold, replied innocently, 'Then will you have a little fire?'

'Fire?' said the Sachette with a strange accent – 'and will you make a little, also, for the poor little one who has been beneath the sod for these fifteen years?'

Her limbs shook, her voice trembled, her eyes flashed. She raised herself upon her knees; suddenly she stretched her thin white hand towards the child, who was looking at her in surprise. 'Take away that child!' she cried, 'the Egyptian woman is about to pass by.'

Then she fell with her face to the ground, and her forehead struck the floor with the sound of one stone upon another. The three women thought her dead. But a moment later she stirred, and they saw her crawl upon her hands and knees to the corner where the little shoe was. Then they dared not look; they no longer saw her, but they heard a thousand kisses and sighs, mingled with heartrending cries and dull blows, like those of a head striking against a wall; then, after one of these blows, so violent that they all three started, they heard nothing more.

'Has she killed herself?' said Gervaise, venturing to put her head in at the aperture. 'Sister! Sister Gudule!'

'Sister Gudule!' repeated Oudarde.

'Ah, good heavens! she no longer stirs!' exclaimed Gervaise – 'Is she dead, think you? – Gudule! Gudule!' Mahiette, whose utterance had been choked until then, now made an effort. 'Wait,' said she; and then, bending down to the window, 'Pâquette!' she cried, 'Pâquette la Chantefleurie!' A child who thoughtlessly blows upon the ill-lighted fuse of a petard, and makes it explode in his face, is no more terrified than was Mahiette at the effect of this name thus suddenly flung into the cell of Sister Gudule.

The recluse shook all over; sprang upon her feet, and bounded to the window with eyes so flaming that Mahiette and Oudarde and the other woman and the child retreated to the parapet of the quay.

But still the forbidding face of the recluse appeared pressed against the bars of the window. 'Oh, oh!' she cried, with a frightful laugh, ' 'tis the Egyptian who calls me!'

At this instant the scene which was passing at the pillory caught her wild eye. Her forehead wrinkled with horror – she stretched out of her den her two skeleton arms, and cried out, in a voice that resembled a death-rattle: – 'So, 'tis thou once more, daughter of Egypt – 'Tis thou who callest me, stealer of children! Well, be thou accursed! accursed! accursed! – '

IV

A Tear for a Drop of Water

THESE WORDS WERE, so to speak, the connecting link between two scenes which, until that moment, had been simultaneously developing themselves, each upon its particular stage – the one, that which has just been related, at the Trou aux Rats; the other now to be described, at the pillory. The former was witnessed only by the three women whose acquaintance the reader has just made; the latter had for spectators the whole crowd which we saw some time since collect upon the Place de Grève, around the pillory and the gibbet.

This crowd, which the four sergeants posted from nine o'clock in the morning at the four corners of the pillory had inspired with the hope of some sort of an execution – not a hanging, probably – but a whipping, a cutting off of ears, something in short – this crowd had increased so rapidly that the four sergeants, too closely besieged, had been obliged more than once to 'press it,' as they expressed it, by sound blows of their whitleather whips and the haunches of their horses.

The populace, well accustomed to wait for public executions did not manifest great impatience. It amused itself looking at the pillory – a very simple sort of structure, consisting of a cubical mass of stonework, some ten feet high, and hollow within. A very steep flight of steps, of unhewn stone, called by distinction the 'ladder,' led to the upper platform, upon which was seen a horizontal wheel of solid oak. The victim was bound upon this wheel, on his knees, and his arms pinioned. An upright shaft of timber, set in motion by a capstan concealed inside the little structure, gave a rotary motion to the wheel, which always maintained its horizontal position, thus presenting the face of the culprit successively to each side of the Square in turn. This was called 'turning' a criminal.

It is evident that the pillory of the Grève was far from possessing all the attractions of the pillory of the Markets. There was nothing architectural, nothing monumental. There was no iron-cross roof – no octagonal lantern – there were no slender columns, spreading out at the edge of the roof into capitals composed of foliage and flowers – no fantastic and monster-headed gutter-spouts – no carved woodwork – no delicate sculpture cut deep into the stone.

They were forced to be content with those four rough stone walls, with two buttresses of sandstone, with a sorry stone gibbet, meagre and bare, on one side.

The treat would have been indeed a poor one for lovers of Gothic architecture. It is true, however, that none were ever less interested in architecture than the good cockneys of the Middle Ages, who cared very little for the beauty of a pillory.

At last the culprit arrived, tied to the tail of a cart, and as soon as he was hoisted upon the platform, so that he could be seen from all parts of the Square, bound with cords and straps to the wheel of the pillory, a prodigious hooting, mingled with laughter and acclamations, burst from the assemblage in the Square. They had recognized Quasimodo.

It was he, in fact. It was a strange reverse. Pilloried on the very place where the day before he had been saluted, acclaimed and proclaimed Pope and Prince of Fools, escorted by the Duke of Egypt, the King of Tunis and the Emperor of Galilee. One thing is certain, and that is that there was not a soul in the crowd – not even himself, in turn triumphant and a victim, who could clearly make out in his own mind the connection between the two situations. Gringoire and his philosophy were lacking from this spectacle.

Presently, Michel Noiret, sworn trumpeter to the king, imposed silence on the louts and proclaimed the sentence, pursuant to the ordinance and command of monsieur the provost. He then fell back behind the cart, with his men in livery surcoats.

Quasimodo impassive, did not wince. All resistance on his part was rendered impossible by what was then called, in the language of criminal law, 'the vehemence and firmness of the bonds' – that is to say, that the small straps and chains probably entered his flesh. This, by-the-by, is a tradition of the jail and the galleys which is not yet lost, and which the handcuffs still preserve with care among us, a civilized, mild, and humane people (the guillotine between parentheses).

He had allowed himself to be led, thrust, carried, hoisted, bound and bound again. Nothing was to be seen upon his countenance but the astonishment of a savage or an idiot. He was known to be deaf; he seemed to be blind.

They placed him on his knees on the circular plank; he made no resistance. He was stripped of shirt and doublet to the waist; he submitted. They bound him down under a fresh system of straps and buckles; he let them buckle and strap him. Only from time to time he breathed heavily, like a calf, whose head hangs dangling over the side of the butcher's cart.

'The dolt!' said Jehan Frollo du Moulin to his friend Robin Poussepain (for the two students had followed the sufferer, as in duty bound), 'he understands no more about it than a cockchafer shut up in a box.'

There was a wild laugh among the crowd when they saw, stripped naked to their view, Quasimodo's hump, his camel breast, his callous and hairy shoulders. Amidst all this mirth, a man of short stature and robust frame, in the livery of the City, ascended the platform, and placed himself by the culprit. His name speedily circulated among the spectators – it was Maître Pierrat Torterue, official torturer at the Châtelet.

He began by depositing on one corner of the pillory a black hourglass, the upper cup of which was filled with red sand, which was filtering through into the lower receptacle. Then he took off his parti-coloured doublet; and there was seen hanging from his right hand a slender whip with long, white thongs, shining, knotted, braided and armed with points of metal. With his left hand he carelessly rolled his right shirt-sleeve up to his armpit.

Meanwhile Jehan Frollo shouted, lifting his curly, blond head above the crowd (he had mounted for that purpose on the shoulders of Robin Poussepain), 'Come and see – messieurs! mesdames! – they're going to peremptorily flagellate Master Quasimodo, the bell-ringer of my brother monsieur the Archdeacon of Josas – a knave of oriental architecture, who has a back like a dome, and legs like twisted columns!'

And the people laughed, especially the boys and young girls.

At length the executioner stamped with his foot. The wheel began to turn; Quasimodo staggered under his bonds. The amazement suddenly depicted upon his deformed visage redoubled the bursts of laughter all around him.

All at once, at the moment when the wheel in its rotation presented to Maître Pierrat Quasimodo's humped back, Maître Pierrat raised his arm, the thin lashes hissed sharply in the air like a handful of vipers, and fell with fury upon the poor wretch's shoulders.

Quasimodo made a spring as if starting from his sleep. He now began to understand. He writhed in his bonds. A violent contraction of surprise and pain distorted the muscles of his face; but he heaved not a sigh. Only he turned his head backward to the right, then to the left, balancing it as a bull does when stung in the flank by a gadfly.

A second stroke followed the first – then a third – then another – and another – and so on and on. The wheel did not cease to turn, nor the blows to rain down.

Soon the blood spurted; it streamed in countless rivulets over the swarthy shoulders of the hunchback; and the slender thongs in their rotary motion which rent the air sprinkled drops of it upon the crowd.

Quasimodo had relapsed, in appearance at least, into his former apathy. At first he had striven, silently and without any great external effort, to burst his bonds. His eye had been seen to kindle, his muscles to stiffen, his limbs to gather all their force and the straps and chains stretched. The effort was powerful, prodigious, desperate – but the old shackles of the provostry resisted. They cracked; and that was all.

Quasimodo sank down exhausted. Amazement gave place in his countenance to an expression of bitter and deep discouragement. He closed his only eye, dropped his head upon his breast, and seemed as if he were dead.

Thenceforward he stirred no more. Nothing could wring any motion from him – neither his blood, which continued to flow; nor the blows which fell with redoubled fury; nor the rage of the executioner, who worked himself up and became intoxicated with the execution; nor the noise of the horrid lashes, keener and sharper than the stings of a wasp.

At length an usher of the Châtelet, clothed in black, mounted on a black horse, and stationed by the side of the steps from the commencement of the punishment, extended his ebony wand toward the hourglass. The executioner stopped. The wheel stopped. Quasimodo's eye slowly reopened.

The flagellation was finished. Two assistants of the official torturer bathed the bleeding shoulders of the sufferer, anointed them with some kind of unguent, which immediately closed all the wounds, and threw over his back a sort of yellow cloth cut in the form of a chasuble. Meanwhile Pierrat Torterue let the blood that soaked the lashes of his scourge drain from them in drops upon the ground.

But all was not yet over for Quasimodo. He had still to undergo that hour on the pillory which Maître Florian Barbedienne had so judiciously added to the sentence of Messire Robert d'Estouteville – all to the greater glory of the old physiological and psychological play upon words of Jean de Cumène – *Surdus absurdus* (a deaf man is absurd).

The hour-glass was therefore turned, and the hunchback was left bound to the plank, that justice might be fully satisfied.

The populace, particularly in the Middle Ages, is in society what the child is in a family. So long as they remain in that state of primitive ignorance, of moral and intellectual minority, it may be said of them as of a child,

'That age is a stranger to pity.'

We have already shown that Quasimodo was generally hated – for more than one good reason, it is true. There was hardly a spectator among that crowd but either had or thought he had some cause of complaint against the malevolent hunchback of Notre-Dame. The joy at seeing him appear thus in the pillory had been universal; and the harsh punishment he had just undergone, and the piteous plight in which it had left him, far from softening the hearts of the populace, had but rendered their hatred more malicious by arming it with the sting of mirth.

Accordingly, 'public vengeance,' as the legal jargon still styles it, once satisfied, a thousand private spites had now their turn. Here, as in the Great Hall, the women were most vehement. All bore him some grudge – some for his mischievousness, others for his ugliness. The latter were the more furious.

'Oh! thou phiz of Antichrist!' exclaimed one.

'Thou broomstick-rider!' cried another.

'What a fine tragical grin!' bawled a third, 'and one that would have made him Fools' Pope if to-day had been yesterday.'

' 'Tis well!' chimed in an old woman. 'This is the pillory grin; when is he to give us the gallows grin?'

'When art thou to have thy big bell clapped upon thy head a hundred feet under ground, thou cursed ringer?' shouted one.

'And to think 'tis this devil rings the Angelus!'

'Oh! thou deaf man! thou one-eyed creature! thou hunchback! thou monster!'

'A face to make a woman miscarry, better than all the drugs and medicines.'

And the two students, Jehan du Moulin and Robin Poussepain, sang at the top of their lungs, the old popular refrain –

> *A halter for the gallows rogue!*
> *A fagot for the witch!*

Countless other insults rained upon him, and hootings, and imprecations, and laughter, and now and then a stone.

Quasimodo was deaf, but his sight was good; and the public fury was not less forcibly expressed on their faces than by their words. Besides, the stones that struck him explained the bursts of laughter.

He bore it for a time. But, by degrees, that patience which had resisted the lash of the torturer relaxed and gave way under these insect stings. The Asturian bull that has borne unmoved the attacks of the picador is irritated by the dogs and the banderillas.

At first he slowly rolled around a look of menace at the crowd. But, shackled as he was, his look was powerless to chase away those flies which galled his wound. He then struggled in his bonds; and his furious contortions made the old wheel of the pillory creak upon its timbers. All which but increased the derision and the hooting.

Then the poor wretch, unable to break the collar which chained him like a wild beast, once more became quiet; only, at intervals, a sigh of rage heaved the hollows of his breast. On his face there was not a blush nor a trace of shame. He was too far from the social state, and too near the state of nature, to know what shame was. Moreover, with such a degree of deformity, is infamy a thing that can be felt? But resentment, hatred, despair, slowly spread over that hideous visage a cloud which grew darker and darker, more and more charged with electricity which burst forth in a thousand flashes from the eye of the cyclops.

However, that cloud was lightened for a moment as a mule passed through the crowd, bearing a priest on his back. As far away as he could see that mule and that priest, the poor sufferer's countenance softened. The fury which convulsed it gave way to a strange smile, full of ineffable sweetness, gentleness, tenderness. As the priest approached this smile became more pronounced, more distinct, more radiant. It was as if the unfortunate creature hailed the arrival of a deliverer. But the moment the mule was near enough to the pillory for its rider to recognize the sufferer, the priest cast down his eyes, wheeled about, clapped spurs to his beast, as if in haste to escape a humiliating appeal, and by no means desirous of being known and addressed by a poor devil in such a situation.

This priest was the Archdeacon Dom Claude Frollo.

Quasimodo's brow was overcast by a darker cloud than ever. The smile was still mingled with it for a time; but bitter, disheartened and profoundly sad.

Time passed. He had been there at least an hour and a half; lacerated, abused, mocked, and almost stoned to death.

All at once he again struggled in his chains, with redoubled desperation, that shook the whole framework that held him; and, breaking the silence which he had hitherto obstinately kept, he cried in a hoarse and furious voice, which was more like a bark than a human cry, and which drowned the noise of the hooting, 'Water!'

This exclamation of distress, far from exciting compassion, heightened the mirth of the good people of Paris who surrounded the pillory, and who, it must be admitted, taken as a whole and as a multitude, were at this time scarcely less cruel and brutal than that horrible tribe of Truands, to whom we have already introduced the reader, and who were simply the lowest stratum of the people. Not a voice was raised around the unhappy victim, except to jeer at his thirst. Certainly he was at this moment more grotesque and repulsive than he was pitiable – with his face purple and dripping, his wild eye, his mouth foaming with rage and suffering, and his tongue lolling half out. It must also be stated that had there even been any good, charitable soul of a townsman or townswoman among the rabble, who might have been tempted to carry a glass of water to that miserable creature in pain, so strong an idea of shame and ignominy was attached to the infamous steps of the pillory as would have sufficed to repel the good Samaritan.

In a few minutes, Quasimodo cast a despairing look upon the crowd, and repeated in a still more heart-rending voice, 'Water!'

Everyone laughed.

'Drink this!' cried Robin Poussepain, flinging in his face a sponge which had been dragged in the gutter. 'There, deaf scoundrel, I am thy debtor!'

A woman threw a stone at his head, saying: 'That will teach thee to waken us at night with thy cursed ringing!'

'Well, my lad!' bawled a cripple, striving to reach him with his crutch, 'wilt thou cast spells on us again from the top of the towers of Notre-Dame?'

'Here's a porringer to drink out of,' said one man, hurling a broken pitcher at his breast. ''Tis thou that, with only passing before her, made my wife be brought to bed of a child with two heads!'

'And my cat of a kitten with six paws!' yelped an old crone as she flung a tile at him.

'Water!' repeated Quasimodo for the third time, panting.

At that moment, he saw the populace make way. A young girl, fantastically dressed, emerged from the throng. She was followed by a little white goat with gilded horns, and carried a tambourine in her hand.

Quasimodo's eye sparkled. It was the gypsy-girl whom he had attempted to carry off the night before, for which piece of presumption he had some confused notion that they were punishing him at that very moment – which, in point of fact, was not in the least the case, since he was punished only for the misfortune of being deaf and of being tried by a deaf judge. He doubted not that she, too, was come to take her revenge, and to deal her blow like all the rest.

Thus, he beheld her rapidly ascend the steps. He was choking with rage and vexation. He would have liked to crumble the pillory to atoms; and could the flash of his eye have dealt death, the gypsy would have been reduced to ashes before she could have reached the platform.

Without a word, she approached the sufferer, who writhed in a vain effort to escape her; and detaching a gourd from her girdle, she raised it gently to the poor wretch's parched lips.

Then in that eye, hitherto so dry and burning, a big tear was seen to start, which fell slowly down that misshapen face so long convulsed by despair. It was possibly the first that the unfortunate creature had ever shed.

Meanwhile, he forgot to drink. The gypsy-girl made her little pout with impatience; and smiling, pressed the neck of the gourd to the tusked mouth of Quasimodo.

He drank deep draughts. His thirst was burning.

When he had done, the poor wretch put out his black lips, undoubtedly to kiss the fair hand which had just succoured him; but the young girl, who, remembering the violent attempt of the preceding night, was perhaps not without some mistrust, drew back her hand with the frightened gesture of a child afraid of being bitten by some animal.

Then the poor deaf creature fixed upon her a look of reproach and unutterable sorrow.

It would have been a touching sight anywhere – this beautiful, fresh, pure, charming girl, who was at the same time so weak, thus piously hastening to the relief of so much wretchedness, deformity and malevolence. On a pillory the spectacle was sublime.

The very populace were moved by it, and clapped their hands, shouting, 'Noël, Noël!'

It was at that moment that the recluse caught sight from the loophole of her cell of the gypsy-girl on the pillory, and hurled at her her sinister imprecation, 'Accursed be thou, daughter of Egypt! accursed! accursed!'

V

End of the Story of the Cake

ESMERELDA TURNED PALE, and with faltering step descended from the pillory, the voice of the recluse pursued her still. 'Get thee down! get thee down! Egyptian thief! thou shalt go up there again!'

'The Sachette is in one of her humours,' said the people, grumbling – and that was the end of it. For that sort of woman was feared, which rendered them sacred. Nobody in those days was willing to attack any one that prayed day and night.

The hour had come to release Quasimodo. He was unbound, and the crowd dispersed.

Near the Grand Pont, Mahiette, who was going away with her companions, suddenly halted.

'By-the-by, Eustache,' said she. 'what hast thou done with the cake?'

'Mother,' said the boy, 'while you were talking to that lady in the hole, there was a great dog came and bit of my cake – and then I bit of it too.'

'What, sir!' cried she, 'have you eaten it all?'

'Mother, it was the dog. I told him so; but he would not listen to me. Then I bit a piece too – that's all.'

' 'Tis a terrible child,' said the mother, smiling and scolding at the same time. 'Look you, Oudarde – he already eats by himself all the fruit from the cherry-tree in our croft at Charlerange. So his grandfather says he'll be a captain. Just let me catch you at it again, Master Eustache. Get along, you fat, little pig!'

BOOK SEVEN

I

On the Danger of Confiding
One's Secret to a Goat

SEVERAL WEEKS HAD PASSED. IT WAS NOW the beginning of March. The sun, which Dubartas, that classic ancestor of periphrasis, had not yet named 'the grand duke of the candles,' was none the less cheerful and radiant. It was one of those days of the early spring which are so mild and beautiful that all Paris turns out into the squares and promenades and celebrates them as if they were Sundays. On days so brilliant, so warm, and so serene, there is one hour in particular, at which one should go and admire the portal of Notre-Dame. It is the moment when the sun, already sinking in the west, almost exactly faces the cathedral. Its rays, becoming more and more horizontal, withdraw slowly from the pavement of the Place, and climb along the pinnacled façade, causing its thousands of figures in relief to stand out from their shadows, while the great central rose-window glares like a cyclops' eye lighted by reflections from his forge.

It was just that hour.

Opposite the lofty cathedral, reddened by the setting sun, upon a stone balcony, over the porch of a handsome Gothic house, at the corner of the Place and the Rue du Parvis, some lovely young girls were laughing and chatting gracefully and playfully. By the length of the veil which hung from the peak of their pointed coif, twined with pearls, down to their heels – by the fineness of the worked chemisette which covered their shoulders, revealing, according to the engaging fashion of that time, the swell of their fair virgin bosoms – by the richness of their under petticoats, still more costly than the upper skirt (admirable refinement!) – by the gauze, the silk and the velvet, with which the whole was loaded – and above all, by the whiteness of their hands, which proved that they led a life of idle ease – it was easy to divine that they were noble and wealthy heiresses. They were, in fact, Damoiselle Fleur-de-Lys de Gondelaurier, and her companions, Diane de Christeuil, Amelotte de Montmichel, Colombe de Gaillefontaine, and the little De Champchevrier, all damsels of good birth, assembled at that moment at the house of the widowed lady of De Gondelaurier, on account of Monseigneur de Beaujeu and madame his wife, who were to come to Paris in the month of April, there to choose maids of honour for the

Dauphiness Marguerite, on the occasion of her reception in Picardy, at the hands of the Flemings. Now, all the gentry for thirty leagues around were seeking this honour for their daughters, and a goodly number had already brought or sent them to Paris. The damsels in question had been entrusted by their parents to the care of the discreet and venerable Madame Aloïse de Gondelaurier, widow of a former master of the king's cross-bowmen now living in retirement with her only daughter, at her house in the Place du Parvis-Notre-Dame, at Paris.

The balcony on which these young girls were opened into an apartment richly hung with fawn-coloured Flanders leather stamped with golden foliage. The beams that ran across the ceiling diverting the eye with a thousand fantastic carvings, were painted and gilded. Splendid enamels gleamed here and there upon carved chests; and a boar's head made of pottery crowned a magnificent sideboard, the two steps of which showed that the mistress of the house was the wife or widow of a knight banneret. At the farther end by a high fireplace, covered with armorial bearings and escutcheons from top to bottom, sat in a rich crimson velvet armchair, the lady of Gondelaurier, whose fifty-five years were as plainly written in her dress as on her face.

By her side stood a young man of imposing though somewhat vain and swaggering mien, one of those handsome fellows about whom all women agree, though the grave and discerning men shake their heads at them. This young cavalier wore the brilliant uniform of a captain of the archers of the household troops – which too closely resembled the costume of Jupiter, which the reader has already been enabled to admire in the first book of this history, for us to inflict upon him a second description.

The damsels were seated, partly in the room, partly on the balcony; some on cushions of Utrecht velvet with gold corner-plates; others on oaken stools carved with flowers and figures. Each of them held on her lap a portion of a large piece of tapestry on which they were all working together, while a good part of it lay on the matting which covered the floor.

They talked together in that whispering tone, and with those half-stifled laughs, peculiar in an assembly of young girls in whose midst there is a young man. The young man, whose presence served to set in play all these feminine wiles, appeared, himself, to care very little about it; and, while these lovely girls were viewing with each other to attract his attention, he seemed to be chiefly absorbed in polishing the buckle of his sword-belt with his doeskin glove.

From time to time, the old lady addressed him in a low voice, and he replied as best he could, with awkward and forced courtesy. From the smiles and significant gestures of Madame Aloïse, from the glances she threw toward her daughter Fleur-de-Lys as she spoke low to the captain, it was evident that there was here a question of some betrothal concluded, some marriage near at hand, no doubt, between the young man and Fleur-de-Lys. And from the cold embarrassed air of the officer, it was easy to see that on his side at least there was no question of love. His whole manner expressed constraint and weariness, which a modern French subaltern on garrison duty would admirably render by the exclamation, 'What a beastly bore!'

The good lady, infatuated, as any silly mother might be, with her daughter's charms, did not perceive the officer's want of enthusiasm, but exerted herself in a low voice to attract his attention to the infinite grace with which Fleur-de-Lys plied her needle or wound a skein of silk.

'Do look now, cousin,' said she, pulling him by the sleeve that she might speak in his ear. 'Look at her! see, now she stoops.'

'Yes, indeed,' answered the young man, and he relapsed into his cold abstracted silence.

Shortly after, he had to lean again, on Dame Aloïse saying:

'Did you ever see a more charming lightsome face than that of your betrothed? Can anyone be more fair or more lovely? Are not those hands perfect? and that neck, does it not assume every graceful curve of the swan's? – How I envy you at times! and how happy you are, in being a man, wicked rogue that you are! Is not my Fleur-de-Lys adorably beautiful? and are you not passionately in love with her?'

'Assuredly,' answered he, while his thoughts were occupied elsewhere.

'Speak to her, then,' said Madame Aloïse, pushing him by the shoulder; 'say something to her; you're grown quite timid.'

We can assure the reader that timidity was neither a virtue nor a defect of the captain. He endeavoured, however, to do as he was bid.

'Fair cousin,' said he, approaching Fleur-de-Lys, 'what is the subject of this tapestry which keeps you so busy?'

'Gentle cousin,' answered Fleur-de-Lys, in a pettish tone, 'I have already told you three times; it is the grotto of Neptunus.'

It was evident that Fleur-de-Lys saw more clearly than her mother through the cold, absent manner of the captain. He felt that he must needs make conversation.

'And for whom is all this fine Neptune-work intended?' asked he.

'For the abbey of Saint-Antoine des Champs,' said Fleur-de-Lys, without raising her eyes.

The captain took up a corner of the tapestry: 'And pray, my fair cousin, who is that big gendarme blowing his trumpet till his cheeks are bursting?'

'That is Triton,' answered she.

There was still an offended tone perceptible in the few words uttered by Fleur-de-Lys. The young man understood that it was indispensable he should whisper in her ear some pretty nothing some gallant compliment – no matter what. He accordingly leaned over, but his imagination could furnish nothing more tender or familiar than this: 'Why does your mother always wear that petticoat embroidered with her arms, like our grandmothers of Charles VII's time? Pray tell her, fair cousin, that it's not the fashion of the present day, and that her hinge (*gond*) and laurel (*laurier*) embroidered upon her dress make her look like a walking mantelpiece. 'Pon honour, no one sits under their banner in that way now, I do swear.'

Fleur-de-Lys raised her fine eyes toward his reproachfully:

'Is that all you have to swear to me?' said she in a low tone.

Meanwhile the good Dame Aloïse, delighted to see them thus leaning over and whispering to each other, exclaimed, playing all the while with the clasps of her prayer-book: 'Touching picture of love!

'The captain, more and more embarrassed, returned to the subject of the tapestry. 'It is really a beautiful piece of work!' he cried.

At this juncture, Colombe de Gaillefontaine, another beautiful white-skinned blonde, in a high-necked gown of blue damask, ventured timidly to put in a word, addressed to Fleur-de-Lys, but in the hope that the handsome captain would answer her: 'My dear Gondelaurier, did you ever see the tapestries at the Hotel de la Roche-Guyon?'

'Is that not the hotel where the garden is attached to the linen-maker of the Louvre?' asked Diane de Christeuil, laughing; for, having fine teeth, she laughed on all occasions.

'And near that great old tower of the ancient wall of Paris?' added Amelotte de Montmichel, a pretty, curly-haired, rosy-cheeked brunette, who had a habit of sighing, as the other of laughing, without knowing why.

'My dear Colombe,' said Dame Aloïse, 'are you speaking of the hotel which belonged to Monsieur de Bacqueville in the reign of Charles VI? There is indeed magnificent tapestry there, of the high warp.'

'Charles VI! King Charles VI!' muttered the young captain curling his mustache. 'Mon Dieu! what a memory the good lady has for by-gone things!'

Madame de Gondelaurier continued: 'Superb tapestry indeed! So superior that it is considered unique!'

At this moment, Bérangère de Champchevrier, a little sylph of seven years of age, who was gazing into the square through the trefoils of the balcony railing, cried out, 'Oh! do look, dear god-mamma Fleur-de-Lys, at that pretty dancing-girl who is dancing on the pavement, and playing the tambourine among the people yonder!'

'The sonorous vibration of a tambourine was, in fact, heard by the party.

'Some gypsy-girl from Bohemia,' replied Fleur-de-Lys, turning nonchalantly toward the square.

'Let us see! let us see!' cried her lively companions, running to the front of the balcony, while Fleur-de-Lys, musing over the coldness of her affianced lover, followed slowly; and the latter, released by this incident, which cut short an embarrassing conversation, returned to the farther end of the room with the satisfied air of a soldier relieved from duty. And yet no unpleasing service was that of the lovely Fleur-de Lys; and such it had once appeared to him; but the captain had by degrees become weary of it, and the prospect of an approaching marriage grew less attractive to him each day. Besides, he was of a fickle disposition; and, if the truth must be told, rather vulgar in his tastes. Although of noble birth, he had contracted, under his officer's accoutrements, more than one of the habits of the common soldier. He delighted in the tavern and its accompaniments, and was never at his ease save amidst coarse witticisms, military gallantries, easy beauties, and as easy conquests. He had notwithstanding received from his family some education and polish; but he began his career too young, had too early kept garrison, and each day the varnish of the gentleman became more and more worn away under the friction of the gendarme's baldric. Though still continuing to visit her occasionally, prompted by some small remnant of common respect, he felt doubly constrained with Fleur-de-Lys. In the first place, because he distributed his love so promiscuously that he had but little left for her; and in the second, because, surrounded by a number of stately, starched and modest ladies, he was constantly in fear lest his tongue, accustomed to the language of oaths, should inadvertently break through its bounds and let slip some unfortunate tavern-slang. The effect may be imagined!

And yet, with all this were mingled great pretensions to elegance in dress and noble bearing. Let these things be reconciled as they may – I am but the historian.

He had been for some minutes thinking, or not thinking, but leaning in silence against the carved mantelpiece, when Fleur-de-Lys turning suddenly, addressed him – for after all, the poor girl only pouted in self-defence:

'Gentle cousin, did you not tell us of a little gypsy-girl you saved from a parcel of thieves a month or more ago, as you were on the night patrol?'

'I believe I did, fair cousin,' said the captain.

'Well,' rejoined she, 'perhaps it is that very gypsy-girl who is now dancing in the Parvis. Come and see if you recognize her, cousin Phœbus.'

A secret desire of reconciliation was perceptible in the gentle invitation she gave him to draw near her, and in the care she took to call him by his name. Captain Phœbus de Chateaupers (for it is he whom the reader has had before him from the beginning of this chapter) with tardy steps approached the balcony. 'There,' said Fleur-de-Lys tenderly, placing her hand on his arm, 'look at that little girl, dancing there in the ring! – Is that your gypsy?'

Phœbus looked, and said:

'Yes – I know her by her goat.'

'Ah! – so there is! – a pretty little goat, indeed!' said Amelotte, clasping her hands with delight.

'Are its horns really gold?' asked little Bérangère.

Without moving from her fauteuil, Dame Aloïse inquired:

'Is it one of those gypsy-girls that arrived last year by the Porte Gibard?'

'Mother,' said Fleur-de-Lys gently, 'that gate is now called Porte d'Enfer.'

Mademoiselle de Gondelaurier knew how much the captain's notions were shocked by her mother's antiquated modes of speech. Indeed he was already beginning to sneer and muttering between his teeth: 'Porte Gibard! Porte Gibard! That's to make way for King Charles VI.'

'Godmamma,' exclaimed Bérangère, whose eyes, incessantly in motion, were suddenly raised toward the top of the towers of Notre-Dame, 'who is that black man up there?'

All the girls raised their eyes. A man was indeed leaning with his elbows upon the topmost balustrade of the northern tower, overlooking the Grève. It was the figure of a priest; and they could clearly discern both his costume and his face resting on both his hands. He was motionless as a statue. His steady gaze was riveted on the Place.

There was in it something of the immobility of the kite when it has just discovered a nest of sparrows and is looking down upon it.

'It is monsieur the Archdeacon of Josas,' said Fleur-de-Lys.

'You have good eyes if you know him at this distance,' observed La Gaillefontaine.

'How he looks at the little dancing-girl,' remarked Diane de Christeuil.

'Let the Egyptian girl beware,' said Fleur-de-Lys; 'for he loves not Egypt.'

' 'Tis a great shame that man stares at her so,' added Amelotte de Montmichel, 'for she dances delightfully.'

'Fair cousin Phœbus,' said Fleur-de-Lys, suddenly, 'since you know this little gypsy-girl beckon to her to come up. It will amuse us.'

'Oh, yes!' exclaimed all the young girls, clapping their hands.

'Why! 'tis not worth while,' replied Phœbus. 'She has no doubt forgotten me; and I know not even her name. However, since you wish it, ladies, I will try.' And leaning over the balustrade of the balcony, he began to call out – 'Little one!'

The dancing-girl was not at that moment playing her tambourine. She turned her head toward the point whence this call proceeded; her brilliant eyes rested on Phœbus, and she stopped short suddenly.

'Little one,' repeated the captain, and he beckoned to her to come in.

The young girl looked at him again; then blushed as if a flame had risen to her cheeks; and, taking her tambourine under her arm, she made her way through the midst of the gaping spectators, toward the door of the house where Phœbus was, with slow, faltering steps, and with the agitated look of a bird yielding to the fascination of a serpent.

A moment or two after, the tapestry door hanging was raised, and the gypsy appeared on the threshold of the room, blushing, confused, breathless, her large eyes cast down, and not daring to advance a step farther.

Bérangère clapped her hands.

Meanwhile, the dancer stood motionless at the entrance of the apartment. Her appearance had produced a singular effect upon this group of young girls. It is certain that all of them were more or less influenced by a vague and indefined desire of pleasing the handsome officer, that the splendid uniform was the object at which all their coquetry was aimed; and that, ever since his entrance, there had been a certain secret suppressed rivalry among them, which they scarcely acknowledged even to themselves, but which broke forth none the less in their gestures and remarks. Nevertheless, as they all possessed nearly the same degree of beauty, they contended with equal arms, and each might reasonably hope for victory. The arrival of the gypsy-girl suddenly destroyed this equilibrium. Her beauty was so rare that, the moment she appeared at the entrance of the apartment, it seemed as though she diffused a sort of light peculiar to herself. Within this enclosed chamber, surrounded by its dusky hangings and wainscotings, she was incomparably more beautiful and radiant than in the public square. She was as the torch suddenly brought from the midday light into the shade. The noble damsels were dazzled by it in spite of themselves. Each felt that her beauty had in some degree suffered. Hence their battle-front (if we may be allowed the expression) was changed immediately, though not a single word passed between them. But they understood each other perfectly. The instincts of women comprehend and respond to each other more quickly than the understandings of men. An enemy had arrived in their midst; all felt it – all rallied. One drop of wine is sufficient to redden a whole glass of water: to tinge a whole company of pretty women with a certain degree of ill humour, it is only necessary for one still prettier to make her appearance – especially when there is but one man in the party.

Thus the gypsy-girl's reception proved mightily freezing. They eyed her from head to foot; then exchanged glances; and all was said – they understood each other. Meanwhile the young girl was waiting to be spoken to, in such emotion that she dared not raise her eyelids.

The captain was the first to break silence.

'Upon my word,' said he, with his tone of brainless assurance 'here is a charming creature! What think you of her, fair cousin?'

This remark, which a more delicate admirer would at least have made in an undertone, did not tend to dissipate the feminine jealousies which were on the alert in the presence of the gypsy-girl.

Fleur-de-Lys answered the captain with a simpering affectation of disdain – 'Not bad.'

The others whispered together.

At length, Madame Aloïse, who was not the less jealous because she was so for her daughter, addressed the dancer:

'Come hither, little one,' said she.

'Come hither, little one!' repeated, with comical dignity, little Bérangère, who would have stood about as high as her hip.

The gypsy advanced toward the noble dame.

'My pretty girl,' said Phœbus, with emphasis, taking several steps towards her, 'I do not know whether I have the supreme felicity of being recognized by you.'

She interrupted him with a look and smile of infinite sweetness.

'Oh! yes,' said she.

'She has a good memory,' observed Fleur-de-Lys.

'Well, now.' resumed Phœbus, 'you escaped nimbly the other evening. Did I frighten you?'

'Oh! no,' said the gypsy.

There was, in the intonation of that 'Oh! no,' uttered after that Oh! yes,' an ineffable something which wounded Fleur-de-Lys.

'You left me in your stead, my beauty,' continued the captain, whose tongue became unloosed while speaking to a girl from the streets, 'a rare grim-faced fellow, humpbacked and one-eyed, the ringer of the bishop's bells, I believe. They tell me he's an archdeacon's bastard and a devil by birth. He has a droll name too; they call him Quatre-Temps (Ember week), Pâques-Fleuries (Palm Sunday), Mardi-Gras (Shrove Tuesday), I don't know what! – the name of some bell-ringing festival, in short. And so he thought fit to carry you off, as if you were made for such fellows as beadles! That is going a little too far. What the deuce could that screechowl want with you? Hey, tell me!'

'I do not know,' she replied.

'What insolence! a bell-ringer to carry off a girl, like a viscount! a lout poaching on the game of gentlemen! a rare piece of assurance, truly! But he paid pretty dear for it. Maître Pierrat Torterue is as rough a groom as ever curried a rascal; and your ringer's hide – if that will please you – got a thorough dressing at his hands, I warrant you.'

'Poor man!' said the gypsy-girl – the scene of the pillory brought back to her remembrance by these words.

The captain burst out laughing. 'By the bull's horns! here's pity about as well placed as a feather in a pig's tail. May I have a belly like a pope, if . . .'

He stopped suddenly short. 'Pardon me, ladies – I fear I was about to let slip some nonsense or other.'

'Fie, monsieur!' said La Gaillefontaine.

'He speaks to this creature in her own language,' added Fleur-de-Lys in an undertone, her irritation increasing every moment. This irritation was not diminished by seeing the captain, delighted with the gypsy, and most of all with himself, turn round on his heel and repeat with coarse, naïve and soldierlike gallantry: 'A lovely girl, upon my soul!'

'Very barbarously dressed!' said Diane de Christeuil, with the smile which showed her fine teeth.

This remark was a flash of light to the others. It showed them the gypsy's assailable point; as they could not carp at her beauty, they fell foul of her dress.

'Very true,' said La Montmichel. 'Pray, little girl, where did you learn to run about the streets in that way, without either neckerchief or tucker?'

'That petticoat is so short that it makes one tremble!' added La Gaillefontaine.

'My dear, you will get yourself taken up by the sumptuary police for your gilded girdle,' continued Fleur-de-Lys, with decided sharpness.

'Little girl, little girl,' resumed Christeuil, with an implacable smile, 'if you had the decency to wear sleeves on your arms they would not get so sun-burned.'

It was a sight worthy a more intelligent spectator than Phœbus, to watch how these fair damsels, with their envenomed and angry tongues, twisted, glided and writhed, as it were, around the street dancer; they were at once cruel and graceful; they searched and pried maliciously into her poor silly toilet of spangles and tinsel. Then followed the laugh, the ironical jest, humiliations without end. Sarcasms, haughty condescensions, and evil looks rained down upon the gypsy-girl. One might have fancied them some of those young Roman ladies that used to amuse themselves with thrusting golden pins into the bosom of some beautiful slave or have likened them to elegant greyhounds, turning, wheeling with distended nostrils and eager eyes, around some poor hind of the forest which their master's eye prevents them from devouring.

After all, what was a poor dancing-girl of the public square to those high-born maidens? They seemed to take no heed of her presence; but spoke of her, before her, and to herself, aloud, as of something unclean, abject, and yet at the same time passably pretty.

The gypsy-girl was not insensible to these pin-pricks. From time to time, a glow of shame, or a flash of anger inflamed her eyes or her cheeks – a disdainful exclamation seemed to hover on her lips – she made contemptuously the little grimace with which the reader is already familiar – but remained motionless; she fixed on Phœbus a sad, sweet, resigned look. There was also happiness and tenderness in that gaze. It seemed as if she restrained herself for fear of being driven away.

Phœbus laughed and took the gypsy's part, with a mixture of pity and impertinence.

'Let them talk, little one,' repeated he, jingling his gold spurs 'doubtless, your dress is a little wild and extravagant; but in a charming girl like you, what does that signify?'

'Dear me!' exclaimed the blonde Gaillefontaine, drawing up her swan-like throat with a bitter smile, 'I see that messieurs the king's archers take fire easily at bright gypsy eyes.'

'And why not?' said Phœbus.

At this rejoinder, uttered carelessly by the captain, like a stray stone whose fall one does not even watch, Colombe began to laugh as well as Amelotte, Diane, and Fleur-de-Lys, into whose eyes a tear started at the same time.

The gypsy, who had dropped her eyes on the floor as Colombe and Gaillefontaine spoke, raised them beaming with joy and pride, and fixed them once more on Phœbus. She was very beautiful at that moment.

The old dame, who was watching this scene, felt offended without understanding why.

'Holy Virgin!' cried she suddenly, 'what's that about my legs? Ah! the villainous beast!'

It was the goat which had just arrived in search of its mistress, and which, in hurrying toward her, had entangled its horns in the load of drapery which the noble dame's garments heaped around her when she was seated.

This made a diversion. The gypsy disentangled its horns without saying a word.

'Oh! here's the little goat with golden hoofs,' cried Bérangère, jumping with joy.

The gypsy crouched upon her knees, and pressed her cheek against the caressing head of the goat. It seemed as if she were asking its pardon for having left it behind.

Meanwhile, Diane bent over and whispered in Colombe's ear:

'Ah! good heavens! how is it I did not think of it before? 'Tis the gypsy with the goat. They say she's a sorceress, and that her goat performs very marvellous tricks.'

'Well,' said Colombe, 'let the goat amuse us now in its turn, and perform us a miracle.'

Diane and Colombe eagerly addressed the gypsy: 'Little one, make your goat perform a miracle.'

'I do not know what you mean,' said the dancing-girl.

'Why, a miracle – a conjuring trick – a feat of witchcraft.'

'I do not understand.' And she turned to caressing the pretty animal again, repeating, 'Djali! Djali!'

At that moment Fleur-de-Lys noticed a little bag of embroidered leather hung round the goat's neck.

'What is that?' she asked of the gypsy.

The girl raised her large eyes toward her, and replied gravely, 'That is my secret.'

'I should like to know your secret,' thought Fleur-de-Lys.

Meanwhile, the good dame had risen angrily. 'Come, come, gypsy, if neither you nor your goat have anything to dance to us, what are you doing here?'

The gypsy directed her steps slowly toward the door without making any reply. But the nearer she approached it, the slower were her steps. An irresistible magnet seemed to retard her. Suddenly, she turned her eyes moistened with tears toward Phœbus, and stood still.

'Zounds!' cried the captain, 'you shall not go away thus. Come back and dance for us something. By-the-by, my beauty, what's your name?'

'Esmeralda,' said the dancer, without taking her eyes off him.

At this strange name the young women burst into an extravagant laugh.

'A formidable name indeed, for a girl,' said Diane.

'You see,' remarked Amelotte, 'that she's an enchantress.'

'My dear,' exclaimed Dame Aloïse, solemnly, 'your parents never fished that name for you out of the baptismal font.'

Meanwhile, Bérangère, without attracting attention, had, a few minutes before, enticed the goat into a corner of the room with a piece of nut-cake. In an instant they had become good friends; and the curious child had untied the little bag which hung at the goat's neck, had opened it, and spread the contents on the matting; it was an alphabet, each letter being inscribed separately on a small tablet of wood. No sooner were these toys displayed upon the matting, than the child saw, with surprise, the goat (one of whose miracles, doubtless, it was) select with her gilded hoof certain letters, and arrange them in a particular order by gently pushing them together. In a moment they formed a word which the goat seemed practised in composing, so slight was her hesitation; and Bérangère suddenly cried out, clasping her hands with admiration:

'Godmamma Fleur-de-Lys – do see what the goat has been doing!'

'Fleur-de-Lys hastened to look, and suddenly started. The letters arranged on the floor formed this word,

PHOEBUS

'Did the goat write that?' she asked, with a faltering voice.

'Yes, godmamma,' answered Bérangère.

It was impossible to doubt her; the child could not spell.

'Here's the secret!' thought Fleur-de-Lys.

Meanwhile, at the child's exclamation they had all hurried forward to look; the mother, the young ladies, the gypsy, and the officer.

The gypsy saw the blunder the goat had committed. She turned red – then pale – and began to tremble like a culprit before the captain, who regarded her with a smile of satisfaction and astonishment.

'*Phœbus*!' whispered the girls, in amazement, 'that's the captain's name!'

'You have a wonderful memory!' said Fleur-de-Lys to the stupefied gypsy. Then bursting into sobs: 'Oh!' stammered she tearfully, hiding her face between her two fair hands. 'she is a sorceress!' while she heard a voice yet more bitter whisper from her inmost heart, 'she is a rival!'

She fell fainting to the floor.

'My child! my child!' cried the terrified mother. 'Begone, you fiendish gypsy!

Esmeralda gathered together the unlucky letters in the twinkling of an eye, made a sign to Djali, and quitted the room at one door as Fleur-de-Lys was being carried out through the other.

Captain Phœbus, left alone, hesitated a moment between the two doors; then followed the gypsy.

II

Showing that a Priest and a Philosopher Are Different Persons

THE PRIEST WHOM the young ladies had observed on the top of the northern tower, leaning over toward the Square, and so attentive to the gypsy-girl's dancing, was, in fact, the Archdeacon Claude Frollo.

Our readers have not forgotten the mysterious cell which the archdeacon had appropriated to himself in this tower. (I do not know, let me observe by the way, whether it is the same cell, the interior of which may be seen to this day through a small square window, opening toward the east, at about the height of a man from the floor, upon the platform from which the towers spring, a mere hole, now naked, empty, and falling to decay; the ill-plastered walls of which are to-day *decorated* here and there with a parcel of sorry yellow engravings representing cathedral fronts. I presume that this hole is jointly inhabited by bats and spiders, and, consequently, a double war of extermination is carried on against the flies).

Every day, an hour before sunset, the archdeacon ascended the staircase of the tower and shut himself up in this cell, where he sometimes passed whole nights. On this day, just as he had reached the low door of his retreat, and was putting into the lock the complicated little key, which he always carried with him in the purse suspended at his side, the sound of a tambourine and castanets reached his ear. This sound proceeded from the Square in front of the cathedral. The cell, as we have already said, had but one window, looking upon the back of the church. Claude Frollo had hastily withdrawn the key, and in an instant was on the summit of the tower, in that gloomy, thoughtful attitude in which the young ladies had first seen him.

There he stood, grave, motionless, absorbed in one sight, one thought. All Parrs lay at his feet; with her thousand spires and her circular horizon of gently rolling hills; with her river winding under her bridges, and her people flowing to and fro through her streets: with the cloud of her smoke; with the mountainous chain of roofs pressing about Notre-Dame range upon range. But, in all that city, the archdeacon saw but one spot on its pavement, the Place du Parvis; in all that crowd, but one figure, that of the gypsy.

It would have been difficult to say what was the nature of that glance, or whence arose the flame that issued from it. It was a fixed gaze, but full of tumult and perturbation. And yet from the profound quiescence of his whole body, scarcely shaken now and then by an involuntary shiver, as a tree by the wind, from the rigidity of his arms, more marble-like than the balustrade on which they leaned; from the petrified smile which contracted his countenance, one might have said that no part of Claude Frollo was alive but his eyes.

The gypsy-girl was dancing, twirling her tambourine on the tip of her finger, and tossing it in the air as she danced Provencal sarabands; agile, light, joyous and unconscious of the formidable gaze which fell directly on her head.

The crowd swarmed around her, from time to time, a man tricked out in a red and yellow coat, went round to make them keep the ring; then returned, seated himself in a chair a few paces from the dancer, and took the goat's head on his knees. This man appeared to be the companion of the gypsy. Claude Frollo, from his elevated post, could not distinguish his features.

From the moment that the archdeacon perceived this stranger his attention seemed divided between the dancer and him, and his countenance became more and more sombre. All at once he started up, and a thrill shook his whole frame. 'Who can that man be?' he muttered between his teeth. 'Until now I have always seen her alone.'

He then plunged down under the winding vault of the spiral staircase, and once more descended. In passing the door of the belfry, which was ajar, he saw something which struck him; he beheld Quasimodo, who, leaning out of one of the apertures in those great slate eaves which resemble enormous blinds, was likewise gazing into the Square. He was so absorbed in profound contemplation that he was not aware of his adoptive father passing by. His wild eye had a singular expression; it was a charmed, tender look. 'Strange!' murmured Claude; 'can it be the Egyptian at whom he is thus looking?' He continued his descent. In a few minutes the moody archdeacon sallied forth into the Square by the door at the base of the tower.

'What has become of the gypsy?' said he, mingling with the group of spectators which the sound of the tambourine had collected.

'I know not,' answered one of those nearest him; 'she has but just disappeared. I think she is gone to dance some of her fandangos in the house opposite, whither they called her.'

In the place of the gypsy-girl, upon the same carpet whose arabesques but a moment before had seemed to vanish beneath the fantastic figures of her dance, the archdeacon saw no one but the red and yellow man, who, in order to earn a few testers in his turn, was parading around the circle, his elbows on his hips, his head thrown back, his face red, his neck outstretched, with a chair between his teeth. On this chair he had tied a cat, which a woman of the neighbourhood had lent him, and which was spitting in great affright.

'By Our Lady!' cried the archdeacon, just as the mountebank, perspiring heavily, passed in front of him with his pyramid of chair and cat; 'what does Maître Pierre Gringoire there?'

The harsh voice of the archdeacon threw the poor devil into such commotion that he lost his equilibrium, and down fell the whole edifice, chair and cat and all, pell-mell upon the heads of the bystanders in the midst of inextinguishable hootings.

It is probable that Maître Pierre Gringoire (for he indeed it was) would have had a sorry account to settle with the neighbour who owned the cat, and all the bruised and scratched faces around him, if he had not hastened to profit by the tumult to take refuge in the church, whither Claude Frollo had motioned to him to follow.

The cathedral was already dark and deserted; the transepts were full of shadows, and the lamps of the chapels twinkled like stars, so black had the arched roofs become. Only the great rose-window of the façade, whose thousand tints were steeped in a ray of horizontal sunlight, glistened in the dark like a cluster of diamonds, and threw its dazzling reflection to the other end of the nave.

When they had proceeded a few steps, Dom Claude leaned his back against a pillar and looked steadfastly at Gringoire. This look was not the one which Gringoire had dreaded, ashamed as he was at being surprised by so grave and learned a personage in that merry-andrew garb. There was nothing mocking or ironical in the priest's glance; it was serious, calm and searching. The archdeacon was the first to break silence.

'Come, now. Maître Pierre,' said he, 'you are to explain many things to me. And first of all, how comes it that you have not been seen these two months, and that now one finds you in the public squares, in rare guise, i' faith, half red, half yellow, like a Caudebee apple?'

'Messire,' said Gringoire, piteously, 'it is in sooth a monstrous garb, and behold me about as comfortable in it as a cat with a calabash clapped on her head. 'Tis wrong, I admit, to expose messieurs, the sergeants of the watch, to the liability of cudgelling, under this cassock, the shoulders of a Pythagorean philosopher. But what could I do, reverend master? 'Tis the fault of my ancient jerkin, which basely forsook me at the beginning of the winter, under the pretext that it was falling into tatters, and that it required repose in the basket of rag-picker. What was to be done? Civilization has not yet arrived at the point where one may go stark naked, as ancient Diogenes wished. Add to this, that the wind blew very cold, and the month of January is not the time that one can successfully attempt to make humanity take this new step. This garment offered itself – I took it, and left off my old black frock, which, for a hermetic like myself, was far from being hermetically closed. Behold me, then, in my buffoon's habit, like Saint Genest. What would you have? It's an eclipse. Apollo, you know, tended the swine of Admetus.'

' 'Tis a fine trade you've taken up,' replied the priest.

'I confess, my master, that it's better to philosophize and poetize – to blow the flame in the furnace, or receive it from heaven – than to wear cats as a coat-of-arms. So, when you addressed me, I felt as foolish as an ass before a roasting-jack. But what was to be done, messire? – one must eat every day; and the finest Alexandrine verses are not so toothsome as a piece of Brie cheese. Now, I composed for the Lady Margaret of Flanders, that famous epithalamium, as you know; and the town has not paid me for it, saying that it was not of the best – as though one could give a tragedy of Sophocles for four crowns. Hence, I was near dying of hunger. Happily, I found that I was rather strong in the jaw; so I said to this jaw: "Perform some feats of strength and equilibrium – find food for thyself – *Ale te ipsam*." A pack of vagabonds, who are become my good friends, taught me twenty different kinds of Herculean tricks; and now I give to my teeth every night the bread they have earned during the day by the sweat of my brow. After all, *concedo*, I grant that it is but a sorry employ of my intellectual faculties, and that man is not made to pass his life in playing the tambourine and biting chairs. But, reverend master, one must not only live, but also gain a livelihood.'

Dom Claude listened in silence. All at once his hollow eyes assumed an expression so sagacious and penetrating that Gringoire felt himself, so to speak, searched to the bottom of the soul by that look.

'Very good, Maître Pierre; but how comes it that you are now in company with that gypsy-dancer?'

'I'faith,' said Gringoire, ' 'tis because she is my wife and I am her husband.'

The dark eye of the priest flashed fire.

'And hast thou done that, miserable man?' he cried, seizing Gringoire's arm with fury; 'and hast thou been so abandoned by God as to lay thy hand upon that girl?'

'By my hope of Paradise, monseigneur,' answered Gringoire, trembling in every limb, 'I swear to you that I have never touched her – if that be what disturbs you.'

'But what speakest thou, then, of husband and wife?' said the priest.

Gringoire eagerly related to him, as succinctly as possible, what the reader already knows – his adventure of the Cour des Miracles, and his marriage by the broken jug. It appeared, moreover, that this marriage had led to no results whatever, and that each evening the gypsy-girl contrived to cheat him of his nuptials as she had done on the first night. ' 'Tis a mortification,' he said in conclusion; 'but that comes of my having had the misfortune to wed a virgin.'

'What mean you?' asked the archdeacon, whose agitation had gradually subsided.

' 'Tis rather difficult to explain,' answered the poet. ' 'Tis a superstition. My wife is, according to what an old thief, who is called among us the Duke of Egypt, has told me, a foundling – or a lostling, which is the same thing. She wears on her neck a amulet, which it is affirmed will some day cause her to find her parents again, but which would lose its virtue if the young maid were to lose hers. Hence it follows that both of us remain quite virtuous.'

'So,' resumed Claude, whose brow cleared more and more, 'you believe, Maître Pierre, that this creature has not been approached by any man?'

'What chance, Dom Claude, can a man have against a superstition? She has got that into her head. I assuredly esteem as a rarity this nun-like prudery which is preserved untamed amid those gypsy-girls, who are so easily brought into subjection. But she has three things to protect her: the Duke of Egypt, who has taken her under his safeguard, reckoning, perchance, that he shall sell her to some gay abbé; her whole tribe, who hold her in singular veneration, like an Our Lady; and a certain tiny poniard, which the sly minx always wears about her in spite of the provost's ordinances, and which darts forth in her hand when you but clasp her waist. 'Tis a fierce wasp, I can tell you.'

The archdeacon pressed Gringoire with questions.

La Esmeralda was, in Gringoire's opinion, an inoffensive, charming, pretty creature, with the exception of the pout peculiar to herself – an artless and warm-hearted girl, ignorant of every thing, and enthusiastic about everything, not yet aware of the difference between a man and a woman, even in her dreams; just simple like that; fond, above all things, of dancing, of bustle, of the open air – a sort of a woman bee, with invisible wings on her feet, and living in a perpetual whirl. She owed this disposition to the wandering life she had always led. Gringoire had contrived to ascertain that, while quite a child, she had traversed Spain and Catalonia to Sicily; he believed that she had even been taken by the caravan of Zingari, to which she belonged, to the kingdom of Algiers – a country situated in Achaia – which country adjoins on one side Lesser Albania and Greece, and on the other the Sicilian sea, which is the road to Constantinople. The gypsies, said Gringoire, were vassals to the King of Algiers, in his capacity of chief of the nation of the white Moors. Certain it was that La Esmeralda had come into France while yet very young, by way of Hungary. From all those countries the girl had brought with her fragments of fantastic jargons, foreign songs and ideas, which made her language as motley as her costume, half Parisian, half African. For the rest, the people of the quarters which she frequented loved her for her gaiety, her gracefulness, her lively ways, her dances and her songs. In all the town, she believed herself to be hated by two persons only, of whom she often spoke with dread: the Sachette of the Tour-Roland, a miserable recluse, who bore a secret grudge against gypsy-women, and who cursed the poor dancing-girl every time she passed before her loophole; and a priest who never met her without casting upon her looks and words that affrighted her. The mention of this latter circumstance disturbed the archdeacon greatly, though Gringoire scarcely noticed his perturbation; the two months that had elapsed having been quite sufficient to make the heedless poet forget the singular details of that night when he had first met with the gypsy-girl, and the presence of the archdeacon on that occasion. Otherwise the little dancer feared nothing. She did not tell fortunes, and so was secure from those prosecutions for magic that were so frequently instituted against the gypsy-women. And then, Gringoire was as a brother to her, if not as a husband. After all, the philosopher very patiently endured this kind of Platonic marriage. At any rate he was sure of food and lodging. Every morning he set out from the headquarters of the Truands, generally with the gypsy-girl; he assisted her in the crossways to gather her harvest of targes (an ancient

Burgundian coin) and petits-blancs (an ancient French coin). Every evening he returned with her under the same roof, let her bolt herself in her own little chamber, and slept the sleep of the just – a very agreeable existence on the whole, said he, and very favourable to reverie. And then, in his heart and conscience, the philosopher was not very sure that he was madly in love with the gypsy. He loved her goat almost as much. It was a charming, gentle, intelligent, clever animal; a learned goat. Nothing was more common in the Middle Ages than those learned animals which excited general wonder, and which frequently brought their instructors to the stake. However, the witch-craft of the goat with the gilded hoofs were very harmless tricks indeed. Gringoire explained them to the archdeacon, whom these particulars seemed to interest deeply. In most cases it was sufficient to present the tambourine to the goat in such or such a manner, in order to obtain from it the trick desired. It had been trained to that by the gypsy, who possessed, in these delicate arts, so rare a talent that two months had sufficed to teach the goat to write with movable letters the word 'Phœbus.'

'Phœbus!' said the priest. 'Why Phœbus?'

'I know not,' replied Gringoire; 'perhaps it is a word which she believes endowed with some magical and secret virtue. She often repeats it in an undertone when she thinks she is alone.'

'Are you sure,' rejoined Claude, with his penetrating look, 'that it is only a word and not a name?'

'Name of whom?' said the poet.

'How should I know?' said the priest.

'That is what I am thinking, messire; these gypsies are a sort of Guebres, and worship the sun – hence Phœbus.'

'That does not seem so clear to me as to you, Maître Pierre.'

'After all, that does not concern me. Let her mumble her Phœbus to her heart's content. One thing is certain. Djali loves me almost as much as she does her.'

'Who is this Djali?'

'The goat.'

The archdeacon dropped his chin into his hand and appeared to reflect for a moment. Then suddenly turning to Gringoire:

'And thou wilt swear that thou hast never touched her?'

'Who?' said Gringoire. 'The goat?'

'No – that woman.'

'My wife? I swear to you I have not.'

'And you are often alone with her?'

'Every evening for a good hour.'

Dom Claude knit his brows.

'Oh, ho! *Solus cum sola non cogitabuntur orare Pater Noster.*' (He alone with her [alone] will not think of saying paternosters.)

'Upon my soul, I might say the *Pater*, and the *Ave Maria*, and the *Credo in Deum patrem omnipotentem* (I believe in God the Father Almighty), without her taking any more notice of me than a hen does of a church.'

'Swear to me by thy mother's womb,' repeated the archdeacon violently, 'that thou hast not so much as touched that creature with the tip of thy finger.'

'I could also swear it by my father's head, for the two things have more than one affinity. But, my reverend master, permit me a question in my turn.'

'Speak, sir.'

'What concern is it of yours?'

The pale face of the archdeacon crimsoned like the cheek of a girl. He kept silence for a moment, then answered with visible embarrassment:

'Hearken, Maître Pierre Gringoire. You are not yet damned, so far as I know. I take an interest in you, and wish you well. Now, the least contact with this Egyptian child of the devil would make you a vassal of Satan. 'Tis the body, you know, which ruins the soul. Woe to you, if you approach that woman. That is all.'

'I tried once,' said Gringoire, scratching his ear; 'it was the first day, but I got stung.'

'You had that effrontery, Maître Pierre?'

And the priest's brow darkened again.

'Another time,' continued the poet, smiling. 'before I went to bed, I peeped through the keyhole, and I beheld the most delicious damsel in her shift that ever made a bed creak under her bare foot.'

'Get thee gone to the devil!' cried the priest, with a terrible look; and pushing the amazed Gringoire by the shoulders, he plunged with long strides beneath the darkest arches of the cathedral.

III

The Bells

SINCE HIS MORNING on the pillory, the inhabitants in the neighbourhood of Notre-Dame thought they noticed that Quasimodo's bellringing ardour had grown cool. Formerly the bells were going on all occasions – long matin chimes which lasted from primes to complines; peals from the belfry for high mass; rich scales running up and down the small bells for a wedding or a christening, and mingling in the air like a rich embroidery of all sorts of delightful sounds. The old church, vibrating and sonorous, was in a perpetual joyous whirl of bells. Some spirit of noise and caprice seemed to sing continuously through those mouths of brass. Now that spirit seemed to have departed. The cathedral seemed gloomy and wilfully silent. Festivals and funerals had the simple peal, bare and unadorned – what the ritual demanded, nothing more; of the double sound proceeding from a church, that of the organ within, and of the bells without, the organ alone remained. It seemed as if there was no longer any musician in the steeples. Quasimodo, nevertheless, was still there; what had happened to him, then? was it that the shame and despair of the pillory still rankled in his heart, that the lashes of his tormentor's whip reverberated unceasingly in his soul, and that his grief at such treatment had wholly extinguished in him even his passion for the bells? Or was it rather that Marie had a rival in the heart of the ringer of Notre-Dame, and that the big bell and her fourteen sisters were neglected for something more beautiful and pleasing?

It happened that in the year of Our Lord 1482, the Annunciation fell on Tuesday, the 25th of March. On that day the air was so pure and light that Quasimodo felt some returning affection for his bells. He therefore went up into the northern tower, while the beadle below threw wide open the doors of the church, which were then enormous panels of strong wood, covered with leather, bordered with nails of iron gilt, and framed in carvings 'most cunningly wrought.'

Having reached the high loft of the belfry, Quasimodo gazed for some time, with a sorrowful shake of the head, on his six songstresses, as if lamenting that some other object had intruded into his heart between them and him. But when he had set them in motion – when he felt that cluster of bells moving under his hand – when he saw, for he did not hear it, the palpitating octave ascend and descend that sonorous scale like a bird hopping from branch to branch – when the demon of music, that demon who shakes a glittering quiver of stretti, trills and arpeggios, had taken possession of the poor deaf creature, then he became happy once more; he forgot everything, and his heart expanding made his countenance radiant.

He went and came, he clapped his hands; he ran from rope to rope, he encouraged the six chimes with voice and gesture, as a leader of the orchestra spurs on intelligent musicians.

'Go on, Gabrielle,' said he, 'go on, pour forth all thy sound into the Square; 'tis a festival to-day. No laziness, Thibauld. What! thou'rt lagging! Get on with thee. Art grown rusty, lazybones? That is well! – quick! quick! – let not thy clapper be seen. Make them all deaf like me. Bravo! Thibauld. Guillaume! Guillaume, thou art the biggest, and Pasquier is the smallest, and Pasquier does best. I'll lay anything that those that can hear, hear him better than thee. Good! good! my Gabrielle – harder! harder! Hey! you there, The Sparrows, what are you both about? I don't see you make the least noise. What's the meaning of those brazen beaks of yours, that seem to be gaping when they ought to be singing? Come – work away! 'tis the Annunciation. The sun is fine, the chime must be fine also. Poor Guillaume – thou art quite out of breath, my big fellow!'

He was wholly absorbed in goading on his bells, which were all six leaping, each better than the other, and shaking their shining haunches like a noisy team of Spanish mules urged forward by the apostrophizings of the muleteer.

All at once, letting his glance fall between the large slate scales which cover, at a certain height, the perpendicular wall of the belfry, he descried on the Square a young girl fantastically dressed, who stopped, spread out on the ground a carpet on which a little goat came and placed itself, and around whom a group of spectators made a circle. This view suddenly changed the course of his ideas, and congealed his musical enthusiasm as a breath of air congeals melted rosin. He stopped, turned his back to the bells, and crouched behind the slate eaves, fixing on the dancer that thoughtful, tender and softened look which had already astonished the archdeacon on one occasion. Meanwhile, the forgotten bells died away abruptly and all together, to the great disappointment of the lovers of chimes who were listening to the peal in good earnest from off the Pont-au-Change, and who went away dumbfounded, like a dog who has been offered a bone and given a stone.

IV

'Ανάγκη *

IT CHANCED THAT UPON one fine morning in this same month of March – I think it was on Saturday, the 29th, St. Eustache's day – our young college friend, Jehan Frollo du Moulin, perceived, as he was dressing himself, that his breeches, which contained his purse, emitted no metallic sound. 'Poor purse!' said he, drawing it forth from his pocket. 'What! not one little parisis! How cruelly have dice, beer-pots and Venus depleted thee! Behold thee empty, wrinkled and limp! Thou art like the throat of a fury! I ask you, Messire Cicero and Messire Seneca, whose dog's-eared tomes I see scattered upon the floor, what profits it me to know better than a governor of the mint, or a Jew of the Pont-aux-Changeurs, that a gold écu stamped with the crown is worth thirty-five unzains at twenty-five sous eight deniers parisis each; and

* Doom

that an écu stamped with the crescent is worth thirty-six unzains at twenty-six sous six deniers tournois apiece, if I have not one miserable black liard to risk upon the double-six? Oh! Consul Cicero! this is not a calamity from which one extricates one's self with periphrases – by *quem-ad-modums* ('after-the-manner-in-whiches') and by *verum-enim-veros* ('but-indeeds').

He dressed himself sadly. A thought struck him as he was lacing his boots, but he at first rejected it; nevertheless, it returned, and he put on his waistcoat wrong side out, an evident sign of a violent internal struggle. At last he dashed his cap vehemently on the ground, and exclaimed: 'Be it so! come what may, I'll go to my brother. I shall catch a sermon, but I shall also catch a crown.'

He then hastily donned his fur-trimmed jacket, picked up his cap, and rushed out like a madman.

He turned down the Rue de la Harpe, in the direction of the City. Passing the Rue de la Huchette, the odour from those admirable spits, which were incessantly going, tickled his olfactories, and he cast an affectionate glance toward that cyclopean cookshop which one day drew from Calatagirone, the Franciscan, the pathetic exclamation: *Veramente, queste rotisserie sono cosa stupenda!* (Verily, these cook-shops be stupendous places!) But Jehan had not the wherewithal to buy a breakfast; and he plunged, with a profound sigh, under the gateway of the Petit-Châtelet, that huge, double trefoil of massive towers which guarded the entrance to the City.

He did not even take the time to throw a stone in passing, as it was then customary, at the wretched statue of that Perinet Leclerc who had given up the Paris of Charles VI to the English, a crime which his effigy, the face battered with stones and soiled with mud, expiated during three centuries, at the corner of the streets de la Harpe and de Bussy, as in a perpetual pillory.

Crossing the Petit-Pont, and striding down the Rue Neuve-Sainte-Geneviève, Jehan de Molendino found himself in front of Notre-Dame. Then all his indecision returned, and he walked about for some moments around the statue of M. Le Gris, repeating to himself with anguish, 'The sermon is sure, the crown piece is doubtful.'

He stopped a beadle who was coming from the cloisters – 'Where is monsieur the Archdeacon of Josas?'

'I believe he is in his cell in the tower,' said the beadle; 'and I would not advise you to disturb him there unless you come from some one like the pope or the king himself.'

Jehan clapped his hands.

'By Satan! here is a splendid opportunity for seeing the famous sorcery-box!'

Being brought to a decision by this reflection, he boldly entered through the little, dark doorway, and began to ascend the winding staircase of Saint Gilles, which leads to the upper stories of the tower. 'I shall see!' he said, as he proceeded. 'By the ravens of the Holy Virgin! it must needs be a curious thing, that cell which my reverend brother hides so secretly! 'Tis said that he lights up the kitchens of hell there, and cooks the philosopher's stone over the blaze. Egad! I care as little for the philosopher's stone as for a pebble; and I'd rather find an omelet of Easter eggs fried in lard on his oven than the biggest philosopher's stone in the world!'

Reaching the gallery of little columns, he stopped to breathe a moment, swearing against the interminable staircase by we know not how many million cart-loads of devils; he then continued his ascent by the narrow door of the northern tower, which is now closed to the public. Just after he had passed the cage of the bells he came upon a little landing-place, built in a lateral recess, and under the arch, a low pointed door; while a loophole opposite, in the circular wall of the staircase, enabled him to discern its enormous lock and strong iron bars. Persons desirous of visiting this door at the present time may recognize it by this inscription, in white letters, on the black wall: J'ADORE CORALIE. 1829. Signé, Ugène. (I adore Coralie. 1829. Signed, Ugène.) 'Signé ' is in the original.

'Whew!' said the scholar. ' 'Tis here, no doubt.'

The key was in the lock. The door was close to him; he pushed it gently, and put his head through the opening.

The reader has without doubt seen some of those admirable sketches by Rembrandt – that Shakespeare of painting. Among many marvellous engravings there is one especial etching which is supposed to represent Doctor Faustus, and at which it is impossible to look without being dazzled. It represents a gloomy cell, in the middle is a table, loaded with hideous objects – death's heads, spheres, alembics, compasses, hieroglyphic parchments. The doctor is at this table, clad in his coarse great-coat, and covered to the very eyebrows with his fur cap. Only half of his body is seen. He has half risen from his immense armchair, his clenched fists rest on the table, and he is gazing with curiosity and terror at a luminous circle, formed of magic letters, which gleams from the wall in the background like the solar spectrum in the camera obscura. This cabalistic sun seems to tremble before the eye, and fills the wan cell with its mysterious radiance. It is horrible and it is beautiful.

Something very similar to Faust's cell appeared to Jehan when he ventured to put his head in at the half-open door. It was a similar, gloomy, dimly-lighted retreat. There also was a large armchair and a large table; compasses; alembics; skeletons of animals suspended from the ceiling; a globe rolling on the floor; hippocephali pell-mell with glass jars in which quivered leaf gold; skulls placed on parchments scrawled over with figures and letters; thick manuscripts piled up, all open, without any pity for the cracking corners of the parchment; in short, all the rubbish of science; dust and cobwebs covering the whole heap; but there was no circle of luminous letters, no doctor in ecstasy, contemplating the flaming vision as the eagle gazes at the sun.

And yet the cell was not deserted. A man sat in the armchair, bending over the table. Jehan, to whom his back was turned, could only see his shoulders and the back of his head; but he had no difficulty in recognizing that bald head, which Nature had provided with an everlasting tonsure, as if wishing to mark, by this outward symbol, the archdeacon's irresistible clerical vocation.

Jehan accordingly recognized his brother; but the door had been opened so gently that Dom Claude was not aware of his presence. The inquisitive student availed himself of the opportunity to examine the cell for a few moments at his leisure. A large furnace, which he had not at first observed, was to the left of the armchair, beneath the dormer-window. The ray of light which penetrated through this aperture made its way through the circular web of a spider, which tastefully inscribed its delicate rose in the arch of the window, and in whose centre the insect architect hung motionless, like the nave of this lace wheel. On the furnace were heaped in disorder all sorts of vessels – earthenware flasks, glass retorts, coal mattresses. Jehan noticed with a sigh that there was not a single saucepan. 'The kitchen utensils are cold!' thought he.

In fact, there was no fire in the furnace, nor did it appear to have been lighted for a considerable time. A glass mask, which Jehan noted among the alchemist's tools, and doubtless used to protect the archdeacon's face when handling any dangerous substance, lay in a corner, covered with dust, and apparently forgotten. Beside it lay a pair of bellows, equally dusty, the upper side of which bore this motto encrusted in letters of copper – *Spira, spera!* (Blow, and hope!)

Other mottoes were, according to the custom of the hermetic philosophers, written on the walls in great number; some traced in ink, others engraved with a metallic point. There were, moreover, Gothic, Hebrew, Greek and Roman characters, pell-mell together; inscriptions overflowing at random, one upon the other, the newest effacing the oldest, and all entangled together like the branches in a thicket, or pikes in an affray. It was, in fact, a confused medley of all human philosophy, thought and knowledge. Here and there one shone out above the rest like a banner amid the spear-heads. Generally, it was some brief Latin or Greek device, such as the Middle Ages knew so well how to formulate: *Unde? Inde?* (Whence? Thence?) *Homo homini monstrum!* (Man a marvel to man.) *Astra, castra, nomen, numen.* (Thy stars, my camp thy name, my power.) Μέγα βιβλίον μέγα κακόυ (A great book, a great evil.) *Sapere aude.* (Dare to know.) *Fiat ubi vult.* (It bloweth whither it listeth.) Etc. Sometimes a word apparently devoid of all meaning, as Ἀναγκοφαγία (Hard fare) – which perhaps concealed some bitter allusion to the monastic system; sometimes a simple maxim of clerical discipline, set forth in a regular hexameter:

Cælestem dominum, terrestrem dicito domnum.

There were also Hebrew hieroglyphics, of which Jehan, who as yet knew even little Greek, understood nothing; and the whole was crossed in all directions with stars, figures of men or animals and triangles intersecting each other; which contributed in no small degree to liken the daubed wall of the cell to a sheet of paper over which a monkey has been dragging about a penful of ink.

The general appearance of the cell, in short, was one of neglect and ruin; and the sorry condition of the utensils led to the conjecture that their owner had for some time been distracted from his labours by other cares.

This master, however, bending over a vast manuscript, adorned with singular paintings, seemed tormented with a thought which mingled constantly with his meditations. At least, so Jehan judged from hearing him exclaim, with the pensive pauses of a dreamer, who thinks aloud:

'Yes; so Manou asserted and Zoroaster taught! the sun is born of fire; the moon of the sun. Fire is the soul of the universe; its elementary atoms are diffused and in constant flow throughout the world, by an infinite number of channels. At the points where these currents cross each other in the heavens they produce light; at their points of intersection in the earth they produce gold. Light – gold; the same thing. From fire to the concrete state. The difference between the visible and the palpable, the fluid and the solid, in the same substance – between steam and ice – nothing more. These are not mere dreams; it is the general law of Nature. But how are we to wrest from science the secret of this general law? Why! this light which bathes my hand is gold! these same atoms expanded in harmony with a certain law only require to be condensed in accordance with a certain other law! And how? Some have thought it was by burning a sunbeam. Averroës – yes it was Averroës – Averroës interred one under the first column to the left in the sanctuary of the Koran, in the great mosque of Cordova; but the vault may not be opened, to see if the operation be successful, until eight thousand years have passed.'

'The devil!' said Jehan to himself, 'here's a long while to wait for a crown.'

'Others have thought,' continued the archdeacon, musing, 'that it would be better to operate upon a ray of Sirius. But it is difficult to obtain one of his rays pure, because of the simultaneous presence of other stars, whose rays mingle with it. Flamel esteemed it more simple to operate upon terrestrial fire. Flamel! there's predestination in the name! *Flamma!* – Yes, fire. That is all. The diamond is in charcoal; gold is in fire. But how to extract it? Magistri affirms that there are certain feminine names which possess a charm so sweet and mysterious that it suffices to pronounce them during the operation. Let us read what Manou says on the matter: "Where women are honoured, the divinities rejoice; where they are despised, it is useless to pray to God. A woman's mouth is ever pure; it is like running water, like a sunbeam. A woman's name should be pleasing, soft and fanciful, should end with a long vowel, and resemble words of benediction." Yes, the sage is right; in truth. Maria – Sophia – Esmeral . . . Damnation! Again that thought.'

And he closed the book with violence.

He passed his hand across his brow, as if to drive away the idea which possessed him; then he took from the table a nail and a small hammer, the handle of which was curiously painted in cabalistic characters.

'For some time,' said he, with a bitter smile, 'I have failed in all my experiments; one idea possesses me, and sears my brain like a red-hot iron. I have not even been able to discover the secret of Cassiodoros, whose lamp burned without wick or oil – and yet a simple matter.'

'A plague upon it!' said Jehan through his teeth.

'A single wretched thought, then,' continued the priest, 'is enough to make a man weak or mad! Oh! how Claude Pernelle would laugh at me – she who could not for a moment turn aside Nicolas Flamel from his pursuit of the great work! What! I hold in my hand the magic hammer of Ezekiel! At every blow which the formidable rabbi, from the depths of his cell, struck upon this nail with this hammer, that one of his enemies whom he had condemned, were he two thousand leagues off, sank a cubit's depth into the earth, which swallowed him up. The king of France himself, in consequence of having one evening inconsiderately knocked at the door of the thaumaturgus, sank up to the knees in the pavement of his own city of Paris. This happened three centuries ago. Well! I have the hammer and the nail, and yet these implements are no more formidable in my hands than a club in the hands of a maker of edged tools. And yet it is only necessary to discover the magic word which Ezekiel pronounced as he struck upon the nail.'

'Nonsense!' thought Jehan.

'Come, let us try,' resumed the archdeacon, eagerly. 'If I succeed, I shall behold a blue spark flash from the head of the nail. *Emen-hetan! Emen-hetan!* That's not it. *Sigeani! Sigeani!* May this nail open the grave for whosoever bears the name of Phœbus! . . . A curse upon it! still, again, eternally the same idea!'

And he flung the hammer from him angrily. Then he sank so deep into his armchair and over the table that Jehan lost sight of him behind the high back of the chair. For some moments he saw nothing but his fist convulsively clenched upon a book. All at once, Dom Claude arose, took a pair of compasses, and silently engraved upon the wall, in capital letters, this Greek word:

ΑΝΑΓΚΗ

'My brother is mad,' said Jehan to himself; 'it would have been much simpler to have written *Fatum* – every one is not obliged to know Greek.'

The archdeacon resumed his seat in his armchair, and leaned his head on both his hands, like a sick man whose brow is heavy and burning.

The student watched his brother in surprise. He, who carried his heart in his hand, who observed no other law in the world but the good old law of Nature, who allowed his passions to flow according to their natural tendency, and in whom the lake of powerful emotions was always dry, so assiduous was he every morning in making new channels to drain it – he knew not how furiously the sea of the human passions ferments and boils when all egress is denied to it, how it accumulates, how it swells, how it overflows, how it hollows out the heart, how it breaks forth in repressed sobs and stifled convulsions, until it has rent its dykes and burst its bed. The austere and icy exterior of Claude Frollo, that cold surface of rugged and inaccessible virtue, had always misled Jehan. The jovial student had never dreamt of the lava, deep and furious, which boils beneath the snowy crest of Ætna.

We know not whether any sudden perception of this kind crossed his mind; but, feather-brain though he was, he understood that he had seen what he ought not to have seen, that he had surprised the soul of his elder brother in one of its most secret attitudes – and that he must not let Claude perceive it. Seeing that the archdeacon had relapsed into his former immobility, he withdrew his head very softly, and made some noise with his feet outside the door, like some one just arriving and giving notice of his approach.

'Come in,' cried the archdeacon from the interior of his cell. 'I was expecting you; I left the key in the door purposely; come in, Maître Jacques.'

The student entered boldly. The archdeacon, much annoyed by such a visit in such a place, started in his chair. 'What! is it you, Jehan?'

' 'Tis a J, at any rate,' said the student, with his ruddy, merry and impudent face.

The countenance of Dom Claude resumed its usual, severe expression.

'What brings you hither?'

'Brother,' replied the student, endeavouring to assume a decent, serious and modest demeanour, twirling his cap in his hands with an air of innocence, 'I am come to ask of you –'

'What?'

'A little moral lecture, of which I have great need.' Jehan dared not add aloud, 'and a little money, of which I have still greater need.' This last part of his sentence remained unuttered.

'Sir,' said the archdeacon in a cold tone, 'I am greatly displeased with you.'

'Alas!' sighed the student.

Dom Claude turned half around in his chair and looked steadily at Jehan: 'I am very glad to see you.'

This was a formidable exordium. Jehan prepared for a rough encounter.

'Jehan, I hear complaints of you every day. What affray was that in which you beat with a cudgel a certain little viscount, Albert de Ramonchamp?'

'Oh!' said Jehan; 'a vast thing that! a scurvy page amused himself with splashing the students by making his horse gallop through the mire.'

'How about that Mahiet Fargel, whose gown you tore? *Tunicam dechiraverunt*, (They have torn the robe,) saith the complaint.'

'Pshaw! a sorry Montaigu hood! that's all.'

'The accusation says *tunicam* – not *cappettam*. Do you know Latin?'

Jehan made no answer.

'Yes,' continued the priest, shaking his head, 'this is what study and letters are come to now! The Latin tongue is scarcely understood; the Syriac unknown; the Greek so odious that it is not considered ignorance in the most learned to skip a Greek word without reading it, and to say: *Græcum est, non legitur.*' (It is Greek, it is not read.)

The student raised his eyes boldly. 'Monsieur my brother, doth it please you that I shall explain in good French vernacular that Greek word which is written yonder on the wall?'

'What word?'

' 'Ανάγκη.'

A slight flush spread over the high cheekbones of the archdeacon, like the puff of smoke announcing externally the secret commotions of a volcano. The student hardly noticed it.

'Well, Jehan,' stammered the elder brother, with an effort, 'what is the meaning of yonder word?'

'FATE.'

Dom Claude turned pale again, and the student pursued :

'And that word below it, graven by the same hand, 'Αναγνεία, signifies impurity. You see I know my Greek.'

The archdeacon remained silent. This Greek lesson had set him musing.

Master Jehan, who had all the cunning of a spoiled child, judged the moment a favourable one to venture his request. Assuming, therefore, a particularly soft tone, he began:

'My dear brother, do you hate me so, then, as to look grim at me on account of a few paltry cuffs and blows dealt, in fair fight, amongst a pack of boys and marmosets, *quibusdam marmosetis?* You see I know my Latin, brother Claude.'

But all this fawning hypocrisy had not its accustomed effect on the severe elder brother. Cerberus did not bite at the honey-cake. The archdeacon's brow did not lose a single wrinkle.

'What are you driving at?' said he, dryly.

'Well, in point of fact, this,' answered Jehan, bravely, 'I need money.'

At this bold declaration the archdeacon's face assumed quite a pedagogic and paternal expression:

'You know, Master Jehan, that our fief of Tirechappe only brings in, including both the quit-rents and the rents of the twenty-one houses, thirty-nine pounds eleven pence six Paris farthings. It's half as much again as in the time of the brothers Paclet; but it is not much.'

'I need money,' said Jehan, stoically.

'You know that the official decided that our twenty-one were held in full fee of the bishopric, and that we could only redeem this homage by paying to his reverence the bishop two marks of silver gilt, at six Paris pounds each. Now these two marks I have not yet been able to get together. You know it.'

'I know that I need money,' repeated Jehan, for the third time.

'And what would you do with it?'

This question caused a flash of hope to gleam before Jehan's eyes. He resumed his demure, caressing manner.

'Hark you, dear brother Claude – I would not come to you with any evil intention. It is not to cut a dash in the taverns with your money, or to parade the streets of Paris in gold brocade trappings, with my lackeys – *cum meo laquasio*. No, brother; 'tis for a good work.'

'What good work?' asked Claude, somewhat surprised.

'Two of my friends wish to purchase an outfit for the infant of a poor Haudriette widow – it is a charity – it will cost three florins, and I should like to contribute my share.'

'What are the names of your two friends?'

'Pierre l'Assommeur and Baptiste Croque-Oison.' (Peter the Slaughterer and Baptist Crack-Gosling.)

'Humph!' said the archdeacon; 'those are names as fit for a good work as a catapult for the high altar.'

It is certain that Jehan had chosen very badly the names of his two friends. He realized it too late.

'And then,' continued the shrewd Claude, 'what sort of an infant's outfit is it that is to cost three florins, and that for the child of a Haudriette? Since when have the Haudriette widows taken to having brats in swaddling-clothes?'

Jehan broke the ice once more. – 'Well, then, I want some money to go and see Isabeau la Thierrye, to-night, at the Val d'Amour.'

'Impure wretch!' exclaimed the priest.

' 'Αναγνεια!' (Impurity!) said Jehan.

This quotation, which the student borrowed, perhaps mischievously, from the wall of the cell, had a singular effect upon the priest. He bit his lip, and his wrath was extinguished in a crimson flush.

'Begone!' said he to Jehan; 'I am expecting some one.'

The scholar made one more effort.

'Brother Claude, give me, at least, one little farthing for something to eat.'

'How far have you got in the decretals of Gratian?' asked Dom Claude.

'I've lost my copy-books.'

'Where are you in the Latin humanities?'

'Somebody has stolen my copy of Horatius.'

'Where are you in Aristotle?'

'I' faith, brother, what father of the Church is it who says the errors of heretics have ever found shelter amid the thickets of Aristotle's metaphysics? A fig for Aristotle! I'll never mangle my religion with his metaphysics.'

'Young man,' continued the archdeacon, 'at the king's last entry there was a gentleman, named Philippe de Comines, who wore embroidered on the housings of his horse this device, upon which I counsel you to meditate: *Qui non laborat non manducet.*' (He who labours not eats not.)

The student remained silent a moment his finger in his ear, his eyes bent on the ground, and an angry countenance.

All at once he turned toward Claude with the brisk motion of a water-wagtail.

'So, good brother, you refuse to give me a penny to buy me a crust at the baker's?'

'*Qui non laborat non manducet.*'

At this answer of the inflexible archdeacon, Jehan hid his head between his hands, like a woman sobbing, and exclaimed, with an expression of despair ' 'Ο τοτοτοτοτοι!' (An exclamation indicative of despair.)

'What does all this mean, sir?' asked Claude, amazed at this outburst.

'What, indeed?' said the student, and he looked up at Claude with impudent eyes, into which he had been rubbing his fists, to make them look as if they were red with tears; 'it is Greek – 'tis an anapest of Æschylus which expresses grief perfectly.'

And here he burst into a laugh, so droll and so ungovernable that the archdeacon could not help smiling. It was in fact Claude's fault: why had he so spoiled this boy?

'Oh, good brother Claude,' continued Jehan, emboldened by this smile, 'see now my broken buskins. Can any tragedy in the world be more pathetic than boots whose soles are hanging out their tongues?'

The archdeacon had quickly resumed his former sternness. 'I will send you new boots, but no money.'

'Only one poor little penny, brother,' persisted the supplicant Jehan. 'I'll learn Gratian by heart – I'll believe well in God – I'll be a perfect Pythagoras of science and virtue! Only one little penny, for pity's sake! Would you have me devoured by famine whose jaws are gaping before me, blacker, deeper and more noisome than Tartarus or than a monk's nose?'

Dom Claude shook his wrinkled head – 'Qui non laborat . . .'

Jehan did not let him finish.

'Well, then,' cried he, 'to the devil! Now for a joyous time! I'll go to the tavern – I'll fight – I'll break pots, and go and see the wenches!'

Thereupon he hurled his cap at the wall, and snapped his fingers like castanets.

The archdeacon eyed him with gloomy look.

'Jehan, you have no soul.'

'In that case, according to Epicurus, I lack a something, made of another something, which has no name.'

'Jehan, you must think seriously of reform.'

'Oh, come now,' cried the student, looking alternately at his brother and at the alembics on the furnace, 'everything's atwist here; I see – ideas as well as bottles.'

'Jehan, you are on a very slippery, downward path; know you whither you are going?'

'To the tavern,' said Jehan.

'The tavern leads to the pillory.'

' 'Tis a lantern like any other, and 'twas perhaps the one with which Diogenes found his man.'

'The pillory leads to the gallows.'

'The gallows is a balance which has a man at one end and the whole world at the other. 'Tis fine to be the man.'

'The gallows leads to hell.'

'That's a rousing fire.'

'Jehan, Jehan! The end will be bad.'

' 'Twill have had a good beginning.'

At this moment the sound of a footfall was heard on the stairs.'

'Silence!' said the archdeacon, putting his finger to his lip; 'here is Maître Jacques. Hark you, Jehan,' added he, in a low tone, 'beware of ever speaking of what you have seen and heard here. Hide yourself quickly under this furnace, and do not breathe.'

The student crept under the furnace, and there a happy thought struck him.

'By the way, brother Claude – a florin for not breathing!'

'Silence! I promise it.'

'You must give it to me.'

'Take it, then!' said the archdeacon, throwing him his pouch angrily. Jehan crept under the furnace again, and the door opened.

V

The Two Men in Black

THE PERSONAGE WHO ENTERED wore a black gown and a gloomy mien. What, at the first glance, struck our friend Jehan (who, as may well be supposed, so placed himself in his corner as to be able to see and hear everything at his good pleasure) was the perfect sadness of the garb and the countenance of this newcomer. A certain meekness at the same time overspread that face; but it was the meekness of a cat, or of a judge – a sort of affected gentleness. He was very gray and wrinkled, bordering on sixty; his eyes blinked, his eyebrows were white, his lip pendulous and his hands large. When Jehan saw that it was nobody – that is, probably, only a physician or a magistrate – and that this man's nose was at a great distance from his mouth, a sign of stupidity, he ensconced himself in his hole, in despair at having to pass an indefinite length of time in such an uncomfortable position, and in such poor company.

The archdeacon, meanwhile, had not even risen to receive this person. He motioned to him to be seated on a stool near the door and after a few moments' silence, during which he seemed to be pursuing a previous meditation, he said, to him in a somewhat patronizing tone, 'Good-day, Maître Jacques.'

'Greeting, Maître,' replied the man in black.

In the two ways of pronouncing, on the one hand, this *Maître Jacques*, and, on the other, this *maître* by itself, the difference being my lord and sir, between *domine* (sir) and *domne* (sire). It clearly bespoke the teacher and the disciple.

'Well,' resumed the archdeacon, after another silence, which Maître Jacques took good care not to break, 'are you succeeding?'

'Alas! maître,' said the other with a sorrowful smile; 'I keep on blowing. Plenty of ashes, but not a spark of gold.'

Dom Claude made a gesture of impatience.

'I was not talking of that, Maître Jacques Charmolue, but of the trial of your magician – is it not Marc Cenaine that you call him? – the butler of the Court of Accounts? Does he confess his sorcery? Have you been successful with the torture?'

'Alas, no!' replied Maître Jacques, still with his sad smile, 'we have not that consolation. That man is a stone; we might boil him at the Pig-market before he would say anything. However, we spare no pains to get at the truth. He has already every joint dislocated. We are trying everything we can think of, as saith the old comic writer Plautus:

> *Adversum stimulos, laminas, crucesque, compedesque,*
> *Nervos, catenas, carceres, numellas, pedicas, boias.* *

But all to no purpose – that man is terrible; I lose my labour with him.'

'You have found nothing further in his house?'

'I'faith, yes,' said Maître Jacques, fumbling in his pouch; 'this parchment. There are words in it which we do not understand. Monsieur the criminal advocate, Philippe Lheuiler, knows, however, a little Hebrew, which he learned in that affair of the Jews of the Kantersten Street, at Brussels.'

So saying, Maître Jacques unrolled a parchment.

'Give it here,' said the archdeacon. And casting his eyes over the scroll, 'Pure magic, Maître Jacques!' cried he. '*Emenhetan!* that is the cry of the witches as they appear at their Sabbath. *Per ipsum, et cum ipso, et in ipso!* (Through Him, and with Him, and in Him!) that is the command which chains the devil down in hell again. *Hax, pax, max!* that has to do with medicine. A spell against the bite of mad dogs. Maître Jacques! you are king's attorney in the ecclesiastical court – this parchment is abominable.'

'We will put the man to the torture again. Here again,' added Maître Jacques rummaging again in his bag, 'is something we found at Marc Cenaine's.'

It was a vessel belonging to the same family as those which covered the furnace of Dom Claude. 'Ah!' said the archdeacon, 'a crucible for alchemy!'

'I confess to you,' replied Maître Jacques, with his timid and

* Against the whips, the searing-irons, and the crosses and the fetters,
The cords, the chains. the prisons, the stocks, the shackles, the collars.

constrained smile, 'that I have tried it over the furnace; but I have succeeded no better with it than with my own.'

The archdeacon set about examining the vessel. 'What has he engraved on his crucible? – *Och! och!* – the word to drive away fleas! This Marc Cenaine is an ignoramus. I can easily believe you will not make gold with this! it will do to put in your alcove in the summer, and that is all.'

'Since we are talking of errors,' said the king's attorney, 'I have just been studying the figures on the portal below, before ascending, hither. Is your reverence quite sure that the opening of the work of physics is there portrayed on the side toward the Hotel-Dieu, and that, among the seven nude figures at the feet of Our Lady, that which has wings on his heels is Mercurius?'

'Yes,' replied the priest; ' 'Tis Augustin Nypho who writes it, that Italian doctor who had a bearded demon that acquainted him with all things. But we will go down, and I will explain to you from the text.'

'Thanks, my maître,' said Charmolue, bowing to the ground. 'By-the-way, I was on the point of forgetting! When doth it please you that I shall apprehend the little sorceress?'

'What sorceress?'

'That gypsy-girl, you know, who comes and dances every day on the Parvis, in spite of the official's prohibition. She has a goat with devil's horns, which is possessed; it reads and writes, understands mathematics like Picatrix, and would suffice to hang all Bohemia. The prosecution is all ready; 'twill soon be got through with. A pretty creature, I warrant on my soul, that dancer – the handsomest black eyes! – two Egyptian carbuncles! When shall we begin?'

The archdeacon was excessively pale.

'I will let you know,' he stammered, in a voice scarcely articulate; then he resumed with an effort, 'Look you to Marc Cenaine.'

'Never fear,' said Charmolue, smiling; 'when I get back I'll have him buckled on the bed of leather again. But he's a devil of a man – he wearies Pierrat Torterue himself, who hath hands larger than my own. As the excellent Plautus saith –

Nudus vinctus, centum pondo, es quando pennes perpedes.' *

'The torture of the wheel! That is the best we have; he shall take a turn at that.'

Dom Claude seemed absorbed in gloomy reverie. He turned toward Charmolue.

'Maître Pierrat . . . Maître Jacques, I mean – look to Marc Cenaine.'

* Bound naked, thou art a hundred weight when thou hangest by the feet.

'Yes, yes, Dom Claude. Poor man! he will have suffered like Mummol. But what an idea! a butler of the Court of Accounts, who must know the text of Charlemagne, *Stryga vel masca*, (Witch or vampire,) to attend the witches' sabbath. As for the girl – 'Smeralda, as they call her – I will await your orders. Ah! as we go through the portal, you will explain to me the gardener painted in fresco, that one sees on entering the church – the Sower, is it not? Eh, maître, what are you thinking about?'

Dom Claude, plunged in his own thoughts, heard him no longer. Charmolue, following the direction of his eye, saw that it was fixed mechanically on the large spider's web stretched across the small window. At this moment, a giddy fly, attracted by the March sun, flew into this net and became entangled in it. Upon the vibration of the web, the enormous spider made a sudden rush from his central cell; then at one bound sprang upon the fly, which he bent double with his fore-antennæ, while with his hideous proboscis he scooped out its head. 'Poor fly!' said the king's attorney of the ecclesiastical court; and he raised his hand to save it. The archdeacon, as if starting out of sleep, held back his arm with convulsive violence.

'Maître Jacques,' cried he, 'meddle not with fate!'

The king's procurator turned in alarm. It seemed as if his arm were held by iron pincers. The eye of the priest was fixed, haggard, wild, and remained glaring on the horrible little group of the spider and the fly.

'Oh! yes,' continued the priest, in a voice which seemed to issue from his very bowels; 'there is the universal symbol! She flies – she is joyous – she emerges into life – she courts the spring, the open air, liberty! Oh! yes, but she strikes against the fatal network – the spider issues from it, the hideous spider! Poor dancer! poor predestined fly! Maître Jacques, I do not interfere! 'tis fate! Alas! Claude, thou art the spider! Claude, thou art also the fly! Thou didst hasten on in search of knowledge, of light, of the sun. Thy only thought was to reach the pure air, the broad day of eternal truth; but, in rushing toward the dazzling loophole which opens upon another world – a world of brightness, of intellect, of science – infatuated fly! insensate sage! thou didst not see the subtle web suspended by destiny between the light and thee. Thou didst madly dash thyself against it, wretched maniac – and now thou dost struggle, with crushed head and mangled wings, between the iron antennæ of fate! Maître Jacques, Maître Jacques, let the spider do its work!'

'I assure you,' said Charmolue, who looked at him without comprehending, 'that I will not touch it. But let go my arm, Maître, for mercy's sake! you have a hand like a vice.'

The archdeacon heard him not. 'Oh! fool!' continued he, without taking his eyes off the window. 'And even couldst thou have broken through that formidable web, with thy frail wings, thoughtest thou to have attained the light? Alas! that glass beyond – that transparent obstacle – that wall of crystal harder than brass, which separates all philosophy from the truth – how couldst thou have passed beyond it? Oh! vanity of science! how many sages have come fluttering from afar, to dash their heads against it! How many systems come buzzing to rush pell-mell against this eternal window!'

He was silent. These last ideas, which had insensibly brought back his thoughts from himself to science, appeared to have calmed him. Jacques Charmolue brought him back completely to a sense of reality by addressing to him this question: 'Come now, my maître, when will you come and help me to make gold? I long to succeed.'

The archdeacon shook his head with a bitter smile. 'Maître Jacques, read Michael Psellus, *Dialogus de energiâ et operatione dæmonum*. (Dialogue – philosophical – on the power and agency of evil spirits). What we are doing is not altogether innocent.'

'Speak lower, maître! I fear you are right,' said Charmolue.

'But one must practise a little hermetic philosophy when one is but a poor king's attorney of the ecclesiastical court, at thirty crowns tournois a year. Only, let us speak low.'

At that moment the noise of jaws in the act of mastication proceeding from under the furnace, struck upon the anxious ear of Charmolue.

'What is that?' he asked.

It was the student, who, very cramped and uneasy in his hiding place, had managed to discover a stale crust and a corner of mouldy cheese, and had begun to eat, without further ceremony, by way of consolation and breakfast. As he was very hungry, he made a great noise, laying strong emphasis on each mouthful, and this it was that had startled and alarmed the king's attorney.

' 'Tis a cat of mine,' said the archdeacon, quickly, 'regaling herself under there with a mouse.'

This explanation satisfied Charmolue.

'Why, indeed, maître,' answered he, with a respectful smile 'every great philosopher has his familiar animal. You know what Servius says *Nullus enim locus sine genio est.*' (For there is no place without its genius.)

Meanwhile Dom Claude fearing some new prank of Jehan reminded his worthy disciple that they had some figures on the portal to study together; and they both quitted the cell, with an exclamation from the student who began seriously to fear that his knees would bear the mark of his chin.

VI

The Effect which Seven Oaths Produce in the Open Air

'*Te Deum laudamus!*' (We praise thee, O God!) exclaimed Master Jehan, issuing from his hole, 'the two screech-owls are gone at last. *Och! och! – Hax!, vax! max!* – fleas! mad dogs! the devil! I've had enough of their conversation! My head rings like a belfry. Mouldy cheese into the bargain! Whew! let me get down and take the big brother's purse to convert all those coins into bottles.'

He cast a glance of tenderness and admiration into the precious pouch; adjusted his dress; rubbed up his boots; dusted his poor furred sleeves, all gray with ashes; whistled an air; cut a caper; looked around to see if there was anything else in the cell that he could take; scraped up here and there from the furnace some amulet of glassware by way of trinket to give to Isabeau la Thierrye; finally pushed open the door which his brother had left unfastened as a last indulgence, and which he in turn left open as a last piece of mischief; and descended the winding stairs, skipping like a bird.

In the midst of the darkness of the spiral way he elbowed something which drew aside with a growl. He presumed that it was Quasimodo, and it struck him as so droll that he descended the rest of the stairs holding his sides with laughter, and was still laughing when he got out into the Square.

He stamped his foot when he found himself again on the ground. 'Oh!' said he, 'good and honourable pavement of Paris! Cursed stairs, fit to put the angels of Jacob's ladder out of breath! What was I thinking of to thrust myself into that stone gimlet which pierces the sky, and all to eat bearded cheese and to look at the steeples of Paris through a hole in the wall!'

He advanced a few steps, and caught sight of the two screech-owls, that is to say, Dom Claude and Maître Jacques Charmolue, contemplating one of the carvings on the portal. He approached them on tiptoe, and heard the archdeacon say in a whisper to Charmolue: 'It was William of Paris who had a Job engraven on that stone of the hue of lapis-lazuli, gilded on the edges. Job represents the philosopher's stone, which must be tried and tortured in order to become perfect, as saith Raymon Lulle – *Sub conservatione formæ specificæ salva anima.*' (Under the preservation of a specific form save your souls.)

'That is all one to me,' said Jehan; ' 'Tis I who have the purse.'

At that moment he heard a powerful and sonorous voice behind him pour forth a formidable volley of oaths: – '*Sang-Dieu! Ventre-Dieu!*

Bé-Dieu! Corps de Dieu! Nombril de Belzébuth! Nom d'un pape! Corne et tonnère!' (By the blood of God! by the belly of God! by God! by the body of God! by the belly of Beelzebub! by the name of the pope! horns and thunder!)

'My life for it,' exclaimed Jehan; 'that can be none other than my friend Captain Phœbus.'

This name of Phœbus reached the ears of the archdeacon just as he was explaining to the king's attorney the dragon hiding his tail in a bath from whence issued smoke and a king's head. Dom Claude started, stopped short, to the great astonishment of Charmolue, turned round, and saw his brother Jehan accosting a tall officer at the door of the Condelaurier mansion.

It was, in fact, Captain Phœbus de Chateaupers. He was leaning against the corner of the house of his betrothed, and swearing like a Turk.

'By my faith, Captain Phœbus,' said Jehan, grasping his hand, 'you swear with a rare fancy.'

'Blood and thunder!' replied the captain.

'Blood and thunder yourself!' rejoined the student. 'How now gentle captain? Whence comes this overflow of fine phrases?'

'Pardon me, good comrade Jehan,' cried Phœbus, shaking him by the hand: 'a galloping horse cannot stop short. Now, I was swearing at full gallop. I've just left those silly women, and when I come away I always find my throat full of curses; I must spit them out or strangle – blood and thunder!'

'Will you come and drink?' asked the student.

This proposal calmed the captain.

'I fain would, but I have no money.'

'But I have.'

'Nonsense! let's see it.'

Jehan displayed the pouch before the captain's eyes with dignity and simplicity. Meanwhile, the archdeacon, having left Charmolue quite astounded, had approached them, and halted a few paces distant, watching them both without their noticing him, so absorbed were they in looking at the pouch.

Phœbus exclaimed: 'A purse in your pocket, Jehan! 'tis the moon in a bucket of water; one sees it, but 'tis not there; there is nothing but the reflection. Egad! I will wager they are but pebbles.'

Jehan replied coldly, 'Here are the pebbles wherewith I pave my fob.'

And without another word he emptied the pouch upon a neighbouring post with the air of a Roman saving his country.

'True gold!' growled Phœbus – 'Targes! big and little silver pieces! coppers, every two worth one of Tournay! Paris farthings! and real eagle liards. 'Tis dazzling.'

Jehan remained dignified and unmoved. A few liards rolled into the mud; the captain, in his enthusiasm, stooped to pick them up. Jehan withheld him – 'Fie, Captain Phœbus de Chateaupers!'

Phœbus counted the coins; and, turning with solemn look toward Jehan, 'Know you, Jehan,' said he, 'that here are three and twenty Paris pence? Whom did you rifle last night in Rue Coupe-Gueule (cut-gullet)?'

Jehan flung back his blonde, curly head, and said, half closing his eyes disdainfully, 'One may have a brother who is an archdeacon and a simpleton!'

'Horns of the devil!' cried Phœbus, 'the worthy man!'

'Let's go and drink,' said Jehan.

'Where shall we go?' said Phœbus; 'to La Pomme d'Eve?'

'No, captain: let us go to the Vieille-Science – An old woman (*vieille*) who saws (*scie*) a basket-handle (*anse*). 'Tis a rebus, and I like that.'

'A plague on rebuses, Jehan; the wine is better at the Pomme d'Eve; and then, by the side of the door there's a vine in the sun which cheers me while I'm drinking.'

'Very well, then; here goes for Eve and her apple,' said the student, taking Phœbus by the arm. 'By the way, my dear captain, you said just now, Rue Coupe-Gueule (cut-gullet). That is a very bad form of speech; we are no longer so barbarous – we say Rue Coupe Gorge (cut-throat).'

The two friends set out toward Pomme d'Eve. It is needless to say that they first gathered up the money, and that the archdeacon followed them.

The archdeacon followed them haggard and gloomy. Was this the Phœbus whose accursed name, ever since his interview with Gringoire, had been mingled with all his thoughts? He knew not; but it was at least a Phœbus; and that magic name was sufficient inducement for the archdeacon to follow the two heedless comrades with stealthy step, listening to their words and observing their slightest gestures with anxious attention. Indeed, nothing was easier than to hear everything they said, so loud they talked, not in the least concerned that the passers-by were taken into their confidence. They talked of duels, wenches, flagons and frolics.

At the turn of a street, the sound of a tambourine reached them from a neighbouring crossway. Dom Claude heard the officer say to the student, 'Thunder! let us hasten our steps.'

'Why, Phœbus?'

'I am afraid lest the gypsy will see me.'

'What gypsy?'

'The little one with a goat.'

'La 'Smeralda?'

'The same, Jehan. I always forget her devil of a name. Let us make haste: she will recognize me, and I would not wish that girl to accost me in the streets.'

'Are you then acquainted with her, Phœbus?'

Here the archdeacon saw Phœbus chuckle, stoop to Jehan's ear, and whisper a few words in it; Phœbus then burst into a laugh, and tossed his head with a triumphant air.

'For a truth?' said Jehan.

'On my soul!' said Phœbus.

'This evening?'

'This evening!'

'Are you sure she will come?'

'Are you a fool, Jehan? Can there ever be any doubt in such matters?'

'Captain Phœbus, you are a lucky soldier.'

The archdeacon overheard all this conversation. His teeth chattered; a visible shiver ran through his whole body. He stopped a moment, leaned against a post like a drunken man, then followed in the track of the two jolly scamps.

When he came up with them again they had changed the subject; and he heard them singing, at the top of their lungs, the refrain:

> *'The lads the dice who merrily throw,*
> *Merrily to the gallows go.'*

VII

The Spectre Monk

THE CELEBRATED WINE-SHOP of La Pomme d'Eve was situated in the University, at the corner of the Rue de la Rondelle and the Rue du Bâtonnier. It was a very spacious but very low room on the ground floor, with an arched roof, the central spring of which rested on a huge wooden pillar, painted yellow; tables everywhere; shining pewter jugs hung on the wall; always a large number of drinkers; a plenty of wenches; a window on the street; a vine at the door, and over the door a creaking square of sheet-iron, with an apple and a woman painted upon it, rusted by the rain, and swinging in the wind on an iron rod. This kind of weathercock which looked towards the pavement, was the signboard.

Night was falling; the street was dark; the wine-shop, full of candles, flamed from afar like a forge in the darkness; the noise of glasses and feasting, of oaths and quarrels, could be heard through the broken panes. Through the mist which the heat of the room spread over the front casement, a multitude of swarming figures could be seen confusedly; and from time to time a burst of noisy laughter broke forth from it. The passers-by whose business called them that way hastened by this noisy window without casting their eyes on it. Only, now and then, some little ragged urchin would raise himself on tiptoe as far as the window-sill, and shout into the wine-shop the old bantering cry with which it was then the custom to greet drunkards:

> *'Back to your glasses*
> *You drunken, drunken asses.'*

One man, however, paced imperturbably back and forth in front of the noisy tavern, looking at it incessantly, and going no farther from it than a pikeman from his sentry-box. He was cloaked up to the nose. This cloak he had just bought of the old clothes man near La Pomme d'Eve, doubtless to protect himself from the cold of a March night – perhaps also to conceal his costume. From time to time he paused before the dim lattice-leaded casement, listened, looked and stamped his foot.

At length the tavern-door opened. It was for this that he seemed to have been waiting. Two tipplers came out. The ray of light which escaped from the door cast a glow for a moment on their jovial faces. The man in the cloak stationed himself under a porch on the other side of the street.

'Thunder and guns!' said one of the two drinkers, ' 'Tis on the stroke of seven – the hour of my appointed meeting!'

'I tell you,' repeated his companion, with a thick utterance, 'that I don't live in the Rue des Mauvaises Paroles (bad words) – *Indignus qui inter mala verba habitat.* (Unworthy he who lives among bad words). I lodge in the Rue Jean Pain Mollet – *in vico Joannis Pain Mollet* – and you are more horned than a unicorn if you say the contrary. Everybody knows that he that gets once upon a bear's back is never afraid – but you've a nose for smelling out a dainty bit, like Saint James-of-the-Hospital.'

'Jehan, my friend, you are drunk,' said the other.

The other replied, staggering: 'It pleases you to say so, Phœbus; but it hath been proved that Plato had the profile of a hound.'

The reader has no doubt already recognized our two worthy friends, the captain and the student. The man who was watching them in the dark appeared also to have recognized them; for he followed with slow steps all the zigzags which the reeling student forced the captain to describe, who, being a more seasoned drinker, had retained all his self-possession. By listening attentively, the man in the cloak was enabled to catch the whole of the following interesting conversation:

'*Corbacque!* (Body o' Bacchus!) try to walk straight, master bachelor;

you know that I must leave you. There is seven o'clock. I have to meet a woman.'

'Leave me, then! I can see stars and darts of fire. You are like Dampmartin Castle, that's bursting with laughter.'

'By the warts of my grandmother, Jehan, but this is talking nonsense a little too hard. By the way, Jehan, have you no money left?'

'Monsieur the rector, there is no mistake. The little shambles – *parva boucheria* – '

'Jehan – friend Jehan – you know I have promised to meet that little girl at the end of the Pont Saint Michel; that I can take her nowhere but to La Falourdel's, the old crone of the bridge, and that I must pay for the room. The white-whiskered old jade will give me no credit. Jehan, for pity's sake, have we drunk up the whole of the priest's pouch? Haven't you a penny left?'

'The consciousness of having spent the other hours well is a just and savoury sauce for the table.'

'Belly and guts! a truce to your gibberish. Tell me – you devil of a Jehan – have you any coin left? Give it me, by heaven! or I'll search you all over, were you as leprous as Job, and as mangy as Cæsar.'

'Sir, the Rue Galiache is a street with the Rue de la Verrerie at one end of it, and the Rue de la Tixeranderie at the other.'

'Well – yes – my good friend Jehan – my poor comrade – the Rue Galiache – good – very good. But, in the name of heaven, come to your senses. I want but a few pence, and seven o'clock is the hour.'

'Silence to the song and attention to the chorus:

  ' " *When mice have every case devour'd,*
   The King of Arras shall be lord;
   Is frozen o'er at Saint John's tide,
   Across the ice we then shall see
   The Arras men their city flee." '

'Well, scholar of Antichrist, mayst thou be strangled with the guts of thy mother!' exclaimed Phœbus; and he gave the tipsy student a rough push, which sent him reeling against the wall, whence he fell gently upon the pavement of Philip Augustus. With a remnant of fraternal pity which never quite forsakes the heart of a drinker, Phœbus rolled Jehan with his foot upon one of those pillows of the poor man which Providence keeps ready at the corner of every street-post in Paris, and which the rich scornfully stigmatize with the name of dung-heaps. The captain placed Jehan's head on an inclined plane of cabbage-stalks, and forthwith the student fell to snoring in a most magnificent bass. Yet the heart of the captain was not wholly free from animosity. 'So much the worse for thee, if the devil's cart picks thee up as it goes by,' said he to the poor, sleeping clerk; and he went his way.

The man in the cloak ceased following him and stopped for a moment beside the prostrate student, as if agitated by indecision; then heaving a deep sigh, he continued to follow the captain.

Like them, we will leave Jehan sleeping under the friendly watch of the bright stars, and speed after them, if it so please the reader.

On turning into the Rue Saint André des Arcs, Captain Phœbus perceived that some one was following him. As he accidentally glanced behind him, he saw a sort of shadow creeping behind him along the walls. He stopped – it stopped; he went on – the shadow went on again also. This, however, gave him very little concern. 'Ah! bah!' said he to himself, 'I have not a penny about me.'

In front of the College d'Autun he came to a halt. It was at that college that he shuffled through what he was pleased to call his studies; and from a certain mischievous schoolboy habit which still clung to him, he never passed the front of that college without inflicting on the statue of Cardinal Pierre Bertrand, carved on the right hand of the gateway, the affront of which Priapus complains so bitterly in the satire of Horace, *Olim truncus eram ficulnus*. (I was once a fig-tree). He had done this with so much unrelenting animosity that the inscription, *Eduensis Episcopus* (Bishop of Autun), had become almost effaced. Therefore, he halted before the statue according to his wont. The street was utterly deserted. As he was retagging nonchalantly his doublet with his head thrown back, he saw the shadow approaching him slowly – so slowly that he had full time to observe that this shadow had a cloak and a hat. When it had come up to him, it stopped, and remained as motionless as the statue of Cardinal Bertrand. But it riveted upon Phœbus two intent eyes, glaring with that vague light which issues at night from those of a cat.

The captain was brave, and would have cared little for a robber with a rapier in his hand. But this walking statue, this petrified man, made his blood run cold. At that time there were certain strange rumours afloat about a spectre monk, a nocturnal prowler about the streets of Paris in the night-time, and they now came confusedly to his mind. He stood stupefied for a few moments then finally broke silence with a laugh.

'Sir,' said he, 'if you be a thief, as I hope is the case, you're just now for all the world like a heron attacking a walnut-shell. My dear fellow, I am the son of a ruined family. Try your hand hard by here. In the chapel of this college there's some wood of the true cross, set in silver.'

The hand of the shadow came forth from under its cloak, and descended upon the arm of Phœbus with the force of an eagle's grip; at the same time the shadow spoke:

'Captain Phœbus de Chateaupers!'

'What, the devil!' said Phœbus; 'you know my name?'

'I know not your name alone,' returned the man in the cloak, with his sepulchral voice; 'but I know that you have an appointment this evening.'

'Yes,' answered Phœbus, in amazement.

'At seven o'clock.'

'In a quarter of an hour.'

'At the Falourdel's.'

'Exactly so.'

'The old hag of the Pont Saint Michel.'

'Of Saint Michel, the archangel, as the Paternoster saith.'

'Impious man!' muttered the spectre. 'With a woman?'

'*Confiteor*' (I confess).

'Whose name is . . .'

'La 'Smeralda,' said Phœbus gaily, all his heedlessness having gradually returned to him.

At this name the shadow's grasp shook Phœbus's arm furiously.

'Captain Phœbus de Chateaupers, thou liest!'

Any one who could have seen, at that moment, the captain's inflamed countenance – his leap backwards, so violent that it disengaged him from the clutch which held him – the haughty mien with which he clapped his hand on his sword-hilt – and, in the presence of this wrath, the sullen stillness of the man in the cloak; any one who could have beheld this would have been frightened. There was in it somewhat of the combat of Don Juan and the statue.

'Christ and Satan!' cried the captain; 'that's a word that seldom assails the ear of a Chateaupers! Thou durst not repeat it.'

'Thou liest!' said the shadow coldly.

The captain ground his teeth. Spectre monk – phantom – superstitions – all were forgotten at that moment. He now saw nothing but a man and an insult. 'Ha, it is well!' spluttered he in a voice choking with rage. He drew his sword; then, stuttering, for anger as well as fear makes a man tremble – 'Here!' said he. 'on the spot! Come on! Swords! swords! Blood upon these stones!'

But the other did not stir. When he saw his adversary on guard, and ready to lunge, 'Captain Phœbus,' said he, and his voice quivered with bitterness, 'you forgot your assignation.'

The fits of rage of such men as Phœbus are like boiling milk, whose ebullition is calmed by a drop of cold water. These few words brought down the point of the sword which glittered in the captain's hand.

'Captain,' continued the man, 'to-morrow – the day after tomorrow – a month hence – ten years hence – you will find me quite ready to cut your throat. But first go to your assignation.'

'In sooth,' said Phœbus, as if seeking to capitulate with himself; 'a sword and a girl are two delightful things to encounter at a trysting-place; but I cannot see why I should miss one of them for the sake of the other, when I may have both.'

He replaced his sword in his scabbard.

'Go to your assignation,' resumed the unknown.

'Sir,' answered Phœbus, with some embarrassment, 'gramercy for your courtesy. It will, in truth, be time enough to-morrow to chop up father Adam's doublet into slashes and buttonholes. I am beholden to you for allowing me to pass one more agreeable quarter of an hour. I did indeed hope to have laid you quietly in the gutter, and yet be in time for the fair one – the more so as it is genteel to make women wait a little in such cases. But you appear to be a mettlesome chap, and it is safer to put off our game until tomorrow. I will, therefore, betake myself to my appointment. It is for the hour of seven, as you know.' Here Phœbus scratched his ear. 'Ah! by my halidom! I forgot! I have not a penny to pay the price of the garret, and the old hag will want to be paid beforehand; she distrusts me.'

'Here is the wherewithal to pay.'

Phœbus felt the stranger's cold hand slip into his a large coin. He could not help taking the money, and grasping the hand. 'God's truth!' he exclaimed, 'but you're a good fellow!'

'One condition,' said the man. 'Prove to me that I was wrong, and that you spoke truth. Hide me in some corner whence I may see whether this woman be really she whose name you uttered.'

'Oh,' replied Phœbus, ' 'Tis all one to me. We will take the Saint Martha chamber. You can see at your ease from the kennel hard by.'

'Come, then,' rejoined the shadow.

'At your service,' said the captain. 'I know not indeed whether you be not Messer Diabolus *in propria persona* (in person). But let us be good friends to-night; to-morrow I'll pay you all debts, of purse and of sword.'

They set out again at a rapid pace. In a few minutes the sound of the river below apprised them that they were upon the bridge of Saint Michel, then covered with houses.

'I will first let you in,' said Phœbus to his companion; ' then I will go fetch the wench who was to wait for me near the Petit Châtelet.'

That companion made no reply; since they had been walking side by side, he had not uttered a word. Phœbus stopped before a low door and knocked loudly. A light appeared through the cracks of the door. 'Who's there?' cried a mumbling voice.

'By the body! by the belly! by the head of God!' answered the captain.

The door opened instantly, and revealed to the new-comers an old woman and an old lamp, both of which trembled. The old woman was bent double – dressed in rags – with a shaking head, pierced by two small eyes, and coiffed with a dish clout – wrinkled everywhere, on hands and face and neck – her lips receding under her gums – and all round her mouth she had tufts of white hair which gave her the whiskered and demure look of a cat.

The interior of the hovel was no less dilapidated than herself; the walls were of plaster; black rafters ran across the ceiling; a dismantled fireplace; cobwebs in every corner; in the middle of the room a tottering company of maimed stools and tables; a dirty child played in the ash-heap; and at the farther end a staircase, or rather a wooden ladder, led to a trap-door in the ceiling.

As he entered this den, Phœbus's mysterious companion drew his cloak up to his eyes. Meanwhile, the captain, swearing like a Turk, hastened 'to make the sun flash from a crown-piece,' as saith our admirable Régnier.

'The Saint Martha room,' said he.

The old woman addressed him as monseigneur, and deposited the crown in a drawer. It was the coin which the man in the black cloak had given Phœbus. While her back was turned, the ragged, dishevelled little boy, who was playing in the ashes, went slyly to the drawer, abstracted the crown-piece, and put in its place a dry leaf which he had plucked from a fagot.

The hag beckoned to the two gentlemen, as she called them, to follow her, and ascended the ladder before them. On reaching the upper story, she placed her lamp upon a chest; and Phœbus, like a frequenter of the house, opened the door of a dark closet. 'Go in there, my dear fellow,' said he to his companion. The man in the cloak complied without uttering a word; the door closed upon him; he heard Phœbus bolt it, and, a moment afterward, go down-stairs again with the old woman. The light had disappeared.

VIII

The Advantage of Windows Overlooking the River

CLAUDE FROLLO (for we presume that the reader, more clever than Phœbus, has seen in this whole adventure no other spectre monk than the archdeacon himself) Claude Frollo groped about for some moments in the dark hole into which the captain had bolted him. It was one of those nooks such as architects sometimes leave at the junction of the roof and the outer wall. The vertical section of this kennel, as Phœbus had so aptly termed it, would have made a triangle. There was neither window nor skylight, and the pitch of the roof prevented one from standing upright. Claude, therefore, crouched down in the dust and plaster which crumbled beneath him. His head was burning. Feeling about him with his hands, he found on the floor a bit of broken glass, which he pressed to his brow, its coolness affording him some relief. What was passing at that moment in the dark soul of the archdeacon? God and himself alone could tell.

In what fatal order did he arrange in imagination La Esmeralda, Phœbus, Jacques Charmolue, his younger brother, so beloved, yet abandoned by him in the mire, his archdeacon's cassock, his reputation, perhaps at stake at the Falourdel's – all these images, all these adventures? It is impossible to say; but it is certain that these ideas formed a horrible group in his mind.

He had been waiting a quarter of an hour; it seemed to him that he had grown a century older. All at once he heard the wooden staircase creak; some one was coming up. The trap-door opened once more; light reappeared. In the worm-eaten door of his nook there was a crack of considerable width; to this he glued his face. Thus he could see all that went on in the adjoining chamber. The cat-faced old woman appeared first through the trap-door with lamp in hand; then Phœbus, twirling his moustache; then a third person, that lovely, graceful creature, La Esmeralda. The priest beheld her rise from below like a dazzling apparition, Claude trembled; a cloud spread over his eyes, his pulse beat violently; everything swam before him; he no longer saw or heard anything.

When he came to himself again, Phœbus and Esmeralda were alone, seated on the wooden chest, beside the lamp, whose light revealed to the archdeacon's eyes their two youthful figures, and a miserable pallet at the farther end of the garret.

Beside the pallet was a window, broken, through the panes of which, like a cobweb upon which rain has fallen, could be seen a small patch of sky, with the moon in the distance resting on a pillow of soft clouds.

The young girl was blushing, confused, palpitating. Her long drooping lashes shaded her glowing cheeks. The face of the officer, to which she dared not lift her eyes, was radiant. Mechanically, and with a charming air of embarrassment, she traced with the tip of her finger meaningless lines upon the bench, and watched her finger. Her feet were not visible, for the little goat was nestling upon them.

The captain was very gallantly arrayed. At his neck and wrists he had tufts of embroidery, the great elegance of the day.

Dom Claude could only hear with great difficulty what they said to each other, through the humming of the blood that was boiling in his temples.

An amorous chitchat is a very commonplace Sort of thing. It is a perpetual 'I love you,' – a very monotonous and very insipid musical strain to indifferent ears, unless set off with a few flourishes and grace-notes. But Claude was no indifferent listener.

'Oh!' said the young girl, without lifting her eyes, 'despise me not, Monseigneur Phœbus; I feel that what I am doing is wrong.'

'Despise you, my pretty dear,' replied the officer with a consequential and modish air of gallantry; 'despise you, good lack! and why should I?'

'For having accompanied you.'

'On that score, my charmer, we don't at all agree. I ought not only to despise you, but to hate you.'

The young girl looked at him in affright: 'Hate me! What, then, have I done?'

'For requiring so much solicitation.'

'Alas! ' said she, ' 'Tis because I am breaking a vow – I shall never find my parents – the amulet will lose its virtue; but what then? What need have I for father and mother now?'

As she thus spoke she fixed upon the captain her large, dark eyes, moist with joy and tenderness.

'Deuce take me, if I understand you,' exclaimed Phœbus.

Esmeralda remained silent for a moment; then a tear fell from her eye, a sigh from her lips, and she said, 'Oh, monseigneur, I love you.'

Such a perfume of chastity, such a charm of virtue, surrounded the young girl that Phœbus did not feel quite at his ease with her. These words, however, emboldened him. 'You love me!' said he with rapture, and he threw his arm round the gypsy's waist. He had only been waiting for this opportunity.

The priest saw him, and tested with the tip of his finger the point of a dagger concealed in his breast.

'Phœbus,' continued the Bohemian, gently disengaging her waist from the tenacious hands of the captain, 'you are good – you are generous – you are handsome – you have saved me – me, who am but a poor gypsy foundling. I have long dreamed of an officer who should save my life. It was of you that I dreamed, before I knew you, my Phœbus. The officer of my dream had a beautiful uniform like yours, a grand air, a sword. Your name is Phœbus – 'tis a beautiful name. I love your name, I love your sword. Draw your sword, Phœbus, that I may see it.'

'Child!' said the captain; and he unsheathed his rapier with a smile.

The gypsy-girl looked at the hilt, then at the blade; examined with adorable curiosity the cypher upon the guard, and kissed the weapon, saying, 'You are the sword of a brave man. I love my captain.'

Phœbus again took advantage of the situation to imprint on her lovely bent neck a kiss which made the girl start up as red as a cherry. It made the priest grind his teeth in the darkness.

'Phœbus,' resumed the gypsy, 'let me talk to you. Just walk about a little, that I may see you at your full height, and hear the sound of your spurs. How handsome you are!'

The captain rose to comply, chiding her at the same time with a smile of satisfaction. 'What a child you are! By the way, my charmer, have you ever seen me in my state uniform?'

'Alas, no!'

'Ha, that is really fine!'

Phœbus returned and seated himself beside her, but much closer than before.

'Hark you, my dear . . . '

The gypsy gave him a few little taps on the lips with her pretty hand with a childish playfullness, full of gaiety and grace.

'No, no, I will not listen. Do you love me? I want you to tell me if you love me.'

'Do I love thee, angel of my life?' cried the captain, half kneeling before her. 'My body, my blood, my soul – all are thine – all are for thee. I love thee, and have never loved any but thee.'

The captain had repeated this phrase so many times, on many similar occasions, that he delivered it all in a breath, and without making a single mistake. At this impassioned declaration, the gypsy raised to the dingy ceiling a look full of angelic happiness.

'Oh!' murmured she, 'this is the moment when one should die!'

Phœbus thought 'the moment' a good one to steal another kiss, which tortured the wretched archdeacon in his lair.

'Die!' cried the amorous captain; 'what are you talking of, my lovely angel? 'Tis the time to live – or Jupiter is but a scamp. Die at the beginning of so sweet a thing! By the horns of the bull! what a jest! That would not do. Listen, my dear Similar – Esmenarda – Your pardon! but you have so prodigiously Saracen a name that I never can get it straight; I get entangled in it like a brier.'

'Good heavens!' said the poor girl, 'and I thought my name pretty because of its singularity! But, since it displeases you, I would that I were called Goton.'

'Ah! do not weep for such a trifle, my graceful maid; 'tis a name to which one must get used, that is all. When once I know it by heart, 'twill come ready enough. So hark ye, my dear Similar. I adore you passionately; I love you so that 'tis really marvellous. I know a little girl that's bursting with rage about it.'

The jealous girl interrupted him. 'Who?'

'What matters that to us?' said Phœbus; 'do you love me?'

'Oh!' said she.

'Well, that is all. You will see how I love you, too. May the great devil Neptunus spear me if I don't make you the happiest creature alive. We'll have a pretty little lodging somewhere. I'll make my archers parade under your windows; they're all on horseback, and don't care a fig for Captain Mignon's men. There are spear-men, crossbow-men and culverin-men. I'll take you to the great musters of the Parisians at the Grange de Rully. It is very magnificent. Eighty thousand armed men; thirty thousand white harnesses, short coats or coats of mail; the sixty-seven banners of the trades; the standards of the Parliament, of the Chamber of Accounts, of the treasury of the generals, of the assistants of the mint – the devil's own turnout, in short. I will conduct you to see the lions of the king's palace – which are wild beasts. All the women like that.'

For some moments the young girl, absorbed in her pleasing reflections, had been dreaming to the sound of his voice, without heeding the meaning of his words.

'Oh, how happy you will be!' continued the captain, and at the same time he gently unbuckled the gypsy's girdle.

'What are you doing?' she said quickly. This 'act of violence' had roused her from her reverie.

'Nothing,' answered Phœbus. 'I was only saying that you must abandon all this garb of folly and street-running when you are with me.'

'When I am with thee, my Phœbus! ' said the young girl tenderly.

She again became pensive and silent.

The captain, emboldened by her gentleness, clasped her waist without her making any resistance; then began softly to unlace the poor child's bodice, and so greatly disarranged her neckerchief that the panting priest beheld the gypsy's lovely shoulder emerge from the gauze, round and dusky like the moon rising through the mists of the horizon.

The young girl let Phœbus have his way. She seemed unconscious of what he was doing. The bold captain's eyes sparkled.

All at once she turned towards him.

'Phœbus,' said she, with an expression of infinite love, 'instruct me in thy religion.'

'My religion!' cried the captain, bursting into a laugh. 'I instruct you in my religion. Blood and thunder! what do you want with my religion?'

'That we may be married,' she replied.

The captain's face assumed a mingled expression of surprise, disdain, carelessness and licentious passion.

'Bah,' said he, 'why should one marry?'

The gypsy turned pale, and her head drooped sadly on her breast.

'My sweet love,' resumed Phœbus, tenderly, 'what are all these foolish ideas? Marriage is a grand affair, to be sure. Is any one less loving for not having spouted Latin in a priest's shop?'

While speaking thus in his softest tone, he approached extremely near the gypsy-girl; his caressing hands resumed their place around the lithe, slender waist. His eye kindled more and more, and everything showed that Master Phœbus was on the verge of one of those moments in which Jupiter himself commits so many follies that the good Homer is obliged to summon a cloud to his rescue.

Dom Claude meanwhile saw all from his hiding-place. Its door was made of decayed puncheon staves, leaving between them ample passage for his look of a bird of prey. This brown-skinned, broad-shouldered priest, hitherto condemned to the austere virginity of the cloister, was quivering and boiling in the presence of this night-scene of love and voluptuousness. The young and lovely girl, her garments in disorder, abandoning herself to the ardent young man, seemed to infuse molten lead into his veins. An extraordinary agitation shook him; his eye sought with lustful desire to penetrate beneath all those unfastened pins. Any one who could then have seen the wretched man's countenance close against the worm-eaten bars might have thought they saw a tiger's face glaring from the depths of a cage at some jackal devouring a gazelle.

Suddenly, with a rapid motion, Phœbus snatched off the gypsy's neckerchief. The poor girl, who had remained pale and dreamy, started up as if suddenly awakened; she hastily drew back from the enterprising officer; and casting a glance at her bare neck and shoulders, blushing, confused, and mute with shame, she crossed her two lovely arms upon her bosom to hide it. But for the flush that crimsoned her cheeks, to see her thus silent and motionless, one might have thought her a statue of Modesty. Her eyes were bent upon the ground.

But the captain's action had exposed the mysterious amulet which she wore about her neck.

'What is that?' said he, seizing this pretext to approach once more the beautiful creature whom he had just alarmed.

'Touch it not,' she replied quickly; ' 'tis my protector. It will help me to find my family again, if I remain worthy to do so. Oh, leave me, sir! My mother! my poor mother! my mother! where art thou? Come to my rescue! Have pity, Captain Phœbus; give me back my neckerchief.'

Phœbus drew back, and said coldly:

'Oh, young lady, I see plainly that you do not love me.'

'Not love him!' exclaimed the unhappy child, and at the same time clinging to the captain and drawing him to a seat by her side. 'Not love thee, my Phœbus? What art thou saying, wicked man, to rend my heart? Oh, come – take me – take all – do with me as thou wilt – I am thine. What matters the amulet to me now? What matters my mother to me now? Thou art my mother, since I love thee. Phœbus, my beloved Phœbus, dost thou see me? 'Tis I. Look at me. 'Tis that little

233

girl whom thou wilt surely not repulse – who comes, who comes herself to seek thee. My soul, my life, my body, my person, all is one thing – which is thine, my captain. Well, no! let us not marry, since it bothers thee; and then what am I? A wretched girl of the gutters – while thou, Phœbus art a gentleman. A fine thing, truly! a dancer wed an officer! I was mad! No, Phœbus, no; I will be thy mistress – thy amusement – thy pleasure – when thou wilt – a girl who will be only thine. I was only made for that, soiled, despised, dishonoured; but what then – loved! I shall be the proudest and the happiest of women. And when I grow old and ugly, Phœbus – when I am no longer fit to love thee, my lord, thou wilt still suffer me to serve thee. Others will embroider scarfs for thee; I, thy servant, will take care of them. Thou wilt let me polish thy spurs, brush thy doublet and dust thy riding-boots. Thou wilt have this much pity; wilt thou not, my Phœbus? Meantime, take me. Here, Phœbus, all this belongs to thee. Only love me. We gypsy-girls need nothing more – air and love.'

So saying, she threw her arms around the officer's neck; she looked up at him imploringly and smiled through her tears. Her delicate neck rubbed against his cloth doublet with its rough embroidery. She twisted her beautiful, half-naked limbs around his knees. The intoxicated captain pressed his burning lips to those lovely African shoulders. The young girl, her eyes cast upward to the ceiling, her head thrown back, quivered, all palpitating beneath this kiss.

All at once, above the head of Phœbus, she beheld another head – a green, livid, convulsed face, with the look of a lost soul; beside this face there was a hand which held a dagger. It was the face and hand of the priest; he had broken open the door, and he was there. Phœbus could not see him. The young girl was motionless, frozen mute at the frightful apparition – like a dove which chances to raise its head at the instant when the hawk is glaring into her nest with his round eyes.

She could not even utter a cry. She saw the poniard descend upon Phœbus, and rise again reeking.

'Malediction!' said the captain, and he fell.

She fainted.

As her eyes closed, as all consciousness left her, she thought she felt a fiery touch upon her lips, a kiss more burning than the executioner's branding-iron.

When she recovered her senses, she was surrounded by soldiers of the watch; they were carrying off the captain weltering in his blood; the priest had disappeared; the window at the back of the room, looking upon the river, was wide open; they picked up a cloak which they supposed to belong to the officer, and she heard them saying around her:

' 'Tis a sorceress who has stabbed a captain.'

BOOK EIGHT

I

The Crown Changed into a Withered Leaf

GRINGOIRE AND THE whole Court of Miracles were in a state of terrible anxiety. For a whole month no one knew what had become of La Esmeralda, which sorely grieved the Duke of Egypt and his friends the vagrants; nor what had become of her goat, which redoubled Gringoire's sorrow. One night the gypsy had disappeared; and since that time had given no signs of life. All search had proved fruitless. Some malicious 'street tumblers' told Gringoire they had met her that same evening in the neighbourhood of the Pont Saint Michel, walking off with an officer; but this husband after the fashion of Bohemia was an incredulous philosopher, and besides, he, better than any one else, knew to what a point his wife was chaste. He had been able to judge what invincible modesty resulted from the two combined virtues of the amulet and the gypsy, and he had mathematically calculated the resistance of that chastity multiplied into itself. On that score, at least, his mind was at ease.

Thus he could not explain her disappearance. It was a great grief to him. He would have grown thinner upon it, had that been possible. He had forgotten everything else, even to his literary pursuits, even his great work, *De figuris regularibus et irregularibus* (concerning regular and irregular figures), which he intended to have printed with the first money he should procure. (For he raved about printing ever since he had seen the *Didascolon* of Hugues de Saint Victor printed with the celebrated types of Vindelin of Spires.)

One day, as he was passing sadly before the Criminal Tournelle, he perceived a crowd at one of the doors of the Palace of Justice.

'What is there?' he inquired of a young man who was coming out.

'I know not, sir,' replied the young man. ' 'Tis said a woman is being tried for the murder of a man-at-arms. As there seems to be something of sorcery in the business, the bishop and the judge of the Bishop's Court have interposed in the cause; and my brother, the archdeacon of Josas, can think of nothing else. Now, I wished to speak to him; but could not get at him for the crowd – which vexes me mightily, for I am in need of money.'

'Alas! sir,' said Gringoire, 'I would I could lend you some; but, though my breeches are in holes, it's not from the weight of crown-pieces.'

He dared not tell the young man that he knew his brother, the archdeacon, to whom he had not returned since the scene in the church – a negligence which embarrassed him.

The student went his way, and Gringoire followed the crowd going up the staircase of the Great Hall. To his mind there was nothing equal to the sight of a criminal trial for dispelling melancholy; the judges are generally so delightfully stupid. The people with whom he had mingled were moving on and elbowing each other in silence. After a slow and tiresome shuffling along a long gloomy passage, which wound through the Palace like the intestinal canal of the old edifice, he arrived at a low door opening into a hall, which his tall stature permitted him to overlook above the undulating heads of the crowd.

The hall was huge and ill-lighted, which latter circumstance made it seem still larger. The day was declining; the high, pointed windows admitted but a faint ray of light, which faded before it reached the vaulted ceiling, an enormous trellis-work of carved wood, whose countless figures seemed to move confusedly in the shadows. There were already several candles lighted here and there upon tables, and glimmering over the heads of the clerks bending over musty documents. The front of the hall was occupied by the crowd; to the right and left were lawyers in their robes seated at tables; at the farther end, upon a raised platform, were a number of judges, the last rows of whom were lost in the darkness – with immovable and sinister-looking faces. The walls were dotted with innumerable fleurs-de-lis. A large crucifix might be vaguely descried above the judges, and everywhere there were pikes and halberds, which the light of the candles seemed to tip with fire.

'Sir,' said Gringoire to one of his neighbours, 'who are all those persons yonder, ranged like prelates in council?'

'Sir,' answered the neighbour, 'those are the councillors of the High Chamber on the right; and the councillors of inquiry on the left: the masters in black gowns, and the honourables in scarlet ones.'

'Yonder, above them,' continued Gringoire, who is that big red-faced fellow who is perspiring so?'

'That is monsieur the president.'

'And those sheep behind him?' proceeded Gringoire, who, as we have already said, loved not the magistracy – which arose, possibly, from the ill-will he bore the Palace of Justice since his dramatic misadventure.

'They are messieurs, the masters of requests of the king's household.'

'And that wild boar in front of him?'

'That is the clerk to the court of parliament.'

'And that crocodile on the right?'

'Maître Philippe Lheulier, advocate extraordinary to the king.'

'And that great black cat to the left?'

'Maître Jacques Charmolue, king's attorney in the ecclesiastical court, with the gentlemen of the officiality.'

'And now, sir,' said Gringoire, 'what are all those good folk about?'

'They are trying some one.'

'Trying whom? I see no prisoner.'

' 'Tis a woman, sir. You can not see her. Her back is toward us, and she is concealed by the crowd. Stay, yonder she is, where you see that group of halberds.'

'Who is the woman?' asked Gringoire. 'Do you know her name?'

'No, sir; I am but just come. I suppose, however, that there is sorcery in the matter, since the judge of the Bishop's Court is present at the trial.'

'Well,' said our philosopher, 'we will see all these men of the gown devour human flesh. It is as good a sight as any other.'

'Think you not, sir,' observed his neighbour, 'that Maître Charmolue looks very mild?'

'Hum!' answered Gringoire, 'I distrust a mildness which hath pinched nostrils and thin lips.'

Here the bystanders imposed silence on the two talkers. An important deposition was being heard.

'My lords,' an old woman in the middle of the hall was saying, whose face was so concealed beneath her garments that she might have been taken for a walking bundle of rags – 'my lords, the thing is as true as it is true that my name is Falourdel, and that for forty years I have lived on the Pont Saint Michel, and paid regularly my rent, dues and quit-rent. The door is opposite the house of Tassin Caillart, the dyer, who lives on the side looking up the river. An old woman now! a pretty girl once, my gentlemen! Some one said to me but lately, "Mother Falourdel, spin not too much of an evening; the devil is fond of combing the distaffs of old women with his horns. 'Tis certain that the spectre monk that roamed last year about the Temple now wanders in the City. Take care, La Falourdel, that he doesn't knock at your door." One evening I was spinning at my wheel, when there comes a knock at my door. I ask who is there. Some one swears. I open the door. Two men enter – one in black, with a handsome officer. Of the one in black nothing could be seen but his eyes – two coals of fire. All the rest was cloak and hat. And so they say to me, "The Saint Martha room." 'Tis my upper chamber, my lords – my best. They give me a crown. I lock the crown in my drawer, and I say, "This shall go to buy tripe to-morrow at the Gloriette shambles." We go up-stairs. On reaching the upper room, and while my back was turned, the black man disappears. This startled me a bit. The officer, who was as handsome as a great lord, goes down-stairs with me. He leaves the house. In about time enough to spin a quarter of a bobbin, he comes back again with a beautiful young girl – a doll who would have shone like the sun had her hair been dressed. She had with her a goat, a great he-goat, whether black or white I no longer remember. That set me to thinking. The girl – that was no concern of mine; – but the goat! I don't like those animals; they have a beard and horns – it is like a man; and then they smack of the witches' sabbath. However, I said nothing. I had the crown-piece. That was only fair; was it not, my lord judge? I show the captain and the girl into the up-stairs room, and leave them alone – that is to say, with the goat. I go down and get to my spinning again. I must tell you that my house has a ground-floor and a floor above; the back of it looks upon the river, like the other houses on the bridge, and the windows, both of the ground-floor and of the chamber, open upon the water. Well, as I was saying, I had got to my spinning. I know not why I fell to thinking of the spectre monk whom the goat had put into my head again – and then the beautiful girl was rather strangely tricked out. All at once I hear a cry overhead, and something falls on the floor, and the window opens. I run to mine, which is beneath it, and I see a dark mass drop past my eyes into the water. It was a phantom clad like a priest. The moon was shining; I saw it quite plainly. It was swimming toward the City. Then, all of a tremble, I call the watch. The gentlemen of the police come in; and being merry, not knowing at first what was the matter, they fell to beating me. I explained to them. We go up-stairs, and what do we find? My poor chamber all blood – the captain stretched out at full length with a dagger in his neck – the girl pretending to be dead – and the goat all in a fright. "Pretty work!" say I. "It will take more than fifteen days to wash that floor. It must be scraped. It will be a terrible job." They carry off the officer – poor young man, and the girl, all in disorder. But wait. The worst is, that on the next day, when I went to get the crown to buy tripe, I found a withered leaf in its place.'

The old woman ceased. A murmur of horror ran through the audience.

'That phantom, that goat, all that smacks of sorcery,' said one of Gringoire's neigbours.

'And that withered leaf!' added another.

'No doubt,' continued a third, ' 'Tis some witch who has dealings with the spectre monk to plunder officers.' Gringoire himself was not far from considering this combination as alarming and probable.

'Woman Falourdel,' said the president majestically, 'have you nothing further to communicate to the court?'

'No, my lord,' replied the crone, 'unless it is that in the report my house has been called a crazy, filthy hovel – which is an outrageous way of talking. The houses on the bridge are not so goodly as some, because there are so many people there; but the butchers dwell there, for all that, and they are rich men, married to fine, proper sort of women.'

The magistrate whom Gringoire had likened to a crocodile now rose.

'Silence,' said he; 'I beg you, gentlemen, to bear in mind that a poniard was found on the accused. Woman Falourdel, have you brought the leaf into which the crown was changed that the demon gave you?'

'Yes, monseigneur,' answered she; 'I found it. Here it is.'

An usher of the court handed the withered leaf to the crocodile, who, with a doleful shake of the head, passed it on to the president, who gave it to the king's attorney in the ecclesiastical court; and thus it made the circuit of the hall.

'It is a birch-leaf,' said Maître Jacques Charmolue; 'an additional proof of magic.'

A counsellor then began:

'Witness, two men went up-stairs together in your house – the black man whom you first saw disappear, then swim the Seine in priest's clothes, and the officer. Which of the two gave you the crown?'

The old woman considered for a moment, and then said 'It was the officer.' A murmur ran through the crowd.

'Ha,' thought Gringoire, 'that shakes my conviction.'

But Maître Philippe Lheulier, king's advocate extraordinary again interposed.

'I will recall to these gentlemen that in the deposition taken at his bedside, the murdered officer, while admitting that he had a confused idea, at the moment when the black man accosted him that it might be the spectre monk, added that the phantom had eagerly pressed him to keep his appointment with the prisoner; and on his, the captain's, observing that he was without money, he had given him the crown which the said officer had paid La Falourdel. Hence, the crown is a coin from hell.'

This conclusive observation appeared to dispel all the doubts of Gringoire and the other sceptics in the audience.

'Gentlemen, you are in possession of the documents,' added the king's advocate, seating himself, 'you can consult the deposition of Phœbus de Chateaupers.'

At that name the accused sprang up; her head rose above the throng. Gringoire, aghast, recognized Esmeralda.

She was pale; her hair, once so gracefully plaited and spangled with sequins, hung in disorder; her lips were livid; her hollow eyes were terrible. Alas!

'Phœbus!' said she, wildly; 'where is he? Oh, messeigneurs! before you kill me, tell me, for pity's sake, whether he yet lives!'

'Be silent, woman,' answered the president; 'that is no concern of ours.'

'Oh, have mercy! tell me if he is alive,' continued she, clasping her beautiful, emaciated hands; and her chains were heard as they brushed along her dress.

'Well,' said the king's advocate roughly, 'he is dying. Does that content you?'

The wretched girl fell back on her seat, speechless, tearless, white as a wax figure.

The president leaned over to a man at his feet, who wore a gilt cap and black gown, a chain round his neck and a wand in his hand:

'Usher, bring in the second accused.'

All eyes were now turned toward a small door, which opened, and, to the great agitation of Gringoire, made way for a pretty goat with gilded hoofs and horns. The dainty creature paused for a moment on the threshold, stretching out its neck as though, perched, on the summit of a rock, it had before its eyes a vast horizon. All at once it caught sight of the gypsy-girl; and leaping over the table and a registrar's head in two bounds it was at her knees. It then rolled gracefully on its mistress's feet, begging for a word or a caress; but the prisoner remained motionless, and poor Djali itself obtained not a glance.

'Eh, why – 'tis my villainous beast,' said the old Falourdel; 'I recognize the pair of them well enough.'

Jacques Charmolue interposed.

'If it please you, gentlemen, we will proceed to the examination of the goat.'

Such was, in fact, the second prisoner. Nothing was more common in those times than to indict animals for sorcery. Among others, in the accounts of the provost's office for 1466, may be seen a curious detail concerning the expenses of the trial of Gillet-Soulart and his sow, executed 'for their demerits' at Corbeil. Everything is there: the cost of the pen in which the sow was put; the five hundred bundles of short fagots from the wharf of Morsant; the three pints of wine and the bread, the last repast of the victim, in a brotherly manner by the executioner; down to the eleven days' custody and feed of the sow, at eight Paris pence each. Sometimes they even went beyond animals. The capitularies of Charlemagne and Louis le Debonnaire impose severe penalties on fiery phantoms which may presume to appear in the air.

Meanwhile, the king's attorney in the ecclesiastical court cried out: 'If the demon which possesses this goat, and which has resisted all exorcisms, persist in its deeds of witchcraft – if he alarm the court with them – we warn him that we shall be obliged to put in requisition against it the gibbet or the stake.'

Gringoire broke out into a cold perspiration. Charmolue took from a table the gypsy's tambourine, and, presenting it in a certain manner to the goat, he asked the latter:

'What o'clock is it?'

The goat looked at him with an intelligent eye, raised her gilt foot, and struck seven blows. It was indeed seven o'clock. A movement of terror ran through the crowd.

Gringoire could no longer contain himself.

'She'll be her own ruin,' cried he aloud; 'you see that she knows not what she is doing!'

'Silence among the louts at the end of the hall!' said the bailiff, sharply.

Jacques Charmolue, by means of the same manœuvres with the tambourine, made the goat perform several other tricks connected with the day of the month, the month of the year, etc., which the reader has already witnessed. And, by an optical illusion peculiar to judicial proceedings, these same spectators who had probably more than once applauded in the public squares Djali's innocent magic, were terrified at it beneath the roof of the Palace of Justice. The goat was indisputably the devil.

It was still worse when, the king's attorney having emptied on the floor a certain leathern bag full of detached letters which Djali wore about her neck, they beheld the goat sort out with its foot from among the scattered alphabet the fatal name: *Phœbus*. The sorcery of which the captain had been the victim seemed unanswerably proved; and, in the eyes of all, the gypsy-girl, that enchanting dancer, who had so often dazzled the passers-by with her grace, was no longer anything but a frightful vampire.

However, she gave no sign of life; neither the graceful evolutions of Djali, nor the threats of the magistrates, nor the muttered imprecations of the audience – nothing seemed to reach her ear.

In order to arouse her, a sergeant was obliged to shake her unmercifully, while the president solemnly raised his voice:

'Girl, you are of Bohemian race, addicted to deeds of witchcraft. You, in complicity with the bewitched goat, implicated in the charge, did, on the night of the 29th of March last, wound and poniard, in concert with the powers of darkness, by the aid of charms and spells, a captain of the king's archers, Phœbus de Chateaupers by name. Do you persist in denying it!'

'Horrible!' exclaimed the young girl, hiding her face with her hands. 'My Phœbus! Oh, this is indeed hell!'

'Do you persist in your denial?' demanded the president, coldly.

'Do I deny it!' said she, in terrible accents; and she rose with flashing eyes.

The president continued bluntly:

'Then how do you explain the facts laid to your charge?'

She answered in a broken voice:

'I have already told you I know not. It is a priest – a priest whom I do not know – an infernal priest, who pursues me!'

'Just so,' replied the judge; 'the spectre monk!'

'Oh, gentlemen, have pity! I am only a poor girl . . .'

'Of Egypt,' said the judge.

Maître Jacques Charmolue interposed sweetly – 'In view of the sad obstinacy of the accused, I demand the application of the torture.'

'Granted,' said the president.

A shudder ran through the whole frame of the wretched girl. She rose, however, at the order of the halberdiers, and walked with a tolerably firm step, preceded by Charmolue and the priests of the officiality, between two rows of halberds, toward a false door, which suddenly opened and closed again behind her, which produced upon the unhappy Gringoire the effect of a horrible mouth which had just devoured her.

When she disappeared, a plaintive bleating was heard. It was the little goat wailing.

The sitting of the court was suspended. A counsellor having remarked that the gentlemen were fatigued, and that it would be a long time for them to wait before the torture was over, the president answered that a magistrate must be ready to sacrifice himself to his duty.

'What a troublesome, vexatious jade!' said an old judge, 'to get herself put to the question when one has not supped!'

II

Continuation of the Crown Changed into a Withered Leaf

AFTER ASCENDING AND descending some steps in passages so dark that they were lighted in broad day by lamps, Esmeralda, still surrounded by her lugubrious attendants, was pushed forward by the sergeants of the Palace, into a room of sinister aspect. This chamber, circular in shape, occupied the ground floor of one of those great towers which still in our day rise above through the layer of modern structures with which modern Paris has covered the old city. There are no windows to this cellar; no other opening than the entrance, which was low and closed by an enormous iron door. Nevertheless, light was not lacking. A furnace had been constructed in the thickness of the wall; a large fire was lighted in it, which filled the vault with its crimson reflection, and stripped of every ray a miserable tallow-dip placed in a corner. The iron grating which served to close the furnace being raised at that moment only showed at the mouth of the flaming chasm against the dark wall the lower edge of its bars, like a row of sharp, black teeth set at regular intervals, which made the furnace look like the mouth of one of those legendary dragons that spit forth fire. By the light which it cast, the prisoner saw all about the room frightful instruments whose use she did not understand. In the middle was a leathern mattress laid almost flat upon the ground, over which hung a thong with a buckle fastened to a copper ring which a flat-nosed monster carved in the keystone of the vault held between his teeth. Tongs, pincers, large plowshares, were heaped inside the furnace, and were heating red-hot, promiscuously upon the burning coals. The blood-red glow of the furnace illuminated in the chamber only a confused mass of horrible things.

This Tartarus was called simply the question chamber.

Upon the bed was seated carelessly Pierrat Torterue, the official torturer. His underlings, two square-faced gnomes, with leathern aprons and tarpaulin coats, were turning about the irons on the coals.

In vain the poor girl called up all her courage; on entering this room she was seized with horror.

The sergeants of the bailiff of the Palace ranged themselves on one side; the priests of the Bishop's Court on the other. A clerk and a table with writing materials were in one corner.

Maître Jacques Charmolue approached the gypsy with a very sweet smile.

'My dear child,' said he, 'do you still persist in your denial?'

'Yes,' she replied in a faint voice.

'In that case,' resumed Charmolue, 'it will be our painful duty to question you more urgently than we should otherwise wish. Have the goodness to sit down on this bed. Maître Pierrat, give place to mademoiselle, and shut the door.'

Pierrat rose with a growl.

'If I shut the door,' muttered he, 'my fire will go out.'

'Well, then, my good fellow,' replied Charmolue, 'leave it open.'

Meanwhile, La Esmeralda remained standing. That leathern bed, on which so many poor wretches had writhed, frightened her. Terror froze her very marrow; there she stood bewildered and stupefied. At a sign from Charmolue, the two assistants laid hold of her and seated her on the bed. They did her no harm; but when those men touched her – when that leather touched her – she felt all her blood flow back to her heart. She looked wildly around the room. She fancied she saw moving and walking from all directions towards her, to crawl upon her body and pinch and bite her, all those hideous implements of torture, which, as compared to the instruments of all sorts she had hitherto seen, were like what bats, centipedes and spiders are to birds and insects

'Where is the doctor?' asked Charmolue.

'Here,' answered a black gown that she had not observed before. She shuddered.

'Mademoiselle,' resumed the fawning voice of the attorney of the ecclesiastical court, 'for the third time, do you persist in denying the facts of which you are accused?'

This time she could only make a sign with her head; her voice failed her.

'You persist?' said Jacques Charmolue. 'Then it grieves me deeply, but I must fulfil the duty of my office.'

'Monsieur, the king's procurator,' said Pierrat gruffly, 'with what shall we begin?'

Charmolue hesitated a moment, with the doubtful grimace of a poet seeking rhyme.

'With the boot,' said he at last.

The unfortunate creature felt herself so utterly abandoned by God and man that her head fell upon her breast like a thing inert, destitute of all strength.

The torturer and the doctor approached her both at once. The two assistants began rummaging in their arsenal.

At the sound of those frightful irons the unfortunate girl quivered like a dead frog which is being galvanized. 'Oh,' murmured she, so low that no one heard her, 'Oh, my Phœbus!' She then relapsed into her former immobility and petrified silence.

This spectacle would have rent any heart but the hearts of judges. She resembled a poor sinful soul tormented by Satan beneath the scarlet wicket of hell. The miserable body upon which that frightful array of saws, wheels and racks was to fasten – the being whom the rough hands of executioners and pincers were to handle, – was, then, this gentle, fair and fragile creature; a poor grain of millet which human justice was handing over to the terrible mills of torture to grind.

Meanwhile, the horny hands of Pierrat Torterue's assistants had brutally bared that beautiful leg, that little foot, which had so often delighted the by-standers with their grace and loveliness in the streets of Paris.

' 'Tis a pity,' growled out the torturer as he remarked the grace and delicacy of their form.

Had the archdeacon been present he would assuredly have bethought him at that moment of his symbol of the spider and the fly. Presently the poor girl saw through the mist which spread before her eyes the 'boot' approach, soon she saw her foot, encased between the iron-bound boards, disappear in the frightful apparatus. Then terror restored her strength.

'Take off that,' she cried frantically; and starting up all dishevelled, 'Mercy!'

She sprang from the bed to fling herself at the feet of the king's attorney but her leg was held fast in the heavy block of oak and iron-work, and she sank upon the boot more helpless than a bee with a leaden weight upon its wings.

At a sign from Charmolue she was replaced on the bed and two coarse hands fastened round her small waist the leathern strap which hung from the ceiling.

'For the last time, do you confess the facts of the charge?' asked Charmolue, with his imperturbable benignity.

'I am innocent.'

'Then, mademoiselle, how do you explain the circumstances brought against you?'

'Alas, sir, I know not.'

'You deny, then?'

'All!'

'Proceed,' said Charmolue to Pierrat.

Pierrat turned the handle of the screwjack; the boot tightened, and the wretched victim uttered one of those horrible shrieks which have no orthography in any human language.

'Stop,' said Charmolue to Pierrat.

'Do you confess?' said he to the gypsy.

'Everything!' cried the wretched girl. 'I confess! I confess! Mercy!'

She had not calculated her strength when she faced the torture. Poor child! whose life hitherto had been so joyous, so pleasant, so sweet; the first pang vanquished her.

'Humanity forces me to tell you,' observed the king's attorney, 'that, in confessing, you have only to look for death.'

'I hope so,' said she; and she sank back upon the leathern bed lifeless, bent double, suspended by the thong buckled round her waist.

'So, my beauty, hold up a bit,' said Maître Pierrat, raising her. 'You look like the golden sheep that hangs about Monsieur of Burgundy's neck.'

Jacques Charmolue raised his voice:

'Clerk, write. Bohemian girl, you confess your participation in the love-feasts, witches' sabbaths and practices of hell, with wicked spirits, witches and hobgoblins? Answer.'

'Yes,' said she, so low that it was lost in a whisper.

'You confess to having seen the ram which Beelzebub causes to appear in the clouds to call together the witches' sabbath, and which is only seen by sorcerers?'

'Yes.'

'You confess to having adored the heads of Bophomet, those

abominable idols of the Templars?'

'Yes.'

'To having had habitual dealings with the devil in the shape of a tame goat, included in the prosecution?'

'Yes.'

'Lastly, you avow and confess having, with the assistance of the demon and of the phantom commonly called the spectre monk, on the night of the twenty-ninth of March last, murdered and assassinated a captain named Phœbus de Chateaupers?'

She raised her large staring eyes to the magistrate and replied, as if mechanically without effort or emotion:

'Yes.'

It was evident that she was utterly broken.

'Write down, registrar,' said Charmolue; and addressing the torturers: 'Let the prisoner be unbound and taken back into court.'

When the prisoner had been 'unbooted' the attorney of the ecclesiastical court examined her foot, still paralyzed with pain. 'Come,' said he, 'there's no great harm done. You cried out in time. You could dance yet, my beauty!'

He then turned to his acolytes of the officiality.

'At length justice is enlightened! that is a consolation, gentlemen! Mademoiselle will at least bear this testimony, that we have acted with all possible gentleness.'

III

The End of the Crown Changed into a Withered Leaf

WHEN, PALE AND LIMPING, she re-entered the court, a general hum of pleasure greeted her. On the part of the audience, it was that feeling of gratified impatience which one experiences at the theatre, at the conclusion of the last interlude of a play, when the curtain rises and the last act is about to begin. On the part of the judges, it was the hope of supping ere long. The little goat, too, bleated with joy. She tried to run to her mistress, but they had tied her to the bench.

Night had quite set in. The candles, whose number had not been increased, gave so little light that the walls of the hall could not be seen. Darkness enveloped every object in a sort of mist. A few apathetic judges' faces were just visible. Opposite to them, at the extremity of the long hall, they could distinguish a vague white patch against the dark background. It was the accused.

She had dragged herself to her place. When Charmolue had magisterially installed himself in his, he sat down; then rose and said, without exhibiting too much of the self-complacency of success, 'The accused has confessed all.'

'Bohemian girl,' continued the president, 'you have confessed all your acts of sorcery, prostitution and assassination upon Phœbus de Chateaupers?'

Her heart was wrung. She was heard sobbing amid the darkness.

'Whatever you will,' answered she feebly; 'but kill me quickly.'

'Monsieur, the king's attorney in the ecclesiastical court,' said the president, 'the chamber is ready to hear your requisitions.'

Maître Charmolue produced a tremendous roll of paper, from which he began to read, with much gesticulation and the exaggerated emphasis of the bar, a Latin oration, wherein all the proofs of the suit were drawn up in Ciceronian periphrases, flanked with quotations from Plautus, his favourite comic author. We regret that we can not present our readers with this extraordinary composition. The orator delivered it with wonderful action. Before he had finished the exordium the perspiration was starting from his brow, and his eyes from his head.

All at once, in the middle of a finely turned period, he broke off, and his countenance, usually mild enough, and indeed stupid, became black as a thunder-cloud.

'Gentlemen,' cried he (this time in French, for it was not in the scroll), 'Satan plays so large a part in this affair that here he is present at our councils, and making mock of their majesty. Behold him!'

So saying, he pointed to the little goat, which, seeing Charmolue gesticulate, thought it was but right she should do the same, and had seated herself on her haunches, mimicking as well as she could, with her fore-feet and bearded head, the pathetic pantomime of the king's attorney in the ecclesiastical court. This was, it may be remembered, one of her prettiest tricks. This incident, this final proof, produced a great effect. The goat's feet were bound together, and the king's attorney resumed the thread of his eloquence.

It was very long, but the peroration was admirable. The last sentence ran thus – the reader may imagine the hoarse voice and breathless gestures of Maître Charmolue:

'*Ideo, domini, coram stryga demonstrata, crimine patente, intentione criminis existente, in nomine sanctæ ecclesiæ Nostræ Dominæ Parisiensis, quae est in saisina habendi omnimodam altam et bassam justitiam in illa hac intemerata Civitatis insula, tenore presentium declaramus nos requirere primo, aliquandam pecuniariam indemnitatem; secundo, amendationem honorabilem ante portalium maximum Nostræ Dominæ ecclesiæ cathedralis; tertio, sententiam in virtute cujus ista stryga cum sua capella, seu in trivio* *vulgariter dicto* la Grève, *seu in insula exeunte in fluvio Sequanæ, juxta pointam jardini regalis, executatæ sint!'* *

He put on his cap and sat down.

'Alas!' sighed Gringoire, heart-broken- *'bassa latinitas!'* (low latinity!)

Another man in a black gown near the prisoner then rose; it was her advocate. The fasting judges began to murmur.

'Mr. Advocate, be brief,' said the president.

'Monsieur, the president,' replied the advocate, 'since the defendant has confessed the crime, I have only one word to say to these gentlemen. Here is a clause in the Salic law: "If a witch hath eaten a man, and if she be convicted of it, she shall pay a fine of eight thousand deniers, which make two hundred pence in gold." May it please the chamber to condemn my client to the fine?'

'A clause that has become obsolete,' said the advocate extraordinary to the king.

'I deny it,' replied the prisoner's advocate.

'Put it to the vote,' said a councillor; 'the crime is manifest – and it is late.'

The question was put to the vote without leaving the hall. The judges nodded assent; they were in haste. Their capped heads were seen uncovered one after another in the dusk at the lugubrious question addressed to them in a low voice by the president. The poor accused seemed to be looking at them, but her bewildered eye no longer saw anything.

The clerk of the court began to write; then he handed the president a long scroll of parchment.

The unhappy girl then heard a stir among the people, the pikes clash and a chilling voice say:

'Bohemian girl, on such day as it shall please our lord the king, at the hour of noon, you shall be taken in a tumbrel, in your shift, barefoot, with a rope around your neck, before the great portal of Notre-Dame; and there you shall do penance with a wax torch of two pounds weight in your hand; and from thence you shall be taken to the Place de Grève,

---

* Therefore, gentlemen, the witchcraft being proved, and the crime made manifest, as likewise the criminal intention – in the name of the holy church of Our Lady of Paris, which is seised of the right of all manner of justice, high and low, within this inviolate island of the City – we declare, by the tenor of these presents, that we require firstly, some pecuniary compensation; secondly, penance before the great portal of the cathedral church of Our Lady; thirdly, a sentence, by virtue of which this witch, together with her she-goat, shall, either in the public square commonly called *La Grève*, or in the island standing forth in the river Seine, adjacent to the point of the royal gardens, be executed.

where you shall be hanged and strangled on the Town gibbet, and likewise this, your goat; and you will pay to the Bishop's Court three lions of gold, in reparation of the crimes, by you committed and confessed, of sorcery, magic, debauchery and murder, upon the person of the sieur Phœbus de Chateaupers. So God have mercy on your soul!'

'Oh! 'tis a dream!' murmured she; and she felt rough hands bearing her away.

IV

'Leave All Hope Behind'

IN THE MIDDLE AGES, when an edifice was complete, there was almost as much of it under the ground as above it. Unless built upon piles, like Notre-Dame, a palace, a fortress or a church had always a double bottom. In cathedrals it was, as it were, another subterranean cathedral, low, dark, mysterious, blind, mute, under the upper nave which was overflowing with light and resounding night and day with the music of bells and organs. Sometimes it was a sepulchre. In palaces and fortresses it was a prison; sometimes a sepulchre also, sometimes both together. Those mighty masses of masonry, whose mode of formation and slow growth we have explained elsewhere, had not foundations merely; they might be said to have roots branching out under ground in chambers, galleries and staircases, like the structure above. Thus, churches, palaces and fortresses were buried midway in the earth. The vaults of a building were another building into which one descended instead of ascended, and whose subterranean stories extended downward beneath the pile of exterior stories of the edifice, like those forests and mountains which are reversed in the mirror-like waters of a lake beneath the forests and mountains of the banks.

At the fortress of Saint Antoine, at the Palace of Justice of Paris, at the Louvre, these subterranean edifices were prisons. The stories of these prisons, as they went deeper into the ground, grew narrower and darker. They formed so many zones, presenting various degrees of horror. Dante could never have imagined anything better for his hell. These tunnel-like dungeons usually ended in a deep hole, shaped like the bottom of a tub, where Dante placed his Satan, and where society placed those condemned to death. When once a miserable human existence was there interred, then farewell light, air, life, *ogni speranza* (all hope behind); it only came forth to the gibbet or to the stake. Sometimes it rotted there; human justice called that *forgetting*. Between mankind and himself the condemned one felt an accumulation of stones and jailers weighing down upon his head, and the entire prison, the massive fortress, was but one enormous complicated lock that barred him out of the living world.

It was in a dungeon hole of this kind, in the *oubliettes* excavated by Saint Louis in the *in pace* (prison in which monks were shut up for life) of the Tournelle, that – for fear of her escaping, no doubt – Esmeralda had been placed when condemned to the gibbet, with the colossal Palace of Justice over her head. Poor fly, that could not have stirred the smallest of its stones!

Assuredly, Providence and mankind had been equally unjust; such an excess of misfortune and torture was not necessary to crush so frail a creature.

She was there, lost in the darkness, buried, entombed. Any one who could have beheld her in this state, after having seen her laugh and dance in the sun, would have shuddered. Cold as night, cold as death, not a breath of air in her tresses, not a human sound in her ear, no longer a ray of light in her eyes, bent double, loaded with chains, crouching beside a jug and a loaf of bread upon a little straw in the pool of water formed beneath her by the damp oozing of her cell, without motion, almost without breath, she was now scarcely sensible even to suffering. Phœbus, the sunshine, noonday, the open air, the streets of Paris, the dances with the applauses of the spectators, the sweet prattlings of love with the officer; then the priest, the old crone, the poniard, blood, the torture, the gibbet – all this did indeed float before her mind, now as a harmonious and golden vision, again as a hideous nightmare. But it was now no more than a horrible and indistinct struggle veiled in darkness, or than distant music played above on the earth, and which was no longer audible at the depth to which the unfortunate creature had fallen.

Since she had been there she neither waked nor slept. In that misery, in that dungeon, she could no more distinguish waking from sleeping, dreams from reality, than she could the day from the night. All was mingled, broken, floating, confusedly scattered in her mind. She felt nothing, knew nothing, thought nothing; at best she only dreamed. Never did living creature plunge so far into the realm of nothingness.

Thus benumbed, frozen, petrified, had she scarcely noticed the sound of a trap-door which was twice or thrice opened somewhere above her, without even admitting a ray of light, and through which a hand had thrown a crust of black bread. Yet this was her only remaining communication with mankind – the periodical visit of the jailer. One thing alone still mechanically occupied her ear; over her head the dampness filtered through the mouldy stones of the vault, and a drop of water dropped from them at regular intervals. She listened stupidly to the noise made by this drop of water as it fell into the pool beside her.

This drop of water falling into the pool was the only movement still stirring around her, the only clock to mark the time, the only sound that reached her of all the noises made upon the surface of the earth.

Although, indeed, she also felt, from time to time, in that sink of mire and darkness, something cold passing here and there over her foot or her arm, and she shuddered.

How long had she been there? She knew not. She had a recollection of a sentence of death pronounced somewhere against some one; then she was borne away, and she awaked icy cold in the midst of night and silence. She had crawled along upon her hands, then iron rings cut her ankles and chains clanked. She discovered that all around her was wall, that underneath her were flag-stones covered with water, and a bundle of straw; but there was neither lamp nor air-hole. Then she seated herself upon the straw, and occasionally, for a change of position, on the lowest of some stone steps in her dungeon.

At one time she had tried to count the dark moments measured for her by the drop of water; but soon that mournful employment of her sick brain had ceased of its own accord and left her in stupor.

At length, one day, or one night (for midnight and noon had the same hue in this sepulchre), she heard above her a louder noise than that usually made by the turnkey when he brought her bread and jug of water. She raised her head and saw a reddish light through the crevices of the sort of trap-door made in the arch of the *in pace*.

At the same time the heavy lock creaked, the trap-door grated on its rusty hinges, turned, and she beheld a lantern, a hand, and the lower part of the bodies of two men, the door being too low for her to see their heads. The light pained her so acutely that she shut her eyes.

When she reopened them the door was closed, the lantern was placed on a step of the staircase, one man alone was standing before her. The black gown fell to his feet, a cowl of the same hue concealed his face. Nothing was visible of his person, neither his face nor his hands. It looked like a long black winding-sheet standing upright, beneath which something seemed to move. She gazed fixedly for some moments at this sort of spectre. Still neither she nor he spoke. They were like two statues confronting each other. Two things only seemed to have life in the vault: the wick of the lantern, which sputtered from the dampness of the atmosphere, and the drop of water from the roof, which interrupted this irregular crepitation by its monotonous plash, and made the reflection of the lantern quiver in concentric waves upon the oily water of the pool.

At length the prisoner broke silence.

'Who are you?'

'A priest.' The word, the accent, the sound of the voice made her start.

The priest continued in a hollow tone:

'Are you prepared?'

'For what?'

'To die.'

'Oh!' said she, 'will it be soon?'

'To-morrow.'

Her head, which she had raised with a look of joy, again sank upon her bosom.

'That is very long yet,' murmured she; 'what difference would a day make to them?'

'Are you then very unhappy?' asked the priest after a short silence.

'I am very cold,' replied she.

She took her feet in her hands, a habitual gesture with unfortunate creatures who are cold, and which we have already observed in the recluse of the Tour-Roland, and her teeth chattered.

The priest's eyes appeared to be wandering from under his hood around the dungeon.

'Without light! without fire! in the water! It is horrible!'

'Yes,' answered she with the bewildered air which misery had given her. 'The day belongs to every one; why do they give me only night?'

'Do you know,' resumed the priest, after another silence, 'why you are here?'

'I think I knew once,' said she, passing her thin fingers across her brow, as if to assist her memory, 'but I know no longer.'

All at once she began to weep like a child.

'I want to go away from here, monsieur. I am cold – I am afraid – and there are creatures that crawl over my body.'

'Well, follow me'

'So saying, the priest look her arm. The poor girl was chilled to her very vitals, yet that hand felt cold to her.

Oh!' murmured she, ' 'tis the icy hand of death. Who are you?'

The priest threw back his hood; she looked: it was that sinister visage which had so long pursued her – that demon's head which had appeared to her at La Falourdel's over the adored head of her Phœbus – that eye which she last saw glaring beside a dagger.

This apparition, always so fatal to her, and which had thus driven her on from misfortune to misfortune, even to an ignominious death, roused her from her stupor. It seemed to her that the veil which had clouded her memory was rent asunder. All the details of her mournful adventure, from the nocturnal scene at La Falourdel's to her condemnation at the Tournelle, rushed upon her mind at once, not vague and confused as heretofore but clear, distinct, vivid, living, terrible. These recollections, almost obliterated by excess of suffering, were revived at the sight of the sombre figure before her, as the heat of fire brings out afresh upon white paper invisible letters traced upon it with sympathetic ink. All the wounds of her heart seemed to be torn open afresh and bleed simultaneously.

'Ha!' she cried, pressing her hands to her eyes, with a convulsive shudder, 'it is the priest!'

Then she let fall her unnerved arm and remained sitting, with bent head, eyes fixed on the ground, mute, and still trembling.

The priest gazed at her with the eye of a hawk which has long hove red high in the heavens above a poor meadow-lark cowering in the wheat, gradually and silently descending in ever lessening circles, and suddenly swooping upon his prey like a flash of lightning, and holds it panting between his talons.

She began to murmur in a low tone:

'Finish! finish! the last blow!' And her head sank between her shoulders in terror, like a sheep awaiting the blow of the butcher's axe.

'You look upon me with horror, then,' he asked at length.

She made no answer.

'Do you look on me with horror?' he repeated.

Her lips contracted as if she were smiling.

'Yes,' said she; 'the executioner taunts the condemned! For months he pursues me, threatens me, terrifies me. But for him my God, how happy I would be! It is he who has cast me into this abyss! Oh, heavens! it was he who killed – it was he who killed him – my Phœbus!'

Here she burst into sobs, and raising her eyes toward the priest:

'Oh! wretch! who are you? what have I done to you? do you then hate me so? Alas! what have you against me?'

'I love thee!' cried the priest.

Her tears suddenly ceased; she eyed him with the vacant stare of an idiot. He had fallen on his knees and was devouring her with eyes of flame.

'Dost thou hear? I love thee!' cried he again.

'What love!' ejaculated the unhappy creature.

He continued:

'The love of a damned soul!'

Both remained silent for several minutes, crushed under the weight of their emotions – he maddened, she stupefied.

'Listen,' said the priest at last, and a strange calm came over him; 'thou shalt know all. I am about to tell thee what hitherto I have scarcely dared tell myself, when I secretly questioned my conscience, in those dead hours of the night when it is so dark that it seems as though God no longer sees us. Listen. Before I saw thee, young girl, I was happy . . .'

'And I too!' sighed she feebly.

'Interrupt me not! Yes, I was happy; or, at least, I thought so. I was pure; my soul was filled with limpid light. No head was raised more proudly or more radiantly than mine. Priests consulted me on chastity, doctors on doctrines. Yes, science was all in all to me; it was a sister — and a sister sufficed me. Not but that, growing older, other ideas came across my mind. More than once my flesh was thrilled as a woman's form passed by. That force of sex and passion which, foolish youth, I had thought stifled forever, had more than once shaken convulsively the chain of the iron vows which bind me, miserable wretch, to the cold stones of the altar. But fasting, prayer, study, the macerations of the cloister again made the spirit ruler of the body. And then I shunned women. Morever, I had but to open a book, for all the impure vapours of the brain to evaporate before the splendour of science. In a few minutes I saw the gross things of earth flee far away, and I was once more calm and serene, bathed in the tranquil light of eternal truth. So long as the Demon sent only vague shadows of women to attack me, passing casually before my eyes, in the church, in the streets, in the fields, and scarcely recurring in my dreams, I vanquished him easily. Alas! if the victory has not remained with me, it is the fault of God, who made not man and the Demon of equal strength. Listen. One day . . .'

Here the priest paused, and the prisoner heard deep sighs burst from his bosom, each one seeming like the last breath of agony.

He resumed:

'One day, I was leaning on the window of my cell. What book was I reading? Oh! all that is whirling now in my brain. I was reading. The window opened upon a square. I heard the sound of a tambourine and music. Vexed at being thus disturbed in my reverie, I glanced into the square. What I saw, others saw beside myself — and yet it was not a spectacle for mortal eye. There, in the middle of the pavement — it was noon, brilliant sunshine — a creature was dancing, a creature so beautiful that God would have preferred her to the Virgin — would have chosen her for His mother — would have been born of her, had she existed when he was made man. Her eyes were black and lustrous; amidst her raven hair, certain locks, through which the sunbeams shone, were glistening like threads of gold. Her feet moved so swiftly that they appeared indistinct, like the spokes of a wheel revolving rapidly. Around her head, amongst her ebony tresses, were plates of metal, which sparkled in the sun, and formed about her temples a diadem of stars. Her dress, thickset with spangles, twinkled, blue and with a thousand sparks, like a summer night. Her brown and pliant arms twined and untwined about her waist like two silken scarfs. Her figure was of surpassing beauty. Oh! how resplendent that form, which stood out like something luminous even in the very light of the sun itself! Alas! young girl, it was thou! Surprised, intoxicated, charmed, I allowed myself to gaze upon thee. I looked at thee so long that suddenly I shuddered with affright. I felt that the hand of Fate was upon me.'

The priest, oppressed by emotion, again paused for a moment; then continued:

'Already half fascinated, I strove to cling to something and to stay myself from falling. I recalled the snares which Satan had already set for me. The creature before me was of that preternatural beauty which can only be of heaven or hell. That was no mere girl moulded of our common clay, and faintly lighted within by the flickering ray of a woman's spirit. It was an angel, but of darkness – of flame, not of light. At the moment that I was thinking thus, I saw beside thee a goat, a beast of the witches, which looked at me laughingly. The midday sun gilded its horns with fire. Then I perceived the snare of the Demon, and I no longer doubted that thou camest from hell, and that thou camest for my perdition. I believed it.'

Here the priest looked the prisoner in the face, and added coldly:

'I believe it still. However, the charm operated little by little. Thy dancing whirled in my brain; I felt the mysterious spell at work within me. All that should have waked in my soul was lulled to sleep; and, like those who perish in the snow, I took pleasure in yielding to that slumber. All at once thou didst begin to sing. What could I do, wretch that I was? Thy song was still more bewitching than thy dance. I tried to flee – impossible. I was nailed, rooted to the ground. It seemed as if the marble flags had risen to my knees. I was forced to remain until the end. My feet were ice, my brain was boiling. At length thou didst, perhaps, take pity on me: thou didst cease to sing; thou didst disappear. The reflection of the dazzling vision, the reverberation of the enchanting music, gradually faded from my eyes and ears. Then I sank into the corner of the window, more stiff and helpless than a fallen statue. The vesper bell roused me. I rose. I fled; but, alas! something within me had fallen to rise no more; something came upon me from which I could not flee!'

He made another pause and proceeded:

'Yes; from that day forth there was within me a man I knew not. I had recourse to all my remedies – the cloister, the altar, work, books – follies! Oh! how empty science sounds when we beat against it in despair a head filled with frantic passion! Knowest thou, young girl, what I saw ever after between the book and me? Thee, thy shadow, the image of the luminous apparition which had one day passed before me. But that image was no longer of the same hue; it was gloomy, funereal, darksome – like the black circle that long hangs about the vision of the imprudent one who has been gazing steadfastly at the sun.

'Unable to rid myself of it – hearing thy song ever humming in my head – constantly seeing thy feet dancing on my breviary – constantly feeling at night, in my dreams, thy form against my own – I wished to see thee again – to touch thee – to who thou wast – to see whether I should find thee indeed equal to the ideal image that had remained of thee – to dispel, perhaps, my dream with the reality. At all events, I hoped a new impression would efface the first, and the first had become insupportable. I sought thee. I saw thee again. Misery! When I had seen thee twice, I wished to see thee a thousand times, I wished to see thee always! Then – how stop short on that steep descent to hell? Then I was no longer my own master. The other end of the thread which the Demon had tied about my wins was fastened to his foot. I became vagrant and wandering like thyself, I waited for thee under porches, I spied thee out at the corners of streets, I watched thee from the top of my tower. Each night I found myself more charmed, more despairing, more fascinated, more lost!

'I had learned who thou wast – a gypsy, a Bohemian, a gitana, a zingara. How could I doubt the witchcraft? Listen. I hoped that a trial would rid me of the charm. A sorceress had bewitched Bruno of Asti; he had her burned, and was cured. I knew it; I wished to try the remedy. First, I tried to have thee forbidden the square in front of Notre-Dame, hoping to forget thee if thou camest no more. Thou didst not heed. Thou camest again. Then came the idea of carrying thee off. One night I attempted it. There were two of us. Already we had laid hold on thee, when that wretched officer came upon us. He delivered thee. Thus was he the beginning of thy misfortunes, of mine and of his own. At length, not knowing what to do or what was to become of me, I denounced thee to the official.

'I thought I should be cured like Bruno of Asti. I, also, had a confused idea that a trial would deliver thee into my hands; that in a prison I should hold thee, I should have thee; that there thou couldst not escape me; that thou hadst possessed me a sufficiently long time to give me the right to possess thee in my turn. When one does evil, one should do it thoroughly. 'Tis madness to stop midway in the monstrous! The extremity of crime has its delirium of joy. A priest and a witch may mingle in ecstasy upon the straw of a dungeon floor!

'So I denounced thee. 'Twas then that I used to terrify thee whenever I met thee. The plot which I was weaving against thee, the storm which I was brewing over thy head, burst from me in muttered threats and lightning glances. Still I hesitated. My project had its appalling sides, which made me shrink back.

'Perhaps I might have renounced it, perhaps might my hideous thought have withered in my brain without bearing fruit. I thought it would always depend upon me to follow up or set aside this prosecution. But every evil thought is inexorable, and insists on becoming a deed; where I supposed myself all-powerful, Fate was mightier than I.

Alas! alas! 'tis she who has laid hold on thee, and cast thee amid the terrible machinery of the engine I had secretly constructed! Listen; I am nearing the end.

'One day – again the sun was shining brightly – I beheld a man pass me who pronounced thy name and laughed, and who carried profligacy in his eyes. Damnation! I followed him. Thou knowest the rest.'

He ceased.

The young girl could find but one word:

'Oh, my Phœbus!'

'Not that name!' said the priest, seizing her arm with violence. 'Pronounce not that name! Oh! unhappy wretches that we are 'tis that name which has ruined us! or rather, we have ruined each other by the inexplicable play of fate! Thou art suffering, art thou not? Thou art cold; darkness blinds thee; the dungeon wraps thee round; but, perhaps, thou hast still some light shining within thee – were it only thy childish love for that empty being who was trifling with thy heart? while I – I bear the dungeon within me; within me is winter, ice, despair; I have the darkness in my soul.

'Knowest thou all that I have suffered? I was present at thy trial. I was seated on the bench with the officials. Yes, under one of those priestly hoods were the contortions of a damned spirit. When thou wast brought in, I was there; when thou wast interrogated, I was there. The den of wolves! 'Twas my own crime; 'twas my own gibbet they were slowly constructing over thy head! At each deposition, at each proof, at each pleading, I was there; I could count each of thy steps on the road of agony. I was there, again, when that wild beast . . . Oh! I had not foreseen the torture! Listen. I followed thee to the chamber of anguish. I saw thee stripped and handled by the vile hands of the torturer. I saw thy foot – that foot, upon which I would have given an empire to press a single kiss and die; that foot, beneath which I would with rapture have been crushed – that foot I beheld encased in the horrible boot, that boot which converts the limb of a living being into bleeding pulp! Oh! wretched me! while I looked on at that I grasped beneath my sackcloth a dagger with which I lacerated my breast. At the shriek which thou utteredst, I plunged it in my flesh; at a second cry, it would have entered my heart. Look; I think it still bleeds.'

He opened his cassock. His breast was indeed torn as if by a tiger's claws, and in his side was a large, ill-closed wound.

The prisoner shrank back with horror.

'Oh!' said the priest, 'girl, have pity on me! Thou thinkest thyself unhappy. Alas! alas! thou knowest not what misery is. Oh! to love a woman – to be a priest – to be hated – to love her with all the fury of your soul – to feel that you would give for the least of her smiles your blood, your vitals, your reputation, your salvation, immortality and eternity, this life and the other – to regret you are not a king, a genius, an emperor, an archangel, God, that you might place a greater slave beneath her feet – to clasp her day and night in your dreams, in your thoughts, and to see her in love with the trappings of a soldier, and have nothing to offer her but a priest's dirty cassock, which will terrify and disgust her. To be present with your jealousy and your rage while she lavishes on a miserable, blustering imbecile treasures of love and beauty! To behold that body whose form inflames you, that bosom which has so much sweetness, that flesh tremble and blush under the kisses of another! Oh heavens! to love her foot, her arm, her shoulder! to think of her blue veins, of her brown skin, until one writhes for nights together on the pavement of one's cell; and to see all those caresses one has dreamed of end in torture! to have succeeded only on laying her on the bed of leather! Oh, these are the true pincers heated at the fires of hell! Oh happy is he that is sawed asunder between two planks, or torn to pieces by four horses! Knowest thou what torture he feels through long nights? whose arteries boil, whose heart seems bursting, whose head seems splitting, whose teeth tear his hands – fell tormentors which turn him incessantly, as on a fiery gridiron, over a thought of love, jealousy and despair? Mercy, girl! A truce for a moment! A few ashes on this living coal! Wipe away, I beseech thee, the big drops of sweat that trickle from my brow! Child! torture me with one hand, but caress me with the other! Have pity, maiden! have pity on me.'

The priest writhed on the wet pavement and beat his head against the edges of the stone steps. The young girl listened to him, looked at him.

When he ceased speaking, panting and exhausted, she repeated in an undertone:

'Oh, my Phœbus!'

The priest dragged himself towards her on his knees.

'I implore thee,' cried he, 'if thou hast any bowels of compassion, repulse me not! Oh! I love thee! I am a miserable wretch! When thou utterest that name, unhappy girl, it is as if thou wert grinding between thy teeth every fibre of my heart! Mercy! If thou comest from hell, I go thither with thee. I have done everything to that end. The hell where thou art will be my paradise; the sight of thee is more entrancing than that of God. Oh! say! wilt thou none of me, Then? I should have thought the mountains would have been shaken on their foundations the day a woman would repulse such a love. Oh! if thou wouldst . . . Oh! how happy could we be! We would flee; I would help thee to flee; we would go somewhere; we would seek that spot on the earth where the sun is brightest, the trees most luxuriant, the sky the bluest. We would love each other; we would pour our two souls one into the other and we would each have an inextinguishable thirst for the other which we would quench incessantly and together at the inexhaustible fountain of love!'

She interrupted him with a loud and terrible laugh.

'Look, father! you have blood upon your fingers!'

The priest remained for some moments petrified, his eyes fixed on his hand.

'Yes, 'tis well,' he resumed at length with strange gentleness; 'insult me, taunt me, overwhelm me with scorn! but come, come away. Let us hasten. It is to be to-morrow, I tell thee. The gibbet on the Grève, thou knowest! It is ever ready. 'Tis horrible! to see thee borne in that tumbrel! Oh! mercy! Never did I feel as at this moment how dearly I love thee. Oh! follow me. Thou shalt hate me as long as thou wilt. Only come. To-morrow! to-morrow! the gibbet! thy execution! Oh! save thyself! spare me!'

He seized her arm; he was frantic; he strove to drag her away.

She fixed her eye intently on him.

'What has become of my Phœbus?'

'Ah!' said the priest, letting go her arm, 'you have no pity!'

'What has become of Phœbus?' she repeated coldly.

'He is dead!' cried the priest.

'Dead!' said she, still cold and passionless; 'then why do you talk to me of living?'

He heard her not.

'Oh. yes!' said he as if talking to himself, 'he must indeed be dead. The blade entered deep. I believe I touched his heart with the point. Oh! my very soul was in that dagger's point!'

The young girl rushed upon him like an enraged tigress, and thrust him against the flight of steps with supernatural strength.

'Begone, monster! begone, murderer! leave me to die! May the blood of us both mark thy brow with an everlasting stain . . . Be thine! priest? Never! never! nothing shall unite us! not hell itself! Begone, accursed! Never!'

The priest had stumbled to the steps. He silently disengaged his feet from the folds of his cassock, took up his lantern, and began slowly to ascend the steps leading to the door; he reopened the door and went out.

All at once the young girl beheld his head re-appear; his face wore a frightful expression, and he cried to her, hoarse with rage and despair:

'I tell thee, he is dead!'

She fell face downwards on the ground, and no sound was heard in the dungeon save the sob of the drop of water which made the pool palpitate amid the darkness.

V

The Mother

I DO NOT THINK there is anything in the world more gladsome than the ideas which awake in a mother's heart at the sight of her child's little shoe; above all, when it is the holiday, the Sunday, the christening shoe – the shoe embroidered to the very sole, a shoe in which the child has not yet taken one step. That shoe has so much daintiness and grace, it is so impossible for it to walk, that it seems to the mother as though she saw her child. She smiles at it, she kisses it, she talks to it, she asks herself whether there can actually be a foot so tiny; and, if the child be absent, the pretty shoe suffices to bring the soft and fragile creature before her eyes. She fancies she sees it – she does see it – full of life and laughter, with its delicate hands, its round head, its pure lips, its serene eyes, whose white is blue. If it be winter, there it is, crawling on the carpet, climbing laboriously upon a stool; and the mother trembles lest it go too near the fire. If it be summer, it creeps about the yard, the garden, plucks up the grass from between the stones, gazes with artless wonder, and fearlessly, at the big dogs, the great horses, plays with the shell-work, the flowers, and makes the gardener scold when he finds the gravel on the beds and the mould upon the walks. Everything smiles, everything is bright everything is playful, like itself, even to the zephyr and the sunbeam, which sport in rivalry amidst its wanton curls. The shoe recalls all this to the mother, and her heart melts before it as wax before the fire.

But when the child is lost, those thousand images of joy, of delight, of tenderness, which swarmed around the little shoe, become so many sources of horror. The pretty little embroidered shoe is now only an instrument of torture, incessantly racking the heart of the mother. It is still same chord which vibrates, the fibre the most sensitive, the most profound; but instead of its being touched by an angel, it is now wrenched by a demon.

One morning, as the May sun was rising in one of those deep blue skies in which Garofolo loves to picture the descent from the cross, the recluse of the Tour-Roland heard the sound of wheels, the tramp of horses and the clanking of irons in the Place de Grève. She was but little roused by it, fastened her hair over her ears to deaden the sound, and on her knees resumed her contemplation of the inanimate object which she had been thus adoring for fifteen years. That little shoe, we have already said, was to her the universe. Her thoughts were locked up in it, never to be parted from it but by death. What bitter imprecations she had breathed to heaven, what heart-rending complaints, what prayers and sobs about this charming, rosy, satin toy, the gloomy cave of the Tour-Roland only knew. Never was keener anguish lavished upon a thing more charming or more delicate.

That morning it seemed as if her grief was venting itself more violently than usual, and she was heard from without lamenting in a loud and monotonous voice that wrung to the heart.

'Oh! my child,' said she, 'my child! my poor, dear, little babe, I shall see thee then no more! Is it then over? It always seems to me as if it happened but yesterday! My God! my God! to take her from me so soon; it would have been better not to have given her to me! You do not know, then, that our children are of our own bowels, and a mother that has lost her child believes no longer in God? Ah! wretched that I am, to have gone out that day! Lord! Lord! to take her from me thus! You never saw me with her, then, when I warmed her all joyous at my fire, when she laughed at me as I gave her suck, when I made her little feet creep up my bosom to my lips? Oh! if you had but seen that, my God! you would have had pity on my joy; you would not have taken from me the only love that was yet left in my heart! Was I such a wretched creature, then, Lord, that you could not look at me before you condemned me? Alas! alas! there is the shoe, but the foot, where is it? where is the child? My babe! my babe, what have they done with thee? Lord, give her back to me! For fifteen years have I torn my knees in praying to thee, my God! Is that not enough? Give her back to me for one day, one hour, one minute, but for one minute, Lord, and then cast me to the evil one forever! Oh! if I only knew where lay but the hem of your garment, I would cling to it with both my hands, and you would be obliged to give me back my child! Her pretty little shoe, have you no pity on it, Lord? Can you condemn a poor mother to these fifteen years of torture? Good Virgin! good Virgin of Heaven! my infant Jesus has been taken from me; they have stolen it, they have eaten it on the wild heath, they have drunk its blood, they have crushed its bones! Good Virgin! have pity on me! My daughter! I must have my daughter! What care I that she should be in heaven! I'll none of your angel, I want my child! I am the lioness, I want my whelp! Oh, I'll writhe upon the ground, I'll dash my forehead against the stones, I'll damn myself and curse you, Lord, if you keep from me my child! You see how my arms are bitten, Lord! Has the good God no pity? Oh, give me but black bread and salt, only let me have my child to warm me like a sun! Alas! Lord God, I am only a vile sinner, but my child made me pious. I was full of religion for love of her, and I saw you through her smile as through an opening of heaven. Oh, let me only once, once again, but a single time, put this shoe on her pretty, little, rosy foot, and I will die, good Virgin, blessing you! Ah! fifteen years! she would be grown up now. Unhappy child! What! is it true, then, I shall never see her more, not even in heaven? for I shall never go there. Oh, what misery to say, "There is her shoe, and that is all!"

The wretched woman had thrown herself on this shoe, for so many years her consolation and despair, and her heart was rent with sobs as on the first day – for to a mother that has lost her child, it is always the first day. That grief never grows old. The mourning garments may wear out and lose their dye, the heart remains dark. At that moment, fresh and joyous children's voices passed before the cell. Whenever any children met her eye or ear, the poor mother used to rush in the darkest corner of her sepulchre, and seemed as if she would plunge her head into the stone that she might not hear them. This time, on the contrary, she started up and listened eagerly. One of the little boys had just said:

'They're going to hang a gypsy-woman to-day.'

With a sudden bound, like that of the spider which we have seen rush upon a fly at the trembling of her web, she ran to her loophole, which looked out, as the reader is aware, upon the Place de Grève. There, indeed, was a ladder reared against the permanent gibbet, and the hangman's assistant was busy adjusting the chains rusted by the rain. Some people were standing around.

The smiling group of children was already far away. The recluse sought with her eyes some passer-by whom she might interrogate. Close to her cell she perceived a priest, who pretended to be reading in the public breviary, but whose mind was much less occupied with the lattice-guarded volume than with the gibbet, toward which he cast from time to time a stern and gloomy look. She recognized Monsieur the archdeacon of Josas, a holy man.

'Father,' asked she, 'whom are they about to hang yonder?'

The priest looked at her without answering; she repeated the question, and then he said, 'I don't know.'

'There were some children that said it was a gypsy-woman,' continued the recluse.

'I believe it is,' said the priest.

Then Pâquette la Chantefleurie burst into a hyena-like laughter.

'Sister,' said the archdeacon, 'you greatly hate the gypsy-women then?'

'Hate them!' cried the recluse; 'they are witches, child stealers! They devoured my little girl, my child, my only child! I have no heart left, they have devoured it!'

She was frightful. The priest looked at her coldly.

'There is one of them whom I hate above all, and whom I have cursed,' resumed she; 'a young one, who is the age my girl would be if her mother had not eaten my girl. Every time that young viper passes before my cell she makes my blood boil.'

'Well, sister, be joyful,' said the priest, icy as a sepulchral statue; 'that is the one you are about to see die.'

His head fell upon his breast and he moved slowly away.

The recluse writhed her arms with joy.

'I had foretold it to her that she would go up there again. Thank you, priest,' cried she.

And then she began to pace with rapid steps before the bars of her window, her hair dishevelled, her eyes glaring, striking her shoulder against the wall, with the wild air of a caged she-wolf that has long been hungry and feels that the hour of her repast is approaching.

VI

Three Human Hearts Differently Constituted

PHŒBUS, HOWEVER, was not dead. Men of that stamp are hard to kill. When Maître Philip de Lheulier, king's advocate extraordinary, had said to poor Esmerelda, 'he is dying,' it was an error or in jest. When the archdeacon had repeated to the condemned girl, 'he is dead,' the fact was that he knew nothing about the matter, but he believed it, he made sure of it and he had no doubt of it. It would have been too hard for him to give favourable news of his rival to the woman whom he loved. Any man would have done the same in his place.

Not that Phœbus's wound was not severe, but it was less so than the archdeacon flattered himself. The surgeon, to whose house the soldiers of the watch had at once carried him, had, for a week feared for his life, and had even told him so in Latin. However youth triumphed; and as often happens, notwithstanding prognostics and diagnostics, Nature amused herself by saving the patient in spite of the physician. It was while he was still lying upon the leech's pallet that he underwent the first interrogatories of Philippe Lheulier and the official inquisitors, which he had found especially wearisome. Accordingly, one fine morning, feeling himself better, he had left his golden spurs in payment to the man of medicine, and taken himself off. This, however, had not in the least affected the judicial proceedings. Justice in those days cared little about clearness and precision in the proceedings against a criminal. Provided only that the accused was hung, that was all that was necessary. Now the judges had ample proof against La Esmeralda. They believed Phœbus to be dead – and that was the end of the matter.

Phœbus, for his part, had fled to no great distance. He had simply rejoined his company in garrison at Queue-en-Brie, in the Isle of France, a few stages from Paris.

After all, it did not please him in the least to appear in this suit. He had a vague impression that he would play a ridiculous part in it. In fact, he did not very well know what to think of the whole affair. Irreligious and superstitious, like every soldier who is nothing but a soldier, when he came to question himself about this adventure, he was not altogether without his suspicions of the little goat, of the singular fashion in which he had first met La Esmeralda, of the no less strange manner in which she had betrayed her love, of her being a gypsy, and lastly of the spectre monk. He perceived in all these incidents much more magic than love; probably a sorceress; perhaps a devil; a sort of drama, in short; or, to speak the language of that day, a mystery – very disagreeable indeed – in which he played a very awkward part, that of the personage beaten and laughed at. The captain felt abashed at this; he experienced that sort of shame which Lafontaine has so admirably defined:

Ashamed as a fox caught by a hen

Moreover, he hoped that the affair would not be noised abroad; that, himself being absent, his name would hardly be pronounced in connection with it, and that in any case it would not go beyond the court room of the Tournelle. In this he was not mistaken. There was then no *Gazette des Tribunaux*; and as hardly a week passed in which there was not some counterfeiter to boil, some witch to hang, or some heretic to burn, at some of the numberless *justices* of Paris, people were so much accustomed to see at every crossway the ancient feudal Themis, bare-armed, with sleeves turned up, doing her work at the gibbets, the whipping posts and pillories, that they hardly paid any heed to it. The aristocracy of that day scarcely knew the name of the victim who passed by at the corner of the street; and, at most, it was only the populace that regaled itself with this coarse fare. An execution was a common incident in the public highways, like the baker's braising pan or the butcher's slaughter house. The executioner was but a sort of butcher of a little deeper dye than the rest.

Phœbus, therefore, soon set his mind at rest in regard to the enchantress Esmeralda or Similar, as he called her, to the dagger thrust which he had received from the gypsy-girl, or from the spectre monk (it mattered little to him which), and to the issue of the trial. But no sooner was his heart vacant on that score, than the image of Fleur-de-Lys returned thither; for the heart of Captain Phœbus, like the natural philosophy of the day, abhorred a vacuum.

Moreover, he found it very dull staying at Queue-en-Brie, a village of farriers and cow-girls with chapped hands; a long string of poor huts and thatched cottages, bordering the highway on both sides for half a league; a tail (*queue*) in short, as its name imports.

Fleur-de-Lys was his last flame but one – a pretty girl, a delightful dowry. Accordingly, one fine morning, quite cured, and fairly presuming that after two months had elapsed, the affair of the gypsy-girl must be over and forgotten, the amorous cavalier arrived on a prancing horse at the door of the Gondelaurier mansion.

He paid no heed to a somewhat numerous rabble which had gathered in the Place du Parvis, before the portal of Notre-Dame. He recollected that it was the month of May; he supposed it to be some procession, some Whitsuntide or holiday, fastened his horse's bridle to the ring at the gate, and gaily ascended the stairs in search of his fair betrothed.

She was alone with her mother.

Fleur-de-Lys had still weighing upon her heart the scene of the sorceress with her goat and its accursed alphabet, and the lengthened absence of Phœbus. Nevertheless, when she beheld her captain enter, she thought him so handsome, his doublet so new, his baldric so shining, and his air so impassioned, that she blushed with pleasure. The noble damoiselle herself was more charming than ever. Her magnificent fair locks were braided to perfection; she was clad in all that heavenly blue which so well becomes fair people (a bit of coquetry she had learned from Colombe), and her eyes swam in that languor of love which becomes them still better.

Phœbus, who had seen nothing in the line of beauty since he quitted the country wenches of Queue-en-Brie, was intoxicated with the sight of Fleur-de-Lys – which imparted to our officer so eager and gallant an air that his peace was made immediately. Madame de Gondelaurier herself, still maternally seated in her big arm-chair, had not the courage to scold him. As for Fleur-de-Lys's reproaches, they died away in tender cooings.

The young lady was seated near the window, still embroidering her grotto of Neptunus. The captain was leaning over the back of her chair, while she murmured to him her gentle upbraidings.

'What have you been doing with yourself for these two months past, you naughty man?'

'I swear,' replied Phœbus, a little embarrassed by the question, 'that you are beautiful enough to set an archbishop to dreaming.'

She could not help smiling.

'Good, good, sir. Let my beauty alone and answer me. Fine beauty, indeed!'

'Well, my dear cousin I was recalled to the garrison.'

'And where was that, if you please? and why did you not come to bid me farewell?'

'At Queue-en-Brie.'

Phœbus was delighted that the first question had helped him to elude the second.

'But that is quite close by, sir. How happened it that you came not once to see me?'

Here Phœbus was very seriously perplexed. 'Because – the service – and then, charming cousin, I have been ill.'

'Ill!' she repeated in alarm.

'Yes – wounded.'

'Wounded!'

The poor girl was quite overcome.

'Oh, do not be frightened at that,' said Phœbus, carelessly; 'it was nothing. A quarrel – a sword cut – what is that to you?'

'What is that to me!' exclaimed Fleur-de-Lys, lifting her beautiful eyes filled with tears. 'Oh! you do not say what you think when you speak thus. What sword cut was that? I wish to know all.'

'Well, my dear fair one, I had a quarrel with Mahé Fédy, you know, the lieutenant of Saint Germain-en-Laye, and we have ripped open a few inches of skin for each other – that is all.'

The mendacious captain was well aware that an affair of honour always set a man off to advantage in the eyes of a woman. In fact, Fleur-de-Lys looked him in the face with mingled sensations of fear, pleasure and admiration. Still, she was not completely reassured.

'Provided that you are wholly cured, my Phœbus!' said she. 'I do not know your Mahé Fédy, but he is a villainous man. And whence arose this quarrel?'

Here Phœbus, whose imagination was only tolerably active, began to be rather at a loss how to find a means of extricating himself for his prowess.

'Oh, I know not; a mere nothing; a horse; a remark! Fair cousin,' he exclaimed, by way of turning the conversation, 'what noise is that in the square?' He went to the window.

'Oh, heavens! fair cousin, what a great crowd in the Place.'

'I do not know,' said Fleur-de-Lys; 'it appears that a witch is to do penance this morning before the church, and thereafter to be hanged.'

So absolutely did the captain believe the affair of La Esmeralda to be terminated, that he was little affected by these words of Fleur-de-Lys. Nevertheless, he asked her one or two questions.

'What is the name of this witch?'

'I do not know,' she replied.

'And what is she said to have done?'

She again shrugged her white shoulders.

'I know not.'

'Oh, my sweet Saviour!' said the mother, 'there are so many sorcerers nowadays that they burn them, I verily believe, without.

knowing their names. One might as well seek the name of every cloud in the sky. After all, one may be tranquil. The good God keeps his register.' Here the venerable dame rose and went to the window. 'Good Lord!' she cried, 'you are right, Phœbus – there is indeed a great crowd of the populace. There they are, blessed be God! even on the house-tops! Do you know, Phœbus, this reminds me of my young, days – the entry of King Charles VII, when there was also such a crowd. I no longer remember what year it was. When I speak of this to you it produces upon you the effect – does it not? – of something very old, and upon me of something very young. Oh! the crowd was far finer than now. There were some even upon the battlements of the Porte Saint Antoine. The king had the queen on a pillion; and after their highnesses came all the ladies mounted behind all the lords. I remember there was much laughing; for by the side of Amanyon de Garlande, who was very short of stature, there was the Sire Matefelon, a knight of gigantic stature, who had killed heaps of English. It was very fine. A procession of all the gentlemen of France, with their red banners waving in the air. There were some with pennons, and some with banners. Let me see – there was the Sire of Calan, with his pennon; Jean de Chateaumorant, with his banner; the Sire of Coucy, with his banner, and a richer one, too, than any of the others, except the Duke of Bourbon's. Alas! 'tis a sad thing to think all that has existed, and exists no longer.'

The two lovers were not listening to the worthy dowager. Phœbus had returned to lean over the hack of the chair of his betrothed; a charming situation, whence his libertine gaze could invade every opening in Fleur-de-Lys's collarette. This collarette gaped so opportunely, and revealed to him so many exquisite things, and led him to divine so many others, that Phœbus, dazzled by this skin with its gleams of skin, said to himself, 'How can one love any but a fair skin?'

Both were silent. The young girl raised sweet, enraptured eyes to him from time to time, and their hair mingled in a ray of spring sunshine.

'Phœbus,' said Fleur-de-Lys suddenly, in a low tone, 'we are to be married in three months – swear to me that you have never loved any woman but myself.'

'I swear it, fair angel!' replied Phœbus; and his passionate gaze combined with the truthful tone of his voice to convince Fleur-de-Lys. Perhaps indeed, at that moment, he himself believed what he was saying.

Meanwhile, the good mother, delighted to see the betrothed pair on such excellent terms, had left the apartment to attend to some household matter. Phœbus observed it; and this so much emboldened the adventurous captain, that some very strange ideas entered his brain. Fleur-de-Lys loved him; he was her betrothed; she was alone with him;

his former inclination for her had revived, not with all its its freshness, but with all its ardour; after all, there was no great harm in tasting one's fruit before it is harvested. I do not know whether these ideas actually crossed his mind, but so much is certain, that Fleur-de-Lys was suddenly alarmed at the expression of his glance. She looked around and saw that her mother was no longer there.

'Good heavens!' said she, flushed .and uneasy, 'I am very warm!'

'I think, indeed,' returned Phœbus, 'it must be almost noon. The sun is troublesome; We need only draw the curtains.'

'No, no!' cried the trembling damsel; 'on the contrary, I need air.'

And, like a fawn that scents the breath of the approaching pack, she rose, hurried to the window, opened it, and rushed upon the balcony.

Phœbus, considerably vexed, followed her.

The Place du Parvis Notre-Dame, upon which, as we know, the balcony looked, presented, at that moment, a singular and sinister spectacle, which suddenly altered the nature of the timid Fleur-de-Lys's alarm.

An immense crowd, which overflowed into all the neighbouring streets, blocked up the square itself. The low wall, breast high, inclosing the Parvis, would not have sufficed to keep it clear, had it not been lined by dense ranks of the sergeants of the Onze-vingts, and of hack-buteers, culverin in hand. Owing, however, to this grove of pikes and arquebusses, the Parvis was empty. Its entrance was guarded by a body of the bishop's own halberdiers. The great doors of the church were shut, in contrast to the countless windows overlooking the square, which, open up to the very gables, revealed thousands of heads heaped one upon another, something like the balls in a park of artillery.

The surface of this mob was gray, dirty and squalid. The spectacle which was awaiting was evidently one of those which have the privilege of extracting and collecting all that is most unclean in the population. Nothing could be more hideous than the noise which arose from that swarm of soiled caps and unkempt heads. In this crowd there was more laughter than shouting, more women than men.

Ever and anon some sharp, shrill voice pierced the general uproar.

'Hi! Mahiet Baliffre! Is she to be hanged yonder?'

'Simpleton! 'tis here she is to do penance in her shift. The priest will spit a little Latin in her face. That is always done here at midday. If 'tis the gallows you want, you must e'en go to the Grève.'

'I'll go there afterwards.'

'Tell me, Boucanbry, is it true that she has refused a confessor?'

'So it seems, La Bechaigne.'

'Look at that, the heathen!'

'Sir, it is the custom. The Palace bailiff is bound to deliver the malefactor, ready sentenced, for execution; if 'tis a layman, to the provost of Paris; if 'tis a clerk, to the official of the bishopric.'

'Thank you, sir.'

'Oh, heavens!' said Fleur-de-Lys, 'the poor creature!'

This thought filled with sadness the glance which she cast upon the crowd. The captain, much more occupied with her than with that pack of rabble, was amorously fingering her girdle behind. She turned around with smiling entreaty.

'For pity's sake, let me alone, Phœbus! if my mother were to return she would see your hand.'

At that moment, the clock of Notre-Dame slowly struck twelve.

A murmur of satisfaction burst from the crowd. The last vibration of the twelfth stroke had hardly died away, when all the heads surged like the waves before a sudden gale, and an immense shout went up from the pavement, from the windows, and from the roofs, 'There she is!'

Fleur-de-Lys covered her eyes with her hands, that she might not see.

'My charmer,' said Phœbus, 'will you go in?'

'No,' replied she; and those eyes which she had just closed through fear, she opened again through curiosity.

A tumbrel drawn by a strong Norman dray horse, and quite surrounded by horsemen in violet livery with white crosses, had just entered the square from the Rue Saint-Pierre-aux-Bœufs. The sergeants of the watch cleared a passage for it through the crowd by a vigorous use of their whit-leather whips. Beside the tumbrel rode some officers of justice and police, recognizable by their black costume and their awkwardness in the saddle. Maître Jacques Charmolue paraded at their head.

In the fatal cart sat a young girl, her hands tied behind her, and with no priest at her side. She was in her shift; her long black hair (the custom then was to cut it only at the foot of the gibbet) fell in disorder upon her half-bared throat and shoulders.

Athwart that waving hair, more glossy than a raven's plumage, a rough, gray cord was seen, twisted and knotted, chafing her delicate skin and winding about the poor girl's graceful neck like an earthworm around a flower. Beneath that rope glittered a small amulet, ornamented with bits of green glass, which had been left to her, no doubt, because nothing is refused to those about to die. The spectators at the windows could see in the bottom of the tumbrel her naked legs, which she strove to conceal under her as by a final feminine instinct. At her feet lay a little goat, bound. The prisoner was holding together with her teeth her ill-tied chemise. It seemed as if even in her misery she still suffered from being thus exposed almost naked before all eyes. Alas! it was not for such shocks that modesty was made.

'Jesus!' said Fleur-de-Lys hastily to the captain, 'look there, fair cousin – it is that horrid gypsy-girl with the goat.'

So saying, she turned to Phœbus. His eyes were fixed on the tumbrel. He was very pale.

'What gypsy-girl with the goat?' he stammered.

'Why,' rejoined Fleur-de-Lys, 'do you not remember?'

Phœbus interrupted her:

'I do not know what you mean.'

He stepped back to re-enter the room, but Fleur-de-Lys, whose jealousy, already so deeply stirred by this same gypsy-girl, was now re-awakened, cast at him a glance full of penetration and mistrust. She now vaguely recollected having heard a captain mentioned who had been implicated in the trial of this sorceress.

'What ails you?' said she to Phœbus; 'one would think that this woman disturbed you.'

Phœbus forced a sneering smile.

'Me! not the least in the world! Me, indeed!'

'Remain, then,' returned she imperiously, 'and let us see the end .'

The unlucky captain was obliged to remain. He was somewhat reassured by the fact that the condemned girl kept her eyes fixed upon the bottom of the tumbrel. It was but too truly La Esmeralda. In this last stage of ignominy and misfortune she was still beautiful; her great, dark eyes looked larger on account of the hollowness of her cheeks; her pale profile was pure and sublime. She resembled what she had been, as a virgin of Masaccio resembles a Virgin of Raphael's, weaker, thinner, more delicate.

Moreover, her whole being was tossed hither and thither, and, save for her sense of modesty, she had abandoned everything, so utterly was she crushed by stupor and despair. Her body rebounded at every jolt of the cart, like some shattered, lifeless thing; her gaze was fixed and unconscious; a tear still lingered in her eye, but motionless, and as it were frozen.

Meanwhile, the dismal cavalcade had traversed the crowd, amid shouts of joy and stare of the curious. Nevertheless, historical fidelity calls upon us to state that on seeing her so beautiful and so forlorn, many were moved to pity, even among the most hardhearted. The tumbrel entered the Parvis.

Before the central doorway of the church it stopped. The escort drew up in line on either side. The mob was silenced; and amid this silence so solemn and anxious the two halves of the great door turned, as if of themselves, upon their hinges, which creaked like the sound of a fife. Then the deep interior of the church was seen in its whole extent, gloomy, hung with black, faintly lighted by a few wax tapers twinkling afar off upon the high altar, yawning like the mouth of a cavern upon the square resplendent with sunshine. At the farthest extremity in the dusk of the chancel, was dimly seen a colossal silver cross, standing out in relief against a black cloth, which hung from the roof to the pavement. The whole nave was deserted; but heads of priests were seen moving confusedly in the distant choir stalls; and at the moment when the great door opened there burst from the church a loud, solemn and monotonous chant, hurling as it were in gusts, fragments of doleful psalms at the head of the condemned one:

' . . .*Non timebo millia populi circumdantis me; exsurge, Domine: salvum me fac, Deus!*' (. . . I will not fear the thousands of the people gathered about me; arise, O Lord! save me, O my God.)

' . . . *Salvum me fac, Deus, quoniam intraverunt aquæ usque ad animam meam!*' (. . . Save me, O God; albeit the waters have entered, even unto my soul.)

' . . . *Infixus sum in limo profundi; et non est substantia.*' (. . . Behold, I am set fast in the slime of the great deep and there is no ground under my feet.)

At the same time another voice, separate from the choir, intoned from the steps of the high altar, this mournful offertory:

' . . . *Qui verbum meum audit, et credit ei qui misit me, habet vitam æternam, et in judicium non venit; sed transit a morte in vitam.*' (. . . Whoso heareth my word, and believeth in him that sent me, hath life everlasting; he cometh not unto judgment, but from death he passeth unto life.)

This chant, which a few old men, buried in their own gloom, sang from afar over this beautiful creature full of youth and life, wooed by the warm air of spring, and bathed in sunshine, was the mass for the dead.

The people listened devoutly.

The unfortunate girl, bewildered, seemed to lose her sight and her consciousness in the dark interior of the church. Her pale lips moved as if in prayer; and when the hangman's assistant approached to help her down from the cart, he heard her repeating in a whisper, this word: 'Phœbus.'

They untied her hands, made her alight, accompanied by her goat, which was also unbound, and which bleated with joy at finding itself free. She was then led barefoot over the hard pavement to the foot of the steps leading to the portal. The cord about her neck trailed behind her like a serpent pursuing her.

Then the chanting in the church ceased. A great golden cross and a row of wax candles began to move through the gloom. The halberds of the motley dressed beadles clanked, and a few moments later a long procession of priests in chasubles and deacons in dalmatics marched solemnly towards the prisoner, singing psalms as they came into view. But her eyes were riveted upon him who walked at their head, immediately after the cross-bearer.

'Oh!' she said in a low tone with a shudder, ' 'Tis he again! the priest!'

It was in fact the archdeacon. On his left walked the sub chanter; and on his right, the precentor, carrying his staff of office. He advanced with head thrown back, eyes fixed and opened wide, chanting in a loud voice:

'*De ventre inferi clamavi, et exaudisti vocem meam.*' (Out of the bowels of the earth I have called unto thee, and thou hast heard my voice.)

'*Et projecisti me in profundum in corde maris, et flumen circumdedit me.*' (And thou hast cast me into the depths of the sea, and the waters have gone about me.)

When he appeared in the broad daylight, beneath the lofty arched portal, covered with an ample cope of silver, barred with a black cross, he was so pale that more than one amongst the crowd thought that one of the marble bishops kneeling upon the monuments in the choir had risen and had come forth to receive on the threshold of the tomb her who was about to die.

She, equally pale and rigid, hardly noticed that they had placed in her hand a heavy lighted taper of yellow wax. She had not heard the shrill voice of the clerk, reading the fatal lines of the penance; only, when told to answer amen, she said 'Amen!' It was only the sight of the priest making a sign to her guards to retire, and himself advancing toward her, that brought back to her any sense of life and strength.

Then the blood boiled in her veins, and a lingering spark of indignation was re-kindled in that already numb, cold soul.

The archdeacon approached her slowly. Even in this extremity she saw him gaze upon her nakedness with eyes glittering with passion, jealousy and desire. Then he said to her in a loud voice, 'Young woman, have you asked pardon of God for your sins and your offences?' He bent to her ear, and added (the spectators supposed that he was receiving her last confession), 'Wilt thou be mine? I can even yet save thee!'

She looked steadily at him: 'Begone, demon! or I denounce thee!'

He smiled – a horrible smile. 'They will not believe thee. Thou wilt but add scandal to guilt. Answer quickly! wilt thou be mine?'

'What hast thou done with my Phœbus?'

'He is dead,' said the priest.

At this moment the miserable archdeacon raised his head mechanically, and saw, at the opposite side of the square, on the balcony of the Gondelaurier house, the captain standing by Fleur-de-Lys. He staggered, passed his hand over his eyes, looked again, muttered a malediction, and all his features were violently contorted.

'Well, then, die, thou!' said he, between his teeth; 'no one shall have thee!'

Then raising his hand over the gypsy, he exclaimed, in a sepulchral voice, '*I nunc anima anceps, et sit tibi Deus misericors.*' (Go thy way now, lingering soul, and may God have mercy upon thee!)

This was the awful formula with which it was the custom to close that gloomy ceremonial. It was the signal given by the priest to the executioner.

The people knelt.

'*Kyrie Eleison!*' (Lord, have mercy upon us!) said the priests, who remained beneath the arch of the portal.

'*Kyrie Eleison!*' repeated the throng, with that murmur which runs over a sea of heads, like the waves of a troubled sea.

'Amen!' said the archdeacon.

He turned his back upon the prisoner; his head again fell upon his breast; his hands were crossed; he rejoined his train of priests, and a moment later he disappeared with cross, candles and copes beneath the dim arches of the cathedral, and his sonorous voice gradually died away down the choir while chanting these words of despair:

'*Omnes gurgites tui et fluctus tui super me transierunt!*' (All thy whirlpools, O Lord, and all thy waves, have gone over me!)

At the same time, the intermittent clang of the iron butts of the beadles' halberds dying away by degrees among the columns of the nave, sounded like a clock hammer striking the last hour of the condemned.

The doors of Notre-Dame remained open, showing the interior of the church, empty, deserted, draped in mourning, torchless and voiceless.

The condemned girl remained motionless in her place, awaiting her doom. One of the vergers was obliged to notify Maître Charmolue of the fact, who, during all this scene, had set himself to study that bas-relief of the great portal, representing, according to some, Abraham's sacrifice, according to others the great Alchemical Operation, the sun being typified by the angel, the fire by the fagot and the operator by Abraham.

He was with some difficulty withdrawn from this contemplation; but at length he turned, and at a sign from him, two men in yellow, the executioner's assistants, approached the gypsy-girl to bind her hands once more.

The unhappy creature at the moment of re-mounting the fatal cart, and setting out on her last stage, was perhaps seized with some poignant clinging to life. She raised her dry, red eyes to heaven, to the sun, to the silvery clouds, intermingled with patches of brilliant blue; then she cast them around her upon the ground, the people, the houses. All at once, while the man in yellow was pinioning her arms, she uttered a terrible cry, a cry of joy. Yonder, on that balcony, at the corner of the Place, she had just caught sight of him, her friend, her lord, Phœbus, the other apparition of her life!

The judge had lied! the priest had lied! it was he indeed, she could not doubt it. He was there, handsome, alive, dressed in his brilliant uniform, his plume on his head, his sword by his side!

'Phœbus! ' she cried, 'my Phœbus!'

And she tried to stretch towards him arms trembling with love and rapture, but they were bound.

Then she saw the captain knit his brows; a fine young woman, leaning upon his arm, looked at him with scornful lip and angry eye; then Phœbus uttered some words which did not reach her; and then he and the lady both disappeared precipitately through the window of the balcony, which closed after them.

'Phœbus!' she cried, wildly; 'dost thou too believe it?'

A monstrous thought had dawned upon her. She recollected that she had been condemned for the murder of Phœbus de Chateaupers.

She had borne up until now, but this last blow was too severe. She fell senseless upon the ground.

'Come,' said Charmolue, 'carry her to the cart, and make an end of it.'

No one had observed in the gallery of statues of the kings, carved just above the arches of the portal, a strange-looking spectator, who, until now, watched all that passed with such impassiveness a neck so outstretched, a visage so deformed, that, but for his parti-coloured red and violet garb, he might have been taken for one of the stone monsters through whose jaws the long gutters of the cathedral have disgorged themselves for six centuries past. This spectator had missed nothing that had taken place since midday in front of the portal of Notre-Dame. And at the very beginning, without any one noticing him, he had securely fastened to one of the small columns of the gallery a strong knotted rope, the other end of which trailed on the top of the steps below. This done, he began to look on tranquilly, whistling from time to time when a blackbird flitted past.

Suddenly, at the moment when the executioner's assistants were preparing to execute Charmolue's phlegmatic order, he threw his leg over the balustrade of the gallery, gripped the rope with his feet, his knees and his hands; then he was seen to slide down the façade, as a drop of rain slips down a windowpane, run up to the two sub-executioners with the speed of a cat just dropped from a house-top, knock them down with two enormous fists, pick up the gypsy with one hand, as a child might a doll, and leap, at one bound, into the church, lifting the girl above his head, and shouting in a tremendous voice, 'Sanctuary!'

This was done with such rapidity that, had it been night, the whole might have been seen by the glare of a single 'clash of lightning.

'Sanctuary! Sanctuary!' repeated the crowd; and the clapping of ten thousand hands made Quasimodo's only eye sparkle with joy and pride.

This shock restored the prisoner to her senses. She raised her eyelids, looked at Quasimodo, then closed them again suddenly as if terrified at her deliverer.

Charmolue, the executioners and the whole escort were confounded. In fact, within the precincts of Notre-Dame the condemned was inviolable. The cathedral was a recognized place of refuge; all temporal jurisdiction expired upon its threshold.

Quasimodo had stopped under the great portal. His broad feet seemed to rest as solidly upon the floor of the church as the heavy Roman pillars themselves. His big bushy head was buried between his shoulders like the head of a lion, which also has a mane, but no neck. He held the trembling girl, suspended in his horny hands, like a piece of white drapery, but he carried her with as much care as if he feared he should break or injure her. He seemed to feel that a thing so delicate, exquisite and precious was not made for such hands as his. At times he looked as if he dared not touch her, even with his breath. Then, all at once, he would press her close in his arms to his angular breast, as his own, his treasure, as her mother might have done. His gnome-like eye, resting upon her, flooded her with tenderness, grief and pity, and was suddenly lifted, flashing fire. Then the women laughed and wept, the crowd stamped their feet with enthusiasm, for at that moment Quasimodo had a beauty of his own. He was fine; he, that orphan, that foundling that outcast; he felt himself august and strong; he looked full in the face that society from which he was banished, and into which he had so powerfully intervened; that human justice from which he had snatched its prey; all those tigers whose jaws perforce remained empty; those myrmidons, those judges, those executioners, all that royal power which he, poor, insignificant being, had foiled with the power of God.

Then, too, there was something touching in the protection afforded by a being so deformed to a being so unfortunate; in the circumstance of a poor girl condemned to death being saved by Quasimodo. They were the two extremes, natural and social wretchedness, coming into contact and aiding, each other.

However, after a few moments of triumph, Quasimodo plunged abruptly into the church with his burden. The people, fond of any display of prowess, sought him with their eyes under the gloomy nave, regretting that he had so quickly withdrawn from their acclamations. All at once he was seen to reappear at one extremity of the gallery of the kings of France. He ran along it like a madman, holding his conquest aloft, and shouting: 'Sanctuary!' Fresh plaudits burst from the multitude. Having traversed the gallery, he plunged again into the interior of the church. A moment later he reappeared upon the upper platform, with the gypsy still in his arms, still running wildly along, still shouting 'Sanctuary!' and the throng applauded. Finally he made a third appearance on the top of the tower of the great bell: from thence he seemed to show exultingly to the whole city her whom he had saved; and his thundering voice, that voice so rarely heard by any one, and never by himself, thrice repeated with frenzy that pierced the very clouds: 'Sanctuary! Sanctuary! Sanctuary!'

'Noël! Noël!' cried the people in their turn; and that prodigious shout resounded upon the opposite shore of the Seine, to the astonishment of the crowd assembled in the Place de Grève, and of the recluse who was still waiting with her eyes fixed on the gibbet.

BOOK NINE

I

Delirium

CLAUDE FROLLO was no longer in Notre-Dame when his adopted son thus abruptly cut the fatal knot in which the unhappy archdeacon had bound the gypsy-girl and caught himself. On returning into the sacristy, he had torn off the albe, cope and stole; flung them all into the hands of the amazed verger; fled through the private door of the cloister, ordered a boatman of the Terrain to carry him over to the left bank of the Seine, and plunged in among the hilly streets of the University, going he knew not whither; meeting, at every step, parties of men and women hastening gaily towards the Pont Saint Michel, in the hope that they might still 'arrive in time' to see the witch hanged – pale, wild, more troubled, more blind and more fierce than a night bird let loose and pursued by a troop of children in broad daylight. He knew not where he was, what he did, whether he dreamed. He went forward, walking, running, taking any street at random, making no choice, only urged ever by the Grève, that horrible Grève, which he confusedly felt to be behind him.

In this manner he skirted Mount Sainte Geneviève, and finally emerged from the town by the Porte Saint Victor. He continued his flight so long as he could see, on turning, the towered enclosure of the University, and the scattered houses of the faubourg; but when at last a ridge completely hid that odious Paris – when he could imagine himself a hundred leagues from it – in the country – in a desert – he paused, and it seemed to him as if he breathed more freely.

Then frightful ideas rushed upon his mind. He saw once more clear into his soul, and shuddered. He thought of that unfortunate girl who had destroyed him, and whom he had destroyed. He cast a haggard eye over the two winding paths, along which fate had driven their separate destinies, to that point of intersection at which she had pitilessly dashed them against each other. He thought of the folly of eternal vows, the emptiness of chastity, science, religion, virtue, the uselessness of God. He indulged in evil thoughts to his heart's content, and, while plunging deeper into them, he felt as if the fiend were laughing within him.

And, as he thus sifted his soul to the bottom, when he perceived how large a space Nature had prepared there for the passions, he sneered more bitterly still. He stirred up in the depths of his heart all his hatred, all his malevolence; and he discovered with the cool eye of a physician examining a patient, that this hatred, this malevolence, were but vitiated love, that love, the source of every virtue in man, turned to horrible things in the heart of a priest, and that a man constituted as he was, by making himself a priest, made himself a demon. Then he laughed frightfully, and suddenly became pale again, in contemplating the worst side of his fatal passion, of that corroding, venomous, malignant, implacable love, which had driven one of them to the gibbet, the other to hell-fire; her to condemnation, him to damnation.

And then he laughed anew, as he reflected that Phœbus was alive; that, after all, the captain lived, was light-hearted and happy, had finer doublets than ever and a new mistress, whom he brought to see the old one hanged. And he sneered at himself with redoubled bitterness, when he reflected that, of all the living beings whose death he had desired, the only creature he did not hate, was the only one who had not escaped him.

Then his thoughts wandered from the captain to the populace and he was overcome with jealousy of an unheard of kind. He reflected that the people, also, the entire mob, had had before their eyes the woman he loved in her shirt, almost naked. He wrung his hands in agony at the thought that the woman, whose form half seen by him alone in darkness, would have afforded him supreme delight, had been exposed, in broad daylight, at noontide, to the gaze of a whole multitude, clad as for a bridal night. He wept with rage over all those mysteries of love profaned, sullied, exposed, withered forever. He wept with rage, picturing to himself the foul eyes that had been gratified by that scanty covering, that this lovely girl, this virgin lily, this cup of purity and delight, to which he dared not place his lips without trembling, had been converted, as it were, into a public trough, at which the vilest rabble of Paris, thieves, beggars lackeys, had come to quaff together a shameless, impure and depraved pleasure.

And when he strove to picture to himself the felicity which he might have found upon earth, had she not been a gypsy and he not a priest, had Phœbus never existed, and had she but loved him; when he imagined the life of serenity and love which might have been possible for him too; when he thought that there were at that very instant happy couples here and there upon the earth, engaged in sweet converse, in orange groves, on the banks of murmuring streams, in the light of the setting sun, or under a starry sky, and that, had it been God's will, he might have formed with her one of those blessed couples – his heart melted in tenderness and despair.

Oh, she – still she! It was this fixed idea that haunted him incessantly, that tortured him, that turned his brain and gnawed his vitals. He regretted nothing, repented nothing; all that he had done, he was ready to do again; he liked better to see her in the hands of the executioner than in the arms of the captain. But he suffered; suffered so intensely, that at moments he tore out his hair by handfuls to see if it were not turning white.

There was one moment, among the rest, when it occurred to him that, perhaps at that very minute, the hideous chain which he had seen that morning, was drawing its iron noose closer and closer around that slender, graceful neck; this idea made the perspiration start from every pore.

There was another moment when, laughing diabolically at himself, he pictured to his imagination, at one and the same time, La Esmeralda as on the first day he had seen her – lively, careless, joyous, gaily attired, dancing, winged, harmonious – and La Esmeralda of the last day, in her scanty shift, with the rope about her neck, slowly ascending with her naked feet the rough ladder to the gibbet. This double picture was so vivid that he uttered a terrific cry.

While this whirlwind of despair overturned, broke, tore up, bent to the earth, uprooted all within him, he gazed upon nature around him. At his feet some fowls were pecking and scratching about among the bushes, enamelled beetles crawled in the sunshine. Over his head groups of dappled gray clouds sailed over a blue sky. In the horizon, the spire of the abbey of Saint Victor shot up its obelisk of slate above the intervening ridge of ground. And the miller of the Butte Copeaux whistled light-heartedly as he watched the steady-turning sails of his mill. All this active, industrious, tranquil life recurring around him in a thousand forms hurt him. He resumed his flight.

Thus he sped through the country until nightfall. This flight from Nature, life, himself, man, God, everything, lasted the whole day. Sometimes he threw himself face downward upon the earth, and tore up the young corn with his nails. Sometimes he paused in some deserted village street, and his thoughts were so unendurable that he would seize his head in both hands, as if to tear it from his shoulders and dash it on the stones.

Toward the hour of sunset he examined himself again, and found himself almost mad. The storm which had been raging within him from the moment when he had lost all hope and wish to save the gypsy, had left him unconscious of a single sound idea, a single rational thought. His reason lay prostrate, almost utterly destroyed. His mind retained but two distinct images, La Esmeralda and the gibbet, all the rest was black. These two images together formed a horrible group; and the more he fixed upon them such power of attention and thought as he was yet master of, the more they seemed to increase according to a fantastic progression – the one in grace, in charm, in beauty, in light, the other in horror – until, at last, La Esmeralda appeared like a star, the gibbet as an enormous fleshless arm.

It is remarkable that, during all this torture, he never seriously thought of putting an end to himself. The wretch was made thus; he clung to life – perhaps, indeed, he really saw hell in prospect.

Meanwhile, daylight was declining. The living being still existing within him began vaguely to think of returning. He believed himself to be far from Paris; but, on looking around, he discovered that he had only made the circuit of the University . The spire of Saint Sulpice and the three lofty pinnacles of Saint Germain-des-Prés, shot up above the horizon on his right. He bent his steps in that direction. When he heard the challenge of the abbot's men-at-arms around the battlemented walls of Saint Germain, he turned aside, took a path that lay before him, between the abbey mill and the lazaretto of the suburb, and in a few minutes found himself upon the border of the Pré-aux-Clercs. This meadow was celebrated by reason of the brawls which went on there night and day; it was the *hydra* of the poor monks of Saint Germain. *Quod monachis Sancti Germani Pratensis hydra, fuit, clericis nova semper dissidiorum capita suscitantibus.* (Which was the *hydra* of the monks of Saint Germain-de-Prés, the laymen constantly raising some new heads of dissension.) The archdeacon was afraid of meeting some one there; he dreaded any human face; he had avoided the University and the hamlet of Saint Germain; he wished to go through the streets again as late as possible. He passed along the side of the Pré-aux-Clercs, took the deserted path which separated it from the Dieu-Neuf, and at length reached the waterside. There Dom Claude found a boatman, who, for a few farthings, took him up the Seine to the extremity of the island of the city, and landed him upon that uninhabited tongue of land where the reader has already beheld Gringoire musing, and which extended beyond the king's gardens, parallel to the islet of the Passeur-aux-Vaches.

The monotonous rocking of the boat, and the murmur of the water, had somewhat stupefied the unhappy Claude. When the boatman had left him, he remained standing stupidly upon the bank, staring straight before him, and seeing everything in a sort of tremulous mist, which made all seem like a phantasmagoria. It is no uncommon thing for the exhaustion of violent grief to produce this effect upon the mind.

The sun had set behind the lofty Tour de Nesle. It was now the twilight hour. The sky was white; the water of the river was white. Between these two white expanses the left bank of the Seine, on which his eyes were fixed, extended its sombre length, which, gradually diminishing in the perspective, plunged into the gray horizon like a black spire. It was covered with houses, of which nothing was distinguishable but the dark outline standing out in strong relief in the dark from the clear light of the sky and the water. Lights began to glimmer here and there in the windows. The immense black obelisk, thus isolated between the two white masses of sky and river, the latter very broad just here, produced a singular effect on Dom Claude, such as might be felt by a man lying flat on his back at the foot of the Strasburg Cathedral and gazing up at the enormous spire piercing the twilight shadows above his head; only in this case it was Claude who was erect, and the obelisk which was horizontal. But as the river, reflecting the sky, deepened indefinitely the abyss beneath him, the vast promontory seemed to shoot into space as boldly as any cathedral spire, and the impression produced was the same. The impression was made even stronger and more profound; that, although it was indeed the steeple of Strasburg, it was the steeple of Strasburg two leagues high; something unheard of, gigantic, immeasurable; a structure such as no human eye ever beheld; a Tower of Babel. The chimneys of the houses, the battlements of the walls, the fantastically-cut gables of the roofs, the spire of the Augustines, the Tour de Nesle – all these projections which indented the profile of the colossal obelisk – added to the illusion by their odd resemblance to the outline of a florid and fanciful sculpture.

Claude, in the state of hallucination in which he then was, believed that he saw – saw with his bodily eyes – the pinnacles of hell. The innumerable lights gleaming from one end to the other of the fearful tower, seemed to him to be so many openings of the vast furnace within; the voices and the sounds which arose from it like so many shrieks and groans. Then he was terrified; he clapped his hands to his ears that he might not hear, turned his back that he might not see, and fled from the frightful vision with hasty strides.

But the vision was within him.

When he once more entered the streets, the people passing to and fro in the light of the shop-windows appeared to him like an everlasting coming and going of spectres about him. There were strange noises in his ears; extraordinary fancies disturbed his brain. He saw neither houses, nor pavement, nor vehicles, nor men and women, but a chaos of undefined objects blending one into another. At the corner of the Rue de la Barillerie, there was a chandler's shop, which had its sloping roof above the window, according to immemorial custom, hung with tin hoops from each of which was suspended a circle of wooden candles, which shook in the wind and rattled like castanets. He fancied he heard the heap of skeletons at Montfaucon knocking their bones against one another.

'Oh' muttered he 'the right wind dashes them one against another and mingles the clanking of their chains with the rattling of their bones. Perhaps she too is there among them!'

Distracted, he knew not whither he went. Presently he found himself upon the Pont Saint Michel. There was a light in the window of a ground-floor room – he went up to it. Through a cracked pane he saw a dirty room, which awakened confused recollections in his mind. In this room, ill-lighted by a small lamp, there was a young man, fair and fresh-looking, with a merry face, throwing his arms, with boisterous laughter, about a girl very immodestly attired; and near the lamp there was an old woman spinning and singing in a quavering voice. As the young man did not laugh constantly, the old woman's song made its way in fragments to the ear of the priest; it was something unintelligible yet frightful:

'Growl, Grève! bark, Grève!
Spin away, my distaff brave!
　Let the hangman have his cord,
　That whistles in the prison-yard.
Growl Grève! bark Grève!

'Hemp, that makes the pretty rope –
Sow it widely, give it scope –
　Better hemp than wheaten sheaves;
　Thief there's none that ever thieves
The pretty rope, the hempen rope.

'Bark, Grève! growl, Grève!
To see the girl of pleasure brave
　Dangling on the gibbet high,
　Every window is an eye –
Bark, Grève! growl Grève!'

Thereupon the young man laughed and caressed the wench. The old woman was La Falourdel; the girl was a courtesan; the young man was his brother Jehan.

He continued to gaze; as well this sight as another.

He saw Jehan go to a window at the back of the room, open it, cast a glance at the quay, where countless lighted windows gleamed in the distance, and heard him say, as he shut the window again:

'By my soul, 'tis night already! The towns folk are lighting their candles, and God Almighty his stars.'

Then Jehan came back to the wench, and smashing a bottle that stood on a table, exclaimed:

'Empty already, by Jove! and I have no more money. Isabeau, my dear, I shall not be satisfied with Jupiter until he has changed your two white nipples into two black bottles, that I may suck Beaune wine from them day and night.'

This fine piece of wit made the courtesan laugh, and Jehan took his departure.

Dom Claude had barely time to fling himself on the ground, in order to escape being met, looked in the face, and recognized by his brother. Luckily the street was dark, and the student drunk. Nevertheless, he noticed the archdeacon lying on the pavement in the mud.

'Oh! oh!' said he, 'here's a fellow who has been leading a jolly life to-day.'

He pushed Dom Claude with his foot, and the archdeacon held his breath.

'Dead drunk!' resumed Jehan. 'Come! he's full! a very leech loosed from a cask. He's bald,' added he, stooping over him; ''tis an old man – *Fortunate old man!*'

Then Dom Claude heard him move off, saying:

'All the same! reason is a fine thing, and my brother, the archdeacon, is a lucky fellow to be wise and have money!'

Then the archdeacon rose, and ran without halting to Notre-Dame, whose enormous towers he could see rising in the dark above the houses.

When he arrived, panting, at the Place du Parvis, he shrunk back, and dared not lift his eyes toward the fatal edifice.

'Oh,' he murmured to himself, 'is it possible that such a thing took place here to-day, this very morning!'

However, he ventured to glance at the church. The front was dark, the sky beyond it glittered with stars, the crescent moon, in her flight upward from the horizon, at that moment reached the summit of the right hand tower, and seemed to have perched upon it, like a luminous bird, on the edge of the black trifoliated balustrade.

The cloister door was closed; but the archdeacon always carried about him the key of the tower, in which was his laboratory; availing himself of it he entered the church.

He found within it the gloom and silence of a cave. By the heavy shadows falling on all sides in broad masses, he knew that the hangings put up for the morning's ceremony had not been removed. The great silver cross shone from the depths of the gloom, dotted with glittering points, like the milky way of that sepulchral night. The long windows of the choir showed the tops of their pointed arches above the black drapery, their stained glass panes admitting a faint ray of moonlight, had only the doubtful colours of the night, a sort of violet, white and blue, of a tint to be found nowhere else but on the faces of the dead. The archdeacon, seeing these wan spots all round the choir, thought he beheld the mitres of bishops gone to perdition. He closed his eyes; and when he opened them again, he thought they were a circle of pale visages gazing at him.

He fled across the church. Then it seemed to him as if the church itself took life and motion – that each of the great columns was turning into an enormous paw that beat the ground with its big stone spatula, and that the gigantic cathedral was a sort of prodigious elephant, breathing and marching, with its pillars for legs, its two towers for tusks, and the immense black cloth for its housings.

This fever, or madness, had reached such a pitch of intensity, that the external world was no longer anything to the unhappy man but a species of Apocalypse, visible, palpable, terrible.

He had one moment of relief. As he plunged into the side aisles, he perceived a reddish light behind a group of pillars. He rushed towards it as to a star. It was the feeble lamp which burned day and night above the public breviary of Notre-Dame beneath its iron grating. He cast his eye eagerly upon the sacred book, in the hope of finding there some sentence of consolation or encouragement. The volume was open at this passage of Job, over which he ran his burning eye:

'And a spirit passed before my face; and I heard a small voice; and the hair of my flesh stood up.'

On reading this dismal sentence, he felt as a blind man would whose fingers are pricked by the staff which he has picked up. His knees failed him, and he sank upon the pavement, thinking of her who had that day suffered death. Such awful fumes rose up and penetrated his brain, that it seemed to him as if his head had become one of the mouths of hell.

He must have remained long in this posture – neither thinking, nor feeling, helpless and passive, in the hands of the demon. At length some strength returned to him; it occurred to him to take refuge in the tower, near his faithful Quasimodo. He rose; and, as fear was upon him, he took the lamp of the breviary to light him. This was a sacrilege; but he had ceased to heed such trifles.

He slowly climbed the stairs of the towers, filled with a secret dread, which must have been shared by the few passers-by in the square, who saw the mysterious light of his lamp moving at that late hour from loophole to loophole, to the top of the tower.

All at once he felt a breath of cool air on his face, and found himself under the doorway of the upper gallery. The night was cold; the sky was streaked with hurrying clouds, whose large, white masses drifted one upon another like river ice breaking up after a frost. The crescent moon, stranded in the midst of them looked like a celestial vessel caught among those icebergs of the air.

He lowered his gaze and contemplated for a moment through the railing of slender columns which unites the towers, afar off, through a light veil of mist and smoke, the silent throng of the roofs of Paris, steep, innumerable, crowded and small as the ripples of a calm sea on a summer night.

The moon gave but a feeble light, which imparted to earth and sky an ashy hue.

At this moment the Cathedral clock raised its shrill, cracked voice. Midnight rang out. The priest thought of mid-day. Twelve o'clock had come again.

'Oh,' he whispered to himself, 'she must be cold by this time.'

Suddenly a puff of wind extinguished his lamp, and almost at the same instant there appeared, at the opposite corner of the tower, a shade, a something white, a shape, a female form. He started. By the side of this female form was that of a little goat, that mingled its bleat with the last sound of the bell.

He had strength enough to look – it was she!

She was pale, she was sad. Her hair fell over her shoulders as in the morning, but there was no rope about her neck, her hands were no longer bound; she was free, she was dead.

She was clad in white, and over her head was thrown a white veil.

She came toward him slowly, looking up to heaven. The unearthly goat followed her. He felt as if turned to stone, and too heavy to escape. At each step that she advanced he took one backwards, and that was all. In this way he retreated beneath the dark arch of the stairway. He froze at the thought that she might perhaps enter there too; had she done so, he would have died of terror.

She did, in fact, approach the staircase door, paused there for some moments, looked steadily into the darkness, without appearing to perceive the priest, and passed on. He thought she looked taller than when she was alive. He saw the moon through her white robes; he heard her breathe.

When she had passed on, he began to descend the stairs as slowly as he had seen the spectre move, imagining himself a spectre also – haggard, his hair erect, his extinguished lamp still in his hand – and, as he descended the spiral stairs, he distinctly heard in his ear a mocking voice repeating: 'And a spirit passed before my face; and I heard a small voice, and the hair of my flesh stood up.'

II

Hunch-backed, One-eyed, Lame

EVERY TOWN in the Middle Ages, and up to the time of Louis XII, every town in France had its places of refuge, or sanctuaries. These sanctuaries, amid the deluge of penal laws and barbarous jurisdictions that inundated the state, were like so many islands rising above the level of human justice. Any criminal that landed upon them was saved. In each district there were almost as many of these places of refuge as there were of execution. The abuse of a privilege went side by side with the abuse of punishment – two bad things endeavouring to correct each other. The royal palaces, the mansions of princes, and especially the churches, had right of sanctuary. Sometimes an entire town which stood in need of repopulation was made temporarily a place of refuge for criminals; thus Louis XI made all Paris a sanctuary in 1467.

When once he had set foot within the asylum, the criminal was sacred; but he must beware of leaving it; one step outside the sanctuary, and he fell back into the flood. The wheel, the gibbet, the strappado, kept close guard around the place of refuge, watching incessantly for their prey like sharks around a vessel. Condemned persons thus rescued have been known to grow gray in a cloister, on the staircase of a palace, in the garden of an abbey, in the porch of a church; in this way the sanctuary itself was but a prison under another name. It sometimes happened that a solemn ordinance of the Parliament violated the sanctuary and gave up the condemned to the hands of the executioner, but this was a rare occurrence. The parliaments stood in fear of the bishops; for when there was friction between these two robes, the gown had but a poor chance against the cassock. Occasionally, however, as in the case of the assassins of Petit-Jean, the headsman of Paris, and in that of Emery Rousseau, the murderer of Jean Valleret, justice overleaped the Church and passed on to the execution of its sentences. But, except by virtue of a decree of Parliament, woe to him who violated a place of sanctuary! Everone knows the fate of Robert de Clermont, marshal of France, and Jean de Châlons, marshal of Champagne; and yet the case in question was merely that of one Perrin Marc, a money-changer's man, a miserable assassin; but the two marshals had forced the doors of Saint Méry; therein lay the crime.

Such was the respect with which sanctuaries were invested, that, according to tradition, it occasionally extended even to animals. Aymoin relates that a stag, chased by Dagobert, having taken refuge at the tomb of Saint Denis, the hounds stopped short, barking.

Churches had usually a small retreat prepared for the reception of the suppliants. In 1407 Nicolas Flamel had built for them upon the arches of Saint Jacques-de-la-Boucherie, a chamber which cost him four pounds sixpence, sixteen Paris farthings.

At Notre-Dame it was a tiny chamber, situated on the roof of the side aisle beneath the flying buttresses, precisely at the spot where the wife of the present keeper of the towers has made a garden, which compares with the hanging gardens of Babylon, as a lettuce with a palm tree, or as a porter's wife with a Semiramis.

Here it was that, after his wild and triumphal race along the towers and galleries, Quasimodo deposited La Esmeralda. So long as that race lasted, the damsel had not recovered her senses, half stupefied, half awake, having only a vague perception that she was ascending in the air, that she was floating, flying there, that something was carrying her upward from the earth. From time to time she heard the loud laugh and the harsh voice of Quasimodo at her ear. She half-opened her eyes; then beneath her she saw, confusedly, Paris all checkered with its countless roofs of tile and slate, like a red and blue mosaic, and above her head Quasimodo's frightful but joy-illumined face. Her eyelids fell she believed that all was over, that she had been executed during her swoon, and that the misshapen spirit which had presided over her destiny had laid hold of her and was bearing her away. She dared not look at him, but surrendered herself to fate.

But when the breathless and dishevelled bell-ringer laid her down in the cell of refuge; when she felt his clumsy hands gently untying the cord that had cut into her arms, she experienced that kind of shock which startles out of their sleep those on board a ship that runs aground in the middle of a dark night. Her ideas awoke also, and returned to her one by one. She saw that she was in Notre-Dame; she remembered having been snatched from the hands of the executioner; that Phœbus was living, that Phœbus loved her no longer; and these two ideas, one of which imparted so much bitterness to the other, presenting themselves at once to the poor girl, she turned to Quasimodo, who remained standing before her, and whose aspect frightened her, and said to him: 'Why did you save me?'

He looked anxiously at her, as if striving to guess what she said. She repeated her question. He then gave her another look of profound sadness, and fled.

She was amazed.

A few moments later he returned, bringing a bundle, which he laid at her feet. It contained apparel which certain charitable women had left for her at the threshold of the church.

Then she looked down at herself, saw that she was almost naked, and blushed. Life had returned.

Quasimodo seemed to participate in this feeling of modesty. Covering his eye with his broad hand, he again departed, but with lingering steps.

She hastily dressed herself. It was a white robe with a white veil, the habit of a novice of the Hôtel-Dieu.

She had scarcely finished before Quasimodo returned. He carried a basket under one arm and a mattress under the other. This basket contained a bottle, bread and some other provisions. He set the basket on the ground, and said, 'Eat.' He spread out the mattress on the flag-stones, and said, 'Sleep.'

It was his own meal, his own bed, that the bell-ringer had brought her.

The Egyptian lifted her eyes to his face to thank him, but could not utter a word. The poor fellow was absolutely hideous. She drooped her head with a thrill of horror.

Then he said to her:

'I frighten you. I am very ugly, am I not? Do not look at me, only listen to me. In the daytime you will stay here; at night you can walk about all over the church. But stir not a step out of it, either by night or by day. You would be lost. They would kill you, and I should die.'

Moved by his words, she raised her head to reply, but he was gone. Alone once more, she pondered on the singular words of this almost monstrous being, and struck by the tone of his voice, so hoarse and yet so gentle.

She then began to examine her cell. It was a little room, some six feet square, with a small window and a door upon the slightly sloping roof of flat stones. A number of gutter-spouts, terminating in figures of animals, seemed bending over her, and stretching their necks to look at her through the window. Beyond the roof she discerned many chimney-tops, from which issued the smoke of all the fires of Paris, a sad spectacle for the poor gypsy-girl, a foundling, condemned to death – an unfortunate creature, with neither country, family nor home.

Just as the thought of her forlorn situation wrung her heart more keenly than ever, she felt a hairy, shaggy head push between her hands upon her lap. She started (everything alarmed her now), and looked down. It was the poor goat, the nimble Djali, who had escaped with her when Quasimodo scattered Charmolue's men, and who had been lavishing caresses on her feet for nearly an hour without obtaining a single glance. The gypsy covered it with kisses. 'Oh, Djali,' said she, 'how I have forgotten thee! And yet thou thinkest of me. Oh, thou art not ungrateful!'

At the same time, as if an invisible hand had lifted the weight which had so long held back her tears, she began to weep; and as her tears flowed, she felt the sharpest and bitterest of her grief depart with them.

When evening came she thought the night so beautiful, the moonlight so soft, that she made the circuit of the gallery which surrounds the church. It afforded her some relief, so calm did the earth appear when viewed from that height.

III

Deaf

ON THE FOLLOWING MORNING she perceived, on awaking, that she had slept. This strange fact amazed her; she had been so long unaccustomed to sleep! A bright beam from the rising sun came in at her window, and shone in on her face. But with the sun, she saw at the window an object that frightened her – the unfortunate face of Quasimodo. She involuntarily closed her eyes again, but in vain, she fancied that she still saw, through her rosy lids, that gnome's mask, one-eyed and gap-toothed. Then, still keeping her eyes shut, she heard a rough voice saying, very gently:

'Do not be afraid. I am your friend. I came to watch you sleep. It does not hurt you, does it, that I should come and see you sleep? What does it matter to you if I am here when you have your eyes shut? Now I am going. Stay, I have placed myself behind the wall; now you may open your eyes again.'

There was something still more plaintive than these words; it was the tone in which they were uttered. The gypsy, touched by it, opened her eyes. He was no longer at the window. She went to it and saw the poor hunch-back crouching in a corner of the wall, in a sad and resigned attitude. She made an effort to overcome the repugnance with which he inspired her. 'Come hither,' she said to him, gently. From the motion of her lips Quasimodo thought she was bidding him to go away; then he rose up and retreated, limping, slowly, with drooping head, not venturing to raise to the young girl his face full of despair. 'Come hither, I say,' cried she; but he continued to move off. Then she darted out of the cell, ran to him, and took hold of his arm. On feeling her touch, Quasimodo trembled in every limb. He lifted a beseeching eye; and finding that she was trying to draw him with her, his whole face beamed with joy and tenderness. She tried to make him enter her cell; but he persisted in remaining on the threshold. 'No, no,' said he, 'the owl enters not the nest of the lark.'

Then she threw herself gracefully upon her couch, with her goat fast asleep at her feet. Both were motionless for several minutes, contemplating in silence – he, so much grace – she, so much ugliness. Every moment she discovered in Quasimodo some additional deformity. Her eye wandered from his crooked legs to the hump on his back, from the hump on his back to his one eye. She could not understand how a being so awkwardly fashioned could be in existence. But withal there was so much sadness and gentleness about him that she began to be reconciled to it.

He was the first to break silence. 'So you were telling me to return.'

She nodded affirmatively, and said, 'Yes.'

He understood the motion of her head. 'Alas!' said he, as though hesitating whether to finish, 'I am – I am deaf.'

'Poor man!' exclaimed the gypsy-girl, with an expression of kindly pity.

He smiled sorrowfully.

'You think that was all I lacked, do you not? Yes, I am deaf. That is the way I am made. It is horrible, is it not? And you – you are beautiful.'

There was so deep a sense of his wretchedness in the poor creature's tone, that she had not the courage to say a word. Besides, he would not have heard it. He continued:

'Never did I see my ugliness as now. When I compare myself with you, I do indeed pity myself, poor unhappy monster that I am. I must look to you like a beast, eh? You – you are a sunbeam, a dewdrop, a bird's song. As for me – I am something frightful, neither man nor beast – something harder, and more trodden under foot, and more unshapely than a flint-stone.'

Then he began to laugh, and that laugh was the most heartbreaking thing in the world. He went on:

'Yes, I am deaf, but you will speak to me by gestures, by signs. I have a master who talks to me that way. And then, I shall, very soon, know your wish from the movement of your lips, and from your look.'

'Well then,' replied she, smiling, 'tell me why you saved me.'

He watched her attentively as she spoke.

'I understand,' he answered, 'you ask me why I saved you. You have forgotten a poor wretch that tried to carry you off one night – a poor wretch to whom you brought relief, the very next day, on their infamous pillory; a drop of water and a little pity. That is more than I can repay with my life. You have forgotten that poor wretch, but he remembers.'

She listened to him with deep emotion. A tear started in the bell-ringer's eye, but it did not fall; he seemed to make it a point of honour to repress it.

'Listen,' he resumed, when he no longer feared that this tear would fall. 'We have here very high towers; a man who should fall from one would be dead before he touched the pavement; when it shall please you to have me to fall, you will not have to even utter a word, a glance will suffice.'

Then he rose. This odd being, unhappy as the gypsy was, still aroused some compassion in her breast. She motioned to him to remain.

'No, no,' said he, 'I must not stay too long, I am not at my ease. It is out of pity that you do not turn away your eyes. I will go where I can see you without your seeing me; it will be better so.'

He drew from his pocket a small metal whistle. 'There,' said he; 'when you want me, when you wish me to come, when you do not feel too much horror at the sight of me, use this whistle. I can hear this sound.'

He laid the whistle on the ground and fled.

IV

Earthenware and Crystal

TIME WENT ON. Calm gradually returned to the soul of La Esmeralda. Excessive grief, like excessive joy, is a violent thing, which is of short duration. The human heart cannot long remain in either extremity. The gypsy had suffered so much that surprise was now the only emotion of which she was capable.

With the feeling of security, hope had returned to her. She was out of the pale of society, out of the pale of life; but she vaguely felt that it might not perhaps be impossible to return to them. She was like one dead, keeping in reserve a key to her tomb.

She felt the terrible images which had so long beset her gradually fading away. All the hideous phantoms, Pierrat Torterue, Jacques Charmolue, vanished from her mind – all, even the priest himself.

And then, Phœbus was alive; she was sure of it; she had seen him. To her the life of Phœbus was everything. After the series of fatal shocks which had laid waste all within her, she found but one thing intact in her soul, one sentiment – her love for the captain. Love is like a tree; it shoots of itself; it sends its deep roots through all our being, and often continues to flourish over a heart in ruins.

And the inexplicable part of it is that the blinder this passion the more it is tenacious. It is never stronger than when it is most unreasonable.

No doubt La Esmeralda could not think of the captain without a tinge of bitterness. No doubt it was frightful that he too should have been deceived; that he too should have deemed such a thing possible; that he too should have conceived of a dagger's thrust coming from her who would have given a thousand lives to save him. But, after all, she must not blame him too severely; for had she not acknowledged her crime? had she not yielded, weak woman as she was, to the torture? The fault was all her own; she ought rather to have let them tear the nails from her feet than such an avowal from her lips. But then, could she but see Phœbus once more, for a single minute, a word, a look, would suffice to undeceive him, to bring him back. She had no doubt of it. She also strove to account to herself for many singular things; for the accident of Phœbus's presence on the day of her penance, and for his being with a young lady. It was his sister, no doubt – an explanation by no means plausible, but with which she contented herself, because she must needs believe that Phœbus still loved her, and her alone. Had he not sworn it to her? And what stronger assurance did she require, simple and credulous as she was? And, furthermore, in the sequel of the affair, were not appearances much more strongly against herself than against him? Therefore she waited and hoped.

We may add that the church itself, the vast edifice which enveloped her upon every side, protecting her, guarding her, was a sovereign tranquilizer. The solemn lines of its architecture, the religious attitude of all the objects by which the girl was surrounded, the pious and serene thoughts escaping, as it were, from every pore of those venerable stones, acted upon her unconsciously. The structure had sounds, too, of blessedness and such majesty, that they soothed that suffering spirit. The monotonous chant of the performers of the service, the services of the people to the priests, now inarticulate, now in thundering loudness; the organs bursting forth like the voice of a hundred trumpets; the three bell-towers humming like hives of enormous bees – all that orchestra, with its gigantic gamut, incessantly ascending and descending from the voice of the multitude to that of the tower, overruled her memory, her imagination and her sorrow. The bells especially soothed her. It was like powerful magnetism which those vast machines poured in large waves over her.

Thus each sunrise found her less pale, calmer, and breathing more freely. In proportion as her internal wounds healed, grace and beauty bloomed again on her countenance, but more retiring and composed. Her former character also returned – something even of her gaiety, her pretty pout, the fondness for her goat, her love of singing, her feminine bashfulness. She was careful to dress each morning in the corner of her little chamber, lest some inhabitant of the neighbouring garrets should see her through her window. When her thoughts of Phœbus allowed her leisure, the gypsy-girl sometimes thought of Quasimodo. He was the only link, the only means of communication with mankind, with the living, that remained to her. Poor child! She was even more out of the world than Quasimodo himself. She knew not what to make of the strange friend whom chance had given her. Often she reproached herself for not having a gratitude sufficient to shut her eyes; but, positively, she could not reconcile herself to the sight of the ringer; he was too ugly.

She had left the whistle he had given her lying upon the ground. This, however, did not prevent Quasimodo from reappearing, from time to time, during the first days. She strove hard to restrain herself from turning away with too strong an appearance of repugnance when he came to bring her the basket of provisions or the pitcher of water; but he always perceived the slightest motion of the kind, and went away sorrowful.

One day he came at the moment she was caressing Djali. For a while he stood, full of thought, before the graceful group of the goat and the gypsy; at length he said, shaking his heavy and misshapen head:

'My misfortune is, that I am still too much like a man – would that I were wholly a beast, like that goat.'

She raised her eyes towards him with a look of astonishment.

To this look he answered, 'Oh, I well know why!' and went his way.

Another time he came to the door of the cell (which he never entered) at that moment when La Esmeralda was singing an old Spanish ballad, the words of which she did not understand, but which had lingered in her ear because the gypsy-woman had lulled her to sleep with it when quite a child. At the sight of that ugly face, which made its appearance so abruptly in the middle of her song, the girl broke it off with an involuntary gesture of alarm. The unhappy bell-ringer fell upon his knees on the threshold, and with a beseeching look clasped his clumsy, shapeless hands. 'Oh!' said he, sorrowfully, 'go on, I pray you, and send me not away.' She was unwilling to pain him; and so, trembling all over, she resumed her song. By degrees her alarm subsided, and she abandoned herself wholly to the expression of the plaintive air she was singing. He, the while, remained upon his knees, with his hands joined as in prayer, attentive, hardly breathing, his gaze riveted upon the gypsy's brilliant eyes. It seemed as if he was reading her song from her eyes.

On another occasion he came to her with an awkward and timid air. 'Listen,' said he, with an effort; 'I have something to say to you.' She made him a sign that she was listening. Then he began to sigh, half opened his lips, seemed for a moment to be on the point of speaking, then looked at her again, shook his head, and slowly withdrew, his hand pressed to his brow, leaving the gypsy stupefied.

Among the grotesque figures carved upon the wall, there was one for which he had a particular affection, and with which he often seemed to exchange fraternal glances. Once the gypsy heard him say to it: 'Oh! why am I not of stone like thee!'

At last, one morning, La Esmeralda had advanced to the verge of the roof, and was looking into the Place over the pointed roof of

Saint-Jean-le-Rond. Quasimodo was there behind her. He used to so place himself of his own accord, in order to spare the young girl as much as possible the unpleasantness of seeing him. Suddenly the gypsy started; a tear and a flash of joy sparkled simultaneously in her eyes; she knelt down on the edge of the roof, and stretched out her arms in anguish toward the Place, crying out 'Phœbus! oh, come! come hither! One word! but one word, in heaven's name! Phœbus! Phœbus!' Her voice, her face, her gesture, her whole person had the heart-rending aspect of a shipwrecked mariner making the signal of distress to some gay vessel passing in the distant horizon in a gleam of sunshine.

Quasimodo leaned over and saw that the object of this tender and agonizing prayer was a young man, a captain, a handsome cavalier, glistening with arms and accoutrements, prancing across the end of the square, and saluting with his plume a beautiful young lady smiling at her balcony. The officer, however, did not hear the unhappy girl calling him, for he was too far off.

But the poor deaf man heard it. A deep sigh heaved his breast. He turned round. His heart was swollen with the tears which he repressed; his convulsively clenched fists struck against his head, and when he withdrew them there was in each of them a handful of red hair.

The gypsy was paying no attention to him. He said, in an undertone, grinding his teeth:

'Damnation! That is how one ought to look then! One need but have a handsome outside!'

Meanwhile she remained kneeling, crying with extraordinary agitation:

'Oh, there! he alights from his horse. He is going into that house. Phœbus! He does not hear me. Phœbus! Oh! that wicked woman, to talk to him at the same time that I do! Phœbus! Phœbus!'

The deaf man was watching her. He understood this pantomime. The poor ringer's eye filled with tears, but he let none fall. All at once he pulled her gently by the border of her sleeve. She turned round. He had assumed a look of composure, and said to her: 'Shall I go and fetch him?'

She uttered a cry of joy.

'Oh, go! go! Run! quick! – that captain, that captain! bring him to me! I will love thee!'

She clasped his knees. He could not help shaking his head sorrowfully.

'I will bring him to you,' said he, in a faint voice. Then he turned his head, and plunged hastily down the staircase, his heart bursting with sobs.

When he reached the Place, he found only the handsome horse fastened at the door of the Gondelaurier mansion; the captain had just gone in.

He looked up at the roof of the church. La Esmeralda was still there, on the same spot, in the same posture. He made her a melancholy sign of the head; then set his back against one of the posts of the porch of the mansion, determined to wait until the captain should come forth.

In the Gondelaurier house it was one of those gala days which precede a marriage. Quasimodo saw many people enter, and no one come out. From time to time he looked up at the roof of the church; the gypsy did not stir any more than he. A groom came and untied the horse, and led him to the stable of the household.

The entire day passed thus – Quasimodo against the post, La Esmeralda upon the roof, Phœbus, no doubt, at the feet of Fleur-de-Lys.

At length night came; a dark, moonless night. In vain did Quasimodo fix his gaze upon La Esmeralda; she was but a white spot in the twilight, then nothing was to be seen. All had vanished, all was black.

Quasimodo saw the front windows from top to bottom of the Gondelaurier mansion illuminated. He saw the other casements in the Place lighted one by one; he also saw them extinguished to the very last, for he remained the whole evening at his post. The officer did not come forth. When the last passers-by had returned home, when the windows of all the other houses were in darkness, Quasimodo remained entirely alone, entirely in the dark. There were at that time no lamps in the square of Notre-Dame.

But the windows of the Gondelaurier mansion continued lighted, even after midnight. Quasimodo, motionless and attentive, beheld a throng of lively dancing shadows pass athwart the many coloured painted panes. Had he not been deaf, in proportion as the murmur of slumbering Paris died away, he would have heard more and more distinctly, from within the Logis Gondelaurier, a sound of feasting, laughter and music.

Towards one o'clock in the morning the guests began to take their leave. Quasimodo, wrapped in darkness, watched them all pass out through the porch; none of them was the captain.

He was full of melancholy thoughts; at times he looked up into the air, like one weary of waiting. Great black clouds, heavy, torn split, hung like ragged festoons of crape beneath the starry arch of night.

In one of those moments he suddenly saw the long folding window that opened upon the balcony, whose stone balustrade projected above his head, mysteriously open. The frail glass door gave passage to two persons, then closed noiselessly behind them. It was not without difficulty that Quasimodo, in the dark, recognized in the man the handsome captain, in the woman, the young lady whom he had seen in the morning welcoming the officer from that very balcony. The square was quite dark, and a double crimson curtain, which had fallen behind the glass door the moment it closed, allowed no light to reach the balcony from the apartment.

The young man and the young girl, as far as our deaf man could judge without hearing a word they said, appeared to abandon themselves to a very tender tête-a-tête. The young lady seemed to have permitted the officer to make a girdle for her waist of his arm, and was gently resisting a kiss.

Quasimodo looked on from below this scene, all the more interesting to witness, as it was not intended to be seen. He contemplated, with bitterness, that happiness, that beauty. After all, nature was not silent in the poor fellow, and his vertebral column, wretchedly distorted as it was, quivered no less than another's. He thought of the miserable portion which Providence had allotted to him; that woman, love and its pleasures, would pass forever before his eyes without his ever doing anything but witness the felicity of others. But what pained him most of all in this spectacle what mingled indignation with his chagrin, was the thought of what the gypsy would suffer could she behold it. True it was that the night was very dark, that La Esmeralda, if she had remained at the same place, as he doubted not she had, was at a considerable distance, and that it was all that he himself could do to distinguish the lovers on the balcony; this consoled him.

Meanwhile their conversation grew more and more animated. The young lady seemed to be entreating the officer to ask nothing more from her. Quasimodo could only distinguish the fair clasped hands, the mingled smiles and tears, the young girl's glances directed to the stars, and the eyes of the captain lowered ardently upon her.

Fortunately, for the young girl was beginning to resist but feebly, the door of the balcony suddenly reopened, and an old lady made her appearance; the young beauty looked confused, the officer annoyed, and all three went in.

A moment later a horse was prancing under the porch, and the brilliant officer, enveloped in his night cloak, passed rapidly before Quasimodo.

The bell-ringer allowed him to turn the corner of the street, then ran after him, with his ape-like agility, shouting: 'Hi! captain!'

The captain halted.

'What does the rascal want with me?' said he, espying in the dark that uncouth figure running toward him limping.

Quasimodo, however, had come up to him, and boldly taken his horse by the bridle: 'Follow me, captain; there is one here who desires to speak with you.'

'By Mahound's horns,' grumbled Phœbus, 'here's a villainous ragged bird that I fancy I've seen somewhere. Hello! sirrah! leave hold of my horse's bridle!'

'Captain,' answered the deaf man, 'do you not ask me who it is?'

'I tell thee to let go my horse,' returned Phœbus, impatiently. 'What means the rogue hanging thus from my bridle rein? Dost thou take my horse for a gallows?'

Quasimodo, far from releasing the bridle, was preparing to make him turn round. Unable to comprehend the captain's resistance, he hastened to say to him:

'Come, captain; 'tis a woman who is waiting for you.' He added, with an effort, 'a woman who loves you.'

'A rare varlet!' said the captain, 'who thinks me obliged to go after every woman that loves me, or says she does – and if perchance she resembles thee with thy face of a screech-owl? Tell her that sent thee that I am going to be married, and that she may go to the devil.'

'Hark ye!' cried Quasimodo, thinking to overcome his hesitation with a word; 'come, monseigneur; 'tis the gypsy-girl that you know of.'

This word did, in fact, make a great impression on Phœbus, but not that which the deaf man expected. It will be remembered that our gallant officer had retired with Fleur-de-Lys several moments before Quasimodo had rescued the condemned girl from the hands of Charmolue. Since then, in all his visits at the Logis Gondelaurier, he had taken care not to mention that woman, the recollection of whom was besides painful to him; and Fleur-de-Lys, on her part, had not deemed it politic to tell him that the gypsy was alive. Hence, Phœbus believed poor *Similar* dead a month or two ago. Add to this, for some moments the captain had been thinking of the extreme darkness of the night, the supernatural ugliness and sepulchral voice of the strange messenger that it was past midnight; that the street was as solitary as the night that the spectre monk had accosted him, and that his horse panted as it looked at Quasimodo.

'The gypsy!' he exclaimed, almost frightened. 'How now! Art thou come from the other world?' And he laid his hand on the hilt of his dagger.

'Quick! quick!' said the deaf man, endeavouring to drag the horse along; 'this way!'

Phœbus dealt him a vigorous kick in the breast.

Quasimodo's eye flashed. He made a movement as if to fling himself upon the captain. Then, checking himself; he said: 'Oh, how happy you are to have some one who loves you!'

He emphasized the words 'some one,' and leaving hold of the horse's bridle, said:

'Begone!'

Phœbus spurred on in all haste, swearing. Quasimodo watched him disappear in the misty darkness of the street

'Oh!' said the poor deaf creature to himself, 'to refuse that!'

He returned to Notre-Dame, lighted his lamp, and climbed up the tower again. As he expected, the gypsy-girl was still at the same spot.

The moment she perceived he was coming she ran to meet him.

'Alone!' she cried, clasping her pretty hands in anguish.

'I could not find him again,' said Quasimodo coldly.

'You should have waited for him all night,' returned she passionately.

He saw her angry gesture, and understood the reproof.

'I'll watch him better another time,' said he, hanging his head.

'Get you gone,' said she.

He left her. She was dissatisfied with him. He would have preferred being chided by her than to cause her pain. He had kept all the grief for himself.

From that day forward the gypsy saw him no more; he ceased coming to her cell. Now and then, indeed, she caught a distant glimpse of the ringer's countenance looking mournfully upon her from the top of some tower; but as soon as she perceived him, he would disappear.

We must admit that she was but little troubled by the voluntary absence of the poor hunch-back. At the bottom of her heart she felt grateful to him for it. Nor was Quasimodo himself under any delusion upon this point.

She saw him no more, but she felt the presence of a good genius about her. Her provisions were renewed by an invisible hand while she slept. One morning she found upon her window-sill a cage of birds. Over her cell there was a piece of sculpture that frightened her. She had repeatedly evinced this feeling in Quasimodo's presence. One morning (for all these things were done in the night) she saw it no longer; it had been broken off. He who had climbed to that piece of carving must have risked his life.

Sometimes, in the evening, she heard the voice of one concealed behind the great blind of the belfry, singing, as if to lull her to sleep, a melancholy and fantastic song, verses without rhyme or rhythm, such as a deaf man might make:

> *Oh, look not on the face,*
> *Young maid, look on the heart:*
> *The heart of a fine young man is oft deformed;*
> *There are some hearts will hold no love for long.*
> *Young maid, the pine's not fair to see,*
> *Not fair to the eye as the poplar,*
> *Yet it keeps its leaves in winter-time.*
> *Alas! it's vain to talk of this;*
> *What is not fair ought not to be –*
> *Beauty will only beauty love –*
> *April looks not on January.*

> *Beauty is perfect,*
> *Beauty wins all,*
> *Beauty alone exists not by half.*

> *The crow flies but by day;*
> *The owl flies but by night;*
> *The swan flies night and day.*

On waking one morning, she saw in her window two jars full of flowers; one of them a glass vessel, very beautiful and brilliant, but cracked; it had let all the water escape, and the flowers it contained were faded. The other vessel was of earthenware, rude and common, but it had kept the water, so that its flowers were fresh and blooming.

I do not know whether she did it intentionally, but La Esmeralda took the faded nosegay and wore it all day in her bosom.

That day she did not hear the voice from the tower singing. She felt little concern about it. She passed her days in caressing Djali, watching the door of the Logis Gondelaurier, in talking low to herself about Phœbus, and crumbling her bread to the swallows.

She had altogether ceased to see or to hear Quasimodo. The poor ringer seemed to have departed from the church. One night, however, as she lay wakeful, thinking of her handsome captain, she heard a sigh, near to her cell. She rose up affrighted, and saw by the moonlight, a shapeless mass lying before her door. It was Quasimodo sleeping there upon the stones.

V

The Key of the Red Door

MEANWHILE PUBLIC RUMOUR had acquainted the archdeacon with the miraculous manner in which the gypsy-girl had been saved. When he learned this, he felt he knew not what. He had reconciled his mind to the thought of La Esmeralda's death, and thus he had become calm; he had touched the depths of possible grief. The human heart (and Dom Claude had meditated upon these matters) cannot contain more than a certain quantity of despair. When the sponge is thoroughly soaked, the sea may pass over it without its imbibing one tear more.

Now, Esmeralda being dead, the sponge was filled to its utmost; all was over for Dom Claude upon this earth. But to feel that she was alive, and Phœbus also – that was the recommencement of torture, of pangs, of vicissitudes, of life – and Dom Claude was weary of all that.

When this piece of intelligence reached him, he shut himself in his cloister cell. He appeared neither at the conferences of the chapter, nor at the services in the church. He closed his door against every one, even the bishop. He kept himself thus immured for several weeks. He was thought to be ill, and so indeed he was.

What was he doing, shut up thus? With what thoughts was the unfortunate man contending? Was he making a final struggle against his formidable passion? Was he combining some final plan of death for her and perdition for himself?

His Jehan, his cherished brother, his spoiled child, came once to his door, knocked, swore, entreated, announced himself ten times over. Claude would not open.

He passed whole days with his face pressed against the casement of his window. From that window, situated in the cloister, he could see the cell of Esmeralda; he often saw herself, with her goat – sometimes with Quasimodo. He remarked the assiduities of the ugly deaf man, his obedience, his delicate and submissive behaviour to the gypsy-girl. He recollected – for he had a good memory, and memory is the tormentor of the jealous – he recollected the singular look which the ringer had cast upon the dancing-girl on a certain evening. He asked himself what motive could have urged Quasimodo to save her. He was an eye-witness to a thousand little scenes which passed between the gypsy and the ringer; where, in their gestures, as seen at that distance and commented on by his passion, appeared to him most tender. He distrusted woman's capriciousness. Then he felt confusedly arising within him a jealousy such as he had never imagined; a jealousy which made him redden with shame and indignation. 'As for the captain,' thought he, 'that might pass – but this one!' And the idea overpowered him.

His nights were frightful. Since he knew the gypsy-girl to be alive, those cold images of spectres and the grave, which had beset him for a whole day, had vanished from his spirit, and the flesh began again to torment him. He writhed upon his bed at the thought that the dark-skinned damsel was so near him.

Each night his delirious imagination represented to him La Esmeralda in all the attitudes that had most strongly excited his passion. He beheld her stretched across the body of the poniarded captain, her eyes closed, her fair neck crimsoned with the blood of Phœbus; at that moment of wild delight when the archdeacon had imprinted on her pale lips that kiss of which the unfortunate girl, half dying as she was, had felt the burning pressure. Again he beheld her undressed by the savage hands of the torturers, letting them thrust her little foot naked into the horrid iron-screwed buskin, her round and delicate leg, her white and supple knee; and then he saw that ivory knee alone appearing, all below it being enveloped in Torterue's horrible apparatus. He figured to himself the young girl, in her slight chemise, with the rope about her neck, with bare feet and uncovered shoulders, almost naked, as he had seen her upon the last day. These voluptuous images made him clench his hands, and sent a shiver through his frame.

One night in particular, they so cruelly inflamed his priestly virgin blood, that he tore his pillow with his teeth, leaped from bed, threw a surplice over his night-robe, and went out of his cell with his lamp in hand, half naked, wild, with flaming eyes.

He knew where to find the key of the red door, opening from the cloister into the church; and, as the reader is aware, he always carried about him a key of the tower staircase.

VI

Sequel to the Key of the Red Door

THAT NIGHT LA ESMERALDA had fallen asleep in her little chamber, full of forgetfulness, of hope and of happy thoughts. She had been sleeping some time, dreaming, as usual, of Phœbus, when she thought she heard some noise about her. Her sleep was light and restless – the sleep of a bird; the slightest thing awakened her. She opened her eyes. The night was very dark. Yet she discerned at the little window a face regarding her; there was a lamp which cast its light upon this apparition. The moment that it perceived itself to be observed by La Esmeralda, it blew out the lamp. Nevertheless, the young girl had caught a glimpse of its features; her eyelids dropped with terror. 'Oh!' said she in a faint voice, 'the priest!'

All her past misfortune flashed upon her mind, and she fell back frozen upon her bed with horror.

A moment after, she felt a contact the whole length of her body, which made her shudder so violently that she started up in bed wide awake and furious. The priest had glided to her side and clasped her in his arms.

She strove to cry out, but could not.

'Begone, monster! begone, assassin!' said she, in a voice low and faltering with anger and horror.

'Mercy! mercy!' murmured the priest, pressing his lips to her shoulders.

She seized his bald head with both her hands by the remaining hairs, and strove to repel his kisses, as if he had been biting her.

'Mercy!' repeated the wretched man. 'Didst thou but know what is my love for thee! 'Tis fire! 'tis molten lead! 'tis a thousand daggers in my heart!'

And he held back both her arms with super-human strength. Quite desperate, 'Let me go,' she cried, 'or I spit in thy face!'

He released her. 'Vilify me, strike me, be cruel, do what thou wilt, but have mercy! love me!'

Then she struck him with the fury of a child. She drew up her beautiful hands to tear his face. 'Begone, demon!'

'Love me! love me! have pity!' cried the poor priest, rolling upon her and answering her blows with caresses.

All at once she felt that he was overpowering her. 'There must be an end of this,' said he, grinding his teeth.

She was conquered, crushed and quivering in his arms. She felt a lascivious hand wandering over her. She made a last effort, and shrieked: 'Help! help me! A vampire! a vampire!'

But nothing came. Only Djali was awake and bleated piteously.

'Silence!' said the panting priest.

Suddenly, in the midst of her struggles, as the gypsy retreated upon the floor, her hand came in contact with something cold and metallic. It was Quasimodo's whistle. She seized it with a convulsion of hope, put it to her lips, and blew with all her remaining strength. The whistle sounded clear, shrill, piercing.

'What is that?' said the priest.

Almost at the same instant he felt himself lifted by a vigorous arm. The cell was dark; he could not clearly distinguish who it was that held him thus; but he heard teeth clenching with rage, and there was just light enough mingled with the darkness for him to see shining over his head a large cutlass.

The priest thought he could discern the form of Quasimodo. He supposed it could be no other. He recollected having stumbled, in entering, over a bundle that was lying across the doorway outside. Yet, as the new-comer uttered no word, he knew not what to think. He threw himself upon the arm that held the cutlass, crying, 'Quasimodo!' forgetting, in that moment of distress, that Quasimodo was deaf.

In the twinkling of an eye the priest was thrown upon the floor, and felt a knee of lead weighing upon his breast. By the angular imprint of that knee he recognized Quasimodo. But what was he to do? how was he to make himself known to the other? Night made the deaf man blind.

He was lost. The young girl, devoid of pity, as an enraged tigress, did not interfere to save him. The cutlass approached his head; the moment was critical. Suddenly his adversary appeared to hesitate. 'No blood upon her!' said he, in an undertone.

It was, in fact, the voice of Quasimodo.

Then the priest felt the great hand dragging him by the foot out of the cell; it was there he was to die. Luckily for him, the moon had been risen for a few moments.

When they had cleared the door of the chamber, its pale rays fell upon the features of the priest. Quasimodo looked in his face; a tremor came over him; he relaxed his hold of the priest and shrank back.

The gypsy having come forward to the threshold of her cell, was surprised to see them suddenly change parts; for now it was the priest who threatened, and Quasimodo who implored.

The priest, heaping gestures of anger and reproof upon the deaf man, violently motioned to him to withdraw.

The deaf man bowed his head, then came and knelt before the gypsy's door. 'Monseigneur,' said he, in a tone of gravity and resignation, 'afterwards you will do what you please but kill me first.'

So saying, he presented his cutlass to the priest; and the priest, beside himself, rushed forward to grasp it; but the girl was quicker than he. She snatched the cutlass from Quasimodo's hand, and burst into a frantic laugh. 'Approach!' said she to the priest.

She held the blade aloft. The priest hesitated. She would certainly have struck. 'Thou durst not approach now, coward!' she exclaimed. Then she added, in a pitiless accent, and well knowing that it would be plunging a red-hot iron into the heart of the priest: 'Ha! I know that Phœbus is not dead!'

The priest overthrew Quasimodo with a kick, and plunged trembling with rage, under the vault of the staircase.

When he had gone, Quasimodo picked up the whistle that had just saved the gypsy. 'It was growing rusty,' said he, as he gave it to her, and then he left her alone.

The young girl, overpowered by this violent scene, fell exhausted upon her couch, and burst into a flood of tears. Again her horizon was growing overcast.

As for the priest, he had groped his way back into his cell.

'Twas done. Dom Claude was jealous of Quasimodo. He repeated pensively to himself his fatal sentence: 'No one shall have her!'

BOOK TEN

I

Gringoire has a Succession of Bright Ideas in the Rue des Bernardins

FROM THE TIME that Pierre Gringoire had seen the turn that this affair was taking, and that torture, hanging and various other disagreeables were decidedly in store for the principal personages in this comedy, he no longer felt any desire to take part in it. The Truands, amongst whom he had remained, considering that, after all, they were the best company in Paris – the Truands had continued to feel interested in the gypsy. This he found very natural in people who, like herself, had nothing but Charmolue and Torterue in prospect, and who did not, like himself, soar into the regions of imagination between the two wings of Pegasus. He had learned from their discourse that his bride of the broken pitcher had found refuge in Notre-Dame, and he was glad of it. But he did not even feel tempted to go and see her there. He sometimes thought of the little goat, and that was all. For the rest, by day he exerted his wits to get his bread; and by night he lucubrated a memorial against the Bishop of Paris, for he remembered being drenched by his mill-wheels, and he bore him malice therefor. He occupied himself also with a commentary upon the fine work of Baudry-le-Rouge, Bishop of Noyon and of Tournay, de *Cupa Petrarum*, which had given him a violent inclination for architecture, an inclination which had supplanted in his breast his passion for hermetics, of which, too, it was but a natural consequence, seeing that there is an intimate connection between the hermetic philosophy and masonry. Gringoire had passed from the love of an idea to the love of the form of that idea.

One day he had stopped near the church of Saint-Germain-l'Auxerrois, at the corner of a building called *le For-l'Evêque*, which was opposite another called *le For-le-Roi*. There was at this For-l'Evêque a beautiful chapel of the Fourteenth century, whose apsis was on the street. Gringoire was examining devoutly its external sculptures. It was one of those moments of selfish, exclusive and supreme enjoyment in which the artist sees nothing in the world but his art, and the world itself in that art. All at once, he felt a hand fell heavily on his shoulder; he turned round – it was his old friend, his old master, monsieur, the archdeacon.

He was quite confounded. It was long since he had seen the archdeacon; and Dom Claude was one of those grave and ardent beings, a meeting with whom always disturbs the equilibrium of a sceptical philosopher.

The archdeacon maintained silence for some moments, during which Gringoire had leisure to observe him. He found Dom Claude much altered, pale as a winter morning, with hollow eyes and hair almost white. The priest was the first to break this silence, by saying in a calm but freezing tone: 'How do you do, Mâitre Pierre.'

'As to my health,' answered Gringoire, 'eh! eh! one can say both one thing and another on that score. Still it is good, on the whole. I do not take too much of anything. You know, master, the secret of keeping well, according to Hippocrates: *Id est: cibi, potus, somni venus, omnia moderata sint.*' (That is: love of food, drink slumber, let all things be in moderation.)

'You have no care, then, Maître Pierre?' resumed the archdeacon, looking steadily at Gringoire.

'Faith, not I!'

'And what are you doing now?'

'As you see, master. I am examining the cutting of these stones and the style in which this bas-relief is executed.'

The priest began to smile with that bitter smile which raises only one corner of the mouth. 'And that amuses you?'

' 'Tis paradise!' exclaimed Gringoire. And, leaning over the sculptures with the fascinated air of a demonstrator of living phenomena: 'Now, for example, do you not think that that metamorphosis, in bas-relief, is executed with a great deal of skill delicacy and patience? Look at that small column, was ever capital entwined with leaves more graceful or more exquisitely touched by the chisel? Here are three alto-relievos by Jean Maillevin. They are not the finest specimens of that great genius. Nevertheless, the simplicity, the sweetness of those faces, the sportiveness of the attitudes and the draperies, and that undefinable charm which is mingled with all the imperfections, render the small figures very light and delicate – perchance even too much so. You do not find it interesting?'

'Oh, yes!' said the priest.

'And if you were to see the interior of the chapel!' continued the poet, with his loquacious enthusiasm. 'Carvings everywhere! 'Tis as thickly clustered as the heart of the cabbage! The apsis is of a very devout fashion, and so peculiar that I have never seen anything like it anywhere else!'

Dom Claude interrupted him: 'You are happy, then?'

Gringoire replied with conviction: 'On my honour, yes! First, I loved women, then animals; now I love stones. They are quite as amusing as animals or women, and less treacherous.'

The priest passed his hand across his brow. It was his habitual gesture.

'Indeed!'

'Hark you,' said Gringoire, 'one has one's enjoyments.' He took the arm of the priest, who yielded to his guidance, and led him under the staircase turret of the For-l'Evêque. 'There's a staircase!' he exclaimed. 'Whenever I see it I am happy. That flight of steps is the most simple and the most uncommon in Paris. Every step is chamfered underneath. Its beauty and simplicity consist in the circumstance of the steps, which are a foot broad, or thereabout, being interlaced, mortised, jointed, enchained, enchased, set one in the other, and biting into each other, in a way that is truly firm and admirable.'

'And you desire nothing?' said the priest.

'No!'

'And you regret nothing?'

'Neither regret nor desire. I have arranged my mode of life.'

'What man arranges,' said Claude, 'circumstances disarrange.'

'I am a Pyrrhonian philosopher,' answered Gringoire, 'and hold everything in equilibrium.'

'And how do you earn your living?'

'I still write, now and then, epics and tragedies; but that which brings me in the most is that certain industry of mine, of which you are aware, master – carrying pyramids of chairs on my teeth.'

'A scurvy trade for a philosopher!'

'It is still equilibrium,' said Gringoire. 'When one has an idea, one finds it in everything.'

'I know that,' replied the archdeacon.

After a short silence, the priest resumed:

'You are, nevertheless, poor enough?'

'Poor? Yes, but not unhappy.'

At that moment the sound of horses was heard; and our two interlocutors saw filing off at the end of the street a company of the king's archers, with their lances raised, and an officer at their head. The cavalcade was brilliant, and its march resounded on the pavement.

'How you look at that officer!' said Gringoire to the archdeacon.

'I think I know him!' was the reply.

'How do you call him?'

'I believe,' said Claude, 'his name is Phœbus de Chateaupers.'

'Phœbus! a curious sort of a name! There's Phœbus, too, Count of Foix. I recollect I knew a girl once who never swore but by Phœbus.'

'Come hither,' said the priest; 'I have something to say to you.'

Since the passing of the troop, some agitation was perceptible under the frozen exterior of the archdeacon. He walked on. Gringoire followed him, being wont to obey him, like all who had once approached that commanding personality. They reached in silence the Rue des Bernardins, which was almost deserted. Dom Claude stopped.

'What have you to say to me, master?' asked Gringoire.

'Do you not think,' answered the archdeacon, with an air of profound reflection, 'that the dress of those cavaliers, whom we have just seen, is handsomer than yours and mine?"

Gringoire shook his head.

'I' faith, I like better my red and yellow jerkin than those scales of iron and steel. A fine sort of thing, to make a noise in going along like an iron quay in an earthquake!'

'Then, Gringoire, you have never envied those fine fellows in their warlike hacquetons?'

'Envied what, monsieur the archdeacon? their strength, their armour, their discipline? Give me rather philosophy and independence in rags. I would rather be the head of a fly than the tail of a lion.'

'That is singular,' said the musing priest. 'A fine uniform is a fine thing, nevertheless.'

Gringoire, seeing him absorbed in thought, quitted him to go and admire the porch of a neighbouring house. He returned, clapping his hands.

'If you were less occupied with the fine clothes of men of war monsieur the archdeacon, I would beg you to go and see that doorway. I have always said it; the Sieur Aubry's house has the most superb entrance in the world.'

'Pierre Gringoire,' said the archdeacon, 'what have you done with that little gypsy dancer?'

'Esmeralda? You change the conversation very abruptly.'

'Was she not your wife?'

'Yes, by virtue of a broken pitcher. We were in for it for four years. By-the-by,' added Gringoire, looking at the archdeacon with a half-bantering air, 'you think of her still, then?'

'And you – do you no longer think of her?'

'Very little. I have so many things! Good heavens! how pretty the little goat was!'

'Did not that Bohemian girl save your life?'

' 'Tis true, pardieu.'

'Well, what became of her? what have you done with her?'

'I cannot tell you. I believe they have hanged her.'

'You believe?'

'I am not sure. When I saw there was hanging in the case, I kept out of the business.'

'And that is all you know of it?'

'Stay. I was told she had taken refuge in Notre-Dame, and that she was there in safety; and I am delighted at it; and I have not been able to discover whether the goat escaped with her, and that is all I know about the matter.'

'I will tell you more,' cried Dom Claude; and his voice, till then low, deliberate and hollow, became like thunder. 'She has, indeed, taken refuge in Notre-Dame. But in three days justice will drag her again from thence, and she will be hanged at the Grève. There is a decree of the Parliament for it!'

'Now, that is a shame,' said Gringoire.

The priest in a moment had become cool and calm again.

'And who the devil,' continued the poet, 'has taken the trouble to solicit a decree of reintegration? Could they not leave the Parliament alone? Of what consequence can it be that a poor girl takes shelter under the buttresses of Notre-Dame, among the swallows' nests?'

'There are Satans in the world,' answered the archdeacon.

'That's a devilish bad piece of work,' observed Gringoire.

The archdeacon resumed, after a short silence:

'So then, she saved your life?'

'Yes, among my good friends the Truands. I was within an inch of being hanged. They would have been sorry for it now.'

'Will you not do something for her, then?'

'I should rejoice to be of service, Dom Claude; but if I were to bring a bad piece of business about my ears!'

'What can it signify?'

'The deuce! what can it signify! You are very kind, master! I have two great works begun.'

The priest struck his forehead. In spite of the composure which he affected, a violent gesture betrayed from time to time his inward struggles.

'How is she to be saved?'

'Master,' said Gringoire, 'I will answer you – *Il padelt* – which means, in the Turkish, "God is our hope." '

'How is she to be saved?' repeated Claude, dreamily.

Gringoire, in his turn, struck his forehead.

'Hark you, master; I have some imagination. I will find expedients for you. What if we were to entreat the king's mercy?'

'Mercy! of Louis XI!'

'Why not?'

'Go take from the tiger his bone!'

Gringoire began to seek fresh expedients.

'Well, stay. Shall I address a memorial to the midwives, declaring that the girl is with child?'

At this the priest's sunken eyeballs glared.

'With child! Fellow! do you know anything about it?'

Gringoire was terrified at his manner. He hastened to say:

'Oh, not I. Our marriage was a regular *forismaritagium*. I'm altogether out of it. But, at any rate, one would obtain a reprieve.'

'Madness! infamy! hold thy peace!'

'You are wrong to be angry,' muttered Gringoire. 'One gets a respite, that does no harm to anybody, and it puts forty deniers parisis into the pockets of the midwives, who are poor women.'

The priest heard him not.

'She must leave there, nevertheless,' murmured he. 'The decree is to be put in force within three days. Otherwise, it would not be valid. That Quasimodo! Women have very depraved tastes!' He raised his voice: 'Maître Pierre, I have well considered the matter. There is but one means of saving her.'

'And what is it? For my part, I see none.'

'Hark ye, Maître Pierre; remember that you owe your life to her. I will tell you candidly my idea. The church is watched day and night; no one is allowed to come out but those who have been seen to go in. Thus you can go in. You shall come, and I will take you to her. You will change clothes with her. She will take your doublet, and you will take her petticoat.'

'So far, so good,' observed the philosopher; 'and what then?'

'What then? Why, she will go out in your clothes, and you will remain in hers. You may get hanged, perhaps, but she will be saved.'

Gringoire scratched his ear with a very serious air.

'Well!' said he, 'there is an idea that would never have come into my head of itself.'

At Dom Claude's unexpected proposal, the open and benign countenance of the poet had abruptly clouded over, like a smiling Italian landscape when an unlucky gust of wind throws a cloud across the sun.

'Well, Gringoire, what say you to the plan?'

'I say, master, that I shall not be hanged perhaps, but that I shall be hanged indubitably.'

'That concerns us not.'

'The deuce!' said Gringoire.

'She saved your life. 'Tis a debt you are discharging.'

'There are many others which I do not discharge.'

'Maître Pierre, it must absolutely be so.'

The archdeacon spoke imperiously.

'Hark you, Dom Claude,' answered the poet, in great consternation. 'You hold to that idea, and you are wrong. I don't see why I should get myself hanged instead of another.'

'What have you, then, which attaches you so strongly to life?'

'Ah! a thousand reasons.'

'What are they, pray?'

'What are they? The air, the sky, the morning, the evening, the moonlight, my good friends the Truands, our jeers with the old hags, the fine architecture of Paris to study, three great books to write, one of them against the bishop and his mills; more than I can tell. Anaxagoras used to say he had come into the world to admire the sun. And then, I have the felicity of passing the whole of my days, from morning till night, with a man of genius – who is myself – which is very agreeable.'

'A head fit for a mule bell!' muttered the archdeacon. 'Speak, then this life that thou findst so charming, who preserved it for thee. To whom art thou indebted for the privilege of breathing that air, of seeing that sky, of being still able to amuse thy linnet-head with humbugs and follies? Had it not been for her, where wouldst thou be? Thou wilt have her die then, she through whom thou livest, thou wilt have her die, that creature so lovely, so sweet, so adorable – a creature necessary to the light of the world, more divine than divinity itself, whilst thou, half sage, half fool, a mere sketch of something, a sort of vegetable which fancies it walks and thinks, thou wouldst continue to live with the life thou hast stolen from her, as useless as a taper at noonday! Come, Gringoire, a little pity! be generous in thy turn; she has set the example.'

The priest was vehement. Gringoire listened to him, at first with an air of indecision, then became moved, and concluded with making a tragical grimace which made his wan countenance resemble that of a new-born child in a fit of the colic.

'You are pathetic!' said he, wiping away a tear. 'Well! I will think about it. 'Tis an odd idea of yours.' . . . 'After all,' pursued he, after a moment's silence, 'who knows? perhaps they'll not hang me; there's many a slip between the cup and the lip. When they find me in that box, so grotesquely muffled in cap and petticoat, perhaps they'll burst out laughing. . . And if they do hang me, what then? The rope – 'tis a death like another. Or, rather, 'tis not a death like another. 'Tis a death worthy of the sage who has wavered all his life; a death which is neither fish nor flesh, like the mind of the true sceptic; a death fully marked with Pyrrhonism and hesitation, which holds the medium between heaven and earth, which leaves you in suspense. 'Tis a philosopher's death, and I was predestined thereto, perchance. It is magnificent to die as one has lived – '

The priest interrupted him: 'Is it agreed?'

'What is death, after all?' pursued Gringoire, with exaltation. 'A disagreeable moment, a turnpike-gate, the passage from littleness to nothingness. Some one having asked Cercidas of Megalopolis whether he could die willingly: "Why should I not?" answered he; "for after my death, I shall see those great men Pythagoras among the philosophers, Hecatæus among the historians, Homer among the poets, Olympus among the musicians."'

The archdeacon held out his hand to him. 'It is settled, then? you will come to-morrow?'

The gesture brought Gringoire back to reality.

'Faith, no!' said he, with the tone of a man just awaking. 'To get hanged! 'tis too absurd. I will not.'

'Farewell, then;' and the archdeacon added between his teeth, 'I will find thee again.'

'I do not want that devil of a man to find me again,' thought Gringoire; and he ran after Dom Claude. 'Stay, monsieur the archdeacon,' said he; 'old friends should not fall out. You take an interest in that girl – my wife, I mean. 'Tis well. You have devised a scheme for getting her out of Notre-Dame, but your plan is extremely unpleasant for me, Gringoire. Now, if I could suggest another, myself! – I beg to say, a most luminous inspiration has just occurred to me. If I had an expedient for extracting her from her sorry plight, without compromising my neck in the smallest degree with a slip-knot, what would you say? would not that suffice you? Must I absolutely be hanged before you are content?'

The priest was tearing the buttons from his cassock with impatience. 'Stream of words! What is thy plan?'

'Yes,' resumed Gringoire, talking to himself, and clapping his forefinger to his nose in sign of deep cogitation; 'that is it! The Truands are fine fellows! The tribe of Egypt love her! They will rise at the first word! Nothing easier! A bold stroke! Under cover of the disorder, they will easily carry her off! To-morrow evening. Nothing would please them better.'

'The plan! – speak!' said the priest, shaking him.

Gringoire turned majestically toward him: 'Let me alone! you see that I am composing!' He reflected a few moments more, then began to clap his hands at his thought, exclaiming: 'Admirable! success is sure!'

'The plan!' repeated Claude, angrily.

Gringoire was radiant.

'Come hither,' said he; 'let me tell you this in your ear. 'Tis truly a gallant counterplot, which will get us all out of the scrape. Egad! you must admit that I am no fool!'

He stopped short.

'Ah! by the way, is the little goat with the girl?'

'Yes – the devil take thee!'

'They would have hanged it also, would they not?'

'What is that to me?'

'Yes, they would have hanged it. They hanged a sow last month. The executioner likes that; he eats the animal after. Hang my pretty Djali! poor little lamb!'

'A curse upon thee!' cried Dom Claude. 'The hangman is thyself. What means of safety hast thou found, fellow! Wilt thou never be delivered of thy scheme?'

'Softly, master! You shall hear.'

Gringoire bent towards the archdeacon, and spoke very low in his ear, casting an anxious look from one end of the street to the other, though no one was near. When he had done, Dom Claude took his hand, and said, coolly: ' 'Tis well. To-morrow.'

'To-morrow,' repeated Gringoire; and while the archdeacon withdrew one way, he went off the other, saying low to himself: 'This is a grand affair, Monsieur Pierre Gringoire. Never mind – it's not to be said that because one is of little account one is to be frightened at a great undertaking. Biton carried a great bull on his shoulders; wagtails, linnets and buntings traverse the ocean.'

II

Turn Vagabond!

ON RE-ENTERING THE CLOISTER, the archdeacon found at the door of his cell his brother, Jehan du Moulin, who was waiting for him, and who had beguiled the tedium of waiting by drawing on the wall, with a piece of charcoal, a profile of his elder brother, embellished with a nose of immoderate dimensions.

Dom Claude scarcely looked at his brother; his thoughts were elsewhere. That merry scamp's face, whose radiance had so often cleared away the gloom from the physiognomy of the priest, was now powerless to dissipate the cloud which each day gathered thicker and thicker over that corrupt, mephitic and stagnant soul.

'Brother,' said Jehan, timidly, 'I am come to see you.'

The archdeacon did not so much as raise his eyes toward him.

'Well?'

'Brother,' continued the hypocrite, 'you are so good to me, and give me such wise counsel, that I always return to you.'

'What next?'

'Alas! brother, you were very right when you used to say to me: "Jehan! Jehan, *cessat doctorum doctrina, discipulorum disciplina*. (Cease the doctrine of the doctors, the discipline of the disciples.) Jehan, be prudent. Jehan, be studious. Jehan, pass not the night outside of the college without lawful occasion and leave of the master. Cudgel not the Picards. *Noli, Joannes, verberrare Picardos*. (Beat not the Picards.) Rot not like an unlettered ass, *quasi asinus illiteratus*, upon the straw seats of the schools. Jehan, allow yourself to be punished at the discretion of the master. Jehan, go every evening to chapel, and sing an anthem with verse and orison to our lady, the glorious Virgin Mary." Alas! how excellent was that advice!'

'And then?'

'Brother, you see before you a culprit, a criminal, a miscreant, a libertine, a reprobate! My dear brother, Jehan hath made of your counsels straw and dung to trample under foot. Well am I chastised for it – and God Almighty is exceeding just. So long as I had money, I feasted and led a joyous, foolish life. Oh! how grim-faced and vile behind is debauchery which is so charming in front! Now I have not a coin left; I have sold my table-cloth, my shirt and my towel. A merry life no longer! the bright taper is extinguished, and nothing is left me but noisome tallow dip, which stinks under my nostrils. The girls mock at me. I drink water. I am tormented with remorse and creditors.'

'The rest?' said the archdeacon.

'Alas! my very dear brother, I would fain lead a better life. I come to you full of contrition. I am penitent. I confess my faults. I beat my breast with heavy blows. You are very right to wish I should one day become a licentiate and sub-monitor of the Torchi College. At the present moment I feel a remarkable vocation for that office. But I have no more ink – I must buy some, I have no more pens – I must buy some; I have no more paper, no more books – I must buy some. For these purposes I am greatly in need of a little money, and I come to you, brother, with my heart full of contrition.'

'Is that all?'

'Yes,' said the student. 'A little money.'

'I have none.'

The student then said, with an air at once grave and decided: 'Well, brother, I am sorry to be obliged to tell you that I have received from other quarters very advantageous offers and proposals. You will not give me any money? No? In that case I will turn Truand.'

On pronouncing this monstrous word, he assumed the mien of an Ajax expecting to see the thunderbolt fall on his head.

The archdeacon said coldly to him: 'Turn Truand then.'

Jehan made him a low bow, and descended the cloister stairs whistling.

As he was passing through the court-yard of the cloister, beneath the window of his brother's cell, he heard that window open, raised his head, and saw the archdeacon's stern face looking through the opening. 'Get thee to the devil!' said Dom Claude; 'here is the last money thou shalt have of me.'

So saying the priest flung Jehan a purse, which made a great bump on the student's forehead, and with which Jehan set off, both vexed and content, like a dog that is pelted with marrow bones.

III

Long Live Mirth!

THE READER has probably not forgotten that a part of the Court of Miracles was enclosed within the ancient walls of the Town, a goodly number of whose towers were beginning, even at that epoch, to fall into decay. One of these towers had been converted into a pleasure resort by the Truands. There was a dram-shop on the lowest floor, and the rest was carried on in the upper stories. This tower was the point the most alive, and consequently the most hideous of the whole outcast den. It was a sort of monstrous hive, which was humming day and night. At night, when the remainder of the rabble were asleep, when not a lighted window was to be seen in the dingy fronts of the houses bordering the square, when not a sound was heard to issue from its innumerable families, from those ant-hills of thieves, loose women, and stolen or bastard children, the joyous tower might always be distinguished by the noise which proceeded from it, by the crimson light which, gleaming at once from the air-holes, the windows, the crevices in the gaping walls, escaped, as it were, from every pore.

The cellar, then, formed the public-house. One entered it through a low door and down a staircase as steep as a classic Alexandrine. Over the door, by way of a sign, was a marvellous daub representing new-coined sols and dead chickens, with this punning inscription underneath: *Aux sonneurs pour les trepasses*. ('The ringers for the dead.')

One evening, at the moment when the curfew was ringing from all the belfries in Paris, the sergeants of the watch might have remarked, had they been permitted to enter the formidable Court of Miracles, that more tumult than usual was going on in the Truands' tavern; that they were drinking deeper and swearing louder. Without, in the square, were numerous groups, conversing in low tones, as if some great plot was hatching; while here and there a knave squatted down, whetting some wicked-looking blade upon the pavement.

Meanwhile, within the tavern, wine and gaming so powerfully diverted the minds of the Truandry from the ideas which occupied them that evening, that it would have been difficult to have divined from the conversation of the drinkers what was the affair in hand. Only they had a gayer air than usual, and between the legs of each some weapon was seen glittering, a pruning-hook, a hatchet, a large bludgeon, or the crook of an old hackbut.

The apartment, of a circular form, was very spacious; but the tables were so close together and the tipplers so numerous, that the whole contents of the tavern, men, women, benches, beer-jugs, the drinkers, the sleepers, the gamblers, the able-bodied, the crippled, seemed thrown pell-mell together with about as much order and arrangement as a heap of oyster shells. A few tallow dips were burning upon the tables; but the real light of the tavern, that which sustained in the pot-house the character of the chandelier in an opera house, was the fire. That cellar was so damp that the fire was never allowed to go out, even in the height of summer; an immense chimney, with a carved mantel, and thick-set with heavy iron dogs and kitchen utensils, had in it, then, one of those large fires composed of wood and peat, which, at night, in a village street, bring out in red relief the windows of some forge upon the opposite wall. A large dog, gravely seated in the ashes, was turning before the glowing fire a spit loaded with meat.

In spite of the confusion, after the first glance, one might distinguish amid this multitude, three principal groups, pressing around three several personages with whom the reader is already acquainted. One of these personages, fantastically bedizened with many an Oriental trinket, was Mathias Hungadi Spicali, Duke of Egypt and Bohemia. The old rogue was seated on the table, with his legs crossed and his finger in the air, while in a loud voice he explained his skill in white and black magic to the many gaping faces which surrounded him. Another crowd was gathered thick around our old friend, the valiant King of Tunis, armed to the teeth; Clopin Trouillefou, with a very serious air and in a low voice, was superintending the pillage of an enormous cask of arms, staved wide before him, from which were issuing in profusion axes, swords, bassinets, coats of mail, lance and pike heads, crossbow bolts and arrows, like apples and grapes out of a cornucopia. Each one was taking something from the heap; one a head-piece, another a long rapier, and a third, the cross-handled misericorde or small dagger. The very children were arming; and even the cripples in bowls were barbed and cuirassed, and moved between the legs of the drinkers, like large beetles.

And lastly, a third audience, the most noisy, the most jovial, and the most numerous of all, was crowding the benches and the tables, from the midst of which a flute-like voice, haranguing and swearing, escaped from under a heavy suit of mail, complete from casque to spurs. The individual who had thus screwed himself up in full panoply, was so hidden by his warlike trappings that nothing was seen of his person but a red, impudent, turned-up nose, a lock of fair hair, a red mouth and two daring eyes. His belt was full of daggers and poniards; a large sword hung by his hip; a rusty cross-bow was on his left, and an immense wine-pot before him, without counting a strapping, dishevelled wench who was seated on his right. All the mouths around him were laughing, swearing and drinking.

Add to these twenty secondary groups; the waiters, male and female, running backward and forward with pitchers on their heads; the gamesters stooping over taws, *merèlles*, dice, *vachettes*, the exciting game of the tringlet (a kind of backgammon); quarrels in one corner – kisses in another; and some idea may then be formed of the whole collective scene; over which wavered the light of a great flaming fire, making a thousand grotesque and enormous shadows dance upon the wall.

As for the noise, it might be likened to the interior of a bell in full peal.

The dripping-pan, in which a shower of grease was crackling from the spit, filled up, with its continuous snapping, the intervals of those thousand dialogues which crossed each other in all directions from one side to another of the great circular room.

Amidst all this uproar there was, on one side of the tavern, upon the bench within the great open fireplace, a philosopher meditating, with his feet in the ashes, and his eyes upon the burning brands. It was Pierre Gringoire.

'Be quick! make haste! get under arms! we must march in an hour,' said Clopin Trouillefou to his Argotiers.

A wench was humming an air:

> *Father and mother, good-night;*
> *The latest up rake the fire.*

Two card players were disputing. 'Knave,' cried the reddest faced of the two, shaking his fist at the other, 'I'll mark thee with a club. Thou might go and take Mistigri's place in messeigneur the king's own card party.'

'Ugh!' roared a Norman, easily known by his nasal accent 'we're all heaped together here like the saints of Pebbletown!'

'My children,' said the Duke of Egypt to his auditory, speaking in a falsetto voice, 'the witches of France go to the sabbath without ointment, broomstick, or anything to ride on, with only a few magic words. The witches of Italy have always a he-goat that waits for them at their door. All of them are bound to go out up the chimney.'

The voice of the young scamp armed from head to foot was heard above the general hum.

'Noël! Noël!' cried he. 'My first day in armour! A Truand! I'm a Truand, ventre de Christ! Fill my glass. Friends, my name is Jehan Frollo du Moulin, and I'm a gentleman. 'Tis my opinion that if God were a guardsman he'd turn robber. Brethren, we go upon a noble expedition. We are valiant fellows. Besiege the church, force the doors, bring away the pretty girl, save her from the judges, save her from the priests; dismantle the cloister, burn the bishop in his house; we will do all that in less time than a burgomaster takes to eat a spoonful of soup.

Our cause is just; we'll plunder Notre-Dame, and that's all about it. We'll hang Quasimodo. Do you know Quasimodo, mesdemoiselles? Have you seen him puffing upon the great bell on a Pentecost festival? By Beelzebub's horns, it is very fine. You'd take him for a devil astride of a ghoul. Hark ye, my friends, I'm a Truand from the bottom of my heart, I'm a vagabond in my soul, a cadger born. I was very rich, and I have spent my all. My mother wanted to make me an officer; my father, a sub-deacon; my aunt, a councillor of the inquests; my grandmother, king's prothonotary; my great aunt, treasurer of the short robe; but I would make myself a Truand. I told my father so, and he spit his malediction in my face. I told my mother so, and she, poor old lady, began to cry and chatter like yonder fagot on the iron dogs there. Let's be merry! I'm a real Bicêtre. Barmaid, my dear, more wine! I've still some money left. But mind, I'll have no more of that Surène wine – it hurts my throat. I'd as lief gargle myself, cor-bœuf, with a basket!'

Meanwhile the rabble applauded with boisterous laughter; and, finding that the tumult was redoubling around him, the scholar exclaimed:

'Oh, what a glorious noise! *Populi debacchantis populosa debacchatio!*' (The ravings of the people, popular fury.) Then he began to sing out, with an eye as if swimming in ecstasy, and the tone of a canon leading the vesper chant: '*Quæ cantica! quæ organa! quæ cantilenæ! quæ melodie hic sine fine decantantur! Sonant melliflua hymnorum organa, suavissima angelorum melodia, cantica canticorum mira!*' (What songs, what instruments, what chants here without end are sung! Here sound sweet-toned instruments of hymns, most sweet melodies of angels, wonderful song of songs!) He broke off. 'Hey, you there, the devil's own barmaid! give me some supper!'

There followed a moment of comparative silence, during which the shrill voice of the Duke of Egypt was heard in its turn, instructing his Bohemians.

'The weasel,' said he, 'goes by the name of Aduine, a fox is called Blue-foot or the Woodranger; a wolf, Gray-foot or Gilt-foot; a bear, the Old one or the Grandfather. A gnome's cap makes one invisible, and makes one see invisible things. Whenever a toad is to be christened, it ought to be dressed in velvet, red or black, with a little bell at its neck and one at its feet. The godfather holds it by the head, and the godmother by the hinder parts. 'Tis the demon Sidragasum who hath the power to make wenches dance naked.'

'By the mass,' interrupted Jehan, 'I should like to be the demon Sidragasum!'

Meanwhile, the Truands continued to arm themselves and whisper at the other end of the tavern.

'That poor Esmeralda!' exclaimed one of the gypsy-men; 'she is our sister; we must release her.'

'Is she still at Notre-Dame?' asked a Jew-looking peddler.

'Yes, pardieu!' was the reply.

'Well, then, comrades,' cried the peddler, 'to Notre-Dame! All the more because there in the chapel of Saints Féréol and Ferrution there are two statues, the one of Saint John the Baptist, the other of Saint Anthony, of solid gold, weighing together seventeen gold marks and fifteen esterlins; and the pedestals, of silver gilt, weigh seventeen marks five ounces. I know that; I am a goldsmith.'

Here they set Jehan's supper before him. He exclaimed, as he threw himself upon the bosom of the girl that sat by him:

'By Saint-Voult-de-Lucques, called by the people Saint Goguelu, I am perfectly happy! I see a blockhead there, straight before me, that's looking at me with a face as smooth as an archduke. Here's another, at my left hand, with teeth so long that one can't see his chin. And then, I'm like the Maréchal de Gié at the siege of Pontoise; I've my right resting upon a hillock. Ventre-Mahom! comrade! you look like a tennis-ball merchant! and you come and sit down by me! I am noble, my friend. Trade is incompatible with nobility. Get thee away. Hello! you there! don't fight! What! Baptiste Croque-Oison! with a fine nose like thine! wilt thou go and risk it against that blockhead's great fists? You simpleton! *Non cuiquam datum est habere nasum.* (Not to everyone is it given to have a nose.) Truly, thou'rt divine, Jacqueline-of-the-Red-Ear! it's a pity thou hast no hair on thy head! Hello! My name is Jehan Frollo, and my brother's an archdeacon! the devil fly away with him! All that I tell you's the truth. By turning Truand I've given up one-half of a house, situate in Paradise, which my brother had promised me – *dimidiam domum in paradiso* (half a dwelling in Paradise) – those are the very words. I've a fief in the Rue Tirechappe, and all the women are in love with me, as true as it is that Saint Eloi was an excellent goldsmith, and that the five trades of the good city of Paris are the tanners, the leather dressers, the baldric-makers, the purse-makers and the cordwainers; and that Saint Laurence was broiled over egg-shells. I swear to you, comrades,

> For full twelve months I'll drink no wine,
> If this be any lie of mine!

'My charmer, 'tis moonlight. See yonder, through the air-hole, how the wind rumples those clouds, just as I do thy gorgerette! Girls, snuff the candles and the children. Christ and Mahom, what am I eating now, in the name of Jupiter? Hey, there, old jade! the hairs that are not to be found on thy wenches' heads we find in the omelets. Do you hear, old woman? I like my omelets bald. The devil flatten thy nose! A fine tavern of Beelzebub is this, where the wenches comb themselves with the forks?' And thereupon he broke his plate upon the floor and began to sing with all his might:

> *'And for this self of mine,*
> *By the Blood Divine!*
> *No creed I crave,*
> *Nor law to save:*
> *I have no fire,*
> *I have no hut,*
> *Nor faith to put*
> *In sovereign high*
> *Or Deity!'*

Meanwhile, Clopin Trouillefou had finished his distribution of weapons. He approached Gringoire, who seemed absorbed in profound reverie, with his feet on an andiron.

'Friend Pierre,' said the King of Tunis, 'what the devil art thou thinking about?'

Gringoire turned to him with a melancholy smile:

'I love the fire, my dear lord. Not for the trivial reason that fire warms the feet or cooks the soup, but because it throws out sparks. Sometimes I pass whole hours in watching the sparks. I discover a thousand things in those stars that sprinkle the dark background of the chimney-place. Those stars are also worlds.'

'Thunder, if I understand thee,' said the Truand. 'Dost know what o'clock it is?'

'I do not know,' answered Gringoire.

Clopin then went up to the Duke of Egypt.

'Comrade Mathias,' said he, 'this is not a good time we've hit upon. King Louis XI is said to be in Paris.'

'The more need to get our sister out of his clutches,' answered the old gypsy.

'You speak like a man, Mathias,' said the King of Tunis. 'Moreover, we will act promptly. No resistance is to be feared in the church. The canons are like so many hares, and we are in force. The Parliament's men will be finely balked to-morrow when they come to seek her. Guts of the Pope! I would not have them hang the pretty girl!'

Clopin went out of the tavern.

Meantime, Jehan was shouting in a hoarse voice: 'I drink! I eat! I'm drunk! I'm Jupiter! Hey! you there, Pierre the Slaughterer! look at me like that again and I'll fillip the dust off your nose.'

Gringoire, on the other hand, roused from his meditations, had begun to contemplate the wild and noisy scene around him, and muttered between his teeth: '*Luxuriosa res vinum et tumultuosa ebrietas.* (Wine is a thing of luxury, drunkenness of tumult.) Alas! what good reason I have to abstain from drinking! and how excellent is the saying of Saint Benedict: *Vinum apostatare facit etiam sapientes!*' (To abjure wine also makes wise men.)

At that moment Clopin re-entered, and shouted in a voice of thunder, 'Midnight!'

At this word, which produced the effect of a call to boot and saddle on a regiment at halt, all the Truands – men, women and children – rushed in a mass from the tavern with great noise of arms and iron implements.

The moon was now obscured.

The Court of Miracles was entirely dark. Not a light was to be seen; but it was far from being deserted. A crowd of men and women talking in low tones could be distinguished. They could be heard buzzing, and all sorts of weapons were glittering in the darkness. Clopin mounted upon a large stone.

'To your ranks, Argot!' cried he. 'Fall into line, Egypt! To your ranks, Galilee!'

A movement began in the darkness. The immense multitude seemed to be forming in column. In a few minutes the King of Tunis again raised his voice:

'Now, silence! to march through Paris. The password is, *Petite flambe en bagnenaud.* (Little light in a bladder-nut.) The torches must not be lighted till we reach Notre-Dame. March!'

Ten minutes later the horsemen of the watch fled in terror before a long procession of men descending in darkness and silence toward the Pont-au-Change, through the winding streets that intersect in every direction the close-built neighbourhood of the Halles.

IV

An Awkward Friend

THAT SAME NIGHT Quasimodo slept not. He had just gone his last round through the church. He had not noticed, at the moment when he was closing the doors, that the archdeacon had passed near him and had displayed some degree of ill-humour at seeing him bolt and padlock with care the enormous iron bars which gave to these closed portals the solidity of a wall. Dom Claude appeared even more preoccupied than usual. Moreover, since the nocturnal adventure of the cell, he was constantly ill-treating Quasimodo; but in vain he used him harshly, even striking him sometimes; nothing could shake the submission, the patience, the devoted resignation of the faithful ringer. From the archdeacon he could endure anything – insults, threats, blows – without murmuring a reproach, without uttering a complaint. At most he would follow Dom Claude anxiously with his eye, as he ascended the staircase of the towers; but the archdeacon had of himself abstained from again appearing before the gypsy-girl.

On that night, accordingly, Quasimodo, after casting one look toward his poor forsaken bells, Jacqueline, Marie, and Thibault, mounted to the top of the northern tower, and there, placing his well closed dark-lantern on the leads, took a survey of Paris. The night, as we have already said, was very dark. Paris, which, comparatively speaking, was not lighted at that period, presented to the eye a confused heap of black masses, intersected here and there by the whitish curve of the Seine. Not a light could Quasimodo see except from the window of a distant edifice, the vague and gloomy profile of which was distinguishable, rising above the roofs in the direction of the Porte Saint Antoine. There, too, was some one wakeful. While his only eye was thus hovering over that horizon of mist and darkness, the ringer felt within him an inexpressible uneasiness. For several days he had been upon the watch. He had seen constantly wandering around the church men of sinister aspect, who never took their eyes from the young girl's asylum. He feared lest some plot might be hatching against the unfortunate refugee. He fancied that she was an object of popular hatred as well as himself, and that something sinister might probably happen soon. Thus he remained on his tower, on the lookout, 'dreaming in his dream-place,' as Rabelais says, his eye alternately directed on the cell and on Paris, keeping faithful watch like a trusty dog, with a thousand suspicions in his mind.

All at once, while he was reconnoitring the great city with that eye which nature, as if by way of compensation, had made so piercing that it almost supplied the deficiency of other organs in Quasimodo, it struck him that there was something unusual in the appearance of the outline of the quay of the Vielle-Pelleterie, that there was some movement at that point, that the line of the parapet which stood out black against the whiteness of the water was not so straight and tranquil as that of the other quays, but that it undulated before the eye like waves of a river, or the heads of a crowd in motion.

This appeared strange to him. He redoubled his attention. The movement appeared to be towards the city. No light was to be seen. It remained some time on the quay, then flowed off it by degrees, as if whatever was passing along was entering the interior of the island; then it ceased entirely, and the line of the quay became straight and motionless again.

Just as Quasimodo was exhausting himself in conjectures, it seemed to him that the movement was reappearing in the Rue du Parvis, which runs into the city perpendicularly to the front of Notre-Dame. In fact, notwithstanding the great darkness, he could see the head of a column issuing from that street, and in an instant a crowd spreading over the square, of which he could distinguish nothing further than that it was a crowd.

This spectacle was not without its terror. It is probable that that singular procession, which seemed so anxious to conceal itself in profound darkness, observed a silence no less profound. Still some sound must have escaped from it, were it only the tramping of the feet. But even this noise could not reach the deaf watcher; and this great multitude, of which he could see scarcely anything, and of which he could hear nothing, though it was marching and moving so near him, produced on him the effect of an assemblage of dead men, mute, impalpable, lost in vapour. He seemed to see advancing toward him a mist peopled with men, to see shades moving in the shade.

Then his fears returned; the idea of an attempt against the Egyptian presented itself again to his mind. He had a vague feeling that he was about to find himself in a critical situation. In this crisis he held counsel with himself, and his reasoning was more just and prompt than might have been expected from a brain so ill-organized. Should he awaken the Egyptian? assist her to escape? Which way? The streets were beset; behind the church was the river; there was no boat, no egress! There was but one measure to be taken: to meet death on the threshold of Notre-Dame; to resist at least until some assistance came, if any were to come, and not to disturb the sleep of Esmeralda. The unhappy girl would be awakened soon enough to die. This resolution once taken, he proceeded to reconnoitre the *enemy* more calmly.

The crowd seemed to be increasing every moment in the Parvis. He concluded, however, that very little noise was made, since the windows of the streets and the square remained closed. All at once a light flashed up, and in an instant seven or eight lighted torches were waving above the heads, shaking in the darkness their tufts of flame. Quasimodo then saw distinctly surging, in the Parvis, a frightful troop of men and women in rags, armed with scythes, pikes, pruning-hooks, partisans, the thousand points of which all glittered. Here and there black pitchforks formed horns to those hideous visages. He had a confused recollection of that populace, and thought he recognized all the heads which, a few months before, had saluted him Pope of the Fools. A man holding a torch in one hand and a club in the other mounted a stone post and appeared to be haranguing them. At the same time the strange army performed some evolutions, as if taking post around the church. Quasimodo picked up his lantern and descended to the platform between the towers, to obtain a nearer view and to arrange his means of defence.

Clopin Trouillefou, having arrived before the principal door of Notre-Dame, had, in fact, ranged his troops in order of battle. Although he did not anticipate any resistance, yet, like a prudent general, he wished to preserve such a degree of order as would, in case of need, enable him to face a sudden attack of the watch or of the guardsmen. He had accordingly stationed his brigade in such a manner that, seen from on high and at a distance, it might have been taken for the Roman triangle of the battle of Ecnoma, the pig's head of Alexander, or the famous wedge of Gustavus Adolphus. The base of this triangle was formed along the back of the square, so as to bar the entrance to the Rue du Parvis; one of the sides looked toward the Hôtel-Dieu, the other toward the Rue Saint-Pierre-aux-Bœufs. Clopin Trouillefou had placed himself at the point, with the Duke of Egypt, our friend Jehan, and the boldest of the scavengers.

An enterprise such as the Truands were now attempting against Notre-Dame was no uncommon occurrence in the cities of the Middle Ages. What we in our day call police did not then exist. In populous towns, in capitals especially, there was no central power, sole and commanding all the rest. Feudality had constructed those great municipalities after a strange fashion. A city was an assemblage of innumerable seigneuries, which divided it into compartments of all forms and sizes. From thence arose a thousand contradictory establishments of police, or, rather, no police at all. In Paris, for example, independently of the hundred and forty-one lords claiming concive or manorial dues, there were twenty-five claiming administration of justice and quitrent from the Bishop of Paris, who had five hundred streets, to the Prior of Notre-Dame-des-Champs, who had only four. All these feudal justiciaries recognized only nominally the authority of their suzerain, the king. All had right of superintendence of highways. All were their own masters. Louis XI, that indefatigable workman, who had commenced so effectively the demolition of the feudal edifice, carried on by Richelieu and Louis XIV to the advantage of the royalty, and completed by Mirabeau to the advantage of the people – Louis XI had indeed striven to burst this network of seigneuries which covered Paris, by throwing violently athwart it two or three ordinances of general police. Thus, in 1465, the inhabitants were ordered to light candles in their windows at nightfall, and to shut up their dogs, under pain of the halter; in the same year they were ordered to close the streets in the evening with iron chains, and forbidden to carry daggers or other offensive weapons in the streets at night. But in a short time all these attempts at municipal legislation fell into disuse. The townspeople allowed the candles at the windows to be extinguished by the wind, and their dogs to stray; the iron chains were only stretched in time of public disturbance; and the prohibition against carrying daggers brought about no other change than that of the name of the Rue Coupe-gueule into Rue Coupe-gorge [Cut-jaws into Cut-throat?], which, to be sure, was a manifest improvement. The old framework of the feudal jurisdictions remained standing – an immense accumulation of bailiwicks and seigneuries, crossing one another in all directions throughout the city, straitening and entangling each other, interwoven with each other, and projecting one into another – a useless thicket of watches, under-watches, counter-watches, through the midst of which the armed hand of brigandage, rapine and sedition was constantly passing. Hence, in this state of disorder, deeds of violence on the part of the populace directed against a palace, a hôtel, or an ordinary mansion, in the most thickly populated quarters, were not unheard of occurrences. In most cases, the neighbours did not interfere in the affair unless the pillage reached themselves. They stopped their ears against the report of the musketry, closed their shutters, barricaded their doors, and let the struggle exhaust itself with or without the watch; and the next day it was in Paris, 'Last night, Etienne Barbette was broken open;' or, 'The Maréchal de Clermont was seized, etc.' Hence, not only the royal residences – the Louvre, the Palais, the Bastille, the Tournelles – but such as were simply seigneurial, the Petit-Bourbon, the Hôtel-de-Sens, the Hôtel d'Angoulême, etc., had their battlemented walls and their machicolated gates. The churches were protected by their sanctity. Some of them, nevertheless, among which was Notre-Dame, were fortified. The Abbé of Saint-Germain-des-Prés was fortified like a baron, and there was more weight of metal to be found in his house in bombards than in bells. His fortress was still to be seen in 1630. To-day barely the church remains.

To return to Notre-Dame.

When the first arrangements were completed – and we must say, to the honour of Truand discipline, that Clopin's orders were executed in silence and with admirable precision – the worthy leader mounted the parapet of the Parvis, and raised his hoarse and surly voice, his face turned toward Notre-Dame, and brandishing his torch, whose flame, tossed by the wind and veiled at intervals by its own smoke, made the glowing front of the church by turns appear and disappear before the eye:

'Unto thee, Louis de Beaumont, Bishop of Paris, councillor in the court of parliament: thus say I, Clopin Trouillefou, King of Tunis, Grand-Coësre, Prince of Argot, Bishop of the Fools: Our sister, falsely condemned for magic, has taken refuge in thy church. Thou owest to her shelter and safe-guard. But now, the court of parliament is to take her thence, and thou consentest to it; so that tomorrow she would be hanged at the Grève, if God and the Truands were not on hand. Therefore, we are come to thee, bishop. If thy church is sacred, so is our sister; if our sister is not sacred, neither is thy church. Wherefore we summon thee to give up the girl, if thou wilt save thy church; or we will take the girl and plunder the church. Which will be good. In witness whereof, I here plant my banner, and God have thee in his keeping, Bishop of Paris.'

Quasimodo, unfortunately, could not hear these words, which were uttered with a sort of sullen, savage majesty. A Truand presented the standard to Clopin, who gravely planted it between two of the paving-stones. It was a pitchfork, from the prongs of which hung a bleeding quarter of carrion.

This done, the King of Tunis turned about, and cast his eyes over his army, a ferocious multitude whose eyes flashed almost like the pikes. After a moment's pause:

'Forward, my sons!' cried he. 'To your work, locksmiths.'

Thirty stout men, fellows with brawny limbs and the faces of blacksmiths, sprang from the ranks, with hammers, pincers and iron crows on their shoulders. They advanced toward the principal door of the church; ascended the steps; and directly they were to be seen stooping down under the pointed arches of the portal, heaving at the door with pincers and levers. A crowd of Truands followed them, to assist or look on; so that the whole eleven steps were covered with them.

The door, however, stood firm. 'Diable! but she's hard and head-strong,' said one. 'She's old, and her gristles are tough,' said another 'Courage, my friends!' cried Clopin. 'I'll wager my head against a slipper that you'll have burst the door, taken the girl, and undressed the great altar, before there is one beadle awake. Stay! I think the lock is giving way.'

Clopin was interrupted by a frightful noise which at that moment resounded behind him. He turned round; an enormous beam had just fallen from on high, crushing a dozen of the Truands upon the church steps, and rebounding upon the pavement with the sound of a piece of artillery; breaking legs here and there in the crowd of vagabonds who sprang aside with cries of terror. In a twinkling the narrow precincts of the Parvis were cleared. The locksmiths, though protected by the deep arches of the portal, abandoned the door, and Clopin himself fell back to a respectful distance from the church.

'I have escaped fine!' cried Jehan; 'I felt the wind of it, by the head of the bull! but Pierre the Slaughterer is slaughtered!'

It is impossible to describe the astonishment mixed with dread which fell upon the bandits with this beam. They remained for some minutes gazing fixedly upward, in greater consternation at this piece of wood than they would have been at twenty thousand king's archers.

'Satan!' growled the Duke of Egypt, 'but this smells of magic!'

' 'Tis the moon that throws this log at us,' said Andry-le-Rouge.

'Why,' remarked François Chanteprune, 'they say the moon's a friend of the Virgin.'

'A thousand Popes!' exclaimed Clopin, 'you are all imbeciles!' Yet he knew not how to account for the fall of the beam.

All this while nothing was distinguishable upon the grand front of the building, to the top of which the light from the torches did not reach. The ponderous piece of timber lay in the middle of the Parvis; and groans were heard from the miserable wretches who had received its first shock, and been almost cut in two upon the angles of the stone steps.

At last the King of Tunis, his first astonishment over, hit upon an explanation which his comrades thought plausible.

'God's throat!' said he, 'are the canons making a defence? To the sack, then! to the sack!'

'To the sack!' repeated the mob with a furious hurrah. And they made a general discharge of cross-bows and hackbuts against the front of the church.

This report awoke the peaceable inhabitants of the neighbouring houses; several window-shutters were seen to open, and nightcaps and hands holding candles appeared at the casements.

'Fire at the windows!' cried Clopin. The windows were immediately shut again, and the poor citizens, who scarcely had time to cast a bewildered look upon that scene of glare and tumult, went back shaking with fear to their wives, asking themselves whether the witches' Sabbath was now held in the Parvis Notre-Dame or whether there was an assault by the Burgundians, as in the year '64. Then the husbands dreamt of robbery, the wives of violence and all trembled.

'To the sack!' repeated the Argotiers; but they dared not approach. They looked first at the church and then at the marvellous beam. The beam lay perfectly still; the edifice kept its calm and solitary look; but something froze the courage of the Truands

'To your work, locksmiths!' cried Trouillefou. 'Come! force the door!'

Nobody advanced a step.

'Beard and belly! ' said Clopin; 'here are men afraid of a rafter!'

An old lock-picker now addressed him:

'Captain, it is not the rafter that we care about; 'tis the door that's all sewed up with iron bars. The pincers can do nothing with it.'

'What should you have, then, to burst it open with?' asked Clopin.

'Why, we should have a battering ram.'

The King of Tunis ran bravely up to the formidable piece of timber, and set his foot upon it. 'Here's one! ' cried he; 'the canons have sent it to you.' And he made a mock reverence to the cathedral. 'Thank you, canons,' he added.

This bravado had great effect; the spell of the wonderful beam was broken. The Truands recovered courage; and soon the heavy timber, picked up like a feather by two hundred vigorous arms was driven with fury against the great door which had before been attacked. Seen thus, by the sort of half light which the few scattered torches of the Truands cast over the Place, the long beam borne along by that multitude of men rushing on with its extremity pointed against the church, looked like some monstrous animal, with innumerable legs, running, head foremost, to attack a stone giantess.

At the shock given by the beam, the half metal door sounded like an immense drum. It was not burst in, but the whole cathedral shook, and in its deepest recesses could be heard rumblings. At the same moment, a shower of great stones began to fall from the upper part of the façade upon the assailants.

'The devil!' cried Jehan, 'are the towers shaking down their balustrades upon our heads?'

But the impulse was given. The King of Tunis stuck to his text. It was decidedly the bishop making a defence. And so they only battered the door the more furiously, in spite of the stones that were fracturing their skulls right and left.

It must be remarked that these stones all fell one by one; but they followed one another closely. The Argotiers always felt two of them at one and the same time, one against their legs, the other upon their heads. Nearly all of them took effect; and already the dead and wounded were thickly strewn, bleeding and panting under the feet of the assailants, who, now grown furious, filled up instantly and without intermission the places of the disabled. The long beam continued battering the door with periodical strokes, like the clapper of a bell, the stones to shower down, the door to groan.

The reader has undoubtedly not waited till this time to divine that this unexpected resistance which had exasperated the Truands proceeded from Quasimodo.

Accident had unfortunately favoured but too well the brave deaf mute.

When he had descended upon the platform between the towers, his ideas were all in confusion. He ran to and fro along the gallery for some minutes, like one insane, beholding from above the compact mass of the Truands ready to throw themselves against the church, demanding of the devil or of God to save the gypsy. He once thought of mounting the southern steeple, and sounding the tocsin; but before he could have set the bell in motion, before Marie's voice could have uttered a single sound, was there not time for the door of the church to be forced ten times over? It was precisely the time when the lock-pickers were advancing toward it with their tools. What was to be done?

All at once he recollected that some masons had been at work all day, repairing the wall, the timber-work and the roofing of the southern tower. This was a flash of light. The wall was of stone; the roof was of lead; the timber-work of wood. (That prodigious timber-work was so dense that it went by the name of 'the forest.')

Quasimodo ran to this tower. The lower chambers were, in fact, full of materials. There were piles of rough blocks of stone, sheets of lead rolled up, bundles of laths, heavy beams already notched with the saw, heaps of rubbish; in short, an arsenal complete.

Time pressed. The pikes and hammers were at work below. With a strength multiplied tenfold by the sense of danger, he seized one of the beams, the heaviest and longest. He managed to push it through one of the loopholes; then, grasping it again outside the tower, he shoved it over the outer angle of the balustrade surrounding the platform, and launched it into the abyss.

The enormous beam, in this fall of a hundred and sixty feet, grazing the wall, breaking the carvings, turned several times on its centre, like the arm of a windmill, flying off alone through space. At last it reached the ground; the horrible cry arose, and the black beam, as it rebounded from the pavement, was like a serpent making a leap.

Quasimodo saw the Truands scattered by the fall of the beam, like ashes at the breath of a child. He took advantage of their fright, and while they fixed their superstitious gaze upon the immense log fallen from heaven, and while they peppered the stone saints of the portal with a discharge of bolts and bullets, Quasimodo was silently piling up rubbish, rough blocks of stone, and even the masons' bags of tools, on the edge of that balustrade from which the beam had already been hurled.

Thus, as soon as they began to batter the great door, the shower of blocks of stone began to fall, and it seemed to them that the church was demolishing itself over their heads.

Any one who could have seen Quasimodo at that moment would have been frightened. Independently of the missiles which he had piled up on the balustrade, he had collected a heap of stones on the platform itself. As fast as the blocks heaped on the outer edge were exhausted, he had recourse to this latter heap. Then he stooped, rose, stooped and rose again, with incredible agility. He thrust his great gnome's head over the balustrade then there dropped an enormous stone, then another, then another. Now and then he followed some big stone with his eye; and when it did good execution, he ejaculated: 'Hum!'

The beggars, meanwhile, did not lose courage. The massive door which they were so furiously assailing had already trembled more than twenty times beneath the weight of their oaken battering-ram, multiplied by the strength of a hundred men. The panels cracked, the carvings flew in splinters; the hinges, at each shock, leaped from their hooks; the planks were forced out of their places, the wood was falling in dust, ground between the sheathings of iron. Fortunately for Quasimodo, there was more iron than wood.

Nevertheless he felt that the great door was yielding. Although he did not hear it, each stroke of the battering-ram reverberated in the caverns of the church, and within him. From above he beheld the Truands, full of exultation and rage, shaking their fists at the dark front of the edifice; and he coveted, for the gypsy-girl and himself, the wings of the owls that were flocking away affrighted over his head.

His shower of stone blocks was not sufficient to repel the assailants.

At this moment of anguish he noticed a little below the balustrade from which he had been crushing the Argotiers, two long stone gutters which disgorged immediately over the great door. The inner orifice of these gutters was on a level with the platform. An idea struck him. He ran to his bell-ringer's lodge for a fagot; laid over the fagot many bundles of laths and rolls of lead – ammunition of which he had not yet made any use; and having placed this pile in front of the hole of the two gutters, he set fire to it with his lantern.

While he was thus employed, since the stones no longer fell, the Truands ceased to gaze into the air. The brigands, panting like a pack of hounds baying the wild boar in his lair, pressed tumultuously round the great door, all disfigured and shapeless from the blows of the ram, but still erect. They awaited with a thrill of impatience the last grand blow, the blow which was to burst it in. Each was striving to get nearest, in order to be the first, when it should open, to rush into that well-stored cathedral, a vast repository in which had been successively accumulating the riches of three centuries. They reminded one another, with roars of exultation and greedy desire, of the fine silver crosses, the fine brocade copes, the fine silver gilt monuments, of all the magnificence of the choir, the dazzling holiday displays, the Christmas illuminations with torches, the Easter suns, all those splendid solemnities, in which shrines, candlesticks, pyxes, tabernacles, and reliquaries, embossed the altars as it were with a covering of gold and jewels. Assuredly, at that hopeful moment, thieves and pseudo-sufferers, doctors in stealing and vagabonds, were thinking much less of delivering the gypsy-girl than of pillaging Notre-Dame. Nay, we could even believe that, for a goodly number among them, La Esmeralda was only a pretext – if thieves needed a pretext.

All at once, at the moment that they were crowding about the battering-ram for a final effort, each one holding in his breath and stiffening his muscles, so as to give full force to the decisive stroke, a howl more frightful still than that which had burst forth and expired beneath the beam, arose from the midst of them. Those who did not cry out, those who were still alive, looked. Two jets of melted lead were falling from the top of the edifice into the thickest of the rabble. That sea of men had gone down under the boiling metal, which, at the two points where it fell, had made two black and smoking holes in the crowd, like hot water thrown on snow. There were to be seen dying wretches burned half to a cinder, and moaning with agony. Around the two principal jets there were drops of that horrible rain which scattered upon the assailants, and entered their skulls like fiery gimlet points. It was a ponderous fire which riddled the crowd with a thousand hailstones.

The outcry was heart-rending. They fled in disorder, hurling the beam upon the dead bodies – the boldest as well as the most timid – and the Parvis was left empty a second time.

All eyes were raised to the top of the church. They beheld there an extraordinary sight. On the crest of the highest gallery, higher than the central rose window, was a great flame ascending between the two towers, with whirlwinds of sparks; a great flame, irregular and furious, a tongue of which, by the action of the wind, was at times borne into the smoke. Underneath that flame, underneath the trifoliated balustrade showing darkly against its glare, two monster-headed gutters were vomiting incessantly that burning shower, whose silver stream shone out against the darkness of the lower façade. As they approached the earth, these two jets of liquid lead spread out into myriads of drops like water sprinkled from the many holes of a watering-pot. Above the flame the huge towers, two sides of each of which were visible in sharp outline, the one wholly black, the other wholly red, seemed still more vast by all the immensity of shadow which they cast even into the sky. Their innumerable sculptured demons and dragons assumed a formidable aspect. The restless, flickering light from the unaccountable flame, made them seem as if they were moving. There were griffins which seemed to be laughing, gargoyles to be heard yelping; salamanders puffing fire, tarasques sneezing in the smoke.* And among the monsters, thus awakened from their stony slumber by this unearthly flame, by this clamour, there was one who walked about and who was seen from time to time passing across the glowing front of the pile like a bat before a torch.

Assuredly, this strange beacon-light must have awakened the woodcutter far away on the Bicêtre hills, terrified to behold the gigantic shadows of the towers of Notre-Dame quivering over his heaths.

A terrified silence ensued among the Truands; during which nothing was heard but the cries of alarm from the canons, shut up in their cloisters and more uneasy than horses in a burning stable, the furtive

* A fictitious animal solemnly drawn in processions in Tarascon and a few other French towns. – J. C. B.

sound of windows hastily opened, and still more hastily closed, the stir in the interior of the houses and of the Hôtel Dieu, the wind agitating the flame, the last groans of the dying, and the continued crackling of the shower of boiling lead upon the pavement.

Meanwhile the principal Truands had retired beneath the porch of the Logis Gondelaurier, and were holding a council of war. The Duke of Egypt, seated on a stone post, was contemplating with religious awe the phantasmagoric pile blazing two hundred feet aloft in the air. Clopin Trouillefou was gnawing his huge fists with rage.

'Impossible to get in!' muttered he between his teeth.

'An old church enchanted!' growled the old Bohemian, Mathias Hungadi Spicali.

'By the Pope's whiskers!' added a gray-headed scamp of a soldier, who had once been in service, 'here are two church gutters that spit molten lead at you better than the fortifications at Lectoure!'

'Do you see that demon, going back and forth before the fire?' cried the Duke of Egypt.

'Par-Dieu!' said Clopin, ' 'tis the damned ringer – 'tis Quasimodo.'

The Bohemian shook his head. 'I tell you, no; 'tis the spirit Sabnac, the great marquis, the demon of fortifications. He has the form of an armed soldier, with a lion's head. Sometimes he rides a hideous horse. He turns men into stones, and builds towers of them. He commands fifty legions. 'Tis he, indeed. I recognize him. Sometimes he is clad in a fine robe of gold, figured after the Turkish fashion.'

'Where is Bellevigne-de-l'Etoile?' demanded Clopin.

'He is dead,' answered a Truandess.

Andry-le-Rouge laughed idiotically.

'Notre-Dame makes work for the hospital.'

'Is there then no way of forcing this door?' said the King of Tunis, stamping his foot.

The Duke of Egypt pointed sadly to the two streams of boiling lead, which continued to streak the black front of the building like two long phosphoric distaffs.

'Churches have been known to defend themselves so,' observed he with a sigh. 'St. Sophia's, at Constantinople, forty years ago, hurled to the ground, three times in succession, the crescent of Mahound, by shaking her domes, which are her heads. William of Paris, who built this one, was a magician.'

'Must we then slink away pitifully, like so many running foot men?' said Clopin. 'What! leave our sister there, for those hooded wolves to hang to-morrow!'

'And the sacristy – where there are cart-loads of gold!' added a rascal, whose name we regret that we do not know.

'Beard of Mahound!' exclaimed Trouillefou.

'Let us try once more,' rejoined the Truand.

Mathias Hungadi shook his head.

'We shall never get in by the door. We must find the defect in the old elf's armour, a hole, a false postern, some joint or other.'

'Who's for it?' said Clopin. ' I'll go at it again. By-the-by, where's the little student, Jehan, who was so incased in iron?'

'He's dead, no doubt,' answered some one, 'for no one hears him laugh.'

The King of Tunis knit his brows. 'So much the worse!' said he. 'There was a stout heart under that ironmongery. And Maître Pierre Gringoire?'

'Captain Clopin,' said Andry-le-Rouge, 'he slipped away before we had got as far as the Pont-aux-Changeurs.'

Clopin stamped his foot. '*Gueule-Dieu!* 'Tis he who pushed us on hither, and then leaves us here just in the thick of the job. Cowardly chatterer, with a slipper for a helmet!'

'Captain Clopin,' cried Andry-le-Rouge, looking up the Rue de Parvis, 'yonder comes the little student!'

'Praise be to Pluto!' said Clopin. 'But what the devil is he dragging after him?'

It was in fact Jehan, coming as quick as he found practicable under his ponderous knightly accoutrements, with a long ladder, which he was dragging stoutly over the pavement, more breathless than an ant harnessed to a blade of grass twenty times its own length.

'Victory! *Te Deum!*' shouted the student. 'Here's the ladder belonging to the unladers of Saint Landry's wharf.'

Clopin went up to him.

'Child, what are you going to do, *corne-Dieu!* with this ladder?'

'I have it,' replied Jehan, panting. 'I knew where it was. Under the shed of the lieutenant's house. There's a girl there, whom I know, who thinks me a Cupid for beauty. I made use of her to get the ladder, and now I have the ladder, *Pasque-Mahom!* The poor girl came out in her shift to let me in.'

'Yes, yes,' said Clopin; 'but what are you going to do with this ladder?'

Jehan gave him a roguish, knowing look, and snapped his fingers like castanets. At that moment he was sublime. He had upon his head one of those overloaded helmets of the fifteenth century which daunted the enemy by their monstrous-looking peaks. His was jagged with no less than ten beaks of steel, so that Jehan might have disputed the formidable epithet of ten beaks with the Homeric ship of Nestor.

'What am I going to do with it, august King of Tunis?' said he. 'Do you see that row of statues there, that look like blockheads, over the three portals?'

'Yes. Well?'

' 'Tis the gallery of the Kings of France.'

'What is that to me?' said Clopin.

'Wait a bit. At the end of that gallery there's a door that's always on the latch. With this ladder I reach it, and I am in the church.'

'Boy, let me go first.'

'No, comrade; the ladder is mine. Come, you shall be the second.'

'Beelzebub strangle thee!' said surly Clopin. 'I'll be second to no one.'

'Then, Clopin, find a ladder.'

Jehan set off on a run across the Place, dragging his ladder, and shouting: 'Follow me, boys!'

In an instant the ladder was raised and placed against the balustrade of the lower gallery, over one of the side doorways. The crowd of Truands, uttering loud acclamations, pressed to the foot of it for the purpose of ascending. But Jehan maintained his right, and was the first to set foot on the steps of the ladder. The way was somewhat long. The gallery of the Kings of France is, at this day, about sixty feet from the ground; to which elevation was, at that period, added the height of the eleven steps of entrance. Jehan mounted slowly, much encumbered with his heavy armour, with one hand upon the ladder and the other grasping his cross-bow. When he reached the middle of the ladder he cast a melancholy glance upon the poor dead Truands strewn upon the steps of the grand portal. 'Alas!' said he, 'here is a heap of dead worthy of the fifth book of the Iliad!' Then he continued his ascent. The Truands followed him. There was one upon each step of the ladder. To see that line of cuirassed backs thus rise, undulating, in the darkness one might have imagined it a serpent with steely scales, rearing itself up to assail the church. Jehan formed the head, and whistled shrilly; this completed the illusion.

The student at length reached the parapet of the gallery, and sprang lightly over it, amid the applause of the whole Truandry. Thus master of the citadel, he uttered a joyful shout, but stopped short, suddenly petrified. He had just discovered, concealed behind one of the royal statues, Quasimodo, his eye glittering in the shadow.

Before another of the besiegers had time to gain foothold on the gallery, the formidable hunch-back sprang to the head of the ladder, seized, without saying a word, the ends of the two uprights with his powerful hands; heaved them away from the edge of the balustrade; balanced for a moment, amid cries of anguish, the long bending ladder, crowded with Truands from top to bottom; then suddenly, with superhuman strength, he threw back that clustering mass of men into the square. For a moment or two the most resolute trembled. The ladder thus hurled backward, with all that living burden, remained perpendicular for an instant; then it wavered; then, suddenly describing a frightful arc of eighty feet radius, it came down upon the pavement, with its load of brigands, more swiftly than a drawbridge when its chains give way. There arose one vast imprecation; then all was still, and a few mutilated creatures were seen crawling from under the heap of dead.

A mingled murmur of pain and resentment among the besiegers succeeded their first shouts of triumph. Quasimodo, unmoved, his elbows resting upon the balustrade, was quietly looking on, with the mien of some old long-haired king looking out at his window

Jehan Frollo, on the other hand, was in a critical situation. He found himself in the gallery with the redoubtable ringer – alone, separated from his companions by eighty feet of perpendicular wall. While Quasimodo was dealing with the ladder, the student had run to the postern, which he expected to find on the latch. Not so. The ringer, upon entering the gallery, had fastened it behind him. Jehan had then hidden himself behind one of the stone kings, not daring to draw breath, but fixing upon the monstrous hunch-back a look of wild apprehension, like the man who, making love to the wife of a menagerie-keeper, and going one evening to meet her by appointment, scaled the wrong wall, and suddenly found himself tête-a-tête with a white bear.

For the first few moments the hunch-back took no notice of him but at length he turned his head and started, for the scholar had just caught his eye.

Jehan prepared for a rude encounter, but his deaf antagonist remained motionless; he had only turned toward the scholar, at whom he continued looking.

'Ho, ho!' said Jehan, 'why dost thou look at me with that one melancholy eye of thine?'

And so saying, the young rogue was stealthily adjusting his cross-bow.

'Quasimodo,' he cried, 'I'm going to change thy surname. They shall call thee the blind.'

The arrow parted and whistled through the air, burying its point into the left arm of the hunch-back. This no more disturbed Quasimodo than a scratch would have done his stone neighbour King Pharamond. He laid his hand to the dart, drew it out of his arm, and quietly broke it over his big knee. Then he dropped, rather than threw, the two pieces on the ground. But he did not give Jehan time to discharge a second shaft. The arrow broken, Quasimodo, breathing heavily, bounded like a grasshopper upon the scholar, whose armour was flattened against the wall by the shock.

Then, through that atmosphere in which wavered the light of torches, was dimly seen a terrible sight.

Quasimodo had grasped in his left hand both the arms of Jehan, who made no struggle, so completely did he give himself up for lost. With his right hand the hunch-back took off, one after another, with ominous deliberation, the several pieces of his armour – the sword, the daggers, the helmet, the breastplate, the arm-pieces – as if it had been a monkey peeling a walnut. Quasimodo dropped at his feet, piece after piece, the scholar's iron shell.

When the scholar had found himself disarmed and undressed, feeble and naked, in those terrible hands, he did not offer to speak to his deaf enemy; but he fell to laughing audaciously in his face, and singing, with the careless assurance of a boy of sixteen, a popular air of the time:

> *'She is clad in bright array*
> *The city of Cambray;*
> *Marafin plundered her one day . . . '*

He did not finish. Quasimodo was seen standing upon the parapet of the gallery, holding the scholar by the feet with one hand only, and swinging him round like a sling over the abyss. Then a noise was heard like a box made of bone dashing against a wall; and something was seen falling, which stopped a third part of the way down, being arrested in its descent by one of the architectural projections. It was a dead body which hung there, bent double, the loins broken, and the skull empty.

A cry of horror arose from the Truands.

'Vengeance!' cried Clopin. 'Sack!' answered the multitude. 'Assault! assault!'

Then there was a prodigious howling, mixed with all languages, all dialects and all tones of voice. The poor student's death inspired the crowd with a frantic ardour. They were seized with shame and resentment at having been so long kept in check, before a church, by a hunch-back. Their rage found them ladders, multiplied their torches, and in a few minutes Quasimodo, in confusion and despair, saw a frightful swarm ascending from all sides to the assault of Notre-Dame. Those who had not ladders had knotted ropes; and those who had not ropes climbed up by means of the projections of the sculpture. They clung to one another's rags. No means of resisting this rising tide of frightful visages. Fury seemed to writhe in those ferocious countenances; their dirty foreheads streamed with perspiration; their eyes flashed; all these varieties of grimace and ugliness beset Quasimodo. It seemed as if some other church had sent her gorgons, her dogs, her mediæval creatures, her demons, all her most fantastic carvings, to assail Notre-Dame. It was a coat of living monsters covering the stone monsters of the façade.

Meanwhile, a thousand torches had kindled in the square. This scene of disorder, buried until then in thick obscurity, was wrapped in a sudden blaze of light. The Parvis shone resplendent, and cast a radiance on the sky, while the beacon that had been lighted on the high platform of the church still burned and illumined the city far around. The vast outline of the two towers, projected afar upon the roofs of Paris, cast amid that light a deep shadow. The whole town seemed to be roused. Distant tocsins were mournfully sounding; the Truands were howling, panting, swearing, climbing; and Quasimodo, powerless against so many enemies, trembling for the gypsy, watched those furious faces approach nearer and nearer to his gallery, and implored a miracle from heaven, as he wrung his arms in despair.

V

The Retreat in which Monsieur Louis of France says his Prayers

THE READER HAS probably not forgotten that Quasimodo, a moment before he perceived the nocturnal band of the Truands in motion, while looking over Paris from the height of his belfry, saw but one remaining light, twinkling at a window in the topmost story of a lofty and gloomy building close by the Porte Saint Antoine. That building was the Bastille, and that twinkling light was the candle of Louis XI.

Louis XI had, in fact, been two days in Paris. He was to set out again the next day but one for his citadel of Montilz-les-Tours. His visits to his good city of Paris were rare and short, as he did not there feel himself surrounded by a sufficient number of trap-doors, gibbets and Scottish archers.

He had come that day to sleep at the Bastille. His great chamber at the Louvre, five toises * square, with its huge chimney-piece loaded with twelve great beasts and thirteen great prophets, and his grand bed, eleven feet by twelve, were little to his taste. He felt himself lost amidst all those grandeurs. This burgher king preferred the Bastille with a chamber and a bed of humbler dimensions. Besides, the Bastille was stronger than the Louvre.

This little chamber which the king reserved for himself in that famous state prison was also tolerably spacious, occupying the topmost floor of a turret in the keep. This retreat was circular in shape, carpeted with mats of shining straw; ceiled with wooden beams decorated with raised fleurs-de-lys of gilt metal, with coloured spaces between them; wainscoted with rich carvings interspersed with rosettes of white metal, and painted of a fine light green made of orpiment and fine indigo.

---

* An ancient long measure in France, containing six feet and nearly five inches English measure. – J. C. B.

There was but one window, a long pointed casement, latticed with iron bars and brass wire, still further darkened with fine glass painted with the arms of the king and queen, each pane of which had cost two-and-twenty sols.

There was but one entrance, a modern door with an overhanging arch, covered inside with a piece of tapestry, and outside with one of those porches of Irish wood, frail structures of curious cabinet-work, which were still to be seen abounding in old French mansions a hundred and fifty years ago. 'Although they disfigure and encumber the places,' says Sauval in despair, 'yet our old gentlemen will not get rid of them, but keep them in spite of everybody.'

In this chamber was to be seen none of the furniture of ordinary apartments; neither benches, nor trestles, nor forms, nor common box stools, nor fine stools supported by pillars and counter pillars, at four sols a-piece. There was only one folding arm-chair, very magnificent; the wood was painted with roses on a red ground, the seat was of scarlet Spanish leather, garnished with long silken fringe and studded with abundance of gold-headed nails. This solitary chair testified that one person only was entitled to be seated in that apartment. By the chair, and near the window, there was a table, the cover of which was figured with birds. On this table stood an ink-horn, spotted with ink, some scrolls of parchment, some pens and a large goblet of chased silver. A little further on were a brazier, and, for the purpose of prayer, a praying-stool of crimson velvet embossed with studs of gold. Finally, at the extreme end, a simple bed of yellow and pink damask, with neither tinsel nor lace, having only an ordinary fringe. This bed, famous for having borne the sleep or the sleeplessness of Louis XI, was still to be seen two hundred years ago, at the house of a councillor of state, where it was seen by the aged Madame Pilou, celebrated in the great romance of 'Cyrus' under the name *Arricidie* and of *La Morale Vivante*.

Such was the chamber which was called 'the retreat where Louis of France says his prayers.'

At the moment when we have introduced the reader, this retreat was very dark. The curfew had sounded an hour before; night was come, and there was but one flickering wax candle set on the table to light five persons variously grouped in the chamber.

The first upon whom the light fell was a seigneur splendidly attired in a doublet and hose of scarlet striped with silver, and a loose coat with half sleeves of cloth of gold with black figures. This splendid costume, as the light played upon it, glittered flamingly at every fold. The man who wore it had upon his breast his arms embroidered in brilliant colours – a chevron accompanied by a deer passant. The escutcheon was flanked on the right by an olive branch, on the left by a stag's horn. This man wore in his girdle a rich dagger, whose hilt, of silver gilt, was chased in the form of a helmet, and surrounded by a count's coronet. He had a forbidding air, a haughty mien and a head held high. At the first glance one read arrogance in his face; at the second craftiness.

He was standing bareheaded, a long written scroll in his hand, behind the arm-chair, in which was seated, his body ungracefully doubled up, his knees thrown one across the other, and his elbow resting on the table, a person in shabby habiliments. Imagine, in fact, on the rich seat of Cordova leather, a pair of crooked joints, a pair of lean thighs poorly clad in knitted black worsted, a body enveloped in a cloak of fustian with fur trimming, of which more leather than hair was visible, and, to crown all, an old greasy hat of the meanest cloth, bordered with a circular string of small leaden figures. This, together with a dirty skull-cap, which allowed scarcely a hair to straggle from beneath it, was all that could be seen of the sitting personage. He held his head so bent upon his breast that nothing could be seen of his face thus thrown into shadow, excepting the tip of his nose, on which a ray of light fell and which was evidently long. The thinness of his wrinkled hand showed it to be an old man. It was Louis XI.

At some distance behind them were conversing in low tones two men habited after the Flemish fashion, who were not so completely lost in the darkness but that any one who had attended the performance of Gringoire's mystery could recognize in them two of the principal Flemish envoys, Guillaume Rym, the sagacious pensionary of Ghent, and Jacques Coppenole, the popular hosier. It will be recollected that these two men were concerned in the secret politics of Louis XI.

And quite behind all the rest, near the door, in the dark, there stood motionless as a statue, a stout, brawny, thick-set man, in military accoutrements, with an emblazoned surcoat, whose square face, with prominent eyes, slit with an immense mouth, his ears concealed each under a great mat of hair, and with scarcely any forehead, partook at once of the dog and the tiger.

All were uncovered except the king.

The nobleman standing near the king was reading over to him a sort of long memorial, to which his majesty seemed to listen attentively. The two Flemings were whispering.

'By the rood!' muttered Coppenole, 'I am tired of standing. Is there never a chair here?'

Rym answered by a negative gesture, accompanied by a discreet smile.

'By the mass!' resumed Coppenole, quite wretched at being obliged thus to lower his voice, 'I feel a mighty itching to sit myself down on the floor, with my legs across, hosier-like, as I do in my own shop.'

'Beware of doing so, Maître Jacques!'

'Hey-day! Maître Guillaume – must one only remain here on one's feet?'

'Or on his knees,' said Rym.

At that moment the king's voice was raised. They were silent.

'Fifty sols for the gowns of our valets, and twelve pounds for the cloaks of the clerks of our crown! That's it! Pour out gold by the ton! Are you mad, Olivier?'

So saying the old man raised his head. The golden shells of the collar of Saint Michel could be seen to glitter about his neck. The candle shone full upon his gaunt and morose profile. He snatched the paper from the other's hands.

'You are ruining us,' cried he, casting his hollow eyes over the scroll. 'What is all this? What need have we of so prodigious a household? Two chaplains at the rate of ten pounds a month each, and a chapel clerk at a hundred sols! A valet-de-chambre at ninety pounds a year! Four head cooks at six score pounds a year each! A spit-cook, an herb-cook, a sauce-cook, a butler, an armoury-keeper, two sumpter-men, at ten pounds a month each! Two turnspits at eight pounds! A groom and his two helpers at four-and-twenty pounds a month! A porter, pastry-cook, a baker, two carters, each sixty pounds a year! And the farrier six score pounds! And the master of our exchequer chamber twelve hundred pounds! And the comptroller five hundred! And how do I know what else! 'Tis monstrous! The wages of our domestics are laying France under pillage! All the treasure in the Louvre will melt away in such a blaze of expense! We shall have to sell our plate! And next year, if God and Our Lady' (here he raised his hat from his head) 'grant us life, we shall drink our potions from a pewter pot!'

So saying, he cast his eye upon the silver goblet that was glittering on the table. He coughed, and continued:

'Maître Olivier! princes who reign over great estates, as kings and emperors, should not let sumptuousness be engendered in their households, for 'tis a fire that will spread from thence into their provinces. Therefore, Maître Olivier, consider this said once for all. Our expenditure increases every year. The thing displeases us. Why? Pasque-Dieu! until the year '79, it never exceeded thirty-six thousand pounds; in '80, it rose to forty-three thousand six hundred and nineteen pounds; I have the figures in my head. In '81, it came to sixty-six thousand six hundred and eighty; and this year, by the faith of my body, it will reach eighty thousand pounds! Doubled in four years! Monstrous!'

He paused, breathless, then resumed vehemently:

'I behold around me only people who fatten upon my leanness. You suck crowns from me at every pore!'

All kept silence. It was one of those fits of passion which must have its run. He continued:

''Tis like that Latin memorial from the gentlemen of France, requesting that we re-establish what they call the great offices of the crown. Charges, indeed! charges that crush! Ha! messieurs, you tell us that we are no king to reign *dapifero nullo, buticulario nullo*. (With no steward, no butter.) We will let you see, Pasque-Dieu! whether we are not a king.'

Here he smiled in the consciousness of his power; his ill-humour was allayed by it, and he turned to the Flemings:

'Look you, Compère Guillaume, the grand baker, the grand butler, the grand chamberlain, the grand seneschal, are not worth the meanest valet. Bear this in mind, Compère Coppenole; they are of no service whatever. Standing thus useless around the king they put me in mind of the four evangelists that surround the face of the big clock of the Palace, and that Philippe Brille has just been renovating. They are gilt, but they do not mark the hour, and the hands can get on without them.'

He remained thoughtful for a moment, and then added, shaking his aged head:

'Ho, ho! by Our Lady, but I am not Philippe Brille, and I will not regild the great vassals. Proceed, Olivier.'

The person whom he designated by this name again took the scroll in his hands, and began again reading aloud:

'To Adam Tenon, keeper of the seals of the provostry of Paris, for the silver, workmanship and engraving of the said seals, which have been made new, because the former ones, by reason of their being old and worn out, could no longer be used, twelve pounds parisis.

'To Guillaume, his brother, the sum of four pounds four sols parisis, for his trouble and cost in having fed and nourished the pigeons in the two pigeon-houses at the Hôtel des Tournelles, during the months of January, February and March of this year, for the which he has furnished seven sextiers of barley.

'To a gray friar, for confessing a criminal, four sols parisis.'

The king listened in silence. From time to time he coughed; then lifted the goblet to his lips, and swallowed a draught, making a wry face.

'In this year have been made,' continued the reader, 'by judicial order, and to sound of trumpet, through the squares of Paris, fifty six proclamations. Account to be paid.

'For search made in divers places, in Paris and elsewhere, after treasure said to have been concealed in the said places, but nothing has been found, forty-five pounds parisis – '

'Burying a crown to dig up a sou!' said the king.

'For setting in the Hôtel des Tournelles six panes of white glass, at the place where the iron cage is, thirteen sols. For making and delivering, by the king's command, on the day of the musters, four escutcheons, bearing the arms of our said lord, and wreathed all round with chaplets of roses, six pounds. For two new sleeves to the king's old doublet, twenty sols. For a box of grease to grease the king's boots, fifteen deniers. A new sty for keeping the king's black swine, thirty pounds parisis. Divers partitions, planks and trap-doors, for the safe keeping of the lions at the Hôtel Saint Pol, twenty-two pounds.'

'Costly beasts, those!' said Louis XI. 'But no matter; 'tis a seemly piece of royal magnificence. There's a great red lion that I love for his pretty ways. Have you seen him, Maître Guillaume? Princes must have those wondrous animals. For dogs we kings should have lions, and for cats, tigers. What is great befits a crown. In the time of the pagans of Jupiter, when the people offered up at the churches a hundred oxen and a hundred sheep, the emperors gave a hundred lions and a hundred eagles. That was very wild and very fine. The kings of France have always had those roarings about their throne. Nevertheless, this justice must be done me that I spend less money in that way than my predecessors, and that I have a more moderate stock of lions, bears, elephants and leopards. Go on, Maître Olivier. We had a mind to say thus much to our Flemish friends.'

Guillaume Rym made a low bow, while Coppenole, with his gruff countenance, looked much like one of the bears of whom his majesty spoke. The king did not observe it; he had just then put the goblet to his lips, and was spitting out what remained in his mouth of the unsavoury beverage, saying, 'Foh! the nauseous herb tea!' He who read continued:

'For the food of a rogue and vagabond, locked up for these six months in the lodge of the slaughter-house till it is settled what to do with him, six pounds four sols.'

'What's that?' interrupted the king. 'Feeding what ought to be hanged? Pasque-Dieu! I'll not give a single sol toward such feeding. Olivier, arrange that matter with Monsieur d'Estouteville and this very night you'll make preparations for uniting this gentleman in holy matrimony to a gallows. – Go on.'

Olivier made a mark with his thumb-nail at the rogue and vagabond article, and went on:

'To Henriet Cousin, executioner-in-chief at the justice of Paris, the sum of sixty sols parisis, to him adjudged by monseigneur the provost of Paris, for having bought, by order of the said lord the provost, a large broad-bladed sword, to be used in executing and beheading persons judicially condemned for their delinquencies and had it furnished with a scabbard and all other appurtenances as also for repairing and putting in order the old sword which had been splintered and jagged by executing justice upon Messire Louis of Luxemburg, as will more fully appear – '

Here the king interrupted him. 'Enough,' said he; 'I allow the sum with great good will. Those are expenses which I do not begrudge. I have never regretted that money. Proceed.'

'For having made over a great cage – '

'Ha!' said the king, grasping the arms of his chair with both hands, 'I knew well I came hither to this Bastille for some purpose. Stop, Maître Olivier, I will see that cage myself. You shall read me the cost while I examine it. Messieurs the Flemings, you must come and see that; 'tis curious.'

He then rose, leaned on the arm of his interlocutor, made a sign to the sort of mute who stood before the door to precede, to the two Flemings to follow, and left the chamber.

The royal train was recruited at the door by men-at-arms ponderous with steel, and slender pages bearing torches. It proceeded for some time through the interior of the gloomy donjon, intersected by staircases and corridors even in the very thickness of the walls. The captain of the Bastille went first, and directed the opening of the wickets before the bent and aged king, who coughed as he walked.

At each wicket all heads were obliged to stoop, except that of the old man bent with age.

'Hum!' said he, between his gums, for he had no teeth left. 'We are already quite prepared for the door of the sepulchre. A low door needs a bent passer.'

At length, after making their way through the last door of all so loaded with locks that a quarter of an hour was required to open it, they entered a vast and lofty chamber, of Gothic vaulting, in the centre of which was discernible, by the light of the torches, a huge cubic mass of masonry, iron and wood-work. The interior was hollow. It was one of those famous cages for state prisoners which were called familiarly *les fillettes du roi*. (Little daughters of the king.) In its walls there were two or three small windows, so closely trellised with massive iron bars as to leave no glass visible. The door consisted of a large flat stone slab like those on tombs – one of those doors that serve for entrance only. Only here the occupant was alive.

The king began to walk slowly round the small edifice, examining it carefully, while Maître Olivier, following him, read aloud the memoranda:

'For making anew a great cage of wood of heavy beams, joists and rafters, measuring inside nine feet long by eight feet broad, and seven feet high between the planks; mortised and bolted with great iron bolts, which has been fixed in a certain chamber of one of the towers of the Bastille of Saint Antoine; in which said cage is placed and detained, by command of our lord the king, a prisoner, who formerly inhabited an old, decayed and worn-out cage. Used, in making the said new cage, ninety-six horizontal beams and fifty-two perpendicular; ten joists, each three toises long. Employed, in squaring, planing and fitting all the said wood-work, in the yard of the Bastille, nineteen carpenters for twenty days – '

'Very fine heart of oak,' said the king, striking the wood-work with his fist.

'There were used for this cage,' continued the other, 'two hundred and twenty great iron bolts, nine feet and a half long, the rest of a medium length, together with the plates and nuts for fastening the said bolts, the said irons weighing altogether three thousand seven hundred and thirty-five pounds; besides eight heavy squares of iron, serving to attach the said cage in its place, with clamps and nails, weighing altogether two hundred and eighteen pounds; without reckoning the iron for the trellis-work of the windows of the chamber in which the said cage has been placed, the iron bar of the door of the chamber, and other articles – '

'A great deal of iron,' observed the king, 'to restrain levity of spirit.'

'The whole amounts to three hundred and seventeen pounds, five sols, seven farthings.'

'Pasque-Dieu!' cried the king.

At this oath, which was the favourite one of Louis XI, some one appeared to rouse up in the interior of the cage. The sound of chains was heard grating on the floor, and a feeble voice was heard, which seemed to issue from the tomb, exclaiming: 'Sire, sire! mercy, mercy!' The one who spoke thus could not be seen.

'Three hundred and seventeen pounds, five sols, seven farthings!' repeated Louis XI.

The voice of lamentation which had issued from the cage chilled the blood of all present, even that of Maître Olivier. The king alone looked as if he had not heard it. At his command Maître Olivier resumed his reading, and his majesty coolly continued his inspection of the cage.

'Besides the above, there has been paid to a mason for making the holes to fix the window-grates and the floor of the chamber containing the cage, because the other floor would not have been strong enough to support such cage by reason of its weight, twenty-seven pounds fourteen Paris pence – '

The voice began to moan again:

'Mercy, sire! I swear to you that it was Monsieur the Cardinal of Angers who committed the treason, and not I!'

'The mason is high,' said the king. 'Proceed, Olivier.' Olivier continued:

'To a joiner for window-frames, bedstead, close-stool and other matters, twenty pounds two Paris pence – '

The voice also continued:

'Alas, sire! will you not listen to me? I protest it was not I who wrote that matter to Monseigneur of Guyenne; it was monsieur the

Cardinal Balue.'

'The joiner is dear,' quoth the king. 'Is that all?'

'No, sire. To a glazier for the window-glass of the said chamber, forty-six pence eight Paris farthings.'

'Have mercy, sire! Is it not enough that all my property has been given to my judges, my plate to Monsieur de Torcy, my library to Maître Pierre Doriolle, and my tapestry to the Governor of Roussillon? I am innocent. For fourteen years I have shivered in an iron cage! Have mercy, sire! and you will find it in heaven!'

'Maître Olivier,' said the king, 'what is the sum total?'

'Three hundred and sixty-seven pounds, eight pence, three Paris farthings.'

'Our Lady!' exclaimed the king. 'Here's a cage out of all reason.'

He snatched the account from the hands of Maître Olivier, and began to reckon it up himself upon his fingers, examining, by turns, the paper and the cage. But the prisoner could be heard sobbing. It was lugubrious in the darkness. The faces of the bystanders turned pale as they looked at one another.

'Fourteen years, sire! Fourteen years now! since the month of April, 1469. In the name of the Holy Mother of God, sire, hearken to me. During all this time you have enjoyed the warmth of the sun; shall I, poor wretch, never again see the light? Mercy, sire! be merciful! Clemency is a noble virtue in a king, that turns aside the stream of wrath. Does your majesty believe that at the hour of death it will be a great satisfaction to a king to have left no offence unpunished? Besides, sire, it was not I that betrayed your majesty; it was Monsieur of Angers. And I have a very heavy chain to my foot, and a great ball of iron at the end of it, much heavier than is needful. Eh, sire, have pity on me!'

'Olivier,' said the king, shaking his head, 'I perceive that they put me down the bushel of plaster at twenty sols, though it's only worth twelve. You will make out this account afresh.'

He turned his back on the cage, and began to move toward the door of the chamber. The wretched prisoner judged from the receding torches and noise that the king was taking his departure.

'Sire! sire!' cried he in despair. The door closed. He no longer saw anything, and heard only the hoarse voice of the turnkey singing in his ears a popular song of the day:

> *Maître Jehan Balue*
> *Has lost out of view*
> *His good bishoprics all:*
> *Monsieur de Verdun*
> *Cannot now boast of one;*
> *They are gone, one and all.*

The king reascended in silence to his retreat, and his suit followed him, terrified by the last groans of the condemned man. All at once his majesty turned to the Governor of the Bastille.

'By-the-way,' said he, 'was there not some one in that cage?'

'Par-Dieu, yes, sire!' answered the governor, astounded at the question.

'And who, pray?'

'Monsieur the Bishop of Verdun.'

The king knew this better than any one else. But it was a mania of his.

'Ah!' said he, with an air of simplicity, as if he thought of it for the first time, 'Guillaume de Harancourt, the friend of Monsieur the Cardinal Balue. A good fellow of a bishop.'

A few moments later, the door of the retreat had opened again, then closed upon the five personages whom the reader found there at the beginning of this chapter, and who resumed their places, their attitudes and their whispered conversations.

During the king's absence, several dispatches had been laid upon the table. He himself broke their seals. Then he began to read them over diligently one after another; motioned to Maître Olivier, who seemed to act as his minister, to take up a pen; and, without communicating to him the contents of the dispatches, he began, in a low voice, to dictate to him the answers, which the latter wrote, in an uncomfortable position, on his knees before the table.

Guillaume Rym was on the watch.

The king spoke so low that the Flemings heard nothing of what he was dictating, except here and there a few isolated and scarcely intelligible fragments, as thus:

'To maintain the fertile places by commerce, the sterile ones by manufactures. To show the English lords our four bombards, the Londres, the Brabant, the Bourg-en-Bresse, the Saint Omer – It is owing to artillery that war is now more judiciously carried on – To our friend Monsieur de Bressuire – Armies cannot be maintained without tribute, etc.'

Once he spoke aloud:

'Pasque-Dieu! Monsieur the King of Sicily seals his letters with yellow wax like a King of France! Perhaps we do wrong to permit him so to do. My fair cousin of Burgundy granted no armorial bearings with field gules. The greatness of a house is secured by maintaining the integrity of its prerogatives. Note this, friend Olivier.'

Another time:

'Oh, oh,' said he, 'the long message! What doth our friend the emperor claim?' Then running his eye over the missive, and breaking his perusal with interjections: 'Certes! Germany is so large and powerful that it's hardly credible! – But we forget not the old proverb:

345

"The finest country is Flanders; the finest duchy, Milan, the finest kingdom, France!" Is it not so, messieurs the Flemings?'

This time Coppenole bowed in company with Guillaume Rym. The hosier's patriotism was tickled.

The last dispatch made Louis XI frown.

'What's this?' he exclaimed. 'Complaints and grievances against our garrisons in Picardy! Olivier, write with all speed to Monsieur the Marshal de Rouault. That discipline is relaxed. That the men-at-arms, the feudal nobles, the free archers, the Swiss, do infinite mischief to the rustics. That the military, not content with what they find in the houses of the farmers, compel them, with heavy blows of cudgel or lash, to go and fetch from the town, wine, fish, spices and other unreasonable articles. That their lord the king knows all this. That we mean to protect our people from annoyance, theft and pillage. That such is our will, by Our Lady! That furthermore, it does not please us that any musician, barber or servant-at-arms should go clad like a prince, in velvet, silk and gold rings. That such vanities are hateful to God! That we, who are a gentleman, content ourselves with a doublet made of cloth at sixteen sols the Paris ell. That messieurs the serving-men of the army may very well come down to that price likewise. Order and command. To our friend, Monsieur de Rouault. Good.'

He dictated this letter aloud, in a firm tone, and in short abrupt sentences. At the moment when he had finished, the door opened, and gave passage to a new personage, who rushed all aghast into the chamber, crying:

'Sire! sire ! there's a sedition of the populace in Paris!'

The grave countenance of Louis XI was contracted, but all visible sign of his emotion passed away like a flash. He contained himself, and said with quiet severity:

'Friend Jacques, you enter very abruptly.'

'Sire, sire, there's a revolt!' repeated Friend Jacques, quite out of breath.

The king, who had risen, seized him roughly by the arm, and said in his ear, so as to be heard by him alone, with an expression of concentrated anger, and a side-long glance at the Flemings:

'Hold thy tongue – or speak low!'

The new-comer comprehended and began in a low tone to give a very terrified narration, to which the king listened calmly, while Guillaume Rym was calling Coppenole's attention to the face and dress of the new arrival – his furred hood (*caputia furrata*) – his short cape (*epitogia curta*) and his black velvet gown, which bespoke a President of the Court of Accompts.

No sooner had this person given the king some explanations, than Louis XI exclaimed with a burst of laughter:

'Nay, in sooth, speak aloud, Gossip Coictier. What occasion have you to whisper so? Our Lady knows we have no secrets with our good Flemish friends.'

'But, sire – '

'Speak up!' said the king.

Gossip Coictier was struck dumb with surprise

So, then,' resumed the king, 'speak out, sir. There is a commotion among the louts in our good city of Paris?'

'Yes, sire.'

'And which is directed, you say, against Monsieur the Bailiff of the Palais de Justice?'

'So it appears,' said the *gossip*, who still stammered, utterly astounded at the sudden and inexplicable change which had taken place in the mind of the king.

Louis XI resumed: 'Where did the watch meet with the rabble?'

'Coming along from the great Truandry toward the Pont-aux-Changeurs, sire. I met it myself as I was coming hither in obedience to your majesty's orders. I heard some of them shouting: "Down with the Bailiff of the Palais! " '

'And what grievances have they against the bailiff?'

'Ah,' said Gossip Jacques, 'that he is their lord.'

'Really?'

'Yes, sire. They are rascals from the Court of Miracles. They have long been complaining of the bailiff, whose vassals they are. They will not acknowledge him either as justiciary or as keeper of the highways.'

'So, so,' said the king, with a smile of satisfaction, which he strove in vain to disguise.

'In all their petitions to the Parliament,' continued Gossip Jacques, 'they pretend that they have only two masters – your majesty and their god, whom I believe to be the devil.'

'Eh! eh!' said the king.

He rubbed his hands, laughed with that internal exultation which makes the countenance beam, and was quite unable to dissemble his joy, though he endeavoured at moments to compose himself. No one understood it in the least, not even Maître Olivier. At length his majesty remained silent for a moment, with a thoughtful but satisfied air.

'Are they in force?' he suddenly inquired.

'Yes, assuredly, sire,' answered Gossip Jacques.

'How many?'

'At least six thousand.'

The king could not help saying, 'Good!' He went on:

'Are they armed?'

'Yes, sire, with scythes, pikes, hackbuts, pickaxes. All sorts of very dangerous weapons.'

The king did not appear in the least disturbed by this list. Gossip Jacques deemed it his duty to add: 'Unless your majesty sends speedy succour to the bailiff, he is lost!'

'We will send,' said the king, with affected seriousness. ' 'Tis well! certainly we will send. Monsieur the bailiff is our friend. Six thousand! They're determined rogues! Their boldness is marvellous, and deeply are we wroth at it. But we have few men about us to-night. It will be time enough to-morrow morning.'

Gossip Jacques exclaimed: 'At once, sire! They'll have time to sack the bailiff's house twenty times over, violate the seigneury, to hang the bailiff. For God's sake, sire, send before to-morrow morning.'

The king looked him full in the face. ' I have told you to-morrow morning.'

It was one of those looks to which there is no reply.

After a pause, Louis XI again raised his voice. 'My Friend Jacques, you should know that. What was . . . ' (he corrected himself). 'What is the bailiff's feudal jurisdiction?'

'Sire, the Bailiff of the Palais has the Rue de la Calandre, as far as the Rue de l'Herberie; the Place St. Michel, and the localities commonly called Les Mureaux, situated near the Church of Notre-Dame-des-Champs' (here the king lifted the brim of his hat), 'which mansions amount to thirteen; also the Court of Miracles, and the lazaretto called the Banlieue, also the entire highway beginning at the lazaretto and ending at the Porte Saint Jacques. Of these divers places he is keeper of the ways – chief mean and inferior justiciary – full and entire lord.'

'So ho!' said the king, scratching his left ear with his right hand, 'that makes a goodly bit of my city! Ah! monsieur the bailiff was king of all that!'

This time he did not correct himself. He continued ruminating and as if talking to himself:

'Very fine, monsieur the bailiff, you had there between your teeth a very pretty slice of our Paris.'

All at once he burst forth: 'Pasque-Dieu! what are all these people that pretend to be highway-keepers, justiciaries, lords and masters along with us, that have their toll-gate at the corner of every field, their gallows and their hangman at every cross-road among our people? so that, as the Greek believed he had as many gods as there were fountains, and the Persian as many as he saw stars, the Frenchman counts as many kings as he sees gibbets. Par-Dieu! this is an evil state of things. I like not the confusion. I should like to be told, now, if it be God's pleasure, that there should be at Paris any other lord than the king – any justiciary but our Parliament – any emperor but ourself in this empire. By the faith of my soul! the day must come when there shall be in France but one king, but one lord, one judge, one headsman, as there is but one God in heaven.'

Here he lifted his cap again, and continued, still ruminating and with the look and accent of a huntsman cheering on his pack: 'Good, my people! bravely done! Down with these false lords! At them! have at them! Pillage, hang, sack them! . . . Ah, you want to be kings, messeigneurs? On, my people, on!'

Here he stopped short, bit his lips as if to catch the thought which had half escaped him, fixed his piercing eye in turn upon each of the five persons around him, and then, suddenly seizing his hat with both hands, and looking steadfastly at it, he said: 'Oh, I would burn thee, if thou didst know what I have in my head!'

Then again casting around him the cautious, uneasy look of a for stealing back to his hole:

'No matter, ' said he, 'we will send succour to monsieur the bailiff. Unfortunately, we have but few troops here at the present moment against such a number of the populace. We must wait till tomorrow. Order then shall be restored in the city; and all who are taken shall be hanged forthwith.'

'Apropos, sire,' said Gossip Coictier, 'I had forgotten this in my first alarm. The watch have seized two stragglers belonging to the band. If it be your majesty's pleasure to see the men, they are here.'

'If it be my pleasure!' exclaimed the king. 'What, Pasque-Dieu! Thou forgettest a thing like that? Run! quick! Olivier, go and fetch them in.'

Maître Olivier left the room, and presently returned with the two prisoners surrounded by archers of the guard. The first of the two had a great, idiotic, drunken and astonished face. He was clothed in tatters, and walked with one knee bent and the foot dragging along. The other had a pallid, smiling countenance, with which the reader is already acquainted.

The king scrutinized them a moment without saying a word; then addressing the first one abruptly:

'What is thy name?'

'Geoffroy Pincebourde.'

'Thy trade?'

'A Truand.'

'What wert thou going to do in this damnable sedition?'

The Truand stared at the king, swinging his arms with a besotted look. His was one of those misshapen heads where intelligence is about as much at its ease as a light beneath an extinguisher.

'I know not,' said he. 'They were going, so I went.'

'Were you not going to outrageously attack and pillage your lord the Bailiff of the Palais?'

'I know they were going to take something at somebody's, that's all.'

A soldier brought to the king a pruning-hook, which had been found upon the Truand.

'Dost thou know this weapon?' asked the king.

'Yes; it is my hook. I'm a vine-dresser.'

'And dost thou know that man for thy comrade?' asked Louis XI, pointing to the other prisoner.

'No, I know him not.'

'Enough,' said the king. And making a sign with his finger to the silent person, who stood motionless beside the door, to whom we have already called the reader's attention: 'Friend Tristan.' said he, 'there's a man for you.'

Tristan l'Hermite bowed. He gave an order in a low voice to a couple of archers, who led away the poor vagabond.

The king, meanwhile, turned to the second prisoner, who was perspiring profusely. 'Thy name?'

'Sire, it is Pierre Gringoire.'

'Thy trade?'

'A philosopher, sire.'

'How durst thou, knave, to go and beset our friend monsieur the Bailiff of the Palais? and what hast thou to say concerning this agitation of the populace?'

'Sire, I was not of it.'

'How now, varlet! hast thou not been apprehended by the watch in this bad company?'

'No, sire, there is a mistake. 'Tis a fatality. I write tragedies, sire. I implore your majesty to hear me. I am a poet. 'Tis the hard lot of men of my profession to roam the streets at night. I was passing that way this evening. 'Twas the merest chance. They apprehended me wrongfully. I am innocent of this commotion. Your majesty saw that the Truand did not recognize me. I entreat your majesty – '

'Hold thy tongue,' said the king, between two draughts of his potion; 'you split our head!'

Tristan l'Hermite stepped forward, and, pointing to Gringoire:

'Sire, may we hang that one, too?' This was the first word he had uttered.

'Bah!' answered the king. carelessly, 'I see no objection.'

'But I see many,' said Gringoire.

At this moment, our philosopher's countenance was more green than an olive. He saw, by the cool and indifferent manner of the king, that he had no resource but in something extremely pathetic; and he threw himself at the feet of Louis XI with a gesture of despair:

'Sire, your majesty will vouchsafe to hear me. Sire, let not your thunder fall upon so poor a thing as I. God's great thunderbolts strike not the lowly plant. Sire, you are an august and most powerful monarch – have pity on a poor honest man, as incapable of fanning the flame of revolt as an icicle of striking a spark. Most gracious sire, mildness is the virtue of a lion and of a king. Alas! severity does but exasperate; the fierce blasts of the north wind make not the traveller lay aside his cloak; but the sun granting its rays little by little, warms him so that at length he strips himself to his shirt. Sire, you are the sun. I protest to you, my sovereign lord and master, that I am not a companion of Truands, thievish and disorderly. Rebellion and pillage go not in the train of Apollo. I am not the man to rush into those clouds which burst in seditious clamour. I am a faithful vassal of your majesty. The same jealousy which the husband has for the honour of his wife, the affection with which the son should requite his father's love, a good vassal should feel for the glory of his king. He should burn with zeal for the upholding of his house and the promoting of his service. Any other passion that should possess him would be madness. Such, sire, are my maxims of state; do not, then, judge me to be seditious and plundering because my garment is out at elbows. If you show me mercy sire, I will wear it out at the knees praying for you morning and night. Alas! I am not exceeding rich, it is true; indeed, I am rather poor; but I am not wicked for all that. It is no fault of mine. Every one knows that great wealth is not to be acquired by literature, and that the most accomplished writers have not always a good fire in winter. The gentlemen of the law take all the wheat and leave but the chaff for the other learned professions. There are forty most excellent proverbs upon the philosopher's threadbare cloak. Oh, sire, clemency is the only light that can illumine the interior of a great soul. Clemency carries the torch before all other virtues. Without her they are but blind, and seek God in the dark. Mercy, which is the same thing as clemency, produces loving subjects, who are the most potent body-guard of the prince. What can it signify to your majesty, by whom all faces are dazzled, that there should be one poor man more upon the earth? a poor, innocent philosopher, feeling his way in the darkness of calamity, with his empty purse lying echoing upon his empty stomach. Besides, sire, I am a man of letters. Great kings add a jewel to their crown by protecting letters. Hercules did not disdain the title of Musagetes. Matthias Corvinus showed favour to Jean de Monroyal, the ornament of mathematics. Now, 'tis an ill way of protecting letters, to hang the lettered. What a stain upon Alexander if he had hanged Aristoteles! The act would not have been a patch upon the face of his reputation to embellish it, but a virulent ulcer to disfigure it. Sire, I wrote a very appropriate epithalamium for Mademoiselle of Flanders and Monseigneur the most august Dauphin. That was not like a firebrand of rebellion. Your majesty sees that I am no dunce, that I have studied excellently and that I have much natural eloquence. Grant me mercy, sire. So doing, you will do an act of gallantry to Our Lady, and I swear to you that I am very much frightened at the idea of being hanged!'

So saying, the desolate Gringoire kissed the king's slippers, while Guillaume Rym whispered to Coppenole: 'He does well to crawl upon the floor, kings are like the Jupiter of Crete – they hear only through their feet.' And quite inattentive to the Cretan Jupiter, the hosier answered, with a heavy smile, his eyes fixed upon Gringoire: 'Ah, 'tis well done! I fancy I heard the Chancellor Hugonet asking me for mercy.'

When Gringoire stopped at length out of breath, he raised his eyes, trembling, toward the king, who was scratching with his fingernail a spot upon his breeches' knee, after which his majesty took another draught from the goblet of ptisan. But he uttered not a syllable, and this silence kept Gringoire in torture. At last the king looked at him. 'Here's a terrible brawler,' said he. Then, turning to Tristan l'Hermite: 'Pshaw! let him go.'

Gringoire fell backward, sitting upon the ground, quite thunder-struck with joy.

'Let him go!' grumbled Tristan. 'Is it not your majesty's pleasure that he should be caged for a little while?'

'Friend,' returned Louis XI, 'dost thou think it is for birds like this that we have cages made at three hundred and sixty-seven pounds, eight pence, three farthings apiece? Let him go directly, the wanton [Louis XI affected this word 'wanton,' *paillard* which together with *Pasque-Dieu* was his favourite jest], and send him forth with a drubbing.'

'Oh,' exclaimed Gringoire, in ecstasy, 'this in indeed a great king.'

Then, for fear of a countermand, he made haste toward the door, which Tristan opened for him with a very ill grace. The soldiers went out with him, driving him before them with sturdy blows of their fists, which Gringoire endured like a true stoic philosopher.

The good humour of the king, since the revolt against the bailiff had been announced to him, manifested itself in everything. This unusual clemency of his was no mean proof of it. Tristan l'Hermite, in his corner, was looking as surly as a mastiff balked of his meal.

Meanwhile the king gaily drummed the Pont-Audemer march with his fingers upon the chair arm. Though a dissembling prince he was much better able to conceal his sorrow than his rejoicing. These external manifestations of joy on the receipt of any good news sometimes carried him to great lengths, as, for instance at the death of Charles the Bold of Burgundy, when he vowed balustrades of silver to Saint Martin of Tours, and on his accession to the throne, to that of forgetting to give orders for his father's obsequies.

'Eh, sire!' suddenly exclaimed Jacques Coictier, 'what is become of the sharp pains for which your majesty summoned me?'

'Oh!' said the king, 'truly, my gossip, I suffer greatly. I have a ringing in my ears, and rakes of fire are harrowing my breast.'

Coictier took the hand of the king and felt his pulse with a learned air.

'Look, Coppenole,' said Rym in a low tone. 'There you have him between Coictier and Tristan. That's his whole court – a physician for himself and a hangman for others.'

While feeling the king's pulse Coictier assumed a look of greater and greater alarm. Louis XI watched him with some anxiety. Coictier grew visibly more gloomy. The king's bad health was the worthy man's only farm. He made the most of it.

'Oh! oh!' muttered he at length, 'this is serious, indeed!'

'Is it not?' said the king, uneasily.

'*Pulsus creber, anhelans, crepitans, irregularis*' (quick, short, rattling, irregular), continued the physician.

'Pasque-Dieu!'

'This might carry a man off in less than three days!'

'Our Lady!' cried the king. 'And the remedy, gossip?'

'I am considering it, sire.'

He made Louis XI put out his tongue; shook his head; made a wry face; and in the midst of this grimacing:

'Par-Dieu, sire,' said he, all on a sudden, 'I must tell you that there is a receivership of episcopal revenues vacant, and that I have a nephew.'

'Thy nephew shall have my receivership, Gossip Jacques,' answered the king; 'but take this fire out of my breast!'

'Since your majesty is so gracious,' resumed the physician, 'you will not refuse to assist me a little in the building of my house in the Rue Saint André-des-Arcs.'

'Heugh!' said the king.

'I am at the end of my finances,' pursued the doctor; 'and it would really be a pity that the house should be left without a roof – not for the sake of the house itself, which is quite plain and homely; but for the sake of the paintings by Jehan Fourbault, that adorn its wainscoting. There is a Diana flying in the air, so excellently done, so tender, so delicate, with action so natural, the head so well coiffed and crowned with a crescent, the flesh so white, that she leads into temptation those who examine her too curiously. There is also a Ceres. She, too, is a very beautiful divinity. She is seated upon corn sheaves, and crowned with a gay wreath of ears of corn intertwined with purple goat's-beard and other flowers. Never were seen more amorous eyes, rounder limbs, a nobler air, or a more gracefully flowing skirt. She is one of the most innocent and most perfect beauties ever produced by the brush.'

'Tormentor!' grumbled Louis XI, 'what art thou driving at?'

'I must have a roof over these paintings, sire; and, although it is but a trifle, I have no more money.'

'What will thy roof cost?'

'Well . . . a roof of copper, embellished and gilt . . . not above two thousand pounds.'

'Ha! the assassin!' cried the king. 'He never draws me a tooth but he makes a diamond of it.'

'Shall I have my roof?' said Coictier.

'Yes, the devil take you! but cure me.'

Jacques Coictier made a low bow, and said

'Sire, it is a repellent that will save you. We will apply to your loins the great defensive, composed of cerate, Armenian bole, white of eggs, oil and vinegar. You will continue your potion, and we will answer for your majesty.'

A lighted candle never attracts one gnat only. Maître Olivier perceiving the king to be in a liberal mood, and deeming the moment propitious, approached in his turn: 'Sire!'

'What next?' said Louis XI.

'Sire, your majesty knows that Maître Simon Radin is dead.'

'Well?'

'He was king's councillor for the jurisdiction of the treasury.'

'Well?'

'Sire, his place is vacant.'

While thus speaking, Maître Olivier's haughty countenance had exchanged the arrogant for the fawning expression. It is the only change which ever takes place in the countenance of a courtier. The king looked him full in the face and said, in a dry tone: 'I understand.'

He resumed:

'Maître Olivier, Marshal de Boucicault used to say, "There's no good gift but from a king; there's no good fishing but in the sea." I see that you are of the marshal's opinion. Now, hear this. We have a good memory. In the year '68, we made you groom of our chamber; in '69 castellan of the bridge of Saint Cloud, with a salary of a hundred pounds tournois – you wanted them parisis. In November, '73, by letters given at Gergeaule, we appointed you keeper of the Bois de Vincennes, in lieu of Gilbert Acle, esquire; in '75, warden of the forest of Rouvray-les-Saint-Cloud, in the place of Jacques Le Maire; in '78, we graciously settled upon you by letters-patent sealed on extra label with green wax, an annuity of ten pounds parisis, to you and your wife, upon the Place-aux-Marchands, situated at the Ecole Saint Germain. In '79, we made you warden of the forest of Senart, in room of that poor Jehan Daiz; then captain of the castle of Loches; then governor of Saint Quentin; then captain of the bridge of Meulan, of which you call yourself count. Out of the fine of five sols paid by every barber that shaves on a holiday, you get three, and we get what you leave. We were pleased to change your name of "Le Mauvais" ("the bad") which was too much like your countenance. In '74, we granted you, to the great displeasure of our nobility, armorial bearings of a thousand colours, which give you a breast like a peacock. Pasque-Dieu! are you not surfeited? Is not the draught of fishes fine and miraculous enough? And are you not afraid lest a single salmon more may sink your boat? Pride will ruin you, my gossip. Pride is ever pressed close by ruin and shame. Consider this and be silent.'

These words, uttered in a tone of severity, caused Maître Olivier's countenance to resume its former insolent expression.

'Good!' muttered he, almost aloud. ' 'Tis plain enough that the king is ill to-day; he giveth all to the leech.'

Louis XI, far from being irritated at this piece of presumption, resumed, with some mildness: 'Stay – I forgot to add that I made you ambassador to Madame Marie at Ghent. Yes, gentlemen,' added the king, turning to the Flemings, 'this one hath been an ambassador. There, my gossip,' continued he, again addressing Maître Olivier, 'let us not fall out, we are old friends. 'Tis now very late. We have finished our labours. Shave me.'

Our readers have doubtless already recognized in Maître Olivier that terrible Figaro, whom Providence, the great dramatist of all, so artfully mixed up in the long and bloody comedy of Louis XI's reign. We shall not here undertake to portray at length that singular character. This royal barber had three names. At court he was called politely Olivier-le-Daim (from the daim, or stag, upon his escutcheon), among the people, Olivier the Devil. His real name was Olivier-le-Mauvais, or the Bad.

Olivier-le-Mauvais then stood motionless, looking sulkily at the king, and askance at Jacques Coictier. 'Yes, yes – the physician!' he said between his teeth.

'Well, yes – the physician!' retorted Louis XI with singular good humour; 'the physician has more credit than thou. 'Tis very simple. He has got our whole body in his hands; and thou dost but hold us by the chin. Come, come, my poor barber, there's nothing amiss. What wouldst thou say, and what would become of thy office, if I were a king like King Chilperic, whose gesture consisted in holding his beard with one hand. Come, my gossip, fulfil thine office, shave me. Go fetch thine implements.'

Olivier, seeing that the king was in a laughing humour, and that there was no means even of provoking him, went out, grumbling, to execute his commands.

The king rose, went to the window, and suddenly opening it in extraordinary agitation:

'Oh, yes!' exclaimed he, clapping his hands; 'there's a glare in the sky over the city. It's the bailiff burning; it cannot be anything else. Ha! my good people, so you help me, then, at last, to pull down the seigneuries!'

Then turning to the Flemings: 'Gentlemen,' said he, 'come and see. Is it not a fire which glows yonder?'

The two men from Ghent came forward to look.

'It is a great fire,' said Guillaume Rym.

'Oh,' added Coppenole, whose eyes suddenly sparkled, 'that reminds me of the burning of the house of the Seigneur d'Hymbercourt. There must be a stout revolt there.'

'You think so, Maître Coppenole?' said the king; and he looked almost as much pleased as the hosier himself. 'Don't you think it will be difficult to resist?' he added.

'By the Holy Rood! sire, it may cost your majesty many a company of good soldiers.'

'Ha! cost me! that's quite another thing,' returned the king. 'If I chose – '

The hosier rejoined boldly: 'If that revolt be what I suppose, you would choose in vain, sire.'

'Friend,' said Louis XI, 'two companies of my ordnance, and the discharge of a serpentine, are quite sufficient to rout a mob of the common people.'

The hosier, in spite of the signs that Guillaume Rym was making to him, seemed determined to hold his own against the king.

'Sire,' said he, 'the Swiss were common people, too. Monsieur the Duke of Burgundy was a great gentleman, and made no account of the rabble. At the battle of Grandson, sire, he called out, "Cannoneers, fire upon those villains!" and he swore by Saint George. But the advoyer, Scharnactal, rushed upon the fine duke with his mace and his people; and at the shock of the peasants, with their bull-hides, the shining Burgundian army was shattered like a pane of glass by a pebble. Many a knight was killed there by those base churls; and Monsieur de Château-Guyon, the greatest lord in Burgundy, was found dead, with his great gray horse hard by in a marshy meadow.'

'Friend,' returned the king, 'you're talking of a battle; but here's only a riot, and I can put an end to it with a frown, when I please.'

The other replied, unconcernedly:

'That may be, sire. In that case the people's hour is not yet come.'

Guillaume Rym thought it time to interfere. 'Maître Coppenole,' said he, 'You are talking to a mighty king.'

'I know it,' answered the hosier, gravely.

'Let him speak, Monsieur Rym, my friend,' said the king; 'I like this plain speaking. My father, Charles VII, used to say that truth was sick! For my part I thought she was dead, and had found no confessor; but Maître Coppenole undeceives me.'

Then laying his hand familiarly upon Coppenole's shoulder: 'You were saying, then, Maître Jacques – '

'I say, sire, that perhaps you are right; that the people's hour is not yet come with you.'

Louis XI looked at him with his penetrating eye: 'And when will that hour come, Maître?'

'You will hear it strike.'

'By what clock, pray?'

Coppenole, with his quiet and homely self-possession, motioned to the king to approach the window.

'Hark you, sire,' said he; 'here there are a donjon, an alarm-bell, cannon, towns-people, soldiers. When the alarm-bell shall sound; when the cannon shall roar; when, with great clamour, the donjon walls shall crumble; when the townspeople and soldiers shall shout and kill each other – then the hour will strike.'

The countenance of Louis XI became gloomy and thoughtful. He remained silent for a moment; then tapping gently with his hand against the massive wall of the donjon, as if patting the haunches of a war-horse: 'Ah, no, no!' said he, 'thou wilt not so easily be shattered, wilt thou, my good Bastille?'

Then, turning with an abrupt gesture to the bold Fleming: 'Have you ever seen a revolt, Maître Jacques?'

'I have made one,' said the hosier.

'And how do you set about it,' said the king, 'to make a revolt?'

'Oh!' answered Coppenole, ' 'tis not very difficult. There are a hundred ways. First of all, there must be discontentment in the town. That is not uncommon. And then, the character of the inhabitants. Those of Ghent are easy to stir into revolt. They always love the son of the prince, the prince, never. Well! one morning, we will suppose, some one enters my shop, and says, Father Coppenole, there is this and that; as that the Lady of Flanders wishes to save her ministers; that the high bailiff is doubling the toll on vegetables, or what not – anything you like. Then I throw by my work, go out into the street, and cry: *To the sack*! There is always some empty cask at hand. I mount it, and say in loud tones the first words that come into my head, what's uppermost in my heart, and when one belongs to the people, sire, one has always something upon one's heart. Then a crowd assembles; they shout, they ring the tocsin; the people get arms by disarming the soldiers; the market people join in, and they fall to. And it will always be thus so long as there are lords in the manors, burghers in the towns and peasants in the country.'

'And against whom do ye thus rebel?' inquired the king. 'Against your bailiffs, against your lords?'

'Sometimes. That's as it may happen. Against the duke, too, sometimes.'

Louis XI returned to his seat, and said, with a smile : 'Ah! here they have as yet only got as far as the bailiffs.'

At that instant Olivier-le-Daim re-entered. He was followed by two pages who bore the king's toilet articles; but what struck Louis XI was that he was also accompanied by the provost of Paris and the knight of the watch, who seemed to be in great consternation.

The rancorous barber also wore an air of consternation; but satisfaction lurked beneath it. It was he who spoke first.

'Sire, I ask your majesty's pardon for the calamitous news I bring.'

The king, turning sharply round, scraped the mat on the floor with the feet of his chair.

'What does this mean?' said he.

'Sire,' returned Olivier-le-Daim, with the malicious air of a man rejoicing that he is about to deal a violent blow, 'it is not against the Bailiff of the Palais that this popular sedition is directed.'

'Against whom, then?'

'Against you, sire.'

The aged king rose, erect and straight, like a young man:

'Explain thyself, Olivier, and look well to thy head, my gossip, for I swear to thee, by the cross of Saint Lô, that if thou liest to us at this hour, the sword that cut the throat of Monsieur of Luxemburg is not so notched but it shall saw thine as well.'

The oath was formidable. Louis XI had never but twice in his life sworn by the cross of Saint Lô.

Olivier opened his mouth to reply. 'Sire – '

'On thy knees!' interrupted the king, violently. 'Tristan, look to this man.'

Olivier knelt, and said composedly: 'Sire, a witch has been condemned to death by your court of parliament. She has taken refuge in Notre-Dame. The people wish to take her thence by main force. Monsieur the provost and monsieur the knight of the watch who are come straight from the spot, are here to contradict me if I speak not the truth. It is Notre-Dame that the people are besieging.'

'Ah, ah,' said the king, in a low tone, pale and trembling with wrath; 'Notre-Dame! They are besieging Our Lady, my good mistress, in her own cathedral! Rise, Olivier. Thou art right; I give thee Simon Radin's office. Thou art right; 'tis I whom they are attacking. The witch is under the safeguard of the church; the church is under my safeguard. And I, who thought it was all about the bailiff! 'Tis against myself!'

Then, invigorated by passion, he began to stride up and down. He laughed no longer; he was terrible; he went to and fro. The fox was changed into a hyena. He seemed to be choking with rage; his lips moved, and his fleshless fists were clenched. All at once he raised his head; his hollow eye seemed full of light, and his voice burst forth like a clarion: 'Upon them, Tristan! Fall upon the knaves! Go, Tristan, my friend! Kill! kill!'

This explosion over, he returned to his seat and said, with cold, concentrated rage:

'Here, Tristan! There are here with us in this Bastille the fifty lances of the Viscount de Gié, making three hundred horse, you'll take them. There is also Monsieur de Chateaupers's company of the archers of our ordonnance; you will take it. You are provost-marshal, and have the men of your provostry, you will take them. At the Hôtel Saint Pol, you will find forty archers of Monsieur the Dauphin's new guard; you will take them. And, with the whole you will make all speed to Notre-Dame. Ha! messieurs the clowns of Paris – so you presume to fly in the face of the crown of France, the sanctity of Our Lady, and the peace of this commonwealth? Exterminate, Tristan! exterminate! and let not one escape except for Montfaucon!'

Tristan bowed. ' 'Tis well, sire.'

He added after a pause: 'And what shall I do with the sorceress?'

This question set the king musing.

'Ah,' said he, 'the sorceress! Monsieur d'Estouteville, what would the people with her?'

'Sire,' replied the provost of Paris, 'I fancy that, since the populace is come to drag her away from her asylum in Notre-Dame, 'tis because her impunity offends them, and they desire to hang her.'

The king appeared to reflect deeply; then, addressing himself to Tristan l'Hermite: 'Well, my gossip, exterminate the people and hang the sorceress.'

'Just so,' whispered Rym to Coppenole. 'Punish the people for wishing, and do what they wish.'

'Enough, sire,' answered Tristan. 'If the witch be still in Notre-Dame, is she to be taken despite the sanctuary?'

'Pasque-Dieu! the sanctuary!' said the king, scratching his ear; 'and yet this woman must be hanged.'

Here, as though seized with a sudden idea, he flung himself on his knees before his chair, took off his hat, placed it on the seat, and devoutly fixing his eyes on one of the leaden amulets with which it was loaded: 'Oh,' said he, with clasped hands, 'Our Lady of Paris, my gracious patroness, pardon me. I will only do it this once. This criminal must be punished. I assure you, O Lady Virgin, my good mistress, that she is a sorceress, unworthy your gentle protection. You know, Lady, that many very pious princes have trespassed upon the privileges of churches, for the glory of God and the necessity of the state. Saint Hugh, Bishop of England, permitted King Edward to hang a magician in his church. My master, Saint Louis of France, transgressed for the like purpose in the church of Monsieur Saint Paul, as did also Monsieur

Alphonse King of Jerusalem, in the church of the Holy Sepulchre itself. Pardon me, then, for this once, Our Lady of Paris. I will never again do so, and I will give you a fine statue of silver like the one which I gave last year to Our Lady of Ecouys. Amen.'

He made the sign of the cross, rose, donned his hat once more, and said to Tristan: 'Make all speed, my gossip. Take Monsieur de Chateaupers with you. Sound the tocsin. Crush the populace. Hang the sorceress. That's settled. You yourself will defray the costs of the execution. Report to me upon it. Come, Olivier, I shall not get to bed this night. Shave me.'

Tristan l'Hermite bowed and departed. Then the king, dismissing Rym and Coppenole with a gesture: 'God keep you, messieurs, my good Flemish friends!' said he. 'Go take a little rest. The night is far spent, and we are nearer to morning than evening.'

Both withdrew, and on reaching their apartments, to which they were conducted by the captain of the Bastille, Coppenole said to Guillaume Rym: 'Humph! I've had enough of this coughing king! I have seen Charles of Burgundy drunk; he was less mischievous than Louis XI ailing.'

'Maître Jacques,' replied Rym, ' 'tis because wine renders kings less cruel than does barley-water.'

VI

The Password

ON QUITTING THE BASTILLE, Gringoire ran down the Rue Saint Antoine with the speed of a runaway horse. When he had reached the Porte Baudoyer, he walked straight to the stone cross which rose in the middle of the open space there, as though he were able to discern in the dark the figure of a man clad and hooded in black, sitting upon the steps of the cross.

'Is it you, master?' said Gringoire.

The black figure started up.

'Death and passion! you make me boil, Gringoire. The man upon the tower of Saint Gervais has just cried half-past one in the morning!'

'Oh,' returned Gringoire, ' 'tis no fault of mine, but of the watch and the king. I have just had a narrow escape. I always just miss being hung. 'Tis my predestination.'

'You miss everything,' said the other. 'But come quickly. Have you the pass-word?'

'Only fancy, master. I have seen the king. I have just come from him. He wears fustian breeches. 'Tis a real adventure.'

'Oh, thou word-spinner! What care I for thy adventure? Hast thou the password of the vagabonds?'

'I have it. Make yourself easy. *Petite flambe en baguenaud.*'

' 'Tis well. Otherwise we should not be able to reach the church. The rabble block up the streets. Fortunately, they seem to have met with resistance. We may, perhaps, still be there in time.'

'Yes, master; but how are we to get into Notre-Dame?'

'I have the key to the towers.'

'And how are we to get out again?'

'There is a small door behind the cloister, which leads to the Terrain, and so to the water-side. I have taken the key to it, and I moored a boat there this morning.'

'I have had a pretty escape from being hung,' repeated Gringoire.

'Eh – quick! come!' said the other.

Both then proceeded at a rapid pace towards the city.

VII

Chateaupers to the Rescue

THE READER WILL, perhaps, recall the critical situation in which we left Quasimodo. The brave deaf man, assailed on all sides, had lost, if not all courage, at least all hope of saving, not himself – he thought not of himself – but the gypsy-girl. He ran distractedly along the gallery. Notre-Dame was on the point of being carried by the Truands. All at once a great galloping of horses filled the neighbouring streets, and, with a long file of torches, and a dense column of horsemen, lances and bridles lowered, these furious sounds came rushing into the Place like a hurricane:

'France! France! Cut down the knaves! Chateaupers to the rescue! Provostry! provostry!'

The Truands in terror faced about.

Quasimodo, who heard nothing, saw the drawn swords, the flambeaux, the spear-heads, all that cavalry, at the head of which he recognized Captain Phœbus; he saw the confusion of the vagabonds, the terror of some of them, the perturbation of the stoutest-hearted among them, and this unexpected succour so much revived his own energies that he hurled back from the church the first assailants, who were already climbing into the gallery.

It was, in fact, the king's troops who had arrived.

The Truands bore themselves bravely. They defended themselves desperately. Attacked in flank from the Rue Saint-Pierre-aux-Bœufs, and in rear from the Rue du Parvis, driven to bay against Notre-Dame, which they still assailed and Quasimodo defended, at once besieging and besieged, they were in the singular situation in which, subsequently, at the famous siege of Turin, in 1640, Count Henri d'Harcourt found himself between Prince Thomas of Savoy, whom he was besieging, and the Marquis of Leganez, who was blockading him – *Taurinum obsessor idem et obsessus* (besieger of Turin and besieged), as his epitaph expresses it.

The conflict was frightful. Wolves' flesh calls for dogs' teeth, as Father Matthieu phrases it. The king's horsemen, amid whom Phœbus de Chateaupers bore himself valiantly, gave no quarter, and they who escaped the thrust of the lance fell by the edge of the sword. The Truands, ill-armed, foamed and bit with rage and despair. Men, women and children threw themselves upon the cruppers and chests of the horses, and clung to them like cats with tooth and nail. Others struck the archers in the face with their torches; others thrust their iron hooks into the necks of the horsemen and dragged them down. They slashed in pieces those who fell.

One of them was seen with a large glittering scythe, with which, for a long time, he mowed the legs of the horses. He was frightful. He was singing a song with a nasal intonation, taking long and sweeping strokes with his scythe. At each stroke he described round him a great circle of severed limbs. He advanced in this manner into the thickest of the cavalry, with the quiet slowness, the regular motion of the head and drawing of the breath of a harvester mowing a field of corn. This was Clopin Trouillefou. He fell by the shot of an arquebus.

Meantime the windows had opened again. The neighbours, hearing the shouts of the king's men, had taken part in the affair, and from every story bullets rained upon the Truands. The Parvis was filled with a thick smoke, which the musketry streaked with fire. Through it could be indistinctly seen the front of Notre-Dame, and the decrepit Hôtel-Dieu, with a few pale-faced invalids looking from the top of its roof, studded with dormer windows.

At length the vagabonds gave way. Exhaustion, want of good weapons, the fright of this surprise, the discharges of musketry from the windows, and the spirited charge of the king's troops all combined to overpower them. They broke through the line of their assailants and fled in all directions, leaving the Parvis strewn with dead.

When Quasimodo, who had not for a moment ceased fighting, beheld this rout, he fell on his knees, and raised his hands to heaven. Then, intoxicated with joy, he ran, and ascended with the swiftness of a bird to that cell, the approaches to which he had so gallantly defended. He had now but one thought – it was to kneel before her whom he had just saved for the second time.

When he entered the cell he found it empty.

BOOK ELEVEN

I

The Little Shoe

AT THE MOMENT when the Truands had attacked the church Esmeralda was asleep.

Soon the ever-increasing uproar around the edifice, and the plaintive bleating of her goat, which awoke before her, roused her from her slumbers. She sat up, listened, and looked about her; then, frightened at the light and the noise, she had hurried from her cell to see what it was. The aspect of the square, the strange vision moving in it, the disorder of that nocturnal assault, that hideous crowd leaping like a cloud of frogs, half seen in the darkness; the croaking of that hoarse multitude, the few red torches dancing to and fro in the obscurity, like those meteors of the night that play over the misty surface of a marsh; all together seemed to her like some mysterious battle commenced between the phantoms of a witches' Sabbath and the stone monsters of the church. Imbued from infancy with the superstitions of the Bohemian tribe, her first thought was that she had surprised in their magic revels the strange creatures peculiar to the night. Then she ran in terror to cower in her cell, and ask of her humble couch some less horrible vision.

By degrees, however, the first vapours of terror gradually dispersed; from the constantly increasing din, and from other signs of reality, she discovered that she was beset, not by spectres, but by human beings. Then her fear, though it did not increase, changed its nature. She had dreamed of the possibility of a popular rising to drag her from her asylum. The idea of once more losing life, hope, Phœbus, who still was ever present to her hopes; her extreme helplessness; all flight cut off, no support; her abandonment, her isolation; these thoughts and a thousand others had overwhelmed her. She had fallen upon her knees, with her head upon her couch, and her hands clasped upon her head, apprehensive and trembling; and gypsy, idolatress and heathen as she was, she began with sobs to implore mercy of the God of the Christians, and to pray to Our Lady her protectress. For, even if one believes in nothing, there are moments in life when one is always of the religion of the temple nearest at hand.

She remained thus prostrate for a very long time, trembling, in truth, more than she prayed, her blood turning cold at the nearer and nearer approach of the breath of that furious multitude, ignorant of the nature of this outburst, of what was being plotted, of what they were doing, of what they wanted, but feeling a presentiment of some dreadful result.

In the midst of this anguish she heard a footstep close to her.

She looked up. Two men, one of whom carried a lantern, had just entered her cell. She uttered a feeble cry.

'Fear nothing,' said a voice which was not unknown to her; ' 'tis I.'

'Who are you?' asked she.

'Pierre Gringoire.'

This name reassured her. She raised her eyes again and saw that it was indeed the poet. But there stood beside him a black figure, veiled from head to foot, the sight of which struck her dumb.

'Ah!' continued Gringoire, in a reproachful tone, 'Djali recognized me before you.'

The little goat, in fact, had not waited for Gringoire to announce himself. No sooner had he entered than it rubbed itself gently against his knees, covering the poet with caresses and white hairs, for it was shedding its coat. Gringoire returned the caresses.

'Who is that with you?' said the Egyptian, in a low tone.

'Do not be disturbed,' answered Gringoire; 'it is a friend of mine.'

Then the philosopher, setting his lantern on the floor, squatted down upon the stones, and exclaimed with enthusiasm, clasping Djali in his arms:

'Oh! the charming creature! more remarkable, no doubt, for neatness than for size; but clever, cunning and lettered as a grammarian! Let us see, my Djali, hast thou forgotten any of thy pretty tricks. How does Maître Jacques Charmolue do – '

The man in black did not let him finish. He came up to Gringoire and pushed him roughly by the shoulder. Gringoire rose.

'True,' said he; 'I forgot that we were in haste. But that is no reason, my master, for using folks so roughly. My dear, sweet child, your life is in danger, and Djali also. They want to hang you again. We are your friends and have come to save you. Follow us.'

'Is it true?' exclaimed she, quite overcome.

'Yes, quite true. Come quickly!'

'I am willing,' faltered she; 'but why does not your friend speak?'

'Ah!' said Gringoire; 'because his father and mother were whimsical people, who made him of a taciturn disposition.'

She was obliged to content herself with this explanation. Gringoire took her by the hand. His companion picked up the lantern and walked on in front. Fear stunned the young girl. She allowed herself to be led away. The goat skipped after them, so delighted to see Gringoire again that it made him stumble every moment by thrusting its horns between his legs.

'Such is life,' said the philosopher, every time that he came near falling; 'it is often our best friends who throw us down.'

They rapidly descended the staircase of the towers, crossed the interior of the church, which was all dark and solitary, but reverberated from the uproar without, thus offering a frightful contrast; and went out by the red door into the court-yard of the cloister. The cloister was deserted, the canons having taken refuge in the bishop's house, there to offer up their prayers in common; the court-yard was empty, only some terrified serving-men were crouching in the darkest corners. They directed their steps towards the small door leading from this court-yard to the Terrain. The man in black opened it with a key which he had about him. Our readers are aware that the Terrain was a tongue of land enclosed by walls on the side next the city, and belonging to the chapter of Notre-Dame, which terminated the island eastward, behind the church. They found this enclosure entirely deserted. Here, too, they found the tumult in the air sensibly diminished. The noise of the assault by the Truands reached their ears more confusedly and less clamorously. The cool breeze which follows the current of the river, stirred the leaves of the only tree planted at the point of the Terrain, with a sound that was now perceptible to them. Nevertheless, they were still very near the danger. The buildings nearest to them were the bishop's palace and the church. There was evidently great confusion within the residence of the bishop. Its shadowy mass was flashing in all directions with lights hurrying from one window to another; as, after burning a piece of paper, there remains a dark edifice of ashes, over which bright sparks run in a thousand fantastic courses. Close by, the huge towers of Notre-Dame, seen thus from behind, with the long nave over which they rise, standing out in black relief from the red glare which filled the Parvis, looked like the gigantic uprights of some Cyclopean fire-grate.

What was visible of Paris seemed wavering on all sides in a sort of shadow mingled with light. Rembrandt has such backgrounds to his pictures.

The man with the lantern walked straight to the point of the Terrain. At the very brink of the water, there stood the worm-eaten remains of a fence of stakes with laths nailed across, upon which a low vine spread out its few meagre branches like the fingers of an open hand. Behind this sort of latticework, in the shadow which it cast, a small boat lay hidden. The man motioned to Gringoire and his companion to get in. The goat followed them. The man himself stepped in last of all. Then he cut the rope pushed off from the shore with a long boat-hook, and laying hold of a pair of oars, seated himself in the bow, and rowed with all his might towards mid-stream. The Seine is very rapid at that point, and he found considerable difficulty in clearing the point of the island.

Gringoire's first care, on entering the boat was to place the goat on his knees. He took his seat in the stern; and the young girl whom the stranger inspired with an indefinable uneasiness, seated herself as closely as possible to the poet. When our philosopher felt the boat in motion, he clapped his hands, and kissed Djali between the horns.

'Oh!' cried he, 'now we are all four saved!'

He added, with the air of a profound thinker: 'We are indebted sometimes to fortune, sometimes to stratagem, for the happy issue of a great undertaking.'

The boat made its way slowly toward the right bank. The young girl watched the unknown with secret terror. He had carefully turned off the light of his dark lantern; he was now faintly seen, in the forepart of the skiff, like a spectre. His hood, still down, formed a sort of mask; and every time that, in rowing, he spread his arms, from which hung wide black sleeves, they looked like a pair of enormous bat's wings. Moreover, he had not yet uttered a word, a syllable. No other sound was heard in the boat but the working of the oars, and the rippling of the water against the side of the skiff.

'Upon my soul!' suddenly exclaimed Gringoire, 'we are as gay and merry as owlets! Mute as Pythagoreans or fish. Pasque-Dieu! my friends, I wish some one would talk to me. The human voice is music to the human ear. That is not a saying of mine, but of Didymus of Alexandria, and a great one it is. Of a certainty Didymus of Alexandria is no mean philosopher. One word, my pretty child, say but a word to me, I entreat. By the way, you used to have a droll, odd little pout; do you still make it? Do you know, sweetheart, that the Parliament has full jurisdiction over all places of sanctuary, and that you were in great peril in that little box of yours at Notre-Dame? Alas! the little bird, trochylus maketh its nest in the jaws of the crocodile. Master, here comes the moon again. 'Tis to be hoped that they will not discover us! We are doing a laudable act in saving mademoiselle. And yet they would hang us up in the king's name if they were to catch us. Alas! every human action has two handles. One man gets praised for what another gets blamed for. He admires Cæsar who blames Catiline. Is it not so, master? What say you to this philosophy? I possess philosophy by instinct, by nature, *ut apes geometriam* (as the bees do geometry). Come! no one answers me. What a plague of a humour ye are both in! I talk to myself. 'Tis what we call, in tragedy, a monologue. Pasque-Dieu! I'd have you to know that I have just seen King Louis XI, and that 'tis from him I have caught this oath. Pasque-Dieu! They are still making a glorious howl in the city. 'Tis an ugly, villainous old king. He is all swathed in furs. He still owes me the money for my epithalamium; and he all but hanged me to-night, which would have been most awkward for me. He is niggardly to men of merit. He should e'en read Salvian of Cologne's four books *adversus Avaritiam* (against avarice). In sooth, 'tis a close-fisted king in his dealings with men of letters, and commits very barbarous cruelties. He is a very sponge in sucking up the money drained from the people. His savings are as the spleen, that grows big upon the pining of the other members. And so the complaints of the hardness of the times turn to murmurs against the prince. Under this mild and pious lord gibbets crack with carcasses, blocks stream with gore, the prisons burst like overfull bellies. This king strips with one hand and hangs with the other. He's grand caterer to Dame Gabelle and Monseigneur Gibet. The great are despoiled of their dignities, and the humble incessantly loaded with fresh burdens. 'Tis an exorbitant prince. I love not this monarch. And you, master?'

The man in black let the loquacious poet run on. He was still struggling against the violent and narrow current that separates the prow of the city from the stern of the Island of Notre-Dame, which we call now-a-days the Island of Saint Louis.

'By-the-by, master,' resumed Gringoire, suddenly, 'just as we reached the Parvis through the raging Truands, did your reverence observe that poor little devil, whose brains your deaf man was dashing out against the balustrade of the gallery of the kings? I am short-sighted, and could not distinguish his features. Who might it be, think you?'

The unknown answered not a word. But he suddenly ceased rowing; his arms dropped as though broken, his head fell upon his breast, and Esmeralda heard him sigh convulsively. She started; she had heard sighs like those before.

The skiff, left to itself, drifted some moments with the stream. But the man in black finally roused himself, seized the oars again, and again set himself to row against the current. He doubled the point of the Island of Notre-Dame, and made for the landing place of the Hay-wharf.

'Ah!' said Gringoire, 'yonder is the Barbeau mansion. There, master, look, that group of black roofs, that make such odd angles, there, below that mass of low, streaky, ragged-looking clouds, in which the moon appears smashed and spread about like the yolk of a broken egg. 'Tis a goodly mansion. There's a chapel with a little arched roof, embellished with ornaments excellently cut. Above you can see the belfry with its delicate tracery. There's also a pleasant garden, consisting of a pond, an aviary, an echo, a mall, a labyrinth, a wild-beast house and plenty of thick-shaded walks very agreeable to Venus. And then there's a rogue of a tree which they call "the lewd," because it once favoured the pleasures of a certain princess and a certain constable of France, a gallant and a wit. Alas! we poor philosophers are to a constable of France what a cabbage-plot or a radish-bed is to a grove of laurels. After all, what does it signify? Human life for the great as well as for us is a mixture of good and evil. Sorrow ever waits on joy, the spondee on the dactyl. Master, I must relate to you the history of the Barbeau mansion. It ends tragically. It was in 1319, in the reign of Philip V, who reigned longer than any of the French kings. The moral of the story is that the temptations of the flesh are pernicious and malign. Let us not gaze too long upon our neighbour's wife, however much our senses may be taken with her beauty. Fornication is a very libertine thought. Adultery is a prying into another man's pleasure. Oh! the noise yonder grows louder!'

The tumult was, in fact, increasing around Notre-Dame. They listened. Shouts of victory could very distinctly be heard. Suddenly a hundred flambeaux, that glittered on the helmets of men-at-arms, spread over the church at all heights; on the towers, on the galleries, on the flying buttresses. These torches seemed to be carried in search of something; and soon distant clamours reached distinctly the ears of the fugitives: 'The Egyptian! the sorceress! death to the Egyptian!'

The unhappy creature dropped her head upon her hands, and the unknown began to row furiously towards the bank. Meanwhile, our philosopher reflected. He clasped the goat in his arms, and sidled gently away from the gypsy-girl, who pressed closer and closer to him, as the only protection left her.

It is certain that Gringoire was in a cruel dilemma. He reflected that, as the law then stood, the goat would be hanged too, if she were retaken; that it would be a great pity, poor Djali! that two condemned ones thus clinging to him were too much for him; that, finally, his companion asked nothing better than to take charge of the gypsy. Yet a violent struggle was taking place in his mind; wherein, like the Jupiter of the Iliad, he placed in the balance alternately the gypsy and the goat; and he looked first at one, then at the other, his eyes moist with tears, and saying between his teeth: 'And yet I cannot save you both!'

A shock apprised them that the skiff had reached the shore. The appalling uproar still rang through the city. The unknown rose, came to the gypsy, and offered to take her arm to assist her to land. She repulsed him, and clung to Gringoire's sleeve, who in turn, absorbed in the goat, almost repulsed her. Then she sprang without help from the boat. She was so disturbed that she knew not what she was doing nor whither she was going. She stood thus for a moment stupefied, watching the water as it flowed. When she recovered herself a little, she found herself alone on the landing place with the unknown. It appears that Gringoire had taken advantage of the moment of their going ashore to slip away with the goat among the mass of houses of the Rue Grenier-sur-l'Eau.

The poor gypsy shuddered on finding herself alone with that man. She strove to speak, to cry out, to call Gringoire; but her tongue refused its office, and not a sound issued from her lips. All at once she felt the hand of the unknown upon hers. It was a cold, strong hand. Her teeth chattered. She turned paler than the moonbeam that shone upon her. The man spoke not a word. He began to move towards the Place de Grève with hasty steps, holding her by the hand. At that moment she had a vague feeling that Fate is an irresistible power. No resistance was left in her; she let him drag her along, running while he walked. The quay, at that spot, ascended somewhat before them. Yet it seemed to her as if she were descending a declivity.

She looked on all sides. Not a passer-by was to be seen. The quay was absolutely deserted. She heard no sound, she perceived no one stirring, except in the glaring and tumultuous city, from which she was separated only by an arm of the Seine, and whence her name reached her ear mingled with shouts of 'Death!' The rest of Paris lay spread around her in vast masses of shadow.

Meanwhile the unknown continued to drag her along in the same silence and with the same rapidity. She had no recollection of any of the places that she was passing. As she went by a lighted window, she made an effort, suddenly drew back, and cried out: 'Help!'

The burgher who owned the window opened it, appeared at it in his shirt with his lamp in his hand, looked out with drowsy eyes on the quay, uttered some words which she could not hear and closed his shutter again. It was her last ray of hope extinguished.

The man in black uttered not a syllable. He held her fast, and walked quicker than before. She ceased to resist, and followed him helplessly.

From time to time she mustered a little strength, and said, in a voice broken by the unevenness of the pavement and the breathlessness of their flight: 'Who are you? who are you?' He made no reply.

They arrived thus, keeping still along the quay, at a square of tolerable size. There was then a little moonlight. It was the Grève. In the middle a sort of black cross was visible. It was the gibbet. She recognized all this, and she knew where she was.

The man stopped, turned towards her, and lifted his hood.

'Oh!' faltered she, petrified; 'I knew well that it was he again!';

It was the priest. He looked like the ghost of himself. It was an effect of the moonlight. It seems as if by that light one beholds only the spectres of objects.

'Listen,' said he; and she shuddered at the sound of that fatal voice, which she had not heard for so long. He continued. He spoke with short and panting jerks, which betoken deep internal convulsions. 'Listen. We are here. I have to talk with thee. This is the Grève. This is an extreme point. Fate delivers us up into the hands of each other. I am going to dispose of thy life – thou, of my soul. Beyond this place and this night nothing is to be foretold. Listen to me, then. I shall tell thee . . . First, talk to me not of thy Phœbus.' (As he spoke he paced backward and forward like a man incapable of standing still, dragging her after him.) 'Talk not of him. Mark me, if thou utterest his name, I know not what I shall do, but it will be something terrible!'

Then, like a body which recovers its centre of gravity, he became motionless once more; but his words betrayed no less agitation. His voice grew lower and lower.

'Turn not thy head aside so. Hearken to me. 'Tis a serious matter. First, I will tell thee what has happened. There will be no laughing about this, I assure thee. What was I saying? remind me. Ah! it is that there is a decree of the Parliament, delivering thee over to execution again. I have just now taken thee out of their hands. But there they are pursuing thee. Look.'

He stretched out his arm towards the city. The search, in fact seemed to continue. The uproar drew nearer. The tower of the lieutenant's house, situated opposite to the Grève, was full of noise and lights; and soldiers were running on the opposite quay with torches, shouting: 'The Egyptian! where is the Egyptian? Death! Death!'

'Thou seest plainly,' resumed the priest, 'they are pursuing thee, and that I am not deceiving thee. I love thee. Open not thy lips. Speak not a word, if it be to tell me that thou hatest me. I am determined not to hear that again. I have just now saved thee. First, let me finish. I can save thee absolutely. Everything is prepared. Thou hast only to make it thy wish. As thou wilt, I can do.'

He broke off violently. 'No, that is not what I had to say.'

Then running, and drawing her after him, for he still kept hold of her, he went straight to the gibbet, and pointing to it:

'Choose between us,' said he, coolly.

She tore herself from his grasp, and fell at the foot of the gibbet, grasping that funereal support; then she half turned her beautiful head, and looked at the priest over her shoulder. She might have been a Holy Virgin at the foot of the cross. The priest stood motionless, his finger still raised towards the gibbet, his attitude unchanged, like a statue.

At length the gypsy said to him:

'It is less horrible to me than you are.'

Then he let his arm drop slowly, and cast his eyes upon the ground in deep dejection. 'Could these stones speak,' he murmured, 'yes, they would say, that here stands, indeed, an unhappy man!'

He resumed. The young girl, kneeling before the gibbet, veiled by her long flowing hair, let him speak without interrupting him. His accent was now mild and plaintive, contrasting mournfully with the haughty harshness of his features:

'I love you! Oh, that is still very true! And is nothing, then, perceivable without, of that fire which consumes my heart? Alas! young girl – night and day – yes, night and day! does that deserve no pity? 'Tis a love of the night and the day, I tell you – 'tis torture! Oh, I suffer too much, my poor child, 'tis a thing worthy of compassion, I do assure you. You see that I speak gently to you. I would fain have you cease to abhor me. After all, when a man loves a woman, 'tis not his fault. Oh, my God! What? will you then never pardon me? will you hate me always? and is it all over? 'Tis this that makes me cruel – ay, hateful to myself. You do not even look at me. You are thinking of something else, perchance while I talk to you as I stand shuddering on the brink of eternity to both of us! Above all, speak not to me of the officer! What! Here I to throw myself at your knees! What! I might kiss – not your feet – you would not suffer me, but the ground under your feet. What! I might sob like a child, I might tear from my breast – not words – but my heart and my entrails, to tell you how I love you! all would be in vain – all! And yet naught in your soul but what is kind and tender. You are radiant with the loveliest gentleness, you are wholly sweet, good, merciful, charming! Alas! you have no malevolence but for me alone. Oh, what a fatality!'

He hid his face in his hands. The young girl heard him weeping. It was the first time. Standing thus, erect and convulsed by sobbing, he looked even more wretched and suppliant than on his knees. He wept thus for some time.

'But come,' he continued, these first tears over, 'I have no more words. And yet I had well pondered what I had to say to you. Now I tremble and shiver, I stagger at the decisive moment, I feel that something transcendent wraps us round, and my voice falters. Oh, I shall fall to the ground if you do not take pity on me, pity on yourself. Condemn not both of us. If you could but know how much I love you! What a heart is mine! Oh, what desertion of all virtue! what desperate abandonment of myself! A doctor, I mock at science; a gentleman, I tarnish my name; a priest, I make my missal a pillow of desire, I spit in the face of my God! All this for thee, enchantress! to be more worthy of thy hell! and thou rejectest the damned one! Oh, let me tell thee all! more still! something more horrible! oh, yet more horrible!'

As he uttered these last words, his look became quite wild. He was silent for a moment; then began again, as if talking to himself and in a strong voice, 'Cain, what hast thou done with thy brother?'

There was another silence, and he went on:

'What have I done with him, Lord? I received him, nourished him, brought him up, loved him, idolized him and killed him! Yes, Lord, just now, before my eyes, have they dashed his head upon the stones of thine house, and it was because of me, because of this woman, because of her ...'

His eye was haggard, his voice sinking; he repeated several times, mechanically, at considerable intervals, like a bell prolonging its last vibration: 'Because of her, because of her.'

Then his tongue no longer articulated any perceptible sound though his lips continued to move. All at once he sank down, like something crumbling to pieces, and remained motionless on the ground with his head between his knees.

A slight movement of the young girl, drawing away her foot from under him, brought him to himself. He passed his hand slowly over his hollow cheeks, and gazed for some moments, in vacant astonishment at his fingers, which were wet. 'What?' murmured he, 'have I wept?'

And turning suddenly to the gypsy, with inexpressible anguish:

'Alas! you have beheld me weep, unmoved! Child, dost thou know that those tears are tears of fire? And is it, then, so true that from the man we hate nothing can move us? Wert thou to see me die, thou wouldst laugh. But I – I wish not thy death! One word, one single word of forgiveness! Tell me not that thou lovest me, say only that thou wilt, that will suffice, and I will save thee. If not – Oh, the time flies! I entreat thee, by all that is sacred, wait not until I am become of stone again, like this gibbet which claims thee too. Think that I hold both our destinies in my hand, that I am mad, 'tis terrible, that I may let all go, and that there yawns beneath us, unhappy girl, a bottomless abyss, wherein my fall will pursue thine for all eternity! One word of kindness, say one word, but one word!'

She opened her lips to answer him. He threw himself on his knees before her, to receive with adoration the words, perhaps relenting, which were about to fall from her. She said to him: 'You are an assassin!'

The priest seized her furiously in his arms, and burst into hideous laughter.

'Well, yes, an assassin,' said he, 'and I will have thee. Thou wilt not take me for thy slave; thou shalt have me for thy master. You shall be mine! I have a den, whither I will drag thee. Thou shalt follow me, thou must follow me, or I deliver thee over! Thou must die, my fair one, or be mine – the priest's, the apostate's, the assassin's – this very night; dost thou hear? Come, joy! Come! kiss me, silly girl! The grave! or my couch!'

His eyes were sparkling with rage and licentiousness, and his lascivious lips reddened the neck of the young girl. She struggled in his arms. He covered her with furious kisses.

'Do not bite me, monster!' she cried. 'Oh, the hateful, poisonous monk! Let me go! I'll pull out thy vile gray hair, and throw it by handfuls in thy face!'

He turned red, then pale, then left hold of her, and gazed upon her gloomily. She thought herself victorious, and continued: 'I tell thee, I belong to my Phœbus, that it is Phœbus I love, that 'tis Phœbus who is handsome! Thou, priest, art old! thou art ugly! Get thee gone!'

He uttered a violent cry, like the wretch to whom a red-hot iron is applied. 'Die, then!' said he, grinding his teeth. She saw his frightful look, and strove to fly. But he seized her again, shook her, threw her upon the ground, and walked rapidly toward the angle of the Tour-Roland, dragging her after him over the pavement by her fair hands.

When he had reached it he turned to her:

'Once for all, wilt thou be mine?'

She answered him with emphasis:

'No!'

Then he called in a loud voice:

'Gudule! Gudule! here's the gypsy woman! take thy revenge!'

The young girl felt herself seized suddenly by the elbow. She looked-it was a fleshless arm extended through a loop-hole in the wall, and held her with a hand of iron.

'Hold fast!' said the priest; 'it's the gypsy-woman escaped. Do not let her go. I'm going to fetch the sergeants. Thou shalt see her hanged.'

A guttural laugh from the interior of the wall made answer to these deadly words: 'Ha! ha! ha!' The gypsy-girl saw the priest hurry away toward the Pont Notre-Dame. Trampling of horses was heard in that direction.

The young girl had recognized the malicious recluse. Panting with terror, she strove to disengage herself. She writhed. She made several bounds in agony and despair, but the other held her with superhuman strength. The lean, bony fingers that pressed her were clenched and met round her flesh; it seemed as if that hand was riveted to her arm. It was more than a chain, more than an iron ring; it was a pair of pincers, endowed with life and understanding, issuing from a wall.

Exhausted, she fell back against the wall, and then the fear of death came over her. She thought of all the charms of life – of youth, of the sight of the heavens, of the aspect of nature, of love of Phœbus, of all that was flying from her; and then of all that was approaching, of the priest who would denounce her, of the executioner who was coming, of the gibbet that was there. Then she felt terror mounting even to the roots of her hair, and she heard the dismal laugh of the recluse, saying in low tones: 'Ha! ha! thou'rt going to be hanged!'

She turned with a dying look toward the window of her cell, and she saw the savage face of the Sachette through the bars.

'What have I done to you?' said she, almost inarticulately.

The recluse made no answer, but began to mutter, in a singing, irritated and mocking tone: 'Daughter of Egypt! daughter of Egypt! daughter of Egypt!'

The unfortunate Esmeralda let her head drop under her long flowing hair, understanding that it was no human being she had here to deal with.

All at once the recluse exclaimed, as if the gypsy's question had taken all that time to reach her apprehension:

'What hast thou done to me, dost thou say? Ha! what hast thou done to me, gypsy-woman? Well, hark thee! I had a child – dost thou see? I had a child; a child, I tell thee; a pretty little girl, my Agnès!' she continued wildly, kissing something in the gloom. 'Well, dost thou see, daughter of Egypt, they took my child from me, they stole my child, they ate my child! That is what thou hast done to me!'

The young girl answered, like the lamb in the fable: 'Alas! perhaps I was not then born!'

'Oh, yes,' rejoined the recluse; 'thou must have been born then. Thou wast one of them; she would have been thy age. For fifteen years have I been here, fifteen years have I suffered, fifteen years have I prayed, fifteen years have I been knocking my head against these four walls. I tell thee, they were gypsy-women that stole her from me – dost thou hear that? and who ate her with their teeth. Hast thou a heart? Only think what it is; a child playing, suckling, sleeping; it is so innocent! Well, that is what they took from me, what they killed. God Almighty knows it well. To-day it is my turn. I'm going to eat some gypsy-woman's flesh. Oh, how I would bite thee, if the bars did not hinder me; my head is too big. Poor little thing, while she slept! And if they woke her while taking her away, in vain might she cry. I was not there! Ha! ye Egyptian mothers, ye devoured my child; come now and see your own!'

Then she began to laugh or gnash her teeth. The two things resembled each other in that frantic countenance. Day began to dawn. An ashy gleam dimly lighted this scene, and the gibbet grew more and more distinct in the Place. On the other side, towards the bridge of Notre-Dame, the poor victim thought she heard the sound of the horsemen approaching.

'Madame!' she cried, clasping her hands and falling upon her knees, dishevelled, distracted, wild with fright, 'madame, have pity! They are coming. I have done nothing to you. Would you have me die that horrible death before your eyes? You are compassionate, I am sure. 'Tis too frightful. Let me fly, let me go. Have mercy! I wish not to die thus!'

'Give me back my child!' said the recluse.

'Mercy! mercy!'

'Give me back my child!'

'Let me go, in heaven's name!'

'Give me back my child!'

Again the young girl sank down, exhausted, powerless, with the glassy stare of one already in the grave.

'Alas!' faltered she, 'you seek your child; I seek my parents!'

'Give me back my little Agnès!' pursued Gudule. 'Thou knowest not where she is? Then, die! I will tell thee! I was once a girl of pleasure; I had a child; they took my child; it was the Egyptian women. Thou seest plainly that thou must die. When thy mother, the Egyptian, comes to ask for thee, I will say to her: "Mother, look at that gibbet! or give back my child!" Dost thou know where she is, my little girl? Stay, let me show thee; here is her shoe, all that is left of her. Dost thou know where its fellow is? If thou dost, tell me; and if it is at the other end of the earth, I'll go thither on my knees to fetch it!'

So saying, with her other arm extended through the aperture, she showed the gypsy the little embroidered shoe. There was already daylight enough to distinguish its shape and colour.

The gypsy-girl, starting, said: 'Let me see that shoe. Oh, God! God! God!'

And at the same time, with the hand she had at liberty, she eagerly opened the little bag with green glass ornaments which she wore about her neck.

'Go on! go on!' grumbled Gudule, 'fumble in thy amulet of the foul fiend –'

She suddenly stopped short, trembled in every limb, and cried in a voice that came from the very depths of her heart: 'My daughter!'

The gypsy had taken out of the bag a little shoe precisely like the other. To this little shoe was attached a slip of parchment, upon which was inscribed this *charm*:

> *'When thou the like to this shalt see,*
> *Thy mother'll stretch her arms to thee.'*

Quicker than a flash of lightning the recluse had compared the two shoes, read the inscription on the parchment, and thrust close to the window bars her face, beaming with heavenly joy, crying:

'My daughter! my daughter!'

'My mother!' answered the gypsy-girl.

Here all description fails us.

The wall and the iron bars were between them. 'Oh, the wall!' cried the recluse. 'To see her and not embrace her! Thy hand! thy hand!'

The young girl passed her arm through the opening. The recluse threw herself upon that hand, pressed her lips to it, and there remained, absorbed in that kiss, giving no sign of animation but a sob which heaved her bosom from time to time. Meanwhile, she wept in torrents, in the silence, in the darkness, like rain at night. The poor mother poured forth in floods upon that adored hand the deep, dark well of tears, into which her grief had filtered, drop by drop, for fifteen years.

Suddenly she rose, threw back the long gray hair from her face, and without saying a word, strove with both hands, and with the fury of a lioness, to shake the bars of her window hole. The bars were firm. She then went and fetched from one corner of her cell a large paving-stone, which served her for a pillow, and hurled it against them with such violence that one of the bars broke, casting numberless sparks. A second stroke drove out the old iron cross that barricaded the window. Then, with both hands, she managed to loosen and remove the rusty stumps of the bars. There are moments when the hands of a woman possess superhuman strength.

The passage cleared – and it was all done in less than a minute – she seized her daughter by the middle of her body and drew her into the cell. 'Come,' murmured she, 'let me drag thee out of the abyss!'

When her daughter was within the cell, she set her gently on the ground; then took her up again, and carrying her in her arms as if she were still only her little Agnès, she went to and fro in her narrow cell intoxicated, frantic with joy, shouting, singing, kissing her daughter, talking to her, laughing aloud, melting into tears – all at the same time and vehemently.

'My daughter! my daughter!' she said; 'I have my daughter! Here she is! The good God has given her back to me! Ha! you – come all of you – is there anybody there to see that I've got my daughter? Lord Jesus, how beautiful she is! You have made me wait for her fifteen years, my good God, but it was that you might give her back to me beautiful. So the Egyptians did not eat her! Who said that? My little girl! my little girl! kiss me! Those good Egyptians! I love the Egyptians! Is it really thou? 'Twas then that which made my heart leap every time that thou didst go by. And I took that for hatred! Forgive me, my Agnès, forgive me! Thou didst think me very malicious, didst thou not? I love thee. Hast thou still that little mark on thy neck? Let me see. She has it yet. Oh, thou art beautiful! It was I who gave thee those big eyes, mademoiselle. Kiss me. I love thee. What matters it to me that other mothers have children? I can laugh at them now! They have only to come and look. Here is mine. Look at her neck, her eyes, her hair, her hand. Find me anything as beautiful as that? Oh, I promise you she will have lovers. I have wept for fifteen years. All my beauty has departed, and is come again in her. Kiss me.'

She said a thousand other extravagant things to her, the accent in which they were uttered making them beautiful; disordered the poor girl's apparel, even to making her blush; smoothed out her silken tresses with her hand; kissed her foot, her knee, her forehead, her eyelids; was enraptured with everything. The young girl let her do as she pleased, only repeating at intervals, very low and with infinite sweetness, 'My mother!'

'Look you, my little girl,' resumed the recluse, constantly interrupting her words with kisses, 'look you; I shall love thee dearly. We will go away from here. We are going to be so happy. I have inherited something in Reims, in our country. Thou knowest Reims? Ah, no; how couldst thou know that? thou wert too small. If thou didst but know how pretty thou wert at four months old! Tiny feet, which people came to see all the way from Epernay, five leagues away. We shall have a field and a house. Thou shalt sleep in my bed. Oh, my God! who would believe it? I have my daughter again!'

'Oh, my mother!' said the young girl, gathering strength at last to speak in her emotion; 'the gypsy-woman told me so. There was a good gypsy among our people who died last year, and she had always taken care of me like a foster-mother. It was she that had put this little bag on my neck. She used always say to me: "Little one, guard this trinket well; 'tis a treasure; it will enable thee to find thy mother again. Thou wearest thy mother about thy neck." She foretold it – the gypsy-woman.'

Again the Sachette clasped her daughter in her arms.

'Come,' said she, 'let me kiss thee. Thou sayest that so prettily! When we are in the country, we'll put the little shoes on the feet of an infant Jesus in a church. We certainly owe that to the good, Holy Virgin. Heavens! what a pretty voice thou hast. When thou wast talking to me just now, it was like music. Ah, my Lord God! I have found my child again! But is it credible now – all this story? Surely nothing will kill one, or I should have died of joy.'

And then she clapped her hands again, laughing and exclaiming: 'We shall be so happy.'

At that moment the cell resounded with a clattering of arms and galloping of horses, which seemed to be advancing from the bridge of Notre-Dame, and approaching nearer and nearer along the quay. The gypsy threw herself in agony into the arms of the Sachette: 'Save me! save me! my mother! they are coming!'

The recluse turned pale again.

'Oh, heaven! what dost thou say? I had forgotten. They are pursuing thee. What hast thou done, then?'

'I know not,' replied the unfortunate child, 'but I am condemned to die.'

'To die!' exclaimed Gudule, reeling as if struck by a thunderbolt. 'To die!' she repeated slowly, gazing at her daughter with a fixed stare.

'Yes, my mother,' repeated the young girl, with wild despair, 'they want to kill me. They are coming to hang me. That gallows is for me.

377

Save me! save me! They are coming. Save me!'

The recluse remained for a few seconds in petrified silence, then shook her head doubtingly, and, suddenly bursting into laughter, the old frightful laughter which had come back to her:

'Oh, oh, no! 'tis a dream thou art telling me. Ah! well! I lost her; that lasted fifteen years; and then I find her again, and that is to last but a minute! And they would take her from me again! now that she is handsome, that she is grown up, that she talks to me, that she loves me; it is now they would come and devour her before my very eyes, who am her mother. Oh, no! such things cannot be. God Almighty permits not such things as that.'

Here the cavalcade appeared to halt, and a distant voice was heard saying:

'This way, Messire Tristan. The priest says we shall find her at the Rat-hole.' The tramp of the horses began again.

The recluse started up with a shriek of despair:

'Fly, fly, my child! It all comes back to me. Thou art right. 'Tis thy death! horror! malediction! fly!'

She put her head to the loop-hole, and drew it back again hastily.

'Stay,' said she, in an accent low, brief and doleful, pressing convulsively the hand of the gypsy, who was more dead than alive. 'Stay where you are. Do not breathe. There are soldiers everywhere. Thou canst not get away. It is too light.'

Her eyes were dry and burning. For a moment she said nothing, only paced the cell hurriedly, stopping now and then to pluck out handfuls of gray hair, which she afterwards tore with her teeth.

All at once she said: 'They are coming. I will speak to them. Hide thyself in that corner. They will not see thee. I will tell them thou hast escaped, that I let thee go, i' faith.'

She set down her daughter (for she was still carrying her) in one corner of the cell which was not visible from without. She made her crouch down; arranged her carefully, so that neither foot nor hand should project from the shadow; unbound her black hair, and spread it over her white robe, to conceal it; and placed before her the water-jug and paving-stone – the only articles of furniture she had – imagining that this jug and stone would hide her. And when this was done, she became more calm and knelt down and prayed. The day was only dawning; it still left many shadows in the Rat-hole.

At that moment, the voice of the priest – that infernal voice – passed very near the cell, crying:

'This way, Captain Phœbus de Chateaupers.'

At that name, at that voice, Esmeralda, crouching in her corner made a movement.

'Stir not,' said Gudule.

Scarcely had she said this before a tumultuous crowd of men, swords and horses, stopped around the cell. The mother rose quickly, and went and posted herself at the loop-hole, to cover the aperture. She beheld a large troop of armed men, horse and foot, drawn up on the Grève. The commander dismounted and came toward her.

'Old woman,' said this man, who had an atrocious face, 'we are in search of a witch, to hang her. We were told that thou hadst her.'

The poor mother, assuming as indifferent a look as she could, replied:

'I don't quite know what you mean.'

The other resumed: 'Tête-Dieu! Then what sort of a tale was that crazy archdeacon telling us? Where is he?'

'Monseigneur,' said a soldier, 'he has disappeared.'

'Come, now, old mad woman,' resumed the commander. 'tell me no lies. A sorceress was given you to keep. What have you done with her?'

The recluse, not wishing to deny all, for fear of awakening suspicion, replied, in a sincere and surly tone:

'If you mean a tall young girl that was given me to hold just now, I can tell you that she bit me, and I let her go. There! Leave me in peace.'

The commander made a grimace of disappointment.

'Let me have no lying, old spectre,' he said. 'My name is Tristan l'Hermite, and I am the king's companion. Tristan l'Hermite! Dost thou hear?' he added, casting his eyes around the Place de Grève. ' 'Tis a name that has echoes here.'

'If you were Satan l'Hermite,' rejoined Gudule, gaining hope, 'I should have nothing else to tell you; nor should I be afraid of you.'

'Tête-Dieu,' said Tristan, 'here's a gossip. Ha! so the witch-girl has got away. And which way did she take?'

Gudule answered carelessly: 'By the Rue du Mouton, I believe.'

Tristan turned his head, and motioned to his men to prepare to march. The recluse breathed again.

'Monseigneur,' said an archer all at once, 'just ask the old elf how it is that her window-bars are broken out so?'

This question brought anguish again to the heart of the miserable mother. Still she did not lose all presence of mind. 'They were always so,' stammered she.

'Pshaw!' returned the archer; 'they formed but yesterday a fine black cross that made a man feel devout.'

Tristan cast an oblique glance at the recluse.

'I think the old crone is confused,' said he.

The unfortunate woman felt that all depended on her self possession; and so, with death in her soul, she began to jeer. Mothers possess such strength.

'Bah!' said she, 'the man is drunk. 'Tis more than a year since the back of a cart laden with stones backed against my window and broke the grating. And how I cursed the driver!'

' 'Tis true,' said another archer. 'I was there.'

There are always to be found, in all places, people who have seen everything. This unlooked-for testimony from the archer revived the spirits of the recluse, to whom this interrogatory was like crossing an abyss on the edge of a knife.

But she was doomed to a perpetual alternation of hope and alarm.

'If a cart had done that,' resumed the first soldier, 'the stumps of the bars would be driven inward, whereas they have been forced outward.'

'Ha! ha!' said Tristan to the soldier, 'thou hast the nose of an inquisitor at the Châtelet. Answer what he says, old woman.'

'Good heavens!' exclaimed she, driven to bay, and with tears in her voice in spite of herself, 'I swear to you, monseigneur, that it was a cart which broke those bars. You hear, that man saw it. And besides, what has that to do with your sorceress?'

'Hum!' growled Tristan.

'The devil!' continued the soldier, flattered by the provost's commendation, 'these breaks in the iron are quite fresh!'

Tristan shook his head. She turned pale.

'How long is it, say you, since the cart affair?' he asked.

'A month, perhaps a fortnight, monseigneur. I cannot recollect exactly.'

'She said at first above a year,' observed the soldier.

'That looks queer!' said the provost.

'Monseigneur,' cried she, still standing close to the opening, and trembling lest suspicion should prompt them to thrust in their heads and look into the cell – 'monseigneur, I swear to you that 'twas a cart which broke this grating; I swear it to you by all the angels in paradise. If it was not done by a cart, I wish I may go to everlasting perdition, and I deny my God!'

'Thou art very hot in that oath of thine,' said Tristan with his inquisitorial glance.

The poor woman felt her assurance forsaking her more and more. She was already making blunders, and she perceived with terror that she was not saying what she should have said.

Another soldier now came up, crying:

'Monseigneur, the old elf lies. The sorceress has not gotten away by the Rue du Mouton. The chain of that street has been stretched across all night, and the chain-keeper has seen nobody go by.'

Tristan, whose countenance became every moment more sinister, addressed the recluse:

'What hast thou to say to that?'

She still strove to make headway against this fresh incident. 'That I know not, monseigneur, that I may have been mistaken. In fact, I think she crossed the water.'

'That is in the opposite direction,' said the provost. 'And it is not very likely that she would wish to re-enter the city, where they were making search for her. You lie, old woman.'

'And then,' added the first soldier, 'there is no boat either on this side of the stream or on the other.'

'She must have swum across,' replied the recluse, defending her ground inch by inch.

'Do women swim?' said the soldier.

'Tête-Dieu! old woman! thou liest! thou liest!' exclaimed Tristan, angrily; 'I've a good mind to leave the witch and hang thee. A quarter of an hour's torture will perhaps bring the truth out of thy throat. Come, thou shalt go along with us.'

She caught eagerly at these words:

'As you please, monseigneur. Do it! do it! Torture! I am willing. Take me with you. Quick, quick! let us go directly.' In the meantime, thought she, my daughter will make her escape.

' 'Sdeath!' said the provost, 'what an appetite for the rack. This mad creature is past my comprehension.'

An old gray-headed sergeant of the guard now stepped out of the ranks, and, addressing the provost:

'Mad, in sooth, monseigneur! If she has let loose the Egyptian, 'tis not her fault, for she has no liking for Egyptians. For these fifteen years I have belonged to the watch, and every night I hear her cursing against those Bohemian dames with execrations without end. If the one we are seeking be, as I believe, the little dancing-girl with the goat, she hates that one above all the rest.'

Gudule made an effort, and said:

'That one above all the rest.'

The unanimous testimony of the men of the watch confirmed the old sergeant's words to the provost. Tristan l'Hermite, despairing of getting anything out of the recluse, turned his back upon her, and she, with inexpressible anxiety, watched him go slowly towards his horse.

'Come,' said he, between his teeth, 'forward! we must continue the search. I will not sleep till the Egyptian be hanged.'

Still he hesitated for a while before mounting his horse. Gudule was palpitating between life and death as she saw him cast round the Place that restless look of a hound that feels himself to be near the lair of the game and is reluctant to go away. At last he shook his head and sprang into his saddle.

Gudule's heart, which had been so horribly oppressed, expanded now, and she said in a whisper, casting a glance upon her daughter, whom she had not ventured to look at while they were there, 'Saved!'

The poor child had been all this time in her corner, without breathing or stirring; with the image of death staring her in the face. No particular of the scene between Gudule and Tristan had escaped her; she had shared all the agonies endured by her mother. She had heard, as it were, each successive cracking of the thread which had held her suspended over the abyss; twenty times she thought she saw it breaking asunder, and only now began to take breath and to feel the ground steady under her feet. At this moment she heard a voice saying to the provost:

'Cor-bœuf! monsieur the provost, 'tis no business of mine, who am a guardsman, to hang sorceresses. The rabble of the populace is put down. I leave you to do your own work by yourself. You will permit me to rejoin my company, since it is without a captain.'

The voice was that of Phœbus de Chateaupers. What took place within her was indescribable. He was there, her friend, her protector, her support, her shelter, her Phœbus! She started up; and before her mother could prevent her, she had sprung to the window, crying:

'Phœbus! hither! my Phœbus!'

Phœbus was no longer there. He had just galloped round the corner of the Rue de la Coutellerie. But Tristan was not yet gone. The recluse rushed upon her daughter with the roar of a wild beast; she dragged her violently back, her nails entering the flesh of the poor girl's neck. A tigress mother does not stand on trifles. But it was too late. Tristan had seen.

'Ha, ha,' he cried, with a grin which showed all his teeth, and made his face resemble that of a wolf, 'two mice in the trap.'

'I suspected as much,' said the soldier.

Tristan slapped him on the shoulder:

'Thou art a good cat! Come,' he added, 'where is Henriet Cousin?'

A man who had neither the garb nor the mien of a soldier, stepped forth from the ranks. He wore a dress half gray, half brown, had lank hair, leathern sleeves and a coil of rope in his huge fist. This man always accompanied Tristan, who always accompanied Louis XI.

'Friend,' said Tristan l'Hermite, 'I presume that yonder is the sorceress whom we are seeking. Thou wilt hang me this one. Hast thou thy ladder?'

'There is one under the shed of the Maison-aux-Piliers,' replied the man. 'Is it on this *justice* that the thing is to be done?' continued he, pointing to the stone gibbet.

'Yes.'

'So, ho!' said the man, with a loud laugh, more brutal still than that of the provost, 'we shall not have far to go!'

'Make haste,' said Tristan, 'and do thy laughing after.'

Meanwhile, since Tristan had seen her daughter, and all hope was lost, the recluse had not uttered a word. She had flung the poor gypsy, half dead, into the corner of the cell, and had posted herself again at the loop-hole, both hands resting upon the edge of the stone sill, like two claws. In this attitude her eyes, which had again become wild and fierce, were seen to wander fearlessly over the surrounding soldiers. When Henriet Cousin approached her place, her look was so ferocious that he started back.

'Monseigneur,' said he, turning back to the provost, 'which are we to take?'

'The young one.'

'So much the better, for the old one seemeth difficult.'

'Poor little dancing-girl with the goat!' said the old sergeant of the watch.

Henriet Cousin again approached the window-hole. The mother's eye made his own droop. He said with some timidity:

'Madame – '

She interrupted him in a very low but furious voice; 'What wouldst thou?'

'Not you,' said he, 'but the other.'

'What other?'

'The young one.'

She began to shake her head, crying:

'There is no one! no one! no one!'

'There is,' replied the executioner, 'and well you know it. Let me take the young one; I will not harm you.'

She said with a strange sneer: 'Ah! thou wilt not harm me!'

'Let me have the other, madame. 'Tis the will of monsieur the provost.'

She repeated with an expression of frenzy, 'There's nobody!'

'I tell you there is,' rejoined the hang-man. 'We've all seen that there are two of you.'

'You look, then,' said the recluse, with her strange sneer. 'Thrust your head through the window.'

The hangman eyed the mother's nails, and durst not venture.

'Make haste!' cried Tristan, who had been drawing up his men in a semi-circle round the Rat-hole, and posted himself on horseback near the gibbet.

Henriet once more went back to the provost, quite discountenanced. He had laid his ropes upon the ground, and, with a sheepish look, was turning his hat in his hands.

'Monseigneur,' he asked, 'how must I get in?'

'Through the door.'

'There is none.'

'Through the window, then.'

'It's not wide enough.'

'Widen it then,' said Tristan, angrily. 'Hast thou no picks?'

The mother, from the interior of the cave, was still fixedly watching them. She had ceased to hope; she no longer knew what she wanted, except that they should not have her daughter.

Henriet Cousin went to fetch the box of tools from under the shed of the Pillar House. He also brought from the same place the double ladder, which he immediately set up against the gibbet. Five or six of the provost's men provided themselves with picks and crowbars, and Tristan went with them to the window of the cell.

'Old woman,' said the provost, in a tone of severity, 'give up the girl quietly.'

She looked at him as one who does not understand.

'God's head!' added Tristan; 'what good can it do thee to hinder that witch from being hanged as it pleases the king?'

The wretched woman burst into her wild laugh.

'What good can it do me? She is my daughter!'

The tone in which this word was uttered produced a shudder even in Henriet Cousin.

'I'm sorry for it,' returned the provost; 'but it's the king's pleasure.'

She shrieked, redoubling her terrible laughter, 'What's thy king to me? I tell thee she is my daughter!'

'Make a way through the wall,' said Tristan

To make an opening sufficiently large, it was only necessary to remove one course of stone underneath the window. When the mother heard the picks and the levers undermining her fortress, she uttered a dreadful cry. Then she began to circle with frightful quickness round and round her cell – a habit of a wild beast, which her long residence in the cage had given her. She said nothing more, but her eyes were flaming. The soldiers felt their blood chilled to the very heart.

All at once she took up her paving-stone, laughed and threw it with both hands at the workmen. The stone, ill-aimed (for her hands were trembling), touched no one, but fell harmless at the feet of Tristan's horse. She gnashed her teeth.

Meanwhile, although the sun was not yet risen, it had become broad daylight, and a fine roseate tint beautified the decaying chimneys of the Pillar House. It was the hour when the windows of the earliest risers in the great city open joyfully upon the roofs. A few labouring people, a few fruit-sellers, going to the Halles upon their asses, were beginning to cross the Grève; they stopped for a moment before the group of soldiers gathered about the Rat-hole, gazed at them with looks of astonishment, and passed on.

The recluse had seated herself close to her daughter, covering her with her own body, her eyes fixed, listening to the poor girl, who stirred not, but was murmuring low the one word – 'Phœbus! Phœbus!' In proportion as the work of the demolishers advanced the mother mechanically shrunk away, pressing the young girl closer and closer against the wall. All at once the recluse saw the stones (for she was on the watch, and never removed her eye from them) beginning to give way, and she heard the voice of Tristan encouraging the workmen. Then starting out of the prostration into which her spirit had sunk for some minutes, she cried out – and, as she spoke, her voice now pierced the ear like a saw, then stammered as if every species of malediction had crowded to her lips to burst forth at one and the same time:

'Ho, ho, ho! but this is horrible! You are robbers! Are you really going to take my daughter from me? I tell you she is my daughter! Oh, the cowards! oh, the hangman lackeys! the miserable murdering sutlers! Help! help! fire! And will they take my child from me thus? Who is he, then, whom they call the good God?'

Then, addressing herself to Tristan, with foaming mouth and haggard eyes, on all fours, and bristling like a panther:

'Come, then, and take my daughter. Dost thou not understand that this woman tells thee it's her daughter? Dost thou know what it is to have a child, eh? thou hewolf! Hast thou never laid with thy mate? Hast thou never had a cub by her? And if thou hast little ones, when they howl hast thou no bowels to feel?'

'Down with the stones!' said Tristan; 'they are loose now.'

The crowbars now raised the heavy course of stone. It was, as we have said, the mother's last bulwark. She threw herself upon it, she would fain have held it in its place, she scratched the stones with her nails, but the heavy mass, put in motion by six men escaped her grasp, and fell gently to the ground along the iron levers.

The mother, seeing the breach effected, threw herself on the floor across the opening, barricading it with her body, writhing her arms, beating her head against the flag-stones and crying in a voice, hoarse and nearly inarticulate from exhaustion: 'Help, help! fire, fire!'

'Now, take the girl,' said Tristan, still imperturbable.

The mother looked at the soldiers in so formidable a manner that they had more disposition to retreat than to advance.

'Now for it!' responded the provost. 'You, Henriet Cousin.'

No one stirred a step.

The provost swore. '*Tête-Christ!* my fighting men! Afraid of a woman!'

'Monseigneur,' said Henriet, 'do you call that a woman?'

'She has a lion's mane,' said another.

'Come!' continued the provost; 'the gap is large enough. Go in three abreast, as at the breach of Pontoise. Let's get done with it by the dead

Mahomet! The first man who turns I'll cleave him in two.'

Placed thus between the provost and the mother, the soldiers hesitated a moment; then, making their choice, advanced upon the Rat-hole.

When the recluse saw this, she suddenly reared herself upon her knees, threw aside her hair from her face, then dropped her lean. grazed hands upon her thighs. Great tears started one by one from her eyes, coursing down her furrowed cheeks, like a torrent down the bed that it has worn itself. At the same time she began to speak, but in a voice so suppliant, so gentle, so submissive, so heartrending, that more than one old hardened galley sergeant among those who surrounded Tristan wiped his eyes.

'Gentlemen,' said she, 'sergeants! one word! There's a thing I must tell you. She is my daughter, do you see – my darling little daughter, whom I had lost. Listen; it is quite a story. You must know that I am very well acquainted with messieurs the sergeants. They were always good to me in those times when the little boys used to throw stones at me because I was a girl of pleasure. So you see, you will leave me my child when you know all! I was a poor woman of the town. It was the gypsy-women who stole her away from me. I have kept her shoe these fifteen years. See! here it is. She'd a foot like that. At Reims, La Chantefleurie, Rue Folle-Peine. Perhaps you know all that. It was I. In your youth, in those days, it was a merry time, and there were merry doings. You will have pity on me, won't you, sirs? The gypsy-women stole her from me. They hid her from me for fifteen years. I thought she was dead! Only think, my good friends; I thought she was dead! I've passed fifteen years here, in this cave, without fire in the winter. 'Tis hard, that! The poor dear little shoe! I cried so much that at last God Almighty heard me. This night he has given me back my daughter. It is a miracle of God Almighty's. She was not dead. You will not take her from me, I am sure you will not. If it were myself, now, I would not say no; but to take her, a child of sixteen! Let her have time to see the sun. What has she done to you? Nothing at all. Nor no more have I. If you did but know that I have but her, that I am old, that she is a blessing sent down to me by the Holy Virgin! And then, you are all so kind! You did not know it was my daughter, but you know now. Oh, I love her. Monsieur the great provost, I would rather have a hole in my side than a scratch upon her finger! You look like a good, kind gentleman. What I tell you now explains the thing to you, doesn't it? Oh, if you have had a mother, sir! You are the captain, leave me my child. Only consider that I am praying to you on my knees, as they pray to Christ Jesus! I ask nothing of anybody. I am from Reims, gentlemen; I've a little field there, left me by my uncle, Mahiet Pradon. I am not a beggar. I want nothing, but I must have my child. Oh, I wish to keep my child. God

Almighty, who is master of all, has not given her back to me for nothing. The king – you say the king. It can't be any great pleasure to him that they should kill my little girl. And then, the king is good. It is my daughter, it is my daughter; mine; she's not the king's, she's not yours! I want to go away from here, we both want to go; and when two women are going, mother and daughter, you let them go quietly. Let us go quietly. We belong to Reims. Oh, you are kind sergeants. I love you all. You'll not take my dear little one from me; it is impossible. Is it not, now, quite impossible? My child! my child!'

We shall not attempt to give an idea of her gesture, her accent the tears which she drank while speaking, the clasping and the wringing of her hands, the heartrending smiles, the appealing looks, the sighs, the moans, the agonizing and piercing cries which she mingled with these wild, incoherent and rambling words. When she ceased, Tristan l'Hermite knit his brows, but it was to conceal a tear that was dimmed in his tigerish eye. However, he overcame his weakness, and said, with brief utterance: 'It is the king's will.'

Then he whispered in the ear of Henriet Cousin: 'Get done quickly.' It might be that the redoubtable provost felt his own heart failing him – even his.

The executioner and the sergeants entered the cell. The mother made no resistance; she only dragged up to her daughter and clasped her madly. When the gypsy-girl saw the soldiers approaching, the horror of death revived.

'My mother!' cried she, in a tone of indescribable distress; 'oh, my mother! they are coming; defend me!'

'Yes, my love, I am defending thee!' answered the mother, in a faint voice; and clasping her close to her arms, she covered her with kisses. To see them both thus upon the ground, the mother guarding the daughter, was truly piteous.

Henriet Cousin took the gypsy-girl by the body, just below her beautiful shoulders. When she felt his hands touching her, she cried out and fainted. The executioner, from whose eye big tears were falling upon her drop by drop, offered to carry her away in his arms. He strove to unclasp the embrace of the mother, who had, as it were, knotted her hands about her daughter's waist but the grasp which thus bound her to her child was so powerful that he found it impossible to part them. Henriet Cousin therefore dragged the young girl out of the cell, and her mother after her. The eyes of the mother were also closed.

The sun was rising at that moment; and already there was a considerable collection of people in the square, looking from a distance to see what they were thus dragging over the pavement toward the gibbet. For this was a way of the Provost Tristan's at executions; he had a mania for preventing the curious from coming near.

There was nobody at the windows. Only far away, on the top of that one of the towers of Notre-Dame which looks upon the Grève, two men could be seen who stood darkly out against the clear morning sky, and who seemed to be looking on.

Henriet Cousin paused with the object he was dragging, at the foot of the fatal ladder; and, with troubled breath (so strongly was he moved to pity), he passed the rope round the young girl's lovely neck. The unfortunate girl felt the horrible contact of the hempen cord. She raised her eyelids, and beheld the skeleton arm of the stone gibbet extended over her head. Then she shook off her torpor, and cried, in a loud and agonizing voice: 'No! no! I will not!' The mother, whose head was buried by her daughter's garments, said not a word; but her entire body was convulsed, and she was heard redoubling her kisses upon the form of her child. The executioner seized that moment to unclasp, by a strong and sudden effort, the arms with which she held fast the prisoner, and, whether from exhaustion or despair, they yielded. He then took the young girl upon his shoulder, from whence her charming figure fell gracefully bending over his large head, and set his foot upon the ladder in order to ascend.

At this instant, the mother, who had sunk upon the ground, opened wide her eyes. Without uttering a cry, she started up with a terrific expression upon her face; then, like a beast rushing upon its prey, she threw herself upon the executioner's hand, and set her teeth in it. It was like a flash of lightning. The executioner howled with pain. They ran to his relief, and with difficulty liberated his bleeding hand from the teeth of the mother. She kept a profound silence. They pushed her away with brutal violence, and it was remarked that her head fell back heavily upon the ground. They raised her; she fell back again. She was dead.

The hangman, who had not loosed his hold of the young girl, kept on up the ladder.

II

The Beautiful Creature Clad in White

WHEN QUASIMODO SAW that the cell was empty; that the gypsy-girl was no longer there; that, while he had been defending her, she had been abducted, he took his head between his hands and stamped with rage and astonishment. Then he began to run over all the church, seeking his Bohemian, howling strange cries at every corner, strewing his red hair on the pavement. It was just at the moment when the king's archers were making their victorious entry into Notre-Dame, likewise in search of the gypsy-girl. Quasimodo assisted them, having no suspicion, poor dear creature, of their fatal intentions; he thought that the enemies of the Egyptian were the Truands. He himself took Tristan l'Hermite to every possible hiding-place; opened for him all the secret doors, the double backs to the altars, the inner sacristies. Had the unfortunate girl still been there, he himself would have delivered her up to them.

When the irksomeness of seeking in vain had discouraged Tristan, who was not easily discouraged, Quasimodo continued the search alone. Twenty times, a hundred times over, did he make the circuit of the church, from one end to the other, from top to bottom – ascending, descending, running, calling, shouting, peeping, rummaging, ferreting, putting his head into every hole thrusting a torch under every arch, desperate, mad, haggard and moaning like a beast that has lost its mate.

At length, when he was sure, perfectly sure, that she was gone, that all was over, that she had been stolen from him, he slowly went up the steps of the towers, those steps that he had mounted so nimbly and triumphantly on the day he saved her. He now passed those same places with drooping head, voiceless, tearless and hardly drawing breath. The church was again deserted and silent as before. The archers had quitted it to track the sorceress in the city. Quasimodo, left alone in that vast Notre-Dame, but a moment before besieged and full of tumult, betook himself once more to the cell where the gypsy had slept for so many weeks under his protection.

As he approached it, he could not help fancying that he might, perhaps, find her there. When, at the turn of the gallery which opens on the roof of the side aisle, he could see the narrow little lodging, with its small window and tiny door, sheltered under one of the great buttresses, like a bird's nest under a bough, the poor fellow's heart failed him, and he leaned against a pillar to keep from falling. He imagined that she might have returned thither; that some good genius had no doubt brought her back; that that little chamber was too quiet, too safe, too charming for her not to be there, and he dared not advance a step farther, for fear of dispelling his illusion. 'Yes,' said he to himself, 'she is sleeping, perhaps, or praying; I must not disturb her.'

At last he summoned up courage, approached on tip-toe, looked, entered. Empty! the cell was still empty! The unhappy man paced slowly round it, lifted up her couch, and looked underneath it, as if she could have been hidden between the mattress and the stones; he then shook his head and stood stupefied. All at once he furiously trampled upon his torch, and without word or sigh, he rushed at full speed head-foremost against the wall, and fell senseless upon the floor.

When he recovered his senses he threw himself on the bed, rolled upon it and frantically kissed the place, still warm, where the damsel had lain; he remained thus for some minutes, as motionless as if life had fled; he then rose, bathed in perspiration, panting beside himself, and fell to beating his head against the wall with the frightful regularity of a pendulum, and the resolution of a man determined to dash out his brains. At length he sank exhausted a second time. Presently he crawled on his knees out of the cell, and crouched down opposite the door in an attitude of astonishment.

He remained thus for more than an hour, his eye fixed upon the deserted cell, more gloomy and thoughtful than a mother seated between an empty cradle and a full coffin. He uttered not a word; only at long intervals a sob shook violently his whole body; but it was a sobbing without tears, like summer lightning, which makes no noise.

It appears to have been then that, seeking amid his desolate thoughts to discover who could have been the unexpected abductor of the gypsy-girl, he bethought himself of the archdeacon. He recollected that Dom Claude alone possessed a key to the staircase leading to the cell; he remembered his nocturnal attempts upon La Esmeralda, the first of which he, Quasimodo, had assisted, the second of which he had prevented. He called to mind a thousand details, and soon no longer doubted that the archdeacon had taken the gypsy-girl from him. Yet such was his reverence for the priest, gratitude, devotion and love for that man were so deeply rooted in his heart, that they resisted, even at this dire moment, the fangs of jealousy and despair.

He reflected that the archdeacon had done this thing, and that sanguinary, deadly resentment which he would have felt against any other individual, was turned in the poor deaf man's breast the moment when Claude Frollo was in question, into simply an increase of sorrow.

At the moment that his thoughts were thus fixed on the priest, while the buttresses were beginning to whiten in the dawn, he descried, on the upper gallery of Notre-Dame, at the angle formed by the external balustrade which runs round the apsis, a figure walking. The figure was coming towards him. He recognized it. It was the archdeacon. Claude walked with a slow, grave step. He did not look before him as he went; he was going toward the northern tower, but his face was turned to the right bank of the Seine; and he carried his head erect, as if striving to obtain a view of something over the roofs. The owl has often that oblique attitude. It flies in one direction and gazes in another. In this manner the priest passed above Quasimodo without seeing him.

The deaf man, who was confounded by this sudden apparition, saw him disappear through the door of the staircase of the northern tower. The reader is aware that it is that one which commands a view of the Hôtel-de-Ville. Quasimodo rose and followed the archdeacon.

Quasimodo went up the steps of the tower, to ascend it and to ascertain why the priest went up. The poor ringer knew not what he was going to do (he, Quasimodo), what he was going to say, what he wanted. He was full of rage and full of dread. The archdeacon and the Egyptian came into conflict in his heart.

When he reached the top of the tower, before he issued from the darkness of the stairs upon the open platform, he cautiously observed the whereabouts of the priest. The priest had his back toward him. An open-work balustrade surrounds the platform of the spire. The priest, whose eyes were bent upon the town, was leaning his breast upon the one of the four sides of the balustrade which looks upon the bridge of Notre-Dame.

Quasimodo stole with the stealthy tread of a wolf behind him to see at what he was thus gazing.

The priest's attention was so completely absorbed elsewhere that he heard not the step of the hunch-back near him.

Paris is a magnificent and captivating spectacle, and at that day it was even more so, viewed from the summit of the towers of Notre-Dame, in the fresh light of a summer dawn. The day in question might have been in July. The sky was perfectly serene. A few lingering stars were fading away in different directions, and eastward there was a very brilliant one in the lightest part of the heavens. The sun was on the point of rising. Paris began to be astir. A very white, pure light brought out vividly to the eye all the outlines which its countless buildings present to the east. The gigantic shadows of the spires extended from roof to roof from one end of the great city to the other. Already voices and noises were to be heard from several quarters of the town. Here was heard the stroke of a bell, there that of a hammer, and there again the complicated clatter of a dray in motion. Already smoke was escaping from some of the chimneys scattered over all the surface of roofs, as through the fissures of an immense sulphurous crater. The river, whose waters are rippled by the piers of so many bridges and the points of so many islands, was wavering in folds of silver. Around the town, outside the ramparts, the view was lost in a great circle of fleecy vapours, through which were indistinctly discernible the dim line of the plains and the graceful swell of the heights. All sorts of floating sounds were dispersed over this half-awakened city. And eastward, the morning breeze was chasing across the sky a few white tufts torn from the misty fleece of the hills.

In the Parvis some good women, with their milk-jugs in their hands, were pointing out to one another, in astonishment, the singularly shattered state of the great door of Notre-Dame, and the two congealed streams of lead in the crevices of the stone. This was all that remained of the tempest of the night before. The pile kindled by Quasimodo between the towers was extinct. Tristan had already cleared the square, and had the dead thrown into the Seine. Kings like Louis XI are careful to clean the pavement speedily after a massacre.

Outside the balustrade of the tower, directly under the point where the priest had paused was one of those fantastically carved stone gutters with which Gothic edifices bristle; and in a crevice of this gutter, two pretty wall-flowers in full bloom, shaken and vivified as it were by the breath of the morning, made sportive salutation to each other. Above the towers on high, far above in the sky, were heard the voices of little birds.

But the priest neither saw nor heard any of these things. He was one of the men for whom there are neither mornings, nor birds, nor flowers. In all that immense horizon, spread round him with such diversity of aspect, his contemplation was concentrated on a single point.

Quasimodo burned to ask him what he had done with the gypsy-girl, but the archdeacon seemed at that moment to be out of the world. He was visibly in one of those critical moments of life when one would not feel the earth crumble.

With his eyes steadily fixed on a certain spot, he remained motionless and silent; and in that silence and immobility there was something so formidable that the untamed bell-ringer shuddered at it, and dared not intrude upon it. Only (and this was one way of interrogating the archdeacon) he followed the direction of his eye; and, thus guided, that of the unhappy hunch-back fell upon the Place de Grève.

He thus discovered what the priest was looking at. The ladder was set up against the permanent gibbet. There were a few people in the Place, and a number of soldiers. A man was dragging along the ground something white, to which something black was clinging. This man stopped at the foot of the gibbet. Here something took place which Quasimodo could not clearly see, not because his only eye had not preserved its long range, but a group of soldiers prevented his seeing everything. Moreover, at that instant the sun appeared, and such a flood of light burst over the horizon, that it seemed as if every point in Paris, spires, chimneys, gables, took fire all at once.

Meantime, the man began to mount the ladder. Quasimodo now saw him distinctly again. He was carrying a woman on his shoulder – a young girl clad in white. That young girl had a noose about her neck. Quasimodo recognized her.

It was she!

The man reached the top of the ladder. There he arranged the noose. Here the priest, in order to see better, knelt upon the balustrade.

Suddenly the man pushed away the ladder with his heel, and Quasimodo, who had not breathed for some moments, beheld the unfortunate child dangling at the end of the rope, about two fathoms above the ground, with the man squatted upon her shoulders. The rope made several gyrations on itself, and Quasimodo beheld horrible convulsions run along the gypsy's body. The priest, on his part, with outstretched neck and starting eyeballs, contemplated that frightful group of the man and the girl – the spider and the fly!

At the most awful moment, a demoniacal laugh, a laugh such as can come only from one who is no longer human, burst from the livid visage of the priest. Quasimodo did not hear that laugh, but he saw it.

The ringer retreated a few steps behind the archdeacon, and then, suddenly rushing furiously upon him with his huge hands, he pushed him by the back into the abyss over which Dom Claude was leaning. The priest shrieked, 'Damnation!' and fell.

The spout, above which he stood, arrested his fall. He clung to it with desperate gripe; but, at the moment when he opened his mouth to give a second cry, he beheld the formidable and avenging face of Quasimodo thrust over the edge of the balustrade above his head. Then he was silent.

The abyss was beneath him, a fall of full two hundred feet – and the pavement.

In this dreadful situation the archdeacon said not a word, breathed not a groan. Only he writhed upon the gutter, making incredible efforts to re-ascend; but his hands had no hold on the granite, his feet slid along the blackened wall without catching hold. People who have ascended the towers of Notre-Dame know that the stone-work swells out just beneath the balustrade. It was on this retreating angle that the miserable archdeacon exhausted himself in fruitless efforts. It was not with a wall merely perpendicular that he was dealing, but with a wall that sloped away from under him.

Quasimodo had but to stretch out his hand to draw him from the gulf, but he did not so much as look at him. He was looking at the Grève, he was looking at the gibbet, he was looking at the gypsy.

The deaf man was leaning with his elbows on the balustrade at the very spot where the archdeacon had been a moment before, and there, never turning his eye from the only object which existed for him at that moment, he was mute and motionless, like one struck by lightning, and a long stream of tears flowed in silence from that eye which until then had never shed but one.

Meanwhile the archdeacon was panting; his bald brow was dripping with perspiration; his nails were bleeding against the stones; the skin was rubbed from his knees against the wall.

He heard his cassock, which was caught on the spout, crack and rip with each jerk that he gave it. To complete his misfortune, this spout ended in a leaden pipe, which he could feel slowly bending under the weight of his body. The wretched man said to himself, that when his hands should be worn out with fatigue, when his cassock should tear asunder, when the leaden pipe should yield, he must of necessity fall, and horror thrilled his very vitals. Now and then he glanced wildly at a sort of narrow ledge formed, some ten feet lower, by projections in the sculpture; and he implored heaven from the bottom of his agonized soul, that he might be permitted to spend the remainder of his life upon that narrow space of two feet square, though it were to last a hundred years. Once, he glanced below him into the Place, into the abyss; the head which he raised again had its eyes closed and its hair erect.

There was something frightful in the silence of these two men. While the archdeacon struggled with death in this horrible manner, but a few feet from him, Quasimodo looked at the Grève and wept.

The archdeacon, finding that all his exertions served but to shake the only frail support left to him, at length remained quite still. There he hung, clasping the gutter, scarcely breathing, no longer stirring, without any other motion than that mechanical convulsion of the stomach, which one experiences in a dream when one fancies himself falling. His fixed eyes were wide open with a stare of pain and astonishment. Little by little, however, he lost ground; his fingers slipped along the spout; he felt more and more the weakness of his arms and the weight of his body; the leaden pipe which supported him bent more and more every moment towards the abyss. He saw beneath him, frightful sight, the sharp roof of the church of Saint-Jean-de-Rond, as small as a card bent double. He looked, one after another, at the imperturbable sculptures of the tower, like him suspended over the precipice, but without fear for themselves or pity for him. All about him was stone; before his eyes, the gaping monsters; below, quite at the bottom, in the Place, the pavement; above his head, Quasimodo weeping.

In the Parvis there were several groups of curious good people who were tranquilly striving to divine what madman it could be who was amusing himself in so strange a fashion. The priest could hear them saying, for their voices reached him clear and shrill: 'Why, he'll surely break his neck.'

Quasimodo wept.

At length the archdeacon, foaming with rage and horror, be came sensible that all was in vain. Nevertheless, he gathered what strength remained to him for one last effort. He straightened himself on the gutter, set both his knees against the wall, clung with his hands to a cleft in the stone-work and succeeded in climbing up, perhaps, one foot; but his struggle caused the leaden beak which supported him to give way suddenly. The same effort rent his cassock asunder. Then, finding everything under him giving way, having only his stiffened and crippled hands to hold by, the unhappy wretch closed his eyes and let go of the spout. He fell.

Quasimodo watched him falling.

A fall from such a height is seldom perpendicular. The archdeacon, launched into space, fell at first with his head downward and his arms extended, then he turned over several times. The wind blew him upon the roof a house, where the miserable man broke some of his bones. Nevertheless, he was not dead when he reached it. The ringer could perceive him still make an effort to cling to the gable with his hands, but the slope was too steep, and he had no strength left. He glided rapidly down the roof like a loosened tile, then rebounded on the pavement; there he stirred no more.

Quasimodo then lifted his eye to the gypsy, whose body, suspended from the gibbet, he beheld afar, quivering under its white robe, in the last agonies of death; then he looked at the archdeacon, stretched a shapeless mass at the foot of the tower, and he said, with a sob that heaved his deep breast: 'Oh! all that I have ever loved!'

III

The Marriage of Phœbus

TOWARD THE EVENING of that day, when the judicial officers of the bishop came to remove the mangled body of the archdeacon, Quasimodo had disappeared from Notre-Dame.

Many rumours were circulated concerning this accident. It was considered unquestionable that the day had at length arrived when according to compact, Quasimodo – that is to say, the devil – was to carry off Claude Frollo, that is to say, the sorcerer. It was presumed that he had shattered the body in taking the soul, as a monkey cracks the shell to get at the nut.

It was for this reason that the archdeacon was not interred in consecrated ground.

Louis XI died the following year, in August, 1483.

As for Pierre Gringoire, he succeeded in saving the goat, and obtained considerable success as a writer of tragedy. It appears that after dipping into astrology, philosophy, architecture, hermetics – in short, in every vanity – he came back to tragedy, which is the vainest of all. This he called coming to a tragical end. On the subject of his dramatic triumphs, we read in the 'Ordinary's Accounts for 1483' the following:

'To Jehan Marchand and Pierre Gringoire, carpenter and composer, for making and composing the mystery performed at the Châtelet of Paris on the day of the entry of Monsieur the Legate; for duly ordering the characters, with properties and habiliments proper for the said mystery, and likewise for making the wooden stages necessary for the same, one hundred pounds.'

Phœbus de Chateaupers also came to a tragical end; he married.

IV

The Marriage of Quasimodo

WE HAVE ALREADY SAID that Quasimodo disappeared from Notre-Dame on the day of the death of the gypsy and the archdeacon. Indeed, he was never seen again, nor was it known what became of him.

In the night following the execution of Esmeralda, the executioner's men had taken down her body from the gibbet, and, according to custom, had carried it to the vault of Montfaucon.

Montfaucon, to use the words of Sauval, 'was the most ancient and the most superb gibbet in the kingdom.' Between the suburbs of the Temple and Saint Martin, at the distance of about one hundred and sixty yards from the walls of Paris, and a few bow-shots from the village of La Courtille, was to be seen on the summit of a gentle, almost imperceptibly sloping hill, but on a spot sufficiently elevated to be visible for several leagues round, an edifice of strange form, much resembling a Druidical cromlech, and having, like the cromlech, its human sacrifices.

Let the reader imagine at the top of a chalk hill a great oblong mass of stone-work, fifteen feet high, thirty feet wide and forty long, and having a door, an external railing and a platform. Upon this platform sixteen enormous pillars of unhewn stone, thirty feet high, ranged in a colonnade around three of the four sides of the square supporting them, and connected at the top by heavy beams, from which chains are hanging at short intervals. At each of those chains swing skeletons; not far off, in the plain, are a stone cross and two secondary gibbets, rising like shoots from the central tree, and in the sky, hovering over the whole, a perpetual flock of carrion crows. Such was Montfaucon.

At the end of the fifteenth century this formidable gibbet, which had stood since 1328, was already much dilapidated; the beams were decayed, the chains were corroded with rust, the pillars green with mould, the courses of hewn stone were gaping at their joints, and the grass was growing upon that platform to which no foot reached. The structure made a horrible outline against the sky – especially at night, when the moonlight gleamed upon those whitened skulls, or when the evening breeze stirred the chains and skeletons, making them rattle in the darkness. The presence of this gibbet sufficed to make all the surrounding places gloomy.

The mass of stone-work that formed the base of the repulsive edifice was hollow. An immense cavern had been constructed within it, the entrance of which was closed by an old battered iron grating, and into which were thrown not only the human relics taken down from the chains of Montfaucon, but also the carcasses of the victims of all the other permanent gibbets of Paris. In that vast charnel-house, wherein so many human remains and so many crimes have festered together, many of the great ones of the world, and many of the innocent, have from time to time contributed their bones – from Enguerrand de Marigni, the first victim, and who was one of the just, down to the Admiral De Coligni, who was the last and was of the just also.

As for the mysterious disappearance of Quasimodo, all that we have been able to ascertain respecting it is this:

About a year and a half or two years after the events with which this history concludes, when search was made in the vault of Montfaucon for the body of Olivier le Daim, who had been hanged two days before, and to whom Charles VIII granted the favour of being buried in Saint Laurent in better company, there were found, among all those hideous carcasses, two skeletons, one of which held the other in a singular embrace. One of these skeletons, which was that of a woman, had still about it some tattered fragments of a garment, that had once been white; and about the neck was a string of adrezarach beads, with a little silken bag, ornamented with green glass, which was open and empty. These objects were of so little value that the executioner had probably not cared to take them. The other, which held this one in a close embrace, was the skeleton of a man. It was noticed that the spine was crooked, the head depressed between the shoulders, and that one leg was shorter than the other. Moreover, there was no rupture of the vertebræ at the nape of the neck, whence it was evident that he had not been hanged. Hence the man to whom it belonged must have come thither and have died there. When they strove to detach this skeleton from the one it was embracing it crumbled to dust.

WORDSWORTH CLASSICS

General Editors: Marcus Clapham and Clive Reynard
Titles in this series

DISTRIBUTION

**AUSTRALIA, BRUNEI
& MALAYSIA**
Treasure Press
22 Salmon Street, Port Melbourne
Vic 3207, Australia
Tel: (03) 646 6716
Fax: (03) 646 6925

DENMARK
BOG-FAN
St. Kongensgade 61A
1264 København K

BOGPA SIKA
Industrivej 1, 7120 Vejle Ø

FRANCE
Bookking International
16 Rue des Grands Augustins
75006 Paris

**GERMANY, AUSTRIA
& SWITZERLAND**
Swan Buch-Marketing GmbH
Goldscheuerstrabe 16
D-7640 Kehl Am Rhein, Germany

GREAT BRITAIN & IRELAND
Wordsworth Editions Ltd
Cumberland House, Crib Street,
Ware, Hertfordshire SG12 9ET

Selecta Books
The Selectabook Distribution Centre
Folly Road, Roundway, Devizes
Wiltshire SN10 2HR

HOLLAND & BELGIUM
Uitgeverlj en Boekhandel
Van Gennep BV, Spuistraat 283
1012 VR Amsterdam, Holland

ITALY
Magis Books
Piazza Della Vittoria I/C
42100 Reggio Emilia
Tel: 0522-452303
Fax: 0522-452845

NEW ZEALAND
Whitcoulls Limited
Private Bag 92098, Auckland

NORWAY
Norsk Bokimport AS
Bertrand Narvesensvei 2
Postboks 6219, Etterstad
0602 Oslo

SINGAPORE
Book Station
18 Leo Drive, Singapore
Tel: 4511998 Fax: 4529188

SOUTH AFRICA
Trade Winds Press (Pty) Ltd
P O Box 20194
Durban North 4016

SWEDEN
Akademibokhandelsgruppen
Box 21002,
100 31 Stockholm

DIRECT MAIL
Jay Communications Ltd
Redvers House, 13 Fairmile,
Henley-on-Thames
Oxfordshire RG9 2JR
Tel: 0491 572656 Fax: 0491 573590